Novels by Eugenia Price

WHERE SHADOWS GO

D O U B L E D A Y

New York   London   Toronto   Sydney   Auckland

EUGENIA PRICE

WHERE

SHADOWS

GO

PUBLISHED BY DOUBLEDAY

a division of Bantam Doubleday Dell Publishing Group, Inc.
1540 Broadway, New York, New York 10036

DOUBLEDAY and the portrayal of an anchor with a dolphin
are trademarks of Doubleday, a division of
Bantam Doubleday Dell Publishing Group, Inc.

Book design by Marysarah Garofalo
Map by Martie Holmer

Library of Congress Cataloging-in-Publication Data
Price, Eugenia.
Where shadows go / Eugenia Price. — 1st ed.
p. cm.
Sequel to: Bright captivity.
I. Title.
[PS3566. R47W44   1993]
813'.54—dc20   92-38400
CIP

ISBN   0-385-26702-9
ISBN   0-385-42313-6 (large print)
Copyright © 1993 by Eugenia Price
All Rights Reserved
Printed in the United States of America
May 1993

1   3   5   7   9   10   8   6   4   2

FIRST EDITION

For Tina McElroy Ansa

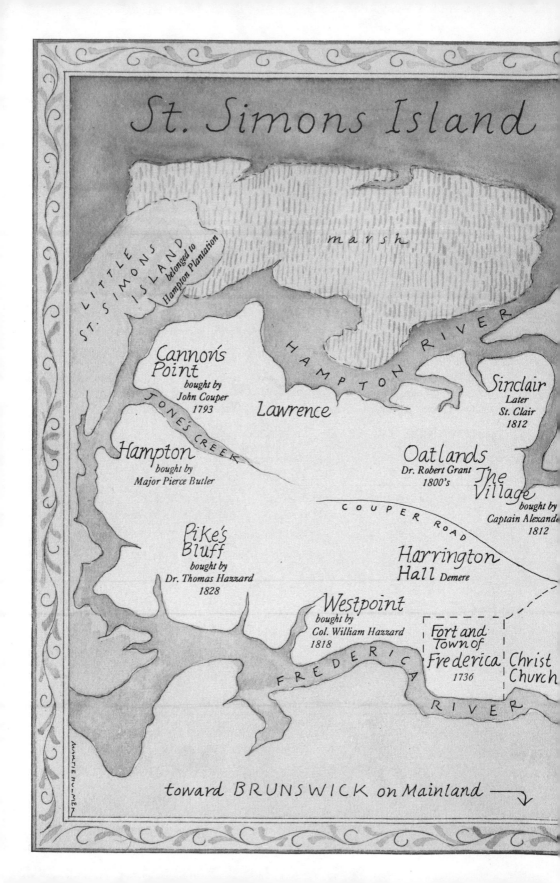

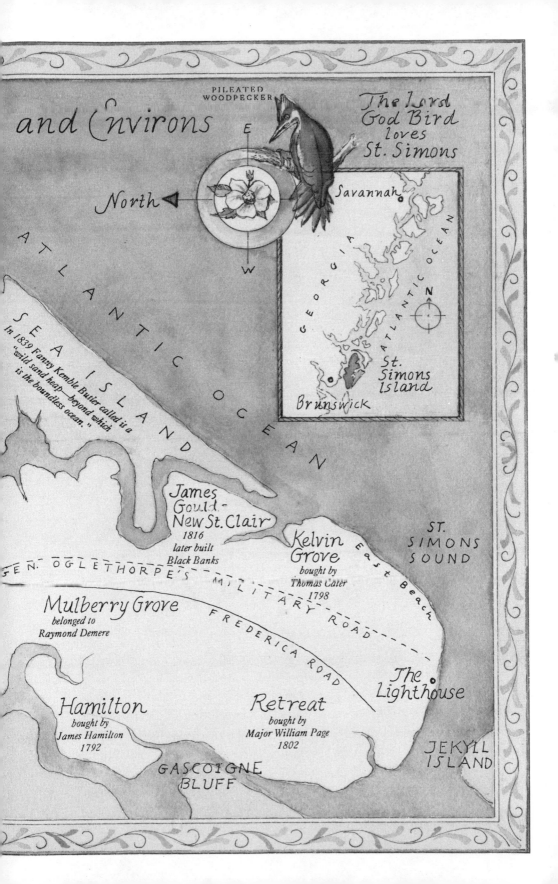

and Environs

PILEATED WOODPECKER

The Lord God Bird loves St. Simons

North

E

W

ATLANTIC OCEAN

SEA ISLAND
In 1839 Fanny Kemble Butler called it a "wild sand heap—beyond which is the boundless ocean."

Savannah

Georgia

ATLANTIC OCEAN

N

Brunswick

St. Simons Island

James Gould—New St. Clair
1816
later built
Black Banks

Kelvin Grove
bought by
Thomas Cater
1798

ST. SIMONS SOUND

GEN. OGLETHORPE'S MILITARY ROAD

Mulberry Grove
belonged to
Raymond Demere

FREDERICA ROAD

EAST BEACH

Hamilton
bought by
James Hamilton
1792

Retreat
bought by
Major William Page
1802

The Lighthouse

GASCOIGNE BLUFF

JEKYL ISLAND

PROLOGUE

MARCH 1825

No one's heart ever beat faster. Anne Couper Fraser was sure of that. The bright March afternoon was too windy and too cold to keep her only child, Little Annie, out on deck with John, as Anne so longed to do. It would be far easier to contain her own excitement outside this stuffy stateroom, where all she could do was sit on a straight chair and watch her daughter sleep. But she was going home. Her heart was racing because after nearly nine years abroad, she was almost back on St. Simons Island.

Despite more than a year of earaches and spells of sore throat before they left London, Little Annie, eight now, had fared so well during the long, rough voyage from Liverpool, this last stretch of water was certainly no time to take chances. March on the Georgia coast could, Anne knew from her own childhood, be warm and mild. Today, March 10, 1825, was cold, even in the sun, as their ship, *Emily,* creaked and groaned its way up the Savannah River toward the busy waterfront. With all her heart, because she herself had waited so endlessly for the moment, she wanted her child to look and act her best when Anne's parents saw their only grand-daughter for the first time. The thought of that happy meeting—surely less than an hour from now—caused her heart to race still more.

Anne glanced at her napping daughter and felt prouder than ever that the thoughtful, sweet-tempered child was her and John's. During the months just past, even when Annie's little throat had been so sore she could not talk, she had whispered words of comfort and encouragement to her mother as they'd waited out the child's illness in Father Fraser's home in London.

For the first two years of Anne's life as Lieutenant John Fraser's wife, she had watched him struggle with his futile, but seemingly unrelenting, effort to rejoin his unit in His Majesty's Royal Navy—the unit that, without a war in progress, no longer needed him. It had been nearly eight years, though, since John vowed he had finally made up his mind to give up trying to return to military life and would go back to Georgia to live with her and Annie in the remodeled little steep-gabled planter's house at Lawrence, which dear Papa had ready and waiting for them. She would certainly do everything in her power to see that John someday learned to love living on St. Simons Island as she loved it.

Little Annie turned over in her sleep, making a soft, contented sound as she snuggled into the thin stateroom bolster. Enjoy being eight years old, her mother thought, and breathed a prayer that her tender, amenable daughter would someday find a *contented* husband to love. Not that Anne Fraser would have changed one single thing about John. The sometimes anxious, even turbulent years of their married life, as John tried to learn to succeed out of uniform, had only found her loving him more and more deeply. The slightest change and he would no longer be John Fraser, her life. He was her life, and what mattered—she still had him with her.

And today was today. They would soon be in Savannah, and Savannah was less than a hundred water miles from her own birthplace, Cannon's Point on St. Simons Island! Her mood brightened, began to soar again. Not only was she eager for Mama and Papa Couper to see her child, Anne felt *she* couldn't wait now for a glimpse of their dear faces, for the glorious moment when Papa would escort the little Fraser family with a flourish—one of Papa's special grand flourishes—across the threshold and into the modest, snug Lawrence cottage as he had long planned.

She fidgeted in her chair. I'm twenty-eight, she thought. John vows I've learned patience being married to him. Well, I haven't. I'm as eager to get off this ship as I hope Annie will be once she wakes up from her nap. Anne knew in her heart that unless something unforeseen had happened, both her parents would be there on the wharf waiting for their ship to dock. If only they didn't have to spend the night in Savannah, pleasant as it was at the old Mackay house with Miss Eliza and her family.

Anne glanced at the gold watch on its ribbon around her neck. Five o'clock. Time for the sun to set. Surely the aging ship, *Emily,* which had brought them this far, would be able to follow the tiny pilot boat up the Savannah River and into port within the hour. It was night in London by now, and Anne breathed another prayer for Father Fraser, hoping he still felt better. Her father-in-law's lumbago and dizzy spells had also detained them. John dared not leave until the older man's health improved. If only Father Fraser would agree to sell the firm and come to Georgia to live! He was always welcome with her and John at Lawrence, but Anne was well aware that the old man would prefer to live with John's brother, Dr. William, married now for almost three years to his adored Frances Anne Wylly, Anne's good friend. William and Frances Anne lived in Darien, Georgia, where Dr. William was doctor in attendance at the new hospital. Even if Father Fraser stayed with William in Darien, he would still be only some eighteen water miles away from John and Anne on St. Simons.

At the porthole, on tiptoe in order to catch a glimpse of her beloved husband out on deck, Anne smiled. There was John, still swapping stories and laughing with an American, a former naval officer against whom he'd fought in the stupid war between their two countries only a few years ago. It had seemed to take forever for John to make up his mind to give up the military and return to Georgia with her, but he *was* John Fraser and wherever he lived, she would enjoy watching him make friends, go on charming people right and left—even recent enemies. Anne's best friend on St. Simons, Anna Matilda Page, married for three months now to a reportedly handsome Northerner named Thomas Butler King, had always vowed that no man could equal John Fraser in sheer charm. Heaven knew, Anne agreed. How soon after they finally reached St. Simons would she be able to visit Anna Matilda for a good long gossip?

Needing to talk to someone, Anne cast an almost impatient glance at her daughter. Asleep, the girl looked more than ever like an angel, but once those dark-fringed lids opened, John's own merry eyes would look up at her. Even when roused from sleep, the child was usually cheerful. "Annie? We're almost in Savannah," Anne said brightly. "Don't you want to splash your eyes and make yourself even prettier before we see our Georgia family at the waterfront?"

Annie opened her eyes. She was only half smiling. "Oh, it's not Katy," she murmured. "It's you, Mama."

"Were you dreaming about your nanny?"

"I guess so. I think I dream about Katy almost as much as about Grandfather Fraser. And"—the gray eyes moved away—"and Samantha. . . ."

Anne reached for the slim, young hand. "My dear, I know you miss your best friend, Samantha. You must miss London, too. I'm —selfish to be so happy to be coming back to *my* childhood home. It isn't yours. I don't think I've thought enough about that."

Annie forced a tiny, hopeless smile. "Do you think Samantha's mother really meant it when she said she'd bring Samantha to Georgia for a visit someday?"

"Oh, I promise she meant it!"

Little Annie is no longer just a child, Anne thought. She thinks too much for an eight-year-old. In what she hoped was a cheery voice, Anne prattled on about how Annie would like to play with Anne's own younger sister, Isabella, and with William Audley, the baby brother Anne had never seen. "Another thing I've just realized is how everyone you'll meet will enjoy your English accent! The Wyllys on St. Simons and several Savannah families are English, too, but your way of speaking is so pert and attractive. My

Eve is going to be simply bewitched by you! I know you miss Katy, but you'll like Eve so much. I promise."

"Does everyone's mother make promises like you and Saman-tha's mother?"

Anne frowned. "Do I make too many promises?"

"Not too many. Just a lot. How close are we to Savannah?"

"Close, close! If old *Emily* ever creeps her way around that big bend I can see in the river out there, we'll be in plain sight of the other ships docked at the wharf. And then you'll get your first glorious glimpse of your very own Georgia grandparents! I can imagine my father pacing up and down the wharf right now pre-tending to inspect bales of cotton, barrels of salt beef—anything to pass the time until our boat is safely there. He may even be up on one of the little iron balconies off Mark Browning's countinghouse on the waterfront—keeping watch. Mr. Browning is Miss Eliza Mackay's friend."

"We stay with Miss Eliza Mackay tonight, don't we? And she has a daughter about my age, named Sallie."

"That's right. Mr. Mark Browning has clerks who often stand out on those iron balconies to watch for incoming sailing ships. I know Grandfather Couper is fidgety to see you. Since the wind is so cold, Grandmother Couper is probably tucked under a warm blanket or a fur robe in the Mackay carriage nearby—waiting too. Annie, you'll feel right at home in Savannah. It isn't nearly as large as London, but it's really quite English. There are even squares with trees and names—as there are in London." She hugged the girl. "Dear heart, you won't be lonely for London very long. Cer-tainly not when you see how magical it is on St. Simons Island, where I was a little girl once."

Anne fell quiet because her daughter, sitting on the side of the narrow stateroom berth now, had begun one of her thinking times. She'd learned to respect the child's tendency to ponder before she finally spoke, especially when what she had to say was important. The habit made John nervous. Almost invariably, he jumped in to tell their daughter what she was thinking. Anne waited.

Finally, Annie said, "I want you to be certain of one thing, Mama. If I know you're happy, I'll be happy too—without Katy or

Grandfather Fraser—even without my best friend, Samantha."
She sighed. "I expect Samantha will be quite grown-up—married,
perhaps, if I ever see her again."

Her daughter's little speech made Anne want to laugh and cry.
She hugged her again, held her for a long moment, then said, "Oh
darling, I don't think either your father or I deserve such a wise,
loving child as you."

"I want Papa to be as happy as you are right now. Do you
think he ever will be?"

"He'll try."

"I know."

"You do know, don't you?"

"I didn't at first," the child said earnestly. "I do now. Papa isn't
always as happy as he pretends. I do like it when he laughs,
though, don't you?"

"Oh yes, yes! Better than almost anything, I like hearing his
laughter."

At that very moment, over the crew's shouts as the *Emily*
neared the wharf, over the straining of the ship, they heard a peal
of John's laughter from on deck. Quick as a squirrel, Little Annie
crawled to the porthole side of her berth and looked out.

"Papa's shaking hands with his gentleman friend. I think he's
saying goodbye. I'm sure he'll be in here with us any minute now!"

The stateroom door burst open on a cold draft and there he
stood, filling the narrow, low entrance, beaming. "Ahoy, mates!"
he all but bellowed, holding out his arms. "Do you realize, wife of
mine, that we're across from Hutchinson Island—about to heave to
at ye old Savannah wharf? Wouldn't surprise me to find half the
city's population on hand to welcome us—*home!*"

Little Annie leaped up into one outstretched arm, kissing his
cheek again and again as though they'd been apart for a year. Anne
moved quickly into the curve of his other arm but said nothing.

"Wife? Didn't you hear my words? I said half the city would
be on hand to welcome us—"

"I heard, John dearest."

"But did you hear me say they'll be there to welcome us
home?"

Quick tears filled Anne's eyes, totally unbidden, and with them a sudden, surprising wave of weakness. He was trying so, so hard. Trying with all his well-meaning heart to convince her that he was almost as glad as she to be nearing St. Simons Island. She knew better.

"Do you really feel we're *all* going home, Papa?" young Annie asked in her direct way. John only laughed. "Don't laugh," the child ordered. "Sometimes you mean something else when you laugh instead of giving me a real answer."

Anne turned to fuss unnecessarily with their already packed belongings and to wipe her eyes, to try to will away the growing dizziness in her head. "Papa's just happy that tomorrow we'll both be able to show you all the beauty on St. Simons, even though there was a hurricane last fall. And you'll finally get to meet Eve and the other people just as soon as our plantation boat docks at Grandpapa Couper's landing."

Sitting beside his daughter on her narrow berth, John lifted the child's face so that he could look directly into her eyes. "Mama's right, Annie," he said. "We're all three going to have the best life ever once we sail from Savannah tomorrow to Mr. Thomas Spalding's wharf on another island, called Sapelo. There, ready with your grandfather's fine, sturdy boat, the *Lady Love,* will be six or eight of his oarsmen all primed to row us straight south to Cannon's Point! And waiting at the Couper dock on St. Simons will be not only your mama's favorite, Eve, but a whole gang of the other Couper people—probably all serenading us as we pull into shore."

Bless you for trying, John, Anne thought, but you're talking too much. Her head still whirled, she supposed because of her own tangled emotions. She felt both relief at what he said and pity.

"I already know Eve's husband, June, will be one of the oarsmen," Annie said. "And that I'm not to say *slaves,* but *people.* I also know the people don't have last names."

"You don't forget anything, do you?" John asked, smiling.

"Heaven knows she's heard my Cannon's Point stories all her life," Anne managed to say in spite of the mounting dizziness.

"Will Eve like me, Mama?"

"Of course she will!"

"Papa, will I like Eve?"

"You're named for your mother," he said, giving Annie a brief hug. "Take your mother's word always."

"Will Eve and I like each other, Mama?"

By now Anne's head spun so, all she could think to say was, "I've already told you she would, dear."

"Will I be allowed to march around the Cannon's Point porch with Grandfather Couper when it's storming?" Annie wanted to know.

"Of course you'll march in the rain with your grandfather, just the way your mother always marched."

When Anne turned away, she stretched out a hand to steady herself on the corner of what passed for a dressing table. John jumped to his feet.

"Anne! Anne, are you—ill?"

Taking her in his arms, he began again—again talking too much. "You're exhausted from such a long, rough voyage," he soothed. "We're almost there, though. It's nearly over. Look! Out the porthole, you can see the Savannah wharf. What a line of ships! There seems to be only one slip remaining for our old *Emily* and we're about to move into it right now."

Both Anne's arms reached to encircle his neck. "John? Annie? Do you both realize my very own parents are right out there waiting to welcome us? To take us—home?"

Anne barely heard herself gasp the word *home,* and from a long way off, her daughter screamed, "Papa! Papa! She's fainting!"

Then, nothing, until Anne felt cold water sloshing over her face. She could also feel her daughter trying to protect her curls from the deluge with a dry towel.

REBECCA   COUPER,   MISS   ELIZA   MACKAY,   AND young Annie stayed upstairs with Anne at the old Mackay house on Broughton Street, while John Couper accompanied Dr. George

Jones to the door and thanked the doctor profusely for coming so quickly to examine his daughter.

"The truth is, mon," Couper said, "I'm grateful most of all for your happy diagnosis! My old head is still agog with joy at the first sight of my only grandchild, little Annie Fraser, and now you tell me there'll be another grandchild this very year. All I can say is glor-ry be! You're sure my lovely daughter Anne will be all right?"

Dr. Jones held out his hand, an amused smile on his face. "I wish I could be as sure about you, Mr. Couper, and perhaps the father-to-be, Mr. Fraser. Gentlemen are often more of a strain on a doctor in a case like this than the mother herself."

Handing Dr. Jones his top hat and gloves, Couper draped the doctor's heavy cape around his shoulders. "My thanks once more, and if I may, I'll trouble you again to assure myself my daughter won't be harmed by a boat trip to St. Simons tomorrow. The little Fraser family is eager to be in their own home on the plantation adjoining mine. Needless to say, my wife and I have waited an eternity for their arrival. In fact, I've planned every festive detail of escorting them to their remodeled house at Lawrence." Couper laughed. "Aye, ther-re'll even be bagpipes!"

On the wide front porch, Dr. Jones promised John Couper that the boat trip would be quite in order, the bagpipes as well. "You should have no problems whatever once she's had a good night's sleep here at Mrs. Mackay's." Again, the men shook hands. "You may have just met your eight-year-old granddaughter for the first time, Couper, but my years of experience tell me she's remarkable and will be on hand every minute—as she is upstairs right now— to help her charming mother. I wish all my house calls were as pleasant and as trouble-free as this one has been."

"I bid you good day, sir," Couper said as the doctor went down the front steps. "And I trust if you happen to see my son-in-law, John Fraser, walking back from the chemist's with fresh smelling salts, you'll inform the young buck that his beloved is in excellent health. I'm sure he's beside himself with joy at the thought of becoming a father again."

"He is indeed," Dr. Jones called, climbing into the driver's seat of his buggy. "And he already knows his wife is going to be just fine. Fraser wouldn't leave until he heard that straight from me. Before he left, I told him he needn't hurry back. It's unlikely Mrs. Fraser will need smelling salts again today. Maybe never. She's a strong young lady."

MARK BROWNING NORMALLY FELT NEITHER SHORT nor frail, but somehow he felt both short and frail when dynamic, wide-shouldered John Fraser knocked briefly, then breezed into his office on Commerce Row just as Mark was about to leave to dress for an evening at the Mackays'.

"Come in, come in, Fraser," Mark said, feeling a bit foolish since the tall, energetic young man was already there, hand out, long, handsome face showing high color from the cold wind outside.

"I'd hoped for a brief talk with you at the Mackays' this evening," John Fraser said in his engaging way, "but I had an errand to do, so I thought I'd drop by to be sure of seeing you alone. I won't require but a few minutes of your time, sir."

"Please take that chair," Mark said, gesturing toward a handsome tapestry-covered armchair beside his desk. "Actually I was just ready to leave for my home on Reynolds Square to make myself presentable for such distinguished company as the Coupers and the Frasers. I'm looking forward to the evening. Miss Eliza Mackay's house, if you remember, is still my second home."

"Indeed I do remember," John answered, crossing his long legs. "You lived with the Mackays, didn't you, when you first came to Savannah as a young man? And"—John swept his hand about the elegantly furnished office—"from the furnishings in this room, I'd wager you have prospered."

"I'm sentimental about them. I had them all sent down from my old family home in Philadelphia."

"Interesting," Fraser said, something else plainly on his mind. "I'm sure we'll find time this evening for pleasant talk, Mr.

Browning. And since my wife learned just an hour ago from Dr. Jones that she is to present me with another child this very year, I must get right back to her."

"Indeed! Then congratulations are certainly in order," Mark said, offering John a cigar, which he refused.

"Thank you. There isn't time. I do need to hurry on, but I have a business proposition to make, Mr. Browning."

"I wish you'd call me Mark. I'd like to call you John."

"Splendid, Mark. Now, on board the old *Emily,* on the voyage from Liverpool, I met a retired American naval officer who told me you were purchasing a new ship to be used in your vast enterprise known as Browning World Shipping."

Mark grinned. "News does travel fast between Savannah and Liverpool. What your shipboard acquaintance told you was true, in fact, until just last week when I came to the firm decision *not* to squander the money on a new ship right now." Mark couldn't help noticing that what had been a persuasive smile was abruptly the deflated look of a child who had just been scolded. "I am curious, though, to know the nature of your proposal."

"It's really not important," John said. "Since you've changed your mind, you could have no interest, but I will explain. You see, I had hoped you'd be confident enough in my long and quite successful experience with the Royal Navy to entrust me with the inspection and purchase of a new ship. I was told the ship you were considering is in Philadelphia. I know how busy you are here in Savannah. I thought perhaps I could spare you a voyage north."

Puzzled, Mark asked, "But aren't you and Mrs. Fraser and your little girl eager to get on down to St. Simons Island to your own home? Miss Eliza Mackay seems to think the entire Couper and Fraser families are most excited by your prospects of becoming a coastal planter. An inspection trip to Philadelphia could require weeks of your time."

In response, John only looked at him, his face still crestfallen. Surprisingly, for a man who talked a lot, he said nothing.

"I do want you to know I appreciate your offer," Mark went on. "Although I admit I don't quite see how the two undertakings would have fit together. I don't doubt your naval expertise, but the trip north could, were I still of a mind to purchase a new ship, take you far past this year's planting time."

On his feet, his natural grace concealing at least some of the unease he evidently felt, John Fraser looked straight at Mark. "I confess I came here today hoping you and I might, even in such a short time, establish a real friendship, sir. You see, I need to tell someone that I realize overseeing the purchase of a ship for you would have caused me to miss cotton planting time on the land Mr. Couper so graciously gave us as a wedding gift."

Mark waited, then asked carefully, "You mean you—hoped for a reason to postpone planting at all this year?"

John's grin was only a bit sheepish. "If I'm honest, I do mean just that. You see, Mark, there are times when I'm painfully aware of my seeming inability ever to be the kind of dependable husband Anne Couper Fraser deserves. For some reason I find honesty fairly easy with you. Heaven knows I've tried to convince myself that by some means, I can—and will—learn how to become the master of a plantation because that's what Anne wants above all else. At times I think I have almost believed I could. I guess I did believe it off and on for months while we were detained in London because of the illness of my father and little daughter." He took a deep breath. "I hated farming so deeply as a boy in Scotland, though, I—I find I need to tell someone that I'm not at all sure I'll ever be good at it." The grin vanished. "I can't abide myself as a failure—in anything. Do I impose on an imagined friendship with you by telling you all this? Imagined from my side?"

"No. You honor me. I know the feeling of having so much to learn. I had to learn everything from Mr. Robert Mackay about how to be a successful factor when I first came here. I understand what you're saying. You simply took me by surprise. I'm quite reserved as a rule. Your directness is good for me. I'd like to be your friend, and I believe your offer to handle the ship purchase for me was—forgive me if this is too blunt—but I feel that offer was a cry for help. How wrong am I?"

"Not wrong at all. I thought I'd admitted that." Both hands out in an almost helpless gesture, John said, "My friend, I'm a veritable battlefield inside. With all my heart I want, first of all, to stop plaguing my beautiful wife."

"Plaguing her?" Mark asked.

"I do plague her. She tries not to let it show and we're blissfully happy, but almost always, running under all I do or say is the dread of failing as a planter. And bolstering that dread is an immature, almost irresponsible yen for adventure." For a moment the two men studied each other. Then John asked, "Need for adventure isn't a problem for you, is it? You're contented right here?"

In response, Mark laughed softly. "I wouldn't want to be anywhere else but Savannah, but I don't lack for adventure, living under the same roof with my amazing two-and-a-half-year-old daughter, Natalie. Granted, she doesn't offer the kind of active life you miss from your years in the military, but there's certainly no predicting the child." Mark turned serious. "I'm not comfortable with what I'm about to say, but if I'm to be a straightforward friend, I'm afraid I'll have to tell you what I really think."

John said nothing, but his look, both apprehensive and eager, freed Mark to go on.

"Last September sent us a devastating hurricane here on the coast. I'm sure you saw some of the damage around Savannah as your ship eased up the river." John nodded. "The destruction at Cannon's Point was severe. Mr. Couper is so prominent, so revered, several stories have been written about his losses in our Savannah newspaper. I understand that the greathearted, kindly gentleman is in rather dire straits financially. Most of his cotton crop was lost. Great walls of water rushed over the Cannon's Point land destroying outbuildings and Negro cabins. His people are so loyal to him, I believe they've done remarkably well at rebuilding their own houses, his horse stables, gin house, blacksmith shop, and so on. But they can't regrow his damaged orange and olive groves or the all-important cotton fields. His son James Hamilton has scheduled a trip abroad for late this summer to study Dutch diking systems, so he won't be nearby to help. The old gentleman is well into his sixties. He's counting on your help, John. Not only is he so pleased to have your little family back on St. Simons, I must em-

phasize he's counting heavily on his young, strong son-in-law—
you."

Still standing as Mark spoke, John strode to a window and
stared out into the darkening evening sky. For a long time, neither
said a word. Finally, just above a whisper, John said, "But I can't
drive a nail without bending it. I can't saw a board evenly. I never
learned how to plow a straight furrow or even to shoe a
horse. . . ."

"You've had years of experience, though, supervising men under you in the Royal Navy. Mr. Couper's people—your people,
once you're master of Lawrence Plantation—will be there to do
the actual work. You'll know how to supervise them."

"I didn't get to stay in the Royal Navy long enough to be
anything higher than a first lieutenant," John said grimly. "I've
taken far more orders than I've given."

"Are you still of a mind to be friends?" Mark asked.

"Yes. Oh yes!"

"Then I have to ask an embarrassing question—embarrassing
for any man to answer. Are you *afraid* of the responsibilities of
becoming a planter?"

John turned slowly from the window to face him. "Yes. Quite
simply—yes. I also hate the idea of owning other people."

"So do I. Owning slaves is the main bone of contention between my dear wife, Caroline, and me."

"But don't you own a Savannah River plantation?"

"No. My wife owns it as an inheritance. I hire the two German
women who are our house servants here in town. I hire the free
man of color who handles the work in our city garden. He also
drives us. You see, I was brought up by a strong abolitionist aunt in
Philadelphia. I love Savannah, Georgia, but my Yankee teaching
about our national Constitution stays with me. I can't forget for a
minute that 'all men are created equal.'" Again, he waited for
John to speak. When his new friend remained silent, Mark added,
"Be that as it may; if our friendship is to get off on the right foot, I
feel I must tell you to think long and hard about the fact that you
also had to learn how to be a fine military man when you were
only a boy, as I recall your telling me soon after we met. You've

agreed to come back to Georgia. You can also learn how to plant the best cotton on the coast. And John, your wife's good father, John Couper, truly needs you now."

AFTER A QUICK, WARM GOODBYE TO MARK BROWN-ing, during which John made a firm promise to give much thought to what his new friend had said, he hurried to the Mackay house on East Broughton Street and headed straight upstairs to the room he would share tonight with Anne.

Unexplainably, each stride he'd taken on his way back to her had seemed to release a new surge of energy. Not just physical energy—*spirit*. He had been right to trust Browning, to speak so freely to him. Best of all, John felt happy surprise in the challenge that John Couper really needed him. He had long admired and respected the good-humored, gracious Scotsman and had believed that Couper genuinely liked him, welcomed him as a son-in-law, but not once had it occurred to John that Couper might be in need of him. From the start, he had believed himself to be merely another fortunate recipient of Couper's hospitality and gracious-ness. Now there might be a chance to give something back to the gentleman everyone so admired and revered. Of course John knew Anne and Little Annie and the barely announced new child would always need him. Why, he wondered, making the last turn in the wide old Mackay stair, had that not been enough until he learned of Couper's dire straits as a result of the hurricane last fall?

Outside the room where Anne was probably still resting, he stopped to collect his thoughts, even felt a touch foolish at his own abrupt shift of mood after having made such a desperate proposal to Mark Browning. Now he felt excited, so full of enthusiasm over his future on St. Simons that he'd forgotten to hang either his top hat or his cloak on the hall tree downstairs. Smiling to himself, he tossed both on a wooden bench outside the bedroom door, squared his shoulders, and trusted his quick wits for the right words to convince Anne that at last, at long last, he knew deep inside that he *could* succeed as a planter.

Softly, he let himself into the quiet, dimly lit bedroom, hoping fervently to find her by herself.

"Anne, my darling, you are alone!" he all but shouted when he saw her sitting at the dressing table, working away on her eternally troubling curls. "I'm so relieved you're feeling better. Look at you, glowing with health and fiddling quite deftly with your hair."

Without a word, she dropped her brush and held both arms out to him. After an eager embrace and a hard kiss on her perfect mouth, he quickly loosened his arms when she began laughing.

"What's so funny?" he demanded.

"You. You're funny, John Fraser. Funny and beautiful and—" She pushed him away. "Let me look at you. You're not only funny and beautiful, you're suddenly much more *fatherly* looking!"

The sheer joy of this first realization together that another child was coming struck them both silent. For what seemed a long, long time, they just stood there looking at each other—beaming.

Then, his face tender with concern, he whispered, "I must remember not to be so rough with you from now on."

"Fiddlesticks! I'm fine!"

"Are you, Anne? Are you really all right? Dr. Jones assured me you probably wouldn't need the fresh smelling salts I bought, but—"

"I won't! I almost fainted only once before, the morning dear Flora McLeod pushed my head down between my knees and saved me—the day *she* discovered Annie was coming." She looked at John in the looking glass. "I'll miss Flora this time," she said. "I know I'll have my own mother nearby and Eve and Papa's Rhyna, the most in demand of all St. Simons Island midwives, but"—she grinned—"no one anywhere is quite like Flora. I hope she and Father Fraser are both all right."

"I guarantee Flora McLeod is all right and Father will be too, if he's obeying his tyrannical housekeeper. But Anne, I—I need to talk about something. Aren't you ever going to finish with your hair?"

He watched her stick one final hairpin into place and test the pile of curls to be sure it held, then he reached quickly to help her to her feet when she laid down the brush. "Careful! You must get up slowly. Anne, you must be careful. We have a long water trip tomorrow."

"What do you need to talk to me about?" she asked a bit nervously. "Is it something serious? Or could we sit side by side on our bed over there and just be close?"

"As far as I'm concerned, Mrs. Fraser, we must always be as close together as possible. But yes, to me it's something serious. Come on."

"You don't need to lead me around. We just found out today that I'm going to have another baby. Look, I'm still flat and stylish. Besides, this isn't the only baby we're going to have. I want lots more because each one will be part of you. And dearest, you're my life. Did you know?"

"Yes," he said, taking her in his arms again as they sat together on the bed. "I know, beloved Anne. I do need to tell you something very important, but I don't think straight when you're so close. You'd better prop up on those pillows and I'll sit in this straight chair beside you. Here, let me lift your feet."

"I don't need to lie down."

"Yes, you do." He pulled up the wooden chair, straddled it, and began to speak in an almost solemn voice. "Anne, do you truly believe I'll ever learn how to be a planter? I don't mean one who just takes orders from your brilliant brother James Hamilton and your father. I mean on my own."

She cocked her head in the manner he so loved and peered at him intently. "John Fraser, you've spent years convincing me that it's all going to work out fine for us once we're back in Georgia. I know you agreed to come partly because of me, but yes, what you tell me, I believe."

"Well, I *didn't* believe until I had a talk with Mark Browning on my way back here from the chemist's."

"You went to see Mr. Browning?"

"I did, and something like a miracle happened inside me. He made me see that your illustrious, generous father really needs me."

Anne's quick little frown showed that he had only puzzled her. "But darling, Papa has always needed us to live nearby. It's going to be the glorious moment of his entire life the first time he takes Little Annie—you and me—to our very own house at Lawrence. Did you think he didn't need us? Did you think he was merely being bighearted to turn Lawrence over to you?"

John thought a minute. Then he decided to tell her everything about his visit to Mark Browning's office—even his now-ludicrous-sounding proposal to make a trip all the way to Philadelphia in order to miss the final date for planting cotton in time for this year's crop, to put off for one more year what had seemed such an impossible ordeal.

For a long time she said nothing. Finally, she reached for one of his hands and held it in her firm little grip. "You—you offered to leave Annie and me to go all the way to Philadelphia so soon after we finally got back to Georgia?"

"Yes," he said. "I did just that. I've never lied to you actually, in so many words. I've just always talked too much, hatched too many crazy schemes in my own head, then hinted to you. That is not the way a dependable husband conducts himself. But Browning somehow got me to admit my downright fear of ever learning how to plant. Admitting that left me bare. He then made me see that without my help your father could go bankrupt."

"Papa?"

"He hasn't recovered from the loss of those sixty slaves to the British. Now the ghastly damage from the hurricane, the loss of most of his crop, has almost finished him. Browning thinks I can help. How I can't imagine, but Anne, *I'm going to try."* He tightened his fingers around hers. "I—I haven't felt needed since I lost my commission in the Royal Navy. My own father made some use of me because I was there, but your father *needs me.* You need a dependable husband. I mean to be just that." A weak grin came. "If I'm not too bumble-fingered ever to learn how to grow cotton . . ."

He saw Anne take a swipe at the tears on her cheeks. Then she said in a curiously guarded voice, "Or too—unwilling to own slaves?"

His grin vanished. "I somehow didn't dream you'd even bring that up," he said hoarsely. "We've rather avoided the subject all these years. You know me even better than I think, don't you?"

"No, John. Every single day I learn something new about you."

For the first time since he'd straddled the straight chair beside the bed where she lay, he looked away from her, searching almost desperately for something light and familiar to say—anything to bridge the sudden distance her words had thrust between them. He didn't want to be a puzzle to Anne! He longed to give her openly every hidden part of him, nothing held back between them. Had he tormented her all these years by being complicated, by indulging himself in what secretly appealed to him? *Appealed* to him? Could tormenting Anne possibly appeal to him? A joke now, a play phrase, would help. He could think of nothing.

"John?"

He turned his face back to her, moved to sit beside her on the bed.

"All that matters right now," she said, "is that I'm giving you another baby. Tell me, sir, do you want a daughter or a son this time?"

Anne had bridged the distance. He grinned. "Do I have a choice?"

"Maybe. Who knows?"

He feigned deep thought. "Let me see, I think I want . . ."

"A son? I do. I want a son who looks exactly like his incomparable father!"

"Poor little fellow," John laughed. "But I've always liked the boy's name Peter. So, let's have a son!"

"Peter? Why Peter?"

"I don't know. I just like the name. I like the nickname Pete. Do I have to have another reason?" He was holding her now, smoothing her hair, and after a long, deep, tender kiss, he asked, "Did you have any real idea that your father was in severe financial difficulties from the hurricane, Anne?"

"No. Oh, Mama wrote about all the outbuildings that blew down or were swept away by high water. Even some of the people's cabins, but when I asked if Eve's house was gone and Mama said no, I guess I stopped worrying too much." He felt her pull away far enough to look him straight in the eyes. "I know I'm twenty-eight," she went on, "but I'm still a little girl where Papa is concerned. I just always expect him to fix everything. Part of the front porch and some of the chimney at our little house at Lawrence were damaged. Mama wrote that Papa had both repaired almost at once, in case we came early."

"That would be like him. He'd certainly have no reason to think I would know how to rebuild a front porch. After all"—he smiled his devilish smile—"he doesn't yet know his son-in-law is suddenly so changed. That he's no longer merely an impetuous adventurer. That from now on he's a man who can shoulder heavy burdens."

"Stop talking as though our life on St. Simons is going to be boring and burdensome! How could it be when we'll be together?" John loved it when she threw both arms about him, not waiting for him to embrace her. "Do you know the moment I'm really waiting for?" she asked. "The moment I've dreamed about more than any other?"

Again feigning deep thought, he mused, "Let me see. . . . You've seen your parents' beaming faces here at the Savannah wharf, and I've already told you I'm a changed man. I give up. What moment, beautiful Anne?"

"You're slow. Annie guessed just before she went downstairs to play with Miss Eliza's little girl Sallie. Can't you guess?"

"Does it have anything to do with your father?"

"You're close. Keep trying."

"I'd rather kiss you again."

"No. I want to tell you that the moment I'm waiting for is when Papa first shows us our very own house at Lawrence! Depending on the tide and when we reach Cannon's Point tomorrow, it could be early the day after tomorrow, but Papa will insist on some kind of ceremony. Wait and see. He'll make an unforgettable game of leading you and Annie and me up the pinestraw path he wrote about, onto the repaired front porch with its new wooden steps, and into the first dear little house to belong only to Mr. and Mrs. John Fraser. Aren't you just popping with excitement at the thought of that moment?"

"Almost as much as the moment I close the door on our first night alone in our very own Lawrence bedroom," he teased.

Anne did not smile. Quite solemnly, she said, "I don't think we'll dare close the door on Annie the very first night."

"*What?*"

"Eve's moving to Lawrence with us, but she'll be in her own new cabin with June. Annie's not used to being alone at night. John, the child misses London. She misses Father Fraser and Flora and Katy and, most of all, her best friend, Samantha. Darling, we're uprooting our little girl from all she's ever known and held dear."

He loosened his arms. "We are, aren't we? But your sister, Isabella, must be nearly ten by now, and the young brother you haven't even seen, William Audley, is only a bit younger than our Annie. And soon she'll have a baby brother named Peter and her own house that will belong to her because it belongs to us and in no time her fragile little arms and legs will be strong and sturdy from swinging on grapevines, swimming in the rivers, and—why, our demure Annie may even turn into a tomboy!"

From downstairs in the Mackay house the supper bell sounded. Anne jumped to her feet, made one final inspection of her curls in the looking glass, and took his arm.

At the top of the stairs that led down to Eliza Mackay's front hall, Anne stopped to look up at him in the flickering yellow candlelight. "I don't ever want you to stop being an adventurer, John. I adored being captured by an adventurer named Lieutenant John Fraser down on Cumberland Island so long ago." Clinging to him, she said, "You know that about me by now, surely. Don't you?"

"Yes, beautiful Anne, I know that about you. I also really know our new adventure on St. Simons is somehow going to turn out all right. I'm not just sure how, but by some means, I'm going to help your father make a good crop, help him avoid bankruptcy. That's my new goal. Part of me still can't believe I'm saying this, but—it's all going to be all right."

PART I

APRIL 1828— DECEMBER 1828

CHAPTER 1

ALL HER LIFE ANNE HAD INSISTED THAT EVERY spring on St. Simons Island there came a day when, as by magic, the very color of the air itself turned from winter gold to crystal white. Papa laughed at the idea; Mama just smiled and now, well into their fourth spring back on the Island, April 1828, John still laughed too. Only Eve, Anne's bright, headstrong servant, seemed able to see the air as Anne saw it.

"Eve's a bit like her Grandmother Sofy," John reminded Anne. "She sees many things that simply are not there."

"Untrue," Anne would snap. "Eve doesn't even like her grandmother most of the time. Your reasoning, sir, gets more like my father's every day."

Living with John at Lawrence, their plantation adjoining her family's Cannon's Point, had probably only given Anne a clearer idea of what both men were really like. Where humor was concerned, they were certainly similar. No one could doubt the men's devotion to each other. No one could doubt that her father, unlike

John, was a patient man—even when John went overboard during their first year back in Georgia and nearly burned the Lawrence cotton barn to the ground after their first year's crops had practically been destroyed by caterpillars. Papa's friend Thomas Spalding, of Sapelo, had urged everyone to prevent a repeat of such a catastrophe by keeping all brush burned. John had not been strict enough with the fieldhands, and in his effort to attract and burn the creatures in moth form, he'd allowed the fire to roar out of control. When John wilted with embarrassment, Papa had merely smiled, reminded his inexperienced son-in-law that he'd at least seen to it that next year's crops would have no ugly worms chewing on them. Then he sent his own carpenters to repair the charred roof of the cotton barn.

Jane Austen's novel *Persuasion* lay open in Anne's lap as she sat on the cottage porch waiting for Eve and the two children, Annie now eleven and red-haired Rebecca two and a half, to return from cutting dogwood blossoms in the woods behind the Lawrence house. Both girls and Eve had skipped off an hour ago, as determined as Anne that the cottage would look cheerful for John's return from an errand to Cannon's Point. Anne's mind was not on the novel. As usual, it was on John himself. Everyone, including dear Mama, made every effort to see that Island life was good for John, whose moods swung wildly from despair at his ineptness to hearty laughter at himself every time he did something he called bumble-fingered and dumb. He was trying, though. How the man was trying to learn how to live a totally new way of life!

Their second and third years spent at Lawrence had been a bit smoother than the first year. John's laughter rang more often through the rooms of their cottage. No father could be more smitten with his daughters, and in the evenings when he felt he'd accomplished something productive, young Annie had no trouble getting him to sing until time for the children to go to bed. John's silvery voice delighted both Annie and feisty little Rebecca, who was learning her numbers under the guidance of Anne's own childhood tutor, William Browne, by counting the days until November, when she would be three. The St. Simons air would have turned gold again by then. Anne remembered its turning over a month before Rebecca was born in the autumn of their first year back in coastal Georgia.

That John had said he wanted a son so he could be named Pete seemed not to matter at all, since anyone could tell that Rebecca was going to be a real tomboy. From the first moment John laid eyes on her scrunched-up, newborn face, he'd called her Pete. Now no one, not even Anne's elegant mother, Rebecca, for whom the girl was named, ever thought of calling her anything but Pete.

The name suited the busy, talkative child, whose curly hair was exactly the same dark red as Papa's. Eve adored Pete, defended her antics at times to the point where Anne wanted to smack them both. Never considered good with children, Eve had an odd bond with young Annie and Pete that somehow pleased Anne, although it made Eve still more independent, almost as though the girls belonged to her in the exact way Anne had always known secretly that she herself was peculiarly Eve's property. At times Eve's possessiveness with the children caused Anne to feel on the outside, almost helpless. Especially in the fall of their first full year back, when Anne had to leave her girls in Eve's care—Anne's mother supervised—while she spent two weeks with her best friend, Anna Matilda King, whose mother, sweet Mrs. Hannah Page, had died suddenly of a stroke.

"Effen you think anybody else but me gonna look after bof your young'uns *anytime,* Miss Anne, you better change your min','" Eve had declared the very day she and Ebo June moved from their cabin at Cannon's Point to the new one at Lawrence, which June had built in his spare time long before Anne and John finally came home from London. "Eve gonna keep on doin' for you, as long as you an' me's alive, but you a grown, bustlin' married woman now an' the young'uns gonna need Eve jus' about all the time!"

Fortunately, young Annie showed no signs of becoming spoiled no matter how Eve pampered her. Not so with Pete, who, even at a tender age, appeared to agree to almost anything Eve wanted, although Anne had often asked her to do the exact same thing five minutes earlier. Most of the time, none of this worried Anne unless Eve grew too uppity or took Pete too often to spend time with Eve's eccentric, spell-casting Gran'maum Sofy. On those days, impressionable, daring Pete might come home decorated with a piece of broken looking glass on a wire across her head and a string of magic herbs around her neck. Even this didn't bother Anne much until Pete began to shush her when she ordered Pete to do something the child didn't want to do. At those times Pete would warn her mother that she'd better be careful not to break Gran'maum Sofy's new spell.

Why Eve persisted in allowing the child to make friends with Sofy Anne had no idea, since Eve really had never seemed to like the old woman, vowing that her grandmother invariably acted in exactly the opposite way from what was natural. So did Pete now and then, but Anne, familiar with the African traits of her father's people, told herself Pete's odd ways were probably only a quirk and would pass. The truth was, Anne had missed Eve so much during the long years in London—had missed her in far more ways than being forced to learn to fix her own brown curls, prepare her own bathwater, and care for her own clothes—that despite Mama's advice, she still gave in far too often to her maid. Anne's mother vowed that she understood Anne's attachment to Eve, but even she seemed not to realize fully that Anne and half-white Eve were, in some deep way, staunch friends.

I need to put this book down. I'm not concentrating on a word I've read, Anne thought. Her old tutor, Mr. Browne, now in his fifties but still making his home at Cannon's Point, had only recently started Anne and Anna Matilda reading Jane Austen, after having spent years cultivating their taste for Walter Scott and Shakespeare. Any thought of Walter Scott, now Sir Walter, invariably set Anne thinking of dear Willy Maxwell, who had given her and John the inestimable gift of a visit to his friend Scott's home, Abbotsford, just before John had finally decided to return to Georgia.

At every opportunity since their return, Mama had engaged Anne in talk of her distant cousin, Willy Maxwell, the present laird (Lord Herries) of her family's ancient castle, Caerlaverock, near Dumfries, Scotland. Mama's life had revolved around Papa for all the years of their marriage, but she was still a Maxwell, and although she'd never even been to Scotland, it had profound meaning for her that Anne, at least, had actually climbed over the magnificent ruins of Caerlaverock.

Anne got to her feet and went to the porch railing to look and listen for the sound of her children's voices from the woods or of John's mare, Ginger, galloping in from Cannon's Point for dinner. From the separate kitchen building out back, she could smell Mina's roast pork and simmering onion soup, the tantalizing aromas mingling on the soft breeze blowing through the woods and across the backyard. Anne's father had given them Mina, their cook, trained (and proud of it) by Papa's own Sans Foix, the only free person of color at Cannon's Point. She had confided her opinion only to Mina, but Anne thought Mina's onion soup superior even to that of Papa's famous chef.

Papa. John had spent the morning helping supervise the all-important manuring of John Couper's main fields with oxcarts of rich, weathered, and cured marsh-mud spread over the gray Island sand so needed to grow what was now being called the superior Sea Island long-staple cotton. Mark Browning had convinced John when their ship first docked in Savannah three years ago that he could actually help Papa escape financial ruin. Knowing this had given John a new reason for trying.

Anne frowned. Help Papa? Until Mark Browning had spoken the hated word *bankruptcy* to John, Anne had lived her life believing that Papa always did the helping! Hadn't he helped her older brother, James Hamilton Couper, in every phase of his life from Yale to full ownership of the fertile, beautifully situated Hamilton Plantation on the southwest side of St. Simons Island? Everyone knew imposing James Hamilton Couper, married only last year to sixteen-year-old, pretty Caroline Wylly, to be excessively brilliant, with interests as wide as the horizon. Without Papa's help and connections, her brother might eventually have made the prestigious name for himself he now enjoyed from the Florida-Georgia border to New England and even in Europe, but certainly not at such a young age. Anne was devoted to James, admired him, but as with her and John, she knew full well that it had been Papa doing the real helping. Now and then she actually felt sorry for her younger brother, William Audley, born while she and John still lived in London. The rather helpless, somewhat idle youngster would have to live his life—no matter what he accomplished— being unfavorably compared with his successful, unusually brainy older brother. Certainly, not yet eleven, William Audley was no help now.

It was true that Papa had suffered enormous losses in the years just past, and because James was away so much, living now at Hopeton Plantation on the mainland—owned jointly by Papa and his friend James Hamilton—Papa needed a man nearby at Cannon's Point and Lawrence. It was certainly true that no one reveled in the mutuality of the friendship between John Fraser and John Couper as did Anne, but she had almost totally put the ridiculous possibility of bankruptcy for her father out of her mind. They had been at Lawrence for three years, and not once had either of her parents mentioned that the John Coupers might be in deep financial difficulty.

If Papa was in money trouble, wouldn't Mama have mentioned it at least once during one of her long talks with Anne? Wouldn't John have brought it up again at some point? Could even her happy-natured father keep something so ruinous to himself and go on acting as though his world was as solid and dependable as ever?

Only once had she asked John outright. He vowed his father-in-law had not mentioned bankruptcy. John sometimes colored his stories or exaggerated, but he didn't lie to her and so she had stopped worrying. Why was she thinking of it today? Did it have anything to do with what her husband said on a heavy sigh just before they got out of bed this morning?

"Anne, if only I could strike the right balance in handling both men and women in Papa Couper's fields and my own! I know I'd be of more real help if I could get the knack of being just strict enough without seeming to order them around as though I were their commanding officer."

No matter how she tried, Anne seemed unable to convince him that all the Cannon's Point people, plus those Papa and her brother James had given or loaned them to work at Lawrence, thought highly of their tall, eager, handsome Mausa John, truly respected him exactly as he was. Invariably he had one response: "One day they respect me, obey me. The next day they take advantage of my soft, muddled heart."

"But I've grown up with fieldhands and house people," she argued. "Don't you think I know what they're thinking?"

"Frankly, I do not believe any white person—even your illustrious brother James Hamilton—knows what any of them is thinking, because we and they think from different points of view. The people look across a chasm at me. I look across at them. Their skin is black, mine is white. They're slaves. I'm the master. How could we possibly know what they are thinking?"

"But has one of them sassed you? Or talked back in any way?"

John laughed wryly. "Most are too canny to do that. Any human being is going to act appropriately and say what appears to better his or her own peculiar condition at the moment, Anne. Even you should know that."

"I hate it when we quarrel!"

"Then stop trying to make me think they all revere me. I know what I know. I'm not in favor of being a slave owner, but apparently I'm not equipped to be anything else at this point in my life." He threw back the covers and sat up on the side of the bed. "I'm not even equipped for planting. I'm a rotten planter, but at least I know when I fail. So don't try flattering. Just stop it, Anne. *Stop it.*"

It had been months since Anne had permitted herself to act on either the anger or the panic she invariably felt when they disagreed. Such self-discipline had not been easy to learn, but she had done it for young Annie's sake. The day she found Annie hidden alone in the hydrangea bushes, crying because she'd overheard her parents arguing and believed they no longer loved each other, had brought home the lesson.

Anne had somehow convinced herself even as she had struggled that day to convince her daughter. "You're grown up enough to understand this, darling," she had explained. "When two people really love each other as your father and I most certainly do, they are honest when they talk. They say what they mean. Do you want Papa to be afraid to tell me about something that bothers him? It makes him feel better to tell me. I can see so much difference between the way he and I talk together now and the way we sometimes tried to fool each other when we all still lived in London at Father Fraser's house. In those days if something worried your papa, he acted most of the time as though nothing was wrong at all. Even as a little girl, you began to sense that. Believe me, Annie, it's much better this way."

Slender young Annie had nodded thoughtfully. She wanted to understand. In her quiet, gentle way, the child had always been a peacemaker, had always seemed to try almost too hard to obey, to accommodate them both. Anne felt sure that briggledy Pete appeared more selfish and demanding simply because Annie had always been sensitive to those around her. The only time Annie made anything resembling a complaint was soon after they returned to St. Simons Island, the day word came that likable young George Abbott, the postmaster at nearby Frederica, had died suddenly. Annie cried then as though her heart would break, because she was sure that in a remote spot like St. Simons, they would never, never again receive a letter from anyone! To Annie, "anyone" meant Grandfather Fraser and her best London friend, Samantha. Now, at age eleven, Annie laughed at her own childishness, because Grandfather Couper had been made postmaster almost at once and handed out mail at Christ Church near the Frederica wharf every Sunday morning.

Annie was always hoping for a letter from London, and her silent heartache when Samantha stopped writing after a year or so was painful to watch. Father Fraser remained faithful in sending his terse, short messages, but Anne could tell that they often only irritated John, much as his father's usually understated conversation had irritated him in London.

"At least the old fellow keeps writing," John said often. "I know it means a lot to Annie. But wouldn't you think he'd sell that wobbly importing business and come here to spend his last days near his grandchildren?"

Anne agreed, although she knew, as did John, that Father Fraser would live with William and Frances Anne at their home on the Ridge in Darien.

When her front porch reverie was broken into by the first

shrill, excited shout from Pete from the direction of the woods behind their cottage, where the girls and Eve were cutting dogwood blossoms, Anne knew they had heard John's horse galloping in from Cannon's Point. The shout was Anne's signal to run to the front steps, pick up the big conch shell, and blow a short, mighty blast, which echoed across their huge front yard and out over Lawrence Creek. Other people used a conch to announce meals or to call for help. John and Anne had established their own custom. A long blast might mean help was needed, but a short, loud toot meant a merry welcome, the announcement of a small or large victory as on the day Pete first managed to walk the length of the porch without falling once. Today Anne's blast meant hurry, hurry, I'm waiting for all of you.

BY THE TIME ANNE COULD SEE JOHN CANTERING along their lane toward the cottage, he'd already scooped Pete up onto his saddle. The child was waving wildly from her lofty perch in front of John, both looking superior atop Ginger, John's high-strung chestnut mare.

"Look at all those glorious dogwood blossoms," Anne called, waving now at Eve and Annie, hurrying to catch up with the two riders. John reined Ginger under the huge oak tree at the foot of the cottage path and lifted Pete to the ground. "Bring the flowers right on in, Eve and Annie," Anne said, "so we can arrange them before Mina calls us to dinner. John, you weren't supposed to get here before we had the dogwood arranged."

They all hurried up the path, Pete pulling her father along by the hand and as usual shouting at the top of her lungs. "But there's a letter, Mama! Papa's got a letter for us!"

"Did someone bring the mail over early from Frederica?" Anne asked John as he kissed her lightly, Pete still swinging on one of his hands. "Today is only Saturday. Papa usually doesn't pick up the mail until just before Sunday service. Who wrote to us? Who brought the letter?"

"Captain James Frewin," John said.

"Who wrote to us?"

"Papa's got a letter from Grandfather Fraser!" Pete yelled.

"He has? Have you read it, John?"

"No," Pete blurted in her most authoritative manner. "He's waiting for us all to read it together. I'm gonna read some of it myself."

"You're not even three yet," Annie scoffed. "How can you read?"

"She kin read if she wants to," Eve said, taking Pete's side as always. "Gimme them flowers, Annie," Eve ordered, then took the dogwood from Annie and headed toward the house. "Pete kin read if Eve's got anything to say about it."

"It seems to me Eve's got everything to say about spoiling Pete," Anne called after her servant. "Now come on, all of you. Eve will arrange the flowers and we're all going to read Father Fraser's letter on the porch this minute."

CHAPTER 2

ANNE'S LONGTIME PROTECTOR AND RIDING ESCORT, Big Boy, the giant Ebo Papa had given John to serve as groom and fisherman, was already leading Ginger in the direction of the stables as the four Frasers settled into chairs—Pete with a big rocker all her own.

While John unfolded the single-page letter, he looked at Pete in mock surprise. "I thought you were going to read some of this," he said. "Don't you want to sit on my lap and try?"

"Nope."

"Why not?" Anne asked.

"Because I can't wait for me. All of you know Grandfather Fraser and I don't. I'm in a hurry to find out when he's coming to live in Georgia with Uncle William and Aunt Frances Anne in Darien, so I can go visit."

"You don't even know Grandfather Fraser's coming at all," Annie said in disgust. "You're just awfully young sometimes, Pete. Read, Papa. Aren't you all prickly to know what he says?"

"Of course. You bet I am," John said, in a tone Anne didn't even try to interpret.

When Pete yelled "Read, Papa!" in a voice that actually hurt Anne's ears, she informed the child that she simply *had* to stop those sudden, piercing shouts.

"Why?" Pete asked.

"Because I said so."

"Why did you say so if you don't know any reason?"

"In the name of heaven, John, do as the child asks. Read!"

"Father wrote this on March twelfth, just over five weeks ago," John said, scanning the single page. "And this is what the old gentleman found to say: 'My dear family, Our weather is as usual for March with a colder wind than a man my age desires, but there are more important matters to be told here. First of all, since I am well aware that you will want to be reassured about Flora McLeod, she seems both sad and eager to be returning to Scotland to live out her days.' "

Stunned, Anne sat up. "Flora is going to leave Father Fraser? She's going back to Scotland to live?"

John was frowning. Plainly, he was reading ahead to himself. When he looked up, she saw the same frightened-boy look she'd seen so often at the dining table in London when his father was abrupt with him. "Aye," John said, his eyes on the letter again. "Flora McLeod is returning to Dumfries to live with her sister."

"Why?" Pete demanded.

"Why do you care?" Annie asked, impatiently for her. "You don't even know Flora McLeod. You don't even know Grandfather Fraser, for that matter."

"But I do," her mother said firmly, "and I too want to know why. John, will you *please* read the remainder of the letter to us?"

With no comment, John read aloud: " 'I made no final plans until Flora and I had settled her journey back to Dumfries and I was certain that she would be able to take up her abode with her sister. The faithful woman has been with us too long for me to pull up stakes and leave to live out my own days in Georgia without first making certain of her well-being.' "

"John!" Anne exclaimed. "Father Fraser's coming! He hasn't responded to any of our attempts to persuade him for a whole year. Now, suddenly, he's coming!"

"Isn't that just like him?" John asked. "In fact, he's probably on the high seas right now, if I'm reading this correctly. He's left it to me to find out, of course, but he gives his possible docking date in Savannah as sometime before the tenth of May."

Annie gasped, "Papa, oh Papa!"

"What is it, Annie dear? You're crying." John did his best to smile easily at his elder daughter. "Annie, are you so happy, you're crying?"

For an instant no one moved. Even Pete was quiet. Anne could see tears running unashamedly down Annie's face, but the girl was smiling, too. And as though mother and daughter had at that moment changed hearts, Anne realized fully how lonely her firstborn had been since the day she'd said goodbye to Father Fraser and the only home she'd ever known, at 2 George Street, London. Eleven was a difficult age at best: the time when a girl reaches ahead to womanhood but also strongly back toward the dear familiarity of being a dependent child. No one could doubt that Annie had been mostly happy living in their snug cottage at Lawrence. Despite her ladylike ways, the girl had plainly loved learning to swim in Lawrence Creek, which wound it's serpentine way past their dock. She liked to climb trees, then swing out and down on thick, twisted bullis grapevines. But how much of Annie had remained restless, isolated, lonely for the sights and smells and sounds of London?

I didn't stop missing the woods, the marshes, the songbirds, and the sun rising out of the ocean in all the years John and I were abroad, Anne thought, watching Annie's eager, tearstreaked face; watching John's face too. No mother could doubt the pure joy welling inside young Annie. But what about John? Is he relieved or distressed that Father Fraser is coming? Or that once here, he will indeed prefer to live with William in Darien? Worse still, is John afraid to face his stern, blunt-spoken parent sooner than we expected? Afraid that my own papa might say something that would let Father Fraser know how much John still has to learn about being a successful planter? Is he afraid that Papa might let slip the fact that last year John *ordered* his fieldhands to make cottonseed beds too close together and mounded up, when they should have been five feet apart and flat, so that some of the crop was lost because it dropped its pods too soon?

Papa had been philosophical about John's costly mistake, but to this day no one dared mention it to John, so great was his humiliation. "It happened," he'd explained to Anne, "on one of those wretched days when I was so determined to be strict enough with the poor Negroes that I went against what they all knew far better than I."

John had never seemed one bit afraid of Anne's father. In fact, all through spring planting this year, she thought her husband had actually begun to enjoy consulting with him as together they made their seed selections and decided which crops to rotate. Of course Anne's father was a born encourager. Father Fraser, she well remembered, had either sat in stony silence or given no more than a satisfied grunt when John managed to add a new client to the Fraser firm's sales listing.

Pete was sitting back in her chair in totally unaccustomed silence, her chubby legs straight out in front of her because the chair was so high. Finally Pete shrilled, "Why is Grandfather Fraser coming here?"

Anne could have hugged her. The abrupt question had seemed to relieve John of whatever had appeared to be almost choking him. He laughed his nearly normal laugh and Anne began to smile too.

"That's an excellent question, Pete," he said. "In fact, I'm proud of you for asking it."

Naturally, Pete cocked her head and wanted to know why.

"Because I was just asking myself the same thing. But let's both hold our curiosity until I've read to the end of his letter. Listen. 'I firmly request that you *not* inform my son William of my arrival because he is a busy doctor and I have no intention of interrupting his practice of medicine to meet me in Savannah when my boat docks. Of course I plan to make my home in Darien, Georgia, with

William and his wife and young son, my namesake, James William, but I would be obliged if you, John, would arrange to meet
my boat at the Savannah wharf near the middle of May. I'm sure
you will be able to find out through your excellent connections
with Mr. John Couper the approximate arrival time. I would be
most pleased for you, Anne, and both children to meet me. In case
you haven't surmised by now, I have sold my firm for enough to
pay my passage and to help William defray my living expenses.' "

For several moments no one said a word. When Annie jumped
up suddenly and excused herself, at least Anne knew that the child
was so overjoyed because Grandfather Fraser was coming, she
simply had to be alone. But with no change in his rocklike expression, John asked, as though thinking aloud, "What's ailing her, I
wonder?"

"Don't you know, dearest?" Anne asked carefully.

"I do not."

"Well," Anne offered, "it makes sense to me that Annie is
afraid we won't understand how happy she really is that Father
Fraser is on his way at last. You know the child has always been
deeply attached to him. John, for our sake, she's tried so earnestly
to act contented since we've been back here."

"I suppose her delight that my father is coming means she'll
want to spend most of her time in Darien once he's up there."

John's remark, edged with sarcasm, was more than Anne
needed to let her know for sure that he was indeed scared, even
willing to feign jealousy over the deep bond that had always existed between his father and his gentle daughter. Her poor John, at
least where Father Fraser was concerned, *was* still immature—a
little boy battling for his parent's approval.

"Pete, go find your sister," Anne said.

"Why, Mama? I don't want her."

Tossing the letter aside, John jumped up, whisked Pete out of
her chair, and lifted her high above his head. "You certainly don't
have to go find your sister, Petey," he said, his forced laugh sounding flat on the afternoon air. "Most of the time I want you to obey
your mother, but right now I'm glad you're here with us. Do you
hear me, young lady?"

Shrieking with laughter, Pete grabbed a handful of John's short, dark hair and whooped, "Do you both want to know why Grandfather Fraser is coming?"

Holding the wriggling child straight in front of him now, John said in mock seriousness, "I most certainly do want to know."

"Because he can't wait a minute longer to see *me!*"

Unable not to smile, Anne said, "We can give thanks daily that our younger daughter is so humble."

John put Pete down and looked straight at Anne. "She's almost as humble as her grandfather Fraser has made me feel," he said, his voice suddenly grim. "This is nothing new, of course, but it would never occur to my father that I might also be busy in the spring of the year. Or that Frances Anne, with a young child to tend, might need to make preparations for his arrival. Naturally, only William's needs have ever been considered first."

CHAPTER 3

FOR THE NEXT FEW DAYS AND NIGHTS, THE ATMO-
sphere between Anne and John when they were alone was so much
like the early years in London that Anne felt caught again in the
old trap of uncertainty about what he was really thinking. Had she
been foolish to believe his decision to return to Georgia freed her
once and for all from feeling shut away from him except when his
lovemaking seemed to unlock the very soul of the man? Was it
possible that John could still fool her as he once did? Had he only
been pretending that he worked the huge fields with a growing
interest?

His lovemaking last night had been, as always, at once stormy
and golden. The same elevating oblivion to everything and everyone else but the two of them invariably brought pure peace once
the bright, wild storm had passed. Why couldn't that peace reach
into the confusion and busyness of the next day? she wondered for
the thousandth time as she sat alone by the dining room window,

making a puckery mess of the lace edging she was stitching onto a new collar for Annie's Sunday dress.

I need desperately to talk to someone, she thought, but I can't worry Mama or Papa. Maybe I am just imagining that John has closed himself away again behind his wit and overcheerfulness because he so dreads Father Fraser's arrival. Flora McLeod would understand, would come up with some sage, no-nonsense piece of advice, but Flora must by now be back in Scotland. I'll probably never see her again on this earth.

I could have Papa's oarsmen row me up to Darien to spend a few days with Frances Anne, but that's a dumb idea. She's married to William, and he, poor man, is contributing to John's strange mood and he isn't even aware that he's doing it, since Father Fraser doesn't want him told yet that he's coming to Georgia to live with him and his family. Frances Anne certainly deserves to know Father Fraser is on his way so that she can set her household in order. But I'm bound to silence by Father Fraser's wishes.

During their first weeks at Father Fraser's George Street house in London, Anne had worked hard to win over her dour, difficult Scottish father-in-law. She'd believed she understood why the older man went on scaring John, making him feel inferior to William, his younger brother. Why, suddenly, was it all such a mystery to her? Papa had fixed everything, hadn't he? John was no longer searching for himself, for a way to earn a living. Thanks to Papa's gift of Lawrence and enough people to work at least part of the land, John had seemed mostly happy, certainly earnest in his efforts to learn how to plant.

Could John still fool her as he once had done? Did he only pretend to like the other Island families—the Wyllys at the Village, the Caters, Captain Frewin at Frederica, grief-stricken Mr. James Gould, still mourning the death of his adored wife, Janie? Even the haughty Hazzard brothers, William and Thomas now living at West Point and Pike's Bluff, thought John exceedingly desirable company. Everyone the Coupers knew held Anne's husband in high esteem. When Anne's picky, brilliant brother James Hamilton held a boat race on the Frederica River, he'd settle for no one less than John Fraser to act as master of ceremonies. Within a year after their return to St. Simons, John Fraser was conducting the festivities at almost every large, social event attended by St. Simons planter families, especially Papa's favorite St. Clair Club meetings. Had John thought he was beginning to enjoy himself in his new work only because he found himself suddenly in demand? Had he been acting when he cultivated Anna Matilda's husband, the polished, slightly arrogant Thomas Butler King?

Anne thought back to the first meeting between John and Thomas King a week after their return. She also remembered with some discomfort a comment John made in the carriage on the way home to Lawrence that evening: "Thomas Butler King's a gentleman all right. Every inch a gentleman, but I can see he's fallen right into being a slave owner despite his having been born in Massachusetts. He's already thinking like a typical Southern planter."

John hated slavery. Was he worried about having to defend the irrefutable fact that he would soon have to attend the slave market in Savannah or Charleston to buy more help to farm each new Lawrence field now being cleared for planting?

Thinking of Anna Matilda's husband sent Anne's thoughts to Anna Matilda herself, these days a sorrow-filled, grown woman. She was still Anne's best friend, but somehow a stranger in her determination to keep on with her mounting duties as the mistress of flourishing Retreat Plantation in spite of the heart-crushing loss of both her parents within months of each other. Anne missed the clinging, naive, pampered child Anna Matilda had once been, missed her very dependence. A year older than her friend, Anne had invariably been the leader, Anna Matilda the willing, even eager follower.

This morning, with her two daughters and John at Cannon's Point, she longed to see Anna Matilda. The two friends were both mothers now. Anna Matilda had a girl, Hannah, only a few weeks older than Pete, and a son, William Page King, not yet two. These days the friends saw little of each other. Anne thought it a waste. The friendship meant too much. Her friend spent much of her time, she knew, seeing to plantation business because Thomas's driving political ambitions often kept him away. Anna Matilda also believed in spending hours with her children. In fact, she had caused Anne to flare a little the last time she'd visited at Lawrence and informed her that she just didn't trust the full care of her own little ones to any of her people. Anne supposed she had resented the remark because day after day she gave in to Eve's demands to look after Annie and Pete most of the time. Eve had walked over to Cannon's Point this morning with the girls, in spite of Anne's insistence that Big Boy could easily have taken them in the wagon. Pete had wanted to walk, so they walked.

Sometimes I think Eve owns me, Anne thought, and it infuriates me. Still, she seems to have improved as a nursemaid. Maybe I just don't want to admit that she has. Maybe I miss her paying attention to me every minute the way it used to be before John and I were married.

Anne took a deep breath, examined the ugly mess she was making of whipping the edging onto the collar, and tossed it aside. On her feet, she hurried out to the porch, where she felt she could think more clearly than shut inside a room on such a bright spring morning.

The day was so clear, so cloudless, she imagined that she could see the needles on the tall, round-topped pines over on Little St. Simons Island, which lay beside the sea, far across tiny, winding Lawrence Creek, beyond the Hampton River and the stretches of brown and green marsh. For a wonder, no one was in sight except Big Boy, fishing alone in a small skiff beyond the second curve in the creek Anne had come to love as her very own because it ran past *her* place on St. Simons Island. The well-repaired tabby cottage at Lawrence, her front yard, and every pine, oak, and cedar were hers. In London she had tried to picture Lawrence Plantation with some of its fertile fields cleared of their tall trees, their tangles of smilax, wild-berry hoops, fallen logs, and palmettos. Cleared and neatly planted. She'd pictured the sagging roof of the old Lawrence house as it was now—sturdy and tightly covered with tin to hold off the rain and the pressing heat of the hot summer sun in July and August. On some overcast, rainy, smoky London days she'd seemed actually to see her cottage as it now was—the porch on which she stood firmly buttressed, its new floor painted a cool, dark green, the white banisters without one missing spindle. She'd almost seen herself, Anne Couper Fraser, standing where she now stood, dressed in the old yellow cotton walking skirt John loved enough for her to have worn it to Caerlaverock on their honeymoon the first day they'd visited there.

She was wearing the same yellow skirt and shirtwaist today. Anne smiled, remembering how carefully Flora had mended the tear in the skirt put there when she'd jumped carelessly from a London carriage just before she and John took the stage for Liverpool to begin their joyful journey back to St. Simons.

Had John really been as joyful as he seemed that day? Had he been relieved to be leaving behind the part of him that had known unease all his life because Father Fraser admitted to favoring even-keeled William?

Now Father Fraser was coming to America! The old gentleman was nearing seventy, as was Anne's own father, so he would be living just eighteen miles or so away from them until he died. "I don't want Father Fraser to die—*ever*," she said aloud. The thought of no more good conversations with the elderly Scotsman brought real pain to Anne's heart as she stood on her pretty front porch with its bright, flowered chair cushions she'd made with her own hands. Her pain now was even sharper than the pain she'd felt when Father Fraser had given her his last affectionate, dry kiss the morning she and John rode away from 2 George Street in a hired London cab. The truth was, Anne loved Father James Fraser with all her heart. Loved him in many of the same ways she loved her own papa. The two had become so close during the years she and John lived in his house, that in an entirely different way from the way she leaned on Papa, Anne had begun to depend on Father Fraser, wanted him always to be a part of her life.

"If only I could tell someone even a little bit of how it hurts me that his coming upsets John—no matter how he pretends."

She spoke aloud freely since there was no one in sight except Big Boy contentedly fishing in his boat out on Lawrence Creek beyond their landing. "How can it make me so happy and John so unhappy? How could he love me as he did last night, though, if he's truly unhappy about anything?"

Had Anna Matilda's late mother been right when she warned both girls that love, even real love, had a different meaning for men? Anne had shrugged off the warning years ago when Mrs. Page had first spoken it. She and John weren't man and wife back then, but Anne knew as firmly as she knew her own name that Mrs. Page had to be wrong, at least about the love *Anne* had found. John had to love her in the same way she loved him. Didn't he prove it each time they filled each other with the stormy glory alone in their room at night? Surely he remembered the next day as she did. Writing a letter, playing with Pete, or in the middle of a discussion with Eve or Annie or Mina—even while doing something dull like sewing—Anne inevitably remembered, could feel her thoughts being invaded by John's love. Surely he did too. Much of his work bored him. No one knew that better than Anne, but even one of Papa's earnest, excited lectures on the wonder of a greening cotton field or the value of crop rotation could possibly keep John's deepest, secret thoughts from being invaded by their shared ecstasy.

"You not by yo'sef, Miss Anne." Eve startled her from the porch doorway. "You been talkin' out loud to yo'sef. I thought you want to know Eve's right here too."

Anne whirled to face the bright-skinned woman who was only a year younger than she but seldom acted young. "What are you doing here, Eve? You're supposed to be with the children—at Cannon's Point!"

Eve stepped out onto the porch. "I be sent home by yo mama."

"Why? What happened?"

Eve only shrugged. Anne was annoyed. "You know I hate it when you don't answer. Something happened and you didn't like it, so tell me what it was."

"How you know I don' lak it?"

"Because you're pouting. Tell me what's wrong. Do you hear me?"

"Co'se I hears you, Miss Anne. Ain' no reason why not." Eve spoke calmly now. "I might look it, but I ain' poutin'. I jus' don' understan' nobody but you."

"But you and Mama got on so well while I was in London! She

was the one who discovered your talent for painting pictures. You're acting most ungrateful. Why did my mother send you back here? Are the girls all right?"

"Yes'm. Pete, she be playin' wif her cornhusk doll Gran'maum Sofy done give her. Miss Annie, she readin' a book lak always. Don' seem lak yo mama she lak me no more now that I lib here at Lawrence wif you an' Mausa John."

"That's ridiculous and you know it. Papa gladly gave both you and June to us. You also know my husband doesn't like it when you call him mausa."

"He be my mausa."

"Well, maybe. I mean—oh, never mind what I mean. Who's going to bring Annie and Pete home after they've had dinner with my parents?"

"Yo mama, she say June, he walk 'em back. He be at Cannon's Point graftin' trees for yo papa. Miz Couper, she say after a big meal a walk be good for Annie an' Pete."

Anne could remember no other area in their lives where she and her mother ever basically disagreed except in handling servants. Her mother had always insisted that Anne, so quick in most things, simply had never grasped how to be firm enough. Well, today was not the time for Mama to pull a teaching trick like this! I'm already too worried about John, she thought. I don't know how to help him because I can't tell for sure how he feels about Father Fraser's arrival. I am not going to waste my energy playing discipline games with Mama! "Eve, are you sure you didn't do something to annoy my mother?"

"No more'n usual."

"What does that mean?"

"Went by to see my own mama an' Gran'maum Sofy."

Then Anne knew. "And did you take Pete with you?"

"Yes'm. I took 'er. She sho lak my Gran'maum Sofy."

"And you know perfectly well that my mother objects to your taking such a young child there!"

"Ain' no law."

"Of course there's no law." Deliberately, she turned her back on Eve and stood looking out over Lawrence Creek, where the gentle giant, Big Boy, had moved his skiff in toward their dock. "Why can't you be pleasant and uncomplicated like Big Boy?" she snapped at Eve.

"'Cause I'm not simpleminded."

Eve spoke so calmly, with such poise, Anne felt herself growing more and more confused. "Can't you tell I'm—upset?" she demanded. "Why are you just standing there acting as though you never lose your temper or irritate anyone, when you're rubbing me so much the wrong way? I'm—I'm worried about—well, about several things, Eve, and I wish you'd go on back in the house and leave me alone. I have to think something through."

"Yo man, he troublin' you, ain' he?"

Surprised, Anne wheeled around to look at her. "Why would you say a dumb thing like that?"

"'Cause you tol' me lotsa times Mausa John, he be happier by far here without the trouble of reachin' after his papa's pat on the head. Everybody knows his papa's on the ocean now headin' this way."

Of course she had told Eve how nearly carefree John had seemed with no contact between him and his father beyond an exchange of letters. Just admitting to herself that she had been the one to confide in Eve irritated her still more. It irritated her now because it proved Mama was right. Anne had allowed Eve to become a friend and that was never a good idea with any servant, no matter how essential that servant may be. Eve wouldn't be sticking in her oar at a time like this otherwise.

"I've had enough," Anne said, turning her back again. "You must have work you need to be doing."

"Oh, I kin allus sponge and freshen your dress-up gowns," Eve said, her voice sounding unusually pleasant. "It allus make Eve glad to be doin' fer you, Miss Anne. Lessen the chu'rn needs me."

"Then I wish you'd go sponge and freshen," Anne said sharply. "I was quite busy when you barged in just now."

"You didn't look busy to me."

"Never mind how I looked to you. I was—*thinking* and I—I need to go on thinking. In fact, I wish you'd lay out my riding clothes first thing tomorrow morning, please. And ask June to send

Big Boy straight to talk to me later today when he brings the girls home. I've just decided to spend tomorrow at Retreat with Anna Matilda. I need to talk to someone who will truly understand."

"Nobody understand you but Eve, Miss Anne."

"Well, you don't understand—*this.*"

"You tellin' me Eve ain't smart enough?"

"I'm telling you you're smart-*aleck.*"

CHAPTER 4

ALTHOUGH THERE WAS A TENDER, LAVENDER SUN-
rise the next morning, the sky was overcast and gray by the time
Eve helped Anne dress in her riding clothes for the trip down the
Island to spend the day with Anna Matilda.

"It won't rain," John assured her when he escorted her out to
the lane in front of their cottage, where Big Boy waited with jet
black Gentleman, Anne's own horse, and Papa's feisty Buck saddled and groomed for himself, ready for their ride. "I guarantee
not one raindrop will fall on you and faithful Big Boy, my love."
John was talking a lot again, saying unnecessary things in a voice
too cheerful to fool her at all. "You know how coastal skies clear,
then cloud over, take on a rainy look," he went on. "But those
aren't rain clouds."

"You've become a coastal expert, haven't you?" she asked,
clinging to his arm, smiling up at him.

He laughed. "If you think so, then I have indeed," he said
lightly. Too lightly.

"John, you're awfully conversational, aren't you?" Her voice was far more serious than she intended. She'd have to think of something lighthearted to say and quickly, or he'd guess how worried she felt. "One thing I do know and that is you're beginning to sound a lot like Papa."

"Then good for me!" He kissed her on the cheek and gestured for Big Boy, who loped up beaming, his big hand out for Anne to use as a mounting block. With his and John's help, Anne now sat her horse.

"What will you be doing today?" she asked John, who had taken her hand.

"Working, milady," he answered with a slight bow. "In fact, your illustrious father and I will be submitting the Lawrence north fields to your equally illustrious, but far more critical, brother James Hamilton for his approval of what we've accomplished this week."

"Don't let James intimidate you, promise? Tell him your work has already been more than approved—by me!"

"I'll tell him first thing," John said, planting a kiss on her hand. Then he waved to Big Boy, who waved back, still beaming because he was the one to be riding along to look after Miss Anne.

"I feel like a young girl again," Anne called as she and Big Boy walked their horses along the lane Papa had years ago lovingly planted with live oaks and cedars—one oak, then one cedar, then another oak, and so on to the point where the Lawrence lane entered Couper Road, which would take them out to Frederica, the Island's one north-south thoroughfare.

At her last sight of him, John still stood waving both arms above his head. Help him today, God, she breathed. I know how nervous he is with my finicky brother here peering and making notes.

After a time, they trotted out the long stretch to Frederica Road and headed south, Big Boy riding Buck a bit in front and to one side of her as he'd always done when protecting her in the old days when she was still just a girl. Typically, he looked back once and smiled, then waved, and off they went down the tree-arched, narrow shell lane at a gallop.

It may be the best idea I've ever had to talk with Anna Matilda today, she thought. John and Annie seemed pleased that I'm going. Even Pete only begged a little to come along.

In no time, as John promised, the sun flashed out, so that Buck, the horse no one but Big Boy and Papa could handle, and Anne's own Gentleman cantered briskly through patches of bright sunlight into black shadow. John is catching on at least to the weather in coastal Georgia, she thought. God help him to learn how to feel at home here. . . .

THEY HAD PASSED MR. JAMES GOULD'S well-cared-for place at New St. Clair and were almost at the northern boundary of Ben Cater's Kelvin Grove Plantation when Anne remembered another day on which she and Big Boy had made the same invigorating ride to Retreat. Another day, back before either was married, when Anna Matilda had seemed much more than a year younger than Anne. In many ways those were carefree times for them both. Anne today, twelve years later, still felt far more experienced, far wiser than her childhood friend. In her reticule that long-ago day, Anne had carried the golden letter from John in which he had asked her to become his wife. The letter had been enclosed in a carefully wrapped package containing his mother's small, twisted gold brooch in a little blue velvet box. To Anne then, and still, it was a breathtakingly beautiful piece. Because she then felt both guilt and maturity, she had mentioned not one word of John's proposal to her parents. The guilt came, she recognized even then, because it was the first time in her entire life she'd kept anything of importance from Mama and Papa.

For Anna Matilda, surely, it had been a far more carefree time, since both her doting parents, affable Mrs. Page and handsome, slightly younger Major William Page, were still alive, still anticipating Anna Matilda's every need and wish. Anne gave thanks that the sun had come out because her own heart grew suddenly heavy when she and Big Boy headed down the Retreat lane today. Dear Mrs. Page would not be out on the veranda with Anna Matilda

waiting for Anne. The Retreat lane was long enough so that somehow Mrs. Page had always managed to assemble all her house
servants to greet Anne, to welcome her . . . lovable Mrs. Page,
merrily fat and cheerful, dressed in spotless white, a cap like snow
on her dark hair, its familiar three blue gauze bows in front.

Anne slowed Gentleman abruptly and when Big Boy slowed
too, she said, "I'm—I'm awfully glad you're with me today, Big
Boy."

The huge black man smiled so tenderly, so expectantly, she
knew she had to think of some special reason to be glad he had
come. "I'm suddenly—terribly sad," she murmured. "Do you realize this is the first time you and I have ridden down here to Retreat
together since Mrs. Page died? Then Major Page just months
later? I'm going to miss them both terribly! Oh, I know I've been
here to see Anna Matilda and her husband, but only with my
parents and John and James Hamilton and, well, they all talked
and thought of the right, sympathetic things to say to Anna Matilda and Mr. King and the servants. Don't you know all the
servants miss them both too? How am I going to know what to say
—all by myself when my own heart feels as though it's breaking in
two?"

They had reined in both horses. Big Boy sat Buck in silence, his
huge, heavily muscled frame straight as a ramrod, but his head
hung down and Anne could see the massive shoulders shake. He
was crying. Big Boy, the gentle Ebo, who had survived the long-
ago suicide attempt made by a boatload of Ebo captives. The sixty
or seventy slaves had been illegally purchased by Anne's own law-
abiding father and the equally respectable Mr. Thomas Spalding of
Sapelo. Proud, freedom-loving Ebo Africans, twelve of whom
managed to drown themselves in Dunbar Creek rather than be
mastered by any white man in Georgia or anywhere else so far
away from their native land. Papa, she knew, still felt deep shame
for the unlawful purchase, especially since he and Spalding had
both signed the Georgia Constitution, which forbade continued
importation of slaves into the state. She knew Papa still thought
about what he had done back when Anne was only six, because
through the years he had told her again and again that Eve's

husband, Ebo June, also a survivor of the tragedy, was solely responsible for the fact that the slow-witted Big Boy had turned out
so well. June had, from the Ebos' first night in the slave pen at
Cannon's Point, taken Big Boy under his personal protection. June
had more or less adopted Big Boy, and June may well be the
smartest, most intelligent slave Papa owned.

I've got to stop doing that, Anne scolded herself, still looking at
the sniffling Big Boy sitting Buck beside her. I've been taught all
my life never to call our people—slaves. I lived in London too
long! Everyone there disapproves of slavery so much, they seem
almost to enjoy calling attention to the word. I've grown too used
to it. I find myself *thinking* the word *slave,* even if I know I
wouldn't dream of saying it out loud.

Big Boy raised his head now and looked right at Anne, something June had certainly taught him never to do. No Negro male
should ever look squarely at a white lady, even if they got along
fine as did Anne and Big Boy. He was looking *at* her, though, and
it was all right with Anne. She had simply touched his great,
loving heart by speaking of how she'd miss Major and Mrs. Page
today.

"I be sorry, Miss Anne," he said brokenly. "Big Boy, he wanta
help so bad. He can' do nuffin' but fish. But he wanta help so bad!"

"You do help, Big Boy. Isn't that what I said to you just now?
Didn't I tell you how glad I am that it's you with me today? Just
knowing you're out there in one of the Retreat skiffs fishing quietly, not complaining if I'm here a long time—that helps me so
much! Thank you. Thank you."

When his broad, dark face lit up, Anne added, "You see, it's
terribly important that I have a good talk with my friend Mrs.
Thomas Butler King today. And you've made that possible. You
know neither my father nor my husband wants me to ride any
distance alone. We all depend on you."

Big Boy said nothing. He only nodded in agreement. He knew
he was dependable. He was.

Anna Matilda had been told by one of the servants that Anne and Big Boy were heading down the Retreat lane, so she was waiting and waving from the veranda with six or seven house servants when the two horses trotted down the lane.

"Now don't fidget, Rutty," Anna Matilda scolded. "I know you want to whip up Miss Anne's favorite dessert, but that can wait. My mother always had all of you out here to greet her and I want you here too."

Lady, who called herself the head, gave Rutty a tap on the arm. "You hear what Missus said, Rutty. Stop squirmin' aroun'. They be plenty ob time fo' you to fix arr'-root puddin' while Missus an' Miss Anne, they doin' they talkin'.'"

"That's right, Lady," Anna Matilda said absently, already curious about the reason for Anne's visit. Because her own life had lately been filled with sorrow, she hoped nothing serious was wrong. Her eyes stung with tears. The mere act of meeting Anne on the veranda caused her to miss her own mother so sharply, Anna Matilda was thankful for once that she was alone. The absences of her husband, Thomas, got no easier. She was proud of him, heaven knew; would never say one word to discourage him in his new political ambitions, but too many people had left her of late. First Mama, then Papa's sudden death from his heart. Thomas's departure yesterday had seemed almost the final straw. A visit today from her best friend meant everything.

Blinking back the tears, she informed her own childhood nurse, Haynie, that she was to keep the two small King children occupied after dinner—outside, if possible—so that there would be uninterrupted time for her to spend with Anne.

Seated in small, handsomely carved rocking chairs near the window of the Retreat master bedroom, the two friends, alone at last after warm greetings, looked at each other for a moment, then tears began to roll down their cheeks.

"I'm—I'm so sorry," Anna Matilda said, drying her eyes in a futile gesture because the tears kept coming. "This is no way to receive you, especially after such a long time apart. But I *do* miss Mama and Papa so much!"

Her friend's silence was so lengthy, Anna Matilda's concern for Anne checked her own weeping. "Anne! Is—is something the matter? Are the children all right? John? Your parents? You've been so quiet. You're not very quiet usually, you know. Did you come today, as you said downstairs, just to pay me a visit?"

Still, Anne said nothing. Instead, she got slowly, almost stiffly, to her feet and went to stand by the window that looked out across the white Retreat sand beach toward the bright, glistening waters of St. Simons Sound, to the Atlantic—the view Anne had always thought so spectacular.

"Anne?"

"Can't you wait a minute?" Anne asked, her voice sounding choked. "I'm the one who should be sorry. Not you! I'm the one. Here I come running to you to—to console me when, compared with yours, there's nothing really wrong in my life at all!" Before Anna Matilda could say anything, Anne's words tumbled on. "I'm only—worried. Both my girls are fine. John is fine. My parents are, except for Papa's rheumatism, very well. And look at you! Oh Anna Matilda, I'm so ashamed of myself. Can you believe me when I tell you how stricken I am because you lost your dear parents within months of each other, that my heart is broken because yours is? Why do you think I began to cry too the minute we sat down here in this handsome, sunny room that used to belong to Major and Mrs. Page? I'm not used to thinking of you as being so grown-up and in charge of yourself. With Thomas away so much, you're in charge of everything! I keep thinking of you the way you always were—a whole year younger, expecting me to have answers for us both. You're truly a grown woman now, aren't you? Even Mama would admire the way you act with your servants."

"What's worrying you, Anne? Stop blathering and tell me."

Anna Matilda saw her friend cock her head in the familiar way that sometimes preceded a sharp retort. Instead, Anne turned from the window, lips trembling. "I—I really miss your parents. How do you get through your days without them? How do you keep walking around?"

Anna Matilda gave her what she hoped was a reassuring smile. "We all do what we have to do, Anne."

Turning abruptly back to the window, Anne asked, "But *how* do we know what to do?"

"You're sounding too philosophical for me, dear friend. More like your erudite brother James Hamilton, not his sister Anne. In grief, especially when one grief follows so closely on another, there is no question about what we do. We go on. Sometimes one hour at a time—even one minute at a time—but we go on. I have no choice. My parents are both—gone." When Anne said nothing, Anna Matilda moved to stand beside her at the window. "You made the ride down here for a reason today, didn't you? For a reason beyond just a friendly visit."

Anne nodded. "Yes. And I'm ashamed of myself! I came to pour out my worries to you. I didn't give enough thought to your broken heart. I'm worried over John because I love him so much and—I love you too, but friends are supposed to help each other and—and here I am still hoping you can tell me which way to turn."

"I knew something was wrong when you behaved in such an absentminded way down on the veranda with the servants."

The two friends held each other, Anna Matilda determined not to let go until she'd made up her mind just how honest, how blunt, she dared be with Anne. If I'm truly her best friend, I'll be truthful, she thought, and after another hug stepped back to look straight into Anne's light blue, troubled eyes. "Did you and John have a row?" she asked.

"No. Oh no. He's—he's even more loving than ever. I've never been shy about telling you what a golden lover John is, even though you've never told me about Thomas."

"I didn't think I needed to tell you. I wouldn't want to live one hour if I weren't Mrs. Thomas Butler King. I've told you that and I think that's enough."

"And you don't mind that he's away from home so much lately?"

"Of course I mind! I die a little every time he rides off."

"Don't you wonder why he leaves you so often?"

"No. He means to be elected from Georgia to the United States Congress someday. As he explains it, he's laying the groundwork now. Making new, influential friends. He knows we're all at his feet around here already. He doesn't have to cultivate any of us. The servants adore him. But the house is painfully empty for me without him. He tries, bless him, to compensate when he is at home and I accept that. I hate it when he goes, but he's my husband. I love him exactly the way he is."

"Does that mean you're still as meek and submissive as I always thought you were?" Anne asked.

Anna Matilda laughed a little. "You have always accused me of that. There was an edge in your voice when you accused me in the old days, though. I didn't hear an edge just now."

"I'm glad, because there wasn't one. I really want to know the truth about being submissive. I know you've never stopped thinking me selfish—at least sometimes."

With no hesitation Anna Matilda answered gently, "That's right, Anne. Oh, you can be generous beyond reason—the way my beloved father always said your papa is—but yes, you can be quite selfish. The very fact that you kept John so aware of your homesickness for St. Simons Island all the while you both lived in London proves it."

Anne's eyes opened in shock. "What? When did being homesick come to mean selfishness?"

"When a woman uses it to force a man into a life he fears. A kind of life he probably doesn't even believe in. Certainly one he dreads. Even you wrote from Scotland how John hated farming when he was a boy."

"Don't you think I know what I wrote in letters back then? He did hate farming, but his father didn't have fieldhands to do the hard work. John and his brother, William, had to do it."

"And now John does have fieldhands, so he's not supposed to hate farming any longer. Is that what you're saying?"

Anne frowned. "I don't know what I'm saying! I wish you'd stop being so high-and-mighty with me. Papa says John is learning fast about planting. Until Father Fraser wrote that he is right now on the high seas on his way to live here in coastal Georgia, I was sure John was learning to love planting almost the way Papa does. He and Papa are really close, Anna Matilda. My father brags on John. Even picky James Hamilton approves of John's supervision of the hands most of the time. But now—now that Father Fraser is actually coming, something has changed."

"I know you'll be glad to have your father-in-law over here, though. Don't you think John will be glad too?"

"That's what's worrying me! I'm not sure. Don't you see? My husband has fallen back into his old London ways. He talks a lot more than usual. He makes too many jokes. He *acts!* And if you don't think by now I know when he's hiding his real feelings behind what he used to call worldly ways, you're wrong. I know John Fraser through and through and I also love him just the way he is."

"Then what's worrying you? Anne, is it his father's disapproval of owning slaves? My dear papa warned me about that twice during the two days he lived after his heart began to fail."

"Major Page—warned about Father Fraser's dislike of our owning slaves in Georgia?"

"Yes. I've thought and thought especially about one good talk he and I had the day before he—went away. He seemed to be trying to assure me that he felt certain Thomas, even though he was born in Massachusetts, realized no Southern gentleman could hope to be successful as a planter without owning people. He impressed on me the truth of Thomas's kind heart. His love for us. He said I needn't worry ever that my husband would grow restless and agitate to sell this land here because of his Northern upbringing. Papa was that certain of Thomas's belief that if an owner treated his people in a kindly manner, owning didn't make all that much difference. He used John—your John—as an example. The two of them had talked it over right after Mama died. Papa knew John didn't believe in owning other human beings, but he thought John had rather resigned himself to it for your sake. John must have told him how his own father disapproved—most of the British do—so I think Papa was, in his way, rather preparing me for this important talk with you."

Back in her rocker again, Anne sat for a long time, silent. Finally she said, "I'm not worried about John and any of our people. I'm worried about John himself. Just when he was starting to become interested in planting, he's acting scared now because Father Fraser is coming. That's the way John is. When he's afraid of something, he talks too much, laughs too often when nothing's very funny. He acts. I know when he's acting and that's what he's doing now. Father Fraser has never even tried to hide the fact that William is his favorite son. John is man enough to have accepted that. He's always known that his father wouldn't live with us at Lawrence, that he'd want to be with William and Frances Anne in Darien. But since my beautiful John is just learning how to be a planter, he's sure deep inside that Father Fraser won't approve of his work at Lawrence and Cannon's Point. He's really been a big help to Papa, you know. This year especially, he seems to be getting better and better at understanding how to hill the cotton, when and how often it needs to be hoed—all that dreary stuff. But Anna Matilda, Father Fraser's approval is the *one thing John has never had.* And I know as sure as that we're sitting here together in these chairs that James Hamilton will slip and say something critical, and Father Fraser will chide John. John will just curl up inside if that happens!" Anne held out both hands in a helpless gesture. "How am I supposed to be in all this? Am I supposed to pretend to John that I think he isn't a bit scared? That he's as happy as I am that his father will be living less than twenty miles away in Darien? Don't you see why I'm upset? You're just sitting there looking so proper, so condescending. And *daring* to tell me I'm selfish when all I'm trying to do is find out how I'm supposed to be with John." Jumping to her feet, Anne demanded, "What *did* you really mean when you called me selfish for wanting to be back in coastal Georgia, where my children can grow up breathing clean air? Where they can put down roots?"

"Your daughter Annie still misses London. She misses her friends there. But Anne, I wasn't thinking of the children when I called you selfish. I was thinking of John."

"He had no way to support us in London! What he was able to earn working with Father Fraser was so little. He tried as hard as any man could try to regain his commission in the Royal Navy, but they didn't need him any longer. John really wants me to be happy, whether you believe it or not. He decided on his own to come back to Georgia. John needs to put down roots too."

The time had come for Anna Matilda to come right out with it. She took a deep breath. "Anne, *you* never once let John forget, the whole time you lived abroad, that you could be happy nowhere else but in coastal Georgia. How much choice did the man really have?" She could see the color drain from Anne's face, but no matter how much she needed her best friend, especially now, Anna Matilda had to be totally honest with her. "I remember picturing you and John during the years you wrote to me from England. I pictured your struggle to understand him when he just kept on trying to regain his commission. You did try. You tried, quite sacrificially, but you also kept him reminded every minute that you were homesick, that you were forever rooted right here on St. Simons Island. Anne, has it ever occurred to you that you're trying to shape John into something he isn't? Has it ever crossed your mind that John might be afraid of being rooted? You've admitted today that you know John is afraid his own father won't be impressed with what he's doing now."

"What does that have to do with John's putting down roots?"

"Only that he might also be *afraid* of being rooted. Have you ever thought of that?"

"No, of course not! Everyone needs roots."

"But even a healthy plant needs time to put them down."

"I suppose so," Anne said, pleating and unpleating the corner of the light scarf she wore. Finally she said, a bit of the old superior tone in her voice, "I expected too much of you, Anna Matilda. I'm sorry."

"What did you expect of me?"

"I need to know how I'm supposed to act with John's putting on such a big show of overdoing everything the way he used to." She got to her feet. "I should go now. You think I'm making a mountain out of a molehill, don't you?"

"No. I find myself wondering often exactly what Thomas is thinking about one thing or another. Exactly how he feels down inside about something. No woman can ever completely know a man, Mama always said."

"She also told us both that unmarried women have a far simpler, easier time of it. At least I remember she said something like that. But I wouldn't want Annie or Pete to miss loving someone as I love their father." When Anna Matilda made no comment, she said with a half-grin, "At least we can both be glad we're not married to my brilliant, strict, disciplined brother James Hamilton. Do you ever feel downright sorry for Caroline Wylly Couper? I do. I know Papa always told James to marry a very young girl so that he could train her to be the kind of wife *he* wanted, but can you ever forget their wedding day last year at the Wyllys'? James looked at his watch right in the middle of the ceremony! The whole wedding party was left behind when *his* scheduled time came for them to leave. Even the young girls giggled. I would have giggled, too, except that I know my brother."

"I know how the younger women pitied Caroline that day," Anna Matilda said, "but she'll always be able to depend on James. She'll always know exactly where he is—even when he's away on business—and when he finishes remodeling that huge old tabby sugarhouse at Hopeton, she'll be the mistress of a splendid plantation mansion. None of this means I'd trade either of our husbands for a successful, brainy gentleman like your brother, even though he's known now on both sides of the Atlantic for his engineering expertise and his planting innovations."

"I certainly didn't ride all the way down here for a lecture on my brother's virtues," Anne said, trying to smile again. "I should have known you'd have no real advice for me."

Anna Matilda laughed softly, almost sadly. "Anne Fraser, I'm just not accustomed to your asking me for advice. You were always the strong one in our friendship." She hugged Anne again. "I wish you wouldn't go yet."

"Why? You must have a hundred things to do around here." Anne returned the hug, then looked straight at Anna Matilda. "I

—I don't mean to be selfish. Will you believe me when I say such a thing had never crossed my mind?"

"Yes, I believe you. Maybe what comes out as selfish now is only the natural result of your always having known exactly what you want. Also what you want of the rest of us."

Anne feigned a shudder. "That sounds beastly, but I hereby promise you that I'll give all you've said a lot of thought. And please forgive me for complaining. I'm sure you're at least a little bit right about my being selfish."

Anna Matilda smiled. "I only meant you're a little bit selfish."

"Do you have any idea how much I admire you, Mrs. Thomas Butler King?"

Anna Matilda felt herself blush. "You—admire me? I've always been the one to admire you, Mrs. John Fraser."

In the downstairs hall at Retreat, Anne said, "You know I've already decided you're absolutely right about my selfishness. I have both my blessed parents. They're reasonably well. John doesn't leave me except for an occasional trip with Papa or James Hamilton to Brunswick or Darien. He's even taking the children and me along when he goes to Savannah to meet Father Fraser. You're not just a little bit right. You're wholly right about me! I'm a spoiled, selfish woman."

"Hush! Anne, I'm so happy Father Fraser is coming to Georgia. I know how fond you are of him. And even though he'll be living in Darien with William and Frances Anne, he can come to St. Simons often and we can all visit him. Maybe John isn't as frightened of his father as you think. Could he just be envious of William's even disposition?"

"John isn't envious of anyone!"

"Maybe not, but he is a complicated man, don't you agree?"

Anne smiled a little. "If I'm perfectly honest, yes, I do. And dear Dr. William is not complicated. He seems to slide through Father Fraser's turbulent moods like a sharp-keeled boat through calm water. John *isn't* easygoing like William." Anne's smile widened as she headed for the front door. "He's just a lot handsomer and has certainly never given me one dull moment."

CHAPTER 5

BY THE FIRST OF JUNE, ANNE, JOHN, AND THE girls had met Father Fraser's ship in Savannah, had spent a pleasant night at the old Mackay house on Broughton Street, and were back on St. Simons—the girls, to John's delight, trying to show their grandfather absolutely everything the first week he was there.

"You simply mustn't fret, Anne," John said as the two finished breakfast alone one morning. "I even overheard Eve scolding you a while ago for stewing over the fact that Annie and Pete could possibly tire my father. He adores being outside with them."

"Eve scolds too much. At least she scolds me too much. And so do you."

He reached for her hand, took the crust of biscuit from it, and kissed each finger slowly and thoroughly. "Eve and I scold you because our lives center around you. Doesn't it ever occur to you that your light-skinned slave adores the very ground you walk on? She wants you to be happy every minute. When she sees you fretting, her first impulse is always to smooth over, or talk you out of, whatever annoys you."

"I'm so glad you've become an authority on servants, Mr. Fraser," Anne said with a glance at the dining room door to make sure Eve didn't see her when she grabbed John's hand and kissed it hard.

"Afraid someone will find out how passionately you love your planter husband?" he teased. "Your slave Eve, at least, already knows. So does my father and so do I."

She let go of his hand. "Everyone who knows me knows I adore you, but I don't like it when you call Eve my slave."

"She is. In all ways. Your father not only gave her to us, along with June, the girl worships the dirt under your sweet feet."

"She loves bossing me around."

"Mark my words, me beauty. When you're an old, old lady, Eve will still be watching out for exactly what's good for Miss Anne. She gives you orders only because she loves you." At that moment John saw Eve appear in the doorway, bringing fresh coffee in the graceful silver pitcher Anne's mother had given them from the family silver collection. "Ah-ha," John said. "Speak of the attractive Eve and she's in full view with just what Miss Anne needs." He got to his feet, bent to kiss Anne's hair. "I don't have time for more coffee, thank you, Eve, but the lady does. By the by, where's my father? Do you know?"

"She knows everything," Anne said, teasing, "and thank you, Eve. I do need another cup. Father Fraser and I sat up talking so late last night, I can't get awake."

"Yo father done gone to spend the day wif Mausa Couper at Cannon's Point," Eve said, creaming Anne's coffee just right. "Them two mens be gettin' tighter'n seeds in a magnolia pod."

Anne brightened. "You're right. And isn't it wonderful? I think Father Fraser's high regard for Papa will mean he'll visit us more often from Darien. Don't you think so, John?"

The smile John had worn, from the moment he and Anne awakened, vanished. For an instant no one spoke. Then, reclaiming his poise behind which he was still taking refuge, he laughed. "Haven't you heard after all these years, Mrs. Fraser, that the laird of Cannon's Point is the magnet of St. Simons Island? Of the entire Southern coast? Far more famous persons than my humble father flock to partake of John Couper's famed hospitality! But wouldn't you love to know what the two of them—our fathers—say to each other?"

"Miss Anne, she knew them two mens would jibe," Eve offered with her flashing smile. "She done tol' me that long befo' Mausa Fraser got chere."

John got to his feet. "Your husband, June, is going to tell me more than I want to hear, Eve, if I don't ride out to meet him in the Lawrence north field. It's almost eight o'clock and I promised June I'd be ready to help him follow the golden maxim of Lord Francis Bacon in commanding nature by obeying her laws."

"June already be there," Eve said, beginning to clear the table.

"I'm sure he is and so I bid you goodbye, wife." John leaned down to kiss her hair again.

"What on earth does Lord Bacon have to do with anything today?" Anne wanted to know.

"You are tempting me, madam," John teased as he reached for his wide-brimmed straw hat. "In plain English, June and I are making crop rotation decisions this morning. We're 'commanding nature by obeying her laws' and that is a direct quote from your illustrious brother James Hamilton, who took it from Bacon."

Anne sipped her coffee. "It sounds like James."

"A direct quotation from his latest essay, to be published in the *Southern Agriculturalist* at some future date, a copy of which I was instructed to study until I could recite it word for word."

"Who instructed you to do that?" Anne asked defensively.

John's smile as he headed for the front door was enigmatic. Intentionally enigmatic. "If you're as smart as Eve, and I believe you to be, you already know, my dear. Your brother himself."

FOR ANOTHER TEN MINUTES OR SO, ANNE SAT alone at her dining room table, wishing Eve would come back from what should have been a short walk to the thick woods behind the Lawrence house, which the girls now called the Park. She was, after all, only taking some fresh-baked cookies to them to enjoy with the lemonade made from the fruit of their very own lemon trees. Making lemonade and cookies so early in the morning had been Eve's idea. A good one, actually, since both girls so adored Father Fraser, nothing less than the promise of a picnic in the Park would have kept them from tagging along with him when he left to spend the day with Anne's father. It had been plain to both Anne and John that Father Fraser wanted to be alone with Papa, so Eve's good idea had been welcome.

Just as Anne finished her coffee, Eve reentered the dining room, picked up the empty cup and its saucer. "You don' need no more coffee, Miss Anne," the girl said firmly. "But Eve need to axe you a question."

"I need to ask you one too. What's yours?"

"You want Gran'maum Sofy to put a spell on Mausa John's father so he won' move all the way to Darien an' leave us?"

Startled, even after all the years she and Eve had been together, Anne jumped up. "I most certainly do *not* want old Sofy to put a spell on Father Fraser for any reason! Why on earth would you think of such a thing? You know I don't even like it that you take Pete to visit her."

"Pete got so she go eben wifout me, she like the ol' woman so much, but jus' cause I don' lak 'er don' mean I wouldn't make use of her spells if I thought it make you happy, Miss Anne, that Mausa John's father be here wif us, stead of way up dere."

"But I've told you from the start that he prefers to live with my husband's brother, Dr. William. That's his choice and we respect it." Anne stopped, wondering how her mother would handle a servant who had just made an offer like Eve's. Well, she thought, I'm not Mama. I'm myself. "But I do thank you for caring about how much I'll miss the dear old fellow once he's no longer here with us."

Eve's hands flew to her hips. "Shoot! Eve carin' 'bout you ain't nothin' new! Yo papa, Mausa Couper, done gib us to each other. Eve gonna look arter you long as you lib!"

"Did June give you any idea at all about what my father might be doing today?"

Eve's bell-like laugh, so unlike the other house women, lit up her face until Anne once again realized how truly beautiful her features were. "My June, he be smart—smarter den any other nigger at Lawrence or Cannon's Point, but eben June, he don' know it all. I axe him 'fore I give him his breakfas' today."

"You already asked June what he thought my papa might be doing today?"

"Eve smart too. Who knows more 'bout how nosy you kin be?"

"I'm nosy sometimes, I grant you. But you continue to surprise me and since I'm the one who taught you to read, I see no reason why you can't learn to pronounce the letter *v* instead of always saying *eben* instead of *even*."

"Since when the way I talk writ down in law?"

"All right, that's enough. I'm tired of that old writ-down-in-law argument. Someday, when—when things calm down a little, I'm going to work on at least your *v*'s and *b*'s so that you'll begin to get them straight."

In response, Eve only shrugged. "June, he say he guess what Mausa Couper want today be to hab a good, long talk wif Mistah Fraser."

"You did it again. You said *hab* instead of *have*."

"But you knowed what I meant. Bof mens be Scotties. Dey jus' lak to talk together the way our old niggers does."

"*Do*. Oh well, never mind, except Father Fraser and my papa are Scottish, not Scotties. Is it as pleasant outside as it looks?" Anne asked.

"Yes'm. Eve git your darnin' an' you get yo'sef out on dat po'ch. Fill yo lungs up wif fresh air."

"Now you're telling me when and where to breathe!"

"That's right, Miss Anne." Eve left the room smiling, only half to herself.

Eve knows how much I want to know what Papa and Father Fraser have to say to each other, Anne thought. Her grapevine never fails unless she wants it to. I could shake her. I'm sure June has overheard something Papa has let slip about why it's so important for those two to talk alone today. Papa tells June a lot of things, I know. Eve knows something. I'm sure of that, or why would she have been so quick to think of a way to keep Annie and Pete from tagging along when Father Fraser rode over to Cannon's Point?

CHAPTER 6

"WELL, JAMES, MY FR-RIEND," JOCK COUPER SAID, tussling awkwardly with the tablecoth his chef, Sans Foix, let the two men have for their own picnic by the Hampton River, "you've already got an idea of Sans Foix's culinar-ry skills in the Cannon's Point dining room, but now I'll demonstr-rate his expertise as a concocter of picnic lunches. If you've ever sunk a tooth into better fr-ried chicken or sampled a tenderer slab of sweet, smoked ham, I demand to hear the full stor-ry!"

Lapsing also into an exaggerated Scottish brogue, James Fraser replied, "Aye, if I have ever exper-rienced the likes, I'll be the fir-rst to let it be known, Jock."

Humming a snatch of "Loch Lomond" as he knelt stiffly to spread and straighten the square cloth, Jock Couper asked, "Would it tr-rouble you too much to pull that corner towar-rd ya just a mite, James?"

"Not at all," Fraser said, giving the cloth an expert flip so that it fell exactly where needed. "I'm not accustomed to but one serrvant, you know. I'm an old hand at helping out. Glad to, glad to, especially since your kind missus infor-rmed me that deep in that basket beside you is also an ample supply of my favor-rite—deviled eggs."

For a time, thoroughly enjoying the mild, soft breeze off the river, the two friends ate heartily, James Fraser pleasing his host not only by his appetite but by his lavish appreciation of Sans Foix's art. When they had quite finished, Jock picked up the bottle of his famous claret and motioned toward the huge live oak tree nearby.

"If you'll join me, sir," Jock said in his most ebullient manner, "I'd like us to sit beneath the gnarled, old branches of the finest live oak left on my property since the United States government took my prize oak as a stern post for the famous warship the USS *Constitution*. Bring your wineglass. I'll fetch mine and the bottle."

"Aye, Jock," James said, admiring the tree, his smile more evident than usual. "You actually had another tree finer than this one?"

"I did indeed," Jock replied proudly. "Even had the other one named. I called it Beloved. Hearts cracked all over Cannon's Point —my people, some of them, even wept—the day Beloved came crashing to the ground, now more than thirty years ago. We were all pr-roud, pr-roud that Beloved had been selected, but hearts br-roke at the sight of her splintering and falling to the ground. Mr. James Gould, still one of my best Island friends, made the decision for the government." Couper laughed his infectious, congenial laugh. "You may or may not be glad to learn that the *Constitution* captured the British *Guerrière* during what is now called the War of 1812."

James Fraser eased himself down onto a wide, flat root at the foot of the great tree trunk. "The war during which our children met each other."

Sitting too, a bit stiffly but careful to protect the claret, Couper laughed again. "The very same war, at the end of which your splendid son fully captured my blessed Anne. And except for Rebecca and me, I've never known two people more in love than those two."

For a time the men sat back against the great tree, sipping their wine and gazing in silence out across the Hampton River toward Little St. Simons Island, to the sea.

Then, his voice low and filled with feeling, Couper began to recite the second stanza of the old Bobby Burns poem "A Red, Red Rose."

> *"As fair art thou, my bonnie lass,*
> *So deep in luve am I;*
> *And I will luve thee still, my dear,*
> *Till a' the seas gang dry."*

Couper felt pleased when James Fraser joined him in the third stanza of the poem every Scotsman knew and loved.

> *"Till a' the seas gang dry, my dear,*
> *And the rocks melt wi' the sun;*
> *And I will luve thee still, my dear,*
> *While the sands o' life shall run. . . ."*

In a moment Couper said, quite solemnly, "I was sur-re ye knew the Burns verse. 'Tis still a favorite of mine for my lovely wife, Rebecca."

"And 'twas for me while I still had my Margaret beside me."

"You recited 'A Red, Red Rose' to her, too?"

"Aye. When my dour, Scottish stiffness didn't prevent."

"Your wife was Scottish, too?"

"Every drop of her precious blood, but unlike me, always able to understand our boy John."

"Do you feel you don't understand him?" Couper asked.

"Your blessed Anne has helped far more than she knows, but aye, I feel I still don't fully understand my elder son beyond knowing for certain that the best thing that ever happened to the lad is —Anne."

Couper splashed more claret in their glasses. "I had another reason for settling us under this great live oak, James."

The two lifted their glasses.

"I recited the old Burns lyric because I'm sure John has many times recited it to Anne, and I moved you to the shade of the branches of this tree because it was always—their tree."

"John and Anne's?"

"To this day I'm not certain they know that my wife and I found out long ago, but back in the days before John came to claim her in marriage, we'd see them flee the house and all its mostly merry occupants to come to the shelter of these spreading old branches here by the river. I say, this time together is turning out to be just fine, isn't it? I find you easy to talk to, James."

"And I you, Jock. I'm flattered, actually, since most find me stuffy and—stiff."

"At our age, we're entitled to a bit of stiffness," Couper joked. "My daughter tells me we're both approaching seventy."

"Aye, Anne told me years back that we were the same age. Blessed we are, too, to be in reasonably good health. I keep thinking I should be quite a bit wiser than I am, though. And more successful. I've never been what a gentleman would call a success. Unlike you, Jock."

Again Couper laughed, but this time somewhat nervously for him, to whom laughter always came easily. "Unlike me?" He turned to face his new friend. "James, you've just made up my mind. I'm going to tell you something I've managed to keep secret from everyone except our lawyer in Brunswick, my son James Hamilton Couper, and my former business partner, Mr. James Hamilton of Philadelphia, for whom my son James was named."

Fraser now looked straight at Jock. "You're going to confide something to me which even your wife and your daughter Anne don't know?"

"Aye. Now and then a mon needs to do that. Needs to gain the objective viewpoint of a trustworthy, near stranger. You and I do have much in common though. And from the fir-rst handshake upon your arrival with the little Fraser family from Savannah, I've felt you a trustworthy, honorable gentleman. The secret should have been plain to both my wife and my daughter Anne, but I fear both hold me in rather prejudiced high esteem. Too high. So, to my knowledge, neither has guessed. My younger son, William

Audley, is not quite eleven and too lazy to have bothered to figure it out. My younger daughter, Isabella, is nearly thirteen, too young to think on such matters. I haven't even found the courage to tell my close friend James Gould, the builder of the St. Simons lighthouse, who now has a vast holding here on St. Simons. I *am* going to tell you, James." Couper took a deep breath. "Though often tolerably successful, after a penniless start, I did suffer reverses. There were embargoes, nonintercourse, and war, all of which interfered with my prospects. Not only were there heavy losses to the British among my people, a devastating hurricane struck in 1824 and wiped out a fine crop that should have brought me close to a hundred thousand dollars."

Fraser whistled softly. "Never saw that much money at once in me whole lifetime!"

"Entire sum lost in twelve hours when the hurricane struck us here. One year later, I nearly lost my crop again to caterpillars. Your son John helped me enormously with them."

"John actually was a help?"

"Don't underestimate the boy. Not ever! He's still learning, but if he could only believe *you* approve of him, he'd turn into a master planter." Telling Fraser of his own financial straits had been harder than Jock anticipated. Fraser's interruptions in the midst of his story were not easy to surmount, but thankful that Anne had told him of John's longing for his father's appreciation, he thought it important to try to elaborate a bit. "Your son William is already one of the most respected men in Darien—a fine doctor, as you know, and rumor has it that he may soon be Darien's mayor. But don't sell John short, friend. I know he's hard to figure at times, but the lad is trying—he's trying earnestly. And he's learning. Even my critical son James Hamilton agrees, and he doesn't agree easily on much since he has always been perfectly aware of his own superior capabilities." When Fraser did not pursue the matter of John, Couper went on with his own story. "After John and I managed to conquer the caterpillar plague, cotton prices then sank with no prospect of improvement. Lands were reduced to one-third their former value, and slaves dropped in value all the way down from four hundred fifty dollars a head to two hundred fifty some as low as two hundred."

"I somehow hoped the subject of slavery would not come up during our talk today, Jock."

"I know you hoped that. It's never been and will never be easy for me to discuss. Deep down under all the layers of my accumulated veneer, I probably feel exactly as you feel about owning other human beings."

"You do?"

"Aye. But I'm a planter and that settles that. Now, if you'll be so good as to allow me to finish my sad story, James, I'll be ever so grateful. Telling even a kind, new friend such as you is far from easy." He refilled their glasses. "So, in short, I saw no hope of paying my debts and retaining my rather large properties scattered about this coastal paradise. I thought it best, after a long conference with myself and the good Lord, to meet the storm. My longtime Philadelphia friend, Mr. James Hamilton, agreed to pay off my debts in return for the surrender of all my property in a lump, except my lands here on St. Simons and one hundred slaves."

A glance at Fraser's long, serious face, turned now toward the river, told Couper nothing, but he decided to plow ahead.

"So on the first day of January last year, 1827, I was thrown on the world without a dollar to support my people or my family and glad to get off so well. My debts gone, I am at least satisfied and relieved from much anxiety. I might add, by way of counting my blessings, that by this event—something like bankruptcy, James— neither my standing in society nor my mode of living has suffered any change whatever. Mr. Hamilton has sold my half of the plantation called Hopeton on the mainland to my son, his namesake. Also my half of the three hundred eighty slaves."

After another deep breath, Couper looked again at James Fraser. The enigmatic Scot was still intent upon the wide-stretching, green-blue vista before him. He said not one word.

"Now then," Couper went on. "If you care to express your views on either my bankruptcy or my being a slave owner, please feel free to do so."

"I think not, Jock. I'm too grateful for your remarkable confidence in me. I feel deeply for your great losses. I do have one question. Why haven't you felt free to tell this story to my son John?"

Couper thought carefully before he answered. "Well, to the best of my knowledge, I believe I haven't told John about my bankruptcy simply because I felt it was too early to burden him with it."

Now Fraser looked squarely at him. "Too early? I don't follow you."

"You really don't, do you?"

James shook his head no. He isn't making this at all easy for me, Jock thought, but he was determined to keep going, to try, if possible, to help John out at least a little with his stiffly reserved father.

"Tell me, James," Couper asked, a new tactic having flashed into his mind, "was your blessed wife of a highly cheerful disposition?"

Still looking out over the river, Fraser answered, "Aye. John is far more like her but devoid of her tact. I expect Margaret was often glum inside. Like John, she could fool me. In fact, she lived out her dear life fooling me, even more successfully than John has ever managed to do. It seems the hardest thing the lad is ever faced with is to speak freely to his own father."

"And do you try to speak freely to him?"

"I try. I also fail almost entirely. At last, once his mother left us, I did decide to be blunt about his brother, William."

"Blunt?"

"Aye. Blunt. At least the lad and I no longer have to pretend with each other. William *is* my favorite."

Couper made no effort to conceal the amazement on his ruddy face. "You—pretended with John all those years he was growing up?"

"Not successfully. He just didn't like me much, I'm afraid. Look here, Jock, I know I've dumbfounded you, and before I say one more word, I want it known that there isn't a father anywhere more proud of his elder son than I. As Lieutenant John Fraser, the lad made a brilliant military record. I'm not a military man. I hate wars. But I was proud of John, I am proud of him. I just don't know how to be with him. We're too different."

"Do you know that he has completely accepted the fact that you favor his brother, Dr. William?"

Without a change of expression, Fraser said, "John told you that, did he?"

"Aye, he did and he accepts it rather gracefully, I'd say."

Draining his wineglass, Fraser said softly, almost sadly, "He is far more comfortable with you, Jock, than with his own father. Which should please you greatly. John is not easy to know."

Jock laughed a little. "Anne tells us both almost daily that we're growing to be more and more alike. Perhaps that's why I find the lad easy to understand. 'Tis me pride, wouldn't you say, James?"

"No, I wouldn't say. 'Tis because you possess the same kind of magnetic charm." Fraser's voice was as matter-of-fact as if he'd just quoted the current cotton prices in Liverpool. "No one had to tell me John has made friends all over St. Simons Island. I already knew it."

"But Dr. William was—is well liked here too. And in Darien."

"Aye."

The one word of agreement told Jock nothing. This puzzling man *was* revealing far more than he knew, though. "You're simply a highly reserved gentleman, James. Far more what is supposed to be the typical Scotsman than I."

"There isn't one of your own children with whom you feel more comfortable?" James asked. "Among the four, isn't there one toward whom you somehow gravitate?"

Since the question had never occurred to Couper, he waited to answer. Finally he said, "I am not aware that I love her any more deeply, but Anne has always been the ver-ry apple of my eye, since you pinned me to a response. It's none of my affair," he went on, "but does your favorite son, Dr. William, even know yet you're in Georgia?"

"Not unless word somehow reached him that my ship docked in Savannah over a week ago. I plan to write to William tonight."

"And does it amuse you to be so hard to figure out, James?"

"Amuse me?"

"Well, do you enjoy being an enigma to most people?"

" 'Tis lonely."

"I see."

"I doubt you've ever been lonely, Jock. I'm told you're the most admired and beloved gentleman in Georgia and beyond."

Couper laughed. "And who, pray, told you such a big fib?"

"My son William wrote it in several letters. Of course, John is your most ardent admirer and with reason. Your generosity with the boy is overwhelming. 'Tis more than overwhelming. 'Tis downright embarrassing to his father."

"Now we'll have none of that. A mon has a per-rfect right to settle a dowry on his charming daughter. Anyway, I needed John."

"He hates farming."

"He's learning to like it. It would mean far more to him than I am evidently able to convince you, James, if you'd let the lad know that you notice how swiftly he's learning to plant."

"What you don't understand, Jock, is what most others have also failed to grasp, and that is that John does *not* need my approval! He's never needed it. Always gone his own way. And before you remind me that it was John who offered his services in my floundering wine import business, aye, it was. But I paid him. I'm sure he kept me from failing those last years in London. He had no knack for business, but he charmed new customers in my direction."

"And did you let John know he'd done good work for you?"

"I kept him on. Wouldn't that inform a man with John's good mind?"

He was getting nowhere with James Fraser and Couper knew it. Why not just give up? If this upstanding, cultivated gentleman almost exactly his own age did not see by now that his elder son would give almost anything for his approval, why did he, Jock, a veritable stranger, expect to convince him?

The two sat in silence for a time; then, after a terse but sincere compliment on Jock's claret, James Fraser said, "I'm more sorry than words can tell about your financial problems. You do seem to have weathered the storm you decided to face in far better shape than I, but I want you to tell John you were forced into bank-ruptcy."

"I intend to tell him someday. Perhaps next year. Barring an-other hurricane or caterpillar plague or a further drop in cotton prices, John's fieldhands should harvest the boy's first profitable crop of cotton—one from which he can go to the market in Savan-nah for the extra hands he needs, on his own, with his own money. Then I plan to tell him. With all my old heart, James, I mean to give the lad a chance to make his mark. His own mark. Once John has done that outside the military, he won't need anyone's ap-proval. He'll have his own." Jock got to his feet. "Undoubtedly I owe you an apology for having been too inquisitive about you and John. If so, I apologize."

James dismissed the apology with a flick of his hand. "You've been too good to the lad, Jock. I now see you've given to him sacrificially. I haven't, but my aging heart burgeons with gratitude to you that you have been so good—that you are so good to John, my difficult and much-beloved son."

Together, they cleaned up after their picnic and began the slow, leisurely walk back toward the Cannon's Point Big House. "Do you think you'll ever be able to *call* John your beloved son?"

"To his face?"

"Of course to his face!"

"With your help, I'll try my best. Perhaps I need you to help me find a way to let him know. Why, even your critical, brilliant son James Hamilton told me day before yesterday that John was learning fast how to plant. My son is far too intelligent ever to believe me if he had the slightest notion that I was forcing myself to—to praise him. I'd rather die leaving him to wonder if he ever really had my approval than to leave him with a false-sounding compliment." Fraser stopped walking and looked straight at Couper. "You see, Jock, I'm going to live with William in Darien, Georgia, for one main reason. 'Tis true I'm more comfortable in his company. William is easygoing, always plain to see. But he's also a doctor and I'm an old man who hasn't been at all well."

Standing together on the river path, the two men looked at

each other for a long time without speaking. Then Couper asked, "You're saying that you've chosen to live up in Darien with William and his family rather than here with all of us because you know you might soon need a doctor near at hand?"

Fraser nodded yes.

"Are you that poorly?"

Fraser shrugged.

"Have you told John your real reason for settling in Darien?"

"He's smart enough to sense it."

Jock shifted the bundle of plates, glasses, and silverware tumbled together in the tablecloth to his left hand and laid his right on Fraser's shoulder. "James, my inestimable new friend, your son John Fraser *is* a highly intelligent, remarkably quick-witted lad, but he isn't the Almighty! It might work wonders if he knew you simply felt safer with a fine doctor right in the house."

"There'll come a time and a way for me to let Johnnie know, Jock," Fraser said as they neared the Big House. "You've given me some help today. But remember, the lad is a smart one. The time and the words must be foolproof. Peculiar, but I expect you to believe me far more readily than Johnnie would." After another short silence, James Fraser laughed softly. "It wouldn't strike you as funny, I know, but twice now in the past minute or so, I've called him Johnnie."

"You've never called him that—even as a little boy?"

"Never. His mother did. My fine Scottish housekeeper, Flora McLeod, never called him anything but Johnnie. I've always called him—John."

Some sense of relief flooded Jock's very being. The gap between his dear son-in-law and his parent was still wide, but with his own ears he had heard James Fraser call the lad—Johnnie.

CHAPTER 7

JUST AS DAWN WAS LIGHTING THE LATE JUNE SKY,
Father Fraser, bathed, shaved, and fully dressed because he was too
excited to stay longer in his bed, walked alone across the yard
toward the Lawrence landing and stood watching the sun return
color to the marsh and trees. Today, he thought, even more surely
than when he'd landed in Savannah a fortnight ago, would mark
the big change in his life. His son William and wife, Frances Anne,
the young lady he'd never seen, were coming this day to St. Simons
Island. Along with their nearly three-year-old son, James William,
Fraser's namesake, they would, after a few days visit at Lawrence
and Cannon's Point, be taking him to Darien to live in their home.
William and his family would make the water trip courtesy of
John's British friend Captain James Frewin, late of the Royal
Navy, now a farmer at Frederica, who also earned part of his
livelihood in the area's growing coasting trade. Frewin, to whom
Father Fraser suspected John hied himself often for the pleasure of

sharing their mutually relished former lives at sea, would be returning to St. Simons today, his small vessel empty of cargo with
room for William's family.

In John's usual offhand way, he had assured his father that
after a good visit on the Island, he, John, would find a means for
him and for William and his wife and son to return to Darien. "I
can surmise the means John will find," Fraser said aloud on the
soft, fresh, early air. "As usual, the lad will turn to his father-in-
law, Jock Couper, who will, if no other conveyance turns up, send
them to Darien by his finest plantation boat, manned by eight
Negro oarsmen."

James Fraser sighed deeply. Try as he continued to do, he still
had trouble reconciling the kind, generous heart of his new,
learned friend, Jock Couper, with that of a slave owner. True, the
Negroes he'd seen about both Cannon's Point and Lawrence did
seem reasonably content. Couper and John allowed them to raise
their own hogs, to fish and hunt once their allotted tasks were over
for the day, but it stuck in James Fraser's craw that Jock and
Fraser's own son John had to *allow* these dark-skinned human
beings to do what any man should be free to do. He had heard of
no whipping at either Cannon's Point or Lawrence. He knew his
son John would sooner die than see another mortal whipped as
though he or she were a dog or a stubborn mule. With his own
ears Fraser had heard three whippings in less than a fortnight—
the actual whistle of the lash, the cries of the victims—all the way
across Jones Creek, which formed the western border of Lawrence
Plantation. The whippings took place, his blessed Anne told him,
either at the hand, or by the order, of manager Roswell King, Jr.,
whose father had also managed both of the late Major Pierce Butler's vast operations—Butler's Island and, across little Jones Creek,
Hampton Point, where the whippings occurred.

"The Kings have both been good neighbors in the practical
sense," Jock Couper had told him, "but never favorites of mine.
Both smart, resourceful, and, to my mind, cruel men. The present
manager, young Roswell, is married to Julia, a pleasant enough
Maxwell relative of Rebecca's. The mild-mannered Julia seems not
to be aware of her husband's treatment of his people. Awkward for

me, the whole marriage arrangement, but certainly none of my affair."

Just as James Fraser sat down stiffly on the Lawrence dock, the better to enjoy the ever-changing colors of the coastal sunrise, he was startled by a woman's musical laughter, a man's affectionate, shouted goodbye, then a burst of galloping hooves. Of course, it was time for the poor slaves to be up and moving about, heading for the fields and plantation shops and gardens, but Fraser had no intention of making small talk with any of them. The mere idea made him highly uncomfortable. Embarrassed him, in fact. Even angered him in spite of his love for Anne, who seemed to take the presence of their people for granted. Slavery angered him in spite of his regard for her father, whom abolitionists in the North would call a "lord of the lash." Well, Jock wasn't. Jock Couper, to Fraser's mind, was more a slave than any of his Negroes. A veritable slave to the hateful system.

Thankful that the Negro who had shouted the warm goodbye had evidently ridden off in the direction of Cannon's Point, Fraser resettled his bones on the dock and leaned his aching back against a piling, ready to resume his own thoughts. A wren shouted from the woods north of the Lawrence cottage. For an instant a smile flickered at the corners of the old man's mouth, then widened a bit when another wren returned the shout with what sounded amusingly like the English words *sweet, sweet.*

The air was sweet. For this moment alone by the winding marsh creek, John's family still in their own house behind him, William's family undoubtedly on the water coming this way, he felt something like sweet peace, himself. His head had whirled only twice since he'd reached St. Simons. Each time, he'd managed to will it right again. His legs ached and his arms and back, but he'd learned long ago to live with that as does any man worth his salt approaching his seventieth birthday.

His concentration on the stricture in his chest, which inevitably came with each wave of longing to share the moment with his beloved Margaret—the longing that came less often with the years but never less painfully—was interrupted by an abrupt sense that someone was nearby.

Then an almost pert "Mawnin', Mausa Fraser" startled him further.

Turning around as best he could without struggling to get to his feet, he saw the quite beautiful, light-skinned slave girl smiling at him from the path beside the dock.

"Mawnin', Mausa Fraser," she said again. "Purty day. You hab yo breakfus so early?"

He knew it was Anne's Eve. In fact, Anne had made a point of introducing him to the girl the very day he reached Lawrence. Introduced him as though Eve was someone special, different from the other slaves on the place. Of course he knew what a time Anne had in London trying to look after herself without Eve to help her, remembered well when John first brought his bride home how Flora McLeod fussed because Anne seemed unable to lift a finger to help herself with her hair, her bath, or her clothes. Of course Flora got over her fuming as soon as she got to know Anne, and at the end in all ways was Anne's mightiest defender.

"I'd as soon you didn't call me—master," he said dryly.

Eve's smile was like the sun coming out of a sea of darkness. "What I suppose to call you, sir?"

"Sir will do fine. I'm certainly no one's master. I take it you're on your way to work for the day."

"That be right, sir. Miss Anne, she so happy yo here to hab breakfus at her house, she want nobody but Eve to serve you." She laughed what he could only think of as a rather condescending but affectionate laugh. "Dat Miss Anne, she mighty partial to Mausa John's papa—you, sir."

"And I to her, Miss Eve."

Now Eve did laugh. Almost the same musical laughter that had so surprised him a moment ago when she told her husband, June, goodbye before he rode off to Cannon's Point.

"I fail to find anything funny," he said.

"Nobody eber call Eve *Miss* Eve! It be funny. Wait till I tell June." Another laugh came. This time low, almost conspiratorial, as though the two of them shared a secret. "In fact, you know what I might do? I might just call June *Mistah* June. See what he say to dat."

When Fraser began to pull himself to his feet by grasping the piling he'd leaned against, Eve rushed to help him.

Standing, he bowed slightly. "Well, thank you very much. I—I appreciate your kindness, Miss Eve."

"Dere you go callin' me dat again!"

For a moment they stood facing each other, Eve's dark, deep-set eyes looking full at him. "I say, there's a question I'd be obliged if you'd answer for me."

"Yes, suh. Jus' axe."

"I come from a country where slavery is deeply frowned upon. In England and Scotland I know of no one who approves of owning other human beings. The whole idea of owning a slave—the whole idea of being a slave—is completely foreign to me. I despise the fact that my son John Fraser is now a slave owner. Would you tell me, please, how it feels to be a slave? How do you feel each morning when you first wake up and realize that you're a slave, Miss Eve?"

The smile vanished from her face. She took one step back, then another. Realizing he had probably asked a clumsy, impossible question, Fraser waited.

The slender girl lifted her chin. "When I wakes up eber day, sir, I feel lak—*Eve!*"

"I see. Even though you resent that my son and his wife own you and your husband, you still are in full possession of your own identity, is that it?"

"What it is," Eve said, standing as straight as a pine, "is dat Eve don' feel no diff'rent washin' her own hair as washin' Miss Anne's hair." After an awkward silence—awkward, at least, for James Fraser—she added, "Scuse me, sir, but how come you lak Mausa Couper the way you does?"

Fraser managed a somewhat relieved smile. "My regard for my new friend John Couper shows, does it, Miss Eve?"

"Yes, sir. It show all right. Effen you so set agin ownin' slaves, how come Mausa Couper lak you?" The infectious smile flashed back. Really a confidential, person-to-person grin, with no hint of submission in it. Once more Fraser thought of the word *conspiratorial.* Were he and Anne's Eve conspiring a bit? Did he dare enjoy it at least in the privacy of his own thoughts? Why not? It was certainly no one's business that he found himself genuinely liking the intelligent, independent spirit of this young woman who called his own son master. "Miss Anne, she skin me alive effen I don' hab yo breakfus fix by the time you ready to eat, sir."

He gave her what for stoic James Fraser was a warm grin. "I'll take my time getting back to the Lawrence dining room, Miss Eve. Don't worry."

"No, sir. Eve don' b'lieve in worry."

"And what do you believe in?"

Over her shoulder as she walked away, she tossed, "I jus' b'lieves in bein' the bes'."

CHAPTER 8

WHEN BIG BOY PROUDLY DREW UP THE AGING BUT well-kept Couper carriage before the Lawrence cottage, Anne ran outside, both girls with her, to greet the William Fraser family and their tall, dark-skinned nurse and housekeeper, Nell. Captain James Frewin had told John his small vessel should reach Frederica before noon, and, of course, faithful Big Boy had been there waiting to drive the Frasers to Lawrence.

After noisy, happy greetings, John, Father Fraser, and Dr. William headed in the carriage for a visit with Anne's parents at Cannon's Point, where William had lived as a welcome houseguest for several years until he and Anne's childhood friend Frances Anne Wylly were married. Eve, as usual, Anne thought, took high-handed charge of Anne's daughters, Nell, and the nearly three-year-old Fraser boy, freeing Anne and Frances to take their first walk together alone since before Anne's marriage some twelve years ago.

Because she knew of a fine, moss-covered fallen log in the

Park, Anne steered her friend around the house and along a tended path that led to the spot where Anne liked to sit anytime she managed some time alone to read or think.

Elaborately brushing off the old leaves and twigs, Anne cleared a place for herself and then, with a flourish, motioned Frances Anne toward her own favorite place, where her friend could sit comfortably, her back against a dead water oak stump nearby.

Counting on Frances's quick humor, Anne then sat down grandly. "One thing you must have noticed, Frances, is that I've turned into a true, ladylike plantation mistress!"

The well-remembered green eyes twinkling, Frances said, "Your elegant mother could not have seated me more graciously in her beautiful Cannon's Point parlor." Both feet up on the log, she hugged her knees and sighed happily. "You know perfectly well that I like being out here far more than I'd like any parlor elegance. For goodness' sake, Anne, start telling me everything!"

"I wrote to you so often from London, you already know a lot about my life there in Father Fraser's house. You know about life here. But we had such a few minutes together at Anna Matilda's mother's funeral, I need to hear about your life now in Darien."

Only half joking, Frances Anne said, "Once you've told me more about Father Fraser himself—how it is living in the same house with him—I'll be able to give you a better idea of what my life might be like from now on. Of course he and I have just met. He does look like an aging John but, as you said, dour. You seemed to be the only person who merited a real smile from the old gentleman a while ago on your front porch. He plainly adores you, Anne."

"Not at first he didn't. I worked at winning him over."

Lifting an eyebrow, Frances Anne asked, "And how long did you have to work?"

Anne laughed. "About an hour at dinner the first night John and I reached 2 George Street. And it wasn't hard. John vows I was shameless, but I honestly liked his father from our initial meeting and found him a challenge. Didn't you think him rather dear when you met just now?"

"Dear? I won't go that far, but William had warned me that

his father's stern exterior isn't the way his heart is. I probably imagined he was receiving the daughter-in-law he'd never seen more graciously than may actually have been the case. Do you think I'm right? Anne, you know I'm not a determined charmer—not like you anyway."

Anne gave her a solemn look. "Father Fraser is John's only living parent. I had to be sure he liked me. The same is true with you, Frances. Besides, William is—his favorite of the two."

Frances's look of surprise was real. "How do you know that?"

"Do you mean William hasn't told you?"

"No, not a word. He and John seem genuinely fond of each other."

"They are! Thank God John has never allowed his father's favoritism to come between him and William. Not in any way that I can see. But Father Fraser makes no bones about it. He'll probably come right out and tell you himself someday. Doesn't the fact that he insists on living with you and William tell you everything?"

"No, because in his letters to us, he's always written that he thinks it better at his age to live in the same house with a doctor."

Anne felt a jolt of panic. "He told you that? Did he say he was ill in some special way? I know he had lumbago or something older people get and we stayed almost a year longer in London with him because he had several dizzy spells, but we also stayed because Annie was having so many sieges of sore throat. Frances Anne, you've frightened me!"

For a long moment Frances studied her. "You really love that old man, don't you? People do sicken and grow feeble when they're his age, you know."

"But he's almost exactly the same age as my papa!"

"Your father has always been an amazing man. I've only just met Father Fraser, but he's a much older-looking man than Mr. Couper. I'm sorry if I've alarmed you."

"Well, you have. Does it worry William?"

"Doctors have what I always call lazy imaginations. William is tender and caring about all his patients, but there's something about being a physician that makes them more realistic than other people. I wouldn't say William is especially concerned over his father's health. But knowing William, he'll keep a close watch over him." Frances took a deep breath. "Anne, it isn't William who's worried, it's his adoring wife. Not that our father-in-law may die anytime soon, but that the nearly perfect idyll William and little James William and I were living out there on the Ridge near Darien will never be the same again."

"You really love William, don't you?"

"Far, far more than I loved him when we were married. What about you and John?"

"Oh yes." Anne smiled at her friend. "I think it's just dawned on me that another woman *could* love a man even half as much as I love John. Even you."

"And Anna Matilda. That girl seems to worship Thomas Butler King."

"I know, but she isn't as blessed as we are. Thomas is always riding off to some political event in another county, some commercial meeting or other. It's pure heaven having John working right here on our own place."

Frances's ready laugh came. "I'm sure you see a lot more of him than I see of William. My husband is undoubtedly the most conscientious doctor on earth. And he never seems to lose patience when some of his sick people send family members to pound on our door at all hours of the night, when most of them could as easily have gone to William's office at the Darien Hospital at a decent hour."

Anne frowned. "What would you do, Frances, if Father Fraser grew ill at night and William was five miles away making a call on someone else?"

"Anne, I'm not that worried about what certainly hasn't happened yet, and furthermore, I don't intend to be." After a time she asked, "You don't like that old gentleman only because he's John's father, do you? You like him for himself too."

"What's wrong with that?"

"Nothing's wrong with it. It's just—unusual."

"I don't see why. Father Fraser and I are friends. He's as

relieved as I am that John couldn't regain his military commission. He and I both hate war."

"Everyone does."

"Not the way Father Fraser and I do!"

Frances laughed. "All right, simmer down. No one hates war as do the two of you."

"Stop treating me like a child. I'm a year older than you. Can you believe we're in our thirties? Next January, I'll be thirty-two."

"But we can both give our husbands more children. Anne, I'm really counting on little James William to help build a bridge between Father Fraser and me. I wanted to name him Alexander after my father, you know. But because William knows his own father so well, I deferred to him. William is a peacemaker at heart."

"You sound as though an ogre is coming to live with you, and it's dear, sweet, warm, lonely Father Fraser."

"Lonely?"

"He's never recovered from having lost his wife, Margaret. He and I had long talks about how a man or a woman is even able to keep breathing when a loved one dies. I couldn't breathe without John. Could you breathe without William?"

"I wouldn't want to. I suppose I—could. I'd certainly try for James William's sake. So would you for the sake of Annie and Pete. Isn't Pete an odd nickname for such a pretty, small girl?"

Anne, her mind still on Father Fraser's health and loneliness, said absently, "Yes, I suppose so. Everyone agrees it's odd, but everyone calls her Pete, and John and I like it just fine." She reached abruptly for Frances's hand. "You will try to learn to like Father Fraser, won't you?"

"Of course. I'd do absolutely anything for William."

"Could I ask you again if you think being in the house with a doctor is the main reason our father-in-law chooses to live with you and William?"

"You've always been able to ask me anything, haven't you? Except maybe whether my sister Heriot is really a little crazy or just determined to live life *her way*."

"I've never even thought of asking you if dear Heriot is crazy!"

"If you haven't thought of it," Frances laughed, "you're the only one. Seriously, Anne, you and your whole family have always been most kind to Heriot, and if you've never wondered about her, *I* certainly have. Do you know what Mama wrote me last week? That on these nice, warm June nights, Heriot sleeps in her garden path! She does. Takes a light blanket out there and goes to sleep talking to her flowers."

"Mama says flowers and plants of all kinds need to be talked to."

"Well, I'm glad to hear your mother believes it too. Makes me feel a little less concerned about Heriot. Honestly, Anne, I think my sister is extremely wise but just doesn't give a fig what people think. Mama worries, but I don't usually feel at all concerned about her. It's her life, and if she has courage enough to live it her way, I say more power to her! Don't you agree?"

"Yes, I do." For a time neither spoke, then Anne asked, "Do you think I'm selfish?"

"No more than the rest of us. Why?"

"Anna Matilda gave me quite a lecture about my being selfish toward John. I flared, but I'm trying to think through what she said."

"What exactly did she say?"

"That John is one of those people who hate being rooted anywhere. That I stayed so homesick during the years he and I lived in London, he had no choice but to give in and do what I wanted. Do you think that's fair?"

"Anne, you and I have been apart for so long, how would I know? I've always thought of you as being the apple of your father's eye, but I don't think I've ever felt you were selfish. That's an ugly word. We're probably all spoiled—all of us whose parents own St. Simons plantations. Do you think I'm selfish to wish that William and I could go on—alone as we have been?"

Anne frowned. "You wish Father Fraser weren't coming to live with you, don't you?"

"And I suppose you think that's beastly selfish of me. Well, maybe it is, but so few women are truly, truly happy in their marriages, I'm not going to feel one bit selfish for wanting ours to go on as blissfully as it has." Frances sighed. "One simply takes in a parent when the time comes. I'd expect William to welcome my mother or my father should one of them be left alone. So, don't worry about your precious friend Mr. James Fraser. We've even named our son for him, and you know I'll do the very best I can to see that he's cared for in his old age."

Anne stood up. "Frances, please do more than that! He's really a sweet man. I know you'll take care of him, see that your servants supply all his needs, but I'm going to pray that you'll come to love him as I do."

"The question is, will he ever come to love me, do you think?" Frances asked, also getting to her feet.

"Yes, if you can remember that because of the way he's lived his long life, you must help him feel free enough to love in return."

"That sounds as peculiar as my sister Heriot."

"Well, it isn't peculiar at all. It's just—Father Fraser."

"I don't coddle people very handily, Anne. I fell in love with William because the man needs less coddling than anyone I've ever known. How about John? Do you have to coddle him? Is he difficult like his father?"

"Neither one of them is difficult. Anyway, real love also loves the difficult. Where would we be if God loved us only at the times we're not difficult?"

"Anne, don't preach. Anyway, I don't believe God coddles us. We're becoming disgustingly solemn. You do coddle John, don't you?"

"Sometimes. He spoils me too. Frances? Does William talk much about his brother?"

"At times quite a lot. Especially about when they were boys. He loves to reminisce about their early days in Dumfries, Scotland. They both loathed farming!"

"I know."

"And still you permitted John to settle in coastal Georgia, into a stratum of life where a man has no choice but to be a planter."

"Are you too calling me selfish?"

"No."

Arm in arm they began to walk back toward Anne's cottage.

"Is John learning to like being a planter?"

"I—I honestly don't know. He tries hard. He tries so, so hard."

CHAPTER 9

A WEEK LATER, ON THE MORNING THEIR GUESTS were to leave for Darien in Papa Couper's plantation boat, the *Lady Love,* John stood with Anne inside the still-closed door to their bedroom. In an almost desperate way, he was holding her close to him.

"Dearest," she whispered, "is something wrong? Or am I undeservedly being given this special treat?"

"Nothing is wrong. Nothing more than usual, anyway. And every day you deserve much more than this. For putting up with me, of course. But there are many other reasons for holding you. You deserve to be held because you're the most beautiful woman on the face of God's earth. And the most sensitive. You truly love my father, don't you?"

"Yes. Maybe almost as much as you love him. Does it make you sad to have him leave this morning?"

He released her but made no move to open the door. "Anne,

did I imagine it or did Father actually call me Johnnie when your parents told us all goodnight last evening?"

Now Anne filled him with the joy he always felt when she threw her arms around him. "You didn't imagine it! I had to bite my tongue last night to keep from asking you if you'd noticed. He did, darling. He called you Johnnie and I vow Papa gave Father Fraser a secret smile of approval!"

"You don't miss a thing, do you."

"Did you also hear Father Fraser admit at the dinner table that if he'd been able to produce crops like yours, he might still be a Dumfries farmer—a successful one?"

"I heard it, but do you honestly think he was speaking of—my fields? He wasn't looking at me when he said that, if you remember."

"No, I don't remember. I was too excited to hear him say it. Dearest husband, make a little room for the poor old fellow, please? If anyone knows by now how hard it is for Father Fraser to praise anyone for anything, you do."

"I do know his face almost cracks when he even tries," John said with a smile.

"You are making room for him. Good for you!" She hugged his neck again. "I'm so proud of you for that. John, I have to tell you something that Frances Anne told me the first day they were here. Father Fraser is going to live with William because he wants a doctor in the house just in case."

A whole new kind of fear gripped John. He knew he was showing it, because Anne quickly dropped her arms from around him. Father must be ill! More ill, John thought, than he'd allowed anyone to know. "Anne, why haven't you told me this before?"

"I—I don't know."

"You don't know?"

She shook her head. "I guess I didn't want to frighten you. Have I frightened you?"

"Yes, but you've also relieved me no end! At least I think you have. I wish they weren't leaving so soon this morning. I need time to sort this out, to think about it." He knew she was, in her sometimes uncomfortably perceptive way, seeing the scared little boy in his look, but this time he didn't care. "Anne, help me. He'll be leaving our dock in half an hour for Cannon's Point. There isn't time for me to think it through, but do you suppose Father might otherwise have chosen to live here with us? God knows Annie's heart will break when he goes, and Pete is also now under the old gentleman's odd, stern spell. Maybe he *is* settling in Darien because William will be there to care for him if he falls ill." He tried to laugh. He failed. "I know that sounds strange, as though I were hoping Father might be more frail than he admits, but you know me better than that."

"This minute I know you better than you know yourself, darling. I know why this relieves you. In a way it relieves me too."

He took her in his arms again. "Anne, Anne, I love you. I love you so much and I'm so grateful that you're exactly as you are. It's even all right that the old boy didn't tell me any of this in the first place."

T HE A LEXANDER W YLLYS, F RANCES A NNE'S PAR-ents, had reached the Lawrence dock by the time Anne and John finished breakfast with their guests, and while Eve saw to a huge picnic basket for the Frasers to enjoy en route home to Darien, Anne took her elder daughter aside to comfort her.

"Don't worry, Mama," Annie said, her face already wet with tears because she had to say goodbye again to Father Fraser. "I won't be a crybaby in public. I'll be very polite to Mr. and Mrs. Wylly and it won't be hard at all to speak nicely to Aunt Frances Anne. I like her. It's—it's just that I wish I knew why Grandfather Fraser doesn't want to stay here with us. He and Pete and I get along fine. Pete's even courteous to him, and you know she hates bothering with courtesy."

"She doesn't hate bothering with courtesy, darling. Pete's just a little tomboy. She'll grow out of it. You'll get over your sadness at saying goodbye to Grandfather Fraser, too, because we'll go often to visit him and Uncle William and Aunt Frances in Darien. And Grandfather Fraser can come here anytime he wants."

Anne longed to tell Annie that the old gentleman had chosen to live with the William Frasers because her Uncle William is a doctor. She dared not. Sensitive Annie would worry all the more if she thought her grandfather even considered that he might fall ill.

Pete and John joined them at the landing as June was overseeing the loading of the last of their guests' valises in John's Lawrence dugout for the short trip to Cannon's Point. Except for Annie, the mood of those gathered on the dock seemed happy enough, Anne thought. Frances Anne was still making her reserved husband, William, laugh. Pete, of course, helped because she loved showing off that she'd just learned from Eve how to stand on her head, sun-browned legs straight up in the air. She not only could perform the trick but could sing "Comin' Through the Rye" at the same time—and did.

Even Father Fraser seemed to laugh rather easily this morning, and Anne had to force herself to make small talk with Mrs. Wylly and Frances Anne when what she wanted to do was eavesdrop on the exchange Father Fraser was having with John, after motioning his son to join him at the far end of the dock.

Anne did overhear the old man say one highly important thing to John: "Son, if I'd had your knack for supervising back when you and William and I were struggling to farm that rocky acreage of ours outside Dumfries, I wouldn't have been so hard on you because you couldn't plow a straight furrow. I believe you should know that it seems to me you've found yourself at last."

Whatever Mrs. Wylly was saying Anne didn't hear, because she was straining every nerve for John's response. He looked so amazed and delighted that he took a long time about it: "Well, Father," he said at last, "at least I can tell you I'm *refinding* myself."

After that, Anne could hear nothing because Pete, both legs in the air again, was once more singing "Comin' Through the Rye" a little off-key and at the top of her lungs.

After the Lawrence boat was loaded and the William Frasers and Father Fraser were seated, John's sudden notion that he and Anne and the girls should go with them as far as Cannon's Point was a welcome one. The Wyllys bid them all a warm farewell, and the boat, riding low in the creek from its overload, set out for the much larger Couper dock and plantation boat.

In sight of the Cannon's Point landing, they could see Rebecca and Jock Couper, Anne's young sister, Isabella, her brother William Audley, her childhood tutor, Mr. Browne, and a knot of Cannon's Point people gathered and waiting.

"NOTHING WOULD DO, DR. WILLIAM," JOCK Couper called as the Lawrence boat neared his dock, "but that these of my people be on hand to wave you off. They hate to see you go as much as I do—as we all do." Everyone waved and waved, including Father Fraser, who had on his initial arrival told Jock he'd never seen such a waving group in his entire life.

He's entered in, Jock thought as he stood waiting for June to steer John's four oarsmen to shore. My new friend, James Fraser, is one of us now. Perhaps a touch overly Scottified yet, but one of us. "We won't keep you!" Jock shouted. "We're just ever so glad for you to use my boat and what a pleasant surprise to see you, John, and Anne and"—he held out both arms to the girls as they climbed excitedly out of the boat—"especially are we happy to see these two young ladies!"

While Anne and the girls chatted and laughed, Jock Couper leaned down from the dock to speak to Father Fraser.

"There was so much to talk about in such a short visit, James, I entirely forgot to inform you that I have fine plans for an important event to take place just as soon as the weather warms in the spring again. An important event having to do with you, sir!"

"Aye? And what could that be, Jock?"

"You will be, because of your pure Scottish blood, inducted at the president's request into the newly formed Society of St. Andrew of Darien! Our Darien chapter was organized only last March and I hereby invite you to become a member."

"But won't the others have some say in the matter? In particular, the president?"

Jock laughed. "He does indeed have a say because I'm the president. My close friend Mr. Thomas Spalding is the vice president, and if our fir-r-st meeting was an indication, you'll be right at home in the society. You see, 'tis made up only of Scottish merchants and planters in the Darien area, and mon, we truly celebrate our heritage! Two or three Scottish daughters prepare the haggis—"

Fraser grinned. "Ah, haggis?"

"Aye, the best you ever tasted and you're more than welcome to join us. You and, of course, Dr. William. John's already a member."

He saw Fraser's grin fade. "John's a member and William isn't?"

"Dr. William was invited, of course," Jock said. "But we met on a day when he had several sick patients, so he couldn't be present. From now on, though, the Darien Society of St. Andrew will be honored by the presence and membership of not one but three Frasers."

"And our illustrious membership welcomes you, Father," John said, so lightheartedly that Jock couldn't help noticing the change in the lad from yesterday. "I swear I wasn't eavesdropping, but I did hear what you said, Papa Couper. And I'm more than pleased, sir. And Father, Mr. Couper's right about the excellence of that haggis. You know I've never liked the mess. What these Scottish daughters prepared was different. Superior!"

For a brief moment Couper caught a certain look on James Fraser's long, normally unanimated face. A look that was both curious and somehow pleasantly surprised. An odd look, but then, as much as Jock Couper liked the man, he would never argue that Fraser wasn't an odd piece. The look, half-mystified and half-pleased, was directed at only John, and John, bless the boy, was beaming back at his father. Had the two, Couper wondered and had to control himself to keep from asking, had a particularly meaningful exchange? Had brittle old James found a way to let John know of his pride in him? Well, Jock thought, seeing June's impatience to start the other oarsmen on their way, no time to learn about any of it now—if indeed there was anything to learn.

John will inform me eventually. The lad and I have plenty of time alone together in our fields.

"We oughta be under way, Mausa Couper," June prodded him, waiting as always for Couper's order.

"We do so hate to see you go, Frances Anne," Anne called. "But take my word for it, all is going to be very well when you reach your own home on the Ridge again."

Couper's alert eyes caught the look between his daughter and her childhood friend Frances Anne. There was more in that look, too, than met his eye. Had something been awry at Dr. William's place in Darien that Couper didn't know? Something Frances Anne had confided to Anne? For the sake of his new and valued friend, James Fraser, he fervently hoped not. Heaven knew the man was already being forced by old age and business failure to make more wrenching changes in his life than anyone nearing seventy should ever have to make.

CHAPTER 10

DURING THE EXTREME HEAT OF JULY AND AUGUST, William thought it wise for his father not to make the trip from Darien to visit John's family and the Coupers, although the old man plainly showed his restlessness.

"And does the heat let up come September?" he asked William and Frances Anne at breakfast one morning during the last week in August. "In London I all but prayed for warm weather. Now I'd give real money for a good, wet, cold English fog off the Thames."

William glimpsed the frustration on his wife's face when she poured more tea for his parent. "We're all doing our very best, Father Fraser, to make your life pleasant," she said, an unmistakable edge in her voice. "You haven't been fishing for weeks. You used to enjoy that, and there's almost always a good breeze on the Darien River."

It never surprised William when his father merely grunted instead of giving a direct answer to a question from either of them, but it seemed always to surprise, even to annoy, Frances Anne.

"Are you not hearing well today?" she asked her father-in-law. "Don't you know it helps you to get out in the fresh air? Don't you like to fish anymore?"

"Does it cool off in September?" the older man repeated, not unpleasantly, but as though Frances Anne had said nothing.

"Sometimes," William said with a grin. "We can't count on it, though, until well into October. Does the Georgia sun bother your head, Father?"

"I'd think it might bother anyone's head. I'll go fishing when I'm of a mind to fish, but it would be pleasing if my son would deign to accompany me now and then."

Now, good-natured William laughed softly. "Oh, I deign to go, Father. In fact, I'd love to go fishing with you every day."

"But you have some very sick patients. I know, I know."

"I'd think you'd be proud that William is now in full charge of the Darien Hospital, Father Fraser," Frances Anne said. "I know I'm certainly proud of him. I'm not only proud of my husband's mounting reputation in the city, I can honestly see my own stature rising among the Darien blue bloods simply because I'm Dr. William Fraser's wife."

"Wait," Father Fraser mumbled, "until he's elected mayor."

"Are you seriously considering accepting the nomination?" she asked, giving William no clue as to how she truly felt about the whole idea.

"Today I'm considering only Father's well-being, this excellent breakfast served to me by my beautiful wife, and the fact that I should have been at the hospital half an hour ago."

"Unless my dear little granddaughter Annie is mistaken, or unless something comes up on his turbulent plantation to delay him, my son Johnnie should be reaching Darien sometime today," Father Fraser said out of the blue.

Standing now, William exclaimed, "John is coming to visit us today, Father? Are you sure?"

"My darling Annie is far more faithful at writing to me than either of her parents, and the gir-r-l is seldom wrong. Is it so surprising that Johnnie be paying his father a visit?"

William and Frances Anne exchanged looks. He had told her soon after his father reached their comfortable frame home on the Ridge near Darien that never before in his entire life had Father Fraser ever called his brother by the endearing nickname Johnnie. William had also told her that he strongly hoped it meant the old gentleman had at last allowed John to share what had, even to the usually philosophical William, been a somewhat suffocating bond between him and his father. All summer long the elder Fraser had, when he'd mentioned John at all, referred to him in the old way as John. Today, within minutes, he had twice called him Johnnie. William was hopeful. Through all the years of his life, he had sincerely longed to be on equal footing in his father's estimation with John—no more favored by their parent, no less. That the two brothers were vastly different William certainly knew, and although he kept hoping their father would find interesting variety in their differences, he had known for many years that Father Fraser felt secure only with him. Still, he took heart now because both he and Frances Anne had heard the old fellow call his brother Johnnie, the affectionate name used in the past only by their late mother and by dear Flora McLeod.

"Do you expect my brother before dinner, Father?" William asked as he reached for his hat.

"If Jock's oarsmen are bringing him, I should think yes."

William grinned. "You and Mr. Couper are already fast friends, aren't you?"

"Aye."

William bent to kiss Frances. Then, heading for the front door, he called back to them both, "If John comes here before he stops at the hospital to see me, will you ask him to be sure he does pay me a visit in my office before time for dinner?"

LEFT ALONE AT THE BREAKFAST TABLE TOGETHER, neither Father Fraser nor Frances looked directly at the other.

For a time, both sat stirring their tea. Stirring far more than necessary.

"And do you have any idea why William needs to see his brother before we dine today, Frances Anne?"

"No, Father Fraser, I most certainly do not have the faintest idea. I'm sure you could tell that I was as surprised as William when you made your announcement about John's arrival." She was using the voice that seemed appropriate in conversation with her father-in-law. It was, first of all, ladylike. It was, she hoped, always kind, but it was also not a tone that encouraged more idle talk than necessary. "I suppose he's coming alone."

"My granddaughter Annie would surely have written were someone else coming with him." The old man cleared his throat, sat straight in his chair, and added, "It's quite possible, you know, that Johnnie means only to be paying his father a visit. It has been a long time since Dr. William has permitted me to see any of my St. Simons family."

On her feet now, clearing the table, Frances Anne said matter-of-factly, "You, of all people, know that William only means you well, sir. He takes his role as your personal physician very seriously. May I ring for Nell to bring you more tea?"

"No, thank you. My son approves of my having only two cups."

"Then, if you'll excuse me, I'll take these dishes to the kitchen. Nell mentioned that she would like to begin her cleaning as early today as possible." She didn't like herself much for forcing him to respond. She did force him, by standing in the doorway to the kitchen, arms full of soiled china. When Father Fraser still said nothing, Frances repeated, "You will excuse me, I hope?"

"I didn't answer you, did I? I'm a discourteous old fool."

Her irritation changed to a wave of pity for the lonely, aging man who quite suddenly—simply by admitting his bad manners—touched her heart. For the first time, she wondered? If I'm honest, yes. But is pity going to be enough to get me through these long, long days shut up here in this house with him when I have no true idea of what he really thinks of me? No wonder Anne's John has always been afraid of his own father! Maybe not so afraid as unsure of what the old gentleman is thinking.

With all her heart, Frances Anne longed for Anne to be with John if indeed he was arriving today.

"NELL? NELL?" THE KITCHEN WAS EMPTY WHEN Frances reached it with her armful of dishes. "Nell! Where are you?" Silence, except for a blue jay squawking in the cedar tree outside the corner kitchen window. "Where in the name of heaven *is* that woman? When I want her out from underfoot, she's always standing there wanting something. When I need her to wash our dishes, she's vanished." Banging the stack of china on the dry sink every bit as recklessly as Nell banged, Frances hurried to the back porch.

"Nell! Nell, I need you. We are probably having a guest for dinner and there are dirty dishes and the house to clean!"

From the yard, off behind a stand of azalea bushes came Nell's South Carolina Gullah answer, "Yas'm. I be out here lookin' arter de boy, ma'am."

"My son, James, is quite all right playing alone in his new sandbox. I need you!"

"Frances? Frances Anne!"

Now, all the way from the dining room—probably still seated at the breakfast table—Father Fraser was calling her. She simply had no time to pamper him as usual this morning, not with John's arriving anytime from St. Simons Island. "What is it, Father Fraser? Can't you come out on the back porch? Better still, walk around to the backyard and talk with your grandson, your namesake, James," she all but shouted. Then she did shout: "Nell! Are you coming in this house or aren't you?"

"Yas'm. Yas'm," Nell said, puffing up the back steps, the strong scent of pipe tobacco following her.

"You've been out behind those bushes having a smoke, haven't you?"

"Yas'm."

"Why do you go on doing that when you know I forbid it?"

"I goes out 'cause you don' 'low nobody but mens to use t'baccy in de house, ma'am. What compny we got comin'?"

"There isn't time to explain everything to you right now. Just get those breakfast dishes in hot, sudsy water at once."

W ITH TWO F REWIN SLAVES HANDLING THE SHEETS, Captain James Frewin's sloop eased in toward the busy wharf at Darien, Georgia, just after three o'clock that afternoon, and John again felt the familiar anxiety at the prospect of seeing his father. Whether he had to walk the three miles to the Ridge, northeast of Darien, where William lived, or could find a ride, he would soon be face-to-face with his father. To calm his nervousness, he reminded himself that the last time parent and son had been together, there had seemed to be changes for the better in his father's attitude toward him. En route with a favorable wind and a smooth trip, John had listened attentively to Frewin's talk of his own future but had made no mention of his parent. Of course Captain Frewin knew John would be seeing his father, but though comfortable friends with the fifty-year-old captain, he had never confided one word about the fact that his father favored William. It was too important that Frewin respect John, too important that John go on making himself likable to all his St. Simons neighbors, to take a chance. Except for Papa Couper, John never spoke confidentially with any Island gentleman.

During the water trip from Frederica—some five or six hours longer by sloop than by plantation boat—Frewin had really done most of the talking. Despite his natural bent to take over conversations, John had found the man's company surprisingly interesting, even absorbing. Captain Frewin understood John's secret rebellion at being forced to leave the Royal Marines. After all, Frewin had served for years in the Royal Navy, had spent most of his life as a mariner. But plainly, that was behind him now. The man had come under the spell of St. Simons Island. To Frewin, as much as he had loved his life at sea, nothing had ever gripped him as did the potential of his future on St. Simons.

"I had a bit of a struggle over owning slaves at the start," Frewin had said. "You know the English attitude on the South's system, but when a man sees the possibilities I see, a kind of mental reorganization takes place."

John knew that James Frewin had come to America from London back about the time he and Anne were married. He also knew that when Frewin became a naturalized United States citizen in Savannah, the man had little capital; he was married now to a quiet-mannered lady named Sarah Dorothy and kept a little battery tavern and store near the Frederica River. John had seen the lots his friend already owned at Frederica; he also had horses, cattle, poultry, hogs, and one riding chair, envied by his less well off neighbors still living near the site of the old colonial town of Frederica on the leeward side of St. Simons Island. Captain Frewin also owned a roomy packet and earned extra income from the coasting trade, mostly in cotton bales he transported to Darien and Savannah from Island plantations.

"I have no intention, Captain, of prying," John said, "but all along our way today you've touched on the subject of your promising future plans. I confess I'm interested. A man's future is all-important when he heads a family. The good Lord knows it took me long enough to discover that."

"But you've discovered it now, Fraser," Frewin said, "and according to your father-in-law, John Couper, a man of excellent judgment, you also have a promising life ahead. As for me, I'm flattered by your interest in my plans, which came about through a plain old stroke of luck. And for you to grasp the importance of what I hope to do, you should keep in mind that I've completely lost my heart to the area around the Old Fort at Frederica. John, there's simply nothing to compare with an Island sunset, flaring flame and gold out over the Frederica River beyond the ruins of James Oglethorpe's once-sturdy tabby fort and parade grounds." Frewin's dark eyes glowed as he talked. "You see, my friend, this very year, this month if I'm fortunate enough today to borrow the money at the Bank of Darien, all that parcel of land at Frederica known as the Old Fort can be mine! That includes the improvements on the land, consisting of a large and commodious dwelling house. Just think of it. And the best part is that I can buy it all at a sheriff's sale for the sum of three hundred dollars!"

John, proud and grateful as he was with Couper's gift of Lawrence, felt his own heart race at the prospect that he too might someday—on his own—be able to risk such a shrewd business undertaking. After all his years of wanderlust, would Anne be able to believe that her unsettled husband could actually *long* to put down roots in a place of his own?

"Your mentor, Jock Couper, informed me just last week, when he rode to Frederica for the post, that you'll have a good crop of cotton this year. A truly profitable crop, which you saw all the way to picking time by your own good efforts. Is that the reason you're bound for Savannah with me on my trusty sloop tomorrow? Seeing your factor, Habersham, up there?"

"Yes," John answered. "Because both Coupers use him, so do I. I'll be calling on him to borrow money on my crop, but"—he looked in the direction of the two Negroes and added just above a whisper—"my main reason for going to Savannah is to attend the slave market."

"Ah-h! Now that is the mark of a successful planter! How many Negroes do you plan to buy?"

Still uneasy with the idea of speaking so bluntly in the presence of Negroes as though the two slaves aboard weren't within hearing distance, John simply held up four fingers. "I don't think Mr. Couper trusts me with the purchase of more on my own." Again he lowered his voice. "I've never bought a slave."

Frewin grinned. "Is Couper testing you by sending you alone?"

"Undoubtedly. So wish me well. I don't look forward to the transaction."

"I remember my first purchase of three slaves. Never easy for an Englishman, but of course I was a United States citizen by then. Three were all I could afford. I did fine, though. So will you, John. Unless I miss my guess, you're finally interested in becoming a good planter."

"It's all so—so different," John said, "so unlike anything I've ever done in my entire life, I hesitate to agree outright, but yes. I do know I'm more interested every day." Again he lowered his voice. "The only thing that has me worried is—is—"

"The slave market."

"Yes. *And* whether or not I should tell my father I'm buying people. He's thoroughly British in his hatred of the institution."

"What of your brother, Dr. William Fraser? I know he's a practicing physician, but he must own a few house people."

"He does. Two." John tried an easy smile. "My father has always approved of anything my brother does. Not always true with me."

"I see."

Perhaps Frewin understood, perhaps not, John thought, but the man meant well. Wanting no more talk of the hateful subject, he began to question Frewin again concerning his own future. "Seeing the high state of your spirits, Captain, I sense my own spirits beginning to rise. You do firmly believe there's a good future on St. Simons, don't you?"

"I do indeed. Glynn County is rich in long-staple cotton land. And the power of the Bank of Darien is nearby for every man in the area to use. That bank is the best friend we have. Coastal planters need capital for everything they undertake, and planting has come to be so lucrative both in our county of Glynn and in McIntosh, Savannah's Planter's Bank was no longer adequate; nor was it convenient enough for prosperous men such as the Coupers, King at Retreat, or Thomas Spalding of Sapelo. Darien's burgeoning prosperity required a bank close by. Now the bank is nurturing Darien itself. The city, by way of its bank, is even a repository for federal funds—in part, at least, because of the increasing cotton market."

"Sounds as though Savannah will need to look to her laurels in the face of what appears to be happening here in Darien," John said, actually beginning to feel a part of the area's business pulse and liking it more than he ever dreamed he might.

"There are those who contend that the Bank of Darien is the largest south of Philadelphia," Frewin mused. "True or not, it is the leading financial institution of the state, if not the entire South."

The two friends were standing in the sloop's bow, taking in the amazing changes evident along the busy Darien waterfront, much of which had, only a few years ago, been burned. John, in particular, was impressed, since he hadn't been north of St. Simons Island in almost a year.

"If I weren't seeing all that with my own eyes, I'd doubt the number and height of those buildings—the busyness along the Darien wharfs!" John exclaimed. "I'd say it could soon rival Savannah's famous Factor's Walk."

For the next half hour or so the two men busied themselves, simply because they both loved the water, supervising the docking of Frewin's sloop. John kept an eye out ashore for a possible ride over the three miles or so between the Darien waterfront and the upper-class residential section called the Ridge, where William's good house stood—the house John had never seen. It would bolster his courage if he could pay a brief visit to William at the Darien Hospital on Broad before he saw their father. A word from William on the health and spirits of their parent might help him decide whether he dared tell Father that he was on his way tomorrow to the Savannah slave market.

As never before, he felt real sympathy for how alone, how foreign, Father Fraser must feel in Darien most of the time. Did the old gentleman know anyone at all who shared his antislavery views? How did he enter into conversations with Southern people who must think him a crank for holding such views? How had their father acted when he learned that William, his favorite, owned two people—a woman in the house and a man who cared for the spacious yard and William's team and carriage?

Thanks to Frewin's good connections, the offer of a ride to the Ridge came before John and Frewin had walked two blocks along the business section near the wharf. In all ways the offer could not have been better for John, and the means by which it came about would, he thought, impress his father. Not far from the Bank of Darien, Frewin introduced him to the new president of the bank, Dr. James Troup, a medical colleague of William's.

"You must be living right, Mr. Fraser," the ebullient Troup said heartily when John told him of his need for a conveyance. "I'm not only about to send one of my most dependable servants to make a delivery at the Ridge, he can take you along and wait for you while you visit with your brother. You'll pass right by the hospital."

"I say, I'm most grateful, Dr. Troup," John said. "My time is a bit limited today and my often-impatient father is expecting me, I'm sure, for a late dinner."

"One thing you should know," Troup said. "My man, Jasper, driver of the wagon and team, is almost stone-deaf. When you need to stop for any reason, just yank on his sleeve. Then hold up one hand. He knows that signal means that he is to stop and wait for you to return to the wagon."

Again, John thanked Dr. Troup and promised Frewin to meet him for the water trip on to Savannah tomorrow morning at seven o'clock sharp. "I also wish you luck at the bank, Captain Frewin," he added with a smile. "In company with the president himself I doubt your need of luck."

"In the market for a loan?" Troup asked Frewin pleasantly.

"I am, sir, and I'll explain fully, but first I'm certain my friend Mr. Fraser needs directions to the wagon and driver. And if your driver's deaf—"

Troup snapped his fingers. "Of course. I forgot. Everyone in town knows my Jasper and my wagon. With your brother about to become our mayor, I don't think of you as a foreigner, Mr. Fraser. My apologies."

John laughed. "I—I am a foreigner, sir. In many ways. But I'm extremely grateful for your kindness."

"We Darien people pride ourselves on kindness and hospitality. Now, do you see the large dray loading lumber in the cobblestone alley alongside that three-story brick warehouse, Fraser?"

"Yes, sir."

"That's your regal conveyance and the darky standing beside it is your driver, Jasper. Come along and I'll instruct him. I know exactly which of his old ears to shout into."

CHAPTER 11

As John was being driven along Broad Street toward the Darien Hospital, he wondered if Jasper's perpetually peaceful expression might be due to the fact that the poor man simply couldn't hear the racket of the other drays and carts, the shouts from the wharf, barking dogs, boat whistles, bells. Now and then, until John fell into a deep reverie, the two exchanged smiles. Not talking was always hard for John, and somehow he found himself more impatient than usual that he couldn't converse with this silent, smiling Negro man. What did Jasper really think about being a slave? Even a man in bondage to a kind gentleman like Dr. Troup must feel resentment that he has no choice but to exist in a mainly choiceless life. A slave owner allowed his property few or no choices. Certainly not in the areas that make a man or a woman feel human.

John sighed heavily and thanked God that his thoughts were not audible to this dignified, dark, warmhearted man on the wagon seat beside him. How could he know that Jasper was a warmhearted person? For all John knew, the old slave may carry a heart twisted with hatred toward all white men. What would stop Jasper from getting through his days merely using that frequent, warm, almost toothless smile as a means of adding a comfort or two to his own dreary existence? A smiling Negro often found himself rewarded by a smiling owner. Papa Couper had told John that his own opinion of himself was formed, in part at least, by his concept of what his people thought of him. "Make a man—any man—feel good and he'll be far more likely to be agreeable to you in return," Papa Couper advised.

"The word is *understanding*," young James Hamilton Couper had counseled John again and again, especially on the days when James visited Lawrence and found John being either too lenient or too strict with his fieldhands. "A well-run plantation is predicated on perfect understanding, John. A perfect understanding between servant and master." When John had asked James Hamilton to elucidate, the tall, stern-faced, disciplined brother of tender Anne had said, "A perfect understanding between a master and a slave means that the slave should know that his master is to govern absolutely and he, the slave, to obey implicitly. That he, the slave, is never for a moment to exercise either his will or his judgment in opposition to the master's positive order. Strict adherence to this perfect understanding will benefit the slave as well as profit the owner. Such perfect understanding spreads peace and harmony."

Out of the corner of his eye, John glanced at Jasper. The old man smiled again.

What degree of "perfect understanding" does Dr. James Troup, such a good-natured, hearty gentleman, have between himself and Jasper? Does it ever occur to Troup that Jasper might not *want* to make this delivery today to the Ridge? Might not want to have me riding along beside him, totally dependent on him because I wouldn't recognize my brother's house or the hospital? Somehow it didn't occur to John that Jasper would not know both buildings. He had found it easy to trust Negroes from the start. "Too easy," Papa Couper sometimes said, with a grin that caused John to suspect that the laird of Cannon's Point may also be too trusting of the human beings he owned.

When Jasper reached to tap him lightly on the arm, then pointed to a large, square, white building about a quarter of a mile ahead, John guessed it must be William's hospital. Was William really running for mayor of Darien? Of course he'd make a good one, but would John ever be able to match such an honor? Did one good cotton crop prove him equal to William? Would the profitable crop impress their father at all? Or did he have to do so well that, like Frewin, John too might be eligible for a loan from the Bank of Darien before Father Fraser would consider his elder son a success?

They had almost reached the hospital. What if William didn't have time for a visit? Why did even a brief talk with his brother before John saw their father seem so important? Did he mean to tell William of his own dread of their father's finding out that he, John, was finally learning how to be a planter? That he was learning to like it most days? Did he mean to tell William of his own dread of their father's finding out that John was about to take part in a slave auction? How had William purchased the two people he owned in Darien? Had he attended the Savannah slave market himself? Or purchased them from a neighbor? Would he tell William not only that he dreaded their father's finding out that John would, of his own free will, bid for the very lives of four other human beings, but that he still had no idea whatever of how he, John, was going to bring himself to do such a hateful thing?

In no way had he been made ready for the obnoxious task ahead by having directly supervised the Lawrence slaves for three years. The memory of those days when he performed as a slave master with the clumsiness and softness of a sentimental fool, allowing them to loaf at their work, to talk him into long rest periods, to feign illnesses, not only caused him embarrassment to this day but also brought a conflicting rush of downright pride in what had seemed his own decency. *How could these contradictory things be true?*

How could he be proud of his own foolish, seemingly decent heart, when that same heart so respects the most skillful of all slave masters, John Couper himself? He had long ago realized that the elder Couper would never profit from his people in quite the same way Anne's brother James Hamilton would profit, but to John there was as much difference between the two men as between sun and rain. He respected James Hamilton's work because it was as brilliant as the sun and as dependable. "My son James Hamilton," Papa Couper had often said, "will always outshine his father in aptitude and talent. The lad is so talented, he must surprise even himself!" All true, John knew, and yet to him, the ideal of true human success was to be found only in John Couper, the laird of Cannon's Point.

John sighed deeply, wonderingly. *The laird of Cannon's Point is also a slave owner.*

Jasper was drawing the loaded dray to one side of the dirt road and reining the team to a stop before the large, white hospital. The slave was smiling broadly at John, exposing three yellow teeth and empty gums. John smiled back, remembering Dr. Troup's instruction to raise one hand so that Jasper would wait.

WILLIAM MET HIM IN THE FRONT HALL OF THE HOS-pital, and the two brothers greeted each other with hearty hugs. "I saw you get out of Dr. Troup's wagon," William said. "I also saw that he'd taught you how to signal deaf old Jasper. And don't worry, the man will wait as patiently as a fence post." He led John down the narrow hallway and ushered him into his tiny, crowded office. "We're not always fancy here in Darien, but we are busy. I'd better warn you I could be called any minute to the ward. I'm quite sure one of my patients won't make it through the day."

William sat behind his cluttered desk, John in the one chair beside it. "I probably should have gone straight to your house," John said, then stopped and studied William's quiet, weary face. "You live a nerve-racking life, don't you, Brother?"

"Any doctor does who's worth his salt. I'm glad you stopped by."

"From all I hear, you're going to be elected mayor of Darien. How can you carry still more responsibility?"

William shrugged, then smiled. "The people of Darien have

been too hospitable, too kind to Frances Anne and me to refuse. I'll find a way—if I'm elected."

"Busy as you are, I really shouldn't have stopped. I'm not quite sure why I did, frankly, except I need a little preparation for seeing Father again. How's his health? I'm sure he's fidgeting for me to get there right now, to the total irritation of poor Frances Anne, I have no doubt."

"I'm also sure he's fidgeting," William said, "but he seems fairly well most days, and now and then I'm convinced my lovely wife is learning how to control herself with him. Our father has never been an easy man to have around. You look in good spirits, Brother."

"I am, thank you. Everyone back on St. Simons is fine, too. By the way, I'm here only overnight. I leave early tomorrow for Savannah."

"I don't believe Annie told Father that in her letter. Do you have to leave so soon? The old boy will be crushed."

John gave a short laugh. "I know he softened a bit toward me while you were all still on St. Simons, but I don't look for him to be crushed."

William sighed. "How can any of us really know what goes on inside our father, John?"

"I've spent most of my life believing you knew. The truth is, he's our father and I'm beginning to believe I love and cherish him more than I've ever been able to admit. It's a good feeling, actually." John stood up. "I should go. It isn't fair to keep Jasper waiting." The two shook hands. "You're needed here at the hospital."

"No one has shouted my name yet. If old Mr. Jones takes a turn for the worst, his daughter will yell like fury—expecting me to make a miracle in a ninety-year-old man with rapidly failing kidneys."

At the door to William's office, John stopped. "William, just to prepare you for what could be a difficult evening at home, I'm going to Savannah to attend a slave auction."

"Sorry to hear you have to do that."

"You own two people, don't you?"

"Yes, but Father assumed Nell and Bob came with my house when I bought it."

"As part of the furniture?"

William grinned weakly. "I suppose so. Will you tell Father what you're aiming to do in Savannah?"

"Should I?"

"Is that why you stopped here first? To ask my advice on an issue like that?"

"I'm not sure. But I am sure I need to go. I'll be there, peacefully or otherwise, by the time you reach—"

John's voice was drowned out by a woman's frantic, shrill scream from the hallway: "Doctah Frasah! *Doctah!* Doctah Frasah! In the name of God, hurry! Papa's goin' fast! You oughta be with him—not in youah office takin' youah ease!"

BACK IN THE WAGON BESIDE JASPER, JOHN MARveled at his brother's dedication and patience. There had never been a time in William's life when he hadn't known that he meant to be a doctor. John hoped the frantic woman's father wouldn't die. William's even disposition and pleasantness seemed never to be broken except when his doctor's heart broke at the loss of a patient.

John and deaf Jasper exchanged smiles again, and John settled back against the straight, wooden seat for the mile or so remaining until they pulled up at William's place. A good thing, he thought, that Jasper knows the house. Frances Anne had written to Anne about it, had seemed pleased with its roominess, and after it received a coat of paint, thought the two-storied frame building most pleasing.

Of course his father had written only that "William has a good, well-built house." John smiled briefly to himself. His father had never been known, so far as he or William could tell, to utter one more word than necessary. With all his heart, he hoped the old gentleman would at least say enough for John to glean some idea of whether he would ever be able to understand that as a coastal Georgia planter, his son had no choice but to buy slaves. Maybe he could count on his parent's regard for Jock Couper. There was no doubt about the high esteem in which he held Anne's father.

Still, John thought, I'm not Jock Couper. I am my father's son, though, and if I'm honest, I have to admit that Anne is right when she vows she can sense that some of the barriers between Father and me have begun to fall down. At least from my side.

His mind flew back to the near hysteria in the voice of the woman shouting at poor William through the closed office door. Father Fraser would sicken and die some day too. It was a shocking thought. There was so much left unsaid, so much left undone between them. Would William's grief be sharper because he and Father had always been close? Should John's be any less sharp because he had never learned how to conduct himself with the man whose approval and blessing had always seemed so out of reach?

Jasper startled John with a light jab on the shoulder. Another big grin on his face, the old Negro pointed to an impressive frame house set back from the road under two great live oaks, flanked by huge magnolia trees.

"Oh," John said. "I see we're here." Remembering he was not being plainly heard, he reached for his valise, jumped to the sandy road, and hurried around to the driver's side of the wagon to shake hands with Jasper and to thank him with an exaggerated nod of his head and then a bona fide Royal Marine salute.

Before Jasper had started the team again, John saw his father sitting with William's small son on the front porch. For a moment he just stood there in the road. His father remained motionless in his chair.

Finally the older man raised a hand in greeting. John ran along the shell driveway that curved from the road to the house and up the three front steps. When Father Fraser stood, John dropped the valise and for the first time in memory, embraced him. Until young James began to tug at John's coat, he held his parent, conscious of the old bones, aware that this stern, stony man was growing frail.

"Father," John said with uncontrollable feeling. "Father, I'm happy to see you looking so fit!" Then, while small James continued to hang on to John's leg—shouting "Man, man!"—John marveled that he'd fallen into the timeworn lie of the young to the old. His father did *not* look fit. Far from it. Oh, the thin arms had gripped John with a hint of their old strength, but within a few months' time his father had aged alarmingly.

Both ended the embrace on a similar, half-embarrassed, awkward movement, and Father Fraser reached for little James. "This isn't just a man, James," he said. "This is your very own Uncle John Fraser. Your father's only brother. Don't you remember when you took a boat ride to St. Simons Island, back when I first came from London?"

The boy laughed. Then hitting John on the thigh, he said, "Sure!"

"Don't let your mother hear you say 'sure,'" John's father admonished. "She'll threaten you with Nell's boo-daddy." Appearing almost to enjoy his role of speaking first to John, then to young James—explaining them to each other—Father Fraser now addressed John. "You see, Son, Frances Anne is trying to bring the boy up to speak proper English. She does *not* approve of 'sure.' Where he got it I haven't the faintest idea."

John tried to laugh. "I'll do my best to set a good example while I'm here this evening."

"Here?" James asked.

"Your mother and father and I haven't seen your uncle for a long time, James. He's an honored and welcome guest in our house." Turning to John again, the older man asked, "Do you mean you're only spending this night with us?"

"I'm afraid that's right. You see, I have to sail on to Savannah early tomorrow. I'm traveling with my neighbor Captain James Frewin, in his coasting sloop."

"Business?"

"Business, Father." Hoping to keep their talk—so far easier than any they'd ever had—on a pleasant note, John asked after Frances Anne.

"I neglected her apologies, Son. William's wife is quilting. It seems that when the Darien ladies decide on a meeting date for

any of their female endeavors, nothing, not even a rare visit by a
family member, alters the plan. I'm sure she gave the woman, Nell,
her orders this morning, and I'm to inform you that Frances will
return for dinner. I urged William to leave the hospital early so
that we might all have time for a good talk together." He motioned John toward a tall-backed, white rocker. "Take that chair.
There's only Nell until William's man, Bob, drives Frances Anne
home in an hour or so. Just leave your valise where it is. Frances
will show you your room later. Bob will carry the luggage." The
old man smiled an almost teasing smile. "I know you're accustomed now to many servants."

For the first time since John had run up onto the porch of
William's house, the two fell into one of their old, awkward silences. Even young James was no help. He had climbed up on his
grandfather's knee and was sitting there as quiet and well-behaved
as any grown gentleman in an English drawing room.

Father Fraser broke the silence by inquiring after the health of
Anne, Pete, and his beloved Annie.

"Fine, I'm thankful to say. All just fine. Anne, of course, sends
undying love to you, as does my daughter Annie. Pete shouted so
many messages as I was readying myself to ride off to meet Frewin
at Frederica, they're all still a jumble in my mind."

"You've done well with your family, Son."

John felt the color rise in his face. Such a small, proper compliment from his father could still cause him to flush like a small boy.
"Father, I'm always happy when I please you." He chuckled a bit.
"The times I've pleased you have been so few, I recall almost every
one, but I do agree. I've done well with my family. Perhaps I
should say they've all done more than well for me—by me." He
stopped smiling. "I never stop marveling at Anne's patience with
me, Father."

"Who's Anne?" the boy wanted to know.

"Anne is your aunt, just as this is your uncle. I might add,
James, that Aunt Anne is one of your grandfather's favorite people
on earth. She and I are true friends. The truest."

"Like Mama?" James asked.

John saw a touch of the old rigidity return to his father's face. "Let's say your mama and I are—friends."

Blunt as always, John thought. I must be watchful at dinner.

"Play with me in my sandpile, Uncle John!"

"Well, now, James, I'm sure we'll find time for that before I have to leave."

"I wanna play now!"

"Later, lad," Father Fraser said. "But I have an excellent idea. Why don't you go on around the house and begin building something you especially want to build, and after a bit, Uncle John can join you."

John felt himself stiffen. He'd counted on the boy as a kind of safeguard against the moment when he'd have to tell his father the nature of his business in Savannah.

Almost at once, James slid from his grandfather's bony knee, ran off the porch, around the house and out of sight. The silence rose around them again.

Finally Father Fraser said, "So, you're sailing to Savannah tomorrow. And will you stop to visit us on your return trip?"

Stalling, John rather elaborately cleared his throat, feigned a slight coughing spell.

As though intentionally coming to his rescue, Father Fraser said, "Various kinds of pollen in the air around here, Jock Couper told me. One type or another most of the year."

John grinned. "So my wife's illustrious brother James Hamilton declares. In fact, he delivered quite a lecture on the subject the last time he paid us a visit at Lawrence. By the way, he's talking now of building a huge sugar mill on his vast holdings called Hopeton."

"I suppose it's to be expected that the man will succeed at whatever he does."

"Yes, sir."

After a time, his father asked, "Young James Hamilton hasn't mentioned anything about his St. Simons plantation to you, John?"

John sat up. "To me, Father? I should say not! He seldom discusses his affairs with me. I'm still a novice in all ways to him. Oh, we get along rather well. I manage to give him an attentive audience when he feels a lecture coming on." He laughed. "At times I think my wife's brother feels lectures overtaking him much the way we average human beings are overtaken by a chill or a stomach cramp."

His father not only smiled, he chuckled audibly. "You're too intelligent not to admire the gentleman wholeheartedly, but you must have to control your—could I say irritation with his almost overpowering good fortune and brains."

"You could say irritation, sir, and find me in total agreement. And I do control myself rather admirably, if I am forced to admit it. I also respect James Hamilton highly."

For a long moment the older man looked straight into John's face. Then he said firmly, "I'm proud of you for that. I commend you for remaining staunch friends with your influential brother-in-law."

Well aware that he must again look like a delighted small boy, John beamed at his father, frowned briefly, then relaxed. "I say, sir, we're having a—a wonderful talk, aren't we? I don't remember ever feeling so—so at home with you before! I even feel as though I should thank you."

As though John had made no comment at all, Father Fraser asked, "You know, don't you, Son, that Jock Couper and I correspond now and then?"

"I'm not surprised. The man is genuinely fond of you. Seldom a day goes by but that he wishes aloud you had chosen to live on the Island with us." He hadn't intended to say that. His father loathed being pushed in a conversation.

Again, as though John had not spoken, Father Fraser mused, "The days are flying by, lad. Far faster than when you and William were boys. Faster than when you and blessed Anne lived with me in London. So fast are they flying that I have come to realize, sitting here on this porch or in my room alone hour after hour, that I have left much unsaid. If your mother was right that there is life after death, I have no doubt that I will live through all eternity wishing I'd been a father to you as I've tried to be to William."

Tears welled in John's eyes. Unbidden. This was not the time for further sentiment. His father had never liked it. He should think of something humorous, should offer his parent an easy way out of his darkening mood. Nothing came.

"Aye," the old man went on, "Jock and I correspond now and then. He did not forbid me to tell you and so, because too much has gone unsaid between us, I think you've a right to know that you are being carefully observed by James Hamilton Couper with the idea that within a few years, when the contract with his present overseer expires, you will be the man he chooses to manage it in full. I believe Hamilton Plantation is quite a bit larger than Lawrence, with many more—slaves. Am I right?"

His voice weak with shock, John could only say, "Aye, sir. It—it's larger by far."

"You are not to count on being offered such an opportunity. As your father, I merely think you deserve to know you're the one man under consideration for Hamilton. 'Twill give you courage and spirit to do an even better job at Lawrence than you may at present be doing."

On his feet because he was too stunned, too nervous, to sit still a minute longer, John asked, *"Papa Couper told you?"*

"However lax I've been as a parent, I've never lied to you, lad."

"I'm not accusing you of—but why would he tell you and not me?"

"I dinna know all there is to know about my new friend Jock. I only ken that he means you well, ver-r-y well indeed. He adores his younger daughter, Isabella, but my blessed Anne holds his old heart."

"Do you think Mr. Couper wanted you to tell me?"

"Aye."

"Is that all you plan to say—just aye?"

"Perhaps he promised his own son James Hamilton not to tell you himself. He wouldn't be breaking that promise now, would he, by telling me?"

"You know the esteemed laird of Cannon's Point very well, don't you?"

"Well enough to trust him with my—my fine planter son's future. My elder son, of whom I'm very proud."

John could only stare at him in silence, almost unable to believe that he had heard correctly.

"You're—*proud* of your planter son, Father?" he managed at last. Then, taking refuge in a small joke, he added, pacing up and down the porch, "You certainly understand Jock Couper's clever mind. That is, if you're right that he meant for you to tell me so I could work still harder." When his father remained silent, John again asked, "Did you mean it when you said you're—proud of your planter son?"

"That isn't what I said. I said I'm proud of my *fine* planter son. Jock tells me that in a year or so you'll be an outstanding coastal planter. And I want you to sit back down and stop walking around like a caged lion. I know why you're going to Savannah, and although I'd rather you struck me in the face than buy a slave, I also know—again Jock has helped convince me—that you cannot remain a planter without owning other human beings as chattel."

John sank back into the big, wooden rocker. "But Father, I'm not sure I can—go through with it!"

"You've been a slave master for three years."

"But they were the fieldhands, our cook, Mina, Big Boy, June, and Anne's favorite, Eve—all the property of one of the Coupers before I began to try to supervise them."

"I doubt that anyone, even Anne, actually supervises Eve. I spoke briefly with the girl one morning alone."

John smiled weakly. "You're right. No one, including Anne, truly bosses Eve. She is somehow different from all the rest."

"My guess is that she's part white. Do you know the name of her father?"

"No, sir. But apparently there's nothing so unusual about that among slaves." Then, both hands out almost beseechingly, John asked, "How am I going to—to *buy* another human being? At first I was deathly afraid even to tell you why I'm headed for Savannah. You helped me with that. Can you help me again? Could *you* bid mere money for the very life of a man like you or William or me? A woman like Anne or my mother?"

Without a moment's hesitation, his father barked, *"No."*

"Then how can I? From the first year of my life, I've known how you and Mother felt about the hideous practice of slavery. You taught me. You brought me up in an English society where men like John Couper and Anne's brother James Hamilton are called lords of the lash!"

"Aye, I did. And you must believe that I would be unable to pay money for the purchase of a living, breathing person. But John, I don't have to do it. I'm not the one who fell hopelessly in love with the tenderhearted, sweet daughter of a slave master. You did that. You are the one who has to conduct himself like the man Anne Couper Fraser loves with all her heart. You are the man who made those marriage vows with Anne. You are the man who accepted almost three hundred acres of fertile land from her slave-owning father and have been making use of the slaves he so generously included in what to him must have been a true, openhearted gift."

Still staring at his parent, John gasped, "I—I don't know what to say to you, sir."

"Don't say anything. Stiffen your spine. You're where you chose to be, so act like it." The old man squared his frail shoulders. "And remember that your father, even if he has to make use of your dear mother's faith, will be praying for you when you're forced to—to look into the eyes of the first Negro on whom you must offer a bid."

After a long silence, John murmured, "Thank you. . . ."

"I want only one promise from you."

"What, sir?"

"Promise me that you *will* look into the eyes of each slave before you buy. Will they be men or women?"

"I'm to buy four men. Three fieldhands and, if possible, a blacksmith."

"Very well. Do as Couper instructed, but look directly into each man's eyes, John. Don't talk to them. You usually say too much. Just look into the eyes of each man."

CHAPTER 12

FOR THE LIFE OF HIM, JOHN COULD NOT STOP thinking of the promise his father so unexpectedly demanded of him. Two days later, standing at the edge of a knot of other white men on the south side of Bay Street in Savannah, where the slave auction was about to begin, the promise to look each man in the eye before he bought him sickened John, but because his father had requested it, he meant to comply. He had never had any trouble looking into the eyes of a single slave among those given him by either Jock or James Hamilton Couper, but looking straight at a man he was about to buy of his own volition would be another matter.

On the strength of one good cotton crop, he was being forced just minutes from now to commit an ugly act that seemed to fit nowhere. Certainly to him, it didn't fit into the otherwise love-filled, genial atmosphere of life in his beloved Anne's cherished St. Simons Island world. Still, Anne's Island world of beauty-drenched sunlight and shadow, of laughter and games, of singing birds and deep woods, of thick vines and vast, glinting expanses of sunlit water, was also the world of hundreds of enslaved human beings. To Anne, this ugly fact seemed as natural a part of daily life as eating and sleeping and making love and rearing children. It was Anne's own familiar world, which, through all their years abroad, she had never stopped missing. Truthfully, it was a world in which John himself had at times been quite happy except for his own periods of failure—his periods of near desperation at the thought of living out his days in one spot, of riding the same fields, of winning the respect of, or causing snickers among, the very men and women he was supposed to be learning how to master.

For more than three years he had made his way by one means or another through each of these swamps of self-doubt, but today, laying them against this moment when he would have to make not one but four other men the property of John Fraser, the recent years of frustration seemed as nothing.

Stiffen your spine, John.

Standing in the hot, sticky summer heat of Savannah, Georgia —a sign before him read VALUABLE SLAVE AUCTION—he struggled as he had struggled through most of two sleepless nights to take it in. Father Fraser still hated slavery. But what went on searing through every bone and muscle in John's body was the still unexplainable fact that his stern, outwardly undemonstrative parent had promised to pray for him when John did what he now had to do or lose his last chance to be the kind of man Anne deserved.

The flash memory of four medals awarded him for courage in battle would have brought a smile, had there been a smile left in him this hot morning as he stood there at the edge of the cluster of bidders for human flesh. There would be no medal for what he meant to do today. Perhaps only he and his father would ever know the enormous courage John would be forced in minutes to find, to make use of, in order to keep Anne happy.

You are the man who made those marriage vows with Anne.

"Go buy your slaves, John," Captain James Frewin had said almost casually as he left to keep an appointment at the Cotton Exchange on Factor's Walk an hour ago. "We're signed out of our boarding house. I'll meet you at the wharf near Mark Browning's pier at eleven o'clock. Just walk your new slaves along on their chain and don't worry that I'll be late. I know this is a new experience for you. You may even be nervous about it. Don't be. Everything will go well."

John had looked out over the Savannah River when he asked, "Frewin, did you say—chain? Will I have to lead them to Browning's pier on a chain? Like cattle?"

John still had trouble believing Frewin's response, but the kindly gentleman had laughed at him. "A little like cattle, I guess. But no one is going to pay one bit of attention to you or your new purchases. See you at eleven. The tide will suit then."

For nearly an hour of the two hours left until time to meet Frewin, John had stood at the back of the group of men—planters and factors, he supposed—because the dread in him was too great to move nearer to where the scrawny, pockmarked auctioneer was selling off one slave after another. First a dark-skinned woman and a mulatto girl; then three strapping men, probably fieldhands; a chunkily built boy of about eleven or twelve. The boy, most likely Annie's age, stood like a real soldier—head up, flinching only once when the auctioneer's toneless voice urged the bidders to observe the lad's wide shoulders, his strong legs and arms, flicking him as he spieled with a riding crop.

John caught his breath. *I should buy that boy,* he thought, *to protect him! I was told not to buy a lad that young, though. I was told to buy only grown men. If Father is right about what Jock Couper confided in him, the supervision of Hamilton Plantation could hang in the balance. Well, at least the men I buy will not be whipped or sold off arbitrarily. If any of them takes a wife, he will never be sold away from her. Neither Jock Couper nor his son believed in breaking up families.*

John took a deep breath and stepped forward as the auctioneer flicked his crop in the direction of a slender but strong-appearing young man probably in his early twenties. John could almost hear the cultivated, gentlemanly words of James Hamilton: "A healthy young man still in his twenties can be turned into an invaluable fieldhand, even a driver."

The flat voice of the auctioneer rattled on about the good health and willingness of young Tiber, standing motionless in his chains even when ordered to turn around. John, fearing the young man might be struck with the whip unless he obeyed, asked his price in a voice that boomed unnecessarily because of his fear.

"Five hundred dollars is a steal for this young buck nigger," the auctioneer said.

John nodded immediate assent, counted out the money he'd borrowed yesterday from his factor, Habersham, handed it over without a word, and then, not knowing what was expected of him next, stepped back.

"Quick to dole out cash today, ain't chu, sir?" the auctioneer said, plainly scornful because John had made no effort to get a lower figure. "Whatsa matter, mister? He's yours. Don't chu want him?" Then he gestured to a helper, who led Tiber to where John stood.

When John took the end of Tiber's chain, he realized with a shock that he had not kept the promise to his father! Almost gently, he turned Tiber around to face him. The two exchanged glances, although Tiber's deep-set eyes held no expression at all and he quickly looked at the ground.

"How do you do, Tiber?" John said, his voice tight. "I'm sure we'll do—just fine."

John stood holding the chain, waiting, while the next slave to mount the low platform, an old woman, brought but two hundred dollars. The next to reach the block was a broad-featured, heavyset man some years older than Tiber. His nervousness growing, John bought the man, almost before the spiel had been completed, for four hundred fifty dollars.

This time, as soon as he'd grasped the chain, John looked squarely into the man's eyes, and wonder of wonders, the man looked back at John. "Will you tell me your name?" John asked.

"George."

James Hamilton would, in a civil voice, have demanded that George address him as sir or master. John didn't even think of it until he'd tried to grin at George and failed. George did grin, but to John's dismay, there was disdain in the grin.

He bought a young man named Peter next and for only one reason beyond the fact that he liked the name Peter: there were no white lash scars on Peter's bare back, a point given particular emphasis by the auctioneer since it was supposed to prove Peter's ready obedience to any master.

"Peter," John said, after handing over four hundred thirty more dollars, "I'd be much obliged if you'd look me right in the eye."

On the young, round face of the fellow called Peter, a surprisingly easy smile appeared, revealing white, strong teeth.

His mind still in wild-swinging turmoil, John hadn't the faintest idea why his promise made to Anne long ago on their honeymoon in Scotland came to mind, but he heard himself ask Peter, "Are you good with dogs?" John had promised Anne that someday he would get her a dog to take the place of Lovey, her childhood house pet, who had died. From their vantage point on an upper floor of the ruins of the old Maxwell castle, Caerlaverock, they had heard a dog bark. It was then he'd made the promise forgotten entirely until this ghastly moment after his purchase of the third man, who answered only, "Yes, sir. I lak dogs."

The fourth was a dark-skinned fellow named Rollie, said to have had some experience as a blacksmith's helper. There were no real smithies available, so for four hundred dollars John bought Rollie. When he looked him in the eye—the squat, heavily muscled Negro had only one—there was no response whatever. No smile, no rebellion—nothing. After the auctioneer's helper interlocked all four chains, then handed one end to John, there seemed nothing to do but begin the dreaded walk toward Mark Browning's pier.

Remembering almost angrily that Browning, a Northerner by birth, had somehow found a way to gain the city's respect without owning a single slave, John strode up Bay Street. His face burned with shame to be leading four human beings along a busy thoroughfare in broad daylight, in full view of coastal citizens Frewin vowed would pay no mind whatever.

Evidently they didn't. And for the entire water trip back to St. Simons, which took almost two full days, the four slaves, except to stretch now and then, sat in puzzling silence. John spoke very little, even to Captain Frewin, but he tried to ask forgiveness from God, who seemed as remote, as helpless, as John felt.

CHAPTER 13

A NNE WAITED IN THEIR BEDROOM ON THE EVENING
of September 1 for John to lock up the four new people he'd
brought in Captain Frewin's boat from Savannah. In her nightgown and cap she stood at an open window, watching for the first
glimpse of her husband after their longest separation since they
returned to St. Simons Island to live. She had pushed back the
curtains to catch a cool breeze off the river, but mostly to give
herself an unobstructed view of their lane. He had been gone five
days. To her it had seemed far longer. Except for seeing to the
security of his new people purchased at the Savannah market, he
would have been in her arms much sooner, she knew. Anne had
heard the team and wagon rattling up their lane, but so far no
sight of John.

She had heard his voice down at the rebuilt slave quarters
where he'd have to lock the new men in a holding cabin until
morning, but there was only silence now, broken off and on by the
sleepy calls of birds and the chickens going to roost for the night.

The heavy September air seemed to be making Papa's Cannon's Point hounds restless. Their barking sounded so close, they might have been Lawrence dogs, except that John didn't care much for hunting. For their daughter Annie's sake, she was glad John wasn't a hunter. The tenderhearted, city-bred girl hated the whole idea of her father's or anyone else's killing even one coon or rabbit or white-tailed Island deer.

To this day Anne rejected every thought that in battle as a Royal Marine, her gentle, laughing John had undoubtedly killed other men, but every man she had ever known hunted animals. At one time she had been a good shot herself. Still, just as she had never felt at home in London, her daughter probably felt less at home among the tall trees and rivers and creeks and the ways of St. Simons people who had spent their lives there. Annie seldom mentioned London any more, but Anne knew the girl still missed city life. Annie had longed to make the water trip with John so that she could visit her grandfather in Darien, but with four new, unbroken Negroes aboard, it was out of the question for John and Captain Frewin to stop for her on their way back from Savannah. As always, Annie had made no big fuss.

Where, she wondered, is John now? Several minutes had passed since she'd heard his voice from the almost windowless cabin where, when there had been disobedience, a man or an occasional woman was jailed for a time. John despised the cabin he called a hut, hated its one tiny window; and she remembered an afternoon when he'd been unusually irritated with himself because there was so much to learn, he vowed never, never to lock a single person in that airless place. But he would have to keep the new people there tonight, at least, and tomorrow Papa would guide John at breaking in the new fieldhands. She hoped it would be Papa and not her brother James Hamilton, whose very presence somehow never failed to discredit John's ability even though Anne knew he didn't intend to do it. James Hamilton had simply never learned how to keep his confidence in his own expertise to himself. Still, he and John seemed to get along all right. Knowing her brother as she did, Anne believed James rather went out of his way to encourage her husband. John thought otherwise, but that was because he had also always excelled in the military and even yet, at times, seemed easily discouraged at the hardships of learning a whole new way of life.

Now she heard his voice again. The quarters were too far away from the Lawrence house for her to understand what he was saying, but he was calling out orders of some kind, probably to June, who would be most helpful with the new men. One thing Anne was sure of, and that was the growing bond between John and June.

"What you expect, Miss Anne?" Eve asked in her cocky way each time Anne mentioned how much John trusted and relied on June. "June smart. He know the people, but most of all, he know Mausa John, know how hard he work an' try an' how much he still hab to learn."

It was good that the person John trusted most, worked with best, was Eve's June.

I'll never know how to manage servants the way Mama does, the way she still thinks I will someday, but how could anyone be any other way than the way I am with Eve when she's the one who ends up doing most of the deciding?

She turned from the window and sat down in her little rocker. Then, in no time she jumped up and went again to the window to watch. The water trip to Savannah, with one night spent at William's house, could, just *could* have been difficult for John, she supposed. He was nervous about having to spend all that hard-earned money on four people without Papa or James Hamilton or anyone experienced there to guide him, but she was sure he did fine. What worried her was the time he spent with Father Fraser.

How can I wait, she thought, to find out if John came right out and told the old dear that he was headed for a slave auction? I don't see how he avoided telling him and I certainly know how Father Fraser feels about owning people. He hates it!

"Why don't you get here, John?" she said aloud, leaning farther out the window, hoping for a glimpse of him striding toward their house. "If only I could see the way he's walking, I'd know a lot," she said, more softly so that the girls wouldn't hear her in the next room. Pete was probably sound asleep, but Annie would be awake. Her sensitive, loving Annie would never drop off to sleep until she knew for certain that her father was safely back in their house.

"Where is he? How could it possibly take so long to lock those men up for the night and order one or two other people to guard them?"

J OHN STOOD OUTSIDE THE LOCKED DOOR OF THE jail cabin, June with him, and for the first time wished he had been alone. His own inner turmoil was so dark and troubled, he wondered how he would be able even to bid June a casual goodnight.

For what must have been a full minute, the two men stood side by side in silence. June must want something, John thought, but what? Why doesn't he tell me goodnight and go on home to Eve?

Finally, his voice low, almost secretive, June asked, "You worried, Mausa John, 'bout keepin' Big Boy up to guard 'em all night cause you think Miss Anne want fish for breakfus?"

The question was so mundane, so commonplace, so far from the reason for John's own turmoil, that he actually laughed a little. "Fish, June? We just locked up four human beings in a stuffy hut with only one high window and you bring up—fish? If Miss Anne planned fish for our breakfast, surely Mina has some ham she can substitute." Night was falling so fast now, John had trouble seeing June's dark face. "I thought it was your idea to make Big Boy the chief guard. The man's size will discourage any attempt at a breakout. But since he's so accustomed to getting up early for his fishing every day, I thought my wife's young brother, William Audley, should stay with Big Boy to keep him awake if he drops off. Big Boy went to get William Audley. They should be back here soon."

"Yes, sir."

"Is something bothering you, June?"

"Look to me lak Big Boy he might hab to keep Mausa William Audley awake. Dat boy a sleeper! He kin drop off settin' on a horse!"

"We'll have to take our chances on that. I don't want any of my fieldhands to lose a night's sleep. There's too much work to be done in that south field tomorrow. Never saw cotton bolls mature so fast, did you? Almost overnight, that field's ready."

"You done turn into a planter, Mausa John. A good 'un, too."

Such a compliment from June was, to John, almost on a scale with a compliment from one of the Coupers. June, he believed, knew cotton as well as, if not better than, most coastal planters would ever know it.

"You want I should stay here an' wait for Big Boy an' young Mausa William Audley?"

"I want you to get back to Eve. You've worked hard today, if your report on both the orchard and the south field isn't in your imagination."

June laughed softly. "No, sir, I ain' make up nothin'. De work be done. You the one, though, needs to git home to Miss Anne. She ain' seed you in five whole days an' four nights. Eve, she skin me 'live effen I don' send you back to Miss Anne now."

"Do you think those new men inside can hear what we're saying? Hear us laugh? Why can't we both just leave them behind that locked door?"

"You barkin' up the wrong tree, Mausa John."

Genuinely puzzled, John asked, *"What?* What are you saying, June?"

"You the mausa ob Lawrence. Dem mens is slaves. We got rules. I knows inside your heart, but I also knows de rules. I done hear Mausa James Hamilton Couper lay the rules down to you afore you make dat Savannah trip. Effen you gib eben one ob dem new mens a notion dat you sof' on de rules, you finished. Dey neber gonna be no good to ya. Scuse me, sir, but June be right."

With a deep, helpless sigh, John said, "I know you're right. I hate it, but I know you're right. And I'm grateful to you for reminding me of my responsibility, June."

"You trus' June."

John knew perfectly well that June had not asked *if* he trusted him. It was not a question. It was a statement of fact. No slave master, according to Alexander Wylly, to the Hazzard brothers, to Thomas Butler King, to Ben Cater, was ever supposed to let a slave know that he was totally trusted. John didn't care. He trusted Ebo June.

In minutes Big Boy rode up with a tousled, droopy-eyed William Audley, and John feared that June had been right. How long could they expect an eleven-year-old boy to stay awake in order to warn Big Boy if a slave tried to escape, should Big Boy doze off? Still, John also trusted Big Boy. Anne had taught him to trust the huge man, whose very size would indeed cause any of the new slaves to think twice before trying to escape. Most important right now, he needed to have them all settled, needed desperately to be with Anne again. To make love to her? Yes, but tonight he mostly needed to talk, to tell her about his time in Darien with his father. He needed to tell her for his own sake, because it was important to know what she thought of the old man's surprising commitment to pray for John—to pray for his courage to take part in what was to the old fellow and to John an ugly, cruel slave auction.

He dared not tell her of his own self-hatred for doing such a thing. He was too weary to risk her not understanding. After all, Anne had lived all her years with slaves as an integral part of daily life. Everyone she knew on St. Simons spent a lifetime with slaves. As close as he and Anne had been for all the years of their married life, he had never risked discussing the subject. He had tried only to adapt outwardly and to keep his true feelings to himself.

Headed at last toward their house, he was almost overcome by weariness. His legs felt wooden, stiff from two days in Frewin's cramped boat. Anne would be watching for him, he knew, and she could always tell a lot from the way he walked, could even detect his state of mind. He would take his time until he was in sight of their second-floor bedroom window, where he was sure she'd be waiting. Then, for her sake, he would summon up his most alert military step.

CHAPTER 14

WEARING ONLY HER NIGHTGOWN BECAUSE THE night was so still and warm, Anne hurried down the stairs, threw open the front door, and fell into his arms.

"John! Oh my darling, you're *home*. How are you? Are you all right? Was it a dreadful trip? Did you get the new people? How did Father Fraser look when you stopped the first night in Darien? Did you tell him all about your fine cotton crop?"

She held him and held him, allowing the magic of being close again to work its wonders in her. His arms somehow felt harder, held her more tightly, seemed to reach for her even as she pressed as hard against him as humanly possible.

"I've got a big slab of Mina's yellow cake and a pitcher of milk upstairs in our room for you," she said, covering his face with kisses as she talked. "I know how you love a party after we're all cozy in our own room at night. Oh John, John . . ."

Then it struck her that he hadn't yet uttered one word. He had only held her, his need painful even for her. "We'll wake the children if we go on standing here like idiots," she whispered, taking his hand, leading him up the stairs, both being as quiet as possible.

When John closed their door, Anne rushed again into his arms and began to kiss him. "No," he said hoarsely. "Not yet, dearest. I —I'll sample Mina's cake first, if you don't mind."

She stood staring at him. Of course he loved Mina's yellow cake, but something was wrong. He wasn't being John at all. They had always made a game of lots of exaggerated hugging and kissing even when he'd only been out of her sight for a single morning, riding the fields with Papa or sneaking an hour or two of fishing with Big Boy.

Without a bite of cake, she watched him strip off his soiled shirt and pour some tepid water into the big china bowl. "Do you have to bathe now?" she asked, knowing full well he would. "I thought we were going to eat some cake, or talk."

In response, he gave her a troubled smile and went right on with his ablutions. "All right," she said, attempting to keep her voice light. "I guess I can wait a little longer." Not wanting to make him more nervous, she sat down in her rocker. "Even counting the time you and Papa went to Savannah and got stuck on a sandbar coming home, do you know this is the longest we've been apart since we moved back to Georgia?"

He toweled his face and chest, then knelt beside her. "Yes, Anne, I realize that and I've missed you every minute. Are the girls all right? Everyone at Cannon's Point?"

"Everyone's fine, but missing you. Papa's ridden over here every single day trying to make sure Annie and Pete didn't miss you too much. Also to confer with June. You know how he trusts him."

"June can do anything he sets his mind to."

"Why are we talking about things like this?" she asked.

He took her hand and moved her from the rocker to their bed, where he sat beside her and began to give her an almost minute-by-minute account of his visit to Darien with William's family and Father Fraser. When he came to the point where Father Fraser had somewhat sternly reminded him that it was he who had made the marriage vows with Anne and that if John were to prove himself a man, he'd have to buy slaves, John was looking at the carpet, apparently unable to look at her.

A kind of numbing fear gripped her so that she dared not trust herself to say a word. Ringing in her ears was Anna Matilda's declaration that Anne had been selfish to let her homesickness for St. Simons show so much that John had no choice but to bring her back to Georgia. With all her being, she had longed only to give to John, never to take from him, never to deprive him.

As they sat side by side on the bed in silence, one question raced back and forth in Anne's mind: How could I have been acting selfish with him all this time and not know it? I'm not stupid, am I? Everyone, including her English tutor, Mr. William Browne, had always called her bright, highly intelligent, quick to learn.

"John?"

"I'm not finished," he said, his voice taut. "Don't say anything yet, Anne. Let me finish."

"But I have to know. Was Father Fraser accusing me of being selfish?"

The quick, puzzled look he gave her indicated that she had scarcely been included in the talk between John and his father, except that it was she whom John had chosen to marry. "What Father told me had nothing to do with you," he said at last. "He was simply challenging me to—to act like a man. A courageous man. Reminding me in that stony way of his that I had entered into an agreement with you for the remainder of my life and that in order to keep that agreement, I had put myself in the position of having to become a slave owner. Of attending an auction with my own money from my own first good crop, because for our future success, I needed at least four new slaves."

Anne also looked down at the carpet while he talked. Then, when he paused, she did her best to think of just the right thing to say. She thought of nothing beyond the fact that somehow John's strange, disturbed mood had directly to do with his purchase of those new people. She knew perfectly well that neither he nor William, nor their father, approved of slavery. She couldn't have lived in England for so long and not known the disdain the British felt for all plantation owners. But what did any of that really have to do with her and John and their happy life on St. Simons Island? Weren't they the happiest married couple either of them knew? Hadn't they laughed and boasted about that in the privacy of their own room time after time? James Hamilton always contended that the whole system of owning people was political, and what on earth could politics have to do with her and John's oneness?

When John said nothing more for such a long time and didn't even reach for her hand, the fear forced her to ask, "Do you—do you understand all of what Father Fraser meant when he spoke of our marriage vows, John?"

He nodded. "All."

"Can you tell me?"

The grin he gave her was more hopeless than tender. "I'm trying, Anne. I have to tell you—my way. Please?"

"Yes, dearest. I'm not nagging. At least that's the last thing I mean to be doing. I just want so much to understand."

He sighed deeply, and to keep from saying the wrong thing, she reached for one of his hands, which he left limply in hers.

"I shouldn't have tried to tell you any of this tonight," he said. "I'm doing a rotten job of it."

"Would some of Mina's cake help?"

Now he laughed almost normally, then reached to take her in his arms. "Maybe I'll do better after all if I'm holding you," he murmured. "Anne, don't ask me to explain what my father meant by this, but the most important thing he said to me—at least as I see it—was that when I was forced to look into the eyes of the first man I bid on, Father would be praying for me! Then the old fellow actually made me promise I'd *look* into the eyes of each man before I bought him."

No one knew better than Anne that John had said some puzzling things to her over the years. Over and over again, she had forced herself not to ask for explanations. But this was different. Any son or daughter should be only happy that a parent had promised to pray. John's feelings concerning what must have struck him as a surprising commitment from his father were a complete mystery to her. Should she ask why Father Fraser made him promise to do such a strange thing as look into the eyes of each Negro he bought?

"Does it make you curious," John asked, "that the old gentleman would ask me to look into each man's eyes?"

Without intending to, John had come to her rescue. "Oh yes! Yes, I'm really puzzled by that. Are you?"

"Yes and no."

"That's no answer." He was still holding her, one hand pressing her head against his shoulder. Anne pulled his hand away and looked at him. "Beloved John, are you—are you as troubled as you seem?"

Again he only nodded yes. And again he was staring down at the carpet.

"Eyes have always been terribly important to you and me," she said, surprising herself. "Do you remember the night at Dungeness on Cumberland Island when you and those noisy, muddy Royal Marines captured James Hamilton, Anna Matilda, me, and all of poor Mrs. Shaw's other houseguests?"

She felt foolish, but evidently her bringing up such an unexpected subject freed John. This time he laughed a truly John laugh. Sometimes she hated it when something she said amused him, because it made her feel as though from his haughty perch as a much-traveled gentleman, he was laughing *at* her. Not this time. His laughter relieved her too. He had been so unlike himself since her first sight of him at the door downstairs, now almost an hour ago.

"Of course I remember the night I captured you," he said, his arms around her again. "How could I possibly forget? I also remember the first moment I saw you in that elegant dining room when we broke into the midst of your eighteenth birthday dinner party."

"Do you? Do you remember that first moment, John? Do you also remember that our eyes seemed to embrace? Almost as though there was no one else in that big dining room but you and me?"

"I'll never forget it, Mrs. Fraser. And that our favorite song is 'Drink to Me Only with Thine Eyes,' but I think you're making some romantic, unreal, whimsical connection between that moment when I looked into your eyes and"—he dropped his arms from around her—"and the altogether odd promise my father extracted from me. Don't do it, Anne. There is no connection. And I'm truly sorry I even told you what Father asked of me."

"Don't be! Please don't be. I love him too, you know. Father Fraser didn't mean anything but good when he asked you to promise that. Maybe he wanted you to take particular notice of the new people's eyes so you'd—so you'd be able to judge their value more clearly."

His tone suddenly bitter, John said, "Look me in the eye, my man, so that I'll be completely sure your entire life is worth my purchasing it for the enormous sum of four hundred fifty dollars! Is that what you mean, Anne?"

She'd said something terribly wrong. But what? John had never given her a look remotely like the one he was giving her now. Then, before she broke into tears of helplessness, he held her close again.

This time his voice was tender, gentle, almost pitying, but not quite. She hated it even when he'd pitied her on their honeymoon because she missed Eve so much as she struggled to fix her own hair. His next words held no pity—only need. The love in his voice when he spoke was as real and compelling as when he sang to her. "I'm a scoundrel, dearest Anne," he said. "Forgive me. And know that you've just rescued me again from myself."

Having no idea what he meant, she asked, "I did?"

"As only you can do. Anne, I still have a lot to sort out. But if you'll bear with me, I will sort it out. That's a promise."

WHEN AT LAST SHE LAY BESIDE HIM, IN HIS ARMS, Anne slept. Not only was he awake, his eyes were wide open, staring into the darkness of their room. What is it that I need to sort out? he asked himself half a dozen times before the answer came: It's nothing new, he thought. The problem has been there from the moment our eyes met at Dungeness those many years ago. He'd known then, at that instant, that he loved her. He'd waited a while to tell her, because even he had trouble believing that there could be the kind of eternal love he felt for Anne Couper on that first, odd meeting. In retrospect, he now knew that she had admitted her love for him far more quickly. On that first night.

I can count to my dying breath on the love of this tender, lovely creature, he told himself, being careful not to tighten his arm for fear of waking her. If everything that tears at me were as simple and true as counting on Anne, I'd be a man without conflict of any kind. Anne is well aware from having lived in London for so long how deep antislavery feelings run there. But does she have any idea that they run so deep in me too? And is there any hope that life lived out in the half-hidden, irregular rhythm of an entire community in human bondage can ever be, to her, anything but *natural*? I know her friendship with Eve is real. I see her gestures of respect for some of her father's older house people, for Big Boy, for Eve's June, for our Mina even on the days when Mina's tempo doesn't suit Anne's. But will my beloved ever come to see the evil in owning these dark-skinned people as one owns a horse or a hog or a cow? Even Anne can't act on what she doesn't see. Will she ever see that the souls of those of us who master are in far more danger than the souls of slaves—slaves only because their skin happens to be dark and ours white?

Father is right. I chose to marry Anne, to give her my love, my energies, my very life, and *she is the daughter of a slave owner.*

He frowned into the blackness. If she ever comes to see the ugly thing clearly—he all but spoke aloud the hopeless words— what will either of us do about it?

CHAPTER 15

JOHN'S TURMOIL AT HAVING BOUGHT FOUR HUMAN beings at auction had been nerve-racking and painful, but his determination not to let Anne see the depth of his loathing of the whole transaction ended up actually helping him get through it. What a man refused to dwell on could not entirely disrupt his daily behavior. He understood himself well enough to know that he'd always fared better, conducted himself in a more normal, casual way, if he simply refused to chew on a problem. His father was right. He had chosen to marry Anne. He, Lieutenant John Fraser, late of the Royal Marines, now owned a plantation *and* the slaves to operate it. The complexity of running such an enterprise was more than enough in itself.

Astride his fiery mare, Ginger, on a bright, blue-skied autumn morning, he firmed his vow to do his very best to ignore the wrong at the heart of the work he had set his mind to master and to spend his every effort on mastering the work itself.

Today, October 20, he was riding to Frederica to meet Captain Frewin, who was to deliver a shipment of lumber and hardware to Hopeton, James Hamilton Couper's splendid plantation on the mainland northwest of Brunswick, Georgia. Couper was his own architect for the massive undertaking of remodeling a huge old tabby sugarhouse into a three-storied mansion. John did not have to pay a visit to his brother-in-law, but Frewin had offered the means of getting there, and if he could make his way, without panic or resentment, through a talk with Anne's efficient, somewhat arrogant brother, he believed he would have helped himself still more.

There were times when he felt some guilt because he had told Anne absolutely nothing of the startling announcement his father had made concerning James Hamilton's idea of someday putting John in control of Hamilton Plantation. Building Anne's hopes too high would not be fair, and evidently the advancement depended on John's success with Lawrence over the next few years. The glorious possibility lay shining at the back of John's mind daily, but he had surprised himself by not dwelling on it. The potential had merely bolstered his courage to try still harder at Lawrence. Today, somehow, he was certain that much of his own future as master of a flourishing place like Hamilton hinged on the way he handled the four new slaves.

Ginger had reached Frederica Road and with the lightest pressure on the rein, turned to gallop past the little new white Christ Church chapel under the giant oaks, toward Old Town, where Frewin would surely be loaded and ready to make the packet trip across the salt creeks and winding rivers to Hopeton.

His heart lifted as it always did when he rode through the bright, sharp sunlight and shadows of St. Simons Island, and he smiled to himself. He had just remembered a full hour's conversation yesterday with Jock Couper, who, for reasons hatched in his own wily mind, had said not one word about the tremendous future happiness John and Anne had a chance to find at beautiful Hamilton Plantation. Papa Couper knew, of course. It had been he who told Father Fraser.

Galloping under the green and scarlet of live oaks and black gum trees, Ginger rounded the curve in the Old Town road and headed for the Frederica dock. Old Jock Couper was obviously going to let James Hamilton himself tell John. He had undoubtedly only mentioned it to John's father in order to give John a chance to compose his emotions before James Hamilton had a chance to tell him in person. How he admired his father-in-law! How deeply he appreciated the old fellow's instincts, especially where John was concerned. Since the year he and Anne had returned to live on St. Simons, some days it had seemed that Jock Couper spent his time figuring out the best means of smoothing John's way.

Slowing Ginger to a trot as the horse approached the old dock, John longed for a way to give thanks that Papa Couper was exactly the kind of man he was, not only because he eased John's way but because he had known how to make what certainly seemed to be an all-important bridge to Father Fraser. On a bright October day such as this, John held real hope that he and his own father could someday be as close and easy with each other.

WELCOMED WARMLY AT HOPETON BY TALL, ALWAYS elegantly dressed James Hamilton Couper, John stood by observing as Couper gave Frewin orders concerning the unloading of the packet of lumber to be used in his mansion, set on rising ground near the bank of the broad canal that ran into the wide Altamaha River a quarter mile away. The old sugarhouse, being remodeled according to James Hamilton's own detailed design, would require, John thought, at least two years in the building, but it would undoubtedly be one of the principal plantations along the entire southeastern coast after equally meticulous and artistic plans had been laid out by the young Hopeton master for landscaping the vast grounds. An unwonted wave of envy swept through John as he stood watching Couper and Frewin instruct Frewin's crew and Couper's slaves—workers and artisans—as to the unloading, which had to be carried out exactly as prescribed on paper in James Hamilton's intricate drawings. If only he could handle workers that way. Every stack of lumber would be piled nearest to the portion of the house where it would eventually be needed. In the entire life of James Hamilton Couper, there was no wasted motion, only precise organization.

By early afternoon, with James's announcement that they would have exactly thirty-five minutes for conversation, John strode along after the graceful Hopeton master to a relatively quiet spot with grass on which to sit.

After John had done his level best to praise not only the setting of the proposed mansion but the design as well, James Hamilton, in his courteous though direct way, asked, "And why, may I inquire, John, did you take the trouble to accompany Captain Frewin to my place today? Your people must still be doing extensive picking at Lawrence and at my father's Cannon's Point too."

"Indeed, James." Then, attempting a pleasant laugh at his own expense, he added, "I'm sure you'll be relieved to know that your often bumbling brother-in-law has learned that ripe boll picking can almost surely go on throughout the month of October." When James didn't even smile, John pushed on: "I assigned tasks just after dawn today and June is at least temporarily acting as my driver. I wish I could spare him for the job full-time."

"And what of your water trip to Savannah last month? I'm sorry my own duties here have prevented a visit to St. Simons since your return with the four new Negroes you bought at auction. You did fill your needs, didn't you?"

The thought flashed through John's mind that it had been John Couper who gave him the Lawrence land, so why did he have to report to young James? He dispelled the annoyance with his most disarming smile. "Rather well, I believe, James, with the one exception that I was unable to purchase a full blacksmith. I did acquire a smithy's helper named Rollie. A man with only one eye, but well-muscled and cooperative enough to be willing to work hard at learning to be my principal smithy."

"I sincerely hope so, but one word of caution. There is no way of being sure with any of these people until a certain amount of time has passed. You must also make certain that he protects his one eye. A blind Negro is of little or no value."

Refusing to feel squelched by such a demeaning lecture, John said, "I quite agree, James."

"And the other three?"

"Each does have a name," John said with the merest edge in his voice. "Peter is superior—young, strong, no scars on his back, which, of course, proves he's obedient. George is surprising me since at the outset he appeared stubborn, to say the least, but now works not only rapidly but, in my judgment, rather well."

"Sometimes the least promising turn out to be most useful," James said, "depending, of course, on your strict application of the plantation rules."

"I know the rules, sir. You taught me well. I've practically memorized the article you wrote on obedience and understanding."

"Dictated by experience," James Hamilton said.

"The fourth new man is Tiber, perhaps the most valuable of all. Young, earnest, shows every sign of being grateful that I permit no whippings at Lawrence."

"And did you tell him of your disapproval of whippings? I certainly hope not!"

"Whippings are not allowed here at Hopeton," John protested.

"Correct, but none of my people has ever heard that from my lips."

"I see."

"What do you see?"

"Simply that you've never told them yourself. I'm sure the recent Lawrence arrivals learned of our humane treatment at the quarters, where all are now living."

"And what of their attitudes when you unlocked the old tabby cabin after their first night with you?"

"According to June, they were simply relieved to be let loose and fed breakfast."

Appearing to ponder all John had said or left unsaid, James Hamilton sat in silence for a brief period, during which John again reminded himself that the possibility of his being one day placed in full charge of Hamilton depended on the whim of this man. Still, he was sure that James Hamilton Couper had probably never done anything on a mere whim. If John were to be offered the handsome manager's salary, which dwarfed the half pay he still received from the Royal Navy, the responsibility, and the large, attractive home for Anne and their children, it would be only because James sincerely believed he would succeed.

James Hamilton looked at his watch. "Our time for conversation is up, John. From what you've told me, you did well with your Savannah purchases. Your picking, of course, *can* easily go on through October. Tell me, do these new fieldhands know how to operate an Eave's gin?"

"Tiber knows," John answered. "For what the others need to learn, I feel I can depend on June's instructions."

"I know you and my father both trust June thoroughly, but you must remember that he is still partly at my father's disposal for the Cannon's Point trees and shrubs. Ginning will have to begin in early November. Perhaps I could lend you the services of my Hamilton overseer, Mr. Bowers, for a few days."

In Frewin's packet en route back to St. Simons Island, John had to curb himself. Frewin both admired and was amused by James Hamilton's precise ways. Of course Frewin knew nothing of the possibility that John himself might one day be in charge of Hamilton. John had told him nothing. He had no intention yet of confiding in Anne, either. She would be sure to dream too much, loving the situation and elegance of Hamilton as she did. Daily, she let John know how happy she was with their small house at Lawrence, but should she give him even one more child, the cottage under the trees set back from Lawrence Creek would be too small. It would be too crowded now if Annie and Pete could not learn their lessons from Anne's childhood tutor, William Browne, still living at Cannon's Point. One day soon the John Frasers would have to find a larger home, with room for a tutor.

After a few hours' sailing, Captain Frewin's packet was now moving along the Frederica River past Hamilton Plantation. John's own admiration for the layout of the handsome, roomy two-storied house, it's carefully tended, spectacular plantings—especially the thick, now snow-white hedge of yucca across the river side—must have been evident as he looked and looked at the well-kept estate. Everyone considered Hamilton one of the finest places on the entire Island.

"Too bad," Frewin said as their packet glided by, "that there is no family to enjoy such a magnificent spot as Hamilton, isn't it, Fraser?"

"Yes. Yes, I quite agree," John answered, again dismissing his concern that as close as the two were, Jock Couper had said not one word to John about the incredible future possibility. Did Papa Couper fear that John might fail to qualify? He had tried hard never to impose on the close bond between him and his father-in-law. He wouldn't impose now. By some means, he'd find a way to wait.

Jock Couper talks almost as much as I do, he thought, with a half-grin. He'll tell me when he thinks the time is right. When I've truly proved myself.

CHAPTER 16

ALTHOUGH JOHN HAD NEVER FOUND JAMES Hamilton Couper particularly easy to like, as autumn wore into winter, he amused himself by making mental notes of every large and small indication that James was indeed still contemplating putting him in charge of the productive St. Simons estate. As it turned out, not only Tiber but George, too, already knew how to operate an Eave's gin. John called the two men aside and confided in them.

"Take my word for this, both of you," he said one mid-November morning as George was cleaning the gin's wooden rollers, which separated the oily black seeds from the long-staple lint without injuring the fiber. "I can plainly see that you men know how to operate this gin. But I'd like to make a deal. Mr. James Hamilton Couper, owner of Hopeton over on the mainland and Hamilton here on St. Simons, is being kind enough to send his Hamilton overseer to teach you." John grinned at them. "I'll be much obliged if the two of you will listen to the overseer, Mr. Bowers, and make

it seem as though you're learning from him. Do you know what
I'm saying?" The more John talked, the guiltier he felt because he
knew full well that it was against all plantation rules even to
suggest to slaves that they take part in any kind of conniving. A
master, James and his father believed, must live an exemplary life
before his people at all times. John was breaking that rule because
he so wanted not to upset James Hamilton, no matter how unnecessary the proffered help of the Hamilton overseer might be. "Do
you understand what I'm saying?" he repeated.

It had been weeks since John had caught even a hint of a
disdainful smile on George's face. The man had seemed to be
reasonably satisfied with conditions at Lawrence. George smiled
now in response to John's question. If there was an inkling of
disdain, John could not see it. George actually looked pleased.

"Ah knows better den you, Mausa Fraser, how to pump up a
white man's pride. Any darkie know dat. I ack like I don' know
nuffin' 'bout Eave's gins!"

"I'd be grateful, just this once," John said lamely. "But don't
try it on me, George, because I'm fairly good at conspiracy myself!"

That, John knew, was the worst thing he could have said, but
he'd said it and all he could do now was hope to catch on if George
attempted the same trick with him. "How about you, Tiber? Will
you allow Mr. Bowers to teach you too? Someday you'll both know
how important this is to me. Can I count on you, Tiber?"

Tiber didn't smile, but the trusting look he gave John made
him feel more guilt than George's apparent delight in such manip-
ulation.

"You know I come down from V'ginny, Mausa Fraser," Tiber
said. "Bein' here wif you, suh, make me feel good lak a dose ob
sulphuh an' 'lasses. I do anything you tells me to do. Fo' as long as
you let me stay wif you, Tiber do anything."

For an embarrassing moment John just stood there, seeing
more clearly for the first time why James Hamilton's obedience
rules—his insistence, along with his father's, that a master live the
good life before his people—rang true. Had he created potential
trouble with George and Tiber in order to better himself? Had he,

without realizing the danger, planted tricky ideas in both the men's minds?

"Well," he said finally, "I think I've learned a valuable lesson from you both. Mr. Bowers will be here tomorrow morning. Right or wrong, my request still holds. And someday maybe you'll understand why I made such a request. I hope so."

"I KNOW IT'S POSSIBLE SOME GINNING CAN GO ON into January of next year," Anne said, trying to alleviate John's boredom one December night after they'd closed the door to their room. "I also know it all gets dreadfully monotonous for you, dearest, but your crop for the year almost past has been pronounced a good one, so—"

"So, I should be satisfied," he said, his voice close to the old sarcasm she so dreaded and had never learned how to respond to. "I know my crop's a profitable one. Even your superior brother has pronounced it so."

"It was excellent. Did you have any trouble borrowing money from Mr. Habersham when you went to Savannah to buy Rollie and Peter and Tiber and George?"

"Of course not. But with ginning still going on, heaven knows when the people will get the trash out and the bags packed for shipment so I can collect." He sighed. "It's just that sometimes it all seems so slow, Anne. Here it is the nineteenth of December. You're right, ginning will be going on into January of 1829, and I had such big plans for taking far better care of you and the girls. For giving you a larger house. What if we had another child? What if we had to retain a tutor? What if we didn't still have free access to the solemn old don, William Browne?"

In her nightgown at the dressing table, she laughed, and shaking her loosed, dark hair down around her shoulders, made an exaggerated leap across the room to where he lay sprawled across the bed, dressed only in his nightshirt. "Husband of mine," she said teasingly, keeping her face serious, "do you realize you haven't made love to me for two nights? I know that's forward of any wife to remind the man she loves of such a thing, but it's absolutely true and I'm lonely for you."

He grinned up at her. "And do you, wife of mine, keep detailed bedroom records in much the same manner in which your eccentric brother keeps copper-scripted plantation records? Do you realize James Hamilton actually expects his records to be used in future centuries as research material? The man's exalted pride in his work will long outlive him, because those works of art he calls plantation records, their pages illustrated with pen-and-ink sketches tinted in pastels and watercolor, will be collected and preserved—by him if by no one else."

Again Anne laughed, then kissed him on his nose. "How do you know all that?"

"The illustrious squire of Hopeton and Hamilton told me so himself."

No longer smiling, Anne turned his face so that he had to look at her. "Don't allow James Hamilton to get under your skin, dearest. Take a lesson from his little wife, Caroline. She's still an object of pity among her friends to this day because as Caroline Wylly, she was always such a cutup. Always loved to play and laugh. But she's learned how to take my brother's intensity. Caroline knows that for some odd reason James Hamilton missed out on learning how to laugh or play." When he said nothing, Anne asked, "He's very hard for you, isn't he?"

John took her in his arms and kissed her until all thought of her brother left Anne's mind. Only later when the peace came, the peace that had followed every storm of passion through all the years of their married life, would she think again. And what she thought brought back what now seemed an almost childlike truth to which she had clung years ago in London after her first exposure to the great British actress Sarah Siddons, in her renowned role as Lady Macbeth. The one line of Shakespeare's tragedy— which Anne had taken, she now realized, entirely out of context— rushed back to her with new insight into *today.* The line to which she had clung then and to which she would cling now was "Only look up *clear.*" Childlike or not, she meant to cling to it. "John?"

"What, beautiful Anne?"

"We're going to be all right. You'll see."

"Was my lovemaking that good?" He was teasing.

"No. I mean yes. It's always perfect, but I'm suddenly just sure about everything."

"And what, dear heart, does everything mean?"

Moving closer to him, she whispered, "I don't know. There aren't always words that describe things I feel."

Into the drowsy, blissful, half-sleepy moment thundered the heavy, urgent sound of galloping horses, louder than horses usually sound because of the extreme quiet of the cold December night air.

John leaped from the bed and began to fumble for a candle. "Don't get up, Anne," he ordered. "It's icy cold in here and I forgot to bank the fire."

"But darling! Who could that be at this hour? It must be after nine o'clock. Did we hear two horses?"

"More than one, I'd say," he mumbled, hitting his bare toe on her rocker as he felt his way to the still-glowing embers by the pale light of a partly burned candle on the bedside table.

"John, something must be wrong at Cannon's Point!" Anne was now out of bed, too, and pulling on her woolen dressing gown. "I'm going downstairs with you, but here." She held out his robe. "You're not going anywhere without your warm robe."

Holding hands, they slipped as quietly as possible into the upstairs hall. A rapid, sharp knock at their front door startled them both, so that they stood rooted on the stairway, hearts pounding.

"Anne? John?" The voice, unmistakably that of Anne's father, called from outside.

"It's Papa!"

"I know," John whispered, helping her by the flickering flame of the candle to the bottom of the stairs. Then he called softly, hoping not to rouse the girls upstairs, "We're coming, Papa Couper. Sometimes it takes me a minute to get this door latch to open."

Panic in her voice, Anne said, "I'll do it, John. I know the trick. Move over."

"Are you alone, Papa Couper?" John called in a sharp whisper as Anne began to unlatch the heavy iron lock.

"No, he isn't alone, John."

"That's William's voice!" John gasped.

"Your brother, Dr. William?"

"I have only one brother, Anne! Here, let me work that door!"

At that moment Anne jerked open the cottage door and hurried to light a candelabra kept on the downstairs hall table.

"William! What are you doing here?" John demanded. "Come in, both of you! What's happened?"

"You look pale as a ghost, Papa," Anne said, sounding almost cross. "Is Mama—is anything wrong with Mama?"

"No, no, Daughter," Jock Couper answered heavily. "Your mother's just fine. She even tried to convince William and me to wait until morning to tell you both."

"To tell us what?" John demanded again. "William! *William.* It's our father, isn't it?"

"Yes, John," William said in a hoarse voice.

"You've—you've been crying, Brother," John said.

William only nodded his head yes.

"John—John and Anne," Papa Couper whispered, "it's far from easy to say, but my new friend, that good mon James Fraser, is—dead."

"William, no!" Anne gasped, then clamped her hand over her mouth, too late, because young Annie was halfway down the stairs, close enough to have heard the heartbreaking news.

Anne hurried, stumbling to where the girl sat on a step—not weeping, not saying a word—just crumpled there like a broken doll in her nightdress and little lace cap.

"Annie, oh Annie!" her mother cried, holding her daughter. "Whatever will you and I do without Father Fraser?"

Still not one sound escaped Annie. In her own panic and desperation, Anne shook her daughter, then began to smooth her back the way she'd always done when Annie had a bad dream.

"I think it's time we all went into the parlor." John spoke in a voice that had no resemblance to his. "Come on, all of you. I'll build up the parlor fire if Rollie didn't forget to replenish our wood basket."

In minutes John had a roaring fire, and by its waving, orange

light they could at least see one another in what otherwise would
have been a dark room, since Anne had left the candelabra in the
hallway. No one sat down. They all stood, warming themselves by
the crackling live oak and pine logs—William looking at no one
and the others staring at William, whose slender shoulders were
now heaving with hard sobs.

Anne saw John slip an arm around his shorter, more slightly
built brother. Finally John said softly, "When you can, Brother, try
to tell us a little something about—Father."

Anne stood holding Annie. Papa Couper's arms were around
them both.

Finally, with no sound in the room but the snapping fire, Anne
felt her daughter stiffen, then heard her ask, "Uncle William, did
Grandfather Fraser cry out, or make any sound when he—died?
Did it hurt him—to die?"

For a brief moment no one spoke. Then Anne saw William
look up, the firelight carving deep shadows in his face. "No, Annie
dear," he said. "He—he just took a deep, deep breath and—left
us."

"Were his eyes closed?" the girl asked.

"No, but I closed them. He looked quite peaceful."

"Perhaps—perhaps you feel up to letting John and his two girls
know where your father's body is right now?" Papa asked William
in such a gentle, sensitive way that Anne began to cry her first tears
since she'd finally gotten the front door unlatched. "Sor-r-ry,
Daughter, if I said the wr-r-ong thing and made you cry."

"No, Papa! No, you didn't. We want to know where our
dearest Father Fraser is—this minute."

"Where is he, William?" John asked. "When did he die? Did
you bury him in Darien?"

William looked at Couper as though needing his help. "I—I
brought Father here."

"I'm honored to say that my friend James Fraser will lie in our
Island cemetery, where he'll be surrounded by all of us someday,"
Papa Couper said, a catch in his voice. "Your father's body is
resting now in his coffin at Captain Frewin's place near the
churchyard, John. I plan to ride back to Frederica with William in

the morning to arrange for the service. Our new rector, young Reverend Motte, is on the Island. I can make the plans with him at Frewin's house, where he rooms. The weather's chilly, so we might wait for the funeral until later tomorrow afternoon. That will give Big Boy enough time to ride to invite the Hazzards, the Caters, the Goulds, and the Kings. The Wyllys know, because Frances Anne is already at her old Village home. William took her there before he came on to Cannon's Point to get me."

Anne went to her father and threw both arms around him. "Papa, what would any of us do without you? Thank you! John and I both thank you, so much. Annie thanks you too. She loved Father Fraser with all her heart." Then she went to John, who had left the warmth of the open fire and stood, his back to all of them, staring out a parlor window into the black night.

When she took his hand, he came willingly, like a child, back to the circle of grieving loved ones still standing in the firelight. "I —I am more grateful than my dumb silence indicates, Papa Couper," he said. "It's just that my heart is full of so much. There are so many questions. Unanswered questions I'll carry now to my own grave." Then, as though needing to speak of more down-to-earth matters, he turned to William. "I suppose, Brother, since you were just elected mayor of Darien last month, you had no trouble finding someone to offer the kindness of a boat to bring him here. No problem either, I'm sure, finding a coffin maker. I say, I am relieved that he'll be here—close by. Did *he* tell you Anne's father had offered the cemetery plot?"

"He did," William answered. "Almost as soon as he came to live with Frances Anne and me in Darien." His tears close to the surface, William added, more to Papa Couper than to John, "I know it was Father's choice to live in Darien, but his final days might have been far more enjoyable here with all of you."

"James Fraser knew his own mind," Papa Couper said. "And you gave him a good home, William, with a wife who respected him and a namesake the mon loved and cher-r-ished. In fact, James was most blessed. Now he can r-rest in our lovely church-yard in his second home on our beloved St. Simons Island, among fr-riends."

For a long moment there was no sound in the room but the spitting fire. Then, as though Anne's daughter could no longer endure the odd stiffness that settles among adults when grief falls, young Annie said, almost to herself, "I wish I could talk to him."

"I know you do," Anne whispered. "So do I. I'd give almost anything just to hear his dear voice again."

"But I have a special question to ask Grandfather Fraser. I'd like so much to know what it's like to—die. And I wish he could tell me what God said to him the very first moment they saw each other. . . ."

PART II

APRIL 1829—
DECEMBER 1831

CHAPTER 17

THE WEATHER WAS SO RAINY AND WINDY ON Thursday, April 23 of the next year, 1829, Jock Couper, now the official St. Simons postmaster, knew there was no point in his riding to Frederica to pick up the mail until it cleared. On such a bad day the bustling, conscientious messenger, Nathaniel Twining of Savannah, wouldn't have dared risk the trip to Newport, where he made regular connections with the Savannah mail boat in his tiny sailing skiff. Of course talkative, self-aggrandizing Nathaniel had every right to take his weekly mission seriously, Jock thought. Every person on St. Simons always hoped for a letter from someone.

The following day, galloping his horse through the rain-washed, sunny Island beauty, he himself was hoping to hear from his lifelong friend and business partner, James Hamilton, in Philadelphia. It had been more than two months since any word had come, and that was not at all like James, who had rescued Jock financially from losing almost everything he owned.

He'd never stopped missing James in all the years since his friend had given his fine Hamilton Plantation to young James Hamilton Couper and moved to far-away Philadelphia, where he had finally taken unto himself a wife to share his old age. Hamilton knew that his namesake, James Hamilton, had in his fertile mind plans to put Lieutenant John Fraser in complete charge of Hamilton Plantation once John had proved himself as a planter to James's satisfaction. Jock's son James had not forbidden his father to share his still-secret plan with Hamilton, and Jock had therefore written his old friend almost at once. In fact, his elder son had not forbidden him to tell anyone but Anne's husband, John. And so, on his own, because he thought the lad had every right to know, Jock had told John's father, the late, still-mourned James Fraser, who had in such a short time become a close friend.

As he trotted his horse now into the old town of Frederica and headed toward the dock, he slowed to a walk for a better, more careful look into the deep, light-shot woods grown up around what had once been General James Oglethorpe's British colonial town of Frederica. The spring sunlight brought a smile as he indulged himself in his longtime habit of actually searching in the light and shadow of the bright, dark woods for the very face of God. How Couper loved the quixotic changes in the St. Simons light! And since talking aloud to God was as natural to him as breathing, he said, "I know You're there somewhere in that light, Lord. There could be no light like that without You nearby. I'm quite aware, Heavenly Father, that You know whether old James Fraser told his son about the possibility of Hamilton before he died. Would I be complaining if I asked why it is You can't tell me? It worries me to watch my son-in-law go through his days on needles and pins. He *must* know. His father must have told him when John spent the night in Darien en route to the slave market in Savannah last year. Otherwise, why would the lad seem so distracted?"

Couper had reached the dock, tied his horse, and listened through a full ten minutes of Nathaniel Twining's boring account of yesterday's blustery weather before he had a chance to stroll off alone to the privacy of a clump of scrub oaks at the far end of the

dock in order to read a letter addressed to him from his friend
James Hamilton's attorney.

> 13 April 1829
> Philadelphia, Pennsylvania
>
> My dear Mr. Couper:
>
>   It is my sad lot to inform you of the death yesterday, Sun-
> day, 12 April, of your friend and former business partner, Mr.
> James Hamilton of this city. His grieving widow, Mrs. Janet
> Wilson Hamilton, and daughter, Agnes, invite friends to their
> home tomorrow at 250 Walnut Street. Hamilton will be buried
> here in Philadelphia on that day. I extend to you, sir, my
> deepest sympathy and assure you that his death was swift and
> apparently as easy as a death can be.
>
> Yours,
> Braxton Burton, Attorney at Law

Couper read and reread the lines, each of which seemed to
swim in the glinting white light off the waters of the Frederica
River—the same river James Hamilton loved to watch from his
waterfront lawn in the old days when he lived down St. Simons
Island at Hamilton Plantation.

Numb from the first heavy rush of disbelief and sorrow,
Couper walked stiffly toward his tethered mount, scrambled into
the saddle, and rode the horse at a walk along a narrow lane to
Christ Church cemetery. Needing comfort, he had considered
finding out if young Reverend Motte was in his room at Captain
Frewin's house, but thought better of it. "Who can comfort me as
well as You, 'the God of all comfort'?" he asked aloud. "I need
comfort, Lord. I'll need comfort for the remainder of my own days
on this beautiful earth, knowing that my revered friend James
Hamilton is no longer here too."

In front of Christ Church, once more he dismounted and
looped the horse's reins around a pine. Slowly he made his way up
the sandy path toward the tiny chapel, walked around the right
side and back to the portion of the cemetery owned by the Coupers

and the Wyllys, to the still-mounded earth where John and William Fraser had recently buried their father, another friend lost to Jock Couper.

He himself had turned seventy last month. How much longer could he expect to live among the myriad beauties of St. Simons Island? And with whom could he talk? "Yes, Lord," he said aloud. "You're right. I have my good friend James Gould. I also have Becca. I have John and my blessed Anne and quiet, tender Isabella and my lovable, lazy son, William Audley. And I still have Hamilton's namesake, my elder son, James Hamilton. It's funny, Lord," he said, "but proud as I am of the lad, words don't come with him as they flowed always with the friend for whom I named him. And it just came to me, Father, that my elder son's insistence that John Fraser not be told yet of his bright future at Hamilton is somehow erecting a wall between my fine son-in-law and me. Lord, that must not be! At seventy years, this old ram should have strength enough to be natural with the lad anyway. It could be John might have to wait for two or three more years. Enlarge my faith, I beg You. Give me the gumption and patience to wait and to keep my mouth shut around John. *It is my son's place to tell him.*"

At Frederica Road in front of the church, he shuffled through the remainder of the mail. Good. There was a letter for his beloved Anne from her friend Anna Matilda, off at the North in Brooklyn, New York. He would ride out to Lawrence so that Anne wouldn't have to wait until he handed out the mail at Sunday service.

The prospect of perhaps finding his daughter at home alone lifted his heart, as always.

He had reached Couper Road when two thoughts struck: He could always tell Anne anything, and Becca wouldn't mind at all if he told their daughter first that he'd lost his best friend. The second thought required that he do some battle. Anne's brother James Hamilton had indeed told him to keep the Hamilton secret from John but had said not one word against telling Anne!

"Lord, You already know I'm a rascal and a very human old man, so there's no use in reminding You." He spurred his horse to a gallop and headed toward the Lawrence turnoff on Couper Road. "You also know that unless You figure out a way to stop me within the next few minutes, I'm going to tell Anne that as soon as her prestigious but stubborn brother feels John thoroughly capable, she will be the mistress of beautiful Hamilton Plantation!"

CHAPTER 18

ANNE HEARD HIM RIDE UP IN FRONT OF HER COT-
tage and hurried outside.

"Papa," she called, running down her front steps. "You're waving a letter! What a wonderful surprise!" She grabbed the enve-
lope and then helped him dismount. "And I'm all alone this morning. We can have one of our real talks for a change." After they
embraced warmly, she said, "Do I embarrass you helping you off
your horse? Tell me I don't. I love to do it. It seems sometimes as
though I never do anything for my wonderful father."

"Anne, Anne," he said, still holding her close. "You've not
stopped doing for me since the day you were born. And today I—I
confess I need one of our real talks."

Anne stepped back to look at him. "You do? Is something
wrong? Mama's all right, isn't she? And Isabella?"

"Yes, yes, everyone's fine. Everyone but your old papa."

"You're not ill, are you?"

"No, thank heaven. But heartbroken, Daughter." She saw him

reach into a pocket, then hand her another letter. "I should give you time to read what Anna Matilda wrote, but lass, I need you. Read my letter first, please."

Once, then a second time, she read the cold, ugly words that robbed Papa of his best friend in all the world outside his family. There were tears in her own eyes, not only for the loss they would all feel, but most of all, tears for her father, because there was nothing anyone could do to help this dear man to whom they'd always turned. It had been a long time since any of the Coupers had even seen Mr. Hamilton, but when she was growing up, he had been almost as much a part of Anne's life as had Papa himself. Wanting with all her heart to find even a few words of comfort for her father, Anne could only throw her arms around him and weep.

Of course he held her, patted her, made small, broken, soothing sounds as he kissed her hair. "There, child, it's going to be all right," Papa murmured. "Old people do—die. It was James's time and he's with God now. In our great loss we simply have to know that. To believe it, to act on it. Who could take better care of him than our heavenly Father?"

"I—I know that! I do know it, Papa, and I'm ashamed of myself. Here you came to me for comfort and I'm taking again— from you!" Struggling a bit, she smiled up at him and said, "Would you like some freshly baked scones and tea? Hitch your horse and sit down on my front porch. I'll go tell Mina to serve us."

"No, no, no, Daughter. Thank you, but I must ride on home. I need to tell your mother about our old friend James Hamilton."

Her father looked so broken, so earnest in his efforts to go on smiling his usual, cheerful smile for her sake, that she pulled a childish trick. She stomped her foot and said, "I absolutely refuse to let you go until you've had a good, strong cup of tea and at least one hot scone! Now, have I made myself clear, sir?"

"Aye," he said, grinning weakly but obeying her. He hitched his mount and followed her meekly up the path to the porch. "My granddaughters are not at home receiving today?"

"They're at your house. Dear Mr. Browne didn't feel up to giving them their lessons yesterday. They went today, Eve escorting them." Anne tried a laugh. "You should have seen the three of them drive off an hour ago. Eve was holding the reins as Eve always does, the girls perched beside her wearing the new dresses you and Mama had Eve's mother make for them. They were both terribly eager to show off their new finery to you."

Sinking thankfully into a porch rocker, he said as cheerfully as possible, "Then, I must get along back to Cannon's Point soon, so as not to disappoint them. But I would relish a cup of tea. Not sure about being able to eat a scone, though."

"Of course you can," Anne called over her shoulder as she hurried inside to give Mina her orders, then came right back to sit with him.

"You didn't see John on the road anywhere, did you?" Anne asked, after she scooted a chair close enough to hold his hand while they talked. "He was riding over to the Hazzards today to borrow some tool or other June needed."

"No. No, I didn't see the lad anywhere. Why couldn't June or one of the other people make that ride?"

For a moment Anne said nothing. She just sat, smoothing the soft red hairs on the freckled back of his hand. "I don't know, Papa. These days I seem not to know very much at all about why John does what he does, or doesn't do."

"Well now, that's a puzzle, isn't it?"

"He's a puzzle to me often, and I'd give almost anything to know why he stays so restless."

"Restless? John's a restless man, Daughter. But is he more restless than usual lately?"

She nodded. "He—he just seems to be—waiting for something. Over and over, he wonders if he'll ever be a real provider for the children and me."

"After such a good crop last year?"

"Oh Papa, I was so sure that good crop would help him calm down. He's proud of his crop. But he's also tired of having me mention it again and again. I've almost run out of ways to buoy his spirits. Do you know something I don't know about John? Has he told you anything that might be worrying him?"

"Lass, you're such a good wife to him!"

"We're not talking about me, we're talking about John! You

two are together a lot; has he told you anything that I should know about, Papa? I'm not going to let go until you tell me, so you may as well do it. You know I can be as stubborn and headstrong as you when I need to know something, and I need to know why John, when he isn't playing like a wild Indian with the girls, is either brooding or only half answering me. Tell me the truth, is he learning how to be a—real planter? He is, isn't he? How could he have had such a fine crop if he weren't?"

"Yes, yes. The lad's learning a year's worth every day of his life. John is already a fine planter."

"Then what's eating him? Why does he have such self-doubts? Why can't he just be—" She broke off, feeling real shame. "How dreadful of me! You've just learned that your best friend has died and here I am yammering at you like a fish wife. Can you ever forgive me?"

He managed a laugh. "No, no, I can't, because there's nothing to forgive. I've spent my life trying hard to be the kind of father to whom you'd run when anything, just anything, went wrong. Something is plainly wrong now—with John. You've told me and you did the right thing because John is your life."

"Yes," she said in a small but firm voice. "He's my life all right. But honestly, I dragged you in here to comfort *you,* to give you tea and scones and—"

With a sizable clatter, Mina kicked the half-closed front door back and with another clatter, set down a tray of tea and still-steaming scones.

"Thank you, Mina. That will be all. Eve, of course, is not here to serve, but I can. I know you have dinner cooking. In fact, I'd love to serve my father. So that will be all."

"Yas'm," Mina said, not unpleasantly but, as always, as though she was dead tired. "You want I should cook mo' hot peppahs dan usual for Mausa John's blackeye peas? Dat man wan' eberthing hot as fiyah. Ain' nuffin' wrong wif Mina's blackeyes de way she fix 'em."

"I know your blackeyed peas are delicious," Anne said, "but humor him just this once more, please?" Then, turning to Papa, she explained, "John still hasn't learned to like our blackeyed peas.

He vows they have no taste at all. Mina tries so hard, though, to please him these days. We all do. And I'm most grateful to you, Mina. He'll—my husband will be his old cheerful self again soon. You'll see."

Still standing in the doorway, hands on hips, Mina grumbled, "I sho hope so, ma'am. Looks lik ain' no pleasin' him no more."

When the big-boned cook had gone back inside the house, Anne said, "Mama still tells me I don't know how to handle servants."

"Your mother is right almost ninety-eight percent of the time, Anne. But tell me, is John so restless it shows even to your servants? He's always been jolly with Mina and Eve."

"I've already talked too much about John. Would you be at all interested in having me read Anna Matilda's letter to you? After I've poured our tea?"

While Anne served them, he sat in deep thought, smoothing the back of his long, dark red hair, graying now at the temples. "I'd be interested to know how your friend Anna Matilda likes it at the North. She's been in her husband's home state of Massachusetts for quite some time, hasn't she? I wasn't prying, but I couldn't help noticing this letter I brought today was from Brooklyn, New York." He thanked her for the tea and scones, immediately took one small bite, then laid it down.

"You're too upset over Mr. Hamilton to eat, aren't you, Papa?"

"I—I don't think so, no. I was still thinking mostly about John, I guess."

"At least drink your tea. You've had a long, hard ride."

"I'm not that old, Daughter!"

She couldn't help smiling at his perseverance when she saw him take another giant bite of Mina's flaky scone. "That's better," she said.

After another sip of tea, he set down the cup. "And Anne, I've just made up my mind about something. Everything will be better once I've told you."

"Told me what?"

Sitting on the edge of her chair, Anne listened while he told her—without apology—that he'd taken it upon himself to write and let Father Fraser know of Anne's brother's plan concerning John and Hamilton Plantation. In fact, he talked until the tea in the pot grew too tepid to drink.

"James Fraser had but one chance to tell John and that would have been the night John spent in Darien on his way to the Savannah market," he said. "The lad has not mentioned one word about any of it to me."

So stunned by what she'd just heard, Anne could only sit there.

"I can see from your little face, Daughter," Papa went on, "that John hasn't told you, either."

"No. No, he hasn't. Papa, do you have any idea why he might —keep such a thing from me?"

"Aye, I have a good idea."

"Then tell me!"

"For one thing, the lad knows he's on trial."

"You're pretty sure Father Fraser told him, aren't you?"

"I am, because I did everything but ask the mon to let John know. I thought it only fair. Your brother's impulse is a generous one, but without realizing it, my son James Hamilton can be cruel."

"Papa! Cruel?"

"Aye. If John has known for all these months that his every move is being watched—his every success and failure probably charted in one of James Hamilton's big record books—why wouldn't the lad be on edge? As you say, restless?"

"Then why did you give Father Fraser freedom to tell him?"

"I repeat that I thought it only fair to John. I've been known to use bad judgment, Anne. Evidently that's exactly what I did."

She patted his hand. "You had only the best intentions, though, Papa. I can certainly see how you'd think it would encourage John to know that James Hamilton, of his own lofty volition, even thought of putting my husband in complete charge of his precious Hamilton Plantation. It's just that, as usual, James Hamilton is thinking only from his own point of view. My brother has no right to make John wait so long! Papa, it's been"—she counted on her fingers from September of last year—"seven whole months."

"Hamilton is your brother's property, Anne. He has a perfect right to do all he can to protect its future profitability."

"Profitability is all my brother thinks about!"

"You know that isn't true. His salary offer of three thousand dollars a year is far from strict business practice. James Hamilton's heart is involved too. He wants you and the children to have everything you need."

"I'm sure my husband can see to that!" She had flared, and that was the last thing her father deserved. "I'm sorry. I shouldn't have said that. But John has done extremely well here at Lawrence this year."

"Better than any one of us had a right to expect, actually. Planting is a difficult profession to learn."

For a long time they sat there on Anne's porch side by side, she still holding on to his hand. Finally she said, "I shouldn't let John know that you told me, should I?"

"No, but I suppose you will."

"My brother could keep him on trial for years!"

"That's possible. And the present overseer does have a three-year contract. James may also have decided that before he turns Hamilton over to John, the lad should have more than one good crop behind him. That isn't unreasonable, you know."

"Maybe not the way a man sees it. John isn't just—any man, though." Papa Couper got to his feet slowly, his old legs plainly bothering him. "You're going, aren't you?" she asked.

"Aye, Daughter. Undoubtedly I've done enough damage."

"You have not. You've helped me more than—more than anyone else could have. At least I know now why John has been acting so jumpy, so downright nervous. I'm sure Father Fraser told him."

"Are you planning to tell John that you know about Hamilton?"

"I don't know yet what I'm going to do. I just know that somehow all this has made me love him even more than ever."

WHEN HER FATHER RODE AWAY, ANNE PICKED UP the still-unread letter from Anna Matilda, hoping with all her heart that nothing was wrong for her friend way up in Brooklyn, New York. As she broke the seal, she couldn't help thinking that were Anna Matilda at home, Anne would visit her for a good long talk. It had been selfish for Anna Matilda's husband, Thomas, to insist that they all make such a long trip north, with Anna Matilda expecting another baby this year. How dreadful if another of her children had to be born in some foreign-sounding northern place like Brooklyn, New York! Little Hannah was born up there. The new baby, Anne knew, was expected sometime in the early fall, and even though Thomas had vowed they'd be home before fall, who could really tell when a man as ambitious as Thomas Butler King would change plans?

Her hands still trembling from what Papa had just told her, Anne ripped the letter trying to get it open, held the torn places together, and began to read.

Dearest Anne,

No place on earth could feel as far from St. Simons Island as Brooklyn, New York, and I'm heartbroken that only this morning Thomas told me that our new child would, like Hannah, be born up here! He is so tender and considerate of me and such a good father that such news, after the difficult time I had when Hannah was born away from Retreat, really hurts me. Wasn't life—all of life—simple and dependable when you and I were girls? Thomas has asked me to understand that he needs to keep certain appointments having to do with the possible purchase of some property in Camden County, Georgia, evidently owned by a gentleman up here. I'm sure what he has in mind is important, but why do men always have to be wanting more property? I'm sorry to complain, but the truth is, I'm taking out on you my deep disappointment that we can't come home until after my baby is born. Thomas is also spending several weeks this summer in Washington City, dealing in some manner with politics. Oh Anne, I miss you and I'm going to stop this and try to be thankful that I'm well so far and hope you are all well too. Remember me to everyone and do remember me in your prayers.

Anne glanced at the remaining few lines almost without seeing them. Papa had done all he knew to do for her by telling her the reason for John's nervousness. There was no chance now of confiding in Anna Matilda. As much as Anne admired and loved her mother, Mama almost always took James Hamilton's side of things. Eve, whose loyalty Anne never questioned, just plain didn't like her older brother. There was no one left to turn to—but John. And John clearly needed her to be strong. She dared not bring up the subject until her own emotions were firmly under control.

Gathering up the half-emptied teacups, she wondered if indeed she *could* control her own emotions should John take offense at being discussed behind his back, even with Papa.

CHAPTER 19

ANNA MATILDA'S BABY, A BOY SHE NAMED THOMAS Butler King, Jr., was born in Brooklyn in September. A letter to Anne and John, written by Thomas King himself, should have relieved Anne far more than it did. Anna Matilda was doing fine, as was the new baby, but Anne definitely was not. She still had not let John know that Papa had told her about Hamilton. She had only stewed and worried, keeping it inside.

"You gittin' jus' lak a cross ol' hen, Miss Anne," Eve said when she brought Anne's breakfast into the Lawrence dining room on a clear November morning. "Dere be somepin' bad wrong an' you hurt me by spectin' Eve to b'lieve day arter day dat nothin' ain' wrong!"

"I never heard anything so silly," Anne said, holding out her coffee cup for Eve to fill.

"Now you addin' on a lie. Where Mausa John dis mornin'? He done in de fiel's?"

"No he isn't and you're being nosy. I'm sorry if I've seemed cross, but I do have the right to act the way I feel in my own house. You wouldn't understand anyway."

Usually careful and quiet when she served, Eve banged down the big silver coffeepot. "Ain' neber been nothin' Eve don' understan' 'bout chu, Miss Anne, an' you knows dat's de truf!"

"When you're upset, your English gets sloppier and sloppier," Anne said, breaking open one of Mina's tender biscuits. "That word is *truth,* not *truf!* Here I thought you were getting so much more careful."

"How I be careful when I so worried? You cross lak dis wif Mausa John? You say yes you cross lak dis wif him an' Eve tell you quick you be sorry some day!"

It shows, Anne thought. I've put off talking to John all summer about my stiff-necked brother's making him wait to learn about Hamilton. It must show because Eve's caught on.

"Mausa John, he ain' eatin' no breakfus today?"

"He had to meet my brother and my father at Cannon's Point early. He's having breakfast up there and I don't think it's any of your business." When Eve only turned her back and said nothing, Anne could have kicked herself. None of what made her upset had anything to do with Eve. None of it was Eve's fault. "Eve," she said, knowing her mother would say she was giving in to her servant too quickly, "I'm sorry. I have been cross and I know you only fuss at me because you care."

When Eve turned around, Anne saw the creamy, light brown cheeks were glistening with tears. "Eve do care."

"*Does,*" Anne corrected.

"Eve does care."

"Thank you, but I don't deserve your caring."

"Yes you does."

"*Do.*"

"Do, does, ain' no law," Eve snapped. Then gentling her voice, she added, "I—I tries to please you, Miss Anne. For all the years you an' me's been together, I tries. An' you does—*do*—deserve me to care. Eve don' always talk right, but outside of June, ain' nuffin' in dis worl' makes no difference to Eve but you, Miss Anne. You an' Mausa John still lovin' each other, ain' you?"

Startled, Anne looked up. "Of course we still love each other!"

"Anybody knows dat," Eve said earnestly, "but what I mean is —real *lovin'!* June love me lots an' no matter how hard we tries, we can't have no baby. But if Mausa John still lovin' you, you gonna be habin a baby again someday and dat chile don' need no crosspatch mama! Annie an' Pete don't neither."

Even with the news of Anna Matilda's new child, Anne had given none of what Eve had just said a single thought. For weeks now, she'd put off letting John know that Papa had told her about Hamilton but had thought about little else. She had not mentioned Hamilton because she was just plain afraid. Afraid of John? How could she be afraid of the dear, beautiful man who was the other half of her very own life?

"What chu skeered of, Miss Anne?"

She stared at Eve. "Scared? What makes you think I'm scared?"

" 'Cause you ack it. Sometimes you put Eve in min' of yo' daughter Annie when she workin' up nerve to climb up to one mo' tree limb. That little thing jus plain skeered 'bout climbin' trees, specially when her baby sister, Pete, she can't hardly wait to git on up higher!"

Not bothering to fold her napkin or to put it in its holder, Anne tossed it on the table and jumped up. "I don't want any more breakfast. I'm all right. I—I just don't have much appetite. I'm going for a walk in the woods and I'm going by myself and I expect you to explain to the girls, when Big Boy brings them home from Cannon's Point after their lessons, that I don't want to be disturbed."

"What you spect Eve to tell 'em?"

"Something. You'll think of—something. I have to have a good, firm talk with myself and I don't want anyone interrupting me!"

ANNE SETTLED HERSELF ON HER FAVORITE FALLEN log in the Park, as the girls liked to call their woods. Because she so hated facing her own fear of how John might react to the kind of talk she knew they needed to have, she stalled by examining the tiny, pale green moss flowers growing on a single fallen twig at her feet. She'd loved the St. Simons lichen and mosses since childhood —especially after the kind of soaking rain they'd had last week, which left the miniature moss-world thicker, more varied, more enchanting than ever. Annie loved every specimen Anne had pointed out to her, too, although she doubted that her older daughter would even have noticed otherwise. Dear, gentle Annie still missed London, and now, with Father Fraser gone, there were times when the girl's loneliness pained Anne almost beyond endurance. With the permission of her parents, because Annie seldom did anything remotely rash, she had begun to ride to Christ Churchyard on the new pony her grandfather Couper had bought as a twelfth-birthday present. She liked to sit beside Father Fraser's grave.

"What do you do there, Annie?" John asked last week at dinner.

"Oh, Grandfather Fraser and I just—visit," the girl said. "He likes my pony a lot."

"Did you tell him why you named her Peggy?" Anne asked.

"I did, Mama. He told me once he always called Margaret, his dead wife, Peggy. I wish my grandmother Margaret Fraser hadn't died so long ago."

"So do I," John said.

The talk had come quickly to an end when Pete, always hating to be left out of anything, especially now that her fourth birthday was coming up next week, broke in with "It won't be fair for Grandpapa Couper not to give me a pony for my birthday too!"

"Oh no, Pete," Anne remembered saying, only half watching a squirrel flip and curl its bushy tail while perched on the tip-top of a pine spike that didn't look nearly sturdy enough to hold its weight. "Oh no, Tomboy Pete," she'd said, "you're still too young for a pony of your own. Besides, you seldom remember to ask permission to do anything." What her parents were giving Pete to celebrate her fourth birthday, Anne knew, was a yellow wagon her father had ordered from an advertisement in the *National Intelli-*

gencer, his favorite newspaper, for which he waited every week.

Her thoughts returned to her present predicament. "All right, Anne Couper Fraser," she said aloud in a firm voice. "You're out here in the woods all alone for the express purpose of giving yourself a good, no-nonsense talk. Why don't you get started?"

The words were no sooner out of her mouth than she heard John's voice calling her, then the crackle and breaking-twig sound of his boots coming toward her, the sound wandering a bit as he called her name, hunting for her solitary spot in the Park.

"Anne! Anne, I know you're out here. Eve told me. Answer me, so I can find you."

Her heart raced. He didn't sound a bit restless or uncertain. His voice sounded like John. Then she heard a dog whine—a puppy! It had to be a puppy's whine and John must be carrying it. "John? Darling, I'm here—over here by the big persimmon tree! Did I hear a puppy?"

A sharp, nervous yap followed. Not a whine this time. It was what passed in a puppy for a bark. She remembered back over all the years to the first day Papa brought Lovey to her, his gift to cheer her as she sat weeping over a dead nonpareil on the front steps of the little old Cannon house when she was about four—Pete's age now. Way back even before the Big House had been started.

"John," she called, jumping to her feet because she could see him now and knew he was indeed carrying an adorable, wiggly, black-and-white pup.

"Anne!" He came toward her, laughing. "Look who's come to belong to you! Could we call him Lovey too? It's not a female like your first Lovey, but—hey, little fellow, hold still until I can make my presentation to the lady."

"Oh John, darling, he's beautiful! Give him to me!"

When John, holding the pup in one arm—or trying to—and reaching to embrace her with the other, attempted a formal, proper presentation, he broke out laughing again. It was a genuine John laugh, the happy, musical peal she had wondered if she'd ever hear again.

"What's wrong? What's so funny?" she demanded.

"Look!" he shouted. "Just take a look at my work shirt and draw your own conclusions, milady."

The doggy had peed freely down the front of John's shirt, all the way to the cuff of his sleeve. "Don't worry about making a fancy speech," Anne said, laughing too. "Just let me hold him!"

He put his own face near hers when he handed the puppy to her and asked, "Do you like the little fellow? I'd say, by the way he's kissing you, he's already smitten with you, and how could he not be? Anne, beautiful Anne, I need to talk. I picked a crazy time to give you a feisty little dog I promised thirteen years ago on our honeymoon, but I need to talk. How can I get a word in edgewise, though, with Lovey carrying on like this? Do you realize I almost never see you alone in the daylight anymore? And by the time we close the door to our room, I'm so tired from a long day's work, I —Anne, Anne, I'm chattering too much again."

Her free arm reaching up to hug him, she said, "You are not! If you had any idea, John Fraser, how I've longed to hear you talk too much again, you'd never stop!" Then, giving the dog a quick smack, she scolded, "Stop that, Lovey, or you won't be honored with the name Lovey at all! Ouch! John, he's got the sharpest little teeth. Why didn't you warn me? He's biting my chin and I'm trying to have a serious talk with my gorgeous husband and—"

"And it's all right that we can't have a serious talk now," he said quickly, taking the dog in order to give her a moment's peace. "There's time tonight for talk, for good talk, and more. . . ." He was laughing again. "Of course we'll have to figure out a place for his highness to sleep, well away from *our* bedroom, to be sure."

"Has Pete seen the puppy? Has Annie? Where did you get him?"

"Neither girl has seen him. They were both closeted with dear old eccentric Mr. Browne, hard at their lessons, I presume, when I got Lovey."

"Where? Where did you get him? Did someone give him to us?"

"Yes, but you have to guess."

"Tell me!"

"Guess!"

"One of Papa's people? Johnson? I know he has a black-and-white dog, but she's part hound. Lovey's no hound dog, John. What is he?"

"He and I apologize for forgetting to bring along his pedigree, milady, but I'm told he's a love dog. The offspring of a good, small terrier and a full-blooded spaniel, neither intended for mating by their owner, but as you can see, both took matters into their own hands."

"I should have guessed at least part spaniel," she said. "Look at that square little muzzle! And of course he's noisy and yaps because he's part terrier."

"You're well versed in dogs, Mrs. Fraser."

"That's because I was born knowing. But John, who gave him to us? And is he really mine?"

"He's yours if you can convince Pete of ownership. Maybe even Annie. Our elder is so quiet, I'm not certain how much she likes dogs, but it's got to be in Pete's very nature. I insist that you guess the name of the donor, though."

"Not Johnson, Papa's butler?"

"No. Not Johnny. Guess again."

"Don't tell me it was Eve's grandmaum, old Sofy! I don't want Sofy to have given us this dog because I feel too uneasy about the time Pete spends with her now."

"Not Sofy, so stop worrying."

"Tell me! Who gave us this handsome, lovable puppy dog?"

John studied her face, still smiling. "I honestly don't think you'd ever guess if you tried for one solid hour."

"Then tell me. It's not becoming for you to be so mean."

Without a word, still holding the squirming pup under one arm, he guided her to her old, moss-covered log. "Sit down. You'll need to be sitting down when I tell you who actually had the warmhearted idea of giving us Lovey."

"All right. I'm sitting." She reached for the pup. "But I want to hold him again. I want to be holding him when you tell me."

"What Lovey wants is to get all four feet on the ground and have himself a good ramble in the woods."

"No! He's going to be a house dog. These woods are still full of fleas and ticks. We haven't had any really cold weather yet." To the dog, she explained, "It's for your own good and comfort, Lovey, for you to sit right here on my lap and be calm. Furthermore, you're going to get frequent baths and spend most of your time indoors and that's for your own protection. These woods are exciting, I know, and full of beauty and all sorts of wild, marvelous smells, but sit! Sit and be quiet and calm. I'm about to find out what good angel sent you to live with us."

John's face had gone serious suddenly. He sat down on the log beside her. Certainly, Anne thought, Lovey's a gift from the last person John ever expected, and then she knew. Of course! John had ridden out early to Cannon's Point because he and Papa and James Hamilton had a business session today. Her usually stuffy, brilliant, stiff-necked, unplayful brother James Hamilton had brought Lovey all the way across the salt marshes and creeks and rivers from Hopeton on the mainland!

As though sensing the odd tension of the moment, the pup eased down between them on the log. Its feistiness abruptly gone, the tiny animal just sat there listening, looking first at John, then at Anne.

"Do you still want me to guess who gave us the puppy?" Anne asked, her voice sounding a little careful.

"Unless I'm mistaken," John said, "you've already guessed. You have seldom failed to read me like one of William Browne's old worn books." For a moment neither spoke, then John said, "Why not try one more time?"

"My brother James Hamilton."

He turned slowly to look directly at her, only half smiling. "Poor old me," he said. "There are times when I truly pity myself. How does one defenseless man bear up day in and day out as I do, under such a shining burden as you?"

Anne was sure he was at least half playing. It had been such a long time since he'd even tried one of their old teasing tricks as a safe way to skirt a difficult moment, she was almost afraid to try to meet him in this one. But why not try, she thought, and did: "I—I rather like the fact that I shine," she said, smiling up at him, "but

I'm not so sure about wanting to be burdensome. Why am I a shining burden, darling?"

"You're too beautiful and you're too intuitive. Even you have to admit to being a bit like quicksilver now and then. Your illustrious and surprising brother James Hamilton did bring us the little dog. Of course he made a brief, proper speech, then began at once to talk business, as though his bringing a playful gift was a daily occurrence."

"Did he say he'd brought it for the girls?"

"No. As I recall, he said the pup, he hoped, would bring 'a world of joy to the entire Fraser family of Lawrence.'"

She grabbed and hugged John's arm, which act so energized Lovey that he began to paw and scratch at John's shirt-sleeve. Then Anne whispered, "My brother James has always had, underneath that formidable, gentleman's exterior, a tender heart, John."

"So you've said."

This, she knew, was the right moment to bring up Hamilton. There would be no better time if she waited another six months or even, God forbid, another year. Still, the old fear kept her silent. Even with the pure joy of these happy, shared moments, with Lovey again sitting attentively between them on the log, she was still afraid that in case John's father had not told him, the news that James Hamilton seemed to be keeping John on trial might spoil everything. She'd allowed her fear to keep her silent for so long, why not just cling to this intimate moment?

"Were the girls coming home after their lessons or did Papa mention their staying for dinner?"

"I have no idea," John said. "The minute I could leave with any grace at all, I bid your father and brother goodbye and hurried home with Lovey. Does it—will it bother you to call him Lovey? I know how much you cared about your other dog."

"Poor old me," she said, imitating him. "How can one lone woman endure such sweetness in a man as I must endure from you, John Fraser?"

"I'm glad I'm sweet," he said, his smile back. "I'm surely not very brave. I'm also not very confident of myself."

"What on earth are you saying? If I'm so beautiful and so

intuitive, doesn't the fact that I love you with more than just all my heart make you confident?"

He sighed. "If you didn't love me in the extravagant way you do, I wouldn't be worth a farthing!"

At that moment, as though he meant to help Anne convince John of his worth, Lovey again started pawing and nuzzling John's sleeve. "See?" she said. "Even Lovey thinks you're wonderful. John, John, I've missed you so much!"

He looked genuinely surprised. "You've missed me? When we've been together every minute I can spare from my infernal work? You've got to explain that, Anne. What do you mean, you've missed me?"

"You've seemed so far away sometimes. Except when we're holding each other in the night, I've felt far away from you. You always did talk a lot and lately you've had so little to say about almost everything. John, there's something I've kept from you. I'll confess I've been afraid to tell you. Now don't get all funny and silent and grim with me. Be you. Please be you, because I don't like not telling you *everything.*" Now the pup was tugging at the lace on Anne's sleeve, nuzzling and kissing her arm.

"Stop that, Lovey," John ordered. "Do you think this pup is going to come between us?" .

"No. No, he most definitely is not. After we've gotten one thing out in the open, we'll both look back on this time here in the woods and see that it was Lovey who fixed everything."

"Anne, what in the name of heaven are you talking about?

"What in the name of heaven has made you so silent and worried and remote for weeks, for months?"

"You tell me what it is you've been keeping from me. You said yourself that there's something you haven't told me because you were afraid I'd get all funny again. What, Anne? What?"

She reached over Lovey to take John's hand. "Did you—did you have time for a talk with Father Fraser the night you spent at William's house in Darien when you were on your way to buy your people at the Savannah slave market?"

Instead of clamming up, withdrawing from her as she was so afraid he might, his smile lit up the woods. Longing to throw both arms around him, she could only stare in sheer wonder. It had been such a long, long time since John had smiled *this* smile, the John smile that shouted merriment, joy, eager delight at being alive on the earth—the John kind of joy that lit not only the woods but all of Anne's heart. It was his honeymoon smile again. They could easily have been sitting side by side in Mr. McDonald's old buggy, rattling merrily across the bridge over the River Nith to spend another happy day at Caerlaverock, Mama's family's ancient castle near Dumfries—both without a care in the world.

Anne didn't throw her arms around him because such a smile had taken her too much by surprise. The months of feeling shut out, of aching over what might be his dark, secret thoughts—the reason for his restlessness—had simply made her helpless. She could only sit there, hoping the puppy wouldn't start to fidget and distract them from the wonder. Because John almost seemed to be enjoying keeping her in suspense, because she so reveled in that smile, because she wanted both to hug him and to smack him, Anne just sat there.

Finally John grabbed Lovey in one hand, jumped nimbly to his feet, and reached his other hand to pull her up, then just stood holding the pup *and* her—laughing into the crisp, clear November air. He was playing like a boy, shouting "ho-ho's" and "yippees" and "huzzahs" with such gusto her mind raced back again to the magical day when, just before their honeymoon ended, dear Cousin Willy Maxwell had ordered his pipers to play the "Fraser of Lovat's Salute" so lustily that John, clad in borrowed kilts, had abruptly begun to march all alone around the ruins of the old Caerlaverock courtyard—for the sheer thrill of it.

His excitement now excited the little dog, of course, and risking ticks and fleas, John put him down. With Lovey pulling at Anne's long skirt, the two of them hugged and hugged, and even though he hadn't answered her question about his visit with Father Fraser, she was laughing, too, because her lover was happy again.

At last he picked up the puppy and almost in the same motion, sat Anne back down on the big, moss-covered log. "I haven't forgotten your question, beloved wife," he said, the smile lingering. "I haven't forgotten it at all. I even know why you asked it. Your wonderful father, who hates keeping a secret as much as I do, told you, didn't he?"

She gave him a half-puzzled, half-smiling look. "Told me what, John?"

"That one blessed future day you and I will leave our cramped little Lawrence house and move—trunks, children, and Lovey—down the Island to live our remaining days in the far roomier, elegantly situated Hamilton place."

Tears welled. She hated a weeping woman, so buried her face on John's shoulder. "Yes, dearest, Papa told me James Hamilton hoped that would happen—someday. But he didn't tell me when, because—"

"—because no one, certainly not your perfect brother, knew *when* your husband would prove himself worthy of such a tremendous undertaking. If I've been detached, Anne, it's because I've been like a prisoner in the dock awaiting the almighty verdict of my judge, James Hamilton Couper!"

The old edge was back in his voice, the edge that was always there when, for almost any reason, he mentioned James Hamilton's name. Anne decided to ignore it. Lifting her head to look straight into his eyes, she said, only half teasing, "Haven't you squeezed the last possible theatrical drop from all this? *Did you talk to Father Fraser that night?* Did he tell you what Papa had told him about James Hamilton's wanting to put you in full charge of his St. Simons holdings? Have you known it all this time and not told me one single word?"

His grin brought one to her face when he mimicked her question: "And haven't *you* known—also from Papa Couper—for months without telling me?"

"Yes."

"And are you just a little bit sorry?"

"I'm also ashamed," she confessed. "Are you sorry too?"

"Aye, that I am, lass." In his excitement John began to play with Lovey with such vigor that this strange, secret tête-à-tête on a fallen log in the Lawrence woods was clearly heading for an abrupt end.

John rose and offered Anne his hand. "Let's put Lovey to a

test, too," he said as they headed along the cleared path toward the cottage. "Heaven knows I've been tested for months on end. Shall I put him down and find out if he likes us enough to follow us home?"

"If you'll examine him for ticks once we get there," Anne said, taking his arm. "Let's try it. Put him down."

Wonder of wonders, the puppy did not fly off into the brambly woods but sat right down on the ground, his tiny pink tongue and black tail waving with delight.

"Come on, boy," John said. "You're going to your very own new home."

"Wait, John," she said. "You've been playing all sorts of games this morning and I'm glad. I love having you happy again. But when do we go to *our* very own new home, Hamilton? Did my brother tell you?"

His face went solemn again. "I haven't been very fair with you, have I? No, he did not tell me. Your brother made a far longer speech when he gave us Lovey than when he finally got around to informing me only today what he had in mind for all the remainder of our earthly lives. James Hamilton is, to me at least, indecipherable. I have no choice but to try my level best to please the man, Anne, but I'll never understand him. I'm elated, excited, and *so* grateful, but it's as though he moves elegantly about in his own rarefied atmosphere, fully expecting his inferiors to follow."

What he had just said truly confused her. To compose herself, she reached down to pick up the dog. "Do you—do you dislike him so much?"

John was playing no games now. His answer was direct, honest, and simple. "No, I don't think I dislike your brother at all. Finally I've come to believe he means us all well, even me. Anne, he couldn't be as cold and unfeeling as I've thought him at times and be the son of your greathearted parents. Before you have to ask me, I want to promise you something."

"What, dearest?"

"That I'll not only do my very best to operate Hamilton as your highly respected brother deserves, I'll also—as from this moment—try to begin to give him the benefit of every doubt. He's just so brainy, it must be hard, even for him, to meet ordinary people on the lowly plane where most of us live."

"I'm sure I love you this minute," she breathed, "more than I've ever loved you."

"Thank you. If you didn't, I wouldn't even *attempt* to please your brother. Should I be able to satisfy his demands on me, much of the credit will have to go to you." He grinned. "Now I may not find the grace to say that ever again, so mark it well, ma'am."

"But did he give you any idea of when all this might happen?" she asked.

"An idea so vague and so infinitesimal, even he may need to look for it under one of his rare and fancy microscopes. I did gather this much from what he said. Now that Mr. Hamilton of Philadelphia is dead, James hopes to buy the deceased's half of Hopeton—the half Hamilton bought from your father when he was in financial trouble. That will take time. It seems that your brother has a contract with his present St. Simons overseer, Mr. Bowers. So it will be a while, at least, before we can move to Hamilton. Can you wait, beautiful Anne?"

"Since all this is out in the open, since there are no secrets between us, yes. I can wait. Is it all right to talk about it? My brother didn't swear you to secrecy, did he?"

John laughed, took the pup from her, and set him down again. "No, I am not sworn to secrecy. Your parents, of course, have known for a long time."

They were almost home now, Lovey scampering and snuffling along beside them, making no effort to wander off. In fact, Anne thought, we'd better warn the girls that he stays so close he could be stepped on. "Annie and Pete don't know we'll be moving some-day, do they? I hope Mama and Papa don't tell them once Mr. Browne is finished with their lessons today. I want us to explain it when we're all together."

"I doubt that either Papa or Mama Couper would deprive us of that," he said. "But from the way Browne acted when I first rode to Cannon's Point this morning, their lessons won't last long."

"Is Mr. Browne ill?"

"I'd say he's quite ill. I never saw a man so weak who was still walking around. Your father is sending for Dr. Tunno. James Hamilton thinks he's in Brunswick today."

Anne stopped walking. "John, I'm worried! Mr. Browne can't be really ill!"

"You mustn't worry until we hear what Dr. Tunno says. I wish William could examine your old tutor."

"So do I, but Dr. Tunno's very good. If we couldn't get William, Dr. John Tunno would be the one I'd want if one of us fell ill. Darling, take care of you! I couldn't bear it if you were sick for any reason." They began to walk again toward home. "What on earth will we do if Mr. Browne can no longer teach our girls? He told me early this fall that my little sister, Isabella, could tutor them should he fall ill. I'm sure she could, except that she's only a year and a half older than Annie. She's awfully bright and patient, though."

"Pete requires patience, even for Belle. Can you believe our young one will be four next week?"

"No, and she'll probably be a grown-up girl of seven by the time we can move down to Hamilton."

"But we will live there," he said in the intimate voice usually kept for whispering love. "I promise you, beloved Anne, that your husband—barring a hurricane or an even worse caterpillar plague—will produce nothing but fine crops. Something else might go wrong for James Hamilton so that we can't go, but it won't be any lack on my part. I've never felt so determined or so sure."

A sharp yap from Lovey caught their attention. The dog had darted off after a squirrel, his shrill, puppy bark sending the tiny animal halfway up a pine tree, where the squirrel stopped, made a short run back down the tree before stopping again out of reach.

When Lovey, startled that the squirrel now faced him, pushed as close to John's boots as possible, they both laughed.

"No wonder I feel confident," John said. "I'm the master of the world's most courageous dog!"

In sight of the cottage, John took her in his arms and kissed her so deeply and for such a long time that Lovey barked again.

Anne pulled half-free of his embrace. "You really don't care if some of our people see us, do you?" she asked.

"Not one iota."

"I hope Eve *did* see us."

"You do?"

"Yes. Sometimes I wish she weren't so smart. I got quite a scolding this morning after you left. She accused me of being a crosspatch with you and with the children and, of course, with her."

"You and I had ourselves nailed up in separate boxes," he said.

"That's right. We did. I hate to admit it, but maybe it's a good thing Eve is so smart. I needed to be scolded. I was—difficult and so were you."

John crossed his heart. "Never again, I swear it. Do you swear it too?"

"Yes. Oh John, yes, yes!"

CHAPTER 20

IN MARCH OF THE NEW YEAR 1830, ANNE made a special trip down the Island to Retreat as soon as she was sure Anna Matilda had reached home again with her new baby, Thomas Jr.

"I know you'll love seeing places you've never been," she told Anna Matilda as they stood saying goodbye on the shuttered front porch of the Retreat cottage—the cottage her husband kept planning to replace with a larger house—"but I wish you weren't going to Europe so soon. I've only seen you this once since your long stay at the North."

"You will never quite believe that anyone else can love the way you love John," Anna Matilda said, "but I do love Thomas every bit as much and he has his heart set on going abroad. He's doing well with the Retreat crops. We can afford it. He's even planning to buy more land in Camden County and build a house there when we get back."

"But you won't be leaving St. Simons, will you?" Anne asked almost wistfully.

"No. Something dreadful would have to happen before I'd ever live anywhere else but my blessed Retreat. And I'm so excited you'll be moving to Hamilton! It's going to be wonderful having you down here on the south end of the Island. Do you realize how much more often we'll see each other?"

"Yes, but what if good Mr. Browne doesn't get well? Dr. Tunno says his circulation is not right, that he has those sinking spells because there isn't enough blood getting to his brain. He's taught us all so much! Somehow I can't bear the idea that you might still be in Europe if—if something happens to him! I know that sounds silly, but our childhood tutor has made his headquarters at Cannon's Point ever since he came to us back in 1803. My girls are doing so well under him. I know you've been tutoring your children yourself, but you can't keep that up much longer if you go on having more babies. I don't even want to start teaching my girls."

"I'm sure Mr. Browne is right that Isabella is perfectly capable of giving Annie and Pete their lessons for a time anyway. You're borrowing trouble, Anne. Mr. Browne is still able to tutor them most days, isn't he?"

"Yes, most days. But people do sicken and die. I get such a sad, sad feeling in the pit of my stomach when I think our faithful, gentle Mr. Browne might die. It—it will be like losing the last bit of our childhood, won't it?"

A N N E ' S   D R E A D   T H A T   W I L L I A M   B R O W N E   M I G H T   D I E while Anna Matilda was away, mentioned to no one but Anna Matilda before she left with her family for Europe in May, came true. Anne's father found the gentle, slender tutor dead in his bed on July 24.

"Not in all the years he lived with us," Papa told Anne when he rode over to Lawrence with the sad news, "was the man ever late for a meal. I went myself to look in on him. He'd been reading

Shakespeare, or trying to, because open on his thin chest lay a copy of *Hamlet.* Beside his bed on his little table was your friend Walter Scott's *Lady of the Lake.* Didn't you and Anna Matilda spend time studying *Lady of the Lake* when you were mere lasses?"

Anne's gaze moved out over the stretch of marsh and river. "We certainly did spend time reading Sir Walter back in those days. Scott and John still correspond occasionally. I'll remind John to tell him in his next letter that my old tutor had his book by his bedside when he died." Fighting tears, she looked at her father. "Papa, I don't think I—really expected Mr. Browne to die—ever. He was just always here studying his books, ready to talk, to teach. What will John and I do now for a teacher? My Annie will keep on studying, but who knows at age four what Pete's interests are going to be? I always counted on Mr. Browne to guide them both the way he guided James Hamilton, Anna Matilda, and me."

"Isabella's only fifteen this year, but William Browne always contended that your sister is perfectly capable of seeing the children through their next few years of study." He sighed. "What I'll do in the short run about your shiftless brother William Audley I dinna ken. That boy would spend every hour of every day with a fishing pole or astride an old plow horse if he had his way. I suppose once we've given our longtime friend Browne a Christian service, I'll have to begin planning for a school at the North for William. The boy needs a firm hand."

Anne frowned. "Papa, do you suppose our new, young rector has had time to reach the Island yet? I do so want Mr. Browne's service to be beautiful. Have you heard anything about the new rector since his ordination up in South Carolina? Wasn't the bishop to let you know his probable arrival time?"

"Aye. And he did, Daughter. I heard last week from the bishop, who also informed me that our former shepherd, Reverend Motte, had reached his home in Maine safely. The Lord watches over us. Young Reverend Theodore Bartow should arrive at Frederica today, the very day our friend Browne took his leave of us. 'Tis fitting that he will read the service for Browne on the Sabbath —tomorrow. James Gould has offered a burial plot. He'll rest in our little cemetery among the families of his many pupils."

TO ANNE, SEATED BETWEEN JOHN AND HER MOTHER in the tiny white chapel at Frederica, the service for William Browne, a quiet, nearly solitary man, was unusually well attended. She knew, of course, that some of those seated along the straight wooden benches wouldn't be there had Mr. Browne not died on a Saturday, but most who attended Sunday services earlier had remained to honor him. She also knew that the congregation of fifteen or sixteen people would have been smaller had it not been twenty-four-year-old Reverend Bartow's first appearance among them. Everyone who knew William Browne regarded him highly, but they were all naturally curious to see the manner in which their new rector comported himself.

No one expected Anne's younger sister, Isabella, to show her sorrow openly. Anne certainly didn't, since Belle had always been so quiet and reserved. No one ever mentioned it, but for all of Belle's life, Anne had held a secret regret because her young sister wasn't what anyone could call pretty. She was the picture of Papa, considered an extremely handsome man, but that meant Isabella had a long nose, a long face—features not thought good in a young lady. Everyone had always loved Belle. Other mothers often irritated their own daughters by setting "that nice, well-behaved Isabella Couper" as an example.

Today was different. About halfway through Reverend Bartow's reading of the service for the dead from the prayer book, Isabella, sitting on the other side of their mother, began to sob. To sob audibly, so that everyone heard, including Reverend Bartow, who paused momentarily to give the weeping girl a tender, comforting glance. Everyone probably noticed that too, Anne thought.

How Anne missed Anna Matilda, who, along with her and James Hamilton, had been among Mr. Browne's earliest pupils. Nothing would seem quite the same again at Cannon's Point with someone else—or no one—occupying their old tutor's room.

During the last prayer, Anne wondered for the first time how old William Browne might be? He'd come to the Couper family as a young man, newly arrived from his native England. To Anne, he had always seemed simply much older—her teacher.

As the knot of parishioners followed the wooden coffin out of the little church and to the freshly dug grave where Mr. Browne would lie, Anne's sorrow was less sharp, less heavy, than last year when they had buried blessed Father Fraser. But her heart ached, and she was still wondering if poor Belle grieved more than anyone else or was just plain scared because, at least for a time, she would have to try to take his place as teacher to both Annie and Pete.

As she walked beside John out into the old cemetery, guilt nagged at her because at thirty-three she had allowed the circumstances of their lives and the difference in their ages to block more than an almost cursory affection for poor Belle. She hadn't intended for this to happen, but being nearly ignored or taken for granted at such close range could hurt Belle most of all.

Standing between John and Papa at the open grave in the Gould plot, Anne shed her own first tears when June, Big Boy, Eve, and Rhyna began to hum, then to sing softly, the old English song "Oh, Willow, Willow, Willow," which Mr. Browne had taught them. They sang it in the odd African rhythm any group of Negroes fell into no matter what the melody, but the deep, quiet reverence in their rich voices caused Anne's tears. She wept for her old tutor, who had brought her the airy beauty of poetry, the path into endlessly opening new worlds to be found in novels written by men like Walter Scott and women like Jane Austen. But her tears flowed also for Isabella, suddenly almost a stranger. The sad truth was that Anne had been too busy fulfilling her own life to pay much attention to Belle's.

As the congregation straggled out of the churchyard and headed for carriages, buggies, and family wagons, she wondered if anyone else noticed that young, sensitive Reverend Theodore Bartow made a point of escorting Belle to the Couper carriage.

CHAPTER 21

ANNA MATILDA KING WAS BACK AT RETREAT IN plenty of time for the arrival of her third son, Henry Lord Page King, born April 25, 1831. Anne, since Anna Matilda's husband was away again, took Isabella and spent a full week with her friend.

"I feel so sorry for her," Belle said as Big Boy drove them home in Papa's carriage. "I know Mr. King expected to be back in time for the baby's birth, but it must be terribly hard for Anna Matilda to go through such a thing without him."

Not only had Belle done extremely well with the girls' lessons, Anne honestly believed that she herself had made a little progress in fulfilling her vow to find a closer relationship with her sister. Belle showed no particular talent for music or dancing or even fancywork, but the girl did love books and was a born teacher. During their stay at Retreat, while Anna Matilda rested, Belle had listened by the hour while Anne told her everything she could remember about her own visit in the home of Sir Walter Scott near

Selkirk, Scotland. She told her also of the nights when Willy Max-well, Lord Herries, had taken her and John to Covent Garden, where they actually saw the world-famous actress Sarah Siddons play Lady Macbeth. Since Belle was a Maxwell descendant through Mama, Anne did her best to describe every crumbled column and fireplace she could remember in every room still standing among the magnificent ruins of the old Maxwell family castle near Dum-fries, Scotland.

Of course Belle asked lots of questions about their distant cousin, Willy Maxwell, who had continued to write to Anne and John during the years since they'd said goodbye to him in London en route to Georgia to live—as John loved to say—"for the re-mainder of our days."

"Willy is probably in his late fifties now, although I don't know his real age," Anne told Belle, "nor can I imagine Willy's ever being anything but slender and gallant and tender and thoughtful and oh so generous. John and I were almost penniless in those days. We depended, except for John's half pay, which he still re-ceives from his regiment, entirely upon Father Fraser. So, when we went out in London's high society, we went through the courtesy and generosity of Willy Maxwell."

"And is he very rich?" Belle wanted to know.

"I suppose so," Anne said and realized that to her, devoted Willy had always been—just Willy, her true friend, John's true friend. "We *are* Maxwell cousins, you know, Belle. I'd give almost anything if he'd visit us here someday. He mentioned it the day John and I left London."

Belle's small hazel eyes lit up. "Do you really think he might come to St. Simons, Anne? Or was Cousin Willy just trying to make the parting easier for everyone? I don't mean he'd lie about it, but I've noticed people do try to—well, sort of smooth things over sometimes."

Anne smiled. "You're a very wise fifteen-year-old, Belle."

"Almost sixteen. I'll be sixteen in September."

"The age Caroline Wylly was when she married our big brother, James Hamilton."

Isabella's face flushed. "Now whatever made you think of that?"

Anne shrugged. "No reason. It's true, though. Our papa has always said a man should marry—"

"—a very young girl so he can train her in his ways," Belle finished for her.

"And do you think that's an odd thing for our father to say?"

A warm smile softened the plainness of Belle's features. "I don't know. If our sweet papa said it, there must be something good about it, but it seems to me that it's awfully general."

"General?"

"Yes. Everyone is different. You and I aren't alike at all, Anne. In fact, I feel as though I'm just getting to know you, and you're my own sister. It may be right for one girl to marry young and wrong for another."

For a time, Anne sat on the carriage seat studying her sister. "No wonder you're a good teacher. You *are* wise. I'm glad we're growing closer all the time, are you?"

"If you're not just pampering me because you may feel sorry for me for some reason."

"Why on earth would I feel sorry for you?

"I'm not pretty, Anne. I can see myself in a looking glass, don't forget. I didn't realize it until I was almost ten or eleven. About the time you and John and Annie came home to live, I guess it was. I —I hadn't seen you since I was a baby. There *are* eighteen years' difference in our ages. When I saw how truly beautiful you are, I knew you took after Mama. Mama's lovely, too. I know I look like Papa, and in a woman that's not considered—pretty." She laughed, Anne thought, rather easily. "Papa says I'm to be proud because I'm so Couperish."

"Do you want to know something absolutely true, Belle?"
"What?"

"You're not only beautiful inside, you have one of the brightest, most honest minds I've ever encountered. In fact, I'm not only quite impressed by you, I think I'm rather in awe of the way you think. You're frowning. Don't you believe me?"

"I believe you all right. I've always had a quick mind. I just doubt that young men go about with Diogenes' lamp looking for intellectually honest and astute women."

"When you're alone, do you think in terms of Greek philosophy? Do you *think* like this but talk down to us lesser mortals?"

Belle laughed. "I don't know."

"I think it's quite possible that you do. But let me tell you, I may not be as brainy as you, still I *am* your older sister and I do know that the right kind of man doesn't want a dumb wife!"

"Who said anything about becoming a wife to the right or wrong kind of man?"

"I did, I guess. But you brought up the fact that young men don't go about searching for honest feminine intellects. You'll find the man absolutely suited to you, Belle."

Without a moment's hesitation and certainly without a hint of embarrassment, Belle said, "I've already found him."

Anne sat up. "What?"

"You heard me. I've found the man with whom I think I want to spend my whole life."

All Anne could think of to say was, *"Who?* Belle Couper, I could shake you!"

Isabella laughed. "I know you could. And maybe you should, but Anne, there hasn't been a real chance to tell you before. You're always so busy and I've been busy trying to keep up with your own bright daughter Annie. Maybe I just didn't feel at ease with you. You were abroad all through the years I was growing up."

"I've been back in Georgia for six years!"

"I don't mean anything snide by this, but I've always assumed you simply didn't notice me much."

"Oh Belle, Belle! You're so straight out with everything, so honest, I have to be too. Don't we all do a lot of dishonest talking to each other?"

"I've thought so at times."

"I've been a rotten big sister, haven't I?"

"No, just a happy, busy big sister. Few women are as happy

with their husbands and children as you, Anne. You must be so grateful to God."

Anne leaned back. "Not grateful enough, but from now on, I promise I'll try to be." She reached for Belle's hand. "Who's the man you've found? Does he like you too?"

"Of course he likes me. He likes my mind anyway. You see, Anne, when you're plain like me, it's hard to be sure. I know our mother wishes I were truly beautiful. She's so proud of your beauty. I think quite rightly proud of her own, too. Mama and I are close, but we don't talk much about things like that. I've always found it easier to talk about really important things with God. Oh, Papa and I laugh together a lot and talk about the horses and his imported flowers and trees, but I came along so late in his life that you were already ensconced in Papa's heart. Now don't worry. I'm not jealous of you. Not a bit. I've just always been rather—alone." She laughed. "The truth is, I've been able to talk to dear Heriot Wylly more easily than to anyone else on earth, and she's called— in a very kind way, of course—crazy Heriot." The laughter faded. "I could also talk to my friend and teacher, Mr. Browne, but only about what I'd found in books, and I always felt free to let him read anything I might write."

"Belle, you're chock-full of secrets! Do you *write* things?"

"Oh yes. I've always scribbled a lot. Don't dare tell Mama or Papa, though."

"Why?"

"Because I don't need them to know now. I told you I've found someone else. Talking with him, which I've done only a few times, is different from talking with anyone else anywhere. Mostly, we exchange writings. Sometimes really personal writings. You see, we have one special—tree."

"Tree? And do you meet there? John and I always had a special tree. Belle, I insist that you tell me this man's name!"

"I'm trying to decide if I should tell you, Anne."

"Is it someone who's lived on St. Simons a long time?"

"No."

"Then, who is it?"

Belle waited. Finally, with a shy smile, she whispered, "To me, he's—Tristan."

"Tristan? And are you Isolde?"

The younger girl nodded. "Until we're ready to let people know, those are the names we use when we leave writings in our partly hollow tree trunk."

"That's all you're going to tell me today, isn't it."

"Yes."

"What if I've already guessed?"

Isabella merely shrugged.

"Will you admit it if I've guessed right?"

"I don't know."

"I'm sure I do know," Anne said. "It's nice Reverend Theodore Bartow. Should I not tell anyone?"

Belle's eyes filled with tears. "Not anyone! I—I hope your knowing won't spoil anything."

"Should I not tell John either?"

"Not yet, Anne, please? Please?"

"All right, I won't tell a single soul, if you'll make a pact with me about a secret of mine."

Isabella turned to her on the carriage seat. "Cross my heart, Anne. Do you have a secret too?"

"I think I do. I'll know for sure by next month, but I—I'm fairly sure I'm going to give John another child. I've missed one time. That's a pretty definite sign. But remember now, it's our secret until I'm certain. With our future looking so bright and the bigger house we'll have to live in at Hamilton, I know John will be terribly let down if I'm wrong about a new baby. He does love children and I want so much to give him a son!"

Anne gave little thought to the probability that Big Boy could hear her over the clatter of the carriage and the horses. Still, if he had heard her beg Belle to keep it a secret, it was the same as Big Boy's swearing on the Bible not to tell either. With all her heart, she hoped it was true. She and Anna Matilda had always dreamed of the day when their homes, headed by the men they loved, could be filled with children. Anna Matilda already had four—with the baby just born—three boys and a girl, Hannah. This time, when

Anne was free to tell John, there would be no reason for him to feel worried, fearful of not being able to support his family. He was going to be in full charge of Hamilton.

"Do you know something?" Anne asked.

"What?"

"Suddenly, I can almost not wait to see John again!" Grinning at Belle, she asked, "Does that sound silly to you? It seems almost odd to be able to tell you something like that. I guess I—I just never thought of telling you *real* things before."

ABOUT HALFWAY HOME IN THE COUPER CARRIAGE, Belle fell back into one of her silences. Oh, she smiled and agreed when, rolling north on Frederica Road, Anne pointed out a riot of spring wildflowers, an especially thick clump of purple roadside violets, a big tree vining with yellow jessamine, but mostly, as she'd always been, Belle was quiet. Lost in her own happy thoughts of the Reverend Bartow, Anne was sure.

Now and then Big Boy would turn a little in the driver's seat and give them his warm smile, raise his hand in the old familiar signal that everything was just fine. Both sisters waved back, and after Belle had waved two or three times, Anne suspected that Big Boy had conspired with Belle before. Perhaps he'd driven her or ridden along with her in hopes of finding a secret message— "really personal writings"—hidden away in the tree she and Theodore Bartow had selected as their own. Where, Anne wondered, was that special tree?

The carriage bumped around the turn off Frederica into Couper Road and began to slow. They must be nearing the tree! When Big Boy turned again and exchanged waves, this time only with Belle, Anne knew for certain. No more than a quarter of a mile up Couper Road, Big Boy pulled the team to one side and stopped beside a huge, jessamine-covered water oak near the right side of the road.

Trying to act as though nothing was at all unusual, Anne hummed a little made-up melody as Belle jumped out and hurried to the tree. Without having to search at all, she reached inside a hollow in its trunk and pulled out a small roll of paper tied with a blue ribbon. Then, without any help from Big Boy, she scampered back onto her seat beside Anne.

The sisters only exchanged smiles. Already the roll of paper was hidden in the folds of Belle's long, pink day dress.

CHAPTER 22

WHEN JOCK COUPER RODE UP TO THE HITCHING
post outside the white picket fence around the Lawrence front
lawn in mid-May, anyone could tell he was excited. Young Annie
saw him first, then Pete. Yelling at the top of her shrill little voice,
Pete called, "Mama! Mama!" and then pushed Annie out of her
way, determined, as always, to be first out the front door and up
into her grandfather's open arms.

Perched on his shoulder, holding on for dear life to his head,
Pete laughed uproariously as his hat fell off and was caught in the
wind off Lawrence Creek.

"Let it go, Grandpapa!" the girl shouted. "Let's watch and see
how far your hat can fly!"

"Not on your life, Petey," the old man said. "That's next to my
Sunday hat and I'm putting you down so you can hurry and catch
it for me." Lowering her to the ground, he called, "Now scoot!"

Annie, who as usual had been standing to one side, waiting out
Pete's attack, held out her arms to her grandfather. He hugged her

and pulled her close enough to whisper, "As postmaster, I'm undoubtedly not supposed to favor my own family, but I've just been to pick up the Island post at Frederica, and right here in my saddlebag I have a surprise for your dear mother. Where is she?"

"Pete yelled so loud when she heard you ride up just now, Mama should be out here any minute. She was upstairs cutting out a new dress for me."

"Ah-ha! And what color will it be?"

"Light green voile," Annie said, "but you don't need to ask me childish questions like that, Grandpapa. After all, I'm fourteen!"

"And what a difference in fourteen-year-olds!" When the girl gave him a puzzled look, he laughed. "You act at least four years older than my son William Audley, I swear. You're going to grow up to be as bright and superior as your mother, lass. Mark my words."

"But I don't like you to make fun of William Audley. I'm glad you think I'm mature, but boys are just different."

"Are they indeed! Ah, here comes your lovely mother now." As though she too were fourteen, he thought, Anne burst from the house to embrace him, her little dog, Lovey, trotting beside her.

"I'm so glad to see you, Papa," she said, hugging him again. "But what brings you here at this hour? Have you been to Frederica to meet Nathaniel Twining with the mail?"

"Aye, and I brought a ver-r-y, ver-r-y special letter from London for you, my dear Anne."

"Just for me? Not John too?"

"I do believe it's addressed also to John, but it's from your cousin, Lord Herries!"

"From dear Willy Maxwell? Where is it? And don't take all day pretending to hunt through your saddlebag, either. I can't imagine why he's writing again so soon. We heard from him just a month ago, you know. Oh Papa! Do you suppose Willy's gotten one of his sudden notions to visit us?"

"Who can say? And would you look at that?" Couper laughed as he watched Lovey scamper up, dragging his hat along with him. "So you beat Pete to it, did you, Lovey? I say, Anne, your lapdog is turning out to be a retriever, a hat retriever!"

Stooping to rescue the hat, she said, "I hope he didn't sink those sharp little teeth into the brim. I honestly think the girls are jealous of me. Some days Lovey seems to prefer being indoors with me rather than out here romping with them."

"Isn't that what you wanted, Mama?" Annie asked. "Pete and I are trying not to let him out much. After all, he sleeps on the foot of your bed at night. You and Papa don't want to get covered with fleas, for heaven's sake."

"We certainly do not," Anne laughed, turning back to her father. "In fact, I think your poor father is growing somewhat desperate because Lovey is so determined to sleep with us."

"He's still a pup," Jock said. "He'll get over that."

"Papa, if you don't get Willy's letter for me this minute, I'm going to scatter all the mail in your saddlebag and find it myself."

Heading back to his mount, he said with mock solemnity, "I'll not only get it for you at once, Daughter, I'll hie myself straight home to Cannon's Point so that you can read it in peace. Your mother will be wondering what took me so long."

ANNE SAT DOWN ON HER FRONT STEPS IN THE MAY sunshine and excitedly broke the seal on Willy's letter. She found only three sheets of elegant, heavy writing paper, but in his packed, small script there would be a lot of news, she was sure. As she had always done—as she'd at least tried to do with letters from John during their times of separation through the years—Anne unfolded the pages slowly, then smoothed and smoothed them, forcing herself to wait and anticipate. Willy had dated the letter nearly six weeks ago and that meant he had probably been in Dumfries, staying in his small, cozy, remodeled quarters facing the crumbling, empty courtyard of Caerlaverock Castle, where she knew he spent this part of each year.

Poor, lonely Willy, she thought. And here I sit on the front steps of my own little house, the mother of two children, the forever wife of the handsomest, most wonderful man in the whole world, my parents nearby, and—she hugged herself—carrying right here in my body another child to give John. This kind of happiness, this sense of belonging, must be what Willy is searching for.

Wanting to share the still-unread letter with John, she ran out to look up the lane that led to the Cannon's Point Road on the chance that he might be galloping home, sneaking in, as he said, a surprise morning visit. He did that lately at every possible chance. The two had never been so close. More so now, by far, than during their first years of married life. From her advanced age of thirty-four, an age that in those early days had to her seemed elderly, she could feel but could never explain the growing depth of her love for him. She depended on him now in a way she'd never done before. Oh, her very life had depended on his being a part of it from the first moment they'd met all those years ago, but John was now not only far handsomer, she could see him daily becoming more confident.

It had been weeks, maybe months, since she'd had to be careful with him for fear he'd withdraw into one of his odd moods when he made too many jokes and talked too much for the sole purpose of pretending he wasn't scared down inside or feeling inferior to James Hamilton. Maybe the best part of all was that John had grown to be as he was now without their ever having had to argue over or discuss his need for it. She and Papa had always laughed over her brother James. Not *at* him but *over* his sometimes foolish-seeming self-discipline and precocious maturity. They'd called him the Old Gentleman when he was eight or nine years of age. James Hamilton, bless him, hadn't changed. John had. Her beloved could now laugh too over James's eccentric ways while, along with every-one else, admiring the tall, usually solemn master of Hopeton and Hamilton. Yes, James still owned Hamilton Plantation, but not only was he going to pay John twice the usual manager's salary to take over its operation as soon as possible, he somehow hadn't caused John to feel overly beholden to him.

John was nowhere in sight and probably wouldn't be home until dinnertime this afternoon. The tender, delicate new cotton plants were up in all his fields, but he'd said at breakfast that two or three acres remained to be thinned and that he'd learned long ago that even the best fieldhands needed supervision while thinning.

Back sitting on her front steps, knowing full well that she couldn't stall one more minute with Willy's letter unread, she gave up on sharing it the first time with John. They could read it together right after dinner—right after she had informed him that it was now definite that he was going to be the father of another child! Belle knew of her hope, but wanting never to disappoint John, Anne had waited to be certain. She had no intention, though, of waiting one more minute to read Willy's letter.

31 March 1831
Dumfries, Scotland

My dear Anne and John,

I imagine you, Anne, have guessed from the address above that I am in my tiny apartment at Caerlaverock, and have been here for more than a fortnight. I continue to roam the world. For what reason, I still cannot say except that I need to pass my days. I do have good friends everywhere I go, although none as close as the human heart seems to need. Invitations abound and I go on being selective, since more and more I enjoy my own companionship and books.

Speaking of books, our dear friend Sir Walter Scott is still his vibrant self to the extent that his worsening health permits. I predict that the man will be struggling to write his books up to the hour of his death. Last year, he suffered an apoplectic attack, which would have proved to a lesser man that his toils were taking their toll. He submitted to a severe regimen and showed enough improvement to begin writing again, although at the end of the year past, he did agree to retire from his legal clerkship at a pension of eight hundred pounds a year, so passed the next months at Abbotsford hard at work finishing *Count Robert of Paris.* Walter seems perpetually involved in his protest of parliamentary reform. At Selkirk, near Abbotsford, a mob of weavers grossly insulted him, so that he was taken away at last amid a shower of stones and cries of insult. I am told that he even seized one rioter with his own hands. As of now, he is, typically, hard at work again on what could well be his last novel, *Castle Dangerous.*

When I left my London flat for Caerlaverock, the great Sarah Siddons, who lives, as you remember, I'm sure, not far from me on Upper Baker Street, was failing fast. With time here at Caerlaverock to weigh facts, I have decided that the famed actress, now in her seventy-sixth year, has always inspired more admiration than affection and it grieves me. Her young niece, Fanny Kemble, who performed so admirably between acts the night the three of us saw Madam Siddons star in *Macbeth,* is now a grown woman of nearly twenty-two years and as amazing and controversial as ever; perhaps even more controversial, since her unquenchable spirit cannot be hidden even beneath the manners of a lady. Fanny and her father, Charles Kemble, who still struggles mightily to keep his Covent Garden theater afloat financially, are extraordinarily close. I have become rather intimate with both Fanny and Charles and enjoy few evenings more than listening to her accounts of their "pleasant days of joyous *camaraderie* and *flânerie*" spent together during her school days in Paris, where everything was new and exciting to Fanny and because of her, new also to her handsome father. Charles is, as you know, elegantly tall, while Fanny is small, high-colored, and high-stepping, with huge, expressive brown eyes.

Now to my explanation for having written at length of the Kembles. At their insistence and because of my lingering desire to see you both again—you and your enchanted St. Simons Island—I have accepted their gracious invitation to sail with them to America, perhaps in the late summer or early fall of next year. You see, Fanny, who wants to do nothing as much as to write greatly, has been captured by both her parents and pushed upon the stage of faltering Covent Garden. She dislikes acting so intensely, she vows fear and nerves make her deaf during performances so that she cannot hear herself even as she enthralls her audiences. She is quite evidently a genius as an actress, in spite of her strong dislike of the theater. She adores her father, Charles, so would, I believe, do anything to help him. Therefore, an American tour is being planned and I shall write at the earliest possible moment with definite dates. I should add that the irrepressible Fanny has also become fast friends with our old host, Sir Walter Scott. I send my deepest regards and true affection to you,

Willy Maxwell, Lord Herries

For a long time Anne sat there on her front step, not really seeing the breathtaking vista of marsh and river and, in the distance, Long Island, against which the sea was pounding to the east. Her mind had, through Willy's newsy letter, flown back to the years in which she and John lived with Father Fraser and Flora McLeod in busy, noisy, smoky London; then to the picturesque Borderland of Scotland, where they had spent their honeymoon in the clear, mostly bright air around Dumfries, John's birthplace. She could almost see the narrow dirt road leading up to the River Nith, which they crossed and recrossed in a borrowed buggy in order to make their many visits to Caerlaverock, her own mother's ancient family castle, in the courtyard of which they had first met kind, elegant Willy Maxwell, her distant cousin. She was excited, of course, that Willy might be paying them a visit on St. Simons next year, but somehow his letter had left her dreaming back, back to their unsettled years abroad, with true affection, almost with nostalgia. Not that she ever meant to leave St. Simons again, even for a visit to their old British haunts. It was just somehow good to remember it all through Willy's newsy letter. John, who had seemed fond of Willy, too, despite his inherited wealth and vast land holdings, would, she knew, be overjoyed that her cousin was planning a visit. John and Willy, both worldly men, both traveled, had seemed to her to be true kindred spirits. Not long after they'd returned to St. Simons, John had confessed to her that he'd told Willy on their first meeting far more than he intended to tell him of himself, of his rebellion at leaving the military, of his unrelieved restlessness. He'd told her, too, that a long talk with Walter Scott had somehow clarified what he must do next.

"I couldn't tell you now, if my life depended on it," John had said several times, "exactly what Scott said to me—even what I said to him—but when I returned to his house at Abbotsford that day during our visit there, I knew I could come back here to Georgia and, by some means, turn my life around."

What had John really meant by turning his life around? Had becoming a St. Simons planter been that disrupting to him? Had it literally turned his life around?

She knew he would be glad to see Willy again. He seldom mentioned the all-important talk between himself and Walter Scott without adding that they—John and Anne—owed Willy Maxwell everything, because it had been Willy who wangled the invitation to the great writer's famous and beloved Abbotsford. One of Anne's dearest treasures was still the signed edition of Scott's novel *Guy Mannering*.

Poor Fanny Kemble, she thought. Then smiled at herself for even thinking such a thing about someone so young and already so famous. But she pitied anyone who, through circumstances beyond her control, could not do the one thing she longed to do above all others. Willy had vowed that young Fanny wanted only to write, but loving her father so deeply, she'd forced herself to turn to acting. Had that also turned *her* life around? Anne hadn't laid eyes on Fanny since her performance between acts as a child of eight, but she would never forget her and wished with all her heart that it might be possible for her and John to go to New York or Philadelphia when Fanny appeared in America next year.

Anne squelched the hope immediately. If all went well, she would, by early fall of next year, be the mother of another child. Her baby, whom John didn't yet know about, should arrive sometime in January 1832.

She refolded Willy's letter and longed for John to come home.

CHAPTER 23

F OR MOST OF AN HOUR ANNE HAD SAT ALONE ON her front steps, lost in thought, waiting for John. When there was no sign of him by half past one, she went again to look up their lane, then impatiently sat back down on the top step. Any other day he'd have been here an hour ago, she thought, determined, as always, to wash up and change out of his work clothes into the clean shirt Eve always had ready and waiting, and even on a hot Georgia day, to slip on a jacket.

Believing herself to be alone, she said aloud, "That man is still British to the core in so many ways."

"Who be, Miss Anne?"

Without getting up, she whirled around to see Eve standing behind her on the porch. "Did you say 'whobee'? Whobee sounds like a bad imitation of an owl!"

"You knows what I said," Eve snapped, but her velvety laugh ran under the sharp voice. "You talkin' to yousef again, jus' lak Gran'maum Sofy, I swear."

"There's no better way to shut my mouth than to say a thing like that, Eve. By the way, how is Sofy these days? I know Mama's been taking Papa's special liniment to her for her rheumatism. Is it helping any?"

"She be mean as eber, if dat what you axe."

"Well, it wasn't, but never mind. I have nothing against Sofy as long as she agrees to stop teaching Pete about charms and hexes and other dumb voodoo stuff. You're not taking Pete to see her much anymore, are you?

"Don' have to take er. Pete go on her own legs." ·

"She's still visiting Sofy? Do you know that for a fact or are you just plaguing me?"

"I knows for a fack. But Gran'maum Sofy she don' teach her no more hexin', she teach Pete how to do ring-plays an' to sing songs."

"African songs?"

Eve leaned against a porch post. "Songs my people sings. You kin call 'em African, I reckon. Pete, she ketch on real fast."

"Couldn't you say *catch* just as easily as *ketch?*"

"No'm."

"I see. Why is it, Eve, that some days you speak rather well and other days you seem to enjoy butchering the King's English?"

"Maybe 'cause I don't know no kings, ceptin' Miss Anna Matilda."

"Very funny."

"It ain' funny to Eve that you actin' so jumpy today. You keepin' a secret hid from me?"

"What?"

"You never ack funny like today lessen you got somepin hid down inside you. I seen Mausa Couper stop by today. Did he tell you somepin that's got you all jumpy like a frog?"

"Eve, I swear to you, there isn't another woman on the face of the earth like you!"

"You think they be another 'oman on the face ob the earth like *you?*"

"That word is *woman,* not *'oman,* and you know it perfectly well. Don't you want to speak better?" Anne asked, looking straight at her. "Does it really make you angry when I try to help you with words?"

"Why I oughta talk different to you den I talks to June? I'm axin' you. Why?"

"Well, I—I'd just think you'd be grateful that I care so much about you."

"Be you grateful dat I care so much 'bout you, Miss Anne?"

"Of course I am! That's a silly question, and whatever you are, you're not dumb."

"You an' June got all my love."

Now Anne got up and went to where Eve stood by the porch post. "Thank you for saying that. I know you love me, but today especially, I'm glad you told me."

"Your Papa, he done upset you?"

"No! He just brought me a very important letter from a wonderful man we knew when John and I lived in London. A sweet, generous, kind gentleman named Maxwell."

"Like yo' mama was a Maxwell?"

"You don't forget anything, do you?"

"It don' pay 'roun you, Miss Anne. Who dis man be?"

"A very, very distant cousin of my mother's—and mine. Just someone who was extremely good to me when I was living abroad."

For a long moment Eve studied her. "He be in love wif you?"

"What?"

"Dis man who be so good to you. Is he sweet on you too?"

"Eve! That's the craziest thing I ever heard you say. Where did you get such a wild idea?"

Now Eve looked out over Lawrence Creek and the marshes. "It jus'—come to me."

"Well, get rid of it this minute. Willy Maxwell is a good and cherished friend to both John and me—a distant relative and nothing more."

"Be dat why you so jumpy today?"

"No, it is not! I'm—I'm simply eager for John to get home so he can read Willy's letter too. It's full of news about people we both know, or saw abroad. Two persons, in fact. One is now a famous

English actress named Fanny Kemble. Do you know what an actress is, Eve?"

"I reckon it mus' hab to do wif de way somebody acks."

"Well, yes, partly. But in big cities, plays—stories, really—are spoken as well as read and actors and actresses speak the stories and make certain, sometimes grandiose gestures, or cry or laugh or curse. Sometimes they perform murders or weep because someone they love has been killed or has sickened and died. You know, stories about people. Sometimes there's dancing too."

Eve had been listening intently. Finally the young woman asked, "You mean lak ring-shouts an' ring-play dances?"

"Well, something like that, yes. But such plays as young Fanny Kemble performs—and I understand she is drawing raves and long, long applause everywhere she performs—are stories that a fine writer has set down. The actors and actresses memorize their parts—they learn them by heart—then speak the words on a stage."

Her lithe, brown body beginning to sway, her heels beating a slow, primitive rhythm, Eve started to sing the low, almost garbled words to "Buzzard's Lope." Fascinated as always, Anne watched and listened, tried in vain to follow Eve's motions. When Eve finished, Anne applauded enthusiastically and asked for "Knee-bone, I Call You, Knee-bone Bend."

But at that moment she heard John's horse galloping up their lane and ordered Eve to go help Mina, hoping for at least a few minutes alone with her husband before dinner was served. If his mood was good and confident, she might even spring her surprise, might even tell him quickly and lightheartedly that she was carrying a new baby. If he seemed troubled, she could wait until they were alone tonight. At least she had Willy's letter to share now, and that would use up some of her own excitement.

STRIDING UP THEIR FRONT PATH, JOHN THOUGHT he'd never seen her look so beautiful. And because she was wearing her old yellow-sprigged day dress, he felt pretty sure that something was afoot—something exciting and happy. He loved every sweet, childlike, sentimental thing Anne did, and although the dress, which he'd adored on their honeymoon, was now probably fifteen years old, she kept it ready to wear on certain days when she had a surprise for him. Or when something special had happened.

On the cottage porch he took her in his arms, apologizing because he was late as usual. His own spirit was soaring, and he was late because of the wonderful news he'd just learned. If he waited to bathe and change clothes, James Hamilton could be there to tell her himself and John had no intention of letting that happen. Anne was going to hear of the glorious certainty of their future straight from John's own lips.

After an initial kiss—the kiss of a man and a woman who had been separated for months instead of hours—in one breath they both said, "Good news! I have good news!" And then they broke into laughter.

"You first, milady," John said.

"No, I want to know your good news first. Tell me, tell me!"

"Very well." He grew almost solemn. "It's happened! Anne, it's happened. The whole thing is definite now. James Hamilton told me less than an hour ago."

"My brother is at Cannon's Point today?"

"He is. And the man seems almost as happy as I about it."

"What, John? Why is he so happy?"

"Your brother is master of all of Hopeton Plantation, and the contract with his Hamilton Plantation manager is up at the end of 1832, so if we're packed and ready to go, you and the girls and Lovey and I will be moving to the finest place on St. Simons Island at least by Christmas of next year!"

She threw both arms around him and shouted with joy, "John! Oh John, I'm so, so proud of you. You did this all on your own. You, *you!*"

He laughed his mischievous laugh. "Don't you think your brother deserves a bit of credit for his generosity?"

"Well, maybe. Yes. Yes, I guess he does, but he'll be getting the management services of the finest planter in coastal Georgia *and* the handsomest! Now's when I have to tell you *my good news* because it all goes together so perfectly." Hugging him still tighter, she whispered, "You and the girls and Lovey and I will be moving to Hamilton, but someone else will be going along too!"

He stared at her. "We're going to have another baby!"

"Fudge!"

"Fudge?"

"Yes. I wanted to tell you first and you beat me to it. There, you see? You'll not only be the finest, the handsomest manager Hamilton ever had, but the smartest. Darling, darling, you are glad about another baby, aren't you?"

He stepped back, beaming. "How do I look?"

"Happy! You look truly happy, my dearest one. And so am I. Besides, I'm praying hard that this time I can give you a son. His name is already John. And no argument, please."

"I wouldn't think of it. But I did forget to tell you Annie and Pete are staying for dinner with Mama and Papa Couper today."

"You mean I get to dine alone with my husband?"

"You do indeed. Pete refused to take the chance that the pork roast Mina's making today might be that little brown-and-white pig the child loved so, until we butchered it."

"Poor baby. I know exactly how she feels. I once felt the exact same way about a pig when I was her age. And you cried when Father Fraser sold your lamb, Malcolm. Remember the day we stood in the road outside the house where you were born in Dumfries and you told me about Malcolm?"

"Of course I remember. I think back on our carefree good times when I'm riding our fields alone or even with Papa Couper riding along with me. He and I enjoy silence now and then"—he laughed—"in spite of the fact that both our wives accuse us of talking a lot."

"I'm going to visit Mama this afternoon. She and I stay so busy running our separate houses, we don't see enough of each other, and there's something terribly important about telling her that she's going to be the grandmother of another little boy. I'm sorry Caroline gave them a grandson before I did. But ours will be special! And John, go wash up for dinner, because now that I know we'll be alone, there's something else to tell you. Papa brought us a letter and in it is something altogether happy. I know Mama will be lyrical about that, too, when I tell her."

"Whatever it is, I can match it," he said haughtily. "I also have something else to tell you of which I'm very proud."

"I want to know now!"

"Your father asked me just this morning to act as host at the next meeting of the St. Clair Club, and that means not only that our Mina provides the meal but that I, my dear Anne, will act as master of ceremonies."

"Well, it's about time. You've been a member for two years, and Anna Matilda told me her Thomas vows you're the most colorful teller of tales of the whole lot of illustrious planters who grace the St. Clair Club table!"

Hearing such an unexpected compliment from a man as particular and as sure of himself as Thomas Butler King gave John still another big reason to be proud of himself.

It's good, he thought as he hurried to wash up for dinner, no longer having to work so hard at *liking* the idea of being a coastal Georgia planter. He would always be bored with the mundane routine of it, he supposed, and he still did secret battle with his own disapproval of slavery, but today he had every reason to congratulate himself, and toweling his chest and arms, he did just that.

CHAPTER 24

DURING THEIR RARE CHANCE TO HAVE DINNER alone, Anne shared Willy's letter and found John as excited at the prospect of his visit as she had hoped. Too excited herself, because of all the marvelous news, to settle down to any kind of work at home, she headed, as soon as John rode off to work, to Cannon's Point on her own horse.

She reined Gentleman in front of her parents' house and was greeted warmly, not only by Big Boy, waiting to drive the girls home from their lessons, but by Papa's groom, Dusty.

"You be a stranger, Miss Anne," Dusty said, pushing ahead of Big Boy to take the reins and offer his hand for her to dismount. "It been a long time since I seen you an' Gentleman!"

"Too long, Dusty," she said. Not wanting Big Boy to feel slighted, she asked him not to hitch Gentleman too far away, since she had to ride back home in an hour. "Where are the girls?"

Both men pointed to the veranda of the Big House. "Pete, she showin' out," Big Boy said, grinning. "Showin' out to her gran'maum. Ol' Sofy done teach Pete some new ring-play. Dat Pete, she eben got her gran'maum an' Rhyna stompin'!"

"I simply can't believe my eyes," Anne gasped, staring at the surprising sight of her sedate, ladylike mother and the stoic midwife, Rhyna, actually trying to step off a Negro ring-play.

Big Boy's grin turned to a giggle. "Miz Couper, she try not to go dancin' 'roun, try not to do no clappin' neither, but—" He shook his woolly head. "Dat Pete, dat Pete!"

"That Pete is right," Anne said, only half laughing as she hurried along the walk and up the steps, still aghast at what she saw. "Pete! Where's Annie?"

"We're busy, Mama!" Pete yelled. "Rhyna's not very good, but Grandmama's learning fast!"

Anne's mother stopped briefly to embrace her, and the embarrassed Rhyna fled quickly into the house. "It's wonderful to see you, Anne dear, but my namesake, Rebecca, and I are quite busy. I had no idea Sofy was such a good teacher." Allowing Pete to grab her hand again and lead her into the intricate swaying and clapping, feet flat, quite out of breath, she called, "You did name her Rebecca after me, Anne, but today she's all Pete!"

"I'd like to know where your sister is, Pete," Anne persisted. "Why isn't she in the circle too?"

Pete, now going on six, stopped long enough to give her mother a quick hug. "Annie's too dumb to do a ring-play," the child scoffed. "She won't even try, will she, Grandmama? Grandmama not only tries with me, she's pretty good, except she can't seem to get the clap at the right time."

"Just watch Pete now," Anne's mother said, still trying to shuffle to the beat. "Go on, Pete, 'step it down' and then you can dance and sing 'Emma You My Darlin'' for your mother. Clap now, but get your rhythm first."

"I need a circle of people around me to do it right," Pete complained. "Don't sit down, Grandmama. Come on, Mama, you too! Now where's Rhyna?"

"I think she made her escape inside the house," Anne said.

"I'm sure she has work to do. Isn't Annie around some-where?"

"Yes, Mama, I'm down here." Annie's voice came from the bushes at the edge of the veranda. "I don't like to do ring-plays. I'm not good at it."

"I'm certainly not either," Anne called. "But weren't you even going to greet me?"

When Annie appeared from behind the shrubbery, her quiet smile meant she was again enduring her younger sister, expecting her mother to understand. "Hello, Mama. We're surprised to see you. Did you come for some special reason?"

"I most certainly did and I want you here to listen while I tell all of you. There's—there's a lot of good news to be told today, believe me!"

Annie climbed the steps, dodging Pete's hand as the younger girl tried to pull her into the ring-play circle.

"Grandmama ordered me to step it down and clap because *she* is smart enough to know I'm just naturally good at ring-play," Pete said loftily.

"Don't be prideful, Pete," Grandmama said. Turning to her daughter, she asked, "What on earth do you have to tell us, Anne? I want to hear. Can't we play another time, Pete?"

"Not till I do one full ring-play. I need the practice. So all of you get in a circle—you too, Annie." Pete began to clap her hands first, explaining that Sofy had told her no one could do the dance right until the clapping was right.

"Did you ever see anything quite like the child, Anne?" her mother asked. "Honestly, I do rather marvel at her. Sofy has taught her well and it should relieve you that the old woman's teaching her something harmless like children's ring-plays."

"I'm ready!" Pete shouted, clapping and beginning to move smoothly, flat-footed, from one foot to the other without shifting her weight. "Can you see I'm not shifting my weight?" she was yelling. "That's the secret, Sofy says. You move from one foot to the other, but you don't shift your weight. And you clap on the third beat, but if you're good like me, you don't need to count, you just clap right the first time."

"Go on, try, Annie," Grandmama said. "I'm sure you can do it too. You're fourteen."

"And I'm also English and *not*—a Georgian," Annie snapped sharply.

Anne and her mother were so surprised to hear Annie snap about anything, they exchanged looks and laughed.

"Now Pete, it's time to sing about Emma," Grandmama ordered.

Clapping in perfect rhythm, Pete began to sing at the top of her voice:

> *"Emma you my darlin';*
> *Oh Emma Oh!*
> *You turn aroun' dig a hole in the groun'*
> *Oh Emma Oh!*
> *Emma you duh bad gal*
> *Oh Emma Oh!*
> *You turn aroun' dig a hole in the groun'*
> *Oh Emma Oh!*
> *Emma you from the country*
> *Oh Emma Oh!*
> *You turn aroun' dig a hole in the groun'*
> *Oh Emma Oh!"*

At the finish of the song Pete went to her knees, moving almost as rhythmically and with as much grace as she'd moved on her feet, and immediately started singing the verse again.

"That's wonderful, Pete," Anne interrupted, "but it's also enough. If you know any other verses and choruses, they can wait. I rode almost three miles over here to tell everyone some marvelous news, and I intend to do it because I have to start home in an hour with your father. Your Uncle James Hamilton is coming to our house with him, and I want to be there for such a special occasion. Do you mind terribly, darling?"

In response, Pete dashed off to find something more exciting to do than talk.

SEATED WITH ANNE AND ANNIE ON THE WIDE CAN-
non's Point veranda, Rebecca Couper had listened and listened,
interrupting Anne's good and happy news only long enough to ask
an occasional question. In all her fifty-six years, she could remember few times when her almost isolated Island life had held such
fine prospects.

In an hour or so, Anne, insisting that she be home for James
Hamilton's visit to Lawrence, had gone, the girls with her. Rebecca
still sat, alone, savoring the glorious news that she and Jock would
again be grandparents and that, wonder of wonders, she might
actually meet her Scottish cousin, Willy Maxwell, Lord Herries.

Of equal importance to her, James Hamilton had finally come
to his always careful conclusion that Anne's John was fully capable
of managing Hamilton. Her son-in-law, hardworking, determined
John Fraser, would finally have a place in their world all his own,
and best of all, he had earned it by the sweat of his brow and by
sheer grit. Surely by the time Willy Maxwell reached St. Simons
next year, plans would definitely be under way for the Fraser
family to move to Hamilton. How she would miss having them on
the adjoining acres! But her joy overruled any thought of sadness.

Rebecca sighed contentedly. All her children seemed really
well and quite happy. William Audley's lack of interest in any
kind of work worried Jock now and then, but the boy was still too
young to have found his place. A year or two away at school could
make a world of difference for her younger son.

Deep in her heart, although the girl had not said one word to
her mother yet, Rebecca felt that her plain, tender, intelligent
daughter Isabella was in love with the new rector, the Reverend
Theodore Bartow. Belle was awfully young to be tutoring Annie
Fraser, too close to Annie's own age, but she was doing it and
doing it well. Any mother would know, as Rebecca knew, that
Isabella was receiving added courage, confidence, poise, from
somewhere outside herself. From *someone* outside herself. The con-

fidence and poise a woman receives as a result of knowing that she is loved by the one man her heart tells her is right for her. Rebecca felt oddly peaceful about Isabella these days. Unlike at any other time in her daughter's nearly sixteen years of life, she was not carrying a secret burden because Belle wasn't as attractive as Anne.

CHAPTER 25

JAMES HAMILTON, BECAUSE OF THE LENGTHY BOAT trip back to Hopeton on the mainland, stayed at Lawrence only long enough to let his sister Anne see how pleased he really was that she and John and their little family would be the new residents at Hamilton Plantation, of which James had always been so proud.

"It's seemed a shame to me, to everyone who's given it much thought," he said as Anne and John walked with him out to the Lawrence lane, "that in all these years since Papa's friend Mr. Hamilton left, no loving family has graced that good Hamilton Big House."

John laughed with delight when Anne, who, despite her brother's stiff reserve, hugged him again and kissed him. "Brother mine," she said, "we will indeed grace the house. And somehow I am going to believe that just watching our happiness grow will demonstrate our gratitude."

Half-embarrassed by her show of affection, James cleared his throat. "Of course, Anne, my dear. Of course. But you mustn't forget that I do not buy a pig in a poke. Your husband has proved beyond doubt to me that he is entirely ready for such a responsible position."

Exactly on the dot set for departure, James Hamilton had ridden off in the Couper carriage, driven by Big Boy, who would proudly take his prominent passenger to Frederica, where James's own sloop was docked.

John and Anne waved as the carriage rolled out of sight, and then, in broad daylight, he swept her into his arms and whirled her around until her long, full skirt made a circle in the sunny air.

"Put me down, John Fraser! Someone will see us, but the truth is," she laughed, "I don't care. So, don't put me down unless you agree not to go back to any old field today, because if you keep holding me like this, I can't let you go!"

"Sorry, darling, but I promised to inspect the south field with June and I'm already half an hour late. I will have one kiss, though."

When he finally forced himself to leave her, he did not rush to mount Ginger but swung into the saddle in a leisurely way and merely trotted, waving the whole time to Anne, who stood waving back until he rounded the bend in their lane.

"Why should we be in a hurry, Ginger?" he asked. "My name isn't James Hamilton Couper, Esquire. You and I do our best, but we do not live by a JHC schedule and now and then a man and his horse need a bit of time for reveling. Do you feel like reveling at all the good and splendid news of this day, Ginger?"

The mare snorted and tossed her handsome head. "In no time at all now, you and I will be running all of Hamilton Plantation! My lovely Anne will be its mistress and our children, including the new little one on its way this very minute, will run and shout over its ample acres and we will make a great success, eh?"

He could tell Ginger was ready for a gallop, but John was not. June had never complained at being kept waiting, and he needed some time to think through the one other possible bit of good news James Hamilton had not even hinted at to Anne when the three were together a while ago.

Earlier today, just as John was saying goodbye to his brother-in-law and his father-in-law en route home for dinner with Anne, James Hamilton had dropped still another bombshell. Jock Couper had seemed as dumbfounded as John felt. In fact, the older man evidently held many reservations, although the pronouncement—and it had been delivered rather as a pronouncement—had come from his highly accomplished son.

"I am leaving fairly soon," the laird of Hopeton had said, "for New Orleans, Natchez, and Mobile. I wanted you both to know, since there's a chance we can all benefit—especially you, John."

Jock had only stared at his tall, imposing son, then asked, "And *why* would you be going to those particular cities, James?"

"Business, Papa. I'm seriously considering an entirely new undertaking—the manufacture of cottonseed oil." Further surprising them both, James had then grinned rather sheepishly, a grin John, at least, had never seen before. "I know the risks, Papa. Know them well. Still, I mean to do it. My plans have advanced beyond the point of mere consideration."

"But Son, you'll never get planters to save and collect their unused seed," Jock had objected. "They're too much in the habit of throwing seed away when not needed. Still, I have always trusted your judgment, James. And you might just be able to bring some form of comfort to my good friend James Gould."

"James Gould?" John had asked.

"Aye, John. Gould's younger son, Horace, expelled last year from Yale, is said to be a purser on a Mississippi River boat out of New Orleans. I'm sure good old James would welcome any word of the boy. The man's worried half-sick."

John had heard the Island gossip about young Horace. He had also heard that the boy had turned abolitionist while at the North, but his thoughts following James Hamilton's startling announcement could not move much beyond the fact that the cottonseed plans might somehow include John himself. "There may indeed be a rather rich opportunity in my plans for you, John," James had said in his usual taunting manner, "For our friend John Wylly, too, if he's interested."

And after that, James had said not another word.

Ginger had brought her master in sight now of the south field, where John could see June rounding up the men for quitting time, checking out their tools, and, on John's orders, commending those who had done a good day's work.

He reached June's side in time to hear him praise Peter, one of the men John had recently bought at the Savannah market, who had been out of the fields for several days with a badly sprained ankle.

"I join June in complimenting you, Peter," John said pleasantly. "And I'm sure your friend Lovey, my wife's little dog, is glad you're able to be back in the fields. You're a good worker and you and Rollie almost washed that dog away while your ankle healed!"

John shook hands with June, bid him goodnight, and without dismounting, his mind still on James Hamilton's mysterious cottonseed plans, turned Ginger toward home just as the sun, a huge fireball, was moving downward in the sky.

How he longed to tell Anne that beyond putting him in charge of Hamilton, the lofty James Hamilton had hinted strongly that by some means John might be included in other future business plans. He dared not tell her. James had ordered secrecy; the women were not to be told. Did that mean he was not even telling his own wife, Caroline, the reason for making the long, hard trip to New Orleans, Natchez, and Mobile?

John shrugged. That surely was none of his affair. When young Horace Gould crossed his mind again, he found himself wishing the boy, if he had really become an abolitionist, would return to St. Simons Island. Since John's first week on the Island in the Lawrence house, he'd bent every effort to make sure that people liked him. Horace Gould, he thought, would undoubtedly be far easier for John to like than some of the other St. Simons neighbors. Except for one of the Hazzard brothers, Dr. Thomas Hazzard, he didn't actively dislike anyone; but beyond the new rector, Theodore Bartow, and of course Jock Couper, he had found himself working rather hard to find interests in common with the others. Truthfully, he had found many of them dull.

James Hamilton Couper dull? He grinned as he hitched Ginger to the Lawrence post where Big Boy would be along later to groom, water, and feed her. John certainly did not find Anne's brother dull. A bit difficult, and now extremely important. James was hard to impress, too, but undoubtedly he would be impressed by a visit from Lord Herries, Anne's cousin. John was truly glad that Willy expected to visit them. No doubt at all that he was a man of the world. Unlike some of the Islanders, Willy Maxwell, at least, didn't laugh unless something was truly funny.

Halfway up the front path, he could hear Pete shout "Papa!" from somewhere inside the house. In seconds she, Annie, and Anne would be rushing out and into his arms.

But before his loved ones appeared, anguished screams came from across Jones Creek! Roswell King, Jr., now in charge of the late Major Pierce Butler's Hampton Point Plantation, was having another black man flogged. Anne would try to act as though nothing had happened. Lately, John had been trying, too, but with no success.

CHAPTER 26

To attend to his many projects at Hopeton, James Hamilton returned from his first trip to New Orleans, Natchez, and Mobile in time to attend the lavish autumn barbecue given by Anna Matilda and Thomas Butler King, at which time they formally presented their recently born son, Henry Lord King, to their Island neighbors. The Coupers and the Frasers had attended, making the trip to Retreat, as did the Goulds, Wyllys, and Caters, in plantation boats. John had, for the first time, enjoyed the eventful, social evening without reservation. He'd even made a point of finding time alone with James Hamilton, hoping that gentleman might inform him a bit more about his own future possibilities in the new cottonseed oil business. James told him nothing, but John did learn that he had seen Mr. James Gould's son Horace and that the young man was indeed a purser on a Mississippi River boat. By now, December 1, James Hamilton was back in Mobile, so only heaven knew when John would have a chance to learn more.

William and Frances Anne, with their small son, James, had

come down from Darien for the Kings' social event, and although
William would return to his hospital soon, Frances and the boy
planned to stay through Christmas with William's in-laws, the
Wyllys. John and William did visit their father's grave in Christ
Churchyard and spoke freely of the separate ways in which they
missed the old man. John talked at length about other events and
concerns in his life as well. He had indeed felt a part of Anne's St.
Simons world at the Kings', and somehow it seemed important
that William know that he did.

"Considering some of the uncomplimentary remarks I've made
in the past about Anne's older brother, especially, I probably have
no reason to think you'll believe this," John said to William as, on
the evening before his brother left, they stood in the yard outside
the old St. Clair Clubhouse, "but I'm fairly sure I've come to be
rather fond of Mr. James Hamilton Couper."

William's soft laugh was scarcely audible over the laughter and
talk of the members already assembled inside the clubhouse for the
early December meeting. "You're only *fairly* sure, Brother? If you
don't know, who does?"

"The man has always been hard for me. Anne knew it. I knew
it. Papa Couper knew it. So did James Hamilton, I suppose, but
who knows exactly what that distinguished gentleman really
thinks? At least tonight, *I* am conducting the meeting of this exclu-
sive St. Simons club, and when he learns of that, he should be
convinced that I've been more than merely accepted by my Island
neighbors. Now, before you lecture me, I know that sounded peevish. What amazes me is that I don't really feel peevish any longer
where my brother-in-law is concerned. Some time ago he even took
me into his confidence—in a measure, at least—about his new venture in New Orleans, Natchez, and Mobile: his cottonseed oil enterprise."

"Just what does he hope to do?" William asked.

Laughing, John answered, "Well, he didn't take me entirely
into his confidence, except to say that his new business is no longer
a secret. He does plan to put me in charge of his rich place at
Hamilton here on the Island in the near future, and for now I'll
settle for that."

"I'm sure your lady love is filling the ears of my wife with high-and-mighty plans for the day when Anne Couper Fraser becomes the mistress of Hamilton Plantation," William said. "Frances misses Anne. I wish they could see more of each other. I think my Frances has always felt she held second place to Anna Matilda King in your Anne's affections, but the two seem quite close now, don't you think?"

"I do and I'd give almost anything to eavesdrop on what they're saying to each other this evening. I'm a little afraid Anne's going to miss living at Lawrence."

"You'd give up your coveted spot as master of ceremonies at the St. Clair Club tonight?" William teased.

"I said *almost* anything. No sir. My beloved father-in-law is the speaker at this meeting, and introducing him means far more to me than I'd feel free to tell even my only brother."

AFTER SEEING THEIR HUSBANDS OFF TO THE PLANT-ers' meeting, the two young wives sat in the cozy, cheerful parlor of the Lawrence cottage, just talking.

"I'm glad neither of us is fiddling with a piece of fancywork," Frances Anne said, "because it seems years since we've had a really heart-to-heart conversation. I miss you, Anne. Do you miss me half as much?"

"Especially when something happens to remind me of those wonderfully free days when we were girls here together without a care in the world."

"You still don't seem to have any cares. In fact, I haven't seen you so happy since you and John came back from London. Aren't you absolutely lyrical you're going to live at that gorgeous spot on the Frederica River down at Hamilton? Tell me again when you think his excellency, your brother, will be ready to have you move?"

Anne looked down at Lovey asleep on her lap. Because another child was due soon, there was barely room for the little dog. "Not this year," she said, "thank heaven. Probably not until the end of next year. The date is up in the air yet. My baby is due in about six weeks, William thinks, so with all the work I'll have to do packing this dear little house filled with our furniture and all our other possessions, it's just as well to wait."

After a moment, Frances Anne said, "This cottage is filled with much more than your furniture and clothing and cooking utensils. I've never been in a house with so much downright cheer. It's truly a welcoming place. Do you take the time to realize that?"

"Yes. It has always been welcoming. I love this little cottage. I'll never forget the first moment Papa brought John and Annie and me here the day after we reached St. Simons. We stayed the first night at Cannon's Point because it was nearly dark when we docked, but bright and early the next morning, the old darling took us each by the hand and actually led us like children up the front steps and into what to me was truly—home. My first home. I honestly hate to leave Lawrence."

"Does John know that?"

"Oh no! The whole idea of his being put in charge of such a place as Hamilton Plantation means far too much to him. I'd never, never give him the faintest idea that it will break my heart the day I say goodbye to this room—the day I see it empty and swept out for the last time. Poor little house will probably stand here alone for who knows how long."

"You don't think John will try to go on managing Lawrence with all of Hamilton on his hands, do you?"

"I most certainly know that he means to. Sometimes I worry about it, too. He'll have to ride from Hamilton all the way up here three or four times a week, but Frances, when that man makes up his mind, that's it. John, bless him—and God protect him—has decided to be one of the best planters on the coast."

"Why do you worry about that when you so longed to come home to St. Simons the whole time you two lived abroad?"

"I worry for fear he'll overdo. He turned forty in October. Don't you ever worry about William's spending such long hours at the hospital, then having his rest broken into when someone rides up to your house needing a doctor at all hours?"

"William's still only thirty-seven, but yes, I know he seldom gets really rested. Somehow he doesn't show his tiredness. The man's so even-tempered no matter what he does or doesn't do. Do you sometimes wish John weren't so—so volcanic by nature?"

Anne laughed. "No. Well, no and yes. I think I'd worry more if he didn't show it when he's exhausted or elated. He was really elated to be conducting the meeting of the St. Clair Club tonight, wasn't he? I'd love to hear him introduce Papa. I know it means a lot to John that William will be there to hear him. Maybe next to having Father Fraser himself, he'll be proud for William to see him perform. Frankly, I'm sorry my brother James left for Mobile so soon again. It's odd about John and James. I don't think they liked each other much for the first few years."

"There are other gentlemen in the area," Frances Anne said, "who find your elegant brother a bit hard to take. He's just so successful at everything he does, I wonder sometimes how my little sister Caroline copes with being married to him. I do know how she does it, though, and so do you."

Anne nodded. "Her sense of humor. Caroline's always laughed a lot and seldom seemed to have to work at it. That very fact puzzles me, though, where James is concerned, because he can be such a sour pickle!"

"You said that, I didn't. I know my brother John has always found James Hamilton a little—shall I say stiff?"

"Why not? He is much of the time."

"Still, your brother vows he intends to allow my brother John to buy an interest in his peculiar cottonseed oil project in New Orleans and Mobile and Natchez."

"He's allowing John Wylly to buy into it?" Anne asked.

"He is, if John decides he wants to do it. He's not as well traveled or quite as polished in his manners as your husband, but he's somewhat temperamental, too, you know. If he thinks even the great James Hamilton Couper isn't undertaking a wise thing in

Alabama and Mississippi and Louisiana, nothing will influence John Wylly to touch it. He can be even more explosive than your husband."

"I don't think my John has a hot temper at all. Sometimes I wish he did, because when something irritates him or when he's frightened, he doesn't explode, he—performs."

"Performs?"

"He could have been a marvelous actor!"

"Well, I suppose you're right . . . yes," Frances mused. "I can picture John striding the boards. And speaking of the theater, Mama read in my father's *National Intelligencer* today that the famous British actress Sarah Siddons died back in June."

Anne sat up so suddenly, Lovey jumped, with a sleepy growl, onto the floor. "My father must not have gotten his *Intelligencer,* because he didn't mention a word about that, and John and I watched Madam Siddons play Lady Macbeth the very first night I saw a real play in London! Oh dear, but I—I guess she *was* getting old and Willy Maxwell did write that she hadn't been well."

"By the way, could I extend an invitation now—a whole year in advance—to you, John, and your Lord Herries to visit us in Darien when he comes to America with Madam Siddons's now equally famous niece, Fanny Kemble? I'd be the envy of the whole of McIntosh County if I had a real Scottish lord in my home!"

"*If* dear Willy really comes," Anne said, snapping her fingers for Lovey to jump back up on her lap. "A year from now is a long time. John and I saw Fanny Kemble that same night on stage with her Aunt Sarah Siddons. She was only about eight years old, but I can still see her—perfectly at ease before a large audience, reciting Shakespeare. Willy tells me Fanny Kemble dislikes the theater, but she adores her father, Charles Kemble, and he needs the money to keep his Covent Garden theater afloat, so she's making the American tour with him." Anne sighed. "I wish I thought John and I could take the water trip to New York. I'd give almost anything to see her act. She's the toast of London—of much of Europe, already."

"Isn't your cousin, Lord Herries, rich?"

"Yes, but there's a baby coming, John and I are not rich, and that's enough of that." Lovey had just gotten settled again in Anne's crowded lap when once more he gave a startled growl and jumped to the floor. "Lovey! What *is* our baby doing?"

"Do you really think your baby kicked so hard it startled the dog?" Frances asked.

"I know it did! I felt it too, and this child isn't due for over a month so far as I know. Whew!" Anne began to writhe in her chair. "Oh, Frances!"

Frances hurried to her. "Are you in pain? You look so pale suddenly." When Anne began to hold her distended stomach with both hands and moan, Frances dragged over a footstool for Anne's feet.

"I'm—I'm afraid I'm in labor, Frances," Anne gasped. "It's—it's so early!"

"Don't try to talk. Just breathe, breathe, breathe. I'll grab my cloak and run to the quarters for Big Boy. He can ride to Cannon's Point and bring Maum Rhyna."

"No! Don't leave! Even the children are at Mama's."

"Hush, do you hear me? Don't move until I come back and I'll be back," Frances called, hurrying out the front door, "just as soon as possible! Just sit there!"

When the front door banged, Lovey scampered to Anne's chair, crawled under it, and began to cry. "Don't do that, Lovey," she breathed. "Don't—just—crawl out of sight and cry. I need you."

Minute after minute dragged by, the pains coming sharper. Cautiously, the little dog had wriggled from under her chair where she could see him again. This time, though, he made no effort to hop onto her lap. "That's a good doggie," she gasped. When she screamed into the empty house, Lovey stopped whining, lifted a soft foot up onto one of her legs, and pressed gently.

After what seemed unending pain-racked moments, still clutching her stomach with one hand, she reached for Lovey's silky head with the other. "All right, Lovey," she breathed. "I'll—I'll mind Frances. I'll do my—level best to wait for her. To be calm, at least until someone gets here to—help me."

BIG BOY, CARRYING A FLAMING PINE KNOT, RODE through the darkness as hard as he could ride to Cannon's Point and to the Couper quarters, where he roused Rhyna, the midwife. Then he raced furiously—Rhyna holding on for dear life behind him—back to Lawrence.

"You got here just in time!" Frances Anne shouted as he and Rhyna hurried up the front walk, not bothering this time to go around to the back door.

"Thank you, Big Boy, but don't leave! You'll have to help Rhyna and me get her upstairs to her own bed."

THE NEW BABY HAD COME EARLY, SO EARLY THAT William appeared more than embarrassed that he'd misjudged the time. Rhyna strutted for days.

"Rhyna's far better at birthing than I'll ever be," William told John at the Lawrence dock when he left to return to Darien to his patients. It may have been better for Anne that I was at the St. Clair Club with you. Frances tells me Rhyna's knife thrown under the bed to cut the pain worked wonders."

Still shaken by the unexpected but remarkably easy time Anne had without him or William present, John sighed deeply. "What matters, Brother, is that Anne is fine and so is our little girl. By the way, Anne named her rightly—for your wife—and I've already begun to call her Fanny."

"I doubt my wife will be easy to live with from now on," William laughed. "She's so proud that the child she helped bring into this world is named Frances Anne. The experience our two wives shared has created a still-deeper bond between them. I'm glad, because my bond with Anne Fraser's husband grows stronger every day. I must tell you again, Brother, what a magnificent job you did conducting the meeting. Your introduction of old Mr. Couper was one every man there will always remember."

"I—I'm too choked up by all that's happened so fast," John said in a surprisingly self-conscious way, "to find the words, but hearing you say that has given an enormous lift to my spirit."

Taking John's outstretched hand, William said, "You're on your way, Brother. From now on, especially as master of Hamilton, I'll wager that you'll be more in demand at social functions than ever. Do you believe our father knows how well you're doing, wherever he is now?"

In a choked voice, John answered simply, "I hope so. I really hope he knows."

PART III

APRIL 1832—
NOVEMBER 1832

CHAPTER 27

IN AN EARLY APRIL SHOWER SO LIGHT IT SEEMED more like drops of airy mist falling than rain, Anne stood at her front parlor window just looking out, making small wagers with herself on exactly how long it would be before the sun really broke through again.

What a perfect moment for a walk, if one loves mist and rain as I do, she thought, wishing as she did many times during almost every day that John were home to walk with her. There was plenty of time. Eve had taken the girls to Cannon's Point for their lessons. Everyone was happy and well. Her whole world was good, good. Mina's lemon cake baking in the oven on one side of her open fireplace and a duck roasting filled the cottage with fragrances that not only caused her to feel foolishly welcome in her own house, but made her smile.

Fanny, now almost four months old, though small of bone and delicate, seemed to be a completely healthy, contented child, plainly delighted to have come early into Anne's own enchanted world of

St. Simons. Although the baby was still being propped up with pillows in her crib and supported when Anne held her on her lap, she not only showed marked interest in her big, handsome father and in young Pete, but laughed at them both. Anne vowed the infant had even pointed today when Anne showed her the resurrection ferns growing on the big oak tree right outside the parlor window. The child lay gurgling now in her crib near where Anne stood, trying to contain the rushes of new joy that kept welling up inside her these nearly perfect days.

Her thoughts, as close to a silent prayer as thoughts could be, moved from gratitude to the exhilarating, recurring picture of what fun it would be for them all when, later this year of 1832, dear Willy Maxwell might actually set foot for the first time on her beloved Island. She had lost count of how many times she'd pictured the moment he would land at the Cannon's Point dock after a water trip from Savannah. Of course she knew he'd have sailed first to New York with his friends Fanny Kemble and her father, Charles. Willy would come South to Savannah alone and then to St. Simons. According to his latest letter, he and the Kembles should reach New York sometime in September.

How wonderful, she thought, if he could see my Island for the first time when our leaves have begun to turn color! Nothing surpassed those unexpected turnings toward autumn on St. Simons, when God decorated the cedars and the many-colored sweet gums with bright, yellow ropes of golden bullis grapevines and scarlet creeper. Undoubtedly, October and November were her two favorite Island months, because autumn colors on the southern coast were subtle, mingling among the always green pines and live oaks and waving banners of thick, gray Spanish moss. *Tillandsia,* Papa and James Hamilton called it, after an old Finnish botanist named Elias Tillands, her brother said. To Anne the gray moss, which turned sage green in the rain, was there purely as ornament, although she knew their people used it to stuff pillows and mattresses.

Festoons of greenish moss waved today in the soft rain—to her mind, in sheer celebration of her happy life. Time spent alone these days brought thoughts of only glad happenings, with no more than the small problems any woman, especially a new mother, had to think about.

Most likely it would be October by the time Willy reached the Island, if his journey really came about, and she was going to begin right now to *think* autumn. The contented gurgling song from the crib had stopped. Fanny was sound asleep. There were socks to darn and buttons to sew on the girls' dresses, but she could do both later. This was Anne's own time to be wholly herself and grateful.

Idly, she noticed that it had taken more time than she'd guessed for the sun to peek out again, but it was beginning this minute to light the woods of the Park, to make tiny round, rainbow prisms in the droplets of rainwater clinging to newly opening spring sweet gum leaves and chartreuse pine flowers. She'd looked for those rainbow colors as a child and still loved finding them.

Her thoughts went to the fun-filled, happy evening spent with John and her children in this very room last night after she had put Fanny to sleep. No matter how loud Anne played the new pianoforte Papa had given her for Christmas or how raucously the girls sang when she played, no matter how many old Scottish ballads or sea chantics John sang, the new baby now slept through most of every night. Last evening had been almost magical. Noisy because Pete was there and John had seemed to want to go on singing song after song for as long as Anne would play, but today in her memory a special enchantment hung over it. She should have shared the experience with her parents or with the Wyllys or with still-lost, lonely James Gould and his family, but she kept such evenings close to her own heart. Who ever knew in advance when such an evening might happen anyway? Still, it was far past time for her and John to have at least a few of their neighbors over for a musical hour or two. Anne kept excusing herself from doing it by remembering how small the cottage parlor really was.

There was time for only a touch of passing guilt, because making her way along the path in the woods toward Anne's house, stooping to pick Anne's own flowers, came Heriot Wylly, the sun glinting off the raindrops in her wet, dark hair. As usual, she was seemingly unaware of rain or sun, of heat or cold. Being outdoors and with flowers—her own or anyone else's—formed the framework of Heriot's entire life as far as Anne knew. In a kindly way or otherwise, depending on who was talking, people whispered or said outright that Heriot was peculiar, strange, not like other Islanders. Well, she wasn't, but as Eve would say, "Where is it written down" that she had to be exactly like everyone else? If twenty-four-year-old Heriot preferred her own company most of the time, that was surely her right.

For a moment Anne just watched her easing along through the jonquil bed, filling her arms with the yellow blooms, a smile of pure happiness on her face. Heriot didn't come often for a visit, and there was no sign so far that she had come to talk today. Anne would have to wait to find out.

Finally, after she'd added a dozen or so hyacinths to the bouquet, Heriot stood smiling down at the flowers, taking in both their beauty and their scent. Then, looking around as though examining her own garden, she ambled up the Fraser path toward the cottage, where Anne was waiting on her porch with a welcoming smile.

"Come in, come in, Heriot," she called. "You can't imagine how glad I am to see you. Did you get very wet walking the two miles from your house?"

Heriot's oddly pointed face was far from blank as she stood, about halfway up the path, looking at Anne. Her expression was aglow and distant, but Heriot always looked as though she was seeing afar, enjoying whatever appeared in her distant vision. There was no sign in her manner that she'd just picked all those flowers from Anne's own garden, nor was there a hint of having helped herself without asking when she came up the path and onto the porch.

"I see you admire my garden too," Anne said. "Sit down, please. You and I haven't had a good talk by ourselves for a long time."

"Good morning, Anne," Heriot said. "Thank you." Then, holding out the flowers, she added, "I brought you a present. Aren't they beautiful? I brought these to you because you're Isabella's sister and she and I are friends. In fact, even though we don't see each other every day, we've come to be special friends.

Belle's the only real friend I've ever wanted to have. Did you know that?"

"Well," Anne said carefully, "yes, I did know you and Belle were friends." How would Anne not know after the carriage ride from Retreat with her younger sister, when Isabella had confided not only that she and the Reverend Bartow left secret messages for each other in the old hollow water oak, but that Heriot Wylly had come to be her friend, who now and then delivered a message for her. "In fact, Belle herself told me of your special friendship, Heriot. She's exceedingly fond of you."

"I know she is." Then Heriot suddenly handed the bouquet to Anne. "I picked these for you. I thought they'd brighten your cottage until you and Lieutenant Fraser move down to Hamilton to live. The Hamilton house is much bigger and sunnier than this one."

"How nice of you!"

"I don't particularly like being called nice."

"You don't?"

"No. I like to be called Heriot. I guess Belle also told you about the messages for Reverend Theodore Bartow I sometimes deliver to the tree for her."

"Uh—yes, she did."

"How do you like him?" Heriot asked.

"Oh, fine. He's a splendid young man. Everyone seems to like him."

"I guess that will be the next Island wedding and don't worry about my telling it around. Except for you, anything Belle tells me is dropped into a secret well. Frankly, I'm like a secret well."

"You—you may be right about the wedding. Theodore Bartow does call on Belle at home now. My parents have him for dinner often."

"I don't take dinner at other people's houses much. I like it at home best. But since I plan to get some orange blossom honey from your Lawrence grove, I might like to eat dinner with you and your family today. I haven't seen little Fanny since she was two months old."

"Then come right inside with me while I get Mina to put these lovely flowers in a vase of water. Fanny's sound asleep in her crib in the parlor."

"I won't wake her, so don't worry. Babies like me."

In the parlor, before she crossed the room to have a good look at Fanny, Heriot sniffed the fragrance from Mina's dinner. "Smells like your Mina's roasting a duck. Duck's my favorite."

"I'm glad," Anne said, laying the bouquet aside for a moment to lift the coverlet and give her guest a look at Fanny. "There she is, Heriot. A very good child, if I do say so. She not only sleeps all night now but almost never cries unless there's a good reason for it."

"Little bitty thing, isn't she? I'd say she'll look a lot like her papa. Got his long nose. Wonder if she'll have a dimple in her chin like his when she's a month or two older?"

"I hope so!" Anne smoothed Fanny's light, fine hair. The baby opened her eyes and looked solemnly up at Heriot, bending above her. Then Fanny smiled and grabbed Heriot's finger.

"See?" Heriot asked. "She likes me. I like you too, Fanny Fraser. I'm in a way related to your family. Your Uncle James Hamilton married my little sister, Caroline, and your Uncle William married my older sister Frances Anne. We're cousins or nieces or something. I have another older sister named Anne Frances. She's Frances Anne's twin. Confusing, isn't it? I'm glad you're only one baby, though. I wouldn't want to be one of twins. I'd much rather be Heriot. That way I can sleep in my garden path if I want to and there's no sister to nag me about it. I hope your mama won't nag you when you get older. Mine doesn't. None of my family nags. They know I can do just fine anywhere on St. Simons, so they let me go my way."

NOT ONLY DID HERIOT STAY FOR DINNER, SHE WAS still there in the happy midst of another music- and laughter-filled evening with the whole Fraser family.

The extravagant compliments for her crispy roast duck and the cake, which Heriot and John were still sampling at eight o'clock that night, had left usually stolid Mina in such a good mood that she could be heard joining the singing as she passed the open parlor window on her way to her cabin in the quarters for the night.

Anne had been playing "Oh, Willow, Willow, Willow," one of her favorites, when they heard the back door bang behind Mina. Immediately Anne swung into the old African shout, which she'd known since childhood, called "Rockah Mh Moomba"; at least she approximated it on the keyboard as close as anyone could expect. And with Annie, Pete, and Heriot dancing about the room, John, who had actually worked at learning the words from June, began to sing. From outside the window, Mina joined in:

> *"Rockah mh moomba*
> *Cum bo-ba yonda*
> *Lil-aye tambe*
> *I rockah mh moomba*
> *Cum bo-ba yonda*
> *Lil-aye tambe*
> *Ashawilligo homasha* banga
> *L'ashawilligo homasha* quank!
> *Ashawilligo homasha* banga
> *L'ashawilligo homasha* quank!"

Every time John and Mina shouted "quank!" Pete yelled with laughter and Heriot danced harder, then jumped.

"You have to jump way over on *quank!*" Heriot called across the room to Pete when John again shouted the word *"quank!"*

"You seem to know all about 'Rockah Mh Moomba,' " Anne said to Heriot at the end of the song.

"All my life," Heriot replied, pausing only long enough to catch Pete by the hand and step into the rapid tempo of an old English ditty, which Anne really knew how to play and John to sing:

> *"It was a lover and his lasse,*
> *With a haye, with a hoe and a haye nonie no,*

That o're the green corne fields did passe
In spring time, the onely prettie ring time,
When birds do sing, hay ding a ding a ding,
Sweete lovers love the spring."

When Anne finished off the accompaniment and John, trying nobly to be serious, had ended the first stanza, Pete yelled, "You sang it wrong, Papa!"

"I did not," John objected, sweeping Pete into the air above his head.

"Yes you did!" the child shouted. "You sang *one*-ly instead of only!"

"But that's the way Shakespeare is *supposed* to have written it," Anne declared.

"What do you mean, Mama?" Annie asked from her straight chair, where she'd been listening and watching all the foolishness. "Did Shakespeare write it or didn't he?"

Anne shrugged. "Who knows? Mr. Browne always told Miss Anna Matilda and me that it's thought William Shakespeare wrote the lyrics."

"It does look as though someone would know one way or the other," Heriot said.

John stood Pete back on her feet and pulled Anne from the chair at the pianoforte. "Things aren't always the way they look, Heriot, my dear," he laughed, still with an arm around Anne. "I say, can you spend the night with us? Or would you like me to have you driven back to the Village to your own bed? I can go for Big Boy to hitch up our buggy. Have you had a chance to ride in the new buggy I just bought in Brunswick?"

"No, Lieutenant Fraser," Heriot said, "I haven't, but it's quite unnecessary to speak to me as though I'm a child or—crazy, the way people say. I can not only speak and understand the English language perfectly, but if you'd be interested, I can recite every word you just sang after having heard the song only once."

Even Pete fell silent. And when the silence grew awkward, Anne asked, "Then, you will stay here tonight, Heriot? We'd love to have you and you are most welcome to sleep on the main mattress of Pete's trundle bed."

Anne not only saw, she felt, Heriot studying her. "Anne, that's kind of you, but have you looked out the window in the past hour? The moon's out full, the sky clear as a big, dark bluebell. I thought you knew me better, but I suppose such things take time. I wouldn't *dream* of not strolling home in all that magical moonlight! Haven't you noticed how friendly the St. Simons woods are at night?"

IN THEIR ROOM AT LAST, HERIOT GONE TO WANDER toward the Wylly house in the Village some two miles away, the children in bed, prayers said, John took Anne in his arms the minute she slipped her nightgown over her head.

"I'm sure average people would comment on the odd but fascinating behavior of our welcome, though uninvited, guest, Miss Wylly," John said, "but I have no time for such things. I'm far too happy, far too proud of myself, far too vain about my family, far too much in love with my beautiful wife, to concentrate on anything beyond finally having you all to myself, especially on a night when Heriot vows the moon casts such a spell." He pulled her down onto the bed. "I'm relieved I didn't have to see to Heriot's trip home, aren't you?"

Both arms reaching for him, she breathed, "Yes! Oh yes. And she's right. Our woods are more than friendly under a full moon. . . ."

"Hush, woman," he whispered hoarsely. "Don't say another word. Just kiss me!"

Through his long kisses, she murmured, "John, dearest John, someday I *am* going to give you—a son."

CHAPTER 28

THE FOLLOWING MAY, JOCK COUPER WAS WAITING
when his young friend, Dr. John C. Tunno left Anne's house and
joined him on the Fraser dock over little Lawrence Creek.

"Mr. Couper, I see you decided to wait," Tunno said pleasantly
as he walked out onto the clean boards of John's newly repaired
dock.

"Aye and what did you expect, Doctor?" Couper asked nervously. "How is my daughter? There's no chance she'll lose the
baby, is there? And she is again with child, isn't she?"

"As nearly as a mortal doctor can tell, she'll bear Lieutenant
Fraser another child sometime around Christmas. These difficult,
confusing periods sometimes come, but I've examined her thoroughly and she's in excellent health. My guess is that she's been
carrying the baby since sometime in March. This is mid-May, so
the fates should smile on you once more before the year is out, Mr.
Couper. You're a fortunate man."

"Indeed, I'm a blessed mon, Doctor, and I thank you for riding all the way up from Retreat to calm my fears. My daughter Anne was sure she was fine. So was her mother, Rebecca, but I get fidgety. Fathers and grandfathers are like that, they tell me. And I'm some of both."

"I'm honored that you bothered to send your man down to Retreat to fetch me. I make the boat trip to St. Simons once a month or so to look in on the Kings and their people. Anything else I can do for you now that I'm up here on your end of the Island?"

"Beyond taking dinner with us at Cannon's Point and spending the night, I don't know of a thing. Mrs. Couper and I would be honored. In fact, she remembered your fondness for Lady Baltimore cake and a fine one is waiting from the expert hand of my chef, Sans Foix. If you'll join me in yonder carriage, Lieutenant Fraser's man, Big Boy, will drive us to Cannon's Point."

In the carriage, jolting over the three miles or so from Lawrence to Cannon's Point, Couper and Dr. Tunno arrived at an arrangement that assured Couper that from now on, Tunno would add a visit at both Lawrence and Cannon's Point to each medical call at the Kings' Retreat Plantation.

"I'll simply feel more secure if you see my daughter Anne on a regular basis, Doctor," Couper explained as the carriage rounded the curve in Couper Road that brought the Big House in sight. "I'm not as young as I once was, you know. My people need attention too on occasion, and although Mrs. Couper is several years younger than I, it may ease her mind a bit as well." Jock chuckled. "By the way, you're rolling along in a springed carriage right now mainly because my old bones and joints don't do too well astride a horse these days."

"You don't ride anymore, sir?"

"Oh yes. I still ride my fields when my fine son-in-law deems it needful, but thanks to him and my own son James Hamilton, I'm more or less a gentleman planter these days. Rebecca vows I'm growing fat from so much carriage riding."

Tunno turned in the tufted seat to look Jock over. "You look the same to me. But I do hear it rumored that Lieutenant Fraser is becoming an expert planter. There were those who doubted a man with his somewhat adventurous background could ever make the bridge to Island life and farming. He must also be happy that still another child is on the way."

"Aye, the man is lyrical! He's always sung like an angel. He sings, my people tell me, through most of his days now that he finally believes he's accomplishing his mission here in Georgia. Even my finicky son James is impressed with John. You know, of course, that the Fraser family will be moving down to Hamilton sometime next year. I'll miss them, heaven knows, but the trust of a successful gentleman like my son seems to have given Lieutenant Fraser the biggest of all boosts. The lad's in Darien today, actually, doing some buying for Anne and the children. He doesn't know I sent for you, by the way. I realize I get fussed at nothing. Wouldn't want to worry John, so I've asked Anne not to tell him you were here."

SOME MONTHS LATER, TOWARD THE MIDDLE OF October, John rode to Frederica to inspect and duly praise a small, new cotton warehouse his friend James Frewin had just added to his expanding property. Frewin, along with other Couper and Fraser friends, knew that the family hoped for word that a distant cousin of Mrs. Couper's would soon be visiting from New York. Everyone knew that this was no ordinary cousin, but a titled Scotsman, Lord Herries. Pete, fascinated by their expected guest's long name—Willy Maxwell, Lord Herries—had let it be known far and wide that a real lord might soon be arriving.

"We'll make short work of my pride in the new warehouse, John," Frewin said when John offered to take the Island post directly to the postmaster, Jock Couper. "The long-awaited letter is here at last, and if I'm any judge of people, the old fellow will want to hand it to his daughter Anne himself. I'm not normally nosy, but I know how eager she's been to hear from Lord Herries. His letter's here. Be a shame if, after all this time, the gentleman can't grace our Island with his presence."

Riding hard a short time later out the Couper Road toward

Cannon's Point, John could think of little else and wished Frewin hadn't planted the idea that of course there was always a chance Willy couldn't make the long water trip.

"From what you've both told me about Lord Herries," Jock said, beaming his anticipation when John tucked the small packet of mail into his father-in-law's saddlebag, "I feel sure he wouldn't allow Anne to hope as she is hoping and then fail to come. I say, John, you're pampering me by riding out of your way just so I can give it to Anne myself." Chuckling as he steadied himself on the mounting block beside his horse, Couper added, "And I thank you for not trying to help me mount! Once I'm up here, I do fine. Now let's gallop. I find I can't wait to see Anne's face when she sees that New York postmark!"

WHEN JOHN AND PAPA HAD LEFT TO SIT TOGETHER on the front porch, Anne settled herself alone in her favorite parlor rocker, still holding Willy's long-awaited letter in both hands. I don't know of anything, she thought, that makes me happier than that John is so fond of Papa he'd ride all the way to Cannon's Point so the old darling could hand me this letter. Of course John accuses me of having Willy on a pedestal, but Willy, bless him, will be impressed by John's success as a planter—mystified probably that he seems to like planting—but he'll be impressed and John does love to impress important people like Willy Maxwell.

And to think Willy is in New York in the brilliant company of young Fanny Kemble, her famous theatrical father, Charles, and who knows what other world-known, cultivated friends! One thing is certain: wherever Willy is, he is being respected, genuinely liked, catered to, even though nothing in his gentle makeup demands it.

She glanced down at her body, her stomach again distended with child. Would Willy still think her pretty in this condition? And seven years older? Willy was Willy, though, and not given to fickle affection. They were friends. Through the first difficult, nervous days back on St. Simons, when John was just learning and making big mistakes and needing her as a child needs its mother, Anne had somehow counted on Willy's friendship even across all those miles of ocean.

Trying to control her excitement, she made herself open the letter slowly, breaking the elegantly simple wax seal a little at a time. Then the letter, which would surely tell her if and when he meant to arrive, was spread before her.

> 1 October 1832
> New York City, U.S.A.
>
> My dear Anne and John,
>
> I am ensconced in a rather nice hotel in your native land and feel certain that since so much has been published up here at the North about the Kembles, you must know of our arrival in New York on 3 September and at least something of the quite phenomenal reception of young Fanny Kemble.

Anne stopped reading. Papa, if he'd received his copy of the *National Intelligencer* from Washington City, hadn't said a word to her, but maybe he'd forgotten that Willy was sailing with the Kembles when they made the crossing to begin their American tour.

> The *New York Evening Post* declared: "Never have we seen a more delighted audience nor heard more enthusiastic applause. Fanny Kemble exhibits such an intensity and a truth never exhibited by an actress in America, certainly never by one so young." At a highly social function a few nights after the Kembles opened, I was told by the mayor of New York himself, the Honorable Philip Hone, said to be a leader of upper-class opinion, that he had written in his own diary that he had "never witnessed an audience so moved, astonished, and delighted," and that he had never heard such deafening shouts and applause as for Fanny herself. You have written already to say you absolutely cannot join me in New York and as a rule I can be philosophical about such refusals, but I find it difficult to

accept that the two of you have not been exposed to Fanny Kemble as an adult on stage!

Be that as it may, I am pleased to tell you that, weather permitting, I will sail from New York Friday the fifth and will arrive in Savannah, Georgia, on or near October 17th or 18th. I will from there find a means of transportation south to your enchanted Island. Seven years is an eternity without sight of you, and I still feel the same eagerness to see the one part of the world where Anne Fraser longed above all others to live.

By the way, I mentioned to Fanny Kemble and her father en route from Liverpool that we had seen her perform as a child between acts with her aunt, the late Sarah Siddons. I'm sure you know of her demise in June of last year and of the demise this year on 21 September of my beloved friend, our host, Sir Walter Scott. My last visit with him a year ago at Abbotsford was, as always, pure stimulus, and as long as I live, I will miss the man's being alive in the same world with me.

Anne knew of Sarah Siddons's death in 1831 but not of Scott's last month! The news that her lifelong favorite author had died stunned Anne to such a degree that she couldn't finish the final, rather formal lines of Willy's letter before she raced out to her front porch to tell John and Papa.

John's first reaction was stark silence. Papa tried to comfort her, to comfort them both, but John just sat there, staring out over their yard toward Lawrence Creek and the stretching marshes.

"I can't believe it, can you, dearest?" Anne asked, still clutching the letter and desperately needing to hear him say something. "It just doesn't seem possible that a man so full of life and laughter could—could ever die!" She looked from John's stricken face to Papa. "Papa, poor Mrs. Scott. My heart aches for poor, quiet, sensitive Charlotte Scott. You see, she told me herself that although she wasn't her husband's first love, she had never, ever loved anyone but—Walter Scott." Her eyes back on John's face, she murmured, almost to herself, "That's—that's the way it is with me, John, so my heart is filled with pain for Charlotte."

"I know," John said.

As though Papa weren't even there, she asked, "Do you? Do you really know, dearest?"

"Yes, Anne. I know you've never loved anyone but me. That's where the comparison with the Scotts ends, though. I never loved any woman the way I love you. It's—it's losing Scott himself that fills me with sorrow."

"I knew you enjoyed him, John," Papa Couper said tenderly, "but I didn't realize how much you cared for the gentleman."

For another long moment, John was silent. Finally, without looking at either Anne or her father, he said softly, "Scott undoubtedly forgot the entire incident, but had it not been for one walk into the Scottish hills with him, I quite probably would not be here with the two of you on this front porch today."

Anne felt fear so sharp, so sudden, she reached for John's hand with both of hers. "Darling! Where—where would we have been? Do you mean we might be in some other place? Or—oh John, certainly you don't mean we might not have been together still! John Fraser, you and I wouldn't have been apart, would we? Answer me!"

Gently he kissed her hand. Then, smiling first at her father and up at Anne, who was still standing beside his chair, he said, "No, beautiful Anne. I only meant that Walter Scott, that one day with me out in his beloved hills, somehow made me see that I *could do* what I now believe I've been able to do right here on St. Simons."

On a deep sigh, Anne heard her father say, "Then bless the memory of Sir Walter Scott, I say. Bless the mon's memory forever!"

John stood up. "Now you, Papa Couper, have a good excuse— the excuse of stiff joints—for remaining seated when a lady is among us. I have none. Forgive me, darling? And I strongly urge you to take my impolite place in this chair. In your condition, with our next child due as a Christmas gift, I intend to go on pampering you. So, sit!"

She sat. "I'm not Lovey! I don't respond well to commands, Lieutenant Fraser, but sitting down *is* better. You always know how to take care of me, don't you? Papa, did you ever in your seventy-three years meet another man to equal my husband?"

Both men laughed and John asked, "Is Willy really coming? Do we have an idea of his arrival time in Savannah? Or haven't you finished reading his letter?"

"I guess I didn't quite finish," Anne said. "But he *is* coming and will find his own transportation to St. Simons from Savannah sometime around the seventeenth or eighteenth of this very month."

"He'll do no such thing," Papa declared, pulling himself to his feet. "Your good mother and I will meet her titled cousin, Willy Maxwell, Lord Herries, in Savannah *in person*—just the two of us. It's been a long, long time since Becca and I have taken a pleasure trip to the old city. Don't you think she'll be delighted with the prospect, Anne?"

"I know she will be, Papa, but John, can't you and I go too?"

"We most certainly cannot," he answered, commanding her again. "I've already warned you that your well-being is my very first concern from now until the day our new arrival joins us."

After a big hug, Papa whispered quite audibly to Anne, "I must go along home, Daughter, with the big news for your dear mother, and remember, neither you nor John was invited by me to make the journey."

"But if you and Mama meet Willy, the Mackays or some other Savannah family will entertain for all of you and it will take days longer for us to be able to see him after all this time!"

"Indeed it will," John said, stooping as though he was about to pick her up and carry her into the house.

"Don't you dare pick me up!"

Both men laughed heartily at her, and Papa, limping a little, headed for the steps. "John knows," her father said, "that picking you up as though you were Pete is strictly against Dr. Tunno's orders, but do try to behave yourself, Daughter. And don't envy your mother and me such a rewarding sojourn in the old city up the coast."

CHAPTER 29

AFTER WILLY HAD POSTED HIS LETTER TO ANNE, he hired a carriage and gave the hackman orders to drive to Miss Fanny Kemble's hotel, The American. No further instruction was needed. Every carriage driver in New York knew of the much-discussed Miss Kemble and the exact location of her hotel as well as her fame, which was spreading like wildfire across the city.

Within moments after Willy entered the lobby, Fanny swept down the stair, smartly dressed in a blue riding skirt and jacket, topped by her already famous visored riding cap, which Willy knew their mutual friend Lady Ellesmere had given her.

"Willy, my dear man," Fanny said in her low, always vibrant voice, hand extended in welcome, "rescue me from this dreary hotel, please! It's absolutely a gift from God that you asked me to go riding today. When I awoke this morning in that dreadful cell of a room, I had no such pleasantry to look forward to. After your welcome message, I now have Willy Maxwell, Lord of Herries, and I hope something resembling a real horse in the offing."

From habit, Willy stood holding her hand, giving her ample time for her opening speech, which he always anticipated with amusement. Yesterday he had made a point of stopping by the livery stable nearest her hotel to look over the horses, knowing full well that none would really suit Fanny, who had found no mount in all of New York broken to the standard British gaits. He also knew the lady so adored riding—proper mount or not—that she would endure, even revel in, a good, brisk, long ride.

"I must say that I've accomplished one great feat since our arrival," Fanny said when they were settled into the worn carriage seat.

"By the morning paper, far more than one," Willy laughed, "and you've been performing little more than a fortnight."

"Oh, I don't mean the theater," she said airily. "I mean my accomplishment in behalf of the odd assortment of American women. Their waistlines are small enough while they're young, but they age fast and thicken. Now, thanks to my influence, some won't. Many are already getting into riding skirts and up on horses. There's even a plan for one merchant to begin copying my riding cap!" Her infectious laugh came. "I must let Lady Ellesmere know. Better than the cap's success, though, is the inevitably improved health of these poor women. I truly think a vigorous shaking does a woman good in every way!"

Knowing a response was never necessary with her, Willy leaned against the carriage seat and merely chuckled.

Always at ease in her presence, he enjoyed the pleasant, quiet moments as their carriage rolled through the clear, surprisingly fresh autumn air. The quiet was short-lived. "Sit up and listen to me," Fanny said abruptly. "When we get to wherever it is we're riding today and after a fine, long canter, I must have an answer to a question that whirls day and night in my mind. Will you promise?"

"I'd love to promise you almost anything, my dear lady," Willy mused, "but even with you, I'd have to weigh the question. Do you care to tell me ahead of our arrival? We're having a picnic eventually. I've had one made up. The basket's riding along in the rear luggage rack. What is it you demand to know?"

With an arrestingly solemn look, she turned to face him. "Not yet, sweet old friend. I am not jesting. My question is quite serious and I expect a serious response."

He laughed a little. "I'm always serious with you, Fanny. By the way, we're headed for the ferry and the Brooklyn side of the Narrows. Does that please you?"

"You're not really changing the subject, you know. I intend to force you to answer my puzzling uncertainty."

"The great Kemble uncertain?" he teased.

"I'm in deadly earnest."

He looked at her expressive face. "I believe you are."

AFTER THEIR FERRY RIDE, HORSES IN TOW, THEY took an ample canter along the Narrows bridle path—for Willy, more than ample—then spread and shared their picnic. Now they sat looking out over the expanse of water between Staten Island and the New York Harbor, wineglasses in hand, Willy feeling a bit anxious because she had not yet asked her mysterious question.

In all the years he'd known the Kemble family, he had never failed to enjoy picnics with young Fanny. The two had been sharing rides and packed baskets since she was a child, even before he and Anne and John had seen her perform that memorable night. Memorable? He turned the word in his mind while his companion sat quietly nearby on the grass, her straight, slender back against an elm tree. That night little Fanny had dramatically displayed her innate acting talent. Her late aunt, Sarah Siddons, had again shown herself to be Lady Macbeth incarnate, but to him the night had been memorable because of Anne Fraser. Again and again, Anne had made a point of thanking him for the perfect evening, the first professionally performed Shakespearean play she'd ever attended.

This was not the time to indulge in memories of Anne, though. Even though he'd disciplined himself to shut out thoughts of her for seven years, doing so now somehow made him uncomfortable. It's good being quiet with Fanny, he thought. She has always fallen with ease and grace into silences with me. At times it's almost as though she's known me all her life in a way no one else has ever known me. I'm glad. I trust her. I trusted her when she was a child. I trust her now that she's the champagne toast of New York. I believe I'll always trust Fanny Kemble's heart. She spouts torrents of words, ideas, but then so does her entire family. Often at a loss for words myself, I enjoy Fanny's loquaciousness. She will always be more or less a child to me no matter how far her fame reaches, but the child in her still rings true.

"Are you ready, Willy?"

"Ready?" He reached for their wine bottle and her glass.

"No. No more wine. Acting in New York forces one to work like a slave. One glass is sufficient. Are you ready for my question?"

"What a peaceful moment to pin a friend like a butterfly." His laugh was not convincing.

"I am your friend," she said. "And you're mine. The years give me the right to ask why you've—never married. I'm not at all sure I mean to marry anyone either. But you're in your fifties, Willy. You're trim as a boy. You own great wealth. Aren't you ever lonely?"

"Oh yes," he said quickly. "I think I've always been lonely."

"Then why haven't you given your love to someone? Yours is one of the world's greatest, tenderest hearts, you know."

"No, I didn't know,"

"Yes you did and I must know why you're still alone. Haven't you found what is called—the right person?"

He looked at her a long time, then, without intending to at all, said, "Yes. Yes, Fanny. I found her some fifteen years ago in the ruins of the old courtyard at Caerlaverock, my family's castle near Dumfriesshire."

Fanny, sensitive to him as always, didn't speak at once. Nor did she look at him. Her dark, luminous eyes moved deliberately out over the water. Her complexion under the bright, fall sun was of a dark cast, too long exposed to weather, the outdoors. She was truly diminutive and, for this moment, no matter how assured and spellbinding on stage, appeared totally inadequate to frighten any man.

Certainly a man so much older than she. She had startled Willy by her question. Or, had he shocked himself even more by answering as he did?

"Do I know her?" Fanny asked at last.

"No. She isn't—English. I see no way you'll ever know her."

"But she is still alive?"

Willy's heart skipped.

"Oh yes," he said lamely. "She's—quite alive."

"Is that all you're going to tell me?"

"Yes."

"Then I'll be kind and ask you a totally different question. I know you're still thinking of making that hideous water journey from New York all the way to some godforsaken spot called St. Simons Island in what must be the equally forsaken state of Georgia. *Why?* That isn't being overly curious, is it? They raise cotton down there by the forced labor of hundreds of ill-treated Negro slaves. An English gentleman of your stature could never think of investing money in such an evil undertaking! I care about you, Willy. I'm not nosing into your affairs. I thought perhaps you didn't know what a ghastly kind of place Georgia must be. One of father's Boston friends told me only yesterday about the cruelty on those plantations. He's a dear friend of a well-bred man of the cloth named the Reverend Dr. William Henry Channing, who's just beginning to use his Christian influence against the Southern 'lords of the lash,' as they're called. Willy, a sensitive, gentle man like you will loathe being in such a place as Georgia!"

Again she had pinned him down. He'd never given slavery much thought but, being British, had observed the growing hatred of the system at home. Certainly he had no notion of entering into it in any way and felt equally certain that neither John Fraser, now a quite successful coastal cotton planter, nor lovely Anne's father, John Couper, could ever be a part of such a system.

Fanny was looking directly at him now. Her striking face, he thought quite irrelevantly, could not be called beautiful, although the full chin balanced the Kemble nose, and Fanny herself could appear both whimsical and saucy. She could also, as now, appear almost intimidating. She did know Willy Maxwell. Her knowing pierced the look she was giving him. God forbid, he thought, that she go on with her tirade against slavery! His very being was too tenderly reaching toward Anne. She *could* not approve of cruelty in any form. He would not be shaken from that certainty.

"I've offended you," Fanny said, her voice suddenly young, wistful. Disconcertingly so.

"No, you have not offended me," he said and wondered helplessly what in the name of everything holy and unholy he would think of to say next.

What he did say was exactly what he had vowed to himself never to tell another living person: In a voice he would not have recognized as his own, he heard himself telling Fanny Kemble that the one woman on earth he'd ever loved was the daughter of a planter in coastal Georgia and that *she* was the sole reason for his odd determination to go there.

When he had finished telling her what he'd hinted to no one but God in fifteen endless years, he could not even look at his friend Fanny. But she leaned over and put her face close to his, so that he had to look back at her. She would force the truth while at the same time encouraging him with those great, expressive eyes that seemed to pour the only real comfort into his heart since the long-ago day in London when he first faced the hopeless fact of his love for Anne Couper Fraser.

Strangely, that look gave him comfort. The comfort came illogically and surely, preparing him, giving him confidence to face some future event that awaited him with the violent, tearing force of a cataclysm. The comfort did not promise that what would come would—*could*—be painless. Quite the opposite. The very comfort itself promised pain. Perhaps a lifetime of pain.

After a measureless pause, Fanny asked, "And will you ask her to marry you once you see her again on her own turf, beloved Willy?"

"No."

"But why not? Why else would you endure the horrors of the hateful ocean we just crossed, why would you torture yourself with what will surely be still another miserable water journey south? Does she know that one of the greatest souls God ever created is in love with her?"

"No."

"You've never told her? Never shown her?"

"I've—never—told her," he murmured. "Most likely I've shown her. She's an amazingly perceptive young woman."

"How young?"

"Thirty-five this winter past. January, I believe."

"Not young at all."

"To me, she will always be."

"Not *you*, beloved Willy Maxwell! I won't have it!" Fanny exclaimed. "Not my childhood friend Lord Herries!"

"You must always be my friend, Fanny. Especially must you be now, after this blathering I've done."

She took his hand in hers and sat holding it. Then, after a deep breath, she said—she didn't ask—she simply said, "She's married."

"Yes. The mother of three children and according to her latest letter, expecting a fourth soon. I'm deeply fond of her dashing husband, formerly an officer in the Royal Marines. His name is John Fraser. I met him the same day I—found her. John and I are friends."

After a long silence Fanny asked, "You are not hoping, are you?"

His small laugh was not really a laugh. "No. I swear to you, Fanny, I've never hoped. I've just—loved."

Her fingers tightened on his. "Poor, blessed Willy. . . . But I'm glad you don't hope. Was it some ancient Phoenician, before Christ was born, who said, 'Hope is not to be trusted'?"

"Dear Fanny. I'm sure it was a very wise Phoenician who said that."

CHAPTER 30

As always, when the Coupers were meeting someone at the busy, noisy old Savannah wharf, Jock went first to young Mark Browning's countinghouse on Commerce Row to inquire after the expected ship. This time they were fulfilling a lifelong dream of Becca's. They were meeting her Scottish cousin, Willy Maxwell, Lord of Herries, but Becca had never laid eyes on the man, and the moment of meeting loomed large and bright for her. Whatever made Rebecca happy made Jock happy too.

He had left his wife comfortably seated in the old Mackay carriage, which was stopped on Bay Street near the dock. She was waiting with Miss Eliza Mackay, her friend, and the Mackays' faithful driver to guard them. Wealthy Mark Browning was away from his office, but a clerk had informed Jock that the *Emperor*, down from New York, had already docked at the slip right next to Browning's own. Couper was moving along the iron balcony above Factor's Walk as fast as he could manage, but it seemed to be taking him forever to reach the dock. Thankfully, the October day was bright and blue. The breeze off the Savannah River carried only a mild chill. Brisk, he thought. Stirs a man's blood.

What would Lord Herries be like? A quiet, thoughtful, generous gentleman, Anne and John vowed. Couper would surely like the man because his daughter had been fond of her mother's kin since their first meeting in the courtyard of Becca's family castle in Scotland.

Anne hadn't seen Willy since she and John left London, but both believed him to be somewhere in his fifties. Once he reached the dock, Couper meant to find Maxwell before leading him to Becca and Mrs. Mackay in the carriage, so he wouldn't miss seeing his wife's face. Although as pure-blooded a Scot as Jock himself, Becca had lived in America all her life and had spent much of that life pondering the looks and natures of her Scottish relatives, distantly related, nevertheless lively in her romantic daydreams. Through the years since Anne's return, the blessed lady had insisted on hearing over and over about the ruins of the Maxwell castle near Dumfries, called Caerlaverock, where John and Anne had been entertained in the crumbling old courtyard by the very man for whom Jock was now looking.

Nothing lifted Jock Couper's spirits as did the prospect of a delightful visit from what must be a most-traveled, wordly-wise gentleman. He did his best to move along a bit faster, peering down every few steps in order to keep the location of the Mackay carriage firmly in mind. It seemed almost too good that he, old Jock Couper, would be the one to introduce Becca to her titled kin. Smiling, he tipped his hat to two perfectly strange ladies and their equally unknown escort. Today, everyone was a friend.

The *Emperor* had docked all right. He could see it, could see its passengers disembarking, but from above, his old eyes were too dim to tell if Lord Herries might be among those already on the wharf.

And then, peering down again just before he descended the stairs from Factor's Walk, he saw an elegantly attired, past-middle-aged man standing, top hat in hand, beside the Mackay carriage, already in conversation with the ladies inside.

"I'm a feeble, slow old goat," he muttered to himself. "Lord Herries has found her—without me!"

THROUGHOUT DINNER AT THE MACKAYS' IN THE spacious, hospitable dining room where Rebecca Couper and her family had enjoyed so many delicious meals over the years, Rebecca smiled each time she and Jock exchanged looks. Everyone at the table—Eliza Mackay, her two daughters, Sallie and Kate, even Rebecca's likable though reserved cousin, Willy Maxwell—knew why she kept giving her husband that smile. Maxwell had been told by the Mackays that Jock had long teased her about being tied to her "pr-r-ecious family tree."

"It's a well-known fact," Miss Eliza said to Willy, "that the senior Coupers are devoted to each other. It's known all up and down the coast and probably all the way to St. Augustine in Florida, but right now you're undoubtedly seeing it in a singular way, Lord Herries. Two persons who have been together under the same roof for as long as they've been, and who can still tease and enjoy it, *are* devoted."

"I'm honored," Willy said, "although not at all surprised. You see, Mrs. Mackay, I've listened for long periods of time to their lovely daughter Anne, who believes firmly that her parents, Mr. and Mrs. John Couper, are the two most wonderful anywhere in the world."

"Anne conveys that, does she?" Jock chuckled, plainly pleased, Rebecca thought. "And did Anne also tell you, Lord Herries, that we think she is, without a doubt, one of the finest daughters anywhere?"

"No, sir, Anne didn't tell me that, but she could have no doubt that I've known it from the start. From the moment of our first meeting in the courtyard of our family's old ruined castle, Cousin Rebecca."

"Ah, this is the moment for which my worthy wife has been waiting!" Jock announced in his most ebullient manner. "A face-to-face talk with her long-lost Maxwell cousin about the old family fortress. I hang my head in shame that I've allowed the years to slip by without taking her there, Lord Herries. The lady has entertained fairy-tale dreams of it all her life."

The talk drifted from Willy's brief, almost cursory description of the ancient family ruins to the current price of cotton on the Liverpool market to differently gaited American and English horses, and then, through Willy, back to Anne. "Your daughter Anne, Cousin Rebecca—is she well? I rather think I'd hoped she might have come along to meet my ship. Of course, truthfully, I expected no one to make the journey, with ship's arrival times what they are. She—Anne wrote me that she and Lieutenant Fraser are expecting another child soon."

"Anne's doing splendidly, thank you," Rebecca said, "although I'm afraid she's in a rather awkward stage now. You see, the baby's due sometime around Christmas."

"Our Anne could never be awkward," Jock put in. "And dare we hope you might remain at Cannon's Point as our most welcome guest through the Christmas holidays at least, Lord Herries?"

Almost bluntly, Rebecca thought, Cousin Willy said, "No. Oh no, sir, but I am grateful for the generous offer. You see, I took passage across from England in the company of my friends the Kembles—Fanny and her father, Charles. They have rather elaborate holiday plans in both New York and Philadelphia. I've promised to return before the middle of next month."

"The famous theatrical Kemble family?" Kate Mackay gasped. "Do tell us about Miss Frances Anne Kemble, Lord Herries! I'd give anything I own for one glimpse of that famous lady. Mrs. Couper did tell us you crossed with them, but somehow hearing you say at our very own dinner table that you're spending Christmas in their truly colorful company is—well, it's too exciting! What's she like? Is it true what the *National Intelligencer* says — that she rides a horse almost every day just for the exercise? I almost never heard of a woman's intentionally exercising!"

Laughing, really laughing for the first time, Willy Maxwell said, "Yes, Miss Kate Mackay, what they say is true. Fanny is, I fear, in the vigorous process of reforming and remaking the women of New York. And when she rides, she wears stunning riding skirts and jackets and a quite cocky visored riding cap. The milliners are even duplicating it. Most important, though, the lady can ride. In fact, when she and I spent most of a day together just before I sailed, she rather exhausted me. Thinks nothing of a five- or ten-mile canter. Revels in it, actually."

Staring at Willy, Kate Mackay again gasped, "You—you know her well enough to spend a day of horseback riding with her? Right in her—regal company?"

Now Willy's laugh caused Kate to flush, Rebecca noticed and felt embarrassed for the young woman, who had lived her well-mannered life of twenty-two years in a sheltered Savannah home, mainly among family and family friends.

"I've known Fanny Kemble since she was a child, Miss Kate," Cousin Willy said in a voice so kind, Rebecca admired his quick sensitivity to the girl. But the casual announcement that he and the highly praised actress were close friends had landed like a bomb-shell. Even sixteen-year-old Sallie, who evidently hadn't read as much about Fanny as had Kate, wanted to know more.

"It would please me mightily," Willy said, "to learn more of *you*—all of you—Miss Mackay. I understand your family lived in London for a time."

Disappointed, Sallie said, "Oh, but that was before I was even born!"

"My late husband and I brought the older children back to Georgia when it looked as though our two countries were going to war," Eliza Mackay explained. "And, of course, they did go to war. In 1812."

Rebecca could see Willy brighten. "Wasn't it near the end of that war when Lieutenant John Fraser captured your daughter and you, Cousin Rebecca?"

She laughed. "Captured us at a house party, along with our older son, James Hamilton. On Cumberland Island."

"I'm glad we can all smile about it now," Willy said, lifting his wineglass. "And may our two countries never fight again!"

Everyone joined him, and Rebecca was proud of Jock because he said not one word about his enormous losses to the British. Even when Eliza Mackay began to insist that they remain in Savannah for a large dinner party, Jock stayed firmly behind Rebecca's refusal as she explained how eager Anne was to see their Cousin Willy again.

" 'Tis true, the girl is carrying another child," Jock said, "and we trust you'll understand, Mrs. Mackay—kind as your invitation is—that none of us wants to add even one small anxiety for Anne."

"Of course I understand," Eliza said. "How pleased you both must be to have your grandchildren around you."

"We are truly disappointed, Cousin Willy," Rebecca said, "that you can't stay for Christmas and the baby's birth. I know how much a good long visit with you would mean to Anne."

Willy gave her what she could only think was a surprisingly sad little smile. "Of course I'm pleased to know Anne wants me, Cousin Rebecca, but I doubt if anyone wants me half as much as I would like to stay." For a moment no one said anything; then Willy asked, "Anne—Anne and John are still as happy as ever, aren't they?"

Jock, Rebecca thought, noticed nothing at all unusual about the question, because chuckling, he said in a casual voice, "Still lovebirds, those two. And you're going to be downright amazed at how expert my son-in-law, John Fraser, has become as a planter, Lord Herries."

Did Rebecca imagine that Willy frowned ever so slightly? She thought not.

"I don't know how well you knew my son-in-law, sir," Jock went on, "but to this day I'm sure he's the most surprised of all to find that he's actually beginning to like farming."

"I—I feel I knew Anne a bit better than John," Willy said, "but I was certainly aware that he didn't expect to like planting at all."

CHAPTER 31

WITH ALL HIS MIGHT, WILLY MAXWELL TRIED—AS
John Couper's well-made plantation boat, the *Lady Love,* moved
under the muscle power of eight slaves to the west side of the
Hampton River toward Couper's dock—to concentrate on the en-
trancing, odd, primitive rhythms of the oarsmen as they sang their
way home. Indeed he had found their songs almost as invigorating
and amazing as Anne had described to him once in London, but
today, October 20, after a night spent with Couper's friend
Thomas Spalding and his family on Sapelo Island, he expected
finally to see Anne herself. There was room in his mind for little
else.

The large, wooden plantation boat, with its polished brass trim,
eased in toward the dock, close enough now so that Willy could see
that the tall, white-shirted, wide-shouldered man waving both
arms over his head was John Fraser. Without Anne. The Cannon's
Point dock, as large and well-constructed as was Spalding's on
Sapelo Island, looked crowded with people. Only two, besides

John, were white. One, a girl about fourteen or fifteen, the other younger, with curly red hair. Everyone, including the white girls, sang lustily—in welcome, he supposed.

"They're giving you a rousing welcome, Lord Herries," Couper said happily, his face showing pride in the vigor of the greeting and the impressive panorama before them as the boat reached the dock below Couper's fine, three-storied home. The white frame house was not at all pretentious, but large, comfortable, its grounds elegantly planted, and certainly it commanded a spectacular view of river, marsh, and sea.

"I was sure the tribute was for you and Cousin Rebecca," Willy said after his first long look at the spot Anne loved with all her heart. Cannon's Point Plantation was her birthplace—on her enchanted Island, where great live oaks festooned with thick, gray moss stood among so many varieties of other trees and shrubs that he would surely be forced, by Couper's obvious pride in them, to examine every tree, every plant and evergreen. Along the river, springtime and summer must bring a veritable wave of fragrance, because he could see what had to be an enormous grove of orange trees. Vaguely he remembered that John had told him of the breathtaking fragrance experienced when he and his British Royal Marine comrades had captured Cannon's Point during the late war with America.

For a minute or so there was no chance for more talk while the handsome, heavily muscled slave, curiously called June, looped a heavy rope around a piling to secure the *Lady Love* to the wharf. He appeared to be in charge of the other workers. The singing had turned into a veritable din of clapping and shouts of gladness that the travelers had arrived safely.

When Willy saw the two white girls grab John's hands, he knew they were Anne's daughters. Annie, the older, had been born in London. He had seen her as a child. The younger one was Rebecca, named for Anne's mother, of course, and so far as he could tell from the boat, a feisty one. Unable merely to stand and wave as the others were doing, she was swinging on her father's hand and jumping up and down. Annie was waving joyously, but being older and much more sedate, she showed a kind of dignity that better suited the ladylike nature of his kind, gracious cousin, Rebecca Couper. But her name was Annie. . . . Anne, *Anne.*

Where was she?

In little more than six weeks, she would be giving birth again. Was she ill? Was she for any reason unable to meet him even at her father's place?

"I know you're wondering about my daughter Anne," John Couper said, moving to stand next to Willy in the bow of the boat. "Dr. Tunno, our good friend, who's tending her, has forbidden horseback riding. Any one of my people would gladly have driven her here in my carriage, but it is almost three miles over a rough sand road. She's supposed to stay at home, but it could just be that she's waiting up at the house for us to greet her. One thing sure, the girl is waiting with bated breath to see her cousin, Willy Maxwell!"

He also would wait, through thanking the slaves for their welcome song, through greeting John Fraser and his two girls. He would wait. Willy Maxwell had done nothing but wait since the first moment he laid eyes on Anne.

AFTER JOHN HAD SHAKEN HANDS WITH WILLY AND given him a hearty hug, he explained briefly that their guest would see his wife soon enough and in a special way Anne herself had carefully planned. "Does that amuse you, Willy?" John asked with his sunny smile. "I must say you look both amused and pleased. Don't worry. Anne hasn't changed a bit. Oh, she's not her usual lithe, slim-waisted self these days. It takes her a while to rise from a chair. But she's still Anne. She still adores her cousin, Willy Maxwell, and she's greeting you in her own charming fashion."

"Where will this take place?" Willy asked, walking beside John up the winding Cannon's Point river path toward the Big House. "Here? Or do we make the three-mile ride to your own plantation?"

"It's going to take place right up there in Grandpapa's house!" the younger, noisier of the two girls shouted, running to catch up and grab Willy's hand in hers as they all swung along. "Mama's too excited about seeing you, Cousin Willy Lord Herries, to wait till we could all get to our house at Lawrence. Eve drove us here in Papa's buggy. Are you excited to be here?"

Smiling down at her, holding tight to her small hand, Willy said, "Don't I look excited, Rebecca? Your name is Rebecca, isn't it?"

"Well yes, it is. But everybody calls me Pete."

"Pete?"

"That's right," John laughed. "And after you've known her a while, you'll understand why." Turning to motion for Annie, John called, "Come on and walk with the three of us, darling. You've been itching to see someone from London; now here's one of London's best come to visit us."

"I am glad to see you, Cousin Willy," Annie said, joining them. When Willy took her hand, too, she said with great sincerity, "It has been a very long time since I saw you last, but I find you still quite pleasant and easy as I did when I was a small child in our blessed London."

For the first time John let go with his contagious laughter. "If you don't feel welcome after a proper British speech like that, Lord Herries, you're dead. Plainly, you're quite alive and, I may say, looking fit, sir. It's awfully good to see you again."

"My mama is acting just plain silly about seeing you," Pete yelled up at Willy. "We're having a new baby. We had one last year too. Her name is Fanny. She's named for my Aunt Frances Anne Wylly Fraser. Aunt Frances is married to Papa's brother, Uncle William."

"Is that so?" Willy asked.

"Uncle William and I are good friends besides being kin. He's a doctor in Darien, Georgia."

When the dignified Couper butler, Johnson, came beaming out of the big Cannon's Point front door, John introduced their guest and instructed Johnson to see to having Lord Herries's luggage sent to his room.

"You'll be staying here at Cannon's Point, Willy. Our cottage at Lawrence is so small, it would smother you."

"I see."

"You don't sound glad to be staying here," Pete said to Willy.

"Not so, Pete. Anyone would be glad to stay in such a welcoming place."

John saw Pete eye Willy closely, a habit she'd developed only recently. An annoying habit, her father sometimes thought, but also amusing, since almost everything Pete did made him smile. "Why are you studying Lord Herries so intently, Pete?"

The child shrugged. "I don't know. He just doesn't seem too excited about not going home with us. It's Mama's idea for you to stay here, Cousin Willy Maxwell Lord Herries," Pete announced.

"Whatever your mother says is fine," Willy said, adding, "Do you like calling me by such a long name, Pete?"

"It's what your name is, isn't it?"

"Well, yes, but my friends call me just plain Willy. You could at least try Cousin Willy, couldn't you?"

"John? John, are you out there? Is dear Willy with you?"

It was Anne calling from behind the closed doors of the parlor. John winked at Willy and called back, "Now let me see, my dear. Wait just a minute and I'll look around. I think I saw your illustrious cousin somewhere nearby."

"Should you tease her at a time like this, John?"

"That's right. You don't tease much, do you, Lord Herries?" John joked. "Well, at our house we do, so you may as well accept that."

"Mama got us all up at dawn today so we could be here at Grandpapa's house and so she could have the parlor all decorated by the time you got here, Cousin Willy," Annie said. "Our mother has talked of almost nothing else since the day she received your letter. You see, her delicate condition prevents her from riding horseback or doing much of anything but arranging flowers and leaves and—" The girl's hand flew to her mouth. "I don't think I was supposed to say that, Papa," she whispered.

"Probably not, Annie, but the moment is so close, I'm sure it's perfectly all right," John said. "You see, Willy, my wife wanted her parents' house to be beautiful for you when first you glimpse her in its setting. Actually, what she's done is work out as fine a stage setting as your friends the Kembles ever thought of. The star, of course, will be Anne herself."

"Yes," Willy said, forcing a smile. "And so she should be."

From behind the closed sliding doors of the Cannon's Point parlor, Anne called again, "Stop that, John! I can hear your voices but not what you're saying and that isn't fair! Open the doors and bring Willy in where I can look at him."

"I'm only waiting for my cue," John called back. "I haven't heard it yet."

"Who's in there with her?" Willy whispered to John.

"Not her little dog, Lovey. He's carefully fastened up in the kitchen. A friend is with her," John replied. "Her best friend, I sometimes think. You remember the servant Anne missed so desperately in London?"

"Eve?"

"Anne will be very pleased that you've remembered her name! Eve's been helping her gather all the decorations—fall flowers and smilax vines and magnolia leaves with their scarlet pods, sumac and hickory that have begun to turn color. Wait and see. Those two women have truly created an autumn bower—a masterpiece!"

"John," Willy said with uncharacteristic impatience, "what *is* the cue Anne's supposed to give you?"

"She's supposed to shout 'Caerlaverock!' " Pete said in a loud whisper.

Raising his voice so he could be heard through the heavy sliding doors, John called, "I'm waiting to hear my cue, Anne!"

For a few seconds they all stood in the hall, even Pete listening for the magic word. Finally they heard Anne say in a distressed voice, "Oh dear! Eve, what am I supposed to say? I feel so silly, but I'm too excited to remember the cue!"

"Caerlaverock!" Pete shouted.

"Thank you, Pete," Anne called from the parlor. "You heard the cue, John. Stop playing games!" When the doors remained closed, they all heard Anne's disgusted sigh and then her voice, muffled with laughter: "All right. *Caerlaverock!*"

WHEN THE THICK DOORS SLID OPEN, WILLY STOOD staring into the large, tastefully furnished room. Stood motionless, still in the entrance hall, until first Pete, then Annie, then John began to applaud loudly. He had dreamed that Anne would meet him in Savannah, so that even on a public wharf he could at least hold her hand briefly, bow over it, perhaps kiss it.

And here he stood, struck dumb by the happy noise and confusion and shouts and giggles of Anne's family—her adoring husband pulling Willy by the sleeve into the midst of more downright joy and excitement and affection than he had ever experienced in any house anywhere.

Willy had not hoped. He had never truly hoped. From the moment he'd known and recognized the depth of the love he would always feel for Anne Couper Fraser, he had—not for one instant—allowed himself to do anything but face the hopelessness of his love. How then could it be such a blow to see her again with John, with two of her three children? Why was he barely enduring such unfamiliar, devastating pain at the sight of her once-graceful body carrying still another of John's children?

Anne had obviously arranged herself in a comfortable chair, beneath garlands of autumn leaves and yellow chrysanthemums, all prepared for her first glimpse again of Willy. For his first glimpse, after all these years, of her. She hadn't changed. At least her face and nature held the same bright attraction for him. Anne herself still reached to the very deepest part of his being. Perhaps he could train himself to ignore the awkward, swollen body. Prayer did not come naturally to Willy. His innate reserve had somehow always included God, too, along with most people he met, but as best he could, he struggled now to plead for help in seeing Anne as—not ugly in her body—as he'd always seen all other women carrying unborn children.

The recurring dream of his arm about her tiny waist, the dream he'd had so often it had become almost enough to blot out the hopelessness when he awoke, must be sternly stopped. Brought to an end. Never dreamed again, because he loved her so tenderly, so eternally, how could he ever bear the sight of Anne's body turned ugly, shapeless?

John literally pushed him into the parlor. He stood there helplessly surrounded by Anne's world. For courtesy's sake, he hoped his silence seemed ungallantly long only to him. Not only had John pushed Willy into the room, he had now all but lifted Anne from her chair so that she stood beaming into Willy's face, both arms out to him. Her ease in showing affection had, to him, always been one of her most endearing charms. Was still. He had seldom entered the old Fraser house near Portman Square in London that Anne hadn't embraced him, welcomed him in her direct, childlike way. Sometimes with a light kiss on his cheek.

"Willy, oh Willy!" Anne said. "You're here! Really here!"

She was welcoming him again in that familiar way, but this time the small, frightening creature inside her caused him to feel clumsy, strange, ill at ease, when he tried to return her warm, delighted embrace.

Laughing as he spoke, John said, "Don't worry, Willy, old man. The baby isn't that fragile! Give the woman a big hug. She's waited and waited for this moment. If ever a guest should feel at home in this always welcoming house, it is, as Pete would say, Cousin Willy Maxwell Lord Herries!"

He returned her embrace. Surely his breeding, his natural sense of gentlemanly behavior, had kept anyone from noticing, but what John had just said in apparent jest about the baby she carried repulsed him. Willy had spoken not one word to her. He felt genuinely ashamed but knew the right words would come from somewhere. He would reach back into the endless years of his life, when more times than he could count, he'd said the right thing in the most difficult moments. The words would come.

"Anne," he said, just above a whisper. "It has been such a long, long time. And I've come such a long, long way for this moment."

"Across the whole Atlantic Ocean plus seventy-three water miles from Savannah!" Pete shouted, sounding proud of herself. "How many miles is the Atlantic Ocean, Cousin Willy Maxwell Lord Herries?"

Willy almost managed a laugh. "Pete, I haven't the vaguest idea how wide that ocean is. But I know I'm glad to be here and—" For the first time he noticed a brown-skinned young woman standing, straight as an English poplar, behind Anne's empty chair. "And you must be Eve," Willy said, bowing to her when he had no memory at all of ever having bowed to a servant.

"Yes, sir," Eve said.

"Come here, Eve," Anne urged, "and meet my wonderful, kind, blessed cousin, Mr. Willy Maxwell. He's heard all about you right from me. And Willy, I know you remember how dreadfully I missed Eve when John and I lived with Father Fraser in London."

"I do remember indeed," Willy said when Eve curtsied, not obsequiously but rather, he thought, like a real lady. Surely the rich-skinned creature was beautiful to look at, slim, as graceful somehow as a soaring bird, although she had merely murmured "Yes, sir," quietly, in recognition.

"You're the one who painted Mrs. Fraser's picture of a wood-pecker—the Lord God Bird—and sent it to her in London, aren't you?"

"Yes, sir. I'se the one. You see it?"

"I most certainly did and I can tell you face-to-face now that it made Anne very happy."

When the senior Coupers entered the parlor, the slightly less-ening tension eased still more and Willy felt a measure of control returning. He had not expected more than what Anne had offered —her still-loyal, affectionate friendship. But for a reason he couldn't explain, he had, despite his long discipline, today come frighteningly close to—hope.

Even as the Coupers were making him comfortable as a guest, he remembered Fanny Kemble's face and heard her arresting voice as though she were right there in the Cannon's Point parlor re-minding him that an ancient Phoenician had once said that "hope is not to be trusted."

Praying would for him undoubtedly never come easy, but within himself on this bright autumn day in Anne's parents' home, he offered some kind of thanks that he had never *truly hoped.*

CHAPTER 32

WHEN THE FRASER FAMILY SAID GOODBYE AND SET out for Lawrence on Willy's first night on St. Simons, Anne made him promise to dine with her in her own cottage tomorrow. Of course he agreed gladly.

"Our house isn't as big as Cannon's Point," Pete informed him as the family was about to drive off in the Couper carriage, John leading the way on his own mount, Ginger, "but you'll have a lot of fun with us, Cousin Willy Maxwell Lord Herries. So get ready."

"My Mina's a fine cook," Anne said from the carriage seat where she, her two older daughters, and her servant Eve, with baby Fanny, would ride, "and I'm not going to apologize ahead of time because she isn't as superior as Papa's Sans Foix. You will just have to adjust your elegant taste." For the first time Willy had the chance to kiss her hand in farewell. "Oh thank you, sir," she said playfully, and then the huge, black slave called Big Boy drove them away.

Mr. and Mrs. Couper had not come out to the carriage because of the late hour, and Willy was a bit relieved. He had never in the finest country houses of England been more royally entertained, but he was grateful for the minutes alone as he walked slowly back up the path to the Cannon's Point house in the gathering darkness. Over the years, because he'd never felt really at home anywhere, Willy had learned to acclimate quickly to strange beds, new faces, new servants, vastly differing foods. True, he had never tasted an entrée more succulent than the obviously celebratory turkey Couper's Sans Foix had fashioned for dinner that afternoon—a whole bird, which looked untouched except by mouth-watering seasonings, although it was completely boned.

"Sans Foix permits no one to watch him as he performs his magic in boning the entire fowl," Couper had explained proudly. "The mon works under a clean tablecloth. Even his kitchen helpers never see how the trick's done."

Willy had liked Sans Foix, as well as his culinary expertise. A free person of color, not a slave, he had worked first for Couper's friend Spalding on Sapelo Island upon his arrival in America from Santo Domingo. Evidently Mr. Couper paid him in some fashion for having made dining at Cannon's Point a social event to be coveted by both famous and not-so-famous guests visiting the spacious house. Just as Willy reached the front veranda, he wondered how surprised Fanny Kemble might be to learn that at least one of Anne's father's servants was not a slave, did not belong to him as property.

I must inquire about Couper's butler, Johnson, Willy thought as he mounted the front steps. Johnson's manner when he served dinner held no hint of that expected by most people at home in England from a slave. Nor, for that matter, had Anne's Eve appeared at all cowed. Far from it, in fact. Protective of Anne, surely, but not in any way overtly submissive.

When he reached the wide front door, Couper was waiting. "My lovely wife, your cousin, begs your forgiveness for not being here to bid you goodnight," Couper said affably. "There was absolutely no need for it, but she insisted on inspecting your room upstairs after Eve prepared it for you."

"Eve?" Willy asked. "Anne's Eve prepared my room?"

"Nothing would do Anne but that Eve saw to everything for your comfort, Lord Herries."

Pleased, Willy felt easy enough to ask, "I may sound a bit stupid—I am on such matters—but does Eve belong to you or to Anne and John?"

Couper laughed almost merrily. "To Anne. Legally to John as well, of course, but Anne and Eve are forever inseparable. I assumed you knew that. There's only a year between them in age. A year younger, Eve has looked after Anne's every need since they were children. It was not only my pleasure but my duty to give Eve and her fine husband, June, along with some others among my people, to Anne and John as a wedding gift." Still smiling, Couper added, "There were times during the years Anne lived in England when my wife and I actually worried about Eve. She missed Anne so much, Rebecca was afraid the girl might become ill. That was when she began to encourage Eve to paint her pictures."

"And does she still paint?"

"Not much. She's far too occupied now with caring for Anne and her children. Even Anne, devoted as she's always been to Eve, was afraid the girl was not of a particularly motherly nature. Certainly no midwife, but she's turned out fine as a nurse. After all, the children *are* Anne's. For Eve, that's more than enough."

After a polite refusal of another dollop of Couper's splendid brandy, pleading fatigue, Willy bid his host goodnight and, carrying a lighted candle, started up the wide Cannon's Point stair. About halfway, he turned back. "I say, Mr. Couper, it's good to be here and somehow I don't feel you'll mind too much if, during my visit, I ask an untoward number of questions about life on a coastal cotton plantation. Am I correct?"

"Our lives are an open book," Couper said, his voice still jovial. "Ask away, lad. Oh, excuse me—Lord Herries."

"I'd be even more comfortable if you called me Willy, sir."

"Are you sure? Someone may have slipped my mind, but I'm fairly certain that you're the first titled guest at Cannon's Point, and I was rather enjoying calling you Lord Herries."

On that pleasant exchange, Willy proceeded up the stair and into the room selected for him by his cousin, Rebecca. After such a day of talk and laughter and so much excitement, it was restful to be alone again. For years Anne had invariably seemed nearer when he entered any room alone.

WHEN WILLY AWOKE THE NEXT MORNING, HE LIS-tened and listened for the birdsong Anne told him had wakened her almost every morning at Cannon's Point while she was living in her father's house. Only what he guessed to be a wren could be heard above sounds of the busy day already begun on St. Simons Island. The wren call had not wakened him, though. Rather, a veritable blast from what must be an enormous conch shell rousing the slaves, he supposed, so that they could assemble for the long walk to John Couper's cotton fields, had disturbed the best night's sleep he'd known since he left the familiar noise of New York's city streets. The rumble and rattle of carts and the shouts of vendors in London had kept Anne awake, she'd told him; had prevented her sleeping because she was so accustomed to the underlying silence of river and Island marsh and planted fields and stands of woods. Early-morning plantation noises were spaced farther apart, were certainly more abrupt, more oddly assorted—the shrill and spasmodic shouts of black men and women, snatches of song. Dogs barked in cities, too, but he seldom noticed. He noticed today. The barks were bays by hounds hunting hounds, he hoped, because riding to hounds was the only sport he truly enjoyed.

Bursts of genuine-sounding laughter floated up to the large, well-furnished, spotlessly clean room Rebecca had said would be his anytime he could visit. He'd heard that Negroes laugh often. The thought made Willy smile, still lying in the soft linen sheets under a light cover that had held his body warmth through the night hours. He smiled sardonically because he tried to imagine Fanny Kemble's comment on the subject of a slave's laughter. "A lord of the lash" she had said Anne's father would be called at the North in the United States. Certainly in England. Of course Willy had heard slave masters called that. Watching people respond to one another had always been one of his favorite pastimes. Today he was struck with the amusing, unpredictable potential of watching Fanny Kemble dine in the warm, genteel company of the Coupers and the Frasers in the elegant Cannon's Point dining room. Would she and old John Couper strike sparks off each other? Would Willy's usually reserved, ladylike cousin, Rebecca Couper, remain reserved if Fanny overlooked her manners and made one of her impromptu, sharp-edged speeches about the evils of slavery? Anne had been captivated by the eight-year-old Fanny that long-ago night when Willy had escorted her and John to *Lady Macbeth* at Covent Garden theater, managed by Fanny's father, Charles. But how would Anne take to the adult, highly opinionated Fanny?

He would never know, of course, so why waste another minute of what must be a perfect Island day by lying there wondering?

A light knock on his bedroom door surprised him. How could anyone in the house—host, hostess, or servant—possibly know that he was already awake? Pulling on his robe, he crossed the room and asked through the still-closed door, "What is it, please?"

From the hallway came a soft, low man's voice, speaking more from consideration than deference. "Hot water, sir. And to axe what yo might lak to eat for you' breakfas'."

"Oh, thank you so much," Willy said, opening the door to a tall, familiar-appearing, muscular Negro man carrying a pail of steaming water and a stack of fresh towels.

"Come in, please."

There was no deferential bow, only the merest nod of the rather handsome wooly head and the statement: "Miss Anne, she make me come ober from Law'rnce to see to you, sir. To bring hot water first, den whateber you wants to eat."

Now Willy recognized the tall Negro. He was the head oarsman, ordering the others and steering the *Lady Love* when he and the Coupers reached Cannon's Point from Sapelo Island yesterday. "Weren't you in the plantation boat with us from Sapelo?" he asked.

"Yes, sir. But I b'longs to Mausa Fraser. My wife Eve, she b'long to Miss Anne."

"You're Eve's husband?"

The big man spoke as he arranged the towels beside a bowl into which he poured the hot water. "I be proud to say Eve be my wife," he said, squaring his already square shoulders, a smile playing at the corners of his full mouth.

"And you rode all the way over here because Miss Anne ordered you to bring hot water to me personally?"

The man chuckled a little. "No, sir. Miss Anne she don't order me. She jus' happen to tell Eve she wish I could take care ob you. Eve she done the orderin'. Eve good at orderin' eberbody."

"I see."

"You care to hab ham an' eggs an' biscuits an' coffee? You want corncakes an' surrup? What you care to hab, sir? Miss Anne she tell Eve she want you to hab zactly what you wants. She say maybe you eben want a cup ob tea stead ob coffee, sir."

Willy could only laugh. "Miss Anne said all that, eh?"

"Yes, sir."

"Tell her when you ride back to Lawrence that I asked to be surprised, then bring whatever is already prepared. Or, I can certainly bathe, dress, and come downstairs to eat."

"Oh no, sir. Miss Anne, she don' want you 'sturbed so early." The man chuckled again, totally at ease. "I learn to do zactly what Eve an' Miss Anne tell me. The easy way."

"I see."

"I b'lieve you does see, sir."

"I'm trying very hard to—get into the rhythm of plantation life. Uh—I don't believe I remember your name. Oh but I do! You're June, aren't you?"

"Yes, *sir*. I speak only Ebo the day I come here. Quicker'n any ob de others, I begin to talk English. Month of June. I name mysef June."

"Ebo?"

"A boatload of Ebos git to S'n Simons almos' dark one night many a year ago. Twelve ob my people jump overboard an' kill theirselves. I jus' a young boy back den. No better sense den to lib on."

Willy had tried hard not to conduct himself as a total stranger, but this so stunned him, he knew his face showed the shock of realization that evidently, rather than to be bound into slavery, some of this man's people—stolen with him from his native Africa—had committed suicide. "I—I don't know what to say, June. You—you appear to be rather contented now. Are you sorry you lived?"

Now Ebo June really laughed. "No, sir. Eberthing be worth lovin' my Eve."

"I see."

At the door, ready to leave, June turned back. "You—you by yosef in de worl', sir?"

"Uh—yes. Yes, I'm quite alone. But since I have many, many friends all over the world, I don't really mind."

"That be good you don' mind."

Did June really think it was good that he, Willy Maxwell, enjoyed being alone? June's manner was certainly not impudent. But how could a servant honestly care one way or another?

Instinct told Willy he'd already conversed too freely, so he dismissed the slave and began his morning bath, feeling almost eager to discover just what his surprise breakfast might consist of. If Couper's chef, Sans Foix, had a hand in it, the food would be fit for the gods.

Anyway, Anne herself had insisted that he be given special treatment, and even the thought of Eve amused and rather delighted him. Last night he'd decided to stay no longer than one week at the most. Now he wondered.

Was his mind being changed for him? Or *was* there a kind of magic in the very air of Anne's enchanted Island?

CHAPTER 33

FOR NEARLY TWO INDESCRIBABLE WEEKS, WILLY
Maxwell lived in her world. The daily rides from Cannon's Point
to Lawrence, from Cannon's Point to Christ Church, were, each
one, singular. Astride Anne's jet black mount, Gentleman, which
she insisted Willy think of as his own during his time on St.
Simons, he absorbed the beauty, the mystique, the nearly primitive,
stirring wildness of her Island. His fifty-six years of life had been
spent roaming the civilized world—dining with nobility and
would-be upper-crust people of wealth and near wealth—but he
had never encountered as varied a collection of humanity as Anne's
servants and neighbors. Nor had he found beauty anywhere on any
continent to equal one certain stretch of sun- and shadow-shot
road between the Big House where she was born and the modest,
cheerful, but plain little cottage where she reigned now among her
children and her servants, never hiding the sheer joy she felt in
being loved by John Fraser.

Had he been with certain people from his own society, he

would have found it possible to laugh at himself for allowing his life to revolve around such a hopeless love. Anne had never given him the slightest inkling that her life didn't revolve around John. His foolish heart had led him into a tangled but somehow golden web with no beginning and no end.

He would love Anne Couper Fraser until he died.

And no one on the face of God's earth knew of his love but Fanny Kemble. Knowing her as he surely did meant that she would hold his secret even after he was no longer alive to endure the pain or the joy. Both pain and joy permeated these precious days, each of which promised at least a word with Anne, a sight of her. A part of him—the cultivated, worldly-wise part of his nature —wanted to flee her presence, to get as far away as possible. Another part of his mind and all of his heart dreaded the passage of every moment. One day soon he would again climb into John Couper's plantation boat and tell Anne goodbye forever.

Better for him, he knew. Especially when he realized, with a start, that in every new face of every Island neighbor he met, he found himself searching for someone whom he could trust with his bright-dark secret. There had been no one. There would be no one. For an instant he had thought perhaps that the pretty young wife of Anne's illustrious brother, absent in Alabama on business during Willy's visit, might understand. He had met Caroline Wylly Couper when her parents, Captain and Mrs. Alexander Wylly, entertained for him at dinner during his first week on St. Simons. The extraordinarily attractive, dark-haired young lady had struck him as being highly good-humored, perceptive, even witty. The risk involved in his deep need to tell someone nearby how hopelessly he loved Anne had stopped him, and he knew the next moment that he had been wise. When Caroline had begun to talk at table in the Wyllys' somewhat shabby but tasteful dining room about her own excitement that a new calf had been born at her husband's plantation, called Hopeton, he knew Caroline Couper's life had been even more provincial, more circumspect, than Anne's. At least Anne had lived abroad for almost a decade.

There had been one Wylly daughter who he'd felt might understand, and that was young Heriot Wylly, who seemed as much a misfit at her own parents' table as did Willy. That Heriot not only would understand a hopeless love, but would probably not even think it unusual, he had little doubt. Then he'd heard her own mother tell Rebecca Couper a few minutes later that Heriot was acting more strangely every day. That she had taken to sleeping beside her spectacular flower beds on rainy nights as well as in good weather. Heriot was interesting but evidently not quite right in her mind.

As he was making polite conversation about the current training of young Victoria to become England's queen, with the Anglophile Wyllys, who hung almost pathetically on his every word, Willy's eyes accidentally met John Fraser's. In that revealing instant he was sure John knew!

Oddly, the unexpected conviction did not frighten him. He had given almost no thought, beyond the time in London that John had tried to borrow money from him, to whether the man was trustworthy. He had simply liked him and felt at ease with him. The fleeting look had exposed what Willy suspected was the truth, but not one more word would pass between the two. Willy would see to that.

Of course John knew. How long he had known seemed not to matter. Willy had learned to accept the inevitable, and any man who loved Anne, as both did, would eventually know.

They would both love her forever.

Later when, because of Anne's condition, Caroline Couper played the rickety old Wylly pianoforte, John even sang an old, old tune that left no doubt in Willy's mind whatever. He had heard John Fraser's excellent singing voice before, but never had it torn at his heart as when John sang:

> *"There is a lady sweet and kind,*
> *Was never face so pleased my mind;*
> *I did but see her passing by,*
> *And yet I love her till I die."*

Back in his room at Cannon's Point, in the waking moments while he lay in the comfortable bed, he could still hear John's voice declaring that he too would love her until he died. In a way Willy would never try to understand, John's song comforted him.

EXCEPT DURING HIS MANY VISITS TO WALTER Scott's Abbotsford, Willy had seldom paid much attention to sunrises. Normally, he retired late and slept late each morning. The room he occupied at Cannon's Point overlooked the Hampton River, though, and beyond it acres of marshland stretched toward the Atlantic, above which each morning's sky hung like a celestial canvas with the kind of light-filled, multicolored beauty no artist's brush could ever have captured.

Everyone retired early on St. Simons. So, of course, did he, and opening his eyes to each day's new and surprising glory came to be a time deep with meaning. Each dawn with its vast expanses of color—shell pink blending to gold overlaying the new, blue day waiting to be born—brought responses within him so strange, so foreign, and yet in some way he felt as though he had at last found his own native air. For the past several mornings, once he'd discovered Anne's sunrise, to which she had opened her eyes daily as a child, he'd sprung from his bed eagerly to find what new wonder the sky held. Was this akin to a feeling of true worship? Or had he only fallen victim to the magic of her descriptions and lyrical praises of this unusual strip of sandy land called St. Simons Island?

Or was the sight that caused him to think of worship merely because he knew she was waking, too, scarcely three miles away, to the same unearthly wonder?

How he longed for at least one more span of time alone with her, minus her attractive children, minus John, minus her parents, minus the mounting numbers of planter neighbors he'd been forced to meet and with whom he squandered the fleeting hours. On his first full day on the Island, he and Anne had walked carefully—Willy watching her every slow, faltering step—down her pinestraw path to the modest Fraser dock above little Lawrence Creek. Back on that first day she had, as usual, done most of the talking. Should he be blessed enough to find one more time to be alone with her, she would again talk to him, because he dared not trust himself to spoil her paradise. Spoil it? For Anne, knowing that he loved her as a man loves a woman not only would be beyond her imagination but would damage everything sweet they had ever shared.

Still, the days were flying past, no matter how tedious the evenings of Island hospitality. His boat would sail from Savannah in five days. There remained only three during which he could breathe the same air with her, see the same sunrises. Three more chances to look at her dear face, to hear her voice. Accustomed by now to disciplining himself, he had made a point of learning to look mainly at Anne's face and at the way she carried her head, to study her expressions, for remembering. The sight of her clumsy, distended body still repulsed him. There would be ample time later to decide why. Silly thought. He already knew. She would have been all grace and beauty had the child within her been his.

At least I can admit that, he thought. And marvel of marvels, I don't resent John Fraser!

Watching the sunrise change from deep rose to ashen rose when a mauve cloud stretched briefly over it before the great fireball itself began to move higher in the sky, he laughed dryly to himself—at himself. It was not a mystery that he felt no envy, no jealousy, no ill will for John Fraser.

I would despise the man because she loves him if I could, he admitted to himself, shut away in his own dawn confessional. I don't even want the man to stub his toe because Anne would worry, so how could I resent him? I love her too much . . . I love her far too much. I love her the way I am now convinced John loves her.

"Is that really true, Willy Maxwell?" he softly asked himself. "Yes. Yes, it's altogether—true."

HAPPILY, WILLY HAD ACCEPTED ANNE'S OFFER OF Gentleman to ride from Cannon's Point to Lawrence every day. Astride Gentleman now, after breakfast with the Coupers, he slowed the sleek black horse to a trot, struck again with the sheer beauty of the light and shadows streaking the narrow, sandy road. In London she had told him at length about the singular St. Simons light. Anne had not exaggerated, he now knew, and today, with only two more chances to make the ride, he was in no hurry to move out of the bright-darkness of the woods' shadows into the sunlight that usually bathed her simple cottage.

She would be surrounded by her family anyway, since they had set the day aside to take Willy all the way to the southwestern part of St. Simons to show him the much larger and, for Anne's sake, he hoped, much finer plantation house where the Frasers would live once John was in full charge of her brother's fertile Hamilton place. He had left Cannon's Point more than an hour earlier today because Anne's delicate condition would force them to make the slower journey in the Couper carriage, which Big Boy had driven to Lawrence yesterday.

From an easy trot, Willy halted Gentleman so that he might imprint the almost mystical beauty around him forever in his memory. A squirrel, cheeks bulging with wild nuts, scampered halfway up a gum tree and sat peering down at him, tail flicking in one single, white shaft of sunlight. "Take care of her after I'm gone, little creature," Willy said aloud to the squirrel. "I envy your being able to stay here."

The squirrel scampered up the tree and out of sight, and just as Willy looked off in the direction of Jones Creek, which separated Cannon's Point and Lawrence from a nearby plantation called Hampton, a great blue heron soared up out of the creek bed. At that very moment, frantic screams broke across the wild silence, shattering the spell.

Frozen by the threatening cries and the unmistakable whistle of a thrashing whip, he sat Gentleman in a kind of empty terror. "Lords of the lash," he heard Fanny Kemble's cultivated voice and felt his body break into a cold sweat. Where he had stopped—halfway between Cannon's Point and Lawrence—it was hard for a stranger to tell the exact direction from which the cries and lashes came.

"Not Cannon's Point," he said aloud, reassuring himself because Anne had told him long ago in London that her father allowed no whippings.

"Not Lawrence! Surely, those cries can't be coming from Lawrence. John Fraser is the master there."

Were the tormented cries those of a woman? A woman or a young boy whose voice had not yet changed?

The horror of what he was hearing forced him to prod Gentleman to a gallop, and as hard as he could ride, Willy Maxwell took himself away from the unbearable ugliness.

WITHIN SIGHT OF THE LOW, SHARPLY PEAKED ROOF-line of Anne's cottage, he pulled on the reins to slow Gentleman so that he might regain a measure of control over his flailing emotions. Hearing Fanny Kemble remind him that Georgia coastal planters were often called lords of the lash was one thing. To have heard the agonized screams of a slave actually being beaten—bare back lacerated, bleeding from the stinging whip—was quite another. If only he could ask Anne face-to-face. If only he could ask *someone.* Painfully, he needed to be assured this very minute that the whipping was not taking place at either Lawrence or Cannon's Point!

The cries had changed. They were more distant now that he'd ridden a quarter of a mile or so in what he hoped was the opposite direction. "I—I must be disoriented." He spoke aloud again, his eyes pointlessly searching the woods beside the road where he and Gentleman had once more stopped. Another fraction of a mile and the road would break free of the stand of trees, into the clearing around Anne's cottage where her flower garden grew and John's planted fields began.

I can't just sit here, he thought, because I'm probably already later than I said I'd be. I know Anne and John are eager to begin the carriage ride—over ten miles, as he recalled—down the Island to Hamilton Plantation.

Slowly he began to walk Gentleman in the direction of the Lawrence dock and the red-brown pinestraw path that led from the road to Anne's house. Once more, with no sense of why he did, Willy searched the tangle of trees and wild grapevines to his right and then to his left. "I am disoriented by what I just heard take place," he said aloud to no one, not even to Anne's beloved horse. "But it's almost as though another presence is nearby." His own voice sounded unfamiliar, harsh.

"Mornin', Mausa Maxwell," a black woman's voice had spoken from the one direction he'd neglected to look—behind him.

"Eve! I—I wasn't expecting to see you out here walking alone!"

"No, sir. I reckon you—heard."

She had come alongside Gentleman now, so that Willy could look directly down into her beautiful but distinctly pain-twisted face. "Yes. Yes, Eve, I heard. It was a whipping, wasn't it?"

"Yes, sir. Ain' but one sound ugly as that. Eberbody at Cannon's Point an' here be glad Jones Creek run between Hampton an' us. The Hampton overseer, King, don' 'low their niggers to cross Jones Creek to visit none ob us ober here lessen they be whipped. Somebody must hab tried to cross over for a little visit."

Engulfed by a wave of relief and revulsion, Willy sat for a moment trying to sort out what Eve had just told him. "I know I should have reached Lawrence half an hour ago. I'm late," he said. "Is Miss Anne up to making the long carriage ride down to Hamilton today?"

"Yes, sir," Eve said. "She be all fired up to get goin'."

Could the young woman possibly have grown accustomed to overhearing whippings? he wondered. Did Anne hear from inside her cottage? Could she still be excited over their proposed journey if she had, indeed, heard?

"Eve, you don't have to answer my question if it's impertinent, but—have you ever *seen* a whipping?"

"Yes, sir. One. Mausa Couper an' Mausa John bof 'low us to cross Jones Creek anytime. I seen one ober dere while Miss Anne, she be 'cross the ocean."

His next question was involuntary. "And—does one ever—forget the sight?"

"No, sir, I still see them long, bleedin' puffs on her bare back."

Willy stared at her. "You saw a *woman* whipped?"

"Ol' S'mantha. She dead now an' safe."

"You—saw an old woman whipped?"

"Not very old back then. Maybe fifty."

"What did she do to—be whipped?"

"Stole a poun' ob butter."

For a long moment Willy just sat his horse, unable to think of anything appropriate to say. Eve, he knew, would wait for him to speak next. Anne insisted that with her, Eve didn't always wait, but according to Anne's explanation, slaves were supposed to. Eve had begun to look out over the creek and marshes now. Suddenly he was compelled to ask, "Eve, were you ever whipped?"

She jerked her gaze back to his face and in an almost irritated voice snapped, "No, sir! I b'long to the Coupers all my days!"

"I see."

"Ain' no Couper people gets whipped. Maybe dey hab to do without now an' then effen dey steals or sasses or does somepin ain' right in Mausa Couper's eyes, but no whippin's allowed. All mausas ain' poured in de same mold, Mausa Willy Maxwell."

"Thank you with all my heart for telling me that," he said simply, then added, "But I really prefer that you *not* call me Master Willy Maxwell. Couldn't you just address me as Mr. Maxwell?"

"I kin, sir. But ain' you somepin special like a king or a prince or somepin?"

For the first time he could laugh. "Well, I do have a title. I inherited it down the Maxwell line. I'm properly Lord Herries, but this is America. And my friends call me just plain Willy Maxwell."

Without a change of expression and quite calmly, Eve said, "I couldn't call you Lord nothin', sir. They ain' but one Lord an' He be God." Then her disarming smile flashed, exposing white, perfect teeth. "I reckon I kin call you Mistah Willy, though. I be partial to you 'cause you be partial to Miss Anne. Except for June, she be my life."

Consciously he tucked that sentence into his memory for the years to come. *She be my life.* Then, with what he hoped was a casual smile, he asked, "Would I be too forward if I inquired just why you're out wandering in the woods by yourself today? Won't you be going along with us to Hamilton to look after Miss Anne?"

Eve, with the grace of a lady in a drawing room, tossed back her head and laughed. "Yes, sir, I be goin' 'long! You think I let Miss Anne go wifout me so close to her time, you bes' stir up your brain, Mistah Willy." Reaching into the pocket of her apron, she brought out a handful of green leaves. "I be out pickin' me some mint leaves. She ain' done it lately, but jus' in case Miss Anne get sick to her stomach, Eve kin brew some mint tea to help put it down."

"Splendid idea," he said. "Are you sure there will be room in the carriage for me? I can easily ride along on Gentleman."

"Co'se dey be plenty ob room! Pete, she don't take up no space. She ride up on the driver's seat wif Big Boy."

Feeling more comfortable with her now, Willy dared to ask, "Eve, would you mind telling me what it—feels like to be a slave?"

She cut her eyes from the mint leaves she was stuffing back in her pocket and gave him an almost pitying look. "Somebody else axe me that same thing once."

"Oh? And may I ask who that person was?"

"No harm. It be Mausa John's papa, poor ol' dead Papa Fraser."

"I see. I knew him quite well. And I'm not at all surprised. You see, we who live much of the time in London don't quite understand about slavery. What did you tell him?"

"The same as I tell you. It feel—like Eve!"

CHAPTER 34

FOR THE MOST PART THE CARRIAGE TRIP WAS pleasant, once John convinced Annie, who tended to get sick from riding, to change seats with him so that she did not have to ride backward.

"You're nearly sixteen now, Daughter," John said with his best smile, "and grown women have a perfect right to feel nauseous when grown men like your selfish father don't take proper care of them."

"I'm sorry, Papa," Annie said. "I know you like to sit next to Mama. I thought I'd try riding backward in the same seat with Cousin Willy today just to find out if I might have outgrown that silly childhood habit. This is much better, though. And I do thank you for changing. Will you be all right, Mama, sitting between Eve and me?"

"I'm fine," Anne said, her face proving it. "This way your father can sing to me and I can look right at him. Do you realize how long it's been since you've sung our old song to me, John?"

"I know the song you mean, Mama," seven-year-old Pete yelled down from her lofty perch beside Big Boy up on the driver's seat.

"You're too young to remember," her father said.

"I am not. Mama told me I had a splendiferous memory, and anyway, you sang it for her one night in our parlor when you both thought I'd fallen asleep."

"And what is the song, Pete?" Willy asked.

" 'Drink to Me Only with Thine Eyes,' " Pete shouted back. "I know it too! Papa taught it to me."

"Oh dear," Anne gasped, in pretended dismay. "John, you didn't. Did you?"

Before John could respond, Pete began singing, off-key as usual but at the top of her strong lungs, " 'Drink to me only with thine eyes and I will pledge with mine. Or leave a kiss within the cup and I'll not—' "

"Pete!" Anne called, laughing. "Have mercy! I think it's fine that you know our favorite love song, but if it's all right with you, I'd much prefer that your father sing it to me. Anyway, you're too young to be asking or not asking for wine!"

For much of the carriage ride, John had kept an eye on Willy. He was watching him now from the corner of his eye, since their friend was seated alongside him. Willy was laughing and showing special interest in Eve. At least he appeared to be interested in how a servant reacted to such nonsensical family play. Of course John could easily put himself in Willy's place, having once been as unaccustomed as Willy to being around slaves. Eve was having a marvelous time. Willy could see that. Anyone could see it, because the young woman adored it every time she happened to be present when John sang to Anne. After all, although poor Willy had no way of knowing it, Eve and Anne had both fallen in love with their men at about the same time back when they were girls.

"Whatsa matter, Papa?" Pete yelled back. "If I can't sing, you can and Big Boy and I don't mind how mushy you and Mama get. We're above all that!" Then she broke into gales of raucous laughter.

"Aren't we *above* all that, Big Boy?" she repeated.

Chuckling, Big Boy answered, "I speck so, Miss Pete. I do speck so."

"Sing, John," Anne begged. "For heaven's sake, sing to me!"

As Mausa John was just finishing off their song in his golden, heart-stopping voice, Eve looked hard at Mister Willy. Up to that last line, because she'd known long before Mister Willy ever reached St. Simons Island that he was hard in love with Miss Anne, Eve had made herself look off into the woods while Mausa John was singing.

No reason to make such a nice man as Mister Willy turn red in the face by looking straight at him, she thought. Every word must have been like a knife stabbing into Mister Willy's heart. But she could no longer control herself. Eve looked right at him and saw one big old shiny tear roll down his smooth cheek. Mister Willy made as if Mausa John's voice was just so beautiful, it brought tears to his eyes, but Eve knew better. She'd tried to tell Miss Anne once that she knew plain as day that Mister Willy Maxwell was sweet on Miss Anne, but of course her dearest friend didn't believe a word of what Eve had said.

When Mausa John didn't stop with one verse but went right on into another one, Eve turned her eyes back to the woods and began to pray inside herself that somehow good Mister Willy Maxwell wasn't hurting too bad.

Nothing left but to try to tell her again, Eve thought as they passed the Gould place on Frederica Road, and this time she'd find a way to make Miss Anne believe her so she could know to be more careful with Mister Willy. Even if it made her mistress mad, who cared? Miss Anne and Eve were real friends. Eve meant to stay beside her forever, for as long as they were both alive on this earth, which meant that as always, they'd make it up and be able to laugh together no matter what.

PETE, SITTING ON HER HIGH CARRIAGE PERCH, WAS the first to see Miss Mary Gould beside the road, and of course she yelled the news to the others.

Anne ordered Eve to lean out to make sure it was Mr. James Gould's daughter, Mary, and not some figment of Pete's active imagination.

"Don't you think I know Miss Mary Gould, Mama? Creepers, I've known her since I was born."

"Watch your language, Pete. Is Miss Mary alone?"

"Yes'm, she be all by herself," Eve reported, hanging out the open side of the carriage. "Sittin' on a stump out by her papa's section ob de road. Look like his people dey take good care ob his part ob Frederica Road, don't it? Nice an' smooth. Miss Mary, she see us. She standin' up now."

Ignoring Eve, Anne frowned. "John, how would Mary possibly know we might be coming down this way at this hour? She's waving for us to stop."

"I had an appointment to meet her father to give me some advice on a bit of remodeling at Hamilton," John said, his voice exaggeratedly unconcerned.

"What kind of remodeling, Papa?" Annie asked.

"What kind of remodeling?" Anne repeated.

John laughed. "Is there an echo in this carriage, Willy?"

"It would seem so," Willy said, somewhat absently, Anne thought.

"There is no echo," Anne said, "but I have a right to know what you're scheming in that inventive mind of yours."

"Me too!" Pete shouted. "What, Papa? I have a right, too."

"Of course you do, Pete. And I swear to all of you I only meant to surprise my womenfolk." Turning to Willy beside him, John explained that Mr. James Gould was a fine builder as well as a planter and had offered not long ago to advise John on some work to be done on the old Hamilton house.

"Was Mr. Gould going to ride all the way to Hamilton from

here to meet you, John?" Anne asked. "I thought he was crippled up with rheumatism."

"He is, but the offer was his, and of course I welcome it. Pull the team over to Miss Mary's side of the road, Big Boy," he ordered.

"Maybe Mary wants to ride down with us," Anne said, waving. "Hello, Mary! Isn't it a lovely fall day?"

"It surely is," Mary Gould called. "When you sit for as long as I have on a tree stump, you're thankful it isn't summer."

Mary Gould, tall, slim, her strong, rather handsome features peering up into the carriage, tried to smile. At once Anne knew something was wrong. "What is it, Mary? Will your father be able to meet us at Hamilton? I confess I just learned of the plans he and my husband made. I had no idea you'd be anywhere but right by Mr. Gould's side, riding with him if he felt up to going."

"I would have been," Mary said, her voice sounding weary and worried. With Mary, who had inherited some of her father's New England reserve although she'd been born right on St. Simons, it was sometimes difficult to tell her exact mood. "We were going to make a day of it," she went on, pushing back a stray strand of dark hair off her forehead. "The truth is, John Wylly offered to bring us in his buggy so that Papa wouldn't have to ride. John was coming too. Papa—Papa isn't even well enough for a buggy trip today. He sent me out here to explain to you."

"We're terribly disappointed, Miss Mary," John said. "I not only needed Mr. Gould's expert advice, Eve and Mina packed a huge picnic for us—more than enough to include you and your father. John Wylly too, although I didn't know John was coming."

"Well, Mary, the truth is," Anne said, showing just a touch of irritation with John, "I didn't even know you and your father were coming. Eve and I might have given the picnic a bit more care. I know John Wylly and your father both adore Mina's sponge cake. My husband seems to have been planning one of his—surprises."

"Your husband," John said, grinning, "was merely being his newly reformed, careful self, wife. There seemed no other chance for Willy to meet the Goulds since he's leaving us so soon, and I also have no intention of pulling down a wall at Hamilton until the master-builder, Mr. James Gould, tells me that the wall I want to be rid of is not a support wall."

"The house might have fallen in on us, Mama," Pete yelled. "Papa's no builder. He vows he even has trouble pounding a nail without bending it!"

"And so he does," John laughed. "Willy, I haven't taken leave of all my manners. May I present Miss Mary Gould, our fine neighbor and good friend. Miss Mary, this is a distant cousin of Anne's, Mr. Willy Maxwell, Lord of Herries."

Mary's dark eyebrows shot up. "Did you say—Lord of Herries, John?"

"It is a pleasure, Miss Mary Gould," Willy said, jumping from the carriage to bow over Mary's hand. "It's always good to meet another Islander. And I am sorry you and your father won't be able to accompany us. John Wylly too. I have met him at his parents' home at dinner, and I liked the young man very much. I hope you'll give my regards to him and, of course, to your father."

"I'll—I'll be sure to tell Papa, sir," Mary said. "As for John Wylly, I'm not at all sure when I'll see him. It would have been a real treat for me to have gone with all of you today."

Standing beside Willy and Mary on Frederica Road now, John also bowed over Mary's hand. "I'm sorry you had such a long wait, Mary. It would have been a treat for all of us having you, your father, and John with us. Unfortunately, our friend Lord Herries will be leaving soon, but we'll see that another picnic basket is packed another day with Mina's sponge cake for Mr. Gould and for John Wylly."

"Most likely John won't be with us, but I know Papa will want to spend time with you at Hamilton just as soon as he's well enough to go down. I'll tell him about the sponge cake, Anne. Are you feeling well these days?"

"Better than with any other child so close to my time," Anne said. "But Mary, is Mr. Gould ill in some way other than his rheumatism?"

"I'm not sure you could really say he's sick, Anne. The truth is, even though my dear mother's been dead for twelve years, he still misses her so much. I try. I'm not Mother, though. If he's ill, it's from loneliness—sheer loneliness."

"And do you think he may be just a bit spoiled?" Anne asked. "I've never known another daughter who so lets her life turn around a parent as you do, Mary. I'd love to spend time with you in some good woman talk. Is there a chance of it, do you suppose? Big Boy can come for you in our buggy anytime you say." Laughing lightly, Anne added, "As you can see, I'm not at my best astride a horse these days, or I'd gallop Gentleman down here to your lovely Rosemount."

"When did you name your house Rosemount, Miss Mary?" Annie asked. "It's a pretty name. Is it because you grow such beautiful roses?"

"I suppose so," Mary said. "The truth is, I didn't name it that. Mrs. Mary Abbott did. And yes, because of my roses."

"The baby isn't due until around Christmas," Anne said. "Could you come one day next week, Mary? Cousin Willy will be gone then and I'll certainly need company."

"Thank you, but you've known me long enough to be sure that everything depends on Father. I guess I'd better be getting on back to see to him. He does send his regrets, John, and hopes you'll be able to meet soon at Hamilton. There's nothing he enjoys more than talk of building just about anything."

"But Mary," John added, "can't we drive you home? Annie can climb up beside Pete and Big Boy. We've plenty of room."

"No. I'd rather walk, thank you." As Willy and John climbed back into the carriage, Mary's smile struck Anne as being the weary smile of a woman far lonelier than her father. "You see, I probably enjoy walking alone—enjoy my own thoughts—more than almost anything. It's a good thing, isn't it?"

THE CARRIAGE ROLLED ON DOWN FREDERICA ROAD, then over to Hamilton Plantation, and Eve had her very first startled sight of the beautifully planted, handsomely situated house where she and her beloved Miss Anne would be living by this time next year. Of course she'd said nothing to Miss Mary Gould, only nodding when Mary casually acknowledged her in the carriage; but now, even as overwhelmed as she felt by actually seeing Hamilton at last, so like a dream or a picture, she could not stop thinking of the sad, young Gould woman.

I won't dare mention it to Miss Anne till I'm sure she's feeling good after the new baby's here, Eve thought as Big Boy stopped the team beside the path that led to the Hamilton house—freshly painted and a lot bigger than their cottage at Lawrence—but as soon as I'm sure she won't fly all over me like a chicken, Miss Anne needs to know that her friend Miss Mary Gould is in love with Mr. John Wylly! I know she is, just the same as I know good Mister Willy Maxwell's in love with Miss Anne.

CHAPTER 35

WHILE ANNE RESTED IN THE PARLOR FROM THE long carriage ride, Willy strolled beside John about the impressive grounds of Hamilton Plantation, its people working in the outbuildings and fields, some still picking the last bolls of Sea Island cotton clinging to the productive plants. Dogs barked, a few cattle roamed an adjoining pasture, and as though a planter family already lived in the large, well-kept, comfortable Big House, there were distant saws taking down trees for firewood and a hammer ringing from an anvil in the blacksmith shop behind the rows of slave quarters.

"One would never guess that this is an unoccupied place," Willy said as they ambled toward the low bluff overlooking the Frederica River. "I'm amazed at the way it's been kept up with no one but slaves and the white overseer, Mr. Bowers, here. How long has Hamilton been without occupants in the Big House, John?"

"No whites have lived in it regularly since before Anne's brother James took himself a wife back in 1827, I believe it was.

I'm not surprised that you don't fathom this, Willy, but the Hamilton people take great pride in the place. Some served the original owner, Mr. James Hamilton, long ago. The older slaves see to it that the younger ones, who don't even remember Hamilton himself, tend these beautiful grounds. They make sure the fields remain productive, too. And the house, as you saw, is kept dusted, scrubbed, and cared for as though an entire family lived in it."

After a brief silence while the two looked out over the river and the stretching miles of salt marsh toward the mainland, Willy said, "An entire family will be living here soon again, eh?"

He thought he'd never seen a prouder, happier face than John's when the new master of Hamilton said, "You can wager all the Maxwell property in every part of Scotland and England on that, Willy! And it could be the first time in this century that a real family has occupied the old house. Hamilton, in those days, was a bachelor. Lived alone here with his people. I know that when my Royal Marines captured it back during the 1812 unpleasantness, Hamilton rattled about in the Big House by himself. He and Couper settled on St. Simons in the 1790s."

"I must say the slaves have been faithful," Willy commented as he examined a sword-sharp spike of what the natives called Spanish bayonet, hundreds of which formed a magnificent yucca border surrounding the house. "These yuccas must be spectacular when they're in full bloom."

"Hamilton is famous for that border of waxen, white blossoms," John said. "Poetry could be written about the sight from the river. I've seen it. Hamilton himself had the yuccas planted, as I understand it. Unlike my father-in-law, Couper, he came to St. Simons with plenty of money. Then, in partnership with John Couper, he vastly increased his holdings through the years before he left to live and marry in Philadelphia. I've always thought that in the beginning of that partnership Hamilton must have supplied the funds, my father-in-law the daring and the ideas, although there's no doubt they were both excellent businessmen. Their separate plantations on St. Simons have always been famous, not only for the quality of their Sea Island cotton but as principal cultural centers on the Island. Famous men from all over the world visited both places."

The two friends sat down on the grass atop the bluff and looked out over the Frederica River. Neither spoke for a time, then Willy asked, "Have you reconciled yourself to being a slave owner, John?"

John looked at him for a moment, then back out over the spectacular, peaceful vista, as though deep in thought.

After a time Willy said, "Perhaps I owe you an apology. It's really none of my affair."

"But it is. We're friends. You've been my friend—my surprisingly understanding friend—since the first walk we shared at Caerlaverock all those years ago. I—I simply don't know how to answer your question. I'm not even sure that I've accepted the fact that I am a slave owner. I know only that as nearly as a devoted husband can tell, Anne is happy. Even before she and I returned to London following that memorable visit you arranged at the late Sir Walter Scott's estate, I had made up my mind that Anne's happiness meant far more to me than anything else in life. Because of that, I began to hope that somehow I had the power within me to learn to be a successful planter, to involve myself in a totally foreign way of life. For her sake. You see, to me, the whole world would be strange and empty, even frightening, without Anne in it. Without knowing that she's fulfilled." He swept his arm about the breathtaking spot where they sat. "This is the world she loves and I love her more than my own life." He chuckled a bit sheepishly at such a tender confession. "You see, I love her so, so deeply that I die a hundred deaths each time she gives birth to another child, despite the sheer joy in each newcomer to our family."

When Willy remained silent for an unusually long time, John dared to say, "I—I somehow think you understand more than most men what I've just confided."

Slowly, almost wearily, Willy Maxwell got to his feet and stood looking out toward the distant mainland tree line. At last he looked down at John, still seated on the grass, and said in an almost hollow voice, "You're right. I do understand far more clearly than you know."

Willy was his guest. Common courtesy, friendship, sensitivity to the pain John suddenly knew his friend had carried every moment since he, Willy Maxwell, had recognized his own love for Anne, kept John silent. Once or twice the thought had crossed his mind, but he had pushed it aside, convincing himself that it was quite possible for a man and a woman to love as friends—as he'd chosen to believe of Willy and Anne in their devotion to each other. Now he knew the stark truth. Willy Maxwell, Lord Herries, had been in love with John's wife since the day they'd first met him at Caerlaverock while still on their honeymoon in Scotland!

Heart pounding, John scrambled to his feet and stood facing his friend. "Willy! Willy, you—"

Willy clamped his hand over John's mouth. "John, no! I beg you—*no*. There's no need for you to say it. Both our lives and hers could be ruined forever. No one's life needs to be ruined."

John grabbed Willy's hand and held it warmly. "You're right, friend. Words never spoken never need to be taken back—or denied, do they?"

"They do not," Willy said, his voice firm. "Nothing will change, John. I leave in two days and everything goes on as though —as though you hadn't finally guessed the truth."

John tried a smile. "I think I've known, but only since you've been here. Perhaps I've only now faced it. Still, at the same moment I faced it, Willy, I also knew that I could trust you always. Even if I should die before Anne, I will die trusting you to—watch over her."

A raucous shout from the direction of the house caused both men to turn. It was Pete racing toward them. "Mama sent me to look for you both! She's rested now and says to tell you she's waited as long as she can to give Cousin Willy Maxwell Lord Herries a tour of our big, fine, new house."

As the girl ran nearer, John smiled at Willy. "I hope you agree that my noisy, tomboy daughter arrived at exactly the right moment."

"I agree wholly. And I promise not only to look after Anne for as long as I'm alive but also to remember that Pete is my face-saving good omen!"

BECAUSE IT WAS IMPOSSIBLE TO BARGE QUIETLY through a door with Pete's holding her father's hand in one of hers and Willy's in the other, the three went banging into the wide entrance hall, Pete calling at the top of her voice for Anne.

"In the name of heaven, Pete," Anne called back from the parlor, "your sister and I are right here and neither of us is deaf! John, Willy, I'm so eager to show Cousin Willy every room in our wonderful new house. Isn't this a marvelously spacious parlor, Willy? Dear old Mr. Hamilton left the house beautifully furnished." She pointed to an empty corner. "And right over there is the perfect spot for the tall, handsome desk Father Fraser left us."

Sun streamed through the high-ceilinged, blue-draperied front windows, which faced the spectacular view of the well-planted yard, its picket fence surrounding tended flower beds and grass that rolled out and away toward the thick, spiky yucca border, now more than six feet tall. John, despite his own continuing pain for Willy, stood holding Pete's hand, beaming, his gaze taking in the elegant room with a stirring sense of pride still new to him. Another man had built this great house. Another man owned it now, but it was John himself who had earned the privilege of being its sole proprietor.

"Tell me, dear Cousin Willy," Anne bubbled, "what you think of this room, the beautiful grounds, the whole house. I'm so happy you can see it before you have to leave, because now you can picture us all here—me playing the pianoforte, John singing, the girls fiddling around, little Fanny old enough to join them before we've been here very long. I imagine you'll still be in New York or Boston or Philadelphia with the Kembles when our new baby comes as a Christmas gift to us all."

John cleared his throat noisily. "My dear Anne, do you suppose I could interrupt long enough to invite Willy for a return visit before he sails back to Europe?"

"Oh yes, Cousin Willy Maxwell Lord Herries," Pete piped.

"You have to come back after we've moved here because then you can stay right in our own house with us!"

"You can't even go, Cousin Willy, until you and I have paid Grandfather Fraser a visit up in Christ Churchyard," Annie said urgently. "You promised we'd do that. Just the two of us."

"Why can't I go too?" Pete wanted to know.

"Because you didn't know Grandfather Fraser the way Cousin Willy and I knew him. After all, we're both Londoners."

"Indeed I did promise, dear Annie," Willy said, "and I intend to keep that promise. You and I will ride over to the church first thing in the morning. But John, don't count on my coming back for a visit. I—I am a roamer of the world. But not a boy any longer. Most of my traveling will be on the Continent from now on. But yes, Anne, I'll picture all of you in this room. I'll even try to picture the new member of the family—that is, providing I receive letters from St. Simons giving me all the particulars."

"Ps-h-s-t!" Pete snorted, making the odd, scoffing sound John had noticed her using now and then of late. "You know Mama will write droves of letters just as soon as she's well from having our new baby. But I'll write too and *I'll tell you the truth!* If our new baby's all squidged up and red and ugly, I'll tell you straight out, Cousin Willy Maxwell Lord Herries!"

"Pete," Anne scolded, "where did you get that vulgar sound you just made?"

"Oh, do you mean ps-h-s-t?" Pete asked.

"That's exactly what I mean."

"Sofy does it all the time. It means something like—*nonsense.*"

"I know what it means," Anne said, "but I don't like your using it. Do you hear me?"

Pete changed the subject. "Are we going to take Cousin Willy Maxwell Lord Herries all over our house, or not?"

"We're beginning the tour this minute," Anne said, pushing her awkward body up out of the chair with John's help. "And your father is going to lead the way, not only because he's been here so often lately with your Uncle James Hamilton before he left again for Natchez, but because he's even been to the attic with the carpenters. And John, no surprises. I want you to tell me which wall it is you and Mr. Gould are tearing down."

An arm about Anne to steady her, John laughed. "I'm not even sure we can take down a wall until Mr. Gould agrees it isn't holding anything in place. But I can show you the wall right now if you insist."

"I do."

John pointed to the tiny room they were all trooping past as they made their way to the central stair. "There it is—the far end of that small room old Mr. Hamilton once used as his office, according to Papa Couper. It's too small for me to work in. If we take down the far wall and open it up into the library, it will give me breathing space, don't you agree?"

John glanced at Willy, who was watching Anne's face intently. Pushing back another wave of pity for the man, he thought, how I wish I could tell him this minute that if she doesn't care for my idea, I won't do it for the world! Then he saw Anne's smile. Instantly, Willy smiled too.

"You're a terribly smart husband, John," Anne said. "If Mr. Gould says it's all right, I think enlarging that cubicle will be a fine idea."

When they crossed the entrance hall into the dining room, John saw Willy stop to ponder one corner of the sunny, long room.

"What's on your busy mind, Willy?" he asked, as casually as possible.

"I've seldom been accused of having a particularly busy mind," Willy said rather easily, John thought, "but if I'm not mistaken, I own a magnificent, very old mahogany hutch that should fit perfectly into that corner. It's been in the Maxwell family for at least three hundred years, I'm told, and only stands gathering dust in a London warehouse. Would you accept it, John and Anne?"

"Willy, how sweet and generous of you!" Anne exclaimed. "John, may we accept it? Mama will be green with envy."

"By now, Lord Herries," John said, "you know that if my wife agrees, I do too. We all thank you. And I'll simply work the harder to be able one day to fill it with china exquisite enough for Anne."

The almost peaceful look on Willy's thin face settled John's heart considerably. Willy Maxwell was indeed the high-caliber man he'd always believed him to be. Of high caliber and exceedingly strong and unselfish.

Out by the river half an hour ago, neither man had spoken the words that would audibly expose Willy's hidden, sacred, long-held love for Anne. As far as John was concerned, it would remain Willy's secret. Within himself, he could honestly admit that his own almost calm acceptance of such a startling realization was beyond understanding. Such a realization would once have filled John with fear. Any woman would undoubtedly have been better off with a well-to-do man like Willy, who could have given her every material thing her heart could ever desire plus steady, day-to-day security from worry. John had *not* been as unaware as Anne thought, during the first years of their married life, of the deep anxiety he'd caused her.

It was a near miracle that as he stood there surrounded by his own little family and dear Willy in the house where he and Anne would soon begin to live out their days, John experienced real *peace.*

What if another man did love Anne? That man was Willy Maxwell. Trustworthy, sensitive, honorable Willy. Even now, with so much of life still ahead, some of the peace, John knew, came from the sure knowledge that as long as Willy was in the world, Anne would be cared for and safe.

PART IV

DECEMBER 1832—
AUGUST 1835

CHAPTER 36

THE LITTLE FRASER FAMILY STOOD ON THE CAN-
non's Point dock on the first day of December—a fortnight after
Willy returned to New York—waving off Anne's parents, bound
for Sapelo on the *Lady Love*. There they would board Thomas
Spalding's schooner for a holiday in the old city of Savannah.
Thomas and his wife, Sarah, would go with them to stay several
days while Anne's father and Mr. Spalding consulted with Mr.
Habersham, their factor.

As usual, twenty or so of the Cannon's Point people came to
see them off. Eve and June had ridden along with the Frasers in
John's wagon from Lawrence, not only because Eve refused to let
Anne out of her sight for long but because Papa Couper insisted
that June be the lead oarsman on the *Lady Love*.

"I think Grandmama Couper is worried that you'll have our
new baby while she's gone," Pete said as she hopped and skipped
along beside her parents back up the path toward where their
wagon stood waiting to take them home. "You can tell about

things like that, Eve. Don't you think I'm right that Grandmama Couper has her fingers crossed that she won't miss our new baby's birth?"

"Eve doesn't know when our baby's coming, Pete," John said, mussing his daughter's shiny red hair. "Rhyna's sure it won't be until Christmas, at least. Isn't that right, Eve?"

"Ol' Rhyna, she don' always know eberthing," Eve said quickly. "She jus' think she know. Ain' nobody knows 'bout Miss Anne lak Eve."

"And since this does concern me in some small way," Anne chided, "would it be too much trouble for you to tell me what Eve knows about the birth of my child? Since when did you become a midwife?"

"I ain't one, but friends, dey knows more'n midwives," Eve said, tagging along behind the family with Pete now swinging on her hand.

Anne gave Eve a big smile. "You're right, Eve. Love or loyalty or voodoo or something does tell *you* a lot of things other people don't seem to know. But I don't need voodoo to tell me how heavy your heart is because June will be gone for maybe two whole weeks."

"Can't be he'ped," Eve said. "June hab to go cause Mausa Couper don't think nobody kin do what June can do. Nobody kin!"

"June's also going to do some grafting for Mr. Spalding while he and the other oarsmen wait for your parents to reach Sapelo again," John explained to Anne.

"Grandpapa swears that no one compares with June where trees are concerned," young Annie said in her newly acquired, mature manner. "I think it's most unselfish of Grandpapa to let June go for maybe two whole weeks. How does he know his own trees won't need June's work on them?"

"And what about your unselfish father, Annie?" John asked, winking down at Anne as he steadied her on the walk back to their wagon.

"Yes, Annie," her mother teased. "After all, June belongs to your father now. He's the unselfish one in my opinion."

"He's the scared one," John said, only half teasing. "What if Mr. John Legare reaches St. Simons and finds me here alone, your expert grandfather off in Savannah, and no one to conduct him on his planned reporting tour of the Island plantations for his magazine?"

"What magazine?" Pete wanted to know.

"The *Southern Agriculturist,*" Anne said. "It's the most famous and widely read agricultural journal in the whole South, dear."

"She's too young to remember that our grandfather and Uncle James Hamilton have been writing articles for it for years," Annie said with a superior touch of scorn in her voice. "But Pete always has to get in her two cents' worth."

"That's enough, Annie. And that's enough from you, too, John," Anne said with mock sternness. "Don't let me hear one more time that *you* wouldn't be a marvelous guide for Mr. Legare should he reach the Island while Papa's away."

"She mean that, Mausa John," Eve volunteered. "After all, Miss Anne, she know you the one dat own June. Fudge! You jus' think hard if the man axe you a question you don't know. Most likely you fin' June done splain to you whatever he axe."

Now Anne winked up at John. One of their favorite jokes hinged on Eve's firm conviction that June had taught John most of what he'd learned about being a coastal planter.

"I'll remember that, Eve," John said gallantly. "And now it's time for me to lift you up onto your pallet in the wagon bed, Mrs. Fraser, for the scenic ride back to Lawrence Castle."

"Not till I climb up first," Eve ordered, "an' make sartin eberthing be all right for her."

"Eve," Anne scolded lightly, "that word is *certain,* not *sartin!* You're plenty smart enough to remember that. Some days you do so well pronouncing words and others—like today—you're just plain careless."

"Fudge," Eve grumbled, again making what to John and Anne had come to be comic use of Pete's favorite slang word.

Rhyna, the midwife, had sacrificed her own cherished good-byes to her master and mistress by staying back in the wagon to guard little Fanny, so that the Fraser family could enjoy their own waving off without a worry about the baby, soon to have her first birthday. "Baby Fanny, she be good as gold," Rhyna said when John lifted Anne up onto Eve's padded pallet in the wagon bed. "You feelin' all right, Miss Anne?"

"Fine, Rhyna, thank you. You do think my new baby will wait for Mama and Papa to return from Savannah, don't you?"

"Only the good Lord knows, Miss Anne, but Rhyna, she be knock ober wif a feather if dat baby let out one cry befo' Chris'mus. Two, tree weeks anyway. When Mausa an' Missus be back?"

"Mama vows before the end of two weeks," Anne said.

"Den you be safe. You got time, chile. Jes' take yo' ease."

THE MORNING OF DECEMBER 6 DAWNED GRAY AND rainy. A low, dense sky over the Hampton River and its marshes was layered with fog. And then the rains came. Long, steady showers that kept the people in their cabins, sewing, mending furniture and harness. John was sure Muslim Tom, the Cannon's Point work driver, would be handing out odd jobs cabin to cabin, but he also hoped that between visits from Tom, the people would do what came naturally to those who lived by the power of their arms and backs—sleep an hour longer.

John, still the master of Lawrence, could afford no such luxury, although he and Anne did spend an extra half hour together in bed, doing what she called cozying.

"I'm never more certain than when we're close that you're real, not just a marvelously beautiful dream," she murmured, pushing against his back as they lay spoon-fashion under the light covers. At least, he thought with a smile, she's as close as she can be with our child between us. "You are real, John," she said, reaching for his hand. "You are real and you're right here and you're mine. Did you know I'm yours?"

"Yes," he chuckled. "I knew, beloved Anne. Your big Lord God Bird told me late yesterday just before I started my ride home from our south field."

"I'm glad you're silly."

"Thank you. So am I. Otherwise, I'd be lost in this family."

"Don't even think of getting up yet," she whispered.

"I don't want to think of it, but something tells me we have maybe five more minutes and then I must. I'm the driver here at Lawrence, you know, milady. Not when we move to Hamilton, though. I'll have a fine driver once we're down there. Did I tell you, your father's Tom talked the old gentleman into letting him train his son, Cuffy, to be my driver?"

"I think so."

"You only think so?"

"Women have a few other thoughts besides planting when they're about to give birth to another child, sir."

He tightened his grip on her hand. "You do fool me, don't you?"

"Not intentionally. At least most of the time, not intentionally. When did I fool you lately?"

"Every other minute," he said, still sounding sleepy and cozy, his head half under the covers. "You see, I'm either the most conceited man on earth or you fool me into thinking that you share every thought I have."

"Is that bad?"

"No. It's perfect. Don't stop."

"And don't you get up!"

"I have to, Anne. Even in such a heavy rain, the man of the plantation must make the rounds of the quarters, assign indoor work for the day." He sighed.

"Why did you sigh like that?"

"For a day or two I don't give it a thought," he said, not so sleepily now, "and then I find I'm worried that the editor of that illustrious agricultural journal, the famous John Legare, will show up while your father's in Savannah. Anne, I don't think I know enough to give him all the detailed information he'll be expecting. I saw the letter he wrote Papa Couper. The man's main reason for coming all the way from South Carolina to St. Simons seemed to be for the express purpose of meeting the fabled Scotsman John Couper. I'll be a sorry substitute. Of course I could take him to

Hopeton and turn him over to your intellectually elite brother James."

"You'll do no such thing! And right now, this minute, don't move except to give me your hand." Without another word she placed his warm, strong hand over her tummy, where the baby was actively living out its final weeks of sheltered life.

"Oh Anne," John breathed. "I love you so much. There are moments when I truly marvel because you love me the way you do. . . ."

"And do you think, dear sir, that I, Anne Couper Fraser, would—could—love a 'sorry substitute'?"

He laughed softly. "I guess not. I also think our five minutes are up. June's away. I'm rather lost without him, you know. Almost as lost as you were back in London without Eve."

For a long moment Anne clung to him, not letting him bounce out into the chilly room. "John, do we depend too much on Eve and June? I wouldn't dare mention anything like this to either Mama or Papa, but sometimes I wonder a lot about that. I want you to try to tell me what you think. I know they're both wonderful servants. I get cross with Eve for being so smart-aleck, but June is as steady as a big rock. They're both always there when we need them. Eve and I, I guess, are really friends."

"You only guess?"

"She reminds me often enough!"

"That's because she's genuinely fond of you. It's also because you make her feel free enough to call you a friend."

"Free enough?"

"That's what I said."

"But Eve belongs to me—to us."

"Legally."

"What kind of an answer is that?"

"What kind of an answer did you want?" He was up on one elbow looking down at her. "Anne, are you trying to ask me if I'm a bit more comfortable being a slave owner these days?"

"I don't see anything wrong with discussing it with one's own husband!" She had flared a little and he could see she was sorry.

"Blessed Anne, this is not the time for you to concern yourself with anything like that. There's too much up ahead that's good—good for us all. Eve and June included. If I didn't think June's abilities as a planter and a botanist would be wasted training him as a driver, I'd talk to your father and to James about doing just that. But the man has so many talents. His hands on the grafted branch of a fruit tree seem to draw out growth! Not only does he know how to prepare a field; he understands seed selection, manuring, the intricacies of crop rotation, listing, bedding. I'd give almost anything if I had the funds to buy June a piece of land and make over the title to him. He would make a far more successful planter than I'll ever be!"

"You're trying to tell me you wish June were free, and I'm not sure I want to hear it," she said in a tight voice.

"What?"

"Don't say any more right now, please. Except that you'll love me with every breath you draw until you get back into this bed with me tonight."

He kissed her tenderly. Once, then again. "Anne, I will love you with every breath I draw until I get back into this bed with you tonight."

CHAPTER 37

Swathed in his battered old Royal Marine canvas rain cloak, the wide collar pulled up over his head, John strode out his front door and headed toward the dock. Rain was really coming down, but while he had been with Anne upstairs, the showers had temporarily let up and so he scanned Lawrence Creek for some sign of Big Boy, who seldom let a shower hinder his morning fishing.

John could see only light rain now on the surface of Lawrence Creek and mist so thick one could have spooned it, but no sign of Big Boy. His heavy boots splashing through puddles, he veered south on the creek path toward his blacksmith's shed. If Big Boy couldn't fish, he was often found with his friend Rollie, one of the men John had bought at the Savannah slave market. Big Boy and Rollie had surprisingly taken to each other, as Big Boy said, "like fish to watah. I'se the fish. Rollie's the watah, 'cause I swims in him. Rollie ain't dumb like Big Boy." The giant Ebo

was a touch slow, John thought as he came in sight of the blacksmith shop, its chimney spewing smoke, but certainly not
dumb.

"I come here," Big Boy said, looking up with a grin when John
stomped the sandy mud off his boots and stepped inside the shed,
"to pump de bellows fo' my frien' Rollie, Mausa John. I don' ketch
but one trout b'fore de rain po' down again."

"If fish can be caught," John said pleasantly, "we all know
you'll catch them, Big Boy. And it looks to me as though Rollie's
not only doing a fine job as my main smith now, but also that he
has an able helper. A good helper he'll hate to lose when the rain
stops."

Short, heavy-shouldered Rollie straightened from his forge,
one calloused hand holding a midweight ball peen hammer with
which he'd been flattening a heated bar of iron. "Morning, Mausa
John," Rollie said, squinting the empty socket where his eye used
to be. "Big Boy, he understan' my bellows good. An' "—Rollie
gave John a rare grin—"you done ketch us, sir. Ah hopes you don'
tell Miss Anne."

"Tell her what, Rollie? Are you making a surprise for Miss
Anne?"

"An'irons!" Big Boy announced, as though he'd just handed
John a million dollars. "Miss Anne wanta s'prise you, so we be
'bliged if you don' say nuffin to her."

"Slow down on dat bellows, Big Boy," Rollie ordered quietly.
"Too many sparks set off de dust."

Big Boy was plainly excited, pumping the big leather and wood
bellows too hard, but one word from Rollie slowed the process
immediately.

"You don' tell Miss Anne, Mausa John?" Big Boy pleaded.
"Rollie, he hear her say she want a sartin kin' ob an'irons fo' de
logs in youah fireplace down at Hamilton. Gonna hab hearts in
'em, jus' lak she want!"

"Hearts?" John asked.

Rollie finished bending what appeared to be an andiron base,
then in response, picked up a foot-long rounded iron bar and
pointed at one end shaped like a heart.

"You must have made that tool yourself, Rollie," John said admiringly.

"Yes, sir. I make it. Eve, she draw de heart."

More pleased than he managed to show, since what was really needed today from the blacksmith shop was a new set of horseshoes, John said, "Well, I'll be a son of a gun, Rollie! You did a fine piece of work on that tool." Then he laughed. "Leave it to my wife to think of having a heart design on our andirons, eh?"

Both men chuckled. "Yes, sir, Mausa John," Big Boy said. "A man kin leabe jus' 'bout anything to Miss Anne."

It was, John knew, no secret to anyone who lived and worked on Lawrence Plantation that Big Boy all but worshiped his mistress. Feeling the old dilemma of wavering between demanding out-and-out obedience from his people and his continuing desire to encourage them in any innovation they might want to try, John said, "Miss Anne thinks a lot of you too, Big Boy, and I forgot to tell you, Rollie, that she's most grateful for the new poker you made for Mina's kitchen fireplace." Both men appeared pleased. So John went on: "And speaking of Miss Anne, I know she'll like these splendid new andirons, Rollie, but—"

"You not tell her, Mausa John?"

"No indeed. That's a promise. Not one word. It's just that we have a horse in need of shoes. I was wondering if you could put aside the andirons for a time and make them today."

Rollie looked at his fire, the curved rod of iron turning red across it with the steady help of Big Boy's bellows, and said, "Yes, sir. You de boss. Me an' Big Boy, we does what you say."

Obedience was all John needed to expect. He knew that. He'd been drilled in it by both Jock Couper and James Hamilton—over and over. Never mind if the slave showed disappointment; simply expect obedience and let the matter go. Now and then, especially if John himself was in a hurry, he had found the method fairly easy. Today, although he did need to assign indoor work to the others, he'd hoped foolishly that neither man would show disappointment.

"You see," he went on, talking too much again, "there is a visitor, a Mr. John Legare, coming sometime soon to gather information about Lawrence, Cannon's Point, and the other Island plantations for his magazine, and I'll need my mount, Ginger, well-shod in case I have to take Mr. Legare around the Island. I sincerely hope Mr. Legare does not arrive before the Coupers are home from Savannah. If he does, he'll have to make the rounds with me and you both know I wouldn't be very good at explaining the fine points of planting or harvesting or ginning."

Not only had he talked too much, he had all but forced the two amenable slaves to flatter him. They both did, assuring him, their "master," that he'd do just fine without Couper.

When he'd bought Rollie in Savannah, there had been no expression at all on the dark-skinned face. There was little now, but as John trudged back toward the quarters in the rain, he could think only that both Big Boy and Rollie played their roles as slaves with far more skill than he did as slave owner.

DURING DINNER THAT DAY, JOHN LISTENED WITH A straight face while Anne cautioned him not to poke around Rollie's blacksmith shop unless Rollie was there. Probably, he thought, I kept my face too straight. I should at least have demanded to know why I could not, at any time I chose, enter my own shed.

She laid down her fork and eyed him suspiciously. "You—you didn't poke around in Rollie's shop today, did you?"

"What's in there, I wonder?" Pete asked with mock innocence. Enough feigned innocence so that John knew Pete was also in on the secret andirons meant to surprise him.

"Pete," young Annie said loftily, "you're so stupid."

"That's enough, Annie," Anne said. "I really don't care for the way you've begun to talk to your sister lately, as though she were too young to follow a normal table conversation."

"Sorry, Mama," Annie said, and as always she truly sounded sorry. Annie, John thought, was almost too docile, too sincere, to hold up her end of the kind of family teasing they all enjoyed.

Of course, maybe Anne hadn't been teasing. A big gap had opened between his daughters now that Annie was nearly sixteen, Pete seven. Thanks to Eve, who spent much of her time with them both, they did seem to get along rather well most of the time, but John wondered now and then how things might go once the new baby came. When Anne herself needed Eve, no one—neither of the older girls—could make much of a claim on Eve's time. Anne would always be first with her, and instead of trying to pretend otherwise, Eve boasted about it.

"I noticed last week that our team harness needed some patching up," John said, deliberately changing the subject. "One of our oxen had a bad sore worn on his neck for need of a new yoke. The shower came at a good time, I guess. I set about twenty people to mending various things while the rain's still coming down today."

From the far end of their fairly small dining table, Anne lifted her water glass in a toast. "To my planter husband—my experienced, expert planter husband," she proclaimed. "Do you have any idea how proud I am of you, John? The girls both know it. Even Little Fanny knows it and in no time she'll be talking well enough to tell her handsome papa how proud her mama is of all he's accomplished."

His most impish grin flashing, John said, "If I do say so, milady, I haven't done poorly. What's your studied opinion, Annie?"

"You already know I think you're more than wonderful, Papa!"

John turned to Pete, wiggling, as usual, in her chair. "And you, my dear Pete? Are you proud of your old papa?"

Applauding, Pete yelled, "Yea! You just do awful good every single day!"

"Pete, for heaven's sake," Anne scolded. "We're all sitting right here at the same table together. What does make you shout so?"

"And use such dreadful grammar!" Annie added.

"It's Mama's place or Papa's to correct my grammar," Pete said in a slightly toned-down voice. "I know I should have said that Papa does awfully well." This time Pete only mumbled, head down, into her dress collar.

At that moment Mina, looking a bit harried as always, burst into the room, a dish towel over her head because she had had to cross the backyard in the rain from her separate little kitchen to the house.

"Mina," Anne said. "Is something wrong? Your stuffed trout is delicious. We're not ready for dessert yet."

"Somebody here to see Mausa John."

"Who is it?"

"Cuffy from ober to Cannon's Point."

"Cuffy?" John asked.

"Yas, sir. He say a gent'man got to de Couper dock in a rowboat. Gent'man to see Mausa Couper, but I done tell Cuffy he know good as me dat Mausa Couper, he done be in Savannah dis week. He say he knows dat, but don' know what to do wif dis gent'man."

"Who could it be, John? Do you have any idea?" Anne asked.

His heart sinking all the way down into his house slippers, John said heavily, "Yes, Anne, I'm afraid I do know."

"Well, is there any law against telling me?"

"None. I—I just have a sick feeling it's *the* Mr. John Legare, editor of the *Southern Agriculturist*. He's due sometime soon, but your father was so certain he would be back before Legare got here."

"The editor who writes to Grandpapa Couper?" Annie asked. "The one who's coming here especially to write about planting methods on St. Simons?"

"The same, Annie dear," John said. "Mina, do I need to go back to your kitchen to talk to Cuffy? Couldn't you send him to me?"

"Co'se I kin send 'im here, Mausa John," the big woman said, pulling the dish towel more snugly over her head. "He be at de back do' jus' as soon as I kin git out dere to tell 'im."

"Cuffy almost never runs errands like this," Pete piped when Mina had gone.

"I know, darling," Anne said. "But this is—well, it is very important, isn't it, John?"

"To say the least. Do you realize that with your father away for at least another week, I'll have to ride the Island with the powerful Mr. Legare? That I'm the one he'll be depending on for enough material to write an extended article for his journal concerning the intricacies of planting on St. Simons Island? That I could be gone for three or four days?" On his feet now, feeling like a small, scared boy, he held out both hands to Anne in a helpless gesture. "How am I going to do it? I could give him wrong facts that would end up humiliating your father, to say nothing of James Hamilton, for the remainder of their lives!"

"John, sit down for a minute. Sit down so I can look right at you. It makes me dizzy to look up and talk."

"Anne, Cuffy will be knocking on our back door any minute," John said, but he did sit back down. "What will I tell Cuffy to do?"

"The courteous thing, dearest. Exactly what you'd think of to do if you were thinking like you. He should have Sans Foix and Johnson give Mr. Legare a good meal, show him to whichever room Johnson knows my parents would want him to have, and tell him you'll be at Cannon's Point to meet him first thing tomorrow morning."

"It's raining," John snapped foolishly. "How can we ride the Island in the rain? How can the important Mr. Legare handle a quill and ink in the rain to make his notes of all the wrong things I'm bound to tell him?"

"John Fraser, listen to me. My father must have had at least an inkling that the *Southern Agriculturist* editor might arrive early. He knew, as well as I know, that you will be magnificent! Papa may have wanted to give you a chance to convince yourself. Why, which gentleman planter on St. Simons Island is in demand to speak, to act as master of ceremonies, even to conduct my fussy brother's famous boat races? Which gentleman, John? What's that popular gentleman's name?"

He sighed heavily. "Oh all right, Anne. I'll be there tomorrow morning, rain or shine. Forgive me?"

"There's nothing to forgive, darling," she said gently. "It was perfectly normal for you to have been a little scared right at first."

"You're never scared of anything, Papa," Pete insisted.

"Thank you, Pete, but I am. I'm—I'm scared because I'm just not sure I've had enough experience as a planter to handle such an assignment without Grandpapa Couper beside me."

"He isn't beside you a lot of the time these days, Papa," Annie said brightly. "Grandpapa's too lame many days to ride the fields with you, and he told me that you've had to make a lot of difficult decisions by yourself out in his fields and yours and that you haven't made a single decision he wouldn't have made himself."

"About twenty or thirty minutes ago, you were asking us all if we weren't pretty proud of you, Papa," Pete chimed in, obviously not wanting her sister to encourage him a bit more than she did.

John was laughing now. Anne began to laugh too. It helped, and when Cuffy rapped on the back door of the cottage, John was ready with the message Anne had suggested—almost word for word.

CHAPTER 38

THE NEXT DAY, DECEMBER 7, DAWN BROKE ACROSS the eastern sky in radiant streamers of gold and scarlet. There would be no rain. The day should be perfect for riding wherever Mr. John Legare chose to go. John had slept little, but now, astride Ginger, galloping around the last bend in the road to Cannon's Point, he felt ready. Thanks to Anne's steady encouragement when she kissed him goodbye, he was no longer afraid of failing either her or Papa Couper during the days spent with the editor of the widely read *Southern Agriculturist*.

"I've made up my mind about one thing," he had told Anne just before he left their room an hour ago. "If Legare asks something I don't know, I'm going to be frank about it. No man could have learned all there is to learn in the few years I've been trying. At least I know everyone on our Island plantations, and if you're sure you're feeling well today, I won't worry and I'll make you proud of me." What he hoped was a confident grin had been her last sight of him in the doorway. "If I lack erudition, I'll make up for it in charm, milady. And darling, it is quite possible I could be gone three or four days, especially if I have to take Legare over to Hopeton."

Now, handing his mount to one of Couper's people, he was grateful for his knack for bluffing. The long-practiced use of charm had gotten him through many impossible predicaments. Anne did seem to feel rather well today, at least as much as a man could tell immediately after rousing her from deep sleep.

Striding toward the Cannon's Point veranda, he pictured himself sometime next year striding up the path to the veranda of the tabby Big House at Hamilton Plantation—the master of its fertile acres. The master of one of the finest places on St. Simons Island. Said by Sir Basil Hall, British naval officer and writer, who had visited James Hamilton Couper last year, to be the finest, including Cannon's Point.

Johnson opened the front door to him with a warm welcome.

"I sure am glad you got here, Mausa John," the middle-aged, light-skinned butler whispered. "Mister Legare, he so dis'pointed Mausa Couper ain' home, he in the parlor pacin' up an' down lak a caged coon."

"Legare isn't the only one disappointed, Johnson. I'm *not* John Couper in any way. But I'll do my best."

"You do fine, Mausa John. Eberbody here think you do just fine."

At the parlor window, his eyes on the beauty stretching outside toward the ocean, stood a slightly built, almost birdlike man, who turned slowly to face John, his slender hand out.

"Dis be Mausa John Fraser, sir," Johnson said in his quiet, gentlemanly way. "Mausa John, dis our houseguest, Mr. John Legare."

"Thank you, Johnson, for all I'm sure you've done to make Mr. Legare's stay pleasant so far." Clasping Legare's hand, John said, "No one is able to care for your needs more capably than Johnson. I always say he's right next to Mr. John Couper himself. Welcome to our Island, sir."

"It's good to meet you, Lieutenant Fraser," Legare said. "I'm indeed sorry to take you from your own work. You see, my transportation here was faster than I'd expected. Will it be possible for you to show me a St. Simons plantation or two today?"

"I've made it possible," John said, beaming. "In fact, after the initial surprise that I'd be the one to be interviewed by you, I find I'm delighted in all ways. If you're willing to be shown about by a mere novice, that is."

"But haven't you been planting along with Mr. Couper and his talented son for several years, Lieutenant?"

"I've certainly been trying to learn how to plant, sir. And I'm sure Mr. John Couper would want me to give you his regrets that he's in Savannah. No one was expecting you quite yet, although we've all felt highly honored that you chose to come. Even our weather has brightened. You've had breakfast, I assume." Johnson, who had slipped quietly from the room until he would be needed again, had served Legare Sans Foix's best, John knew, but he was determined to show this prominent guest every amenity.

"I've never enjoyed a better feast. I say, will you orient me a bit, Lieutenant, before we leave, please?"

Jock Couper, John felt sure, would have been quite satisfied with the agrobiological lecture he then delivered to Legare, who was not only of small physique but almost shy in manner. John expounded as well on the general geography of St. Simons, noting especially that the Island lay a few miles back from the sea and was therefore somewhat protected from most storms, except hurricanes, by marshes, high dunes, and two smaller islands.

As John elaborated on the basics he thought would interest the editor of such a well-known journal, his own confidence grew, and after Legare interrupted to ask the approximate size of St. Simons, he began to surprise himself at how much he had actually learned.

"Our Island is some twelve to fifteen miles long," he said, "and on an average, counting the interspersed stretches of salt creeks and marshland, roughly two miles wide." Warming to his subject, he dipped briefly into the Island's history, which, because he had served so long in His Majesty's Navy, especially interested John. "You see, sir, St. Simons was the southernmost general headquarters of the famous founder of the British Colony of Georgia, General James Oglethorpe, whose fortress town of Frederica lies

mostly in ruins now not far from here on the northern section of
the Island. I will gladly take you to see Fort Frederica, or Old
Town, as we Islanders now call it."

Notebook and quill in hand, Legare had seated himself at a
small desk in the Couper parlor and was taking notes rapidly. "I'd
love to see Frederica, Lieutenant, but how much can you tell me of
the history of cotton itself here?"

I must stay on the subject of agriculture, John reminded himself. "Ah, cotton," John went on. "To the best of my knowledge,
the culture of cotton began here in 1791, with Major Pierce Butler
at Hampton. He was soon followed by Mr. James Spalding, father
of Thomas Spalding, whom you probably met on Sapelo Island en
route here. Then by Mr. John Couper and his close friend and
business partner, the late Mr. James Hamilton, for whom Couper
named his brilliant son. Our cotton, as I'm sure you know, is
considered among the best, if not the best, long-staple cotton and is
now known widely as Sea Island cotton. There are fourteen plantations on St. Simons, which yield from five to six hundred bales
annually."

"And the Island's soil has to be a contributing factor to such
a fine yield," Legare said, making still another note, his bright
eyes peering up at John when he was ready for more information.

"You're correct, sir," John said. "Our soil is extremely light and
friable and appears peculiarly adapted to the culture of top-grade
cotton. According to my father-in-law, Mr. Jock Couper, the selection of seed is also of supreme importance." He cleared his throat a
bit self-consciously. "You see, one of the compliments given me by
Mr. Couper that I most cherish is that he believes I have a knack
for seed selection. The truth is, I came new and green to planting.
Spent my early life entirely in the British military, so a good word
from a man of Couper's reputation as a planter has special meaning for me."

"I'm sure it does," Legare said somewhat absently, his mind
plainly leaping ahead to his next question. "Before we ride out,
Lieutenant Fraser, perhaps an idea of the other crops grown here
aside from cotton?"

"Well, we grow corn, potatoes, the usual garden vegetables, and, of course, some sugarcane. But except for cotton, the other crops on St. Simons are mainly for the use of the various persons living on the plantations. I thought, sir, that we might take a short ride around Cannon's Point, then head down Frederica Road, the Island's main thoroughfare, to give you a more detailed look at a fertile piece of land to the southwest called Hamilton, with which I've lately grown quite familiar. Hamilton belongs to Mr. Couper's elder son."

Ready to end this portion of the interview, the intense John Legare had closed the inkwell on the desk and folded the pages on which he'd been writing. "Splendid, Lieutenant," he said, getting to his feet. "As he served me my enviable breakfast, Couper's man, Johnson, happened to mention that you and your family will be moving down to Hamilton sometime next year. That you will be in full charge. I'm not surprised that you've made yourself familiar with the work there."

"Indeed I have tried to do just that," John said, not minding that his pride in such good fortune must be showing. "You see, Mr. Legare, it took me years to reach the point where I was willing even to try to learn how to operate a Georgia coastal plantation. My experience as a boy on my parents' farm in Scotland had turned me devoutly against such work. The truth is, I loathed farming!"

"Is that so?"

Legare's laconic response left John a bit dismayed. If he was to spend the next few days in the company of this man, he vowed that somehow he'd find a way to loosen him up a bit, to extract a little more response from him. Oh, the famous editor was not un-friendly. Far from it. He merely showed no inclination toward the sociable, colorful conversation on which the gregarious John thrived.

After an apology for not inviting Legare to stop at Lawrence to meet Anne, explaining that she was soon to bear him another child, he rang for Johnson, who, John knew, would come bringing a picnic for him and Legare to share as they made their way around the Island. The servants at Cannon's Point had learned true Southern hospitality from one of the most touted hosts in Georgia, John Couper. Johnson and Sans Foix needed few instructions with a guest in the house.

"I know Mausa Couper be sorrowful to miss you, sir," Johnson apologized again, "but Sans Foix, he done fix one ob his bes' picnics for you an' Mausa John to eat on your ride today."

"I'm sure he has prepared something delicious," Legare said. "If Mr. Couper doesn't return before I leave, I will surely write him about the royal treatment I've received at the hands of his servants."

Bowing grandly, Johnson thanked him and wished them a fine day.

BY THE TIME THE TWO MEN HAD GALLOPED BRISKLY out the Couper Road over to Fort Frederica to show Legare the ruins at Old Town, John was warming still more to his responsibility as guide. After a brief visit at Old Town, they slowed the horses to a walk past the picturesque spot where Christ Church stood, tucked back under its great oak trees. Sensing that his guest's attention was focused on planting only, John merely mentioned that Jock Couper was one of the charter members of the Episcopal vestry at the little church, took great pride in it, and lived by the warmest, most authentic Christian principles.

Riding south now on Frederica Road, they neared the northern boundary of James Gould's vast holdings, and even Legare remarked how well the stretch of road bisecting the Gould land was tended.

"You know, I'm sure," John said, "that each plantation owner is liable for the care of our main Island road. Mr. James Gould is still a New Englander at heart. He's fastidious about his stretch of the road. I intend to make a point of getting to know the man better than I've had time to do so far. He's a widower, reserved by nature, and still grieving for his wife. Grieves also over his younger son, off in New Orleans, working on a riverboat after being expelled from Yale some time ago."

"The son isn't interested in working with his father on such a splendid plantation?"

"Two plantations, in fact. One called New St. Clair, the other Black Banks. I don't really know the son Horace. But from what I'm told, he turned against owning slaves during his time in the North at Yale. For that reason alone I'd like to know the young man."

There had been no point in John's even mentioning slavery, and he knew it. Quite evidently, John Legare, born in the South, took the system for granted as the only means by which a man could operate a large plantation at anything resembling a profit. John had fallen into his old habit of saying too much.

"Surely," Legare said after a long pause, "young Gould learned long ago that slaves are as integral a part of planting cotton as oxen or plows and hoes. As cotton gins themselves. By the way, Lieutenant, I'll need to know as much as possible about your ginning methods on St. Simons."

Of course John meant to tell him about ginning. Actually, once he'd spent a day or so with Legare, delving into John's own variation in seed selection, manuring procedures, quarters for the people, and Couper's belief in crop rotation, he had thought of taking their guest to visit James Gould, because his ginning methods were different from most.

John assured Legare that they'd spend the remainder of the afternoon and the night at Hamilton, where he would demonstrate the Couper ginning methods. They would later stop at New St. Clair and Black Banks. John continued, "Perhaps, sir, you'll have a chance to speak at length with Mr. Gould himself, if he's feeling well. On the way from Hamilton on the southwest end of the Island, I thought we'd also swing by the man's light tower on the far south end. It would please him that you actually saw it. You may not know that James Gould is our lighthouse builder."

"No, I don't believe I knew that," Legare said, projecting his light, tenor voice to be sure John heard. "And does Mr. Gould still have charge of the St. Simons lighthouse?"

"Indeed he does." John laughed a little. "The poor man's too crippled with rheumatism to climb the tower any longer, but he sends one of his people down from New St. Clair every day to clean the lenses, trim the light, and so on. Gould still seems justifiably proud of his tower. Building a lighthouse, according to my father-in-law, his close friend, was James Gould's dream since boyhood."

Out of the corner of his eye, John saw Legare look over at him and smile, perhaps the first spontaneous smile since they'd met. "It's—it's good when a man's dream comes true," Legare said. "I know. A dream of mine came true when I was made editor of the *Southern Agriculturist.*"

Ah-ha, John thought, feeling relief that he had finally cracked Legare's detached professionalism. Perhaps now, conversing with the man would be easier. After all, unless Papa Couper returned early, John would be in the editor's company for several days, especially since Legare had already said that he wanted to inspect James Hamilton's Hopeton over on the mainland. At least at Hopeton, James would take over the interview. There'd be no way to stop his brother-in-law, John thought, and smiled to himself because he had actually come to like the man who had intimidated him, at times even irritated him, for all those years.

Legare seemed more than agreeable, since John had concentrated of late on learning as much as possible about Hamilton Plantation, that they make it their centerpiece for his St. Simons article. With a lusty "Follow me, sir," John spurred Ginger to a gallop along a forested shortcut he'd found from the south end of Frederica Road west to the overwhelmingly beautiful spot he and Anne and their children would soon call home.

CHAPTER 39

"ELIZA, CAN YOU BELIEVE IT'S BEEN A WHOLE week since Jock and I left Cannon's Point to indulge ourselves in this totally enjoyable holiday here with you in Savannah?"

"Seems only a day or so," Eliza Mackay said. "I do wish you could visit us more often. My quiet son William is a steady comfort to me, but he's twenty-eight now and will surely marry sweet Virginia Sarah Bryan soon. With all my heart I hope so, but oh, Rebecca, I'll miss him. My girls are good company in the main. They're both old enough now for real conversation, but my dear, pray daily that Jock won't leave you anytime soon. Robert's been gone for sixteen years this past October, and there's still such a void in my life."

"If you hadn't brought it up, I wouldn't have dared ask, but does it help at all that you're the one who could bear such a loss and not Robert? For years I prayed that I'd die first, but I'm beginning to see now that leaving Jock behind would be worse. I—

I love him so much, I mustn't put him through a thing like that. Does it help that you could spare Robert such grief?"

The day was unusually warm for December, so they were having their second cup of coffee on the roomy old front porch, where Rebecca knew Eliza loved to sit alone or with guests. Rebecca put down her cup and saucer and noticed that her friend was studying her with an almost puzzled look. "Did I speak too freely, Eliza?"

"No. Oh no. It's just that now and then I get overcome by God's patience with us. I've tried every kind of prayer, every kind of constructive attitude I could muster through these years, and not once has it occurred to me that I have indeed been able to spare Robert the pain of being left alone. You've helped me, Rebecca."

"My dear friend, I have no reason to believe that I'd be able to carry on as you have, were I to lose my beloved Jock."

"You would. You'd have no choice because of your children. Yours and his." Eliza Mackay's voice lightened. "Do tell me about your two youngest. I know Anne and Lieutenant Fraser are expecting another child almost any time, but what of Isabella and William Audley? You wouldn't have come to Savannah if they weren't both well, but what are your plans for them?"

Rebecca turned toward her, almost eagerly. "I confess I went to sleep last night in that comfortable bed upstairs wondering if I'd actually confide in you this morning about Isabella."

"We've always trusted each other, Becca. I wouldn't pry"—she laughed—"or did I by asking just now? Is Isabella interested in some young Island man?"

"I'd say it's more than interest. You know the girl isn't exactly a beauty. Her father has always said she's too Couperish to be anything but good."

"That sounds like something Jock Couper might say, but I've always thought Belle was rather a handsome girl. So gentle and graceful, with such a pretty, small waist, I can think of a lot of girls her age who might envy her. How old is Belle now?"

"She was seventeen in September, and, Eliza, I do believe the girl is in love with our young rector at the little church at Frederica. The Reverend Theodore Bartow and Belle somehow seem perfectly matched. He's an unusually sensitive, deeply spiritual, but lighthearted young man. He's been with us for two and a half years, and he and Belle have been close friends almost from the start." She laughed. "For months, I now know, they left secret messages in a certain old water oak for each other. Then, Jock and I invited the young man to dinner. After that they let it be known that seeing each other was important. Since then things have been far clearer to Jock and me than even they suspect. My husband said in the boat coming up here that he looked forward to a visit from Theodore any day, asking for Belle's hand."

"How wonderful, Rebecca! Now I see why Belle chose to visit the Wylly girls on the Island while you are up here."

"Yes, and I agree that it's all great, good news for everyone concerned. My dear little Isabella has, although Anne lived so long abroad, been a bit under Anne's shadow, so I'm quite happy for the girl. Theodore is a fine, learned, well-mannered young man, and best of all, he'll never be too busy to give Belle the attention she has always deserved. He quite adores her."

"How I wish my girls—either one or both of them—could find the right young man. Of course I'd rattle around miserably alone except for the servants in this big house. My buoyant son Jack after his fine record at West Point, will probably be stationed in his beloved Army, moving from pillar to post most of the time. He's in Florida somewhere now, helping to build fortifications in case there's really a war with the Seminoles." She shuddered. "He vows his work with the Army engineers will be fairly safe, though. At any rate, Jack loves Army life and his mother will never stand in the way of it."

"Does either Kate or Sarah ever speak of marriage?"

"Neither mentions the subject. Nor do I. I just cherish having them as long as I can." Eliza Mackay refilled their cups. "And what of William Audley in school at the North? Does he like it?"

"Who knows about that boy? I don't think I've seen Jock more worried than he seems sometimes when he thinks of his younger son's future. He vows there's never been as lazy a lad as William Audley. That before he went to Northampton to school, he'd rather walk a mile or race home on a plow horse than open a book for any reason. His letters do sound much more mature now, though. My mother's instinct tells me William Audley will surprise his father one of these days. His school record seems to be improving steadily."

Eliza laughed. "Jock has always exaggerated a little, I've thought. Now let's see, when Anne and Lieutenant Fraser's next child is born this month, Anne will have given you four grandchildren, right?"

"Yes, and the girl has her heart set on a son this time. It doesn't seem to bother John one bit that they have three girls so far, but Anne longs to present him with a son—named John, of course."

"Your husband mentioned at dinner last night that Dr. Tunno makes the trip to St. Simons every two weeks just to be sure Anne's doing well. Is it true that the young doctor has agreed to leave his own home for Cannon's Point a week before Christmas just in case Anne's child comes early?"

"Eliza, don't even think such a thought! But yes, Dr. Tunno will be there. Still, if that child would happen to come while we're up here, my husband would never recover from it. Nor would I!"

"Well, he told me positively that neither the new baby nor the *Southern Agriculturist* editor, Mr. Legare, would arrive while you're here. Jock seems honored that Legare's coming. It is remarkable that such a widely read journal would feature St. Simons plantations, isn't it?"

"It seems to be," Rebecca said, "but I honestly believe that Anne's John could handle the interview even if Jock's still away. John Fraser's an interesting man, Eliza. No one really expected him to learn to *like* planting. My husband was sure John was talented enough to learn, but it must have been a dreadful wrench leaving the military as he had to do. He loved it the way your Jack loves the United States Army."

After a thoughtful silence, Eliza Mackay said, "He must love Anne more."

"He does. And he has certainly proved his love for her. He— he strongly disapproves of slavery, too, you know."

"Is that right?"

"You know the British feelings about our system, Eliza."

"John's a slave owner now, though. And his human property will only grow in numbers when he takes over Hamilton Plantation, if he makes a success of it. Your husband seems to believe he will."

"Oh he will. I haven't the slightest doubt about John. He gives no clue that Anne strikes him *ever* as being selfish, but what the man has done for love of her is, to me, sacrificial."

"You never speak of any of this with Anne, I suppose."

"Not one word. She belongs to him now. John Fraser belongs to her. He's his own man. Difficult as I know it to be—giving up any hope of ever returning to his regiment, forgoing the world travel he'd reveled in since the age of sixteen when he became a Royal Marine—all those choices were his to make."

"And has he ever become an American citizen?"

"No. His brother, Dr. William Fraser, now mayor of Darien, has taken out citizenship, but not John. He's still on half pay from the Royal Marines. I wonder at times, Eliza, if the boy ever thinks about trying to reenlist. He did try, you know, for a long time. There was no war, so they didn't need him any longer."

"In that case, aren't you judging Anne a bit harshly by sometimes thinking her selfish to demand that they come back here to live? If the Royal Marines no longer need John? Not that they might not again someday. You know how men are about having wars."

"I didn't mean to imply that Anne *demanded* that they come back here. I'm sure she just let John know—as anyone close to her would have known—that St. Simons will always be the one place where Anne is happy. But Eliza, you *are* right. In a way, I suppose John had no real choice but to come here and learn to plant. He'd never had another profession outside the military." Rebecca reached to pat Eliza's hand resting on the arm of the rocker next to hers. "Thank you, dear friend. Talking to you has always cleared my thoughts. Did you know that? I've probably been, as you said, judging Anne a bit harshly. John's biggest adjustment undoubtedly was learning to *like* to plant. I honestly believe he does now, although I'm sure he compares himself with James Hamilton much of the time—never an easy comparison for any other planter.

You've given me something to think about and I promise you I will. I'd never dare mention such a thing to Jock, who all but worships Anne. But I truly have thought her a bit selfish with John all this time." After a pause she added, "John Fraser does loathe being a slave owner. I don't discuss that with Jock, either, but I'm certainly aware of it myself."

CHAPTER 40

UP, BATHED, AND SHAVED BY DAWN THE NEXT DAY
—John's first morning to wake up in the Hamilton house—he was
not at all surprised to see Legare dressed also. His compact, well-
fitted traveling desk containing quills, a bottle of ink, and paper
was already strapped by a special contraption to the Cannon's
Point horse he'd ridden down yesterday.

After a substantial breakfast, prepared by the cook James
Hamilton Couper kept ever-ready to entertain guests at his St.
Simons plantation, John, on Ginger, rode alongside Legare, determined to confine himself to the explicit subject of agriculture as
they covered the Hamilton acres. By midmorning Legare knew
that St. Simons cotton was never planted two consecutive years in
the same field, that their principal manure was marsh-mud collected by fieldhands during the entire year. John also explained
weed chopping, the spreading of fennel in the alleys along which
the marsh-mud is spread, a process called listing. John soon caught
on when he had proudly imparted some information Legare al-

ready knew. It did seem of interest to the editor, though, that listing generally takes place during the winter months, as early as possible; also, that a short time before planting, the beds are formed by running a plow near the list and throwing two furrows on each side, hoes following, molding the actual beds.

Now and then Legare asked that they dismount so that he could take time to develop his pages of copious notes in a fine, neat script. Several pages were added just before they ate their picnic lunch, and John amazed even himself that he knew bedding measurements and planting procedures in such detail. But when the subject turned that afternoon to seed selection, he felt especially qualified because Jock Couper himself had declared him a "born seed selector." It had been John who first noticed that seed with a small green tuft produced far more bolls.

Cultivation seasons and methods were covered to Legare's satisfaction by the time the sun began to set over the Frederica River beyond the narrow stretch of marsh grass bordering the property on the west. "My wife and I will have the St. Simons sky drama shifted from dawn to sunset once we're living over here," he told Legare, unable to control the excitement he had felt on every recent visit to Hamilton.

"You must be looking forward to operating this productive place," Legare said as they rested before riding back to the house for the night. "I've heard that simply working a piece of land gives a planter a special sense of ownership. I'm sure you already know this, Fraser, but for Mr. James Hamilton Couper to put a man in complete charge of a valuable place like this is a distinct honor. Frankly, it surprises me."

John laughed. "You couldn't be half as surprised as I, sir," he said. "But if I do say so, the young Mr. Couper is a man of true acumen. I know his need for someone to take over Hamilton, especially since he plans to be in Alabama and Louisiana and Mississippi for long periods of time in the near future. In a way, merely by the offer, he helped me believe I could really do it."

"And a man delivers according to his faith in himself, right?"

"You're a man of acumen too, Legare." John laughed again.

The day's interview over, he held at least a small hope that the

two might by now be well enough acquainted for an evening of
more stimulating conversation.

T HEIR   DINNER   WAS   PREPARED   AND   SERVED   AS
though the staff of house servants performed their tasks daily. As
the two sat sipping brandy, the fine meal ended, Legare remarked
that it was indeed unusual that a Big House empty of all white
occupants—the temporary supervisor, Captain Bowers, away in
Darien on a purchasing mission—should be kept spotless and
dusted, its china on display, as though a family already lived there.
John simply reminded Legare that he had not yet met the fastidious owner, James Hamilton Couper.

"You will tomorrow, though, sir," John added with a grin.
"And my wife's elder brother will live up to everything you've ever
heard about his widely varied interests and accomplishments. You
will also spend your day, once we reach Hopeton, on *his* exact time
schedule. My brother-in-law even allots himself so many minutes
per day for the reading of poetry, so many for the reading of prose,
and so many for dining—even when there are guests."

Now John heard Legare's light laugh for the first time. "Surely
you jest, Lieutenant."

"You'll see. And by the way, I didn't show you the ginning
process here at Hamilton today because James also uses Eave's gins,
and you'll learn far more from his expert dissertation than from
mine."

"Perhaps more than I need to know?"

Legare was human after all. If John had to be away from Anne
with no means of finding out how she felt, if the girls were all
right, and most of all, if the new baby was pulling no surprises, he
could at least give thanks in his lonely bed tonight at Hamilton
that he'd finally found a means of unlocking Legare's reserve. The
two talked easily together until after ten.

One subject John did not broach was James Hamilton's reason
for the planned sojourn in Mississippi and Louisiana and Alabama.

He'd learned long ago that if Anne's brother wanted something known, he much preferred to do the telling himself.

John had come to enjoy Legare's company and was sorely tempted, observing the man's near awe of James Hamilton's spreading fame and reputation as a scientist, planter, engineer, conchologist, ornithologist, and businessman, to boast a bit about James's strong hint that he meant to take John into his cottonseed oil venture in New Orleans and Natchez and Mobile. He said not one word but hoped, as he dropped off to sleep, to stay within hearing distance all day at Hopeton tomorrow, in case James Hamilton might further commit himself. Anything James said that showed confidence in John's ability gave him the self-assurance he'd felt before only when in command of a contingent of Royal Marines in the old days. Not even his own father or Jock Couper could build his self-esteem as could James Hamilton, especially when James seemed unaware that he was doing it.

ANNE HAD NOT BEEN IN THEIR BIG, EMPTY BED more than an hour when the first pain came, so suddenly and so sharp, she sat bolt upright and cried, "No!"

When the second pain struck, she fell back onto the pillows, biting her lips and clutching the covers until her fingers ached. *Eve.* Rhyna was too far away, but Eve was not. Anne knew Eve had never birthed a baby, but she must have heard something about what to do. The cabin where June and Eve lived was only fifty yards or so from the Lawrence cottage. "Annie!" she screamed. "Annie, come quick!"

The pains were not letting up. In fact, they were almost regular now, and she was alone in the house except for baby Fanny, seven-year-old Pete, and blessed Annie, who didn't know one thing about birthing. "Annie!" she cried again and heard bare running footsteps along the short upstairs hall.

"Mama! I'm coming. I'm coming, Mama!"

"Hurry! Please hurry!"

When the door burst open, Annie and Pete both stood there looking terrified in the light of the one candle Anne had been careful to leave burning, just in case.

"Mama," Annie gasped, leaning over her. "Is it—is it the—baby?"

"Yes. Yes, I'm sure it is. Pete! Pete, put your shoes on and run to Eve's cabin. Run and get Eve, Pete, quick! I—I have to have help. I—I—" Unable to hold it back, Anne screamed. "I'm—I'm sorry, Pete. Don't, please don't be afraid."

"Mama, we *are* afraid," Annie was almost sobbing. "Go, Pete! You heard what Mama said. Put on your shoes and run for Eve. And—and tell Big Boy to saddle a horse and ride hard for Rhyna."

"No, Pete," Anne breathed. "Tell Big Boy to—ride bareback. The baby's not going to wait for him to saddle—anything. Hurry, Pete! In the name of heaven, hurry!"

Eyes filled with tears because the pains were so bad, Anne saw Pete seem to fly out of the room. Then her bare feet thumped down the hallway to the stairs, and the front door banged.

"Mama, she's gone. Pete's gone for Eve," Annie said, plainly struggling to keep her voice steady. "Pete's gone to get Eve and Eve will send Big Boy for—Rhyna and in the meantime, I'm here, Mama. I'm here to help. What can I do? Do you know what—it is I'm supposed to do to help you?"

Her breath coming fast, in raspy gasps now, Anne said, "Just—just look—pull the covers back and look, Annie! Can you see the little head—or anything—yet?" She screamed again and tried to apologize to her terrified, solemn daughter. "Do you—do you see anything?"

"I'm—I'm not sure, Mama. Do—do they call it breaking water? Everything's, everything under you—is all wet!"

"O God, help me," Anne moaned. "Please help me! We don't have anyone—to—help us. God, *help me!*"

"Yes, God, help us. Tell me what to do!" Annie cried.

And from outside, her boisterous voice fading away as she ran, Anne could hear Pete giving God orders: "Jesus!" Pete yelled. "Ol' Sofy says sometimes we have to order You! I order you, God, to help my mama!"

Between the now more frequent pains, Anne tried to laugh at Pete. "Listen, Annie, listen to Pete, bossing God!"

"Mama! Mama, I do see something!" Annie gasped, holding the candle closer now. "Do you think it could be our baby's—head I see?"

For what might have been a long or a short time, Anne knew and felt nothing until cold water hit her face and Eve's chilly fingers touched her bare leg. Almost at once she could feel the tiny head emerge as Eve's strong hand took the weight of it into her palm, the other fingers guiding, guiding.

"Pull, Eve," Anne breathed. "Pull—gently, careful, careful! Slow, pull slow." And then, biting her lips until she tasted blood, a hard, heavy rush of relief . . .

"We do it, Miss Anne," Eve whispered hoarsely, sinking down onto the bed herself. "We do it jus' in time! Eve about—to die too! Oh Miss Anne, is you alive? Is you—still breathin'? Tell me you is!"

"Yes, Eve. Yes. Thanks to you, I'm going to be fine. Is—is the baby all right? Is it a boy?"

"I ain' look yet, but I thought once you be dead. You so still. You stop helpin' atall, Miss Anne."

"I—I think you must have fainted, Mama," Annie whispered.

"Annie she done save yo' life," Eve said, her own breath still short and labored.

"I did not," Annie said. "You did, Eve! Oh Eve, I'll love you forever, because you saved my mama's life."

"It be Annie dat did it. She pour col' water ober yo' face. Annie, she save yo' life, Miss Anne!"

"Stop arguing, you two." Anne said weakly. "And Eve, hold the baby carefully. Is it a boy?"

"The way I'm holdin' it, I can't tell," Eve muttered.

"Then place it carefully on my stomach. . . ."

In a moment, as from a long way off, Anne heard her daughter's whisper. "Eve, the baby's a—boy and he's all—covered with blood!"

"Co'se he be all bloody, Annie! What chu think? Babies come from under a rose bush? Miss Anne, lay quiet, you hear me? Big

Boy ride hard. He be here wif Rhyna soon. You do what you got to do. Lay still!"

Anne, sure that Eve and Annie had suddenly gone away, that she was now alone with John, heard her own voice call him. She called in a whisper, so as not to frighten the baby. "John, John, listen to me. You—you tried to have Dr. Tunno here in time. You tried, dearest. You wouldn't have gone yourself—if we'd had—any idea. . . ."

"Somebody got to cut dat cord!" Eve gasped.

"What? Eve, can you do it?" Annie's voice trembled with fright. "Couldn't I hold the baby's head while you get some scissors? Mama's fainted again, I think. We can't wait for Rhyna!"

"Jesus," Eve prayed under her breath. "I knows where Miss Anne, she keep dem scissors, but who gonna cut?"

"You, Eve." Annie slipped both hands under the tiny, squirming body. "See? I can hold the baby on Mama's stomach."

"Sho I sees, but you reckon I kin do it?"

"You have to! Hurry!"

ANNIE SAT ON THE BED BESIDE HER MOTHER'S STILL body for what seemed an eternity. The new baby was alive, because he kept wiggling some, but not much. If he died in her hands, while she was holding him, Annie felt she would die too. Where did Mama keep her scissors? Had Eve run away because for once she didn't know what to do? The last thing Annie ever thought of was that Eve might be scared or feel helpless.

And then her mother began to moan and stir in the bed, to draw up her knees, to say Papa's name. "I'm here, Mama. It's Annie. Eve's coming with the scissors. I know Rhyna will be here too, any minute. Just—any minute."

The thud of horse's hooves galloping up their lane was sheer music! Big Boy was bringing Rhyna. Eve had waited, Annie thought, *pretending* to hunt for the scissors!

"I thought I'd never find 'em," Eve said, bursting into the

room clutching Mama's sewing scissors and a piece of string in her hand. She dropped to her knees beside the bed.

"I thought a dreadful thing, Eve," Annie murmured. "I thought you were scared and just stalling till Rhyna got here. We've waited this long. Maybe we should wait for Rhyna now. She knows exactly how to cut the cord and what to do next."

"I reckon we kin learn," Eve snapped. "Lemme think. Gran'maum Sofy say she an' Rhyna allus tie a string tight aroun' de naval cord firs'." After tying and pulling the knot so hard the baby cried, Eve drew a deep, shaky breath, picked up the scissors and cut.

The baby was loose from Anne's body at last, but because she'd concentrated on doing it for so long, young Annie still knelt, holding the tiny body.

When Rhyna charged into the room, from sheer nerves and exhaustion Annie's mother began to laugh and cry. Rhyna leaned over the bed to listen to what Mama might be trying to say. "Is it— is it really a boy, Rhyna?"

"Lor' dey ain' been time to look yit, Miss Anne," Rhyna said in her low, reassuring voice. "Now I see! Yes'm, he be a fine boy! You done give Mausa John a son, he firs' son! Jus' you wait til dat man come home. He gonna pop he shirt buttons, he be so proud." Hands on hips, Rhyna glared at Eve. "You ain' got no hot water in heah, girl? Dis lil' fella, he need a bath! An he need his tummy bound up. Git, Eve! Git!"

CHAPTER 41

JOHN AND LEGARE REACHED HOPETON IN A SMALL
Hamilton sailing boat just before noon the next day, and wonder
of wonders, James Hamilton was able to work them right into his
schedule. It amused John that even the mighty James appeared
pleased that the editor of the *Southern Agriculturist* would be writing an article about both Hopeton and Hamilton. James was disappointed, naturally, that his father was in Savannah but seemed
satisfied that John had already given Legare a detailed tour of
Hamilton.

The three, on horseback, immediately began what John knew
would be a detailed coverage of the many innovations at Hopeton,
but thoughts of Anne crowded his mind today. He had spoken
freely to Legare in the boat on the way to the mainland of his
wife's almost girllike hopes of giving him their first son; had felt
easy enough with the journalist to confess that while it would be
comforting to a man if his name was carried on into future genera-

tions, he loved Anne so much, any gift from her would only be cherished.

Once or twice during the Hamilton tour, John caught Legare's sly wink when James Hamilton began to expound on the operation of his Eave's gins. He not only enumerated ad nauseum the number of slaves and horses needed, but went on at length about bevel wheels, cogs, king posts, spur wheels, spur pinions, pulleys, band wheels, fans, whippers, and rollers. John, of course, had had to learn the entire operation of an Eave's gin, since every Island planter used them except old James Gould, who still ginned his ample cotton crops by wind power.

When James Hamilton began to elaborate on velocities, declaring that the rollers in his gin will revolve three hundred eighty-three and one-third times for each revolution of the large cog-wheel, John excused himself with the white lie that he wanted to consult with James Hamilton's driver on an important matter.

Every word his brother-in-law was telling poor Legare was of the utmost importance, he knew; every statistic and figure would enhance the authenticity of Legare's extensive article, but John was far too fidgety to listen.

He was always somewhat nervous in the company of her brother, but more so today because Anne was darting in and out of his thoughts in a most disturbing fashion. He could tell James was far from ending his lecture to Legare. Darkness would fall before they could possibly board the Hamilton boat for the water trip back to St. Simons. John and Legare would have to spend the night on the mainland with James and Caroline Couper.

By the time he could be with Anne again after even a brief visit with old James Gould, they'd have been apart three nights and four full days. Anything could have happened to her or to his girls in that length of time.

THEY DINED IN THE MAGNIFICENT MANSION JAMES had created out of a huge old cotton barn. Legare, as did everyone else, found James Hamilton's wife, Caroline, utterly charming, and of course her dinner was a masterpiece as was breakfast the next morning, eaten in the same grandly furnished, light-filled dining room.

As John adjusted the sail on embarking, the James Hamilton Coupers, a handsome couple, waved from their substantial, well-built dock. James, tall, wide-shouldered; Caroline, though heavy with child, small, dark-haired, and exceptionally pretty. John's preoccupation with being away from Anne, so near her time, lessened only a little as they moved smoothly out into the Altamaha River toward St. Simons. If the good wind prevailed, they should reach Gould's place by midafternoon, but John almost wished he hadn't mentioned that James Gould operated both his single and double gins by wind and osnaburg sails rather than by horsepower. But he had brought it up, and the unusual method would give a colorful twist to Legare's article. As though he divined John's thoughts, Legare mentioned incidentally that he thought it would be late in the day to ride all the way to James Gould's light tower on the southeast end of the Island. Stopping by the Gould plantation would satisfy him.

Relieved, John agreed that Legare could freely quote him, John Fraser, that James Gould had built one of the finest lighthouses anywhere on the coast—north or south.

ONCE BACK ON ST. SIMONS, THEY WASTED LITTLE time docking the boat, freshening up a bit at the Hamilton house, and heading their horses at last for the familiar, tree-lined beauty of Frederica Road.

"You're a jolly good sport, Legare," John called from astride Ginger as both he and his new friend galloped north on the Island's only main road. "Your hand is going to be stiff and sore tomorrow, though. I never saw a man write as fast as you did while James Hamilton Couper was bending your ear through all those hours!"

"He's like conversing with an encyclopedia, isn't he?" Legare asked. "Never met a man with such universal interests. But it's you to whom I'm most indebted, Lieutenant. After hearing Mrs. Caroline Couper ask all those questions about the new baby you and Mrs. Fraser are expecting, I realized just how sacrificial you've been with your time. If there's ever a way I can thank you, I hope you'll feel free to let me know."

John laughed. "I certainly feel far freer than I felt with you for the first few hours of our adventure, sir. I wondered if I'd ever break down your reserve with me."

Legare laughed too. "It's my biggest drawback. I thank you for persevering. I wish I had your natural ways."

John slowed Ginger to a canter, then a trot. "We're nearing the Gould road that leads back to New St. Clair, and you've a treat in store, my friend. To me there isn't a prettier sight than Gould's moss- and vine-hung lane on a sunny day like this one—except, of course, the Couper Road back to Cannon's Point."

The beauty of black shadows and white slants of sunlight slowed them still more as John watched the taut muscles in Legare's face begin to ease under the magic of that one stretch of shell road. After the hard ride from Hamilton, both men allowed their bodies to relax in the saddles, exchanged smiles of pleasure at the loveliness John had promised. Leafless bullis grapevines and larger muscadines twined up and over the narrow, winding, secluded palmetto-lined lane. A wren called from somewhere high above their heads.

"We haven't come far along this lane," Legare said, "but I feel almost rested, as though I've had a good night's sleep."

"I promise we won't have to stay long here at Gould's place," John said. "The man's a New Englander to the core. Doesn't talk much. In fact, my father-in-law, John Couper, who does love to talk, vows he'd like to shake Gould sometimes, although the two have been fast friends since Gould's first visit to St. Simons, back before the turn of the century. The gentleman will answer your questions with genuine courtesy and he'll know what he's talking about, but he won't exhaust you, I promise."

GOULD'S DAUGHTER, MARY, RAN OUT TO MEET them when they rode up under Gould's prized magnolia tree to the wide veranda of what appeared to Legare to be a tabby house —two full stories, two tall, stately chimneys. Certainly more like houses he'd seen on his one trip north to Massachusetts than any other place on St. Simons.

As he bowed to acknowledge John's introduction to Miss Mary Gould, Legare couldn't help thinking that the plain but cordial young woman suited the simple, durable lines of her father's house. James Gould, he knew, was a skilled builder, not only of his light tower but also of this home he had designed for his much-beloved wife, who had died and whom he still missed. He and John had spoken at length of the Goulds—of the wayward son who was working on a Mississippi River boat, of an older, married son now living at Black Banks, of Miss Mary, still a spinster at twenty-three. Not pretty, he thought, but her intelligence shone through. Yes, she was marked by intelligence and a quiet, dependable grace.

"I won't take but a few minutes of your father's time, Miss Gould," Legare said when John explained their mission.

"I wish you could both get him to enjoy a nice long visit, Mr. Legare, but I'm afraid Papa isn't too well. He'll be up to showing you his wind-driven gins, though. He's very proud of them."

"Thank you," Legare said, with another half-bow. "And I stand by my promise not to keep him long. After all, my new friend Lieutenant Fraser hasn't seen his wife and children for several days. I know he's eager to get back to Lawrence."

"No new baby yet, John?" Mary asked.

"Not yet. At least not that I know of," John said. "It is true, isn't it, Mary, that your father gets out the whole of his crop by means of his wind-powered gins?"

"Oh yes. Papa swears by his wind power."

The front door of New St. Clair opened and a tall, lean, slightly stooped man, in his sixties, Legare guessed, hobbled out onto the veranda, his hand open to his visitors. "I'm James Gould," he said, addressing Legare. "Welcome. How do you do today,

Lieutenant Fraser? I think you might have invited our guests into the parlor, Mary."

When Legare shook the older man's hand after John stated the purpose of their visit, Gould smiled for the first time. "So, you're especially interested in my wind power, eh?"

"I am indeed, Mr. Gould. I hope it's convenient for you to explain a bit about how it works. Since you're the only Island planter who uses wind, it will add enormously to my rather lengthy article, which I propose to begin publishing in the *Southern Agriculturist* before the year is out. You see, we're just back from a fine demonstration at Hopeton by Mr. James Hamilton Couper."

Now Gould really chuckled. "James Hamilton's a smart man. More successful than any of the rest of us on this Island. If you've already talked with him, I can certainly see why your article may be a mite long."

"Excuse me, gentlemen," Mary Gould said, "but may I serve you coffee, and will you take dinner with us after you've finished speaking with my father?"

"I'm afraid not, Miss Mary," John said. "It's important that I get along home as soon as possible."

Legare saw James Gould's smile vanish as though a cloud had crossed his weathered, aging face. "I certainly understand, Lieutenant Fraser. It's never easy on a man being away from his wife when she's so near her time. When do you expect your new child?"

"I told you this morning, Papa," Mary Gould said. "Sometime around Christmas."

"So you did, Daughter," Gould agreed, turning to Legare. "Now just what is it you want of me, sir? If I don't have to ride too far, I'll do what I can to help you with your article."

"Lieutenant Fraser tells me you're the only planter on St. Simons who powers his gins by the wind. Would it be possible for me to see the actual mechanism while I listen to your reasons for using wind power?"

"I expect so, but I find it easier to walk than to mount a horse, so if you'll both just follow me."

Legare hurried to his saddlebags, took out his small travel

desk, and rejoined Fraser and Gould, both still in conversation with Miss Mary. As they stood in the yard behind the white picket fence, everyone turned at the sound of a galloping horse coming from the direction of the Gould stables at the end of the shady lane.

Astride a handsome, coal-black mare, perfectly groomed, sat a stockily built Negro, his pleasant face glowing with the kind of smile that in itself told them something good was afoot.

"July!" Gould called. "What's up? Why are you exercising my son's mare out here this time of day?"

"Fine news, Mausa Gould. Good news, specially for you, Mausa Fraser." The smile grew brighter. "You the father ob a bran' new baby boy!"

Mary Gould rushed up to the slave on the horse. "July! Are you sure? The Fraser baby wasn't due until Christmas! Who told you? And if you tell me you heard it on the grapevine, I'll—I'll—"

"You'll what, Daughter?" Gould asked, now smiling too.

"I don't know what I'll do, Papa, but I know it's no time for teasing poor John Fraser! John, it must be true! July wouldn't just make up a thing like that."

"No, sir, Mausa Fraser," July said. "Maum Larney don' lie to nobody. My mama, she be a stickler where lyin' goes. It be true. Ol' Rhyna, de midwife, she tell Mama when she done brung ober some fresh eggs from Miz Wylly." July beamed at John, who seemed unable to say a word. "Cat got your tongue, Mausa Fraser?"

"I—I guess so," John said. "But is my wife all right? What did Rhyna say about Anne? Are you sure it's a—boy?"

"Effen ol' Rhyna don' know a baby boy by now, ain' nobody gonna know," July said, laughing. "It be a boy, sir. Your firs' son an' Miss Anne, she be jus' fine. It be nippin' an' frizzin' I reckon for a while till ol' Rhyna she rode ober from Cannon's Point wif Big Boy, but Eve an' your daughter Annie, dey figured out what to do jus' in time, my mama tell me." When the mare began to prance, July said, "I bes' be mindin' Dolly, here. Eben wif Mausa Horace gone, she be the queen ob my stables."

"Hold on a minute, July," Gould ordered, then turned to Fraser. "John, in the name of heaven, man, get on home! I can take

Mr. Legare to my gin house, give him what he needs, then July can ride Dolly with him back to Cannon's Point and show him the way. Go on home this minute to your wife and new son!"

Legare, who'd come to be genuinely fond of John Fraser, agreed at once. They all waved John off, Ginger galloping like the wind, John not even taking time for a proper goodbye.

AT THE FIRST CURVE IN THE NEW ST. CLAIR ROAD, Legare saw John pass a dark-haired young man galloping toward the Gould house at full clip. He also noticed the two wave in passing.

Fully enjoying this intimate view of Island life, he watched the strikingly handsome, well-built young man ride up, rein his stallion, and doff a wide-brimmed green felt hat to Miss Mary Gould.

"John Wylly!" she gasped. "What in the world are you doing here at this time of day?"

"Now what kind of welcome is that for one of our best neighbors and friends, Daughter?" Gould asked. "Good day, Wylly. I hope things go well at the Village, especially for your father. Alexander's no worse, is he?"

"About as usual, Mr. Gould," Wylly said, nodding at Legare.

"Where are our manners, Papa?" Mary asked, plainly flustered by Wylly's arrival. "This is Mr. Legare, the editor of the famous *Southern Agriculturist,* John. He's here to interview Papa concerning his wind-powered gin. Mr. Legare, may I present our neighbor Mr. John Wylly."

Wylly dismounted and the two shook hands. "A pleasure, Mr. Legare," he said.

"Delighted," Legare said. "Would you care to accompany Mr. Gould and me to inspect his gin house apparatus? Perhaps you could also answer one or two of my questions. You're a planter too, I assume."

"He's really the master of all the Wylly property at the Village," Mary offered. "Without Mr. John Wylly, the whole place would go to wrack and ruin."

"You're too kind, Miss Mary," John said, bowing. "And yes, I'd enjoy hearing you ply our famous lighthouse builder with questions about his odd ginning methods."

"Are you sure you wouldn't prefer to rest from your ride and have some coffee and biscuits, John?" Mary asked hopefully. And then, as though she'd stepped out of line, her face reddened.

"Your coffee and biscuits are always a temptation, Mary," Wylly said, "but after the breakfast I had, I couldn't eat a bite. Thank you just the same, though."

"Well, unless you'd prefer to hear Papa's ginning methods again, you're welcome to rest on our veranda." Legare thought Mary Gould seemed unable not to press her invitation. "I don't think the wind is too chilly."

Something in her expression as she spoke to Wylly struck Legare as being a touch desperate, perhaps even sad. Was his writer's imagination dramatizing feelings that weren't there? He thought not, and as he, John Wylly, and Gould walked away from Mary, he glanced over his shoulder. She seemed to be dragging her shapely young body back toward the house, as though forced again to face some defeat—alone. Young Wylly seemed not to notice.

CHAPTER 42

By spring of the next year, 1833, Anne imag-
ined that she could feel her family, all of them—even the handsome new son, John Couper Fraser—beginning to put down roots
at Hamilton. The feeling was reinforced daily because so far she
was following her mother's admonition to keep her diary up-to-
date from the first early April day of the big move from Lawrence
into the splendid tabby house on the southwestern side of St.
Simons Island. Exhausted as she was by the time the sun set over
the Frederica River each evening, she had made herself write
something of the rewards and hard work and frustration of making this exciting, though difficult, new start.

Not particularly proud of what she wrote or of the careless way
she wrote it, Anne had to admit Mama had been right. Rereading
the pages in her little blue diary gave her a chance to relive the
confusion, the newness, and especially the joy she'd found in being
near enough to Anna Matilda at Retreat so that by late May she

could spend a week with her best friend and a new King daughter, Georgia.

Anne's duties at Hamilton were heavier—there were more people to manage—but as John was proud to be the master, she thrived on her challenge as mistress of an already famous Big House. For all the years during which old Mr. James Hamilton had lived there as a wealthy bachelor, even during the years when her brother James had kept the plantation functioning despite his only occasional visits, the place had been widely known. Hamilton Plantation had been discussed, not only up and down the coast but in various parts of Europe, where James had visited to study drainage and diking in Holland, botany in England, and ornithology in France.

"What, I wonder, is so different, even difficult, about being the mistress of Hamilton?" she wrote in her diary on May 31, after a near row with Eve, who for once had shut her mouth and walked away from the obvious conflict between her and Ella, the Hamilton "main woman." For years Ella had looked after the place for James and for old Mr. Hamilton. Ella's pride in her work and her dominance clashed head-on with Eve's. "Lawrence, compared with where we live now, was small and dear and cozy and had Mama and Papa nearby to turn to when something went wrong. I think I'll have to begin praying that Eve will see how much I need her to help me make the big changes I must make here." With that line Anne ended a morning's entry in the new, blue-grosgrain-covered diary. Ended it abruptly, because Eve was calling her from downstairs.

Eve knows perfectly well that she isn't supposed to shout up the stairs at me like that, Anne thought, replacing the lid on the inkwell and blotting what she had written. Something must be wrong. "I'm coming, Eve!" she shouted back. "Where are you? What's the matter?"

By the time Anne reached the top of the stairs, Eve was there, her dark eyes troubled, her high, smooth forehead creased with pity.

"It be bad, Miss Anne. An' Miss Mary Goul', she feel mighty bad about it. That ol' man be dead!"

"Who's dead, Eve? And what does Mary Gould have to do with it? It isn't her father, is it?"

"No'm. It be Cap'n Wylly. Miss Mary, she ride all the way down here herself to tell you they hab his fun'ral tomorrow at the church up by Frederica. Co'se I knows why Miss Mary she so sorrowful. Miss Mary she be lovin' young John Wylly fo' almos' the whole time you been back from 'cross de ocean. Lovin' him somepin fierce!"

"Eve, sometimes I wonder about your sanity! What on earth are you talking about? Do you think what you just said about Miss Mary and John Wylly could possibly be true and I wouldn't know anything about it?"

"Yes'm. Ain' hard to realize dat atall, Miss Anne."

When Anne only stared at her, Eve went on. "You ain' neber knowed how I was de one dat knowed long ago you an' your mama, Miss Rebecca, bof gonna hab yo' babies fore anybody else knowed. You don' eben know why I knows ol' Ella she gonna keep arter me til she turn you against me right today. You ain' neber ketch on to why Eve knows things afore dey happen. It be time you foun' out."

"What, what, *what* are you talking about?" Anne demanded, her temper flaring. "Don't you think I have enough on my mind these days trying to get my family settled into this place, trying to take care of a new baby, trying to keep you and Ella from scratching each other's eyes out? What are you saying to me?"

"Dat I was born wif a caul ober my face!"

"Oh for heaven's sake, is that all? Do you really expect me to believe that you can foresee the future just because you happened to have been born with a caul over your face?"

Eve straightened to her full height. "Yes'm, I spects it. 'Cause it be true. Ol' Sofy, she be right dere when I come outa my mama's body. She seen it wif her own eyes!"

Anne hated it when Eve made her feel at a disadvantage like this. Eve mattered. Mattered terribly and Anne needed her to be easy and warm and not prickly and mysterious. Hadn't Eve once told her that she had *not* been born with a caul over her face? She honestly couldn't remember because it had seemed so unimportant either way. But Eve had brought it up now as the one explanation of why so long ago she had known ahead of both Anne and Mama that they were both going to have babies, back when William Audley and Annie were born. Eve had also vowed she knew before anyone else that Anne and John were coming back to Georgia to live at Lawrence. But to say she had known for several years that poor, lonely, faithful spinster Mary Gould was in love with John Wylly was too much! As long as Eve kept her predictions inside the family, Anne could overlook them. But it would be embarrassing if one of the other planter's families found out that Anne paid attention to a servant. The whole thing was too silly, too African. It struck Anne that Eve was putting on airs. Trying to be different. Eve, who had been born right at Cannon's Point, the same as Anne.

"Did you say Miss Mary Gould rode up here alone to tell us about poor old Mr. Wylly?" Anne asked, hoping to regain control of herself and the conversation. "Did you leave her down there alone?"

"No'm. You knows Eve too p'lite to do a thing like that! She be halfway home by now. She jus' tell me an' ride off."

"Well, did Miss Mary know whether or not Dr. William Fraser and Miss Frances Anne knew Frances's father had died?"

"Miss Mary's papa, he done send July an' them in a boat to Darien to tell 'em. She say they all hope Miss Frances she git here in time fo' the funeral tomorrow. Miss Mary Goul' so in love wif Mausa Wylly's son John, she feel like one ob her own done die!"

"That's more than enough of that," Anne snapped. "Where are the children?"

"Where you tol' me. I been showin' Annie how to draw pitchers on a board. You done n'glek her the way I be n'glekted till Miss Rebecca she let me fin' out I kin draw too. Annie be good at birds an' she also draw one ugly ol' rattler."

"Goodness," Anne said absently. "Couldn't you think of something prettier than a rattlesnake for her to draw?"

Eve shrugged. "She draw what she draw. Pete, she can't hardly draw nothin'!"

"Well, everyone doesn't have the same talent."

"Pete jus' keep tryin' to draw a Indian head, wit feathers."

Despite her annoyance, Anne laughed. "Where on earth did she get an idea like that? Pete never even saw an Indian! Never mind. Go on back to the old toolshed. Is that where the girls are painting their pictures?"

"Yes'm. You want Eve should fix your hair so's you kin go visit at the Wyllys' this afternoon, Miss Anne?"

"Uh—yes. But not yet. I'll want Mina to bake a sweet potato pie first. I'll have to take along something to eat. Oh Eve, poor old Mrs. Wylly! They had a good, long life together, but I've always thought she loved her husband very much. My heart goes out to her."

"Yes'm. You an' me still got Mausa John an' June an' we better give thanks to God."

Anne smiled at her, hoping that one of their exchanged, knowing smiles would bridge the strained conversation.

Eve did not return Anne's smile. "You still be mad wif me ober de caul, Miss Anne?"

"Of course not! How could I possibly be angry with someone I depend on the way I depend on you? And not just to fix my hair and look after my children. I need—*you*. And right now I want you to find June so he can tell my husband that Mr. Wylly is dead."

"You know I done send word to Mausa John!"

"How would I possibly know that?"

"Effen I'm so important to you, somepin like dat got to be mixed into it! I done send Big Boy to tell him."

ONE WOULD THINK, JOHN MUSED AS HE RODE toward Christ Church the next day with James Hamilton Couper, Caroline, and Anne in the fine new carriage bought when he and Anne first moved to Hamilton, that since they were family, these first houseguests would be easy for Anne. Plainly they were not easy for her because they were none other than the finicky, proper owner himself and his young wife, Caroline. Anne, normally hard to ruffle, evidently wanted everything to be perfect. It was James who made her nervous. Caroline, as always, even in grief over the sudden death of her father, was easy to satisfy. On their way to Captain Wylly's funeral, Caroline seemed especially grateful that they'd named their new son, born in February, Alexander Wylly Couper for his late grandfather. As usual, Caroline was doing her best not to be a problem. Only half listening as the four of them rode along over the seven or so miles to Christ Church, John could tell she was reassuring Anne that she'd done a fine job settling into such a different, more demanding way of life.

"I don't know why things seem so different," Anne was saying to Caroline. "I suppose you found it perfectly simple to move from that small overseer's house into your new Hopeton mansion. I'd like to blame Eve for my inadequacies. She's locking horns with Ella on a daily basis, but I know it isn't Eve. It's the overwhelmed mistress named Anne Couper Fraser!"

"James and I have no right to break into woman talk," John said, slipping an arm around Anne's shoulders, "but I feel sure you agree, James, that milady's doing a splendid job of running a much larger house—and keeping harmony among the people you've had at Hamilton for so long and the few we brought with us from Lawrence."

"I do agree, John," James said affably. Affably for James, at least, who seemed to John to be wearing his funeral manner in deference to his adored wife. "My sister Anne, though, has always scattered sunshine, no matter the circumstances around her. Within another month or so, dear Sister, you'll feel as though you've lived at Hamilton all your life. Did I tell you I greatly admire the bright-patterned slipcovers you've had made for the veranda chairs?"

"No, James, you didn't," Anne said. "But you have made me rather happy by saying I scatter sunshine—whatever that means. With the wife you have, you of all men should recognize sunshine when you see it. Tell me, James, do you let Caroline know often enough exactly how superior, how tasteful, how perfect a wife she is to you?"

John hoped his involuntary chuckle was not out of place, today of all days, but he'd always enjoyed Anne's expertise at cutting her patronizing, no nonsense brother down to size. No question but that she tried to please James, even to impress him with the atmosphere she had created in the home he'd entrusted entirely to John. It had always appealed to John that as fond as she was of James, he seemed not to awe Anne the way he did most other people, even his own parents.

"Don't worry, Anne," Caroline said. "I'm not a perfect wife and James is not a perfect husband. But he *is* James and we're happy together, even though I haven't yet learned quite how to live by a strict schedule." She hugged James's arm. "I'll do, won't I, husband dear?"

To John, James Hamilton's face looked as though it might crack, but he liked the man still more when he patted Caroline's hand and gave her what for James passed as a loving smile.

The journey from Hamilton to Frederica by carriage would take nearly two hours, even with Big Boy driving. The time would pass more quickly and easily, John believed, if somehow they kept the subject off the solemn reason for the trip. "I believe, James," he said, "that we may find Mr. John Legare's first installment of his piece on our coastal plantations appearing in a month or so. Didn't you find him a rather likable chap?"

"I did indeed, John," James said. "And while you were off conferring with my driver that day you brought Legare to Hopeton, he spoke highly of your helpful information and expertise. How did he respond to Mr. Gould's wind-powered gins?"

"Have you forgotten, James?" Anne broke in. "John learned just minutes before Mr. Gould was about to demonstrate his wind power that our son, John Couper, had come into the world early. So he rode right home."

"How could you forget such a thing, James?" Caroline wanted to know. "Anne, we do put up with a lot from our gentlemen, don't we?"

"I wouldn't dare speak for Caroline," John laughed, "but I know how much you have to contend with in me, my dear Anne. I feel sure, though, that Gould's osnaburg sails filled with our occasional wind will be included in Legare's article."

"He struck me as being highly impressed with your own dis-

coveries concerning seed selection, too, John," James Hamilton
said, complimenting John still again. "By the way, I also told the
editor of our possible future involvement in cottonseed oil over in
Alabama and in Louisiana and Mississippi."

To have James mention his new interest in such a casual way
delighted John. He tried not to sound too pleased when he asked,
"You told him about that? When do you plan to leave for Natchez
again, James?"

"James," Caroline said, "not anytime soon, I hope!"

"Not until I'm sure you're beginning to recover from your
grief over losing your father, my dear. Don't worry. I'm not going
before the end of this year."

Seated in the carriage seat across from Caroline, John saw her
eyes fill with tears. "Thank you," she said softly. "I'm—I'm trying
hard not to let go of my feelings now. It's just that we're getting
closer to the churchyard and my heart is so heavy for Mama."

"I'm sure it is," Anne said warmly. "Caroline, what would
either of us do if we were—in her place? How could we bear it?
Can you think of anything—anything at all I might do to help
your poor mother? No!" Anne answered herself. "What could
anyone do? What on earth could anyone do for a woman at a time
like that?"

For the first time in memory, John saw a look on James Hamilton Couper's stern, intelligent face that came close to helplessness.
Did women—tender, sensitive women like Anne and Caroline—
love their men in a dependent way no man could ever truly understand? Was there a degree of loss laid upon them as harsh and
unbearable as that he sensed in Anne now? As that James so
obviously sensed in Caroline?

STANDING WITH JOHN AND HER PARENTS BESIDE
the freshly dug grave in the Wylly plot in Christ Churchyard,
Anne kept her eyes averted from those of poor Margaret Armstrong Wylly. Several years younger than her dead husband, Mrs.
Wylly looked bent and old, as though across her slender shoulders

she carried the grief of every sorrowing widow on earth. Frances Anne and William Fraser had arrived in time, in one of Mr. Frewin's boats from Darien, for the family gathering in the churchyard to share the gentle, comforting words of Isabella's Reverend Theodore Bartow beside the open grave. How, Anne wondered, did a young man like Theodore find such beautiful words —his own words for Mrs. Wylly—not included in the prayer book? "He is called of God," Papa would have said, had Anne had a chance to ask him.

With William Fraser and Frances Anne stood Frances's twin sister, Anne Frances, still unmarried. A little apart, near her brothers, was Heriot, looking oddly peaceful, as though she knew something the others didn't. And leaning heavily on the arm of her son John was the widow, Mrs. Wylly.

Across the open grave from where Anne and John stood, Anna Matilda and Thomas Butler King, their two older children between them, nodded in recognition, six-year-old William holding tight to his mother's hand. Just to one side of the Kings, Anne saw Mr. James Gould with his faithful daughter, Mary, full of sorrow. Once Anne thought she'd only imagined that Anna Matilda turned to look at Mary Gould's unusually sad face. Then she knew she hadn't imagined it, when Mary Gould disengaged her arm from her father's and moved forward to stand beside John Wylly—just to stand there.

For an instant Mary's gesture distracted Reverend Bartow from the prayer he was reading. At the same time a nonpareil sent its silver song out over the otherwise silent beauty of the cemetery.

I don't think dear Mary Gould intended to do what she just did, Anne thought, but she's done it now and in front of everybody.

Tall, dark, solemnly handsome John Wylly gave Mary the merest smile, then turned his attention back to his quietly weeping mother.

CHAPTER 43

THAT NIGHT ANNE MOVED CLOSER TO JOHN IN their large, comfortable bed upstairs at Hamilton, pressing her head hard into his shoulder.

"Can't you get any closer?" he teased. "I think you need to try harder."

"Don't ever, ever die," she breathed. "Do you hear me?"

"I hear you, beautiful Anne, but even your incomparable husband could never promise a thing like that. I know I'm wonderful, but—"

"I'm not in the mood for teasing!"

"Sorry," he said. "The truth is, neither am I."

"I don't think it's helping Mrs. Wylly at all tonight that Captain Wylly was old, do you?" Anne asked.

"I'd think no. Perhaps it's even worse."

"There can be no consolation when the person you love most in all the world is gone!"

"My heart went out to Mr. James Gould, too, at the graveside this afternoon. His Janie is buried in Savannah. The man doesn't even have a grave nearby to tend or visit."

She reached to touch his face. "You're not only beautiful outside, John Fraser, you're beautiful inside, too, aren't you?"

"If you say so."

"I do. And did anyone there—any of the Demeres or the Grants or either of my parents or the Caters—did you hear anyone mention what poor Mary Gould did as the service was ending? I know Anna Matilda was watching her. Did Thomas King say anything to you about Mary's going right in front of everyone to stand by young John Wylly?"

"Not a word. No one said anything. She's a puzzling young woman, isn't she?"

"Eve swears Mary's in love with John Wylly."

"What?"

"She told me just yesterday that she *knows* Mary Gould is in love with John Wylly. It was Mary, you know, who rode here to tell us old Captain Wylly had died."

"How in the name of common sense could Eve know something like that?"

"I don't think it has a thing to do with common sense. She also just got around to telling me after all these years that she was born with a caul over her face and that means she knows lots of things other people can't know."

John laughed.

"You think that's funny? I think it's scary! And I don't like for Eve to talk that way. I certainly don't want her to get like old Sofy. But she has known several things ahead of time through the years. She told Mama I was coming back from London long before you and I knew we were!"

"Well, does Miss Almighty Eve know whether John Wylly is in love with Mary Gould or not?"

"She didn't mention that," Anne answered. "I certainly haven't seen or heard any sign of it. Maybe Mary is just truly tender-hearted. She knows losing his father puts an extra heavy load on John, especially with the Hazzards still fighting the Wyllys over their property line. You noticed, I'm sure, that not one Hazzard attended Captain Wylly's service today."

"I guess you're right, although I hadn't given it any thought." For a time neither spoke. Then John asked, "You're giving something a bit of thought this minute. Want to tell me about it?"

"I'm not sure. But I am thinking about something. About someone. You."

"That's appropriate," John said. "And you know perfectly well I'll keep asking until I find out what you're thinking about me."

"Something my peculiar brother said in the carriage on our way to the church."

"You know I'm also going to ask why you call James Hamilton peculiar."

"Because he is. So much goes on inside his fertile head, he doesn't realize that when he says something that makes no sense to anyone else, he's very likely to cause worry."

"Worry, darling?"

"You were both talking about Mr. Legare as though neither Caroline nor I was in the carriage. Suddenly James blurted out that he'd told him about some kind of cottonseed oil project in Natchez, and it sounded to me as though he was including you in what he said. You haven't said one word about such a thing to me!"

"But I can now."

"Why now?"

"I was afraid to mention it earlier for fear James might change his mind. Then you'd have your hopes up only to be dashed down again."

"Don't you know that as long as I have you, almost nothing could bother me?"

"I know that, but I also noted that you said *almost* nothing. Anne, in all these years we haven't properly talked this out, but your husband was aware back in London how much worry and anxiety he caused you hatching one wild scheme after another when all you really wanted was for us to come back here. I know I pretended to be unaware, but I did know. I know how you worried when I simply couldn't give up trying to get back into the Royal Marines. I also know how wild and crazy my big idea of going to the Cape of Good Hope seemed to you. To you, to my father, to Willy Maxwell. I—I used to be tricky, but I wasn't stupid."

"And you're neither one now, so what was my brother talking about?"

"He really hasn't told me much about it, but as you say, his fertile brain is toying with the idea of pressing cottonseed oil from the cast-off seed that planters normally throw away." Up on his elbow in the bed, looking down at her by candlelight, John turned her face toward him. "Anne, James brought all this up out of the blue one day, and if I'm honest, which I find these days I have to be with you, I was so flabbergasted and so pleased that he had already decided to include me in some small way, I was half afraid to tell you for reasons I probably don't even know about yet. I didn't really like your brother much in the beginning, you know."

"I do know. James is a dear, but he's not known for charming people. You like him a lot more now, though. And that isn't a question. I believe you do."

"I do and not only because he's flattered and honored me by putting me in charge here at Hamilton. I'm probably finally allowing myself to get to know him. Oh, I'm still in awe of his many talents and his business expertise, but truly, Anne, James seems almost human like the rest of us where this cottonseed idea is concerned. I can tell you truthfully that somehow I have the feeling now and then that even the mighty James Hamilton is—just a touch unsure about jumping into it as he seems determined to do. It's breaking entirely new ground for him."

"What part will you have in his cottonseed oil plan? Will you need to invest money in it?"

"Perhaps. He's said very little to me actually. Would it bother you if I found a few hundred or so to invest with him?"

"I don't know anything about it, dearest," she said, pulling his face down for a kiss. "I just know that I've never, ever loved you as much, or been as proud of you, as at this very minute. And if you don't think it's terribly irreverent for us to—to make love on the very night poor Mrs. Wylly buried her captain, I need you to love me."

After a long, tender, passionate kiss, John said, his delectable humor still near the surface of his desire, "I'm sure it's exactly the right time for me to make love to you, beautiful Anne," he whispered. "That is, *if* you can guarantee that our splendid son, John Couper Fraser, is going to sleep through the night and not interrupt us again."

Anne pulled him closer. "I promise," she whispered. "I more than promise, I guarantee our son will go on sleeping soundly. It's his mother who needs attention tonight!"

CHAPTER 44

THROUGHOUT THE SOFT, WARM DAYS OF JUNE AND into July, not only did Anne remember each day to write in her diary, she remembered to be thankful because now that she had given John a son, her life lacked absolutely nothing. After a good, straight talk with Hamilton's "main lady," Ella, she even felt that from now on Ella might unbend a bit with Eve so that the day could come when she and Eve stopped locking horns.

"Eve seems to be helping too," she wrote in her diary on Monday, the eighth day of July 1833. "She seems to have stopped trying to best Ella every time a decision needs to be made about baby John Couper. What an extraordinarily handsome infant John Couper is! Mama vows he's inherited the best features of both the Coupers and the Frasers, that when he's a grown man, there won't be a finer-appearing gentleman anywhere on the coast of Georgia. His father, who will always be the handsomest man on earth to me, seems most proud that baby John does sleep through almost every night at such a young age. He was seven months old earlier this month, and that's young to be so well behaved. I'm sure I'm biased because I wanted so much to give John a son, but he does seem to be developing excellent muscle control at a very early age and notices so much. Today he reached for the old gold brooch his father gave me long ago and tried to pull it off my dress! I think John likes, almost more than anything else about him, that his son laughs a lot. Baby John Couper is going to grow up *helping* his parents! Helping both his parents to be stronger, better persons. There is something different about this child. I know already that one day when I'm old and gray, I'll be able to lean on my fine son, John Couper."

Anne's diary entry and the happy reverie it had brought were broken into by Pete's shout from downstairs. Anne jumped to her feet—alarmed. It was not just Pete yelling for her mother to settle some unimportant dispute. *Something was wrong.*

At the top of the stairs, Anne called down to ask.

"It's about Miss Anna Matilda's son William Page King, Mama!" Pete's voice was full of panic. "Hurry down here! There's something bad wrong with William and William and I are best friends. Mama, hurry!"

Right then Eve ran from the parlor into the front hall, where Pete stood staring up at her mother, the child's pinched face white with fear. An arm protectively around Pete's shoulders, Eve called, "Come on down, Miss Anne! Miss Anna Matilda King, she done send Smart flyin' ober here on horseback to get chu. Miss Anna Matilda, she need you quick. Dat's all I know. Smart, he had to ride right back."

"All right, Eve," Anne called, hurrying down the stairs to hold Pete close for a minute. Pete and young William Page King had always adored each other. Her middle daughter, thought of by everyone as "good old Pete," the noisy, carrot-topped tomboy, was suffering her first real heartache because her beloved young friend was ill. "William will be all right, dear," Anne said soothingly, stroking the bright curly hair. "He probably has a bad fever, but both his mother and I know exactly what to do and I think you should ride over with me—behind me—on Gentleman."

"You gonna ride yo' horse all dat way, Miss Anne? Eve comin' too."

"It isn't that far from Hamilton, Eve. We don't live way up at the other end of the Island anymore, for goodness' sake. And don't even think of coming along!"

"I done more than think," Eve snapped. "I'm goin'!"

"No, you are not. I'll feel far easier in my mind if I know you're here looking after—looking after everything."

"Mama," Pete whispered, clinging to Anne. "Mama, thank you for letting me go with you. William won't die, will he?" Then Pete, who prided herself on the fact that she seldom cried, began to sob. "Don't let them put William in the ground the way they did old Captain Wylly. Promise, Mama, promise!"

In the midst of trying to comfort her daughter, Anne looked at Eve, who had taken two or three steps back and stood quietly waiting, as though she had not demanded to go along.

"No, Pete," Anne said almost absently. "William's young and strong." Then she said to Eve, "I suppose you're pouting."

"No'm. I ain't. You got enough on yo' hans, Miss Anne. Eve stay here an' look arter things for you. Ain' I done tol' you one hun'ert times that I always gonna be jus' what you needs me to be?" To Pete, Eve added, "Now scoot, Petey. Run for Big Boy. He got to saddle yo' mama's horse so's the two ob you kin hurry ober to Retreat. Dat way you'll see for y'self dat yo' frien' Master William, he be gettin' better already."

AS SHE AND PETE GALLOPED TOWARD THE RETREAT road, Big Boy leading the way on Buck, Anne wished there had been time to tell John and Annie why she had to leave so fast and that it could well be several days before she would come home again. John was in his fields, and Annie was visiting at Cannon's Point this week.

She could feel Pete's arms tight around her waist, holding on for dear life. The girl was so afraid. Anne was afraid too. There

was only a year between Pete and young William Page King. Poor
Anna Matilda had lost both her parents and, because children did
often die, must not be asked to bear losing the son she'd named for
her beloved father. "As long as my little William is here," Anna
Matilda had told Anne, "I'll always have something of Papa left to
me." Her firstborn, the daughter she'd named Hannah for her
mother, and her father's namesake, William, would, Anne knew,
always hold a special place in her friend's heart.

Anne envied Pete, still refusing even to try to ride sidesaddle as
women rode. They would reach Retreat sooner if only Anne didn't
have to ride like a lady.

"Are you all right, Pete?" she called back over the pounding
hoofs.

"Yes, Mama, but I'm scared for us to get there!"

"I know, darling. Just remember what Eve said. Probably by
the time we reach Retreat, William will be better."

"Eve thinks she's so smart!"

"Sometimes she is. Sometimes, Pete, Eve does know ahead of
time about things."

"I'll never speak to her again if she's wrong about William!"
Pete was shouting, even though Anne knew her daughter was
trying hard to tone down. The child's shouting from fear now,
though, and if I'm any kind of a mother, I won't scold her today. It
must be hard being Pete. I can talk to blessed Annie the way I'd
talk to any other adult. Fanny is still a little girl. Pete must sometimes feel almost squeezed in, but she isn't. She truly isn't.

Up ahead, Big Boy turned in his saddle and waved to them
both. Anne planned to send him riding back to Hamilton with
messages for John and Eve. As soon as she found out exactly how
ill William King was, Big Boy would gladly ride back, then return
for her if by any chance she didn't need to spend a day or two with
Anna Matilda. Her gratitude moved toward the huge Ebo. If anyone knew that there was nothing he wouldn't do for Anne, it was
she.

"Mama, I'm—so scared!"

"Pray for William to be better," Anne called over her shoulder to the child. "It will help William and it will help you too. You won't be so scared if you talk to God while we're riding, Pete."

"I'll—try."

"That's my good girl. We'll be there in a few minutes now. Then we'll know everything about William. It will be much better when we learn what's really wrong with him."

"Don't talk anymore, Mama. I'm trying to pray."

"I   PRAYED   FOR   YOU   TOO,   MAMA," PETE   SAID, clutching Anne's hand as Big Boy led Gentleman to the Retreat stables and the two of them hurried up the path to Anna Matilda's front porch. "I thought you might need God to tell you what to say to William's mama."

"Oh Pete, thank you! That was such a thoughtful thing for you to do when your own heart hurts."

For the first time in Anne's entire life, she was arriving at Retreat Plantation with no one in sight. Not Anna Matilda, not her daughter Hannah, almost eight, no sign of a single servant. He was away so often, Anne gave no thought to the fact that Thomas Butler King was not on hand to greet them. Anna Matilda would not have sent for Anne had he been home. If one of her own children had been ill, Anne would have wanted only John to be with her. Anna Matilda needed her husband.

Hand in hand, Anne and Pete climbed the front steps that led to the shuttered veranda of the Kings' attractive but modest cottage. Anna Matilda complained about its size, but since Thomas had built a larger home at his new acreage called Monticello in Wayne County, they simply hadn't gotten around to enlarging the Retreat house.

"Will we just go on in even if no one invites us, Mama?"

"Yes, dear. With William ill, it's hard to tell where everyone is. I'm sure one of the servants will hear us."

"Lordy, Miss Anne, you hab to come in dis house without nobody to make you welcome!"

It was Lady—Maum Lady—"the head," as she considered herself because she was indeed the servant on whom everyone depended.

"Where is your mistress, Lady?" Anne asked.

"How's William?" Pete demanded. "Is—William dead?"

Stooping down to hug Pete, Lady murmured, "No, Miss Pete, don' you say such a thing! He ain' dead, but he be a pow'ful sick lil boy. He mama, she don' git no more'n dis from he bedside." The woman measured a few inches between her strong, brown hands. "Lordy, Miss Anne, Missus, she gonna be sick herse'f! She ain' slep' in more'n two nights."

"May I go up to her?" Anne asked.

"Me too," Pete piped. "If you go, Mama, so do I. Lady, is William even a little bit better today?"

"Oh chile, no. If anything, he worse. Dat po' lil fella, he burn up wif de fever!"

"See, Mama?" Pete shrilled, starting to cry. "See? Eve was wrong! Eve lied to me. She said he'd be better!"

"Sh. Keep your voice down, darling," Anne whispered. "You wouldn't do one single thing to make William worse, would you? He may be asleep, and hearing you could waken him."

"Does—does he need to sleep this time of day?" Pete whispered.

"Yes, yes, darling. Sleep is the very best thing for him at any time. Come on." Taking Pete's hand, she led the way up to the master bedroom, where Anne was sure Anna Matilda had the boy. "I suppose his father's away," she called softly down to Lady.

"Mausa King, he be gone de whole time. He don' eben know his boy's so sick. Young Miss Hannah, she be visitin' Miss Mary Abbott."

Inside the darkened bedroom, Pete hung back when Anne went quickly to her friend's side. Plainly, Anna Matilda had been dozing, even though she still held William's hand and was sitting up in a straight chair.

"I'm here," Anne whispered. "Pete's here too. She just had to come with me because she and William are such friends."

"Oh Anne! Anne, thank you," Anna Matilda said, her voice weary and hoarse. "He's—he's burning up with fever. But he seems to be sleeping now. Can you tell? Doesn't he seem to you to be sleeping? I'm—I'm so tired, I—I almost can't decide."

At the foot of his parents' big bed, where William lay, stood young Sally, Lady's daughter, keeping watch. Just being there so that Anna Matilda wouldn't have to keep her sorrowful vigil alone.

"Hello, Sally," Anne whispered. "I suppose you've tried to get your mistress to rest."

"Yes'm, I try. Eberbody try. She ain' gonna leabe him till you git here, Miss Anne. Maybe not den. You try?"

Her arm around her childhood friend, Anne leaned down. "Anna Matilda, it does look as though William's sleeping. Now that I'm here, can't you try to do the same? He may need you far more later."

Anna Matilda gave no real sign that she'd even heard what Anne said. Rather, she began to talk softly, her voice flat, almost as though she were already asleep herself. "We've wrapped him in cold compresses for hours at a time. Fever must be gotten down, you know. You know that. Too high a fever for too long can—can damage his brain. Such a good brain. Such a bright boy. There—there just couldn't be a brighter boy than my William. That's one of the many reasons I named him for Papa. Papa was not only very handsome, he was very intelligent. William is his image. Handsome and so bright."

"I know," Anne said, hoping Pete was still praying that her mother would be able to think of something that might help. "How long has it been since the last round of cold cloths, Anna Matilda?"

"Five minutes. No. It must be longer than that. Feel his little forehead, Anne. Does he still feel so hot?"

Her hand on the child's head, Anne drew in her breath sharply. "Yes. Yes, he's still—quite hot. Has Dr. Tunno been here?"

"Yesterday, I think it was. He says it's a bad fever from—something. William didn't seem to have a cold. But Dr. Tunno said he has an infection somewhere—somewhere in his little body to cause such a high fever."

"Well . . ." Anne felt as helpless as she sounded. "It *is* July. Summer is always bad for fevers. Anna Matilda, did you hear me say that Pete's with me? I thought she should be here. She and William are so close."

For the first time Anna Matilda looked up, her eyes searching the shadowy room. "Pete? Where are you?"

"Here. I'm right here. Eve said he would be better by the time Mama and I got here," the child said. "Could I feel his forehead too?"

"Why yes, my dear. Of course you can. William—William will be so happy when he wakes up and finds out you're here too. Go ahead."

Slowly, as though she were reaching toward a total stranger, Pete's hand barely touched the boy's head, then drew back. "He's hot as fire!"

"And I think it's time for his mother to go to another room and lie down if only for ten or fifteen minutes, while you and Sally and I go about the business of more cold cloths. Pete, run downstairs and tell Lady we need a big bucketful of the coldest well water she can find, with a chunk of ice in it." Just giving an order somehow gave Anne strength. "And some more clean cloths. This is something you and I can do for William ourselves and it just might help a lot."

When Pete tore out of the room, forgetting for the moment to tiptoe, Anne lifted Anna Matilda from the chair where she'd sat for so long. "You're going to lie down in another room—*now,* Anna Matilda. And don't give me any back talk. Pete's a big girl, and she and Sally and I—Lady will help if we need her—will begin a fresh round of cold compresses. We'll find a way to get that high fever down."

For a moment Anna Matilda fell into Anne's arms and wept. Anne held her without a word. Sally, Anne noticed, with the often remarkable sensitivity of the African, turned her back in silence, not daring to leave the room but not wanting to intrude into these deep moments when the two friends clung together.

"I take her to the room next door," Sally said when Anna Matilda raised her head from Anne's shoulder.

"Thank you, Sally," Anne murmured and took her place in the hard, straight chair her friend had just vacated.

FOR MORE THAN THREE HOURS ANNE, PETE, AND Sally, with Lady sending up fresh buckets of cold artesian well water, kept William's hot, sturdy body—chest, back, neck, arms, legs—wrapped in what to him, during brief, lucid moments, must have seemed icy-cold cloths. A responsible side of her own daughter showed itself to Anne in a way she'd never even suspected. Pete would someday grow into a truly strong, capable woman. Anne had known, of course, that Pete and William were best friends, at least for the past year, but she also saw with a shudder that even before her eighth birthday, the girl understood love.

Nothing would make Anne happier than for Pete and William to grow up and marry. The shudder came from her own fear of the heartbreak her daughter might know now if William died. And children did die. Children died often of the mysterious, scarcely treatable forms of fever that so frequently attacked them.

When Anna Matilda rushed back into the room in sheer panic that she had actually fallen asleep for a time, Anne longed to be able to tell her that the fever had broken, that William had, for a moment or two, shown signs that he might even be a little better. She couldn't.

"What?" Anna Matilda demanded. "What, Anne? You're just standing there! I know—I can tell from all this pile of wet cloths—that you've been trying, but why can't you tell me something?"

"Maybe, maybe," Pete offered, her face and voice so weary, Anne felt tears sting her own eyes, "maybe he's—not any worse."

Then without another word, Anna Matilda pushed Anne aside, Pete too, and sank again into the chair where she'd kept watch for more hours than anyone had thought to count.

THE DAY WORE INTO EVENING AND THE QUIET house—it was the little, snug cottage at Lawrence in the half-dream through which Anne battled back to consciousness—closed in on her. It seemed to stifle her so airlessly that she found herself sitting bolt upright in the bed trying to rouse Pete, sleeping beside her, when the sound of a galloping horse broke through her exhausted haze.

"Mama," Pete whispered. "What are you trying to do? Stop pulling on me!"

"I—I guess I was dreaming, darling. I thought we were both back at Lawrence, fastened inside some kind of box, without any air to breathe. Pete, I hear someone outside. Someone just rode up on a horse down in the Kings' front yard! Listen. . . ."

Pete leaped from the bed. "It's Papa! I hear Papa's voice down there, talking to somebody. Oh Mama, I'm sure Papa can think of something to do for William, aren't you? Aren't you sure he can think of—something?"

Fully awake now too, Anne smiled weakly, remembering John's utter helplessness each time one of their children had wakened them in the night with a touch of croup or crying from a bad dream.

"Miz Fraser! Miz Fraser, kin you come down a minute?"

The voice—plainly Lady's—came from the first-floor hall. Anne and Pete hurried down the stairs and into John's arms.

"Oh darling," Anne gasped, "I'm so glad you're here! I don't know what you can do. I don't know what anyone can do, but Pete and I are so glad to see you!"

"Yes, Papa," Pete gasped. "Oh Papa! William might—die!"

Giving Pete his full attention, John tried soothing her. "Now Petey, William's a big, strong boy. I'm sure he's on his way to getting completely well and I—"

"John, wait," Anne interrupted. "Don't promise her anything we can't be certain about. Pete's strong inside where it counts. I've watched her through all the long hours she and I were trying to take care of William while poor Anna Matilda got a little sleep. Pete's already grown up enough to—face facts. William *is* a very sick boy."

"Where's Anna Matilda now?" John asked, frowning, his great, tender heart showing in his wonderful face.

"Upstairs with William again. After all," Anne flared a little, "William's father isn't at home—as usual!"

"Where is he this time?" John asked.

"At some Constitutional Convention in Milledgeville, Anna Matilda says."

"That's ended."

"I know, but he's running for the state senate and had to make several stops on his way home for speeches and—oh John! I'm so glad it's you I love!"

"So am I, dearest Anne, but hadn't I better get Smart or one of the other King people to go for Dr. Tunno? I hear he's in Brunswick."

"He was here before Pete and I came. Dear Dr. Tunno's done all he can do."

"We've been wrapping William all over with cold cloths," Pete said, her chin trembling as she struggled not to cry. "It's an awful hot day, but William isn't just hot—he's burning up with fever. He's—he's so sick, Papa. And just last week, *nobody* could climb a tree faster than William! Not even me."

"I CAN'T LET HER GO HOME ALONE," ANNE WHISpered to John two days later as, with their older children and Anne's parents, she and John walked behind Anna Matilda. Anna was carrying her baby, Georgia, and leading the small boys, Henry Lord and Thomas Butler King, Jr., and Hannah through the thick Georgia heat across the churchyard, away from the newly mounded grave in the Page plot to the rear of Christ Church, Frederica.

"Mama," Pete said through sobs, "I—I can't just leave poor William here in the ground all by himself!"

"Sh, darling," Anne said softly. "William is already in heaven with God. That's only his body in that grave. William is fine again. Better than ever."

"But I—I only recognize William in his body, by the way he always looked! By the way his shoulders were, and his hands!"

Pete was nearly eight, but John, without a word, picked her up and carried her until they had all made the long, sorrowful walk down the church path to the spot under the big oak where he'd hitched the team and carriage.

"You know it's fine with me for you to go, darling," John said to Anne. "You need to be at Retreat with Anna Matilda. Pete, Annie, baby John, little Fanny, and I will be waiting for you when you feel free to come home. I'm sure, even with Thomas gone, someone will bring you over to Hamilton. That man may never forgive himself for being away when his son died."

"I can't bear to think of Thomas now," Anne said after she'd hugged Annie and given Pete a kiss. "Of course he had no way of knowing. William was fine when his father left home. I see Anna Matilda being helped into the King carriage. I must go." For a brief moment they squeezed each other's hands. "You know I'll be home as soon as I think I can leave her."

"I do know, darling. And God be with you every minute."

In the carriage beside her friend, Anne realized in an oddly deep way what John had just said to her: "God be with you every minute." They had seldom spoken of God together. She had always assumed that her beloved husband believed in Him. He must, she thought. His heart is too tender, he's too fine inside, not to know where that goodness comes from.

"I had to bring the littlest ones to William's service," Anna Matilda said, looking straight ahead, her tear-choked voice dull, broken. "Someday they'll be old enough to understand that they were right with their mother today. They'll be glad they came to tell their big brother—goodbye."

Quiet, sweet Hannah Page King reached from the seat opposite to pat her mother's hand. The girl was weeping too.

"You did everything—just right—for William," Anne said, fighting her own tears. "I've never admired you, Anna Matilda, as

I do this minute. And I don't want you to feel you have to talk Not now. Not when we get to Retreat. I'll just be on hand. I'll just be there at your house if you need me."

"It's—it's all right with John for you to come home with me?"

"Oh yes!"

For an instant Anna Matilda looked straight at Anne. "John loves you with all his heart." Then she straightened her slender shoulders. "Thomas—loves me too. He really loves me, Anne. His prominence in the state keeps him away so much."

"I know."

"There's something else too. And Thomas has made it possible. Our new, nice house in Wayne County is ready and waiting. You may as well know, Anne. With William—gone, I don't see how I'll ever be able to live at Retreat again. Not ever."

CHAPTER 45

"I ALWAYS THOUGHT CHILDREN FORGOT THEIR hurts in a hurry," Anne wrote in her diary on the morning of December 5 of that year 1833. "At least I did when I was Pete's age, but my tomboy daughter is unlike most children, or her mother is wrong about her. Here it is almost Christmas; we buried Anna Matilda's boy William back in July, and to this day Pete, at every opportunity, visits his little grave. Our house is quieter than usual because she's been at Cannon's Point for a whole week. I'm sure Papa has taken her to the churchyard to be with William. It isn't that she goes about moping much. She's learning to soften her speaking voice, but she still doesn't particularly like dolls and spends almost every hour, when she isn't studying her lessons or struggling to learn to sew, as high up as possible in her favorite live oak tree behind the house. It's the tree she found she could climb before little William King's legs were long enough for him to climb it, so I suppose—and this is only a mother's imagination— that the tree has special meaning for her. William did grow enough to climb it before he died, and I'd give almost anything if I could know exactly what she thinks about, now that the whole hot summer and autumn have passed. Pete is eight, and when I ask what she thinks about up in that tree, she just grins her father's wonderful grin (slightly devilish) and assures me that she is only memorizing Shakespeare or the Bible. I've never caught her in an out-and-out lie, though, and so I choose to believe she's simply getting to be more like John every day and adores teasing me. I'm certainly glad her sister Annie is old enough for real conversation. How I miss my old friend Anna Matilda, now that she's moved away from St. Simons."

Anne closed the little blue diary and went to stand by the bedroom window, which gave her the now-familiar but always heart-catching view of the Frederica River and its brown marshes stretching all the way to the mainland. Marshes that would turn green near the salt creeks when spring came.

I have lived my life, she thought, except for the years in Father Fraser's city house in London, surrounded by beauty. The kind of beauty city-bound folk travel miles to find.

Today, under a clear winter sun, she could see bright, autumn-red tupelo leaves still clinging to the trees on nearby Hawkins Island. There was even more beauty down in her own tended yard, and beyond Hawkins Island there was misty, distant mainland beauty.

I have a surfeit of beauty, she thought. Does so much of it sharpen the ugliness of death, especially the death of a young person? Does all this beauty heighten my own fear that something dreadful could happen to my beautiful son, John Couper—one year old next week? Why is it that I always think of our only son as John Couper and not just John? Is it because I want him to be a Couper or because there is room for only one John—my lover—his father?

For another moment she indulged herself in a familiar exercise of her imagination—one in which she tried and tried to blot out all that had happened, even the coming of her four beloved children, and to transport herself away from her spacious, beautiful home at Hamilton back to her own girlhood at Cannon's Point in the glowing months after she had fallen forever in love with Lieutenant John Fraser.

John.

Now she was the mother of his children and, wonder of wonders, the wife of his heart. And wonder of wonder of *wonders,* John seemed not only contented as a coastal planter but mostly happy in his work, even proud. Especially proud now that her much-lauded brother, James Hamilton, had decided to include him somehow in his very own business venture in far-off Alabama and Louisiana and Mississippi. James was in Natchez now, his young wife, Caroline, alone. Would John have to join James there at some future time? Fervently, she hoped not! Still, no one could deserve what Anne had. No woman deserved to have her husband as nearby as John had been almost every day and night since they'd come back to St. Simons. The thought of Anna Matilda, living now with her children at Monticello in Wayne County, probably climbing into an empty bed night after night because, as she put it, "Thomas's prominence in the state keeps him away so much of the time."

"How much can a wife be comforted by her husband's prominence anywhere?" Anne asked aloud, still looking out at the beauty of her one place to be. "I can only *ever* be comforted, I can only *ever* be warmed, by my husband's arms!"

A light knock startled her. "Who is it?"

The door opened and in stepped Eve with a letter in her hand. "I hear you talkin' an' thought somebody be in here wif you, Miss Anne, so I knock."

"You're supposed to knock anyway."

Eve smiled. "I knows dat."

"Can't you say *I know that?* Come on, try it."

"I know that," Eve said, enunciating like a lady.

"See?"

"Co'se I sees. But you reckon you like me the way you do if I was a white lady?"

"What on earth does that have to do with anything?"

"You want dis letter or not?"

"Of course I want it," Anne answered, now grinning too. "Where did you get it?"

"Tom's son, Cuffy, done come dis mornin' from Cannon's Point to live here an' be Mausa John's driver an' he bring it from yo' papa, Mausa Couper. Mausa Couper say to tell you he know you wait from one letter to the nex' from Mistah Willy Maxwell."

Anne grabbed the letter. "It's from Willy?"

"Why you think I say his name?"

"I know I ask dumb questions sometimes."

"Yes'm."

"You weren't supposed to agree with that, but you may go now. I need plenty of time to linger over any letter from Cousin Willy Maxwell."

When Eve had gone, Anne sat down in her favorite little rocker near the window and studied the unopened letter. It was sent from Boston, Massachusetts. Evidently the famous actress Miss Fanny Kemble and her father were playing a theater there, and Willy, with nothing else to do with his time, had gone along. Only Willy Maxwell could have addressed this, she thought, smiling as she admired his spidery, elegant script: *Lieutenant and Mrs. John Fraser, Hamilton Plantation, St. Simons Island, Georgia.* Then she excitedly broke the heavy red sealing wax and began to read.

> 15 November 1833
> Boston, Massachusetts
> Tremont Hotel

My dear John and Anne,

I know it is past time for me to return to London, but Fanny seems to want me to stay, and since I am a man whose roots go down quickly in any shallow place, I am still in the United States. Or, as Fanny calls it, "That dreadful America."

Dear Fanny's bark is far more attractive and also more dangerous than her bite. I do believe her when she declares that she needs me here for protection. Not only is her father enjoying himself by making money, he enjoys his social life and seems at times almost oblivious to the fact that his remarkable daughter is in a state of perpetual exhaustion simply from being adored by her audiences and a few particular gentlemen among them. One, a callow, sweet son of the socialite Biddles of Philadelphia; another, a highly cultivated musician copiously named Francis Henry Fitzhardinge Berkeley, who urged Fanny and Charles to make friends with a Philadelphia crony of his called Pierce Butler—named, I believe, for his hot-tempered, famous U.S. statesman grandfather, the late Major Pierce Butler.

Anne stopped reading. Major Pierce Butler, owner of Hampton Plantation, across Jones Creek from Lawrence and Cannon's Point, as well as Butler Island rice plantation, was dead but certainly well known and discussed to this day on St. Simons Island!

It seems that young Pierce Butler, evidently an accomplished flutist and an attorney of sorts, is totally smitten, along with many other young gentlemen in Philadelphia, Boston, New York, Washington—wherever the now highly famous Fanny has played—and is literally dogging her footsteps. For months he has been sending flowers, the card reading A Friend, but now they are perhaps more than friends. They ride together almost daily since Pierce—who, if not wealthy now, will be soon—has nothing more interesting to do than to follow in Fanny's footsteps, which he does with pretty-talking grace and, to me, a shallow, vapid character. Perhaps you can see that I find the young man, though delicate and genteel in appearance, *not* especially likable and certainly Fanny's inferior. Alas, who truly understands young love, though, so I go on being a friend to both Kembles and keep my questions to myself. In Washington Fanny bewitched even Justice Joseph Story of the Supreme Court, who ended up composing poetry for her and to her "deathless name."

Since it is now so near the end of the year, it is quite likely that I will succumb to the Kembles' pleading that I remain through Christmas and so will not book passage back to England until the early part of 1834.

Then, in his usual gentlemanly way, Willy asked to be remembered to all her children, to young Annie in particular, and to

Anne's parents, both her brothers and her sister, Isabella, with the promise that if Anne wrote to him at once, he would promise at least two more letters before sailing.

A glance at the gold watch around her neck told her that John would be out in his fields for another two hours or so, and once more she felt engulfed by a wave of loneliness for Anna Matilda. She had told her own daughter Annie everything she could remember about the long-ago night when Anne had seen the eight-year-old Fanny Kemble perform in London, while Annie was still an infant. Since Annie too was visiting at Cannon's Point, taking instruction from Isabella on how to tutor younger children, there would be no one with whom to share Willy's letter until John came home.

Back at the window again, she smiled, then hugged herself as she did so often these days at almost every fresh realization that John would be home eventually. With Pete and Annie gone, she felt lonely for adult talk, but her life was now so good she could at any time of the day miss her older daughters and John happily. Two-year-old Fanny was sound asleep, as was baby John Couper, but they were both right there in the big Hamilton house with her. And both well.

Her heart again reached toward Anna Matilda. It had been more than a month since Anne had heard from her. The house they called Monticello, in Wayne County, northwest of Brunswick, was evidently a good one, roomier than the Retreat cottage. But was Anna Matilda alone in it this week with only her elder daughter, Hannah Page, Pete's age, and the young ones? How did Anna Matilda, still grieving for young William, move through her days with Thomas so often gone? How did she while away the long evenings after the children went to bed?

Could I, Anne thought, ever live through one hour without knowing John was nearby? No, I could not!

CHAPTER 46

THE SPRING MONTHS ON ST. SIMONS FOLLOWED A
mild winter in the year 1834, spreading the woods and Hamilton's
front yard with azalea and wisteria blossoms and bright greens.
Each ride John and Anne took together through the woods behind
the cleared cotton fields to the east grew more magical.

"I'm glad you had this stretch of shadowy road cleared enough
for us to ride it," she called over to John from her perch atop
Gentleman. "Isn't it beautiful in this clear, green-white spring
light? And don't laugh at me for believing the light changes from
winter yellow to spring white, because it does! You'd know it if
you really looked, and you might even admit it if you weren't so
gorgeous and stubborn."

His musical laughter rang in the woodsy silence about them.
Silence that wasn't really silence except for the feel of it, because
nonpareils and towhees and spring warblers and cardinals called
nearby and from off toward the deepening light-struck shadows
where the road turned into still another shadowed and sunlit lane

—the familiar, partially overgrown shortcut Anne used to ride for her weekly visits to Retreat when Anna Matilda and her family still lived there.

"Don't just laugh at me about the light changing. Look at it!" she said, tightening Gentleman's reins enough to slow the spirited mount so that John could give her a handful of yellow jessamine he'd just reached up to pick as his Ginger, skittering as always, passed below an oak limb golden with the fragrant, vining blossoms.

"Slip these behind your ear—right there into that mass of dark curls, milady," he said, his hand touching Anne's cheek.

"Do you love me today?" she asked, tucking the bright flowers in her hair.

"I love you more every day and you're so beautiful on this spring Saturday, I don't even feel one shred of guilt that I'm leaving the work to our fine young Cuffy. The fellow's good. Your father picked exactly the right plantation driver for me. Do you suppose Mr. John Couper, Esquire, postmaster at Frederica, will hand us a letter from Willy at church tomorrow?"

"I hope so! I wrote back to him right after we got his letter about Fanny Kemble and old Major Butler's grandson, Pierce, and we haven't heard one word since. Cousin Willy must be back in London by now. Or maybe he's even in Scotland at Caerlaverock."

"Do you wish we were at Caerlaverock today?" John asked.

"I want to be exactly where we are—on this bright-dark woodsy road with our dear Annie over there in our own handsome house teaching Pete her lessons like a grown-up tutor. My world is right here, especially now that I've finally given you a son. Do you sometimes get a sense that our little square-shouldered John Couper is going to grow up to be almost as high-spirited and handsome as his father?"

"Do you believe that's really possible, wife?" John laughed. "I often think how glad I am that he did not inherit his father's long face. The boy's features are as nearly perfect as a child's face can be! And he has your singular, lovely, pale blue eyes. What do you suppose he and Eve are doing this minute?"

"Probably laughing. Those two seem to find each other extremely funny. Have you noticed? I think Eve would rather play pattycake than John Couper. I don't think she's wasting time when they play so well together, do you?"

"No, I do not think Eve ever actually wastes time. I know she makes you cross when she doesn't always do exactly what you've asked her to do, but she ends up with it done, doesn't she?"

They had reined their horses now and Anne held out her arms to be lifted to the ground. "Let's go find some wood violets. Suddenly I want a bunch of violets in a bowl beside our bed, don't you?"

He lifted her down, kissed her, secured the jessamine, which had slipped down over her ear, and said, "Mind reader. We were discussing Eve's surprising gifts with our son, but all the time what I really wanted to tell you was that night after night I've been dreaming of a bowl of wood violets."

Holding hands, they ran off into the green woods, laughing like children. "Do you know how glad I am that you're so foolish?" She took his face between her hands. "And that you're so glorious and smart and always in demand on this Island? Have you thought about how James Hamilton is honoring you by asking you to handle all the arrangements for his summer boat race on the Frederica while he's away doing his cottonseed business in Natchez?"

John returned her smile. "Indeed I feel honored. Of course I do know a thing or two about boats, but nothing at all about being master of ceremonies at a high-society boat race with people entering boats from as far away as New York. The man's taking a tremendous chance with me."

"James Hamilton Couper never takes a chance," she declared. "Everything he does is carefully thought out, jotted down, charted, measured, and weighed. He knows you'll be magnificent!"

Accustomed as she thought she was to John's mercurial changes of mood, he surprised her by asking quite solemnly, "Has your brother ever failed at anything?"

Just then she spied a thick patch of violets and stooped to begin picking.

"I asked you a question, Anne. Answer, then I'll help you pick.

It's important for me to know if James Hamilton Couper has ever had one project go wrong for him."

Surprised, she stood up, a dozen or so purple violets in her hand. "You're serious, aren't you?"

"Yes."

"I—I honestly don't know, darling. Anyway, what difference does it make?"

His half-smile was not very convincing. "I guess I honestly don't know the answer to that either. So forget it." Another quick mood change and he was now kneeling too, picking flowers along with her. "I was just wondering, I guess, how his highness would act should I have to report that his Hopeton boat, manned by his Hopeton people, did not win the race this summer—providing he's still away and I am saddled with handling the whole event."

Standing, Anne looked down at him on his knees, dutifully gathering the violets she wanted. "My brother doesn't still make you nervous, does he?"

"Did I ever say he did?"

"No, not in so many words. But I do have a woman's intuition. Could I ask you something?"

Kneeling in the violet patch, he looked up and grinned. "I thought you just did."

"Will you have to be away in Natchez or Mobile or New Orleans, too, at any point in this peculiar cottonseed oil deal of James Hamilton's?"

Handing her a sizable bunch of violets, John stood up. "I may sometime in the future. I swear to you I know almost nothing about it. I simply know that the fact that your brother has some-how included me is—think it odd if you like—mightily encouraging to me. I do admire the gentleman, Anne. I've always admired him, rather looked up to him, and disliked doing it much of the time. Somehow I don't mind anymore. I've come to like James. I have no extra money yet to invest in his project, so he must have something in mind for me to do in behalf of it. Would it make you so unhappy if I did have to spend a few months away?"

"Of course it would make me unhappy! But I'd be ever so proud of you because whatever he has in mind for you, you'll do to perfection." Her skirt full of violets, she reached to hug him. "Darling, do I love you too much? Do I—cling? Do you still get sieges of wanderlust? Do you hope James does need you to travel some in behalf of his cottonseed oil?"

"You could never love me too much. I love it when you cling like this and"—he laughed right in the middle of a kiss—"how could I possibly have a siege of wanderlust when I've been all the way to Darien, Georgia, twice in six months?"

"Be serious!"

"I am serious. True, I stayed only long enough to go over some of Father's estate business with William on one Darien adventure, but the next time I actually stayed two whole days!" When Anne laughed and stuck a bunch of violets under his nose, he said, "Now *you* be serious, milady. Anna Matilda's having another baby in July. Don't you want to be with her at Monticello for this one? You know, it might be a very good thing that Thomas Butler King isn't at home much. Have you thought of that? Poor Anna Matilda might not be equal to more visits from the man!"

"Don't be mean."

"That isn't mean. It's factual. I suppose, though, that Isabella and her parson will be getting married about the same time. You'll want to be here. What a lovely matron of honor you'll be! Shall you and I get married again—join in the ceremony?"

"Papa would think that as funny as you evidently do. Somehow I doubt that Mama would. This is to be sweet, gentle Isabella's special time to shine. Mama is adamant about that."

"Those two are planning to enter into the bonds of matrimony in July, aren't they?"

"Do you sometimes feel as though you're in bonds?"

He turned her around so that she faced the woods about them —streaks of clear sunlight picking out a thousand different greens —and commanded her to apologize not only to him but to the very soul of St. Simons.

"Apologize?"

"Apologize. I don't miss the Royal Marines much anymore, but I haven't forgotten how to give a command. I command you to shout—not whisper—shout so that the gulls riding over on the

Frederica River can hear. Go on, admit to being ashamed for even having such a thought."

"Don't hold me so hard. You're breaking my arm!"

"Then say you're deeply sorry."

Instead, she held his face down to hers and kissed him until, only half joking, he began to plead for mercy. "Anne, Cuffy's a— good driver, but I do have work—to do yet today! Mercy, woman, have mercy on your weak, adoring husband! Say you're sorry. . . ."

"Never," she answered, still kissing him. "I want you weak and romantic and never, never restless in our bonds, because I'm in bonds to you, too. Is that clear, sir?"

Holding her away from him, he asked, "Can you imagine that talk of the wedding of quiet Isabella to her reserved, pious parson could stir up a storm like this on such a sunny day?"

"Never mind," she said pertly, giving him another kiss, a mercifully light one this time. "There won't be any sun tonight."

"No," he breathed, "I guarantee it. Look. We dropped your violets!"

"Kind of in a bunch, though. Help me pick them up and I promise not to tease anymore."

Busily helping her retrieve the scattered, now-wilting violets, John reminded her that they'd have to get to bed early tonight if they were going to be on time for church tomorrow. "It does take longer to drive from down here, and there could be a letter from good old Willy."

"Do you suppose that young Pierce Butler Willy wrote about in his last letter might somehow inherit Hampton Plantation across Jones Creek?"

"Should he be one of the old major's heirs, I wouldn't be a bit surprised," John said. "If he does, Willy's Miss Fanny Kemble will have seduced a very, very rich young man. I imagine he would also own all fifteen hundred acres of Butler Island too."

"It wasn't very nice of you to say Fanny Kemble *seduced* him."

He held out one hand for her to step into when she remounted Gentleman. "I may not be nice, milady," he said, smiling. "But oh, I'm charming!"

CHAPTER 47

THE LONG-EXPECTED LETTER FROM WILLY MAX-
well did not reach St. Simons until August, after the birth of Anna
Matilda's third daughter, Florence, at Monticello, and following
Isabella's lovely, simple wedding to the Reverend Theodore Bartow in July.

Papa had handed Willy's letter to Anne in the churchyard
today, Sunday, August 17, and all through the sermon Anne had
fidgeted to read it. The unexpected arrival of Dr. William Fraser
and Frances Anne with their two sons, nine-year-old James and
year-old Menzies, now napping beside them on the Hamilton veranda, prevented her even opening the letter until she and Frances
settled for the afternoon together.

"I'm relieved that our husbands and James wanted to go out in
John's new little sailboat," Frances Anne said as Lovey, less a feisty
pup by now, settled at Anne's feet. "Do you remember what a time
that little dog had finding room on your lap the night your Fanny

was born? I've laughed often over that dear doggie, because there really wasn't room for him. You almost had no lap!"

"I'll never forget that." Anne laughed too. "But there was an even more dramatic night when baby John Couper decided to join us with no one in the house but Eve, Annie, poor Pete, and me!"

"I always thought my young Menzies was the handsomest member of our family, but Anne, your John Couper is a perfectly beautiful child! Is he much trouble?"

"I know this sounds ridiculous," Anne declared, "but he's as good as he is beautiful. I do love to brag about my son, but since you already know about the night in London all those years ago when we saw eight-year-old Fanny Kemble perform at her father's Covent Garden, I simply have to force Willy Maxwell's latest letter on you. I'm sure there'll be at least some news of Fanny Kemble in it. Do you mind?"

"Mind! Anne, I live in Darien, Georgia, don't forget, with the world's sweetest but busiest doctor, and some days boredom is my closest friend. I thought you'd never offer to share your cousin's letter. I'm all ears!"

"I'm sure poor Mama is too," Anne laughed as she broke the heavy seal and smoothed the folds in Willy's two pages. "He's written it from Mama's Maxwell family's ruined old castle near Dumfries, Scotland, and my poor mother would give almost anything she owns—almost anything Papa owns—for one glimpse of Caerlaverock. I did write you that the now-famous Miss Fanny Kemble is in America on tour with her father, Charles, didn't I?"

"You most certainly did. You wrote at length about her tour while Lord Herries was still here on St. Simons, visiting you and John. Just before you moved into this gorgeous Hamilton house."

"I hope Willy's all right. He's very late with this letter. I've been on needles and pins wondering where he went when he left New York early this year; he'd just managed to pique my interest in the romantic life of his friend Fanny Kemble. In his last letter he said the men in the Northeast were at her feet. Even old Major Butler's grandson, Pierce Butler!"

Frances Anne jumped to attention. "Oh yes! You wrote about

the young Pierce Butler. Do you suppose Fanny Kemble married him?"

"How do I know? Hush. I'm going to read."

> "10 July 1834
> Caerlaverock, Dumfries, Scotland

Dear John and Anne,

Although I beg forgiveness for my long silence, I will not bore you with details of why you have not heard from me. I will encapsulate merely by saying I have been in London for weeks and weeks, waiting while my legal manipulators do the dreary things they do in order to buy and sell various of my properties. But now I am healing my stiff emotions by summering at Caerlaverock. Why is it that flowers that bloom out of cracks in ancient walls of a ruin are so beautiful?

"I'm afraid I left my gossip about the Kembles rather in limbo, because your two letters since my last, dear Anne, were filled with questions concerning the famous Fanny. I will, for that reason, home in directly on her latest adventure. She is now firmly *anchored* and in my opinion, not wisely. The world's most talented and magical actress has been married since June 7 to the cultivated, flute-playing, rather pretty young Pierce Butler, grandson of the late Major Pierce Butler, who owned Hampton Plantation (from where I heard the screams of slaves being whipped while I was spending those otherwise enchanted days on St. Simons). I do not believe young, would-be charming Pierce actually owns the two Georgia plantations left by his hot-tempered grandfather, but on the death of an elderly relative, he will become as wealthy as he is arrogant and charming."

"Anne! I simply can't believe what you've just read. Can you?"

"It's true, Frances, or dear Willy wouldn't have written it. I know he's heartbroken, because he most definitely did *not like* young Pierce Butler, who was literally dogging Fanny Kemble's footsteps all over the northeastern coast! Willy thinks young Butler is most certainly not worthy of such a wife as Miss Fanny Kemble."

"Read, read, read! There's more, isn't there?"

"Unfortunately not much, except that Willy, when the Kembles' American tour ended, sailed back to Liverpool with her father, Charles, to whom Fanny gave all her share of the American earnings from nearly two years of performances."

"Well," Frances Anne said, "if her new husband is eventually going to inherit even the old major's two huge Georgia holdings, she certainly won't want for anything! Anne, do you suppose she might come here to visit ever?"

"No, I do not. Where would such a fine English lady as Miss Fanny Kemble live—either at Butler Island or across Jones Creek from Cannon's Point here on St. Simons? There isn't a decent house at either place. Old Major Butler's mansion at Hampton crumbled to ruins long ago. Only a few rooms are livable and Roswell King uses them. There's only a rickety overseer's house at Butler Island. At least it would be rickety to a lady like her!"

"Do you suppose she'll ever act again on the stage?"

"I wouldn't think so. Evidently her snooty young husband won't allow it. Anyway, Fanny Kemble really hates acting."

"Hates acting? As magnificent as she's supposed to be? As talented?"

"She's always wanted to be a writer. Willy told me that long ago. She made her professional stage debut only to keep her beloved father's Covent Garden from financial ruin. She saved his theater. She also saved her father from ruin. I—I wonder why I feel such genuine concern for her? I do, you know. Oh dear, can you think of anything worse than being married to a man as callow and spoiled as Willy declares young Pierce Butler to be?"

Frances Anne gave her a warm, tender smile. "Anne, I can't honestly imagine being married to—anyone but my gentle, calm, good William. Everyone knows how romantically you and your John met—knows that he really did capture you in all ways. William also captured all of me. Because of the Wyllys' long loyalties to anything British, the Royal Marines went rather easy on my dear father back when they took over our Island, but William became my life. I knew it from the moment I spoke briefly with him the day of your wedding to John. You and John may have met on Cumberland in the most romantic circumstances, but William and I love as deeply. I don't help him much by nagging because he works too hard at the hospital in Darien—makes himself too available to everyone in town with a stomach ache—but I love him with my whole being. Do you suppose a woman like Fanny Kemble—I guess I should say Fanny Kemble Butler now—could ever really love a man the way you and I love our men?"

"I don't see why not."

"Because her own life has always been so full and exciting, I guess. I suppose that's what I mean."

"Were you so dissatisfied growing up here on St. Simons, Frances Anne?"

"I was too young to recognize dissatisfaction, and for all we know now, even Fanny Kemble's life may be full of shadows. Shadows and heartache. Who can tell about any other woman by looking at her life only from the outside?"

Anne smiled. "Who would have imagined just a few years ago that my little sister, Isabella, could have found such happiness as she's so plainly found with her Reverend Bartow? She glows inside and out, doesn't she?"

"And your Annie! Am I only imagining that she has found a fortunate young man?"

"My Annie? Oh I don't think so! She's only seventeen, Frances."

"And how old were you back in 1815 when you left in your father's plantation boat for Cumberland Island and Louisa Shaw's house party, where young Lieutenant John Fraser literally captured you?"

"I was nearly eighteen. I met him on my eighteenth birthday!"

"And won't Annie be eighteen early next year?"

Anne frowned. "In February, yes. Frances Anne, don't even *think* of such a thing as Annie's falling in love—not yet!"

"Give me one good reason why not."

"I—I'd miss her too much. Why, there's so much difference in

Annie's and Pete's ages, without Annie when John's out working in his fields, there are hours and hours when I wouldn't have another adult to talk to except Eve."

"Speaking of Eve—"

"Which we weren't."

"Speaking of Eve, have you ever wondered why she and June have never had a child?"

"Yes, I've wondered."

"What does Eve say about it? She wants children, doesn't she?"

"How would I know?"

"You and Eve have always been closer than mistress and servant, Anne. Why do you try to pretend it's not true?"

"I don't try to pretend that. We're just very nearly the same age and—well, you're right. Eve is my friend. I simply have so much trouble trying to follow Mama's instructions about keeping the proper, workable distance between mistress and servant that I—" Anne leaned over to pat Lovey's head. "Why are we discussing Eve?"

"You have to admit she's not like the other people."

"She refuses to stop butchering the English language the way they do!" Anne snapped.

"Does she actually refuse or is it because all darkies speak peculiarly?"

"Eve's half-white, you know."

"Of course I know. Everyone on the Island knows she's half-white. No one seems absolutely sure who her white father really was, but—"

"What made you say my Annie had found a young man to love?"

"I simply said I think she acts as though she has found someone. You're suddenly quite prickly and I'm the one with at least the semblance of a reason to be prickly. You see, I think I'm carrying another child."

Anne shifted to the edge of her chair so quickly, Lovey growled protectively, came awake enough to see that nothing was harming Anne, then stretched full length on the porch floor.

"Never mind, Lovey. Frances Anne just surprised me. Are you really carrying another child? That's the best news ever!"

"William and I think I must be, yes. I missed my time last month." Frances Anne laughed. "Hadn't you noticed that William looks like the cat that ate the canary? Pleased, but a little worried?"

Anne laughed. "I don't know dear William that well. I know he looks tired. I did notice that, but even young Dr. Tunno looked so exhausted the last time we saw him, I guess I just expect all doctors to look pale and a little weary. If you are carrying another baby—when? When might it be here?"

"Next spring sometime, I'd think. Do you hope you and John have another child, Anne? You and I aren't as young as we might be, you know. Are you thirty-seven?"

"Yes, nosy. And you're thirty-six. You don't have any wild ideas about the name of the young man my Annie is supposed to be in love with, do you?"

Frances laughed. "You're a worrywart, Anne. No. I just thought she looked awfully happy."

"The girl *is* happy. She loves teaching Pete and swears her little tomboy sister is going to be a superb elocutionist. Pete always did talk a lot, you know. That girl could talk her way out of a croker sack with a rope tied around it. It's too bad in a way that Pete's a girl. She might have been a great preacher or a senator had she been born a boy. But I do think Annie is a happy young woman. I honestly don't see how a family could be anything but happy with our life here at Hamilton."

"Do you remember telling me the night Little Fanny was born that secretly you hated leaving the cottage at Lawrence?"

"Of course I remember. I still dream about the little Lawrence house because my beloved papa was so happy giving it to John and me. I'll never forget the first day he took us there. Never. Sometimes I still miss the place, standing there empty and silent. But Hamilton has made John sure of himself, proud of his work, and it's always going to be the one place my children call home. Because we're all so happy together here, some days even I have trouble believing it's true."

WHEN THE NEXT YEAR, 1835, ROLLED AROUND, Frances Anne gave birth to another son, named Clarence Brailsford after a Darien patient who had shown William many kindnesses. On May 3, nearly a month after Frances Anne's child came, Jock read in his *National Intelligencer* that the Pierce Butlers of Philadelphia—Fanny Kemble and her young man, who struck Willy as so wrong for her—had a daughter named Sarah. Fanny Kemble Butler, Anne was sure, had named her first child for her world-famous aunt, the great actress Sarah Siddons.

In August Anne was in the midst of writing about the newly born Butler daughter in a letter to Frances Anne when Captain Frewin, of Frederica, arrived with the sad notice of the "death from unknown causes of Clarence Brailsford Fraser, infant son of Dr. and Mrs. William Fraser, of Darien." Burial, Frewin said, would take place tomorrow in Christ Church cemetery on St. Simons Island.

Anne thanked him, offered him lemonade, which he refused, bid him good day, then sat weeping on her veranda until Lovey began to whine and Eve came out to look for her mistress.

"I know something make you sad, Miss Anne," Eve whispered, one hand resting lightly on Anne's shoulder. "Eve wish she could help you."

"Oh Eve, it isn't I who need help. It's—sometimes it seems it's almost everyone else *but* me. How can my life be all perfect when there is so much sorrow and sadness in the world? Even in this little world right around us?"

PART V

APRIL 1836—
APRIL 1839

CHAPTER 48

IN THE MONTHS THAT FOLLOWED, ANNE HAD DONE her level best to write often to Frances Anne, reminding her that not only she, but perhaps even God, was trusting Frances to find a redemptive use for the singular kind of grief she must feel at the loss of such a tiny baby.

"If God is a Redeemer God," Anne wrote on a soft, rainy April morning of the next year, 1836, "surely He will find a way to redeem your every tear. Each time I write such things to you, I pray you are aware that I feel most inadequate within myself, since the years so far in my own life have been undeservedly kind to me. I wish you and William might have been able to attend the beautiful Centennial service at Christ Church on 14 February past, because Papa's old friend Mr. Thomas Spalding gave the address and spoke from his great, tender heart about the one hundred years since Evening Prayers were first said, with General Oglethorpe present, at the very beginning of our congregation on St. Simons. That was on a Sunday, February 15, 1736, but the nearest Sunday one hundred years later fell on February 14 this year. After the service we visited the graves of our loved ones in the cemetery. With John and me were Pete, Annie and her young friend Paul Demere, our little Fanny—your namesake, now four—John Couper in his father's arms, my blessed parents, your mother, and your sisters, Anne Frances and Heriot. All went to the tiny grave of your infant and prayed. Papa prayed that you and William could find strength through your faith because our God is real and ever-mindful of each tear and each heartache."

She had also written to Frances that Anna Matilda, still unable to return to her old home at Retreat, was again the mother of a new baby—another son, Mallery Page King—born at their large, fine home at Waverly in Camden County, south of Brunswick. "Why the Kings don't move to Waverly I don't understand," Anne wrote, "since the house there is so much better than Monticello. Even the closest among us can't always understand, can we? I do try to be patient with Anna Matilda, though, because Thomas is still away so much, even though he evidently makes up for her loneliness when he does finally reach home again.

"And now for my own news: I too am sure I am carrying another child! With all my heart, I hope this does not make you sad because of your own recent tragedy and loss. I am sure you must feel often that I am too blessed, that no one could deserve all I have been given. Frances Anne, should you feel that way, I agree! I can never deserve such joy and fulfillment as I know every day of my life! How do you suppose God decides who suffers and who knows joy like mine? Does William still have his cough? John caught a bad cold last month but seems fine now. I sometimes wonder if both our beloveds—John and William—might, as they grow older, pay up for all the years of exposure and hardship endured during their years of military life? Do try to keep William from working so hard. I realize he feels as called to his medical profession as Isabella's Theodore to the ministry, but if you can, without seeming to nag, try to think of ways to make him rest. My parents are both quite well, considering that Mama, who has always been young and beautiful, is now 61 and dear Papa 77. If he didn't limp from his rheumatism, though, he would, I know, still ride his fields every day.

"Your dear mother looks extremely well and strikes me as being more tranquil every time I see her. It is as though she has made her own peace with losing your father. Making peace with the kind of agony death must bring is a spiritual achievement, it seems to me. I know I could never do it. Last week, when Annie and I called at the Village, your mother told me that gratitude for all she had been given through your dear father was the secret of her tranquillity. Are we grateful enough, Frances Anne? The truthful answer is no. I *feel* I am at my most grateful when I am close to John—close to his dear body and his dear heart. Then I look at my lovely Annie, at Pete, at little Fanny, and at my beautiful John Couper, and I feel lost in gratitude. But my thanks are still too limited to match God's goodness to me.

"One day when my heart is heavy—as it surely will be sometime in my life—will you remind me, beloved friend, of your mother's words about being grateful?"

AT BREAKFAST IN THE CANNON'S POINT DINING room during the first week in September, Jock Couper reached for his wife's hand and sat holding it, his expressive face a mixture of self-deprecatory humor and annoyance. "I plan to say something in a minute, Becca, but not until I've thought it through a bit. I tend to talk too much when an unavoidable contact with our neighbors on the other side of Jones Creek interrupts my day."

"You're crossing the creek to see Roswell King, Jr., my dear? Is it absolutely necessary? I'd hoped you might just sit with me on the veranda until Anne gets here. Did you forget she's visiting us today?"

"I'm old, wife, but not that old! Of course I know our blessed Anne is coming up from Hamilton. With another child due before December, she shouldn't chance a long carriage ride like that, but she's as stubborn as her papa ever was."

"She needs us, Jock. The child knows that after this visit, she really mustn't risk another long ride. Do you want to tell me why you're going over to Hampton today?"

"I was commanded!"

"Commanded? By whom?"

"Old King's son, Roswell Jr. He sent word by poor Robert late yesterday for me to come before noon today. A matter, he vows, of great importance."

"If it's so important, why can't he come to you? He's a lot younger, heaven knows!"

"I'm perfectly able to take a skiff across Jones Creek, Becca! I don't want to go, but I'm perfectly able." He got to his feet. "And if Anne gets here before I'm dismissed by the high-and-mighty Mr. King, assure her that I'll be back as soon as possible. Try to get her to lie down for a short rest."

"Anne will be fine, Jock. You know Eve's right on that carriage seat with her, looking after her every need—if indeed she has any. Our elder daughter knows her way through the vicissitudes of having a baby by now, don't forget. And she's had almost no morning sickness at all with this little one. Don't worry. She and I won't discuss anything you'd mind missing. Just be careful."

"Johnson is going with me, and if you think he won't be watching me like a mother hen, you need to smarten up."

She laughed. "My but you're pert today," she said when he stooped to kiss her hair. "You don't suppose Anne's visit has any-thing to do with her father's briggledy mood, do you?"

WHEN JOHNSON PULLED THE SMALL SKIFF UP ONTO the sand at the Hampton side of Jones Creek and helped his master out, Couper handed him a bundle.

"What this, Mausa John?"

"A little something for Robert. Tell him Sans Foix made it just for him. It's a package of Sans Foix's tarts—the kind for which your friend poor Robert suffered many beatings for sneaking across the creek when old man King was still here."

Johnson took the bundle with a half-smile. "I members, sir. When Robert still be a young boy, he sneak across Jones Creek 'cause he get to the place where he couldn't stan' it one more day without one of Sans Foix's fruit tarts. I give it to him. Want me to walk with you up the path?"

"I do not," Couper said curtly. "I'm perfectly able to walk, Johnny. But after you give Robert his present, stay close to our skiff. I mean to end this highly important consultation at the earliest possible moment."

SEATED WITH PUDGY YOUNG ROSWELL KING ON THE small, carefully swept porch of the manager's house, Jock Couper listened to him launch into a near diatribe against the new Philadelphia owners of both Hampton and Butler Island.

"As of March 1836, Mr. Couper, the two grandsons of the late Major Butler came legally into the ownership of this place and of the enormous holding called Butler Island. Both properties are now owned by John and Pierce Butler. John Butler's letters to me have seemed rather reasonable. I cannot say the same for those from Mr. Pierce Butler. Oh, they are the letters of a cultivated, highly educated gentleman, as you might surmise, but most demanding. I'm sure you are fully aware of the time and efforts of both my esteemed father and me in the management and success of the two Butler plantations. I doubt that any man knows better than you that there are no plantations in the entire area as prosperous as have been Butler Island and Hampton under the care of the Kings."

"I am well aware that your father and you have outearned my own Cannon's Point, if that's what you're driving at, Roswell."

King smacked at a mosquito attacking the fat bulge around his waistline. "Uh—exactly. It has long been clear to me, and I have conferred at length with my father on the subject, that no one man can manage both plantations with the same degree of success, since one supervisor cannot wrest adequate work from over seven hundred niggers. This place is larger than Cannon's Point and Lawrence combined, and Butler Island is fifteen hundred acres, more or less. I am resigning, therefore, as soon as a replacement can be found and have so notified young Mr. Pierce Butler of Philadelphia." Then Roswell laughed in a manner that struck Jock as being both bitter and delighted.

"And you are pleased with yourself, Roswell?" Couper asked.

"Enormously! The wealth-laden young Philadelphia blue blood, Pierce, already had more than enough on his dainty hands —he had those dainty hands full, you might say—in the famous, hard-to-handle person of his new wife, Frances Kemble Butler. The lady, I believe, is visiting now in her native England with their only child, a daughter named Sarah. That she *fled* to England would probably tell the tale far better than to call it a mere visit. Young Butler came to inspect his fortune called Butler Island during her absence and—"

"The new owner visited Butler Island and didn't come over here to Hampton?" Jock asked, surprised.

"I gathered he did not care for our damp weather, so feigned the need to return to Philadelphia, but the truth is he came only to see for himself just how wealthy he really is now and how much wealthier he will become—would have become, that is, had I not decided to resign. I would have either failed with both plantations or killed myself in the process. Those are the exact words I wrote to him, and because you are my closest neighbor, I thought you had a right to know."

As though Roswell King had not made his startling announcement about resigning, Jock, too devilish to resist, made no comment whatever. Chose to ignore it. Instead, he asked, "And why, pray, did young Mrs. Pierce Butler feel she had to *flee* to her native England?"

The effect on Roswell King, Jr., was even better than Couper had hoped. He not only grew red in the face but choked on his snuff and sputtered, "Why—why, the dastardly book she wrote, of course! Do you mean a man who keeps abreast of events as you do hasn't heard that the woman almost broke up her marriage when she surreptitiously allowed her American *Journal* to be published?

I hear it's a scathing, ill-timed, critical piece of writing as vicious as all the other so-called journals penned by any of those haughty Britishers. Vicious against slavery. The publication in 1835 of her *Journal*—published it against her husband's will, she did, in both America and London—was reason enough to flee the country, I'd say! I'm a courageous man, as you well know, Couper, but I did not dare utter one word about that book when her dilettante husband paid his call on Butler Island. He's a slightly built, delicate-appearing fellow, but one look at his eyes and you know he's well named—*Pierce!* Those eyes can pierce, believe me."

Jock needed an answer to only one question and he asked but one: "Do you know who will be replacing you as manager of Hampton, sir?"

"I suggested Mr. James Gowen of this Island, and he's to be handed a well-run and well-organized plantation to manage."

"Oh yes. I know Gowen. A fine fellow."

Jock said his farewells as quickly as he could manage with any tact at all and in no time was sitting on his own veranda, his rocker pulled close enough to Anne's for them to hold hands.

"Don't anyone say a word for a minute," Anne whispered. "I need to be quiet here in this blessed, familiar place. Did either of you know that the silence at Cannon's Point is unlike any other silence—anywhere?"

"How can dat be?" Eve asked, incredulously, and although she was sitting off to one side on a footstool in order to be nearby if Anne needed anything, Jock saw Rebecca's slight frown of disapproval. He knew, of course, that by Becca's rules, servants spoke when spoken to.

"I believe, Eve, that Anne was addressing her father and me," Rebecca said, her voice kind but unmistakably that of mistress to servant.

"Mama," Anne said, a touch sharply. "Do we have to be so—so proper today?"

"Eve's used to living in a house full of talkative children," Jock half apologized for Eve. "She just gets in a word when she can, I'm sure."

"Papa," Anne said, as though there had been no remotely awkward moment between Mama and Eve, "what did Mr. Roswell King, Jr., want to tell you that was so important?"

"Good news," Jock said. "He's resigning."

"*Resigning?*" Rebecca asked. "I know you've never been overly fond of either King, but is that quite neighborly of you to call it good news?"

"Anne's right, Becca. We don't need to be so proper today, and you're right too. I've never been at all partial to either King. Saw their inestimable worth, certainly, but 'twill be good to have them both gone. Can't help but be better for the poor Hampton people too. By the way, Anne, I slipped a bundle of Sans Foix's berry tarts to Robert while I was over there."

"Good," Anne said. "Robert used to dream about those tarts."

"And tasting them again will probably force the boy to sneak across the creek for more. Then you know what will happen to him, Jock."

"Maybe not, Becca, if Roswell King, Jr., is ever really gone. James Gowen is taking over soon, and unless the new young Philadelphia owners, John and Pierce Butler, force him to it, I can't see James Gowen ordering much whipping."

"The new young owners may demand it," Rebecca said.

"If Gowen makes money for them, I doubt how much they'll even learn of what he does in the way of discipline. It seems that King thinks Pierce Butler is the greediest, the most spoiled of the two brothers, probably the most demanding. But Pierce Butler has his hands full, as King said, with a new wife and child. The wife, the much-lauded actress Fanny Kemble, has her husband upset, by the way, with a book she's written titled *Journal*. Seems it's highly critical, not only of American customs but of slavery. She's of the proverbial British antislavery turn of mind and greatly under the influence of the Reverend William Ellery Channing, the Boston abolitionist. King told me that as I was taking my leave."

"Has the *Journal* been published?" Anne wanted to know.

"It has indeed, Daughter, in total disobedience of her husband's wishes. That marriage, while already a famous one, appears also to be a bit rocky."

"Oh dear," Rebecca said, "I feel sorry for poor little mild, conscientious Mrs. James Gowen. It sounds as though her husband will have his hands full, too, at least with young Mr. Pierce Butler."

"The bad part will undoubtedly come in connection with Butler Island," Jock said. "It is too much for one man to operate both places. Gowen will be in charge only of Hampton. Still, no woman could have an easy time of making a home in that decaying Hampton mansion, where old Major Butler once lived in such style and elegance. There are only a few rooms habitable. A good spring freshet could wash away the remainder of the crumbling house."

"I was absolutely smitten with the poise and artistry of Miss Fanny Kemble when John and I saw her at age eight back in London," Anne said. "And Willy declares all of Philadelphia, Boston, and New York were at her feet as an adult. I wonder if she'll ever act again?"

"We don't need to know that today," Rebecca said to Anne. "You made the long carriage ride from Hamilton to visit us, my dear. Have you been well lately and are you sleeping and eating?"

"She be good, Miss Rebecca," Eve piped from her footstool. "Miss Anne she do better wif a new child comin' this time than any ob de others. Eve look arter her good."

Again Rebecca gave Eve a look, but her voice was patient when she said, "I'm sure you do look after her, Eve. This child could come quite easily, Anne. So much depends on the mother's health and peace of mind."

Anne's smile was even sunnier than her father remembered. But he supposed that each time he'd seen this daughter smile, for all the years of her life, had been like a benediction from God Himself. He kissed the back of her hand, which he still held. "I pray the whole blessed event will bring you only joy and a minimum of discomfort, blessed Anne," he said. "If the wholehearted love of your parents can be of any help at all, all will go well."

AFTER MORE GOOD TALK ABOUT HOW SKILLFULLY Anne's John had conducted the boat races on the Frederica River last summer, with James Hamilton away again hard at work on his dream of a successful cottonseed oil business in Mississippi and Louisiana and Alabama, Anne decided to put one haunting question straight to her father.

"Papa, do you suppose it just could be that my brother has bitten off a little more than even he can chew? John has convinced me that there is a good market for cottonseed oil if it can be pressed and shipped properly, but what's taking James so long to find out? Caroline told me, when she came down to Hamilton from her mother's place at the Village last week, that even though James seems to write to her often and in detail about what he's doing over there, she senses that he's beginning to grow restless being away from his family for such long periods of time. I think she wonders now and then if he's really telling her everything."

"Eve, would you mind asking Sans Foix to serve us some tea?" Mama asked. "I'm sure Anne would love one of his crumpets if he's baked them fresh today."

When Eve disappeared inside the house, Papa gave Mama one of his patient but highly amused looks. "You just couldn't bear for us to put any family business on Eve's grapevine, could you, Becca?" he asked.

"You've spoiled Eve, Anne," Mama said, ignoring Papa's jibe. "Our people seem able to read our minds even without eavesdropping on every word we say. Someday you'll find out how right I've been where Eve is concerned. I know the two of you consider yourselves friends, but one does have to keep one's family affairs somewhat private or the first thing you know, all manner of rumors will be flying about the entire Island!"

As they'd always done, Anne and her father exchanged smiles and went right on with their original conversation about James Hamilton and the cottonseed business in which he'd invested not only good money, but so much time and hard work.

"I've always made it a practice, Daughter," Papa said, "of waiting for James Hamilton to inform me first. I know he's been making that hard trip back and forth for over three years. I also know he was most sincere in wanting both your John and young John Wylly to have an interest in the cottonseed oil business almost from the first. I have been intending to ride over to the Wyllys' while my daughter-in-law, Caroline, is on St. Simons visiting her family. What I do know is that while James has successfully received his patents and built his mills, there has been, during his absences when he came back here over the past few years, much mismanagement with his new project. For their small investments, a little something will come to your John and young Wylly if your brother is able to sell. My belief, at least until I talk to Caroline, is that James is trying hard right now to dispose of the entire project."

"Papa, has James Hamilton ever failed at anything?"

"Not that I know of, Anne. But I believe he may have that new experience facing him soon."

"You haven't said a word about this to me, Jock!" Mama gasped.

"I know, my love. But now you've heard it."

"Why didn't it work out, Papa?"

"First, mismanagement. Most men are definitely not your brother's equal. Second, farmers have been so long accustomed to throwing away their extra seed, they found the habit seemingly impossible to break."

"Is this—is this a terrible tragedy, Papa?" Anne asked.

"A terrible business venture, Daughter, but not a tragedy. I'm sure James will be humiliated in the extreme. He will also lose nearly twenty thousand dollars. He's taken quite a fancy to your John and truly wanted to help him out financially with the bonus of an eighth interest. In my opinion, though, your John is a distinct beneficiary anyway."

"Why on earth would you say that, Jock?" Mama asked.

"Have you never seen the look of pride on John Fraser's face at the mere thought that our son wanted him to be a part of this business, Rebecca?"

"I don't believe so," she said.

"Well I have, Mama," Anne said. "As strict and uncompromising and prosperous as James Hamilton has always been, I'll be terribly sorry for him to fail. But his kind heart has given my John the only thing he lacked—faith in himself. It's been a long, long time since I've seen him in one of his doubting moods. I know Papa and I have always snickered at James Hamilton—called him the Old Gentleman—but he's a generous, good man."

"And I'll be so glad if he's coming home to stay," Mama said. "Isabella told me this morning that Theodore is certain James Hamilton's architectural plan for the huge Christ Church Episcopal in Savannah will be the one to be accepted. He needs to be back here. I'm sure they'll want to honor him."

"Now you hadn't told me one word about *that,* Becca!" Papa said, pretending to pout. "Our son's plans were chosen over all those others? Do you realize, wife, that if James is honored thus, you and I will be honored too? After all, he's *our* son."

CHAPTER 49

IN THE HAMILTON PARLOR WITH HIS BROTHER, William, who had come from Darien with Dr. Tunno to be on hand when Anne's baby arrived, John, unable to sit still, paced the floor. Again and again he paced from the tall windows fronting the Frederica River, past William's chair, to the wide hall staircase, and back again.

"There is no set schedule for the birth of a baby, big Brother," William said with a half-smile. "If ever a man had help getting through the birth of a child, you have. Dr. Tunno's an expert, and I've lost count of how many children I've brought into this world. Can't you settle down for a while? You and I haven't had a good talk in months."

"Can't you run upstairs and ask Tunno for some particulars, William? I need some idea of how soon the baby might come."

"I doubt if I've been back downstairs and in this chair for more than five minutes," William said. "I told you Tunno said it could be morning before Anne even goes into labor. She's close, but it isn't pacing time yet, man."

"You're definitely not the comfort our father was to me while Anne was having our first baby, Annie."

"To hear you tell it," William said, "most of the time Father never gave you an ounce of comfort.

"Well, he did that day. He even said he fully intended to ask God someday how even He could come up with such a cruel way of bringing babies into this world. Cruel for the woman."

"Father said that?"

"Aye." John smiled a little. "Just thinking of the old fellow and I say a Scottish *aye*. Father and I were quite close that day in London. I vowed the first time I heard Anne scream that we'd never have another child! The old gentleman understood. Didn't seem a whit surprised. Said he felt the same way the day I was born. But, of course, then our parents had you. And Anne and I have already had four children. I wasn't even here to be near her for the births of our last two. I still haven't forgiven myself."

"They both came quite early," William reminded him.

"What's to stop you from going back upstairs for another word with Tunno?"

"I haven't caught my breath from the first trip yet," William answered simply.

"Are you serious?" John demanded, so surprised that he stopped pacing to look at William's pale face and hands. "One trip upstairs made you short of breath, Brother?"

After a short laugh, William said, "Afraid so. I've been careful about too many trips up any stairs lately. I guess I'm just worn out from long hours at the hospital. I'll go back up in a few minutes, John."

"No, you will not. You'll stay right where you are. I'll go."

At the foot of the stairs, John saw Eve hurrying down. "She be all right so far, Mausa John," Eve said. "De doctor, he say no real pains yet. Calm yo'self. Miss Anne tell me to say calm yo'self."

"She did?" John asked eagerly. "Anne said that? Did she send you down just to tell me to stay calm, Eve?"

"No, sir. I come down to tell Doctah William dat Doctah Tunno he say for him not to keep runnin' up an' down dem stairs no more. Dat he send me effen dere's somepin' to tell."

John whirled to look at his brother. "Tunno knows you're short of breath?"

"The man is a doctor, John," William said.

Over her shoulder as she ran back up to Anne, Eve called, "I come back when dey's a reason to come back, Mausa John."

"It's time we talked, William," John said, sitting down in his favorite armchair near his brother. "You're not well. You've obviously consulted Tunno. I want to know the truth."

"You know heart trouble runs in our family."

"But—but you're only forty-two! I'm forty-five and I feel fine."

"There's no schedule for having heart trouble, any more than there is for birthing," William said calmly. "I've known about my weak heart since I turned forty."

"And you didn't say one word!"

With a grin, William said, "I have now. And if it will keep you occupied for a while, I might as well tell you I'm thinking of going up to New York to take the waters at Saratoga."

"William, will that help?"

His brother only shrugged. "Would you care to go with me?"

"What?"

"You've been looking tired lately too, John. Even if you do feel fine, a short holiday can't do any harm, can it? Be like old times for us to go somewhere, just the two of us."

"When?" John asked. "When will you go?"

"I can't go before June of next year. Is it a deal?"

"Why—why yes. Of course I'll have to reassign a lot of people, make ample plans for cultivation, talk it over with Anne when she's able to talk to me again. But I know she'd want me to look after you."

"I don't need looking after, Brother," William laughed. "I need your company. And don't you dare start pacing again. Anne is going to get along just fine."

SOMETIME AROUND TEN THE NEXT MORNING, November 22, 1836, Eve proudly announced to John and William that Anne had given birth to another daughter. "Purty as a pitcher an' with a head full ob dark, look like might be curly hair, Mausa John. Miss Anne say she hope you still want to name her S'lina, but she done got another name to go wif it. The baby's name be S'lina Tunno Fraser."

"When can I go up to her, Eve? She can name the baby anything she wants if she's just all right."

"Miss Anne, she say she hab a purty easy time. She fine an' so is little S'lina."

SITTING ON THE SIDE OF THEIR BED, JOHN touched Anne's hair, kissed her mouth, asked her to smile so that he could make his own secret check of her actual condition, then looked down into the scrunched-up face of their new daughter, who had so much dark hair on her tiny head, he laughed.

"She'll have to be careful," he joked, "or the birds will build a nest in that pile of curls!"

"You'll never be able to disown Selina, John," Anne said. "Tiny and new as she is, look at the shape of her face. She's so like you!"

"How dare you call my new daughter a horse face?" he teased.

"How dare you call yourself that? You swore you'd never, never again say you had a horse face!"

"I've forgotten her other name aside from Selina." he said.

"Dr. Tunno was so patient, so tender with me, so—so good, I want us to call her Selina Tunno Fraser. It wasn't easy, John, but he made it the best one yet." Anne touched the baby's head. "I think Selina Tunno Fraser sounds quite dignified, don't you?"

John laughed. "I do and someday this little lady may even *look* dignified!"

CHAPTER 50

In June of the next year, 1837, the first edition of the new *Brunswick Advocate* carried a local news item that read: "Lieutenant John Fraser, Esquire, of St. Simons Island, will accompany his brother, Dr. William Fraser, director of the Darien Hospital, to New York by boat from Savannah and thence up the Hudson to Saratoga so that Dr. Fraser can take the healing waters there."

When her father brought her the edition that came across to St. Simons two days after John left, Anne read and reread the news of his leaving, still feeling as though the past two nights in their lonely bed had been a bad dream. Her heart ached for Frances Anne, and over and over she asked herself how she would get through her days if John had been the ill brother and William were taking him to be treated at Saratoga Springs.

Once more someone else, not Anne, was suffering. The thought helped calm her rebellion that John would probably be gone for as long as one or two months, depending on William's condition. She thought a lot about her sister-in-law Caroline, too, who for the past few years had not seen James Hamilton for months at a time. And about Anna Matilda, once so young and happy, now a grown woman with heavy burdens. For the past four months she had longed to live again at Retreat, back on St. Simons, the place she loved as Anne loved it and where she would be nearby, able to tend her son William's grave. Anna Matilda could not move back because not only had her handsome, ambitious, brilliant husband contracted with Mr. Phineas Nightingale to build the Brunswick Canal, he had invested too deeply in other tracts of land and evidently lacked the funds to buy enough people to plant more than the acreage at Monticello, northwest of Brunswick.

Except for Lawrence, which Papa had given to them as a wedding gift, John owned little, but he was succeeding anyway. Even he couldn't doubt his success for the simple reason that James Hamilton considered him so productive. The Frasers were now sharing in the profits John made year after year in operating Hamilton, plus all proceeds from a few of Lawrence's still-productive fields. Even financially, Anne was better off than Anna Matilda, although Thomas Butler King was rather high up in Georgia politics.

I'm grateful, Lord, she prayed as she went slowly and thoughtfully down the wide Hamilton staircase to find Eve, who should have finished ironing Anne's day dresses by now. Eve would know where all the children were on this bright, already warm summer morning. And Anne needed to hear June's opinion on the condition of the newly grafted orange trees in John's grove he hated so to leave. Eve would know that too.

As usual, she didn't have to look for Eve, who appeared, almost as Anne reached the downstairs hall, with a "surprise."

"What kind of surprise?" Anne wanted to know.

"Guess," Eve said, her smile as bright as the sunshine streaming through the open front door.

"I don't want to guess. You're holding something behind your back. What is it?"

"June an' three ob his oarsmen done been to Brumsick an' back. Mausa John, he leave a few dollars wif June to buy things you might need when he go to Brumsick for supplies while Mausa John be gone. Today he brung you dis." Eve held out another weekly edition of the new *Brunswick Advocate.*

"Oh good!" Anne exclaimed. "That was very thoughtful of June. It's wonderful having our own newspaper. But Eve, look at the name of the paper. You can read. Does it really say *Brumsick Advocate?*"

Grinning, Eve said, "No'm. It say *Brunswick Advocate.*"

"You're not a bit hopeless. You're just stubborn, aren't you?"

"*Brumsick* come easier to say, Miss Anne. You want Eve should bring you some lemonade so you can sit on the veranda an' read the paper like Mausa John do?"

"That would be lovely. Thank you. Where's Fanny? She isn't off somewhere by herself nursing another wounded bird, is she? I like it that my daughter's so interested in caring for hurt wild things, but she tends them wherever she finds them, and last week she barely escaped being bitten by a rattlesnake."

"Fanny she be doin' her lessons wif Miss Annie an' Pete. Miss Annie seem to like givin' dem lessons as good as Miss Isabella like 'em. An' Lovey, he like sittin' there like he learnin' too."

"I wish Pete liked to read as much as Fanny does, and poor little Fanny's eyes are really so weak. I don't intend to stop her, though. I'd have missed half of life when I was young if I hadn't kept my nose in a book so much of the time."

When Eve returned with a tall glass of lemonade, Anne, seated in a veranda rocker with the *Advocate,* thanked her, then asked, "You know I broke a Georgia law when we were both young by teaching you to read, Eve, so how much *do* you read these days? Do you keep your promise to me to read something every night before you and June go to bed?"

"Yes'm." Then Eve laughed. "I does lessen June got a better thing for us to do."

Anne smiled at her. "I see, but what do you read? Do you need a new book? Have you finished *Pride and Prejudice?*"

"Yes'm. But I reads the Bible mostly. An' las' night I read that de Lord, He knows when we all gits up an' when we sits down. I thought to tell you dat today, Miss Anne."

"I'm glad you told me and I—I think I can guess why."

"Yes'm. You knows I feels the prickles up an' down your back cause you don' know where Mausa John is—what he's doin'. You used to knowin' all 'bout him. But the Lord He know when Mausa John gits up an' when he sits back down again."

"Oh Eve, thank you." Anne felt her eyes fill with tears. "I'm—I'm all right, so don't worry about me, but I do thank you. That helps more than you know."

"Not more than Eve knows."

ON THURSDAY AFTERNOON, JUNE 29, AFTER TUCK-ing a light blanket around William so he could sit out on deck of the moderately comfortable steamer taking them from New York up the Hudson River toward their destination at Saratoga, John sat nearby, pretending to read from some old issues of the *Southern Agriculturalist*. On the voyage to New York, John had read the back issue containing the St. Simons piece half a dozen times. Worried as he was about William, he couldn't concentrate enough now to read any other item in the copies he'd brought along, and so once more today, he was rereading the old St. Simons piece. It helped some to keep his mind off his brother's growing weakness, but not much. Legare's opening paragraphs had both a good and a bad effect. Reading such a detailed report about St. Simons Island made him miss Anne still more. Reading Legare's flattering words about John himself at the very beginning of the article gave him strength, a measure of confidence that he was man enough to control both his loneliness for Anne and the children and his worry over William. Legare had written:

> We arrived on St. Simons Island late in the evening of the 6th of December at the residence of Mr. John Couper, and it was with feelings of regret that we learned that Mr. Couper was absent. We regretted it because we felt desirous of becoming personally acquainted with such a revered man with whom we had frequently corresponded. Still, we had little cause for

regret for we received from his son-in-law, Lieutenant John Fraser, every attention we could desire. To Lieutenant Fraser, we feel particularly indebted, not only for escorting us around the Island, pointing out such objects as were worthy, but also for furnishing us with every facility for attaining the purpose of our visit.

Again and again John read that paragraph. Finally, smiling inwardly at his own conceit in seeing his name in print in such a prestigious journal and in such glowing terms, he closed the magazine and looked out at the tall, spring-green trees lining the spectacular banks of the wide Hudson. How late the new green appeared in New York after their hard winter, he thought, remembering that back on St. Simons, Anne's gardenias would be covering the bushes by now with fragrant, ivory-white blossoms—flowers almost as sweet as the scent of her skin, almost as silken to the touch.

Gardenia blossoms turned brown, though, if touched too often. Anne's silken beauty was long-lasting, resilient, always fresh, responsive. Anne was strong and would fare, he thought, far better without him than would Frances Anne, should she lose William.

That uninvited thought shocked him. He dared not even think of losing William—not of William's boys' loss. Certainly not of Frances Anne's desperation without him.

For almost an hour William sat motionless under the cotton blanket. Now John saw his eyelids open, noticed the familiar gray eyes returning his hopeful smile.

"I feel much better, Brother," William said, his weak voice almost inaudible over the churning paddle wheel and engine of the steamer taking them ever farther away from the two women they loved more than their own lives.

"I'm glad," John said. "Could I get you some of that newfangled ice cream? It's for sale by the bowl on this fancy ship, you know. A treat, I should imagine, for a couple of country boys like us from coastal Georgia."

"No thanks, but I wish you'd have some," William said, eyes

closed again. "I know the sun is warm, but the chill I had when we first came out on deck is still with me. About where are we, John?"

"At noon in the dining room, I heard someone say we'd pass Croton-on-Hudson by midafternoon. I'm sure we've already passed it. The sun is beginning to drop a bit. I believe the fellow said the city of West Point, New York, would be next."

"I don't suppose there's a doctor on board," William said, plainly trying to sound casual.

"Only the best," John tried a small joke. "His name, I believe, is Dr. William Fraser. Would you like to talk to him?"

William grinned. "Not especially. Doctors can be utterly use-less, you know. I'd much rather tell Dr. Fraser's brother how—how much he means to me." His breath was shallow and fast. "How—proud I am of what he's accomplished. How—brave I think him for digging deep enough to find the courage to turn his life completely around. Not only to turn it around, but to do it with such a flare and with so much—success."

Fear racing now through his big body like fire through a tin-der-dry woods, John stared at William. "Why—why thank you, sir," he said stiffly, his voice showing the fear and little of the real gratitude he intended. Reaching into his shirt pocket, John took out a small bottle. "Frances Anne gave me some smelling salts, Brother. Will it help any?"

"I'll—I'll give it a try." William took one light whiff and turned his head away. "No, John, no help. No—help. Can—can you find out about a doctor in—West Point, and if there's—a chance this—tub would dock there for us?"

Using all his persuasive powers, John not only got the ship's captain to dock at West Point, New York, but made full use of their shared British military backgrounds. Within an hour after the steamer docked, he had William in bed at the United States Military Academy infirmary.

Throughout the long, anxious, unusually chilly night of June

30, John sat beside William's bed—waiting. Waiting, never easy for him, was now pure torture as hour after hour he tried to give himself even a partially comforting reason for sitting up waiting. For what did he wait? For William to open his eyes, smile, throw back the covers, and spring out of bed—wholly well and himself again?

Medical personnel of various ranks came and went, took William's pulse, shook their heads, left. Then, after what seemed an aeon, another entered the long, cot-lined room, silent except for snores and coughs of West Point cadets with various ailments. Once more a hairy, strong hand found William's pulse, looked at a watch and left.

Finally a young medical officer, introducing himself as Lieutenant White, went through the same procedure but didn't leave.

"This is your brother, Lieutenant Fraser?" the slender officer asked.

"Yes," John whispered. "Can't you—can't you tell me—something, sir?"

"Do you really want me to?"

"If you please," John begged.

"Your brother is—dying. His heart is failing. My superior, Major Crumit, who was here a few minutes ago, says there's nothing we can do. He—my superior did not tell me to tell you, Lieutenant Fraser. I did that on my own. You see, I also had a brother. You and your brother were fortunate to have lived to be grown men together. My brother died when I was fourteen." The young doctor laid his hand on William's damp brow. "Tap that bell if you need me, if you think I can do anything to make—anything—easier for you."

On his feet, tears streaming unashamedly down his lean face, John asked, "Is there nothing at all that can be done for him? *Nothing?*"

"Nothing. I'll make my rounds and try to see that you and your brother aren't disturbed until—until I hear you tap the bell, sir."

He shook John's hand warmly and left.

THE SUN WAS JUST PUSHING LONG, MISTY-PINK clouds out of the morning sky when John saw William stir ever so slightly. Then a rattling gasp escaped into the quiet room, its shadows thinning into light. William gasped once more and was still. For a long time John stood as though at attention. Then he kissed William's cheek and pulled the cover over his face.

It was almost morning. Within minutes, nurses and orderlies would be banging about the ward, but for as long as he and William could be alone, John sat there with him.

Then he gave the bell several rapid taps, hoping against hope that the same kindhearted young doctor might still be on duty to answer the summons.

FROM SOMEWHERE JOHN FOUND THE FORTITUDE AND good sense to make the necessary arrangements for William's body to be sent back to St. Simons Island in a sealed lead casket. The understanding young doctor did not answer his summons—he had gone off duty—but the major who informed him just how to go about everything seemed to sense that it was important that William not be left behind to be buried in a strange place.

The necessary papers signed, there seemed nothing left to do to help William but for John to get the casket and himself to Darien, Georgia, as quickly as possible. The major offered to have him driven the mile or two to the dock, where he could buy a ticket back to New York, but John needed time to sort things out. He thanked the officer, saluted, and began to walk along the road, still almost empty, toward the waterfront.

His legs moved. Somehow he was walking, but had Anne seen him, he wondered if even she would have recognized that the strange, tall man pushing his way through a world of total unreality was really John Fraser. All his life he had longed, fought at times, for independence, the liberty to go his own way without the interference, no matter how well-intentioned, of any other living person. Had he not been weeping as he plodded along the unfamiliar road, he might have laughed. This minute—the sun rising in the sky as though nothing unusual had happened—he would have given anything for the sight of one familiar face, the sound of one voice he loved. Words addressed to him from someone who loved him.

In the heat and filth and terror of battle, he had often felt alone in the world, but never as now. He was the only person who loved William, who knew he was dead. Dead. The word had no real meaning yet except that as John had sat beside him, whispering his name, William didn't, couldn't, answer.

A wren, which sounded for all the world like a St. Simons marsh wren, shouted from somewhere in the bushes beside the lonely road. And then, almost at once, he imagined he heard his father's dry, Scottish burr.

Did Father know about William? Anne would say they were already together. But were they? Would they ever be? Would John ever see William again? Their father and mother?

Even the thought of his father seemed to bring John somewhat back to earth, so that for the first time his scattered, numb thoughts went to Anne. *Anne.* If he could bring himself to write to her and post it today, when would she learn that John was moving around in the world all alone? Alone? "I am *not* alone," he said aloud. "Anne is in my world. It isn't all strange. There was so much I wanted to tell William—if there had been time. Anne will know everything I meant to tell him. Anne knows me. I won't feel so alone once she knows William is gone. I suppose a letter could reach her, especially if Frewin happens to be in Savannah with one of his boats, in three weeks' time."

Talking aloud helped some. Even the sound of his own voice. He would buy a ticket back to New York today, then hope for passage at once to Savannah. "I'll still write to Anne, though," he spoke aloud again. "Perhaps she would then have time to get word to Frances Anne in Darien." Feeling was returning and he was relieved for a moment that he was alone, because a man never dared allow anyone hear him sob as John was sobbing now.

CHAPTER 51

WHEN ANNE, ANNIE, PETE, AND LITTLE FANNY met Anne's parents and Isabella in the churchyard before morning services on Sunday, July 9, she could tell from Papa's face that he had brought her a letter from John, along with the July 6 issue of the *Brunswick Advocate*.

The letter had been sent from New York while they were still en route and was so short, she risked being a moment or two late entering the church in order, at least, to scan it: "Our voyage as far north as this city," John wrote, "was mostly uneventful—good weather, so that William could take advantage of resting on deck in the sun and fresh air. I am pacing my boots off with restlessness at being away from you, beautiful Anne, but believe we will both be glad in the future that I came with my brother. He is truly not well enough to have made the trip alone. Being William, of course, he remains pleasant and as cheerful as his draining weakness permits, sure the Saratoga waters will help him. Use your good judgment about what you tell Frances Anne concerning his illness.

That the man is ill I have no doubt whatever. We should reach Saratoga within ten days or so."

He sent his love and kisses to everyone by name and urged June to keep a close watch on the new grafting, and Cuffy, the Hamilton driver, a close watch on the people's hoeing methods in the south field. Throughout the sermon Theodore preached, Anne thought only of the last line of John's letter: "With all I recognize as my heart, soul, and body, beloved Anne, I love you. Only God in His infinite wisdom recognizes, more than I am able to realize, that without you beside me, I am only half a man."

AFTER SHE AND HER LITTLE FAMILY HAD SAID goodbye to her parents beside the Fraser carriage, where Big Boy waited to drive them home to Hamilton after church, Anne told the children as much as she thought they needed to know of her letter from John and wished for twenty-year-old Annie to help keep the young ones occupied. Any serious thoughts of her eldest daughter, Annie, these days left Anne's heart troubled. Troubled when it should have been glad. Frances Anne had been right. Without doubt, gentle, sweet Annie was falling in love with young Paul Demere. Today, out of the blue, she had gone to dine with the Demeres. Anne was not only bereft at the thought of life without Annie in the house, she had never really liked arrogant, handsome, selfish Paul. The Demeres were a fine old Island family, whose two large homes, Mulberry Grove and Harrington Hall, were St. Simons landmarks. But Paul, to Anne's mind, was just not worthy of Annie.

In an effort to get Annie's foolish infatuation out of her thoughts, she would try, if Frederica Road wasn't too rough, to scan the *Brunswick Advocate* for any interesting tidbits. Everyone was still excited that at long last the residents of the Golden Isles area around Brunswick, Georgia, had their very own newspaper, which, just before James Hamilton returned from Natchez to stay, had run a brief article concerning his business loss when his cotton-seed oil enterprise had failed for lack of proper management at the

New Orleans and Natchez mills. "The genius of Mr. J. H. Couper," the article had declared, "might have made the difference between success and the ultimate failure resulting from Couper's necessary absences from the mill sites in order to attend to his valuable Glynn County holdings."

Anne had never been able to talk intimately with her brother James, so asked no questions, even of John, who had borrowed eight hundred dollars for an eighth interest in the doomed cotton-seed oil venture. She had simply prayed that James hadn't been too disappointed and that by some means John would find a way to repay his debt to the Darien Bank. Papa had told her that James was financially able to withstand his own losses and believed the cottonseed oil failure had been the reason James Hamilton became so immediately involved, now that he was back to stay, with Thomas Butler King in the legal maneuvers having to do with their state-granted charter for the Brunswick Canal.

"The lad, despite his lifetime of success," Papa had said, "needs a new interest to conceal his deep disappointment, but don't worry, Anne. Even your brother can learn from failure, and the lad's known only one."

Everyone on St. Simons and in Brunswick wanted the canal so that Turtle River could be connected with the Altamaha, enabling goods to be brought from the interior to the busy Brunswick port.

Briefly, Anne glanced at a long, detailed account of the canal's progress, but found the carriage lurching far too much for reading such fine print. Only back on her own veranda, overlooking the gardens and the Frederica River, did she find time after dinner to read the newspaper. It was quiet. Eve and the girls were making cornhusk dolls, young John Couper was asleep. She not only could read, she could think at her own leisure.

Before she really focused on the paper, her mind went to Frances Anne, alone up in Darien with her sons, James and little Menzies, but without William.

I know, Frances, she thought, as though her friend were there beside her, that William is away so much of the time at the hospital and driving from house to house to help sick patients, but I also know it's different now because he won't be home to sleep beside you tonight. We'll both be in those big, empty beds alone—needing their arms. When, oh when, do you suppose they *will* be back?

Then, in the easy, natural way Anne had always felt free to talk to God, she asked His forgiveness for being concerned with her own desires, and with a determined snap of the *Advocate,* she straightened it over her knees and began to search for something to take her mind off missing John. Off Frances Anne and William. Off any thought of Annie at the Demeres' dinner table in Mulberry Grove across the Island.

One article, too long to read in her present mood, had to do with the Indian fighting in Florida; another with the ever-growing prosperity in Brunswick; and then like a bolt of lightning, she was struck by the name *Fanny Kemble Butler!*

Peering intently, Anne read:

The Star of Seville is the title of a new drama written by Fanny Kemble Butler. Perhaps no lady has ever tested more fully than Mrs. Butler the value of popularity. When she first appeared on the American stage, a most rapturous enthusiasm welcomed her. . . . Caressed and flattered by the educated and wealthy, she evidently forgot that these attentions must be repaid in kind and in an evil moment, published her American *Journal*—a work abounding in splendid writing and showing genius of the highest order. But because she ridiculed slavery and some of the usages of American high life, the tide was turned against her; talent of any kind was denied her, and the very people who had crowded the theaters night after night to applaud her acting declared the *Journal* trash!

Now a word to our American readers: Conceal it as we may, our national sensitiveness continually breaks out and if not stiff-necked, we are a thin-skinned generation. No foreign traveler can please us. If they point out our faults, we attribute it to prejudice; if our institutions, political and social, are lauded, then it is, to us, flattery. Poor Fanny has been punished and her newly published play, *The Star of Seville,* called trash, simply because she dared to criticize our country all the way from its social behavior to the Southern institution of slavery. Whatever may be the real merit of *The Star of Seville,* it can hardly have justice done it in this country, because she chose to publish her much-abused American *Journal* first.

Anne read and reread the piece. The more she read, the angrier she grew. Why? Why, she wondered, do I feel almost protective of Fanny Kemble Butler? I haven't laid eyes on her since I saw her on a London stage when she was eight years old. It must be because Willy likes her so much. His latest letter certainly sounded upset about her marriage, but Mama vows I mustn't allow Willy's mistrust of her young husband, Pierce Butler, to influence my opinion of him. What difference does *my* opinion of the wealthy socialite, Pierce Butler, make to anyone? Dear Mama just can't help trying to mold me into a better person, even if I am forty years old! Will I do that with Annie and Pete and Fanny and John Couper and baby Selina when they begin to think for themselves?

Such a thought made her laugh at herself. Annie is twenty and I am certainly attempting to mold even her romance, for heaven's sake! No mother should ever think of such a thing. Especially a mother whose own parents had welcomed *her* first and only love as they did. Young love, if it is real, should never, never be tampered with. That had been Anne's credo for as long as she could remember. Yet today, with Annie's dining at Mulberry Grove with the family of young Paul Demere, she was doing battle with her own credo.

"I simply don't trust that boy Paul," she said aloud. "I don't trust him any more than Willy trusts Fanny Kemble's husband, Pierce Butler. Willy has no reason for his dislike of the gentleman except that he's callow and unconvincingly pretty-spoken. Well, so is Paul. He's both pretty-spoken and callow and if John were here this minute, he'd be laughing at me, vowing I'm getting more like Mama every day. Well, I'm Mama's daughter."

"You gettin' ol', Miss Anne?" Eve asked from the doorway. "I hear you talkin' to y'self again. You got company comin'. I done see a buggy round de bend in the lane."

"Eve, if you don't stop sneaking up on me like that, I'm going to—to—"

"To what?" Eve asked easily, giving Anne her best smile. "What chu gonna do to me, Miss Anne?"

"You know I don't know. It does look as though a person could be allowed a little thinking time on her own veranda, though, without being spied on! Who do you suppose is coming in that buggy?"

"Miss Annie an' her man!"

Anne jumped to her feet. "What? Did you say Miss Annie and her—*man*? How dare you?"

"Mr. Paul Demere be a man the las' time I seen him," Eve said in her smart-aleck way, the smile still giving her the upper hand.

"Watch your mouth, Eve. And when they hitch the horse, go tell Annie to come here. I—I need to speak with her."

Still grinning, Eve asked, "You already know you wanna talk to Miss Annie befo' I tell you they comin'?"

Anne stiffened. "Of course I did."

Hoping Eve hadn't noticed that her face flushed from the white lie, Anne sat back down and began to think of something special to tell Annie when she appeared on the veranda—alone, she fervently hoped.

Their laughter reached her first, then she saw her daughter and Paul cross the yard. Annie, who had always been so quiet, was laughing like a bell, clinging to the graceful young man's arm, her dark hair blowing in a light breeze off the river. In her hand she carried a bunch of Queen Anne's lace and her Sunday straw hat with its blue ribbons.

"You wanted to see me, Mama?" Annie asked as the two climbed the veranda steps.

"Good afternoon, Mrs. Fraser," Paul Demere said, bowing politely. "Did you ever see such a beautiful summer afternoon? I will say the gnats are out in force, though."

"And the deerflies," Annie added gaily.

"Good afternoon, Paul," Anne said, her hand out to him. "It's a lovely day all right, but it wouldn't be July on St. Simons without both gnats and deerflies, now, would it?"

"No, ma'am. It surely wouldn't. They're not as bad here by the water, though, as at our place in the woods. I guess you get more wind over here on the leeward side of the Island."

"Did you want to see me, Mama?" Annie asked.

"Uh—yes, I did. But if you and Paul have other plans, I'll understand. I need to discuss something with you alone."

"But Mama, Paul and I were going out in Papa's little sailing boat. Is anything wrong?"

The deeply concerned look on her daughter's pretty face caused Anne to feel downright ashamed. "Oh no. That is, it's nothing that can't wait an hour or so. You two go ahead and have your boat ride. Only do be careful. I suppose you're familiar with the Frederica currents, Paul."

"Yes, ma'am. I did grow up on St. Simons."

She had not sent Annie off on her pleasure ride with any grace at all. Without a specific reason to dislike Paul Demere, Anne now felt like a meddling old woman. Much older than Mama and much more meddlesome. What on earth would she find to discuss privately with Annie when they got back? She sat racking her brain, since Annie almost never did or said anything that required discussion. Most of what she had ever talked about with her firstborn had been some problem of her own, or if the truth be known, usually she, the mother, was turning to Annie for advice concerning one of the other children. Annie had almost all her life been, first of all, her mother's friend.

If only John were here, she thought. Even her humor, her ability to laugh at herself, vanished without him. How did Frances Anne manage without a daughter old enough to converse with her when something went awry?

Anne sat up in her chair. *Frances Anne*. Frances needed someone to be with her now of all times! Anne herself could not leave her own small children, but there must be another adult who could be with her while poor William was away at the North—ill.

Her own daughter Annie would be perfect.

I T NEVER OCCURRED TO A NNIE NOT TO BEGIN MAK-
ing plans to leave for a visit with Aunt Frances Fraser in Darien.
After all, Mama had begged her to go, and although she knew full
well that her mother was not fond of Paul, Mama had even agreed
that he could escort her in the Hamilton plantation boat with Eve's
June in charge, not only of the boat and Annie's bundles but of the
five other oarsmen as well. That way, Annie thought, there would
be no time for her and Paul to be alone on the trip up, and he had
promised his parents to return in two days, but maybe somehow, at
Uncle William's house outside of Darien, they would find a few
moments to talk.

We can whisper in the boat on the way, Annie decided, her
heart aching for Aunt Frances but singing for herself and Paul. He
reached Hamilton exactly when he'd promised, at eight on Friday
morning, August 4, and within half an hour, because June had
already loaded her boxes and small trunk, they were both waving
to Mama and the children standing together on the Hamilton
dock.

As usual, the oarsmen sang as they rowed the sturdy boat north
toward Frederica, past Colonel William Whig Hazzard's West
Point Plantation and Dr. Thomas Fuller Hazzard's place at Pike's
Bluff, and headed for the Darien waterfront. Over and over, to
comfort herself, Annie thought of Mama's last words to her: "See
that Paul takes you all the way to Uncle William's house, now. I'm
glad you'll have someone to look after you. There's no time for me
to say more, darling, but you're just terribly important to me."

Maybe Mama didn't like Paul much, but at least Annie took
comfort in the fact that her mother had not only agreed to allow
him to go with her but wanted him to take her all the way to the
Ridge. If Aunt Frances wasn't too upset over Uncle William, she
thought as Paul, seated beside her, smiled and took her hand, she
might be able to tell her aunt that she truly loved Paul Demere. It
could be only wishful thinking, she supposed, but perhaps Aunt
Frances would understand. Might even like Paul. Of course she
would have known him since he was a boy, because everyone on
St. Simons knew the Demeres, but spending a night in her house
would give him and her aunt a chance to get acquainted as adults.

"Did you mind having to say goodbye to your mother, Annie?" Paul asked. "She seemed almost glad to see me this morning, I thought," he said, giving her his devastatingly attractive smile. The smile that always struck Annie as including her in a private, exciting conspiracy of their own.

"I always hate to leave Mama," she said, "but she did want me to come. And yes, I agree she's truly glad you're with me."

He laughed. "I'm not so sure she's glad *I'm* the one who's escorting you, but I'm glad I am." He lifted her hand to his warm, firm mouth and kissed it.

"Don't do that," she whispered, pulling her hand back. "I don't think our people pay much attention, but Mama says they do, because otherwise, how would they hear so much on their famous grapevine?"

"Your mother's quite a lady. A lady with her own mind, I'd say. She may not like me much, but I admire a woman who knows what she thinks."

Before their boat had reached Pike's Bluff, Paul had asked her to marry him just as soon as she returned from her mission of mercy, as he put it, to Darien. Annie, without a moment's hesitation, said yes. But not until he agreed that they'd keep it a secret until she herself had a chance to tell both her parents.

"I'll go through the formality of asking your father's permission once he's home from Saratoga," Paul said lightly. "That's considered only good form." Then, his arm hooked through hers, he pulled her to him. "But we'll know, you and I. And I'll kiss you and hold you and tell you I love you at every opportunity."

"Not in front of people, though."

One arched eyebrow lifted in the way she loved, he said, "We'll see about that, lovely Annie, but watch me find all sorts of ways."

CHAPTER 52

BECAUSE OF THE LACK OF PASSAGE SOUTH TO SA-
vannah, John was detained for nearly ten days in New York City,
as was William's body in its sealed lead casket, so that he did not
reach Savannah until August 5 in the rottenest kind of weather.

Instead of going, as the Coupers usually did, to the home of
Miss Eliza Mackay, John, by now short of funds for a hotel room,
walked in a heavy rain to the Reynolds Square house of his friend
Mark Browning. At nearly ten o'clock at night, he knocked on the
familiar handsome front door and waited.

Within minutes Browning himself greeted him, welcomed him
inside out of the weather, and ordered his German housekeeper to
bring brandy.

"My wife and daughter have already retired," Browning said
as he hung John's soggy cape on a hall tree and led the way to the
drawing room.

"I know elaborate apologies are in order, Mark," John said,

taking the chair Browning offered, "but somehow I hesitated to barge in at night on lone ladies like Miss Eliza and her daughters. I am deeply sorry to disturb you, but I confess to being relieved and glad to find you not only at home but still up. You're most kind. My journey has been—difficult, to say the least."

"Where have you been, John?" Mark asked. "At the North? I happen to know the only boat due to dock after dark was from New York. Were you on it?"

"I was," John said with a weak smile. "And believe me, we were long after dark. I took time only to stow most of my luggage until tomorrow and walk to your house. We docked less than an hour ago."

And then, with Browning's brandy warming him inside and the man's welcome giving his spirit a lift for the first time in days, John told him of his trip with William, of William's death, and some of what lay ahead once he found transportation to Darien tomorrow, weather permitting.

"If tonight is any indication," Browning said, "you won't be able to take any kind of boat anywhere tomorrow, Fraser. But you know you're more than welcome to stay here with us for as long as you need. I'm so, so sorry about your brother. What an ordeal for you to go through all by yourself! With the delays you experienced getting this far south, I don't suppose you have much hope that the letter telling your wife the sad news has reached her on St. Simons."

"That's what worries me," John said, taking another sip of the fine brandy. "I'd hoped I might get at least as far as Darien—about the time my letter did. Now I don't know what to think, although I posted a note to my wife about William's death the day I reached New York. I couldn't book passage, but the letter may have gone ahead on a mail boat. If so, she'll receive it—out of the blue—with its ghastly news of William's passing and I won't be there to comfort her. I'm dreadfully worried about William's wife, Frances Anne, too. I also wrote of his death to her from New York. How can the woman bear to learn that—my brother's gone and she has no one but two young sons to turn to?"

Mark shook his head. "I can't imagine," he said softly. "What kind of woman is Dr. Fraser's wife?"

"A strong, fine lady. Both my brother and I were fortunate enough to find wives who deeply love us. Frances's life will be only part of a life for as long as she's on this earth, I'm afraid. Mark, I— I feel so helpless."

Gale-force winds had begun to blow against Browning's tall, sturdy, brick townhouse, so that not only did the windows rattle, the wind knifed around his strong front door so hard it blew an eerie, hornlike tune, as though the breath of demons were loosed against it.

"A fine New England contractor built this house," Mark said, "but no front door and no windows could be tight enough to withstand wind like that without making noise. You must be exhausted, John. Do you think you can sleep through it tonight? I'm sure Gerta has prepared your room by now."

On a hard, long sigh, John said, "I haven't slept through a single night since William—left me. But thanks to your kindness, I'll at least rest some. I know I have to get aboard something bound for Darien tomorrow."

Mark looked doubtful. "It could blow itself out in the night, of course, and I'll send you in my fastest schooner if it's quiet by morning, but don't count on it, friend. I think we'd better take everything an hour at a time until we can see morning light of some kind in the sky tomorrow."

WHEN THE WIND BEGAN TO BLOW SO FIERCELY SHE couldn't sleep, Annie crept down the stairs in her aunt's Darien house and tried to look out the high front windows of the parlor. From the room upstairs where she was staying during her visit, all she could see were the heavy, whipping top branches of Uncle William's live oaks and magnolia trees in the yard, and they told her nothing. Grandpapa Couper had dozens of stories about the wildness of the wind, the roaring destruction that pounded over

Cannon's Point during the hurricane that struck the coast the year before she and her parents came back from London, and although Annie had never experienced one, she knew that hurricanes did come.

Hands cupped around her eyes to shut out the dim glow of Aunt Frances's candlestand in the front hall, she peered out into the thrashing darkness. Thuds and crashes outside told her that flowerpots and porch furniture and tree branches were being tossed like fury about the yard; shutters upstairs and nearby on the front veranda banged, and so did Annie's heart. She felt thankful, too, though, because Paul had been gone for two days and was surely back home by now at Mulberry Grove, asleep, she hoped. But if the gale-force winds were raising such a ruckus in Darien, some distance from the sea, they must be roaring over St. Simons Island. "We were in its direct path," Grandpapa had told her again and again. "Nothing to protect us from either the wind or the tidal wave that followed."

Were they all safe at home? Mama, thank heaven, and the other children in her own family were on the leeward side of the Island, so they probably wouldn't feel the full brunt of the storm. Papa was too far north, all the way up in New York State.

From upstairs, the sound thin but terrified, she could hear young Menzies crying, and in no time Aunt Frances—Menzies and James right beside her—came hurriedly down the stairs, carrying a candle.

"We were worried about you, Annie," Aunt Frances said as they joined her in the parlor. "I saw your bed was empty and—"

"I came down here hoping to see something," Annie said. "I don't seem to get so frightened if I can see what's going on."

"It might turn into a hurricane," James said, his voice quite grown up for an eleven-year-old.

"Do you mean this *isn't* a hurricane?" Annie gasped.

"It's hard to tell right now," the boy answered. "Do you think it is, Mama?"

"Only when we see the damage by daylight can we be sure," Aunt Frances said, soothing Menzies by rubbing his back while he clung to her. "I just pray all our loved ones are safe. I'm sure William and John don't even know about it way up in New York, but we must pray, pray for those on St. Simons Island—your family and mine, Annie."

TERRIFIED, WITH BOTH JOHN AND ANNIE AWAY, Anne sat in her parlor with her young children, watching the wildness outside, nervously waiting for daylight to come. She held Selina in her arms. Fanny and Pete and the dog sat on the floor at her feet, pressing against her legs for some form of comfort. John Couper, though, now almost five, stood beside her, a strong little arm about his mother's shoulder.

Once it was light enough for the trees to begin to show green again, she would be able to tell more about the might of the gale that had blown all night and seemed now to be gaining in energy. If they still lived at Lawrence, she could at least gauge the intensity by whatever first light might push its way through the dark, roiling sky at sunrise. Hamilton, though, faced west, toward Brunswick. If possible, the havoc must be even more intense at Lawrence and Cannon's Point.

As she'd done through most of the night, Anne prayed again for her parents' safety. She and John had seen with their own eyes the extent of the damage up there from the hurricane that had struck the year before they returned from London.

John . . . John. She didn't want the children to hear her calling him, so she only thought his name, cradling Selina, smiling up at her special son, John Couper, because she so needed the reassuring smile he inevitably gave back to her.

Crazily, Anne thought how much more secure she'd feel if only Eve could be there with her. There was not one blessed thing Eve could do, but Anne needed her and felt guilty for being so selfish. Even Eve wasn't impulsive enough, though, to try to walk from her cabin to the Big House in a storm like this!

As though some great, determined hand had ripped open a

cloud, the first rain began to fall. There had been a seriously long drought. The crops needed rain, but rain in sheets as weighted as this, with such a monster wind, could only destroy crops. John, she thought, your beautiful plants—your beautiful plants! And you've worked so, so hard. . . .

FOR THE FIRST TIME SINCE ISABELLA'S THEODORE Bartow had been the rector, the bell at Christ Church Frederica did not ring on the Sunday morning of August 6, 1837. The doors of the tiny chapel remained locked. Fury stormed from the heavens at about ten o'clock that morning, battering the Georgia coast throughout the Sabbath, and was still raging when darkness fell that night.

Then, sometime after a thin sun tried to rise on Monday morning, Eve appeared—soaked to the skin—and found Anne and the children asleep in the Hamilton parlor.

"Miss Anne? Miss Anne, you been here since de storm strike us?"

"Oh—oh Eve, I'm so glad to see you! You and June are both all right?"

"Gimme dat baby. I knows you been holdin' her an' I knows your arms sounder asleep than you, Miss Anne!"

"Is it—over, Eve?" Pete whispered from the floor where she'd slept, rubbing her eyes and looking around the room as though to make sure everything was still there.

"It be mos' done, Petey," Eve said. "An' effen you trust Eve's cookin', I done make some fried eggs an' ham. Dey might be a lil' wet from carryin' 'em from the kitchen outside, but dey still be eggs an' ham."

"The chickens, Eve! Were you foolish enough to try to gather eggs on a day like this?" Anne demanded. "Are the chickens still there?"

"Where you think I git 'em? Eve don' lay eggs. Not many ob our chickens still alive, but some laid. Git up, all ob you, an' eat! Ain' no milk, but eat!"

ON TUESDAY MORNING, AUGUST 8, MARK CON-
sulted the captain of his fastest, safest small schooner and found
that, with luck, the man thought he would be able to get John to
the Darien dock that day.

Mark stood with his tall, exhausted, anxious friend, John Fraser, on the heavily damaged Savannah wharf and tried to think of
something reassuring to say to the man.

But John spoke first. "I'm sure I don't need to fish around for
words to express my gratitude to you, Browning. This isn't the first
time you've come to my rescue, you know. Back in 1825, when
Anne and I got back from London, you gave me the courage to try
to learn how to plant cotton. Now you're making it possible for me
to deliver the tragic news to my brother's widow myself. I'm not
sure how I'll find the strength to tell her, but I will. Somehow."

"As soon as you're aboard and on your way, John, I promise to
go straight to my friend Eliza Mackay's house and ask her to pray
for you. I'm not sure how you feel about prayers being answered,
but if anyone has God's ear, it's Miss Eliza."

The expression on John Fraser's face changed so swiftly, Mark
marveled. It was as though a light had been lit from inside the
man. "I'm not—at least I've never been quite sure exactly *how* I
feel about praying. I just know that your telling me that has again
given me an odd kind of courage. Thank you."

They watched Mark's own stevedores hoist the heavy lead
casket on board the schooner and stood watching until its big, wide
crate was out of sight in the hold. Then, after a handshake, Mark,
on impulse, gave the big man a hard bear hug.

"Keep the schooner as long as you need it, John," he called as
John waved from the deck. "Have my captain take you and your
brother's family all the way to St. Simons for the burial. You have
far more need of a good, sturdy ship right now than I have."

CHAPTER 53

THE SKY OVER THE DARIEN WATERFRONT WHEN
John stepped from Mark Browning's schooner onto the storm-
wracked wharf was still gray and leaden—almost the color of
William's sealed casket. That the hurricane-force gale wind had
taken its full toll here, too, no one could doubt. Only heaven knew
how far down the coast. Only heaven knew about Anne and the
children. Only heaven knew what destruction lay across the fields
and stands of St. Simons woods. Tears stung John's eyes at the
thought.

After a few words with Browning's captain, John made arrangements to bring William's little family as early as possible
tomorrow morning to board the schooner for Frederica. He had
decided before leaving New York that William should be buried in
Christ Church cemetery near their father. Father would rest easier,
John knew, if his favorite son was beside him or at least nearby.
Before searching for a conveyance to take him out to William's
home at the Ridge, he turned to face the borrowed schooner and

saluted the remains of his beloved brother. "I'll do the best I can with Frances Anne, William," he murmured. "That's the least I can do in your behalf. This is the last time we'll be—together—without other people, Brother. You were the best of brothers to me, always."

IN THE LATE AFTERNOON JOHN TRUDGED WEARILY up the front steps of William's house at the Ridge, and almost at once Frances Anne stood in the open doorway, silhouetted against the candle-lit entrance hall. Without a word, she reached for John's hand. He grasped it warmly and held on.

"You wrote to both Anne and me that William—couldn't come home with you," she said, scarcely above a whisper. "I just told your Annie I felt I'd hear something further from you today. And here you are."

Inside the lighted hall now, John asked, "My Annie is here?"

"Anne sent her to be with me, even—before we knew. Annie's been here more than two weeks." He saw Frances lift her chin. "Anne also sent Eve's June with your oarsmen to bring my sister Heriot to tell me that—William won't—be coming home again." Her composure held until she added the words *"Not—ever."*

"My letter got here ahead of me, didn't it? Anne's too. I was afraid of that. I'm so, so sorry, Frances Anne."

"I guess Anne almost came herself, but Heriot is—is very good at things like this. Far better than my twin sister, Anne Frances."

John held her while she let her broken heart empty itself of the pent-up tears. Finally, when she was a bit calmed, he led her into the parlor toward what he knew to be her favorite chair.

"No, John. Ever since I found out, I've been resting at every opportunity—there in William's big leather chair. It comforts me, somehow. I'll sit in it now."

"William's—William's body is over at the Darien waterfront on a schooner belonging to Mark Browning of Savannah. Miss Eliza Mackay's friend. He's my friend too. Every time I've needed the man, he's been there to help. We'll—you and Heriot and Annie and your children and I will take William back to St. Simons in Browning's schooner as soon as you can get ready. I know Father will want him nearby in Christ Churchyard."

"Thank you, John. You're—you're good and kind—enough for Anne."

He sighed deeply. "I wish I were!"

"You are. And we're packed and ready to leave tomorrow, just as soon as you can find some means for us to get there."

"Frances, didn't you hear me? Browning told me to keep the schooner as long as we need it. William—William will go along right with us."

CHRIST CHURCH WAS FULL TO OVERFLOWING WITH Island friends and neighbors, all of whom remembered Dr. William Fraser warmly. There were more Cannon's Point, Hamilton, and Wylly people there, too, than white Island neighbors. And after Theodore Bartow said his final prayer beside the newly mounded grave, softly, with an awed reverence John had never heard from any cathedral choir anywhere in the world, the people began to hum and sing: "Remember me, remember days past . . . O Lord, do remember me."

As John and William's older son, James, led Frances Anne along the church path to the Wylly carriage, where her brother John Wylly waited to receive her, the people from three plantations, standing back in a protective circle, went on singing.

"I will hear their voices until the day of my own death," Anne said, clinging to John's arm in their own carriage on the way home to Hamilton. "I'll never stop hearing the people the way they sounded today."

"Nor will I, beautiful Anne." And then he lifted her face so that he could look down into her tear-swollen, pale blue eyes. "Do you ever wonder if you and I are lucky? Or are we—really blessed of God?"

"Yes, I wonder all the time," she said. "I know God doesn't

love us one bit more than He loves Frances Anne and William, so I don't know why everything goes on being so perfect for us." She pushed against him on the carriage seat, holding his arm tight, tight. "Right now, I can only try to realize that you're back. You came home to me. Oh John, you—came home to me!"

CHAPTER 54

BY MID-OCTOBER, WORD SPREAD AROUND THE IS-
land like wildfire that young Horace Gould had finally come home
from his years spent in New Orleans as a purser on a palatial
Mississippi River boat. In fact, for months and months the young
son of James Gould, the lighthouse builder, had been—along with
the deepening trouble between the Wyllys and the Hazzards over
their property line—one of the favorite subjects of gossip.

Except to attend a specially called meeting of Island planters at
the Kings' Retreat Plantation with his father, Horace had kept
mostly to himself. And as William's widow, Frances, told Anne
during a visit Anne made to the Wyllys at the Village in early
November, even Horace's doting sister, Mary, was still doing her
best to protect him from wagging tongues.

"Next to my brother John," Frances said as she and Anne
walked along John Wylly's well-tended woods path behind the
house, "Mary seems to be partial to her younger brother. Not to
Jim, the elder Gould son, off now somewhere in Texas, I think, but

Mary Gould does adore Horace, has always been protective of him. Almost as protective as she is of their father."

"You sound as though you've been seeing quite a bit of Mary Gould, Frances," Anne said, stopping to look up into the bright, crimson canopy of black gum leaves above their heads. "I don't want to change the subject too much, but have you ever seen our autumn leaves brighter than they are this year?"

Anne wished she had kept still, knowing perfectly well that any mention of heart-stopping beauty, even colored leaves, reminded Frances of William. That he was gone. Her grief was, of course, still heavy. The new wild azaleas, which Frances Anne had planted herself on William's grave, had barely had time to begin to root. It had been less than three months since they'd buried her true love near Father Fraser and her and William's baby, Clarence, in the churchyard.

Frances tried hard to smile. She always tried, Anne knew, as though it was somehow rude to exhibit her broken heart. "I'm sorry," Frances said. "But William did so love those bright-red gum leaves. I'll never forget the early autumn days—before our marriage—how he would stand and look and look up at them, marveling that they seemed to grow crimson almost overnight." Determined, Anne knew, not to spoil their walk, Frances went quickly back to Anne's question. "Yes, I have seen more of Mary Gould than usual since I've been staying here at Mama's. And I'm always going to be grateful to that young woman, Anne, even if I do know that at least part of her reason for calling so often is her almost desperate hope that she might also see my brother John."

"How long have you known that Mary Gould is so fond of John?"

"Mary is more than fond of my brother. She's deeply in love with him. My own sixth sense told me that long ago."

"What about John? Does he even know it?"

"Yes. I think he knows it and may wish he could reciprocate." After a deep sigh, Frances added, "Who can tell about him these days, though? He was terribly let down that try as he most certainly did when he went to Mobile to help your brother James Hamilton with that cottonseed business, he couldn't really help. He was so pleased that James Hamilton even thought of including him in his big plans."

"So was my John," Anne said. "But that's all finished now."

"I wish I could say the same about the real reason no one can truly tell what my brother John is thinking lately. Sometimes I get quite frantic with worry. The Hazzard brothers seem almost to— to hate us all just because our name is Wylly. And John, because he's fiery and pigheaded, is at the center of their hatred."

"Mama told me last week," Anne said, "that the trouble be- tween the two families is dividing the Island, but at least the Wyllys should feel supported because most people are on the Wylly side."

"I despise all of it," Frances said. "There are so many things far more important than a few acres of land, Anne. Sometimes— sometimes I'd give anything to talk for at least a few minutes with my William! He's—he *was* always so quiet and sane about every- thing. Right now I'll have to say that my peculiar sister Heriot is the sanest member of our family where that stupid boundary line is concerned. To Heriot, all the land belongs to trees and flowers. She vows people—all people—only *think* they own it. Of course I could tell you verbatim exactly what most Islanders would have to say about such an odd belief. Heriot may be closer to the truth than anyone else is, though. John has always adored Heriot, but even she can't seem to reach him where the Hazzards' claim to our land is concerned. I—I do worry, Anne. I worry a lot."

"My brother James says it's a waste of time to do battle over a mere boundary line when the whole coast is in near financial ruin after the hurricane."

Frances Anne sighed. "Yes, I now know there is something far worse, but growing up, I always believed there was nothing quite as sad as ruined crops. John told me Thomas Butler King agrees with him that we all might have made four hundred fifty bags of cotton on St. Simons this year, but now, with the plants flattened or rotting, we'll do well to make a hundred fifty an acre." Frances gave Anne a poignant smile. "There is always another year, though. Crops can be replanted. Plant life—goes on. And don't tell me William's life is going on too, Anne, because I *know* it is. I just need so desperately to know *how* he's living it. What it's really like where William is now."

WHEN ANNE, WITH BIG BOY IN ATTENDANCE AS always, rode home that afternoon, she found John in deep conversation on their veranda with young Horace Gould.

"Our neighbor Mr. Gould has honored me with a good visit," John said when he hurried to follow the dog, Lovey, out to meet her as she turned Gentleman over to Big Boy in the lane beside their Big House at Hamilton.

"Darling, I'm so glad! Lovey, don't jump on me like that. Can Horace stay for tea with us?"

"I think not," John answered, leading her up the path to the veranda. "You did say you can't stay for tea, didn't you, Gould?"

"That's right, sir," Horace said, bowing over Anne's hand. "I'd love to another time, though. It would be difficult for me to tell either of you how much I already value your offer of friendship, Lieutenant Fraser."

"You're looking fit and stylish and so grown-up, Horace," Anne said. "I'm sure your father and Mary are overjoyed to have you home again. I know we are. My husband's wanted for a long time to know you."

A smile flickered on Horace Gould's thin, rather scholarly features. "Undoubtedly his curiosity was piqued by the contrasting stories about me that must have made the rounds of the Island. It's going to take a while to be comfortable here again, but I intend to be. And Lieutenant Fraser has gone a long way toward making me feel a part of things once more. I'd hoped for time to speak alone with him at the planters' meeting at King's Retreat not long ago. There wasn't time, so I took a chance on finding him free today. I must be going, though. My good sister, Mary, canceled an intended visit to the Wyllys' place so our father wouldn't be left at home alone while I rode over here. Mary's so unselfish, a man can take advantage of her and not know he's doing it. It's a pleasure to see you again, Miss Anne. And"—he turned to shake John's hand—"I'm somehow counting on another chance to share our rather foreign ideas on—various things, sir."

"So am I," John said with enthusiasm. "Come again anytime, Horace. But I'd be ever so grateful if you drop the Lieutenant Fraser and just call me John. You and I find too much to agree on for anything short of first names. Do hurry back. It appears our dog likes you too!"

"Thank you," their guest said warmly. "I like your dog and I will come back. I know you're a busy man, but I'd be honored anytime you find it possible to ride up to New St. Clair."

Arm in arm, John and Anne stood watching young Gould swing into the saddle of his tethered horse Anne knew was named Dolly.

They both waved as Horace galloped off up the lane, and John, slipping his arm around her waist, said, "I feel ten years younger after an hour or so with that boy. I needed it."

"What did you talk about? Planting?"

"No. You won't care for this, but we discussed slavery. Horace Gould changed a lot while he was in college at Yale. He wants to find a legal way to free his boyhood playmate July, now his groom —and slave."

Anne's voice was very young, almost timid, when she asked, "You do insist on using that word *slave,* don't you? I don't mean you use it all the time, darling, but you do forget and use it sometimes."

"I guess I do. But wouldn't it be a bit awkward for me to say July is now his groom and—one of his people?"

"You could have said something like—the groom he now owns."

"Yes," he said with almost no expression. "I suppose I could have said that. Look here, Anne, you don't approve of young Horace Gould's being my friend, do you?"

"Where would you get an idea like that? It's just that—"

"That what?"

"That I hate us to—to disagree on anything!"

"But we're both adults. We're bound to disagree on a few things. I'm a slave owner now. I even bought five new ones to send to work my interest in James Hamilton's cottonseed project before it collapsed. I'm doing as well as any other St. Simons planter whose fields were just decimated by a hurricane. What more can I do to please you?"

"Nothing. Nothing at all! And I have to believe that even though you disapprove of owning people, you still like what you're doing." Until now, she hadn't flared at all. She did, a little, when she added, "I don't think it's fair for you even to imply that all the wonderful things you're accomplishing are just to please me!"

He turned her to him and looked down into her face. "Is it too much to believe that we could both be right in this instance? Or that there's probably some rightness in what each of us thinks and feels on the slavery subject?"

"Is it too much to believe that I love you enough so that none of it matters as much as I sometimes act as though it does? Taking our people for granted could just be a *habit* with me. Can you tell me what the planters' meeting the other night at poor Anna Matilda's deserted St. Simons home was all about? You didn't say a word when you came back. I wonder if Anna Matilda even knew her husband called the meeting at Retreat, with her stuck over at Monticello?"

"I don't know about that, but you can certainly write her that their people keep the place spotless and the yards well-tended. I didn't tell you what happened at the meeting because I assumed it wouldn't interest you. I said almost as little at the Retreat gathering as young Horace said, because the thrust of the whole affair was the future welfare of the cotton states. Thomas Butler King may have been born at the North, but he's a dyed-in-the-wool Southerner now. The man's in high dudgeon over the supposed collusion between the federal government and what he calls the despised North. He actually urges that the South establish direct trade with Europe! That, I can tell you, did not set well with young Horace Gould or with his father or with me. Horace, with his family's roots in New England, is a firm believer in the union of all the American states. Even as a British subject, I think I am too. Thomas King seems to have the South off in a corner of the world fending for itself. He accused the federal government of being in cahoots with the economic tyranny at the North. When John Wylly declared that such a thing struck him as a kind of Southern nationalism, I thought Wylly and Dr. Hazzard might exchange blows. Fortunately, young Wylly laughed it off."

"Oh dear," Anne said. "I do hope Mama isn't right that the boundary dispute between the Hazzards and the Wyllys is really dividing the Island."

"I seem to do very well as master of ceremonies for St. Simons boat races and social events," John said, "but deliver me from its divisive issues! I've moved as far in the direction of Georgia coastal planting as I can move. There are so few white persons on this Island, it would seem as though you and I could be left alone just to live and love within the happy boundaries of Hamilton, doesn't it?"

For a moment Anne said nothing. Then, as though they hadn't been discussing anything unusual, she asked, "Do you think Thomas King was on his way back to his wife at Monticello after that planters' meeting at Retreat?"

"I have no idea. Why?"

"Because poor Anna Matilda is supposed to be having another baby this month."

Laughing abruptly, John smacked himself on the forehead. "Mrs. Fraser, you *are* adorable. Have I told you lately?"

"I don't know what you're talking about."

"Adorable and clever and smart and—I do love you!"

"You're supposed to love me. We belong to each other, but what did I say to bring that on?"

"You're not only beautiful, you're the most expert subject changer in the whole wide world."

"When did I change—what subject?"

"We were, I thought, discussing the content of a rather contentious planters' meeting concerning the tyranny of the wicked

North and the federal government. You did deliberately change the subject, you know." He gave her his melting smile.

"I'll change it still further. Let's go inside so you can play our song for me."

"Good old 'Drink to Me Only'?"

"Good old 'Drink to Me Only.' "

CHAPTER 55

WHEN SPRING FINALLY BEGAN TO BRUSH THE IS-
land with its myriad greens, Anne was still going often to the
Village, up near Cannon's Point, to spend time with Frances Anne.
Her sister-in-law was simply unable to face living in her own
house in Darien at the Ridge because everything reminded her of
William, gone almost a year. Spring was so late in 1838 that even
the *Brunswick Advocate* ran stories about the unusually cold
weather, which was holding back every planter's crops. There had
been frost on May 31! Again this year no one expected a full cotton
crop. Last year a hurricane, this year cold weather. No wonder
John was grateful and relieved when they learned that William
had left provision in his will to pay off John's debt of eight hundred dollars at the Bank of Darien.

Riding back down Frederica Road toward her own home early
in June, after a good talk with Frances, Anne felt for the first time
that perhaps her friend was beginning to find her way out of the
hidden shadows with which her life had been darkened since Wil-

liam went away. Visible, sharp black shadows slashed now across the narrow shell road as Anne raised her hand in response to Big Boy's protective wave to her—a kind of silent little game she'd played with her huge, good-natured Ebo escort for much of her life. The almost mystical light in the woods on both sides of the road created those shadows, she thought. Was light truly beginning to break through the shadows among which Frances Anne had groped all these months? When the sunlight spread like a great lamp being turned up in the dark recesses of the friendly St. Simons woods, did it wipe out the shadows? Or only intensify them? Where, she wondered, do shadows go? Into the darkness at night? Into the light by day? Is night one long, dense shadow? If so, not all shadows were a sign of trouble in the heart, because nights beside John meant only joy—awake or asleep.

From his horse just ahead, where he kept an eye out for snakes or deep ruts in the road, Big Boy waved again. When Anne returned his wave, she smiled. And felt like smiling, because Frances Anne had told her some news only minutes before she and Big Boy rode out the Village lane. News that had given Anne hope for her longtime friend. Only a ray of hope, but she truly believed that Frances Anne was seriously considering James Hamilton's generous offer, not only to escort her and five-year-old Menzies on a holiday at the North but to pay her way. James, Frances told her, needed to make the voyage himself in connection with raising funds for the Brunswick Canal and also to select certain lumber he wanted used in the new Christ Church he had designed to be erected in Savannah. Not only would Frances Anne and Menzies be going, but also Mrs. Phineas Nightingale and her infant daughter, Louisa, named for Louisa Shaw, whose houseparty at Cumberland Island had first brought John into Anne's life so many years ago. Frances's elder son, James, was away at school, so why shouldn't she go? Anne had argued. "There's nothing to keep you down here. And if the widely advertised steam packet *Pulaski* is as splendid as it's supposed to be, the voyage itself will do you a world of good. Please go, Frances! My brother James Hamilton seldom has a stupid idea. I know you'll be glad you went. I don't want to get home this evening in the dark, so Big Boy and I have to leave, but before I go, promise you'll make that lovely, restful voyage."

"She wouldn't say for sure," Anne explained to John excitedly when, blessedly alone, with Annie and the older children visiting the Demeres, the two sat down to a light supper that evening. The sunset over the Frederica River threw its light in wide, rose-colored streaks across the dining room floorboards as Anne told him of her talk with Frances. "She did promise to send down a note by one of the Wylly people tomorrow with a definite decision, though. Darling John, don't you wish we could go too?"

With a grin, he reached for another serving of hominy and reminded her of how seasick she was on their voyage from London.

"But James Hamilton and Frances Anne and Mrs. Nightingale will be taking that new, already famous luxury packet, the *Pulaski!* It moves so fast and smoothly, there's only one night at sea, and shipboard on such a water trip when so many prominent people are escaping our damp, hot summer for the North should be a continuous festival!"

He reached for her hand. "With all my heart I wish we could afford to go. We can't, and anyway, with our crop so backward, I have to be here to try to get as much out of the fields as possible."

"I know and I wouldn't dream of going without you. Frances Anne is the one who matters now. And I somehow feel she is going to go."

"I hope you're right, beautiful Anne. I so want Frances to have a change. As long as she's here with her mother on St. Simons, she'll go to William's grave every day the weather permits."

Anne frowned a little. "But it must—help her to do that."

"I wonder."

For a time she sat making little marks on the tablecloth with the handle of her spoon. "We—we don't deserve the unbroken happiness you and I go on having, do we? John, I love you so much more than I loved you in Scotland—on those wonderful days we laughed and climbed our way around Mama's Caerlaverock. I love you so much more than I loved you—even yesterday. Even this morning! I know God loves everybody best. Not just us. How can it be possible for two people to live such a perfect life together?"

"I know I'm brilliant," he said, resorting as he so often did to teasing when a more profound comment wouldn't come. "But even *I* am not brilliant enough to have an answer to a question like that." His soft, musical laugh came. "Except, of course, that you're so beautiful and I'm—utterly charming."

The Village
St. Simons Island
8 June 1838

Dearest Anne,

I have decided to make the voyage to the North under the care and kindness of your brother James Hamilton, and I will leave with Menzies on Captain James Frewin's schooner early tomorrow morning, 9 June, from Frederica. I am sorry not to be able to see you again at church on Sunday, but Captain Frewin departs St. Simons tomorrow and his offer to take Menzies and me as far as Savannah must be accepted. I feel only nervous now, but perhaps once the *Pulaski* is under way, the voyage will calm me a bit. It's just that I have the nagging sense of leaving something behind—someone. My life, dear William. Since in this earthly existence one never knows what's around the next bend, I want you to be certain of my love and enduring friendship whether or not we meet again here. Pray for us and don't worry. All sea voyages are dangerous, but perhaps this one is as safe and fine as advertised. I will stay in Savannah, until the *Pulaski* sails on 13 June, at Miss Eliza Mackay's. I hope you will be able to visit Mother at the Village now and then. She is her usual calm, strong self. Thank you for being my lifelong friend. You, William's beloved brother, John, and your children will be in my prayers and in my heart.

Frances Anne Wylly Fraser

Anne read the note, delivered the next morning by old Mrs.
Wylly's trusted Peter, and longed, not only to have had time to see
Frances again for a proper goodbye, but to be able to tell John—to
read the note aloud to him—*now*. He would be riding in early this
afternoon in time for dinner, though, and because the children
were still at the Demeres, they would again be alone.

Good, she thought. I need to be with him—just him. Not that
I'm going to worry about Frances and her little boy. I'm not. James
Hamilton and pleasant Mrs. Nightingale will make sure she's all
right. As all right as a woman can be with only a half-life. I
wonder if she had time to ride to the churchyard. I know she
wanted to tell William. How I long for the day when she knows
deep down in her heart that William isn't really there under those
churchyard oak trees, that he's not only with God but with Father
Fraser and their baby. Maybe someday it will help her heart, realizing that William no longer has to grieve over baby Clarence
Brailsford because father and son are together again.

Anne had read and reread her friend's note, standing in the
shade of the thick, green wisteria vine that sheltered one end of the
veranda. Its graceful, purple blossom banners were gone now,
but the June-green leaves, casting their flickering shadows across
ceiling and floor, seemed even more comforting. Frances Anne
had spoken often of how thick the shadows were in her life without William, without her baby son. But *did* shadows always
have to mean sorrow? Didn't shadows on a veranda floor or across
a green stretch of grass also mean that light was there to cause
them?

Bring Frances out of the shadows, dear Lord, she prayed silently. Either bring her out of them or show her that they're really
only visible to us because somewhere there is so much light. . . .

ON WEDNESDAY MORNING, 13 JUNE, AT EIGHT
o'clock, the hour when the handsome, white steam packet *Pulaski*
was due to depart Savannah's old waterfront, Anne stood at one of
the windows in Hamilton's master bedroom, where she and John

had shared an especially tender ecstasy last night. There was darning to be done and a letter to Anna Matilda to be written. Eve was busily freshening the bed with clean linens, being remarkably quiet for Eve. Anne was relieved because her thoughts were on what she imagined was the festive sight of the fine packet, decks thronged with passengers waving to family and friends gathered on the Savannah wharf, whistle blowing, flags snapping in the wind. On St. Simons, at least, it was a clear, sunny day. One could never be sure along the coast, but she hoped, for Frances Anne's sake, that the sun was dancing off the waters of the Savannah River, too.

"You could be on dat big, fancy boat wif Miss Frances dis minute," Eve said, tucking in the corners of a bolster slip before smoothing the last wrinkle from the daytime bed covering. "You jus' too stubborn, Miss Anne, to trust Eve wif things here. Look like you learn. You be forty-one. Dat mean Eve be forty years old. Don' I know by now how to mind churn?"

"You know perfectly well how to pronounce the word *children*. The way you say it, you sound as though you're talking about a butter churn! Of course you know how to take care of my children, but that isn't the reason I'm not on that steam packet today."

The final crease smoothed on the bed, Eve stood grinning at her. "Mausa John be the reason."

"When you're right about something I tell you, and yes, he's the reason. John and Pete and Fanny and baby Selina and John Couper and—and you already know my other main reason for staying here."

"You skeered Miss Annie, she get too serious wif her man, Mistah Paul Demere, while you gone."

"And don't tell me you knew that because you were born with a caul over your face, because I've already told you how I feel about Paul Demere. I have no intention of interfering, but I just don't think he's good enough for our Annie. And I can hear what Mama would say if she knew I'd even think of telling you a thing like that!"

"You an' me's different from other folks, Miss Anne. Eve never tell another livin' soul dat you don' like dat boy."

JUST AFTER DAWN ON JUNE 20, JOHN HURRIED downstairs to answer a rapid, urgent knock at the front door of their Hamilton house. In the half-darkness, he recognized young Horace Gould. Even with so little light, he could tell something was horribly wrong.

"Horace! What on earth brings you here almost before daylight?"

"Bad news. Tragic news," Horace gasped, out of breath from his hard ride. "It's the steam packet *Pulaski!* My new friend, Captain Charles Stevens of Frederica, got home late yesterday from Savannah. He brought supplies for us and I met his boat. Stayed the night at Frederica. The whole city of Savannah is in mourning. I don't have any details, John, but the *Pulaski* blew up! Blew up in the dark of night! Word so far is that only seventeen passengers were saved. That's out of a crew of thirty-seven and maybe more than a hundred and fifty passengers."

"Dear God," John breathed. "My sister-in-law, Frances Anne, and her small son were on that ship! And—Anne's brother James Hamilton!"

"I know. I haven't even stopped to tell the Wyllys yet. Rode straight here to you. Hated to rouse old Mrs. Wylly so early. Maybe the worst part is that the *Pulaski* blew up at night. It's more than a man can take in to think of all those people thrown into black water!"

"I suppose the boilers exploded," John said, turning to find the source of the sound he'd just heard on the stairs. "Anne! Oh Anne. Did—did you hear what Horace said?"

Halfway down the steps, pulling her robe around her, Anne stood rooted, unable to move or speak. John raced up the steps and led her down into the dimly lit front hall, where Horace still stood in the open doorway.

"Are—are there any names yet," Anne gasped, "of those who are safe?"

John had just left Gould standing in the doorway. Now, with Anne there, he was able to begin to think a little. "Sorry, Horace. Come in the parlor where we can all sit down at least. Come on, Anne. I forgot my manners. Horace will tell you every single thing he knows."

He led her to her favorite little rocker. "All I heard," she said, looking up at Horace, "was that—the *Pulaski* blew up in the dark. And some were somehow saved. . . ."

"Seventeen are known to be safe so far," Horace said, "and although Captain Steven couldn't be sure, he thought that your brother James might be one of them."

"Dear God, may it be!" Anne breathed. "But what about Frances Anne?" She was staring up hopefully at John now as though he, of all people, would know how to put her heart at some ease.

"Stevens seemed only to have heard the name of James Hamilton Couper mentioned and a Colonel Roberts," Horace said. "There really are few details yet. Everything's only rumor."

"We—we can pray," Anne said flatly, "that if James Hamilton is safe, so are Frances Anne and little Menzies. James had Mrs. Nightingale from Cumberland Island and her infant daughter and a servant under his care too. . . ."

Anne's words simply hung in the stillness of the slowly brightening room. It was going to be a sunny day, John thought, then realized that both he and Horace were still standing. "Take that chair, Horace. We'll get Mina to bring you something to tide you over on your sad mission to the Wyllys. I suppose you'll be stopping at the Village first thing."

Horace's troubled, pale face showed John that he hadn't honestly thought about his next stop. "I—I may go to New St. Clair and tell Papa and Mary since I pass by there on my way to the Wyllys' and Cannon's Point. Say, Miss Anne, would it be any easier at all on Mrs. Wylly and James Hamilton's wife, Caroline, to hear such tragic news from another woman, do you think?"

"Your sister, Mary?" Anne asked.

"Yes. I know it can't be easy hearing it from anyone, but—"

"Mary is tactful and sensitive," Anne murmured, half to herself. "I'm so glad Caroline is over here on the Island, staying at her mother's home while James is away. Poor Caroline . . . not only her sister Frances but her husband, too."

Not knowing anything else to do or say, John stood abruptly. "I'll get you something to eat, Horace. A cup of—"

"No. No thank you, John. There really isn't time for that. Especially if I—if I decide to have Mary break the news to the Wyllys."

When twenty-one-year-old Annie Fraser appeared in the downstairs hall, John told her all they knew of the ghastly tragedy. The look on her pretty, young face was so stricken, her parents and Horace Gould could only stare at her.

"What, Annie?" Anne asked, going to her. "Why are you— looking like that?"

"Oh Mama! Mama, I—I didn't mention it to anyone, but Paul almost went North on the *Pulaski!*"

"Your beau, Paul Demere?" John asked, feeling foolish because he already knew it could be no one else.

"Why would Paul have been going?" Anne asked.

"I'm not exactly sure," Annie said hoarsely. "Some kind of business errand for his brother, Lewis, I think. And—and if his mother could have gone along, he wanted me to go too. Just for a nice holiday."

"And you—you didn't tell your own mother?"

She had asked her blunt, almost cross question at such an inappropriate time and in a voice so unlike her, John turned Anne to face him and said, "I don't think you— meant to ask that kind of question at such an anxious moment, did you, Anne?"

Tears filled her eyes when she finally answered, "No, John. No, Annie. I surely didn't—mean to do that. Can you forgive me? Here we all stand, not knowing which of our loved ones are dead or alive, and I blurt out a thing like that!"

In response, John saw his daughter smile and slip her arm around her mother's waist.

When Horace had gone, Annie asked, "Wasn't it good of Horace Gould to ride all the way down here to tell us—so early in the morning?"

She'd asked, John knew, not only because it was indeed kind of young Horace but because Annie wanted as always to put her mother at ease. Today, of all times, Anne had let it show almost shamefully how much she disapproved of Annie's choice of young Paul Demere.

"It was more than good of Mr. Gould to make that long trip," Anne said. "And Annie, as long as your sweet, good heart is beating, a part of mine will beat too. But yours will be the *better* part."

"Now darling," John said, "you were just terribly upset, as we all are. As we all will be until we have time to learn more about who is still alive and who—drowned."

"Of course we'll be upset until we know," Anne said, a bit of her old spunk showing, "but what I just said is true. Our daughter's heart is far more loving than her mother's—any day."

CHAPTER 56

W HEN THE ONCE-GRAND BUT STILL WELL-PRE-
served Couper carriage rattled up to the pinestraw walk that led to
Hamilton's veranda the very next day, Pete saw her grandfather
first. In her usual way the girl went hurtling out the front door to
throw both arms around him almost before he'd balanced himself
on his trusty walking stick, after Johnson had helped him down
from the high carriage seat.

The old gentleman returned her embrace warmly, but when
Pete had a good look at his face, she let him go, stepped back,
and said, "Grandpapa! Your cheeks are all wet with tears! You've
been crying. How come you're smiling now? I'm sorry I hugged
you so hard, but I was just so surprised and so glad to see you,
I—"

"Sh! Hush, Petey. Don't apologize. It's too good to have you so
happy to see your old octogenarian grandfather. Didn't you ever
feel like crying and laughing at the same time?"

"I guess so, but what does octogenarian mean?"

"Well, I exaggerated a bit. I haven't quite hit eighty, but close enough."

Pete gave a shrill whistle. "Eighty? That's old, isn't it? But I tell people I'm thirteen when I really won't be until fall." Then she hugged him again, a bit less vigorously. "Mama says I'm too grown-up to keep on being so rough." She took his hand and they began to walk slowly, Pete restraining herself, up the path to the veranda, where by now Mama, Annie, Little Fanny, and John Couper, almost six, were waiting for them. "Look who's here, Mama! Grandpapa Couper came to see us and he's been crying!"

After greeting them all with an affectionate hug, he ran his fingers through his dark red hair, still only slightly gray, and tried to smile. "I've brought the best news, Anne," he said. "Your brother's safe and so are Frances Anne and her lad, Menzies, and Mrs. Nightingale and her infant daughter. You and I have laughed at times at James Hamilton's overly serious traits, but Daughter, he's a hero now."

Anne rushed into her father's arms. "Oh Papa, Papa, how can we find a way to thank God that they're all safe? How do you know they are? I thought we'd have to wait a whole week for the next issue of the *Brunswick Advocate. How do you know?*"

"You must have gone very early to Frederica, Grandpapa," Annie said. "Was there a letter from Uncle James?"

"Were you a mon, Annie, you might one day be as smart as your uncle. Uncle James did indeed write to us, and I have been to Frederica, hoping against hope that Twining had made an extra effort to get word to us here. He did." Out of his jacket pocket Grandpapa Couper took not one but two letters. "Your brother wrote, as is his custom, Anne, a long, long account of every move he made from the time he was wakened by the dreadful boiler explosion to the moment of his writing. Also, our dear friend Eliza Mackay wrote to your mother from Savannah. I brought both letters with me."

"Papa, thank you," Anne said. "I hoped Mama wouldn't have to wait a minute longer than necessary."

He smiled broadly now. "You know I went straight to your dear mother. She insisted, in fact, that I come here with both pieces of mail and while I can't stay, I am free to leave them with you. You can all read them."

"I can read some, Grandpapa," John Couper piped.

"That I know, young John Couper," the old man said, bending down to give the boy another squeeze. "And I'm sure you'll be able to read quite a bit of Uncle James's long epistle, but just in case you can't read every single word, we'll blame it on his hasty script and your mama can tell you what it says. Just be sure you keep in mind that Uncle James Hamilton is a true he-r-ro!"

"I might be a hero someday too," the boy said.

"To me, you've got all the makings, son." The old man stood to his full height, handed the two letters to Anne, and said, "Now don't tease me to stay, lass, because I promised your mother I'd come right back. She and I had so little time to talk about the heartbreaking thing that happened. You'll see, when you read Mrs. Mackay's letter, just how tragic it really is. Once more the Heavenly Father has blessed *us.*" He turned his attention again to young John Couper. "How about doing your old grandfather a favor, son? Would you run out and tell Johnson I'll be ready to drive back right away?"

When the child raced off down the path toward where Couper's faithful Johnson waited in the carriage, he turned again to Anne. "I'd advise that you and Annie read the letters—both of them—first alone, Daughter. Then use your judgment in what you feel the other children should know."

"I heard that," Pete said. "I'm going on thirteen. I'm plenty old enough to know about anything."

"The word is, Petey, that your mother makes that decision. Is that clear?"

Pete hung her head for an instant, then grinned up at him. "Yes, sir. Whatever you say, Grandpapa, but you'll have to get used to the idea that I'm not a child any longer."

WHEN PETE BEGAN TO USE ALL HER CRAFTY CHARM to persuade Mama to allow her to be present when she and Annie first read what details the letters contained of the terrible tragedy at sea, Annie interrupted.

"But Pete, in all the long years you've been on earth, I've never known you to break your word to Grandfather Couper. Are you going to break it today of all days?"

"Did I promise him?" Pete asked innocently.

"I thought you did."

"I heard what I said. What I actually said was that I'd agree to let Mama make the decision. Isn't that right, Mama?"

"Yes, Annie. That's what she promised. And my decision is that you're still a little too young, Pete. We don't have any idea yet of all the horror in these letters. It could give you nightmares. I dread to read them myself, but I don't intend to wait a minute longer, so scoot!"

When her sister left the veranda and went to play with Lovey and the younger children, Annie asked if Mama would like her to read the letters aloud to her.

"If you'll promise not to leave anything out. You're always trying to protect me. Where was Uncle James when he wrote? I know Eliza Mackay's letter has to do with people we know in Savannah. Read your uncle's first, please?"

"All right," Annie said, unfolding the thick sheaf of paper. "He wrote this from 'ten miles south of New River Inlet, North Carolina,' and it's dated June 16, 1838. Mama, that's only three days after the *Pulaski* left Savannah!"

"I know," her mother said, her voice strangely tense, Annie thought, as though Mama were experiencing the disaster herself. "That's like James to want to get word to your grandparents as soon as possible. To me too. He knows how close Frances Anne and I have always been. Read, dear. Please read the opening of his letter."

"My dearest Family,

I am writing this as quickly as possible so as to make use of the kindness of a Captain Ganshorn, who departs for Savannah with his steam packet *Emerald* within a few hours. I feel sure someone there, especially in view of such widespread tragedy, will post it to you quickly. One of my heaviest heartaches has been the knowledge that you will learn of the enormous loss of life without assurance that we—Frances Anne and Menzies, Mrs. Nightingale and her infant, Louisa, and I—are all safe after a most miraculous escape from the awful destruction of the *Pulaski*."

"Oh Annie, Annie." Anne interrupted her daughter. "My blessed brother could have stopped right there. How do we reckon with the way God blesses our immediate family? Only seventeen passengers—and maybe that number includes a few crew members —are still alive as far as we know. Still, all our little party, those aboard closest to us, are safe!"

Annie was listening to her mother, but she was also scanning the letter and thought perhaps she'd better explain that the remainder of Uncle James's letter seemed to be his detailed account of the explosion and the ghastly events following. "There will be plenty of time to read the remainder of this," she explained, "because Uncle James made a copy and it will be published in all the newspapers. Would you rather I read Miss Eliza's much, much shorter letter first? We can then spend all the time we need on these long, tightly packed pages Uncle James wrote."

"All right. Whatever you say, Annie."

"Just looking ahead a page or two, I see Uncle James mentions Miss Eliza's son's family in his letter. Mama, we'd better read her letter now, because I don't think Uncle James knew when he wrote this about the fate of Mr. William Mackay's family."

"Miss Eliza's son William's family was aboard?"

"His whole family! Virginia, his wife, and their two children!"

"Oh dear, then do read the other letter. It's too late now to pray, but poor William Mackay is such a quiet, sensitive man, I don't think he'd ever get over it should something happen to his family."

"Listen and I'll read what Miss Eliza wrote to Grandmama Couper," Annie said.

"My dear friend Rebecca,

With a heart choked with sorrow, I feel the desperate need to tell you, although we know few details, that my beloved, tenderhearted William may have suffered the loss of his entire family—Virginia, his little daughter, Delia, and his baby son, William Jr. We know nothing for certain yet, except that only seventeen people have been reported alive—the Mackay name not among them—so the main purpose of this letter is to tell you of my great gratitude to God that we *have* learned of the safety of your fine son James Hamilton, Frances Anne Fraser, Mrs. Nightingale, and the two children under your son's care. When I learn more, and that is likely because I am here in Savannah, I will write at once.

> Your loving friend,
> Eliza Mackay"

When Annie had finished the letter, she asked, "Mama, if God is love, why isn't He *fair,* too? Mr. William Mackay is such a good, kind man. Why should something so dreadful happen to him?"

"We don't know that it did, Annie. He's just waiting now, hoping and praying for good news. I'm sure Miss Eliza will let my mother know, or when our paper comes over from Brunswick next week, we might be able to find out. It's dreadful that it all took place when there was no chance to get anything in our paper, isn't it?"

"Yes it is," Annie said, "but am I sinful to have asked why God isn't fair? If He is love and we believe He is, why do these tragedies happen?"

"Dear heart, I imagine minds far better than ours have been trying to learn the answer to that question since time began." Anne stood up. "I find all this has made me quite tired, as though I might get one of my sick headaches. Your father won't ride in from his fields for another hour. I think I'll go lie down for a while. Will you call me when he comes home? Better still, send him upstairs. I need to be alone with your father for a few minutes before dinner."

A LITTLE AFTER ONE O'CLOCK THAT AFTERNOON, John opened their bedroom door softly in case Anne had fallen asleep. For a moment he stood looking down at her, his heart reaching, his thoughts turning over and over the golden truth: *beautiful Anne . . . beautiful Anne.*

One rounded arm lay palm up on the coverlet. Her pulse throbbed visibly in the most graceful throat any woman ever had. The lovely eyes—shielded now by the eyelids he loved to kiss—would look up at him in a moment and then he would know. He always knew the depth of Anne's need by her strange, pale, revealing eyes.

"Have I ever loved her as much as I love her this minute?" he asked himself. "Will I ever be good enough, strong enough, really to help her when she has need of me? How many men have wondered that? How many have felt the same near helplessness I feel now, simply because she asked Annie to send me to her?"

"Anne?"

Her smile came slowly. "I wasn't asleep," she whispered. "Was that mean of me—to pretend?"

"Dearest, I'm so, so relieved that James Hamilton is safe! And Frances Anne and Mrs. Nightingale and the children. Annie told me." Sitting on the bed, he took her in his arms. "She told me too that you needed to be with me."

Her arms circled his neck. "John, I'm ashamed of myself!"

"Why on earth would you be ashamed?"

"My brother is safe. Frances Anne is safe. Everyone with him is safe somewhere in North Carolina, I suppose. Everyone close to us is safe and here I am, collapsing like a kitten. A weak kitten. Did Annie tell you poor William Mackay may have lost his entire family?"

"Yes, she told me, dearest. I feel helpless, too. This kind of calamity, even when we know so little about it and even when we know our loved ones are all right, knocks the wind out of anyone's sails. Now listen to me. I've promised our Annie that I'll find time in the fields this afternoon to read every word of what James Hamilton wrote in his long, long account."

"I couldn't bear to read it!"

"I know. And I understand. It was asking too much of yourself even to think of reading about the accident in as much detail as"—he smiled gently—"as I'm sure James Hamilton wrote of it. As only a gentleman as composed and articulate as he *could* have made an effort to recount. I see no reason why you need to read it all—ever. I'll read it and then I promise to give you what you can bear hearing. Don't you believe me?"

"Of course I believe you. It's just that Frances Anne had to struggle through it all, John! She had to fight her way through the whole, terrifying experience, and I can't even bear to read what my own dear brother wrote about it. Just the thought makes me half-sick. Am I so much weaker than she is? Than other women are?"

"You've always worked your way through everything hard that's come to you, darling. Blessedly, you were here with me where you belonged. Had you been there, you would have been just as brave as Frances."

"Did you—did Annie tell you she might have been on that steam packet too?"

"She told us both, remember?"

Tears streamed from Anne's eyes now and John felt as though his own blood had turned to water. She needed his strength, and realizing that their Annie might now be dead—somewhere in the waters of the Atlantic—had drained him of everything resembling strength.

Clinging to him, Anne sobbed, "John, John dearest, life is—life is dangerous, isn't it?"

"Now Anne, not all of it is dangerous," he said helplessly.

"The reason I hated so to think of your going back into your marine regiment was that I was afraid, deathly afraid you'd be killed in some stupid battle. And now look how dangerous it is just to live—even in coastal Georgia."

The dinner bell clanged from the downstairs hall, and he began to dry her eyes with his handkerchief. "When Mina rings, we obey, and you know that perfectly well."

"I couldn't swallow a bite of anything."

"Oh yes you can. Now look at me, Mrs. Fraser, and repeat after me: 'I'm hungry and I'm going to go downstairs with my husband and eat every bite of my dinner. I have one of the best cooks on St. Simons, outside of Sans Foix at Cannon's Point, and being named Mina, as she most certainly is, means that when she rings, we march!' "

Tears were still on her cheeks but he'd made her smile, and with an obedience that almost rivaled Annie's when she was a little girl, Anne obeyed.

On their way down the stairs, holding hands, she whispered, "We do have to pray every minute though, John, that gentle William Mackay's little family is safe."

"All right," he agreed. "And don't forget, I promise to read all of James Hamilton's lengthy piece this very afternoon, and tonight I'll have a full report for you."

"Papa told the children when he brought James's letter down that their uncle is now a hero."

In the downstairs hall John gave her an honest, unguarded look when he said, "I doubt that I've found a way to let you know, but the truth is, your brother has been rather a hero to me for a long time."

CHAPTER 57

James Hamilton's letter was so long that John held it for reference as he tried, alone in their room that evening, to tell Anne, as gently as such a horrible event could be described, most of what her brother had written. In his usual meticulous way, James had covered every action from the initial explosion, which took place after the passengers had retired to their staterooms, to what must have been the most frightening moment: After managing to lead Frances Anne, her little boy, and Mrs. Nightingale with her infant to the area of the only two lifeboats on the ship, James Hamilton, holding the Nightingale baby, instructed Mrs. Nightingale to jump ten feet down into one of the two lifeboats. He then tried to follow her with the child. The yawl surged as he sprang down into it, his foot struck the gunwale, and with the baby in his arms, he fell backward into the sea.

"Dear God," Anne breathed, so visibly shaken John vowed to shorten the account if possible. "Don't skip anything," she whispered. "He's my brother and I have a right to know everything he went through. Was Frances Anne already in the lifeboat when James fell?"

"No. She and little Menzies were still on the sinking packet. But James Hamilton, gripping the infant, bobbed up out of the sea, found a way to put the baby within its mother's reach, then climbed into the boat himself. He then shouted up to Frances Anne to throw Menzies down into the boat. James caught the boy, ordered Frances to jump herself, and broke her fall by allowing her to strike his own body."

"I can't believe there were only two lifeboats, John!"

"And that stupidly careless fact must have caused some passengers, by then in the two yawls, moments of unimaginable horror, because James says the night was filled with screams and shouts from others still aboard the tilting *Pulaski,* pleading with them not to shove off without them."

"They—they just left them on the ship—to die?"

"No choice, Anne. The worst part for James Hamilton was seeing, and hearing the pleas of, friends and acquaintances— faces he recognized—begging not to be left to their watery deaths."

"I can't bear to hear any more," she gasped. "Tomorrow maybe. Not now. John, will any of us ever be quite the same? Even those of us who only *heard* about it?"

"But James reached shore safely and so did his charges." He reached for her hand, lifted her out of her rocker and onto the bed. "And you're going to be yourself again, dearest, just as soon as the shock wears off. I will be too." Spreading a light coverlet over her, he leaned down to kiss her forehead. "Eve can bring you some warm milk. Then I'll come back and stop that trembling."

"Eve's gone home to June by now. I don't need any milk. I just need you. I just need you to hold me. And to tell me you're not terribly ashamed of me for being so frail and dependent."

After a quick visit to the children, John came back, stretched out beside her on the bed, and held her until the trembling stopped. He had already decided not to tell her tonight that William Mackay had, so far as James Hamilton seemed to know, lost his entire little family.

EIGHT DAYS AFTER ANNE'S NEAR COLLAPSE AT THE tragic news, she appeared at breakfast for the first time since John had given her the details of what Frances Anne and James Hamilton had gone through.

When the June 28 edition of the *Brunswick Advocate* reached the Island from the mainland, she fully intended to read its account of the *Pulaski* wreck for herself.

Eve thoughtfully took young John Couper, Fanny, and Pete to the woods to gather wild blackberries so that Anne could read the news story with no one around but Annie.

"Do you ever stop to realize, Mama, that Eve may know you better than the rest of us do?"

"Yes, I'm sure she does, and most of the time I take comfort in it," Anne said, reaching for the newspaper just as Annie was about to read it to her. "I know your father did not tell me every terrible thing your uncle James wrote in his long, long letter, so I intend to read this for myself. Move your chair closer to me and we'll read it together. That way you won't have to wait."

Brunswick Advocate, June 28, 1838

LOSS OF THE STEAMER PULASKI AND DESTRUCTION OF MORE THAN ONE HUNDRED LIVES

We give below from the *Wilmington Advertiser,* the first account of this awful calamity. Words are all too weak to give expression to the deep and heartfelt emotions of horror with which we receive this intelligence. Not a circumstance, even of accident, alleviates the grief of the many surviving friends and relatives of those who have perished by this fatal event; not the most minute fact as yet appears in mitigation of the murderous guilt of those whose gross negligence occasioned this widespread destruction. We present the following from the *Wilmington Advertiser,* Extra, which appeared June 18:

HEART-RENDING CATASTROPHE!!

Loss of the steam packet, *Pulaski,* with a crew of 37 and 150 or 160 passengers. On Thursday, 14th. inst. the steamer, *Pulaski,* Captain Dubois, left Charleston for Baltimore. . . . At about eleven o'clock on the same night, while off the North Carolina coast some thirty miles from land, weather moderate and night dark—the starboard boiler exploded and the vessel was lost, with all the passengers and crew except those whose names are enumerated in the list below.

"I simply cannot bear to read all this explanation they have here about what might have happened, whose fault it was," Anne said, interrupting their reading. "My sick headache will come back if I even let myself think that negligence might have caused so much suffering! We still don't know for sure about William Mackay's little family—not a word—and I'm going to look right now for their names in this list of those saved."

"Mama," Annie said gently. "You won't find the names of Mr. Mackay's family."

"How can you possibly know that?"

"Papa read a letter Grandmama Couper received yesterday from Miss Eliza Mackay. William lost his wife and both his small children."

"But—but your father didn't tell me!"

"Mama," Annie said as though speaking to a small child, "You've been really ill with your sick headache. Papa knew it came on because of this ugly tragedy. Do you think he'd add to your heartache by telling you such a terrible thing?"

"The children's grandmother, Miss Eliza, wrote about it?"

"Yes. She knew we'd all be worried."

"Eliza Mackay has already had such dreadful sorrow in her life —a dead child, her husband dead—dear God, I'd never be able to show the kind of strength she's showing now!" Beginning to sob,

Anne buried her face in her hands. "Your mother is weak, weak, weak! And the worst part is that I didn't even know I was."

"That strange older man named Osmund Kott, who was Caroline Browning's overseer at her plantation on the Savannah River, was drowned, too."

Anne raised her head. "Did those nice Browning people have anyone else on the *Pulaski?*"

"Yes and that's the good news. Mama, buck up, there *is* some really good news. The Brownings' only daughter, Natalie—the one Mr. Browning so adores—was on board too. A young man she'd met during the voyage found her in the water after the explosion. It seems they drifted on some debris for something like five days before a ship picked them up."

"And that beautiful Natalie's all right?"

"I think so. She wrote to her parents from somewhere near Wilmington, North Carolina. She and the young man were terribly burned by the sun, but they're safe. Does that cheer you a little bit?"

After a long silence Anne sat up straight in her chair. "Yes. I didn't know the Browning girl well, but it cheers me, darling Annie. Mainly, *you* have stiffened my spine!"

"I have?"

Drying her eyes on a linen napkin, Anne declared, "I'm through giving in to myself. Even though every loss is horrible, I lost no one near and dear to me. I'm truly ashamed."

"There's more good news," Annie said, trying to smile. "Instead of only seventeen people saved, there are now thirty. Does that help some?"

"Yes, yes." Anne stood up. "And I intend to change the atmosphere around here. Your poor, darling, tender father has had to walk on eggshells around me for a whole week. That's over. I'm going upstairs and bathe and put on something pretty to cheer *him* when he rides in this afternoon."

Now on her feet too, Annie threw both arms around her mother. "Oh Mama, you're back! And that makes me happier than even you could guess."

CHAPTER 58

THROUGHOUT THE SUMMER, EVEN THOUGH FRANCES Anne, Menzies, and James Hamilton had been the only passengers from Glynn County aboard the *Pulaski,* a heavy cloud hung over the very spirit of the people of St. Simons, neighboring Jekyll Island, and Brunswick. Almost everyone had known, or was related to, someone who had boarded the doomed packet in such a festive mood last June. Few seemed able to forget that it might easily have been anyone in the immediate area whose earthly remains still washed about in the depths of the treacherous sea off the North Carolina coast.

Even the weather was foreboding. Everyone complained of the unusually cold autumn. Through September and October the *Brunswick Advocate* seldom failed to mention it and in late November published the fact that ice an inch thick had been found on the decks and ropes of a schooner after only a short run from Charleston: "a phenomenon never before witnessed here."

After Frances Anne and Menzies returned to live temporarily

at the Wylly plantation, Anne regained her equilibrium by working more than usual among her flowers. Along with the sturdy,
well-rooted hydrangeas, hibiscus, geraniums, and *Camellia japonica,* she set out dozens of bulbs to bloom in the spring and made a
huge bed of red poppies, larkspur, Ladies in the Green, pinks, and
every variety of sweet william Papa could supply.

Annie and Pete worked along with her most days and did their
best to change the subject when Anne brought up either the *Pulaski* tragedy or the mounting trouble that seemed to worsen by the
day between the Wyllys and the Hazzards over their property line.

"I don't see why I can't discuss what's happening to the poor
Wyllys because of those Hazzard brothers and their determination
to take control of a mile-long, half-acre strip of Wylly land! What
if someone were trying to do that to Papa? To James Hamilton
right here at our home?"

"It's fine if you discuss it," Annie said. "Pete and I just don't
want you to—to get sick again, that's all."

"That's right, Mama," Pete said. "If you don't let it make you
all funny again with a headache like when the *Pulaski*—" The girl
broke off, glanced nervously at Annie, and Anne knew full well
that her eldest daughter and John had warned Pete against even
mentioning the ship's name.

"I want you both to listen to me. I know I lost control of myself
when that violent accident happened. I expect you're both ashamed
of me. I know I'm ashamed of myself, but mothers are human just
like everyone else and have to grow up too. The Wylly trouble not
only is making nervous wrecks out of Frances Anne and her sisters
and poor old Mrs. Wylly, but has utterly changed John Wylly. He
used to be such a carefree young man, as high-spirited as he is
handsome. Now it's as though he's turned almost overnight into an
old man burdened with trouble. They are all burdened with trouble and if I could do something about it, I would. I can't. The only
thing any of us can do is visit them as often as possible and pray.
But I insist that both of you and your father stop treating me as
though I'm one of these delicate plants we're setting out here in the
yard. And tell me every new thing you learn about the Wylly-
Hazzard trouble. I overheard you both whispering with your fa-

ther the other night, and I'd advise you never to let me catch you doing that again! Is that clear?"

Out of the corner of her eye as she looked up from the tulip bulb she was planting, Anne saw their exchanged glances. Neither girl said a word.

"The last time I had Big Boy ride with me up to the Wyllys', Mrs. Wylly herself told me that Dr. Thomas Hazzard had challenged young John Wylly to a duel. You both knew that, didn't you? Your father knew it too, and no one said a word to me about it. Why not?"

"We were telling you the truth, Mama," Pete said stubbornly, "when we said we didn't want you getting sick again. Some women, Papa says, just do that when trouble comes."

"Papa didn't say that critically, Mama," Annie said quickly. "He was just being his sweet, understanding self."

"And I have no intention of letting him know that you told me. He is the gentlest, dearest man on earth, and if anyone knows he only means to be taking care of me, *I* know it. But I've had a lot of time to think and to look honestly at myself during these last months, and I'm changing what I found when I looked. No one was more surprised than I when I—collapsed."

Anne was kneeling on the ground as she worked the soil, and Pete nearly upended her with a big hug from behind. "Oh Mama, thank you! Do you promise never to do it again?"

She got slowly to her feet, trowel in hand, and laid both arms on Pete's shoulders. "No darling, I won't promise not to be sad and upset and headachy again, because no one can promise that. But I do promise to *try* to keep my emotions in balance. The last thing I ever mean to do is upset my family. I also promise to do a much better job of giving thanks for the wonderful life God has given us. Remember what Theodore Bartow said in his sermon last Sunday?"

Annie nodded. "That strength comes from gratitude."

"Exactly. And I intend to prove that from now on."

"Then I think we can tell her, don't you, Pete?"

With a solemn expression on her usually pert face, Pete assumed her mature manner and said, "Yes, Annie. I agree that we should tell Mama what Papa told you and me last night."

"Would you like to be the one to tell her, Pete?" Annie asked, deferring to her younger sister as Anne had so often seen her do.

Pete stood to her full height—as tall as Anne herself now—and said, "Well, it seems that ol' Doc Hazzard has posted his challenge to a duel with John Wylly on trees all over the county so no one will doubt his intention to get his hands on that strip of Wylly land."

Anne stared at her. "What? Why, Dr. Thomas Hazzard is our justice of the peace on St. Simons! Dueling is against Georgia law!"

"That's maybe the worst part of all of it," Annie said. "It's so humiliating to honorable Islanders like Grandpapa Couper and Papa and the Goulds and the Demeres and Dr. Robert Grant, even though he doesn't always live at his Oatlands Plantation. Ben Cater's humiliated, too, Papa says, and Thomas Butler King. Everybody is downright ashamed."

"Did Dr. Hazzard post his dreadful notice on our Island?" Anne demanded.

"Yep," Pete said. "Nailed it to a big pine tree right where Couper Road turns into Frederica. And that's what we haven't told you, Mama."

"What else is there to tell?"

Again the girls looked at each other. Then Annie said, "Papa told us last night that—that someone cut down that same beautiful old pine tree and chopped it up into billets! They're in a big pile on the ground up there right now."

"Who on earth would do a thing like that?" Anne asked.

"The Island's divided all right," Pete said. "But not right down the middle by a long shot. Most everybody's on the Wylly side. So, it had to be some friend of the Wyllys'. But Papa says everybody that's been asked denies knowing a thing about it. On their honor, they all deny it."

Like a flash, Mary Gould popped into Anne's mind. By now, after Eve's prediction and after watching and listening carefully to every word Mary happened to say about John Wylly, Anne found it easy to believe that the reserved, kind, gentle young woman did love John. Still, she told herself, Mary Gould would never, never do a thing like that—would never order one of the Gould people to do it. Mary loves every tree on St. Simons Island as though it were a member of her own family.

"You're thinking awfully hard, Mama," Pete said.

"Yes, but I'm also about to set out the last tulip bulb and then we can get to the hyacinths." On her knees again, Anne smiled up at her daughters. "The important thing is that I thank you both from the bottom of my heart for this good talk we've had. And I want you to know I fully intend to tell your wonderful father the same things I've told you just as soon as he comes home this afternoon."

THERE WAS NO CHANCE TO BE ALONE WITH JOHN until the younger children had said their prayers and gone to bed, but she did tell him every single thing she could remember from her tulip-planting talk with Annie and Pete today. The more she talked, the wider his smile became, until when she'd said her final word about the heart-deep promise she'd made to Pete that she'd try her level best never to lose her self-control again, he was carrying her in his arms toward their bed, where he gave her the tenderest, longest kiss ever.

"We're going to be—just fine, beautiful Anne," he whispered. "Even when you and I stumble, our two older daughters will help pick us up. Mark my words."

"I do mark them, dearest. Every word you utter, I mark. And if I only knew what we'll do when and if Annie marries Paul Demere and leaves us, I'd go to sleep tonight knowing in my bones that I'm the happiest, most blessed woman in the entire country."

Plainly teasing, he asked, one eyebrow cocked, "Has Eve told you that Annie has plans to marry Paul?"

"No."

"Then I wouldn't worry. Even if Eve does see such a thing in our future, there's no need to worry now."

"But Paul Demere's so young! Annie's twenty-one, but he's just an eighteen-year-old boy. How does he know what he really wants?"

"I think he knows all right. He wants to be able to take care of a wife and family, and when Paul reaches twenty-one, he'll come into some money and enough Demere land at Harrington for a house and small farm. I think he's showing some maturity."

"How do you know all that, John?"

"Annie told me several months ago."

"Why would she tell you and not me?"

John's voice was at its gentlest when he asked, "Couldn't you guess if you really tried, my dearest? Our eldest daughter knows I've always rather liked young Paul."

"John, what kind of mother am I to be so selfish with Annie of all people?"

"You don't want her to move away from us, and that's perfectly natural."

"Is it?"

"Whether it is or not," he said, his impish smile playing on his face, "it's foolish to worry today, and if you really do mark every word I say, mark this, beautiful Anne. What on earth would you and I have done if your wise mother had thrown up a barricade against our marrying?"

Both arms circling his neck, she whispered, "Dearest, I don't know. I couldn't even—breathe without you!"

CHAPTER 59

ON DECEMBER 1 OF THAT YEAR, DESPITE THE abnormally cold day, John stopped at the Goulds' place at New St. Clair as he galloped his mare, Ginger, down Frederica Road after a short errand to Cannon's Point. Since the afternoon the young man visited him at Hamilton, he had seen Horace only at church. To-day, in the face of the Wylly-Hazzard trouble and the out-and-out business panic in the country, which had turned the United States economy upside down since last year, he wanted an easygoing talk with someone comfortable.

Horace, he suspected, wasn't much of a business man, but neither was John. Anyway, he felt free to speak openly and honestly with the boy, who also disliked the whole ugly idea of owning other human beings as deeply as John still disliked it. There was a genuine bond between them. Horace made no bones about his antipathy to slavery, and although John knew his father-in-law, Jock Couper, disapproved the "peculiar institution" too, Couper had, through the years, learned how to converse safely around the issue. Horace was still plainspoken.

When possible, John continued to avoid the subject with Anne. Negro slaves had been such an integral part of her entire life, except for their years spent in London, she still seemed almost puzzled by his unease even when he was careful not to use the word. Lately she had seemed in good spirits, except for her understandable concern over the radical change in Frances Anne's brother John Wylly because of his dispute with Thomas Hazzard, and he meant to help her stay that way.

Horace was running out to meet him when John reined Ginger to a stop in front of James Gould's Big House. The two men greeted each other warmly, commented about the unusually cold weather, as did everyone who stepped outside, and went quickly into the wood-paneled reception hall of New St. Clair, then into the parlor, where a roaring live oak fire blazed and snapped in the huge fireplace, its magnificent hand-carved wooden mantle gleaming in the flickering light.

"I hope this is nothing more than a friendly visit, John," young Horace said, ringing for Maum Larney to bring hot tea and a plate of her famous biscuits. "I was beginning to wonder if you'd ever remember your promise to drop by anytime you were up this way. I'm ever so glad to see you."

John took the inviting tapestry-covered chair Horace offered and stretched his long legs before the welcome heat from the fire. "To me it's lots more than just a friendly visit, Horace," he said. "Oh, nothing's wrong in particular. I'm indulging myself in the chance for some honest, unadorned conversation. The people on this Island are the soul of hospitality, but since I'm still a British subject, my ideas don't always jibe with theirs, and now that I know how many things you and I can agree on—well, here I am. And glad to be here. Is your father about? From what you told me, I could feel rather free with him too. I hope he's well these days."

"Except for his painful rheumatism, he is, thank you. But right after we ate, he went back upstairs to his room. My sister, Mary, is at the quarters seeing to a sick child. You and I are alone and free as the breeze." Horace smiled. "You don't need to worry about Maum Larney overhearing when she brings our tea, either. She's the soul of discretion and has been, for most of my life, like a mother to me."

"I know she's certainly respected by every Negro around," John said, then leaned forward to face Horace. "Tell me, have you had a chance lately to hold a decent conversation with young John Wylly? You two must have known each other all your lives."

"We have," Horace said, frowning. "But the way things are now, he's like a stranger. He even *looks* bitter! His face, always so dark and handsome, is these days just dark and angry. I'm glad to say he refuses to break the law by accepting Hazzard's challenge to a duel, but I live in downright fear, John, that something deplorable could happen between those two men. Of course you haven't a clue either about who might have chopped down that big pine tree with Hazzard's notice nailed to it."

"Not a clue, Horace. Someone who obviously meant to be showing support for Wylly, but that's a stupid way of doing it."

"It's odd that you came by today," Horace went on. "On the day after tomorrow, December 3, my father I are taking John Wylly over to Brunswick in our plantation boat. Papa, Thomas Butler King, here from his place at Monticello, Colonel Charles Henry duBignon, Dr. Thomas Hazzard, and John Wylly are to attend an all-important Canal Company meeting at the Oglethorpe House. I know Papa will do all he can to try to convince John to control himself when he comes face-to-face with Hazzard. John vows that something takes hold of him when the man's name is even mentioned. He knows how rage is changing him. Mary is terribly worried about our trip to Brunswick. I don't know what she thinks might happen, but last night she gave Papa quite a lecture about the fact that no matter how much money he and the other members of the Canal Company have subscribed to the new development project, nothing is worth the fury and hatred that could erupt in that meeting."

"Your quiet sister said that to your father?"

"She did. Mary's full of spunk. Don't let that inherited New England reserve fool you about her. Of course, in my mind, she's

one of the great women on earth. She's been more than my faithful, loyal sister through the years of my unsettled life; she's—my
friend."

"Is it true that many of the slaves sent to work on the canal
have revolted? And that the Irish work crew the Boston investors
sent down have taken to the whiskey bottle? Is Thomas Butler
King in as much financial trouble as Island gossip has it?"

"I'm afraid you're right on all counts. The national financial
panic has everyone in a box. King is a fine, skillful planter—so is
his wife, Anna Matilda, by now—but the man's ambition and
talents seem to shove him almost over his head into everything he
tries."

Maum Larney, an ample woman with one of the kindest faces
John had ever seen—white or brown—served their tea and a
linen-covered silver basket of flaky biscuits with her own elder-
berry jam, exchanged a few pleasantries, and left, but not before
she admonished Horace to ring again if he wanted *anything* else.

"That woman plainly worships the ground you walk on, Horace," John said, buttering a biscuit and dipping a spoon into the
jam pot.

"I had so turned against owning slaves when I was expelled
from Yale, I'm afraid I wasn't very nice to dear Maum Larney
when I first got home. Just the sight of her serving me, all but
bowing down to me, angered me so, I think I took my new revulsion at the horrible institution out on her. I regret it to this day."

"She's forgotten it," John said.

"I doubt that, but love forgives. Certainly the kind Larney has
always shown to all of us." Both men sipped their tea in silence for
a moment, then Horace asked, "What's the latest from up at
Hampton Plantation? Someone told Papa that Roswell King, Jr., is
still there. We thought the man was fidgety to let go of such heavy
responsibility. I agree managing Hampton plus Butler Island is too
much for one man, even one as capable as King."

"He is eager to leave Hampton," John said, "but he's still there
because James Gowen's affairs are such that he can't take over yet.
I suppose you know that the two young Philadelphia grandsons of
old Major Butler own it outright now since their aunt died."

"Papa told me." Horace laughed softly. "My father's all crippled up, but he knows most of what goes on in our vicinity. He even heard that one of the Butler boys plans a visit to both places sometime next year."

That piqued John's interest. "Which one, I wonder. My wife, through her distant cousin, Willy Maxwell, Lord Herries, is fascinated by Fanny Kemble, the fairly recent wife of one of the Butler heirs—named Pierce, I believe, for the old major. My wife and I saw Miss Kemble at age eight perform in London."

"Is that so? I've certainly heard of the famous Fanny Kemble Butler," Horace laughed. "Wouldn't it turn this Island upside down if she were to pay us a visit?"

"From what I know of her now, yes. Apparently Fanny Kemble Butler has always caused a stir because of her great acting talent, but she's causing another kind of stir for her husband these days. It seems she's published her *Journal,* in which she not only criticizes Americans but rather blisters the Southern system of slavery. I have to admit, I hope Pierce Butler does come and that his wife is with him. We could use a bit of excitement right now."

"On top of the Wylly-Hazzard trouble?" Horace asked. "You must be bored, John. I suppose I am more worried about John Wylly because I've known and liked him for so long, but for my money—which is actually nonexistent—I'd settle for some plain old peace right now."

TWO DAYS LATER, JUST AS A STARTLING DECEMBER sunset was turning the sky over the Frederica River into an enchanting flame, gold, and almost eerie green panorama of color, Anne heard footsteps hurrying along the upstairs hall and therefore wasn't at all surprised when Eve burst into her bedroom without knocking.

"Miss Anne! Miss Anne! It be turrible! Something turrible happen today in Brumsick. June, he just ride back from takin' dat basket of Mina's cookies an' pies up to Miss Frances Anne an' her folks at de Village. Oh Miss Anne, how'm I gonna git it out?"

"Get what out, Eve? For heaven's sake, calm down so you can put your words together. What happened? What did June learn at the Wyllys' when he went up there?"

"He be such a fine-lookin' young man, too. Such a kind gent'man. What his mama gonna do without him? Oh Miss Anne, what dat pore ol' white lady gonna do wifout Mausa John Wylly?"

Only an outburst such as Eve's could have forced Anne to turn her back on such beauty out over the river and the marshes, but Eve was upsetting her so much now, she not only turned to face her, she gave her a good shaking in the hope that Eve might simmer down enough to tell her what she was jabbering about. "I order you to tell me exactly what it is you're making such a fuss over! Was there an accident of some kind at the Wylly place? *What did June say?*"

"You kin order all you want," Eve said, "but I can't tell ya till I kin git my bref to do it. Dey warn't no accident at de Village, Miss Anne. De accident happen in Brumsick an' it warn't no accident neither! Doctah Hazzard done whip out a pistol an'—an' *kill* pore young Mausa John Wylly! Kill him dead. Mausa James Goul' an' his son, dey brung his body back in der plantation boat an' I speck po' Miss Frances Anne an' her sister, Mausa James Hamilton's purty lil wife, Miss Caroline, dey be washin' off de blood now an' layin' der brother out! Oh Miss Anne, Miss Anne! *Dey be a murder!*"

Anne released her grip on Eve's shoulders gradually and, before she sank into her little rocker, gave Eve a friendly pat on the arm. "I—I'm sorry I ordered you, Eve. Are you sure? Is June absolutely sure that John Wylly is dead?"

"June, he be right dere when the Goul' boat done dock in Village Crick an' June use his big, strong arms to hep lift dat deadweight—dat bloody deadweight outa de boat onto de dock an' into po' Miz Wylly's house!"

Still in her rocker, from somewhere deep down, Anne sensed that the flaming sunset was beginning to turn bronze now. But the eerie green was still there. And from somewhere else in her brain the name Mary Gould rose to the surface. "Eve? Was anyone else at the Wylly dock when the Goulds brought John's body home? Was—Miss Mary Gould there by any chance?"

"Lord hab mercy," Eve gasped. "She wasn't dere an' I done forgot 'bout pore Miss Mary! She neber had nuffin' ob him but her *hope.*"

"As usual, you sound as though you know everything."

"I knows what I knows. Miss Anne, how come I clean forget pore Miss Mary? She ain' purty like you, but she love Mausa John Wylly wif all her woman heart. She done love 'im fer years an' years!"

"I don't feel like ordering you," Anne said, her voice hoarse. "But I need you to make me a promise, Eve."

"Anything you axe, Miss Anne. Eve right chere. Eve always take care ob you long as she knows it be good for you. . . ."

"I want you to promise me you won't say one word about Mary Gould's *hoping* where John Wylly was concerned. Do you hear me?"

"I hears."

"Then will you promise to keep your mouth shut on the subject? It's going to be hard enough for poor Mary as it is, without the whole Island knowing."

"You be sorrier fer her dan fer Mausa John Wylly's sisters an' mama?"

"No! My heart's broken for Frances and her twin sister and Caroline and his brother and dear, odd Heriot and, of course, for Mrs. Wylly. It's just that other people will *know* why they're grieving, and no one will know but you and John and June and me— about Mary."

"You done tell Mausa John?"

"You told June, didn't you?"

"Yes'm."

"Well, that's your answer."

CHAPTER 60

W HEN THE D ECEMBER 6 EDITION OF THE WEEKLY
Brunswick Advocate reached the Island the day after John Wylly
was buried in Christ Churchyard, John, who had tried to piece
together the actual events from Horace Gould, read the news account aloud to Anne:

"MELANCHOLY OCCURRENCE
It is with pain we lay before our readers an account of a fatal
affray, which took place in this city on Monday last, between
Mr. John Wylly and Dr. Thomas F. Hazzard, both of this
county, which resulted in the death of the former. Most of our
readers are no doubt aware that a dispute has existed between
these two gentlemen for some time past. It appears, however,
that Dr. Hazzard had recently addressed a letter to the mother
of the deceased which was the immediate cause of the attack.
They met on the piazza of the Oglethorpe House and after
exchanging words, Mr. Wylly struck Dr. Hazzard with his

cane. Judge Charles S. Henry duBignon, happening to be present, immediately interfered and succeeded in separating them. A short time after, Mr. Wylly again met Dr. Hazzard in the entry of the Hotel and spat in his face, when the latter drew a pistol and fired, the ball of which passed directly through Mr. Wylly's heart. He reeled a moment, at the same time striking at Dr. Hazzard with his cane, then fell and expired instantly. Mr. Wylly was a young man, being in his thirty-third year, and has left an aged mother and numerous connections to mourn his sudden death. Dr. Hazzard was arrested on the spot, and the case immediately laid before the Grand Jury, who, after a patient investigation, returned a charge of voluntary manslaughter."

"Oh John," Anne said when he'd finished reading, "we were there at that sad, tragic funeral in our little church. We heard the sweet words of comfort Isabella's Theodore spoke. We saw all the Wyllys and poor Mary Gould. But somehow it's all still so unreal to me! I've never seen Papa look so downcast, have you?"

"No, darling, I haven't. Always before, when I needed courage, even a look at that wonderful face of John Couper's somehow fortified me. This has crushed him in a strange way. It's crushed the warm, community spirit of our whole Island. I've never seen prouder human beings than St. Simons families, but have you noticed that even the planters' *people* are stricken by what took place?"

"Yes, I know St. Simons Islanders are proud— I'm one of them —but this tears at the stability and trust we have always taken for granted. We've prided ourselves on the fact that Islanders are decent, law-abiding, peaceful citizens. How is everyone going to live with this?"

"In the long run, the blow to our reputation as peaceful, mostly well-meaning folk could be the worst part of it. Not forgetting for one minute the deep, deep sorrow up at the Village among John's family. The Island is truly going to be split now, Anne. I barely had time to exchange a few words with your father at the church, but he's racking his brain to think of something constructive to do for the Islanders to bring everyone together again." He sighed. "Nothing much can be done, I fear, at least until the shock wears off a bit."

"Could I ask you something?"

"Of course, my darling. Anything."

"Have I—have I behaved any better in this terrible tragedy?"

They had been sitting together on the parlor sofa. He reached for her hand. "You've been magnificent. I've wanted to mention it, but I hesitated to bring it up. You're my beautiful, strong Anne, but let's pray that nothing else happens and that eventually we'll all recover somehow from losing a fine young man like John Wylly."

JOCK AND REBECCA COUPER WENT ARM IN ARM down their front steps to inspect the buds on his *Camellia japonica* bushes after a light freeze the week before.

"I've wanted us to do this for days, Becca," he said, assisting her as best he could down the final step and along the path that led to his camellia grove. "I just haven't had the heart or the energy. Am I foolish to be so concerned about the anguish most Islanders feel, not only for the shame of John Wylly's murder but for the Wyllys themselves? What d'ye think, Becca? Is your husband getting old?"

"Neither of us is young anymore, Jock, but I have the same concern you have—for us all. And to think that the man entirely responsible for keeping the peace on St. Simons—our justice of the peace—is the murderer!"

"Aye, wife. That sticks in my craw above all else, I fear. Everyone knows the Hazzards are opinionated men, but both are educated, both gentlemen. Human nature is indeed a mystery. At times I feel it must almost be a mystery to God Himself."

"I don't think so."

"You don't?"

"No. God the Father certainly had a clear idea of the depths to which human nature—all of it, ours included—could sink, or He would never have sent His Son to die on that cross."

Still holding her arm, he gazed down at her. "After all these years, Rebecca, you continue to amaze me! But you're right. It would do our son-in-law, Theodore Bartow, good to take a few lessons in theology from you."

Just before they reached the camellia grove, they heard a man's voice call Jock's name. They turned to see their neighbor from across Jones Creek, Mr. Roswell King, Jr., clambering up the slight rise in the ground from their landing.

"I hope I'm not intruding," King called, walking toward them rather briskly. "Good afternoon, sir. Afternoon, Mrs. Couper."

"You're most welcome, King," Jock said politely. "Mrs. Couper and I were on our way to examine the buds on our *Camellia japonica* bushes after our short freeze. Is anything wrong? Or have you learned the good news that at long last James Gowen is free to take over your duties at Hampton?"

"What Mr. Couper means is that we're well aware that you're eager to be rid of so much work and responsibility, Mr. King," Becca explained and kept an eye on Jock to be sure he didn't smile in a way that might give away the depth of his own relief should King actually be leaving.

"Nothing more than usual is wrong," Roswell King said, "and no, I've heard no such word, Mr. Couper. But I did receive some rather startling news in a letter from Philadelphia—the letter you handed me at church last Sunday. A man under my pressures has little time for idle chat. This is the first chance I've had to come over to tell you."

As usual, with young King or his father, Jock responded with as few words as possible. "Oh?"

"One of the brothers, Mr. Pierce Butler, and his family will reach Butler Island sometime before the year is out!"

Jock's face registered almost nothing, but Rebecca gasped, "His family, too? Does that mean his—his famous wife, Fanny Kemble Butler?"

Showing little interest, Roswell King grunted, "I should imagine, unless he's up and married someone else lately. It's Pierce Butler himself I'm dreading to see again. The work I have up ahead of me all through Christmas is staggering. He's arrogant enough at best, but with *her* along, there'll be no pleasing the man. My poor wife's in a state of nerves. He told me when he came alone some time ago that there would be no place fit for his wife to live, even on a visit."

"I hate to see Northern visitors of their social standing find our Island citizens so divided, so humiliated, over the recent tragedy in the Wylly family," Jock said, shaking his head.

"Well, Mr. Couper, there isn't a thing you and I can do about Doc Hazzard's hot temper."

"Mr. King's right," Rebecca said comfortingly. "We'll just take each day as it comes, Jock, and trust God with the outcome. Even with such famous visitors coming. Can't you do that?"

"Of course I can do it, Becca! It's my sorrow for all Islanders that eats at me. Maybe more than that, it's finding a way to keep my own spirits up. I grieve for the Wyllys—John was a fine, intelligent lad—but equally, I grieve for the shame we all feel. I'm going to *have* to do something to help heal this wound we all suffer so deeply."

WHAT JOHN COUPER DID, IN HIS EFFORT TO LET IT be known that the majority of St. Simons Islanders were indeed mortified at the dastardly act that had taken place in public view on the steps of Brunswick's Oglethorpe House, was to call a meeting of the most respected Island planters—James and Horace Gould, Ben Cater, Thomas Butler King, Dr. Robert Grant, the Demeres, his son James Hamilton, and John Fraser. Everyone who was invited came, except Thomas Butler King, and as John told Anne before he left for the meeting, "Thomas sent word that he was tied up at Monticello but would go along with whatever we decided."

The meeting was held at New St. Clair in the Gould house,

two days before Christmas, and those attending decided to run a paid announcement as soon as possible explaining their reactions to the gross crime that had taken place in their midst.

Some days later, before John read the piece aloud to Anne, he explained that the planters would share the cost of running it as a paid announcement because the *Advocate* was careful *not* to take sides publicly with either the Wyllys or the Hazzards.

"The undersigned landholders and inhabitants of St. Simons Island, comparing the present state of their society with what it has been, feel deeply mortified at its present degradation.

"They have to lament that their former character for respectability has been impaired and that their happiness has suffered a shock of a most fatal nature. The recent evil has become so intolerable that a proper respect for themselves and for public opinion requires that they should, by a public declaration, show their disapprobation of the act that has led to such a degraded state of society. The late-lamented encounter that took place at Brunswick between Mr. John A. Wylly and Dr. Thomas F. Hazzard being now under judicial investigation, the decorous respect due to the laws of the country prevents the undersigned, *at present,* any declaration of opinion with respect to it.

"They cannot, however, repress the expression of their grief that by that act, one of their most respected citizens has been consigned to an untimely fate and a blighting misery inflicted on a most worthy family. They also cannot too pointedly advert to the fact that had the only justice of the peace on this Island discharged his duty, such a misfortune would not have happened. They therefore recommend that he be prosecuted for malpractice in office and neglect of duty, unless he previously resigns his commission.

"We do hereby nominate and appoint John Couper, Robert Grant, and James Gould a standing committee, to watch over and attend to the interests of our Island, with power to call a meeting of the inhabitants whenever they may deem it necessary. And we pledge ourselves to support them in all the legal prosecutions herein recommended."

When John had finished reading, Anne murmured, "John, what can we do to help Papa? He's the one who called that meeting because his good, loving heart is so shattered. I hope it helped him some that so many of his friends are of the same mind. He's very fond of Mr. James Gould and of all the others. You were there. Did it seem to lift Papa's spirits a little?"

"I think so, yes. And especially since last week the grand jury itself, in session when the murder happened, issued a presentment deploring the unfortunate occurrence and joining in condolences for the Wyllys—for all of us, in fact. The grand jury's presentment even included John Wylly's grieving friends left behind."

"Oh dear, I know poor Anna Matilda King would give almost anything to be living here now. She and her parents were always so close to all the Wyllys. She'd want so much to share in our grief. If that Canal Company Thomas heads would either get the work finished or collapse, maybe her husband would find enough money for them to move back to her blessed home at Retreat! She feels she could live here again now."

"With the financial state of the entire country as it is, and his Northern canal investors losing interest," John said on a deep sigh, "your wish may come true. Frankly, I'd be the least surprised person to see Thomas Butler King's big development plan collapse totally—and soon."

"How soon?"

"This year 1838 is almost over. My guess is that you'll have Anna Matilda living right here again by the end of next year."

CHAPTER 61

FOUR DAYS INTO THE NEW YEAR, 1839, EVE HAD heard the news on her grapevine and hurried out to Anne's flower garden, where her mistress was supervising June's January planting of ornamental fruit trees and hydrangea plants.

"Miss Anne! Miss Anne!" Eve shouted, her long, striped skirt flying as she ran across the lawn toward where Anne stood, watching June dig a deep hole in the root-choked, sandy loam. "June, he kin dig wifout you peerin' ober his shoulder. Eve got big news— bigger news dan any ol' Brumsick newspaper!"

Glad Miss Anne's mother was nowhere nearby to keep her from grabbing Miss Anne by the arm and pulling her off to one side of the lawn out of June's hearing, Eve waited before she spoke, determined to have the full attention of her mistress.

"All right, Eve, you've interrupted my morning's work. What has you so excited and short of breath?"

"I tell you what. Dat stage woman, *she be ober on Butler Islan' dis minute!*"

Her mistress stared at her. "What in the name of common sense are you talking about? Or does it have anything whatever to do with common sense? And why couldn't you tell me in front of June?"

"Because June call it gossip an' I ain' no gossiper."

"Well go on. Tell me! *Who* is on Butler Island? And how do you know anyway?"

"I done heard it on the grapevine from Big Boy an' he jus' ride back from Cannon's Point an' you knows Jones Creek don' keep news from travelin' acrost it from Hampton. All I knows is dat Big Boy done cross over de creek an' dey tell him Mausa Butler an' his family be at de ol' tumbledown overseer's house at Butler Islan'. Dat stage lady!"

"Miss Fanny Kemble Butler is down here?" Anne gasped. "Well, are they coming over to spend any time at Hampton?"

"How's Eve gonna know dat?"

"I thought you knew everything."

"I'd be shamed if I'se you, Miss Anne!"

"Why?"

"Eve thought you'd laugh an' be all excited wif de big news!"

"I *am* excited! Can't you tell?"

"No'm."

Eve turned her back and began to count in a half-whisper: "One, two, three, four, five, six, seven, eight, nine, ten—"

"Stop showing off! I know you've learned to count to a hundred, but why are you choosing this moment to do it?"

Facing Anne again, Eve said with her spontaneous smile, "To see how long it take you to grin an' act like you excited."

Smiling now, Anne said, "Before you begin to count again, how's this? Am I smiling enough to suit you?"

"Yes'm, an' it be a purty smile. You tell me you seen Miss Fanny Kembles when she only eight year old, back when you an' Mausa John still lib 'cross de water. You tell me yo'self Mistah Willy, he know her an' ride horses wif her when he done come to dis country."

"That brain of yours doesn't forget anything, does it?"

"Nuffin'."

"The word is *nothing* and listen to me, Eve. I'm not daring to hope that the great Miss Fanny Kemble might even make the trip from Butler Island to visit at Hampton, but should she come, I want you to speak well! You can pronounce words perfectly, *if* you'd only do it. And don't ask me where it's written down that you have to! You have to because I want you to. Miss Fanny Kemble has a lot of funny ideas anyway about the way we all live down here in the South, and I want to prove to her that *my*—that you, at least, are not only fine-appearing, neat and clean and smart, but that you know how to speak the English language. Is that clear?"

Eve grinned. "Petey, she say it be clear as mud. But yes'm, it be clear."

"It *is* clear."

"All right, if it make you feel better, it *is* clear. You know Eve knows how to talk! I just don't want to stick out like a sore thumb with my people." She giggled. "June, he done think I got high-hat effen I goes 'roun sayin' *is* when I oughta say *be*."

"I know, I know. But as quick as your ears and brain are, there's no excuse for you not to speak well should Fanny Kemble Butler just happen to visit us over here on St. Simons. And I don't want to hear one of those noncommittal yes'ms, either."

The grin Eve gave her now was downright devilish. "You want me to act out my white blood, Miss Anne?"

"I want us to change the subject, and I'll be proud of you no matter what you say or how you say it. I know you'll try. I also know it's easy to forget. Sloppy speech is such a habit with you. Right now I want you to tell me everything you heard from Big Boy about the Butlers. When did they reach Mr. Pierce Butler's rice plantation over on Butler's Island?"

"On New Year's Eve. I guess Miss Fanny she don't let nobody forget how bad she feel about beginnin' a new year in such a ramshackle house as she got to live in at Butler's Islan'."

"Oh dear, I wonder if it's as cramped and plain and run-down as old Roswell King used to claim it was."

As usual, when Anne or anyone else happened to mention the father of the man who was still managing Hampton, Eve froze. No one had ever been able to shake Eve's belief that Roswell King, Sr., was her natural father, although she knew that many doubted it.

"All right, I'm sorry I forgot and mentioned his name," Anne said. "Sometimes, though, I think you're almost proud you're half-white."

"You got to know it all, Miss Anne."

"No, I don't have to know it all. I said I'm sorry, didn't I? I forgot, just as you'll probably forget and say ober and Brumsick should Miss Fanny Butler really come to St. Simons."

"You invite her?"

"Of course, if I have the chance! Eve, Eve, it would be such an honor to have a famous lady like Fanny Kemble Butler in our house."

"De nigger dat tol' Big Boy 'bout her say she be a nice white lady, very rosy, clo'es got on so rich, so silky, so shinin'. Rich hat—oh so rich!"

"That doesn't sound much as though you're watching your speech," Anne said.

"I ain't. I tellin' you what the Butler nigger done tol' Big Boy." They walked slowly back to where June was working. "Sometimes you talk before you think, Miss Anne."

"I know I do. And here I am for the second time about to tell a servant that I'm sorry." She laughed. "Poor, dear Mama wouldn't like that, would she?"

Eve grinned knowingly. "No'm, she sho wouldn't like dat."

CHAPTER 62

THE WINTER SUN WAS JUST COMING UP ACROSS THE
Butler Island marshes and one arm of the Altamaha River when
Fanny Kemble awakened. Thick, rough-hewn wooden shutters
covered the windows of their bedroom. Pierce was still sleeping,
his even-featured face handsome, the normal arrogance absent in
sleep. He turned his head away from the light only when she
rushed from the bed to open a shutter, the better to see what
manner of magic the sunrise was making.

"Saffron," she whispered to herself, not daring to speak the
word aloud, since nothing so quieted her soul as to behold beauty
alone. "The sky is almost pure saffron! Those streaks of blush and
scarlet only seem to heighten and point up the nearly pure yellow."
Odd, she thought—not yet ready to rouse him to talk—to see that
shade of saffron yellow in the sky. If only I could find an hour's
privacy once the weird chaos of this plantation begins for the day, I
know I'd be able to capture the beauty in words.

She turned to look at her sleeping husband. He appeared

smaller of stature in bed, under covers, than standing. Even then he was but a few inches taller than Fanny. But beautiful to look upon, she thought. Dear God in heaven, the man is beautiful to see! And his oddly tender lovemaking last night was still as real and immediate today as when she had finally fallen asleep, oblivious of where they were, of the primitive, half-savage place called a coastal Georgia rice plantation. The vast rice holdings failed to impress her because they had made her, as the master's wife, rich from the brutal labor of slaves who couldn't claim ownership of anything on earth beyond the air they breathed.

She looked around the bedroom—plain, whitewashed wooden walls; floor of such old boards, one had to walk carefully or stumble, and no one in her right mind would dare try traversing it barefoot for fear of splinters. The two narrow windows opened onto distant beauty, but because it was slave country, to her it was beauty only because of distance. So far she had found Butler Island drab. Except for the sky today, which *was* breathtakingly lovely— the odd saffron color fading now almost to green-blue—it was a plain place. Sandy, gray land that had never known the protection of snow, she supposed. A rag rug, woven long ago, frayed now and showing only hints of having once been any color, covered the bare floor from the bed to the door leading directly into a cubicle entrance way. She, the two children, their nurse, Marjorie, and Pierce shared this one so-called overseer's house with the new Butler Island overseer, Thomas Oden, recently sent from Cannon's Point, the plantation separated by a creek from Pierce's Sea Island plantation called Hampton.

"With your imagined pity for all slaves," Pierce had said yesterday, "you should like Thomas Oden. He's been trained by one of the most easygoing masters in the area, a Scotsman—rather old now, I believe—named John Couper. I need to have a straight talk with Oden as soon as possible. He will operate Butler Island according to *my* regimen or find another plantation to run."

"And what is your regimen, dear Pierce?" she had asked, feigning innocence. "Surely anyone as tender as you know how to be would never abide lashings or brutish overwork."

"You've been here for three days, Fanny," he had said, making full use of his melting smile. "Suppose you give me your impression of how my people are treated. I know you've been nosing around in their cabins, listening to their talk. I'd like to know what you think, my dear."

"At first," she'd told him, "I thought them sufficiently fed. They may be. Most look reasonably strong. Rather adequately clothed."

He had tossed his almost too handsome head and assured her that not only was that all true, but his people were not sold to other owners, families were never separated, no one was ever hired out to other masters. Only an occasional punishment when required.

Looking at Pierce now, this morning, just beginning to rouse from sleep, she felt certain that unlike other slave owners about whom she'd heard from Northern friends such as the Reverend William Ellery Channing and some of his abolitionist friends, Pierce would not allow them to be barbarously beaten. She fully intended to find out.

Pierce opened one eye, cocking his eyebrow, then he opened the other and immediately he was awake, the mouth, so innocent in sleep, turned almost sulky as he looked across the room at her. "Good morning, gorgeous Fanny Butler," he said playfully. "I missed you, and the pain of the loneliness wakened me. Now aren't you ashamed to have slipped away?"

Crossing the room to sit beside him on the bed, she said, "The sunrise drew me; it was too beautiful. There wasn't time to be ashamed. I would like to be kissed, though, if you're of a notion to kiss me, sir."

His mouth did look sulky most of the time, but the feel of it on hers stirred total ecstasy. There was no explaining it, especially since a kiss from anyone before the mouth had at least been rinsed had never appealed to her. With Pierce, kissing was always distractingly welcome. She welcomed it now, and he went on kissing her until she trembled in his arms and did her best to make a joke of it.

"Sir, are you trying to make me scream for mercy? If you are, pretend I've done it and go for your bath. You told me last night that today you must make a water trip to the metropolis of Darien, Georgia, for supplies."

All she wanted was to fall further into his arms, but she forced herself to jump to her feet and begin tugging at the other ugly, rough shutter. Then, with all her might, she jerked at the poorly glazed window.

"Fanny! It's January. January can be cold even in Georgia, or have you been too busy searching out cruelties to my slaves to notice?"

"I have not visited one cabin, I swear to you! There hasn't been time. Do you realize that I failed to finish even a brief letter yesterday while you and Mr. Oden were doing whatever you did in your rice paddies, because your slaves trooped all day long into this dilapidated shack we're forced to share with your overseer?"

Out of bed now, pulling on his elegant, heavy, silk brocade robe, Pierce asked absently, "Trooped into *this* house? Why on earth were they doing that?"

"I suggest that you tell me. I'm not accustomed to the ways of black slaves. But they came, the poor things, and formed circles around me as I tried to write. They came six to eight at a time, got down on their haunches, and peered at me. Sometimes they giggled, sometimes they nudged each other and pointed or just sat hunched there watching me as though I were some variety of freak."

"And did they talk to you?"

She threw back her long, dark hair and laughed her best theatrical laugh—a crisp, short one. "Wouldn't you like to know, Mausa?"

"I not only would like to know, I demand to know."

"And why is that, sweet husband? Are you afraid they'll tell me something with which I can confront you?" She dropped the drama. "Pierce darling, I shouldn't be flippant with you over such a ghastly thing as owning slaves. I don't mean to be. I'm just so— so horrified at being here. Can you—can you, for my sake, because of the way you truly loved me last night—at least try to understand me in all this?"

"And why should I when you make no effort to understand my position in it? I've never heard you complain about the spacious elegance of Butler Place, our home in Philadelphia. How do you think I come by my wealth, Fanny? How do you think you are enabled to be gowned in silks and satins so lavish they turn men's heads? Do you think our riches fall from the sky? Even your breathtaking sunrise sky, which you preferred to lying close to me in our bed this very day?"

Through gritted teeth Fanny said, "It is the blight on my life that *you* own these poor wretches, that you are the man and not I! That I, because I love and adore you, must receive from your graceful hands the very clothes on my back. I am *sick* that I own even one costly ballgown bought by the blood and sweat of these benighted people whom you own as though they were valuable breeding cattle!"

"How can even an actress of your high caliber pretend to love me when you despise the very source of the luxuries I heap on you?"

"I don't pretend. I love you, Pierce Butler, with a mostly unreasonable love. I love—simply because I can't help loving you." She went to him, slipped both arms around his neck, and pulled his mouth to hers. "I'm addicted to you, quite evidently. And when I return your love, I am not acting—I am not, I am not, I am not! Any woman in her right mind, if she could kiss you—like this— would love you, Pierce."

Again, standing there in the bedroom of the wretched house, locked in passion, they held each other.

"Now to your bath, sir. I'm not quite sure how you'll be able to do it, but you must leave me behind today." She kissed him.

"Fanny," he breathed, "is this a new game? Must you kiss me like that and everlastingly bring up my infernal bath?"

Outside, at the boat landing, but a stone's throw from the overseer's house where they were staying, Fanny could hear men's voices—some singing as though to themselves, others shouting either commands or oaths. Plainly, they were readying the plantation boat in which eight of them would row Pierce and his overseer,

Thomas Oden, to Darien for the day. Monotonous, squeaky clatter reached her from the rice mill, almost adjacent to the landing. Yet over the sounds of the laboring plantation hung an almost mystical silence, the silence that had struck her from the first moment the ogling, pointing, bowing, foolish-acting Negroes had welcomed them when they first landed on New Year's Eve. Even today she could feel the silence, and then it was splintered, shattered as though someone had taken evil aim at her ears.

Three sharp whistles—not a man whistling but a leather thong cutting the air—were followed by scream after scream. A woman's scream. There was no mistaking that.

"Pierce!" Fanny gasped. "Pierce, that's a woman screaming!"

Pierce stood rooted in the middle of the floor. He made no effort at first to stop her when she pulled the sash of her dressing gown around her and ran to open the closed bedroom door.

"Fanny! Fanny, I order you to come back in this room!"

His voice, sharp and angry, stopped her as though he'd jerked a rope tied around her waist.

Her hand still on the doorknob, she cried, "But Pierce! Someone's being terribly hurt! We must go out there at once and find out what—"

"No! I'm your husband and I command you to stay inside this room."

"You—*command* me?"

"I command you!"

Slowly her fingers released the knob and she went numbly past where he stood, all the way to the window and looked out. A woman, somewhere in middle age, she supposed, was hanging, fastened by her wrists to a tree branch so that her feet barely touched the ground. The poor wretch, therefore, had no means of evading the lash, wielded before Fanny's horrified eyes by Thomas Oden himself. The woman's clothes were thrown up over her head and her back was being scored with a leather thong.

When the whistling lashes and the screams finally stopped, Fanny turned slowly to face Pierce. For a long moment she stood there looking at him, marveling that he seemed unable to say a word. His head was down. He was not returning her look.

Finally Fanny heard her own voice—flat, unfamiliar to her in all ways—declaring firmly, "Here I stand, an Englishwoman, the wife of the man who owns these wretches, and I *cannot say that thing shall not be done again. . . .*"

CHAPTER 63

DAY IN AND DAY OUT, UNABLE TO RIDE A HORSE ON Butler Island because of the swampy conditions and Pierce's dismay that she would even suggest trying, Fanny wandered on foot in the daily more pleasing company of "her slave," named Jack. Pierce, his smile showing that he felt magnanimous in the offering, "gave" Fanny the sole services and protection of young Jack, son of a former head driver. Jack's slender, graceful body and dreamy-eyed face told her that except to escort her hither and yon, he was good at little else except to ask repeated questions. When she wasn't roaming tide-soaked, unadorned Butler Island, she read by the hour or composed letters to her abolitionist friends at the North.

"Jack," she wrote to Dr. William Ellery Channing, "is a study in flattery, humor, mental agility, exaggeration, spirituality, and probably rank deceit. But what slave isn't deceitful? What slave would not find it advantageous to fawn and flatter his or her Mausa and Missus? Jack, I might add, is more curious than any three-year-old child! Yesterday he even asked if it rained in London."

One day in early February when the two were fishing from their own special skiff for catfish, which Fanny called "evil, slimy, dangerously spiked beasts," Jack, his sensitive face showing that another question was forthcoming, further piqued her interest.

"Catfish be good 'nuff for niggers, Missus," he said, his half-smile saying far more, Fanny was sure. "Ain't dat de way it be? Don' you 'spect catfish be good 'nuff for niggers but not for white folks, Missus?"

For a few days Fanny was unsure exactly how far she could trust Jack's wry humor, but soon she was convinced that, although only once had she blurted an ill-advised question, the young man *knew* what she truly thought of slavery. Even after little more than a month spent at Pierce's Butler Island rice plantation, she sensed that her question had been a total mistake. "Jack," she had asked out of the blue, "would you like to be free?"

That night, while Pierce was busy on work plans with his overseer, Oden, Fanny wrote to another friend: "Instantly, as I posed that question, a gleam absolutely shot over Jack's countenance—vivid as light. Then he stammered, hesitated, became excessively confused, and at length replied, 'Free, Missus? What for me wish to be free?' "

The fear of offending, of worsening his lot, had caused Jack to lie outright. His desire to conciliate her favor at all cost wounded Fanny more deeply than anything else since their arrival on the Georgia coast, except the revolting sight of that whipping. She could see at once that Jack's pitiful situation was no mystery to the fellow. Jack's value to Pierce and to her was plainly well known to him. He knew, as did every other laborer on Butler Island, that wealthy Pierce Butler would be in financial ruin without them.

He is afraid of offending me, she thought, and was sickened by the idea. We can fish together, I can try to answer his endless questions about the North and London and my life on the stage, but there will always be that barrier of his pretense to convince me of his happiness and welcome acceptance of total bondage to us. Jack will do his utmost to protect me from poisonous snakes, he will teach me to fish these tidal waters and to row, he will protect me with his own life, but he will not be truthful with me on such a subject as his longing to be free. He dares not even try.

In her room alone, pen in hand, tears blurred her writing.

When it was time for Pierce to rejoin her, she composed herself by deliberately turning her thoughts to the rowing lesson Jack had given her that day. In a rush of words she told Pierce of the lesson, thanked him profusely for having given her, as her special means of getting about, the "darling" little skiff, which carried two oars and a steersman and was appropriately named the *Dolphin*. She described the eerie fascination the primal aura of the rice island held for her; the nearly repugnant way in which she felt drawn to the noble river called the Altamaha, full of shoals, banks, mud, and sand bars—a fusion of both earth and water. He might not actually be listening, and there were times when she felt his physical beauty and charm masked an almost shallow mind, but because she loved him with a kind of glad madness, she told him of her day with Jack and that she had actually rowed the *Dolphin* upward of half a mile. She slipped in the news that still another woman, scarcely past childbirth, had been beaten, but before he could find an opening to defend the brutality, she used her way with words to tell him of her delight in the wild creatures that inhabited these primeval, half-formed regions—amphibious creatures, alligators, serpents, and great-winged fowl soaring above what to her was the hasty pudding of land and water.

"Pierce, my love," she said with a look meant to turn his heart toward her undeniable appeal for him, "if no human chisel ever yet cut breath, then neither did any human pen ever write the kind of light flowing over your rice island! The sight of Butler Island light, even without trees to ease it into shadow, is one of your loveliest gifts to me. You have spread before me the glories of the southern heavens and to you, my love, I say thank you. Italy and Claude Lorrain may go hang themselves!"

And then she waited for his laugh, for him to pull her toward him with those perfect-nailed, clean, sensitive hands of a man who could bring music from a silver flute as heavenly as the light.

Before he reached for her, he laughed. She had struck a chord in his underutilized humor by her ridiculous mention of Italy and Claude Lorrain. To Fanny, his laughter was a rare gift. With her father now back in England, she missed laughter. Pierce had never found a way to abandon himself to the human comedy. For a moment he did, and then he reached for her. Fury might tear at her heart, but his touch transcended the fury. She knew her rage sprang from learning that the life of ease in which they both reveled was theirs because of the blood and sweat and weeping of his slaves, and even when he held her, the fury did not vanish. For the golden oblivion of the wonder that inevitably followed Pierce's touch, Fanny's anger was simply crowded more deeply into her heart.

From that touch and the persistence of his wooing, Fanny's life had been turned upside down—turned upside down and inside out by guilt at having married a slaveholder but made wondrous by his love, which had blessed her with two adorable little girls of her own.

Lying in his arms that night, she prayed earnestly that this time they would merely sleep as any two lovers slept after such perfect moments—uncounted, unaccountable in their ecstasy.

Pierce did not sleep. Her pointed remarks, hidden, she now still hoped, within the blaze of enthusiasm she tried to show him for the wild beauties she'd seen that day on the river, had not been hidden from him at all. His need of her satisfied, he pulled away and said, "Before you sleep, Fanny, I must tell you that Harriet was whipped for out-and-out insolence. It has been three weeks since her child was born. She's perfectly well enough to work in the fields. She complained to Oden when he ordered her to join the crew, then threatened to go back in the hospital minutes after she picked up a rice basket and began to work."

"And did she have to lie again on those ghastly hospital mats, Pierce? Was she still too ill to work?"

"I only know she was insolent. She refused an order and that's not allowed."

"Who knows better how she feels? Harriet or Mr. Oden?"

"I'm your husband, Fanny." His voice took on a hard edge. "You seemed just now to be—my wife in all ways. I demand that you stop chastising me for the nature of my business. Do you hear me? I demand it. I forbid you to listen one more time to the lying complaints of these lazy Negro women!"

For an instant Fanny froze. Then, deliberately making use of her most effective stage technique, she said in an almost softly rounded voice, "It so happens, my husband, that I learned of the most recent mistreatment of this woman through one of your highly skilled and trusted men—Harriet's husband, Ned, your engineer at the rice mill, with whom I spoke as Jack and I returned from our outing on the river. Ned freely admits that because he was trained under a kindly master, his life is fairly easy. Not so his beloved wife. She is, as Ned phrased it, 'almost broke in two wif labor.' Do you suspect your reliable mill engineer, Ned, of lying complaints? Does it ever occur to you that he loves his wife as you claim to love me? That his heart aches for her wretched condition as yours, I should hope, would ache for me?"

She glimpsed his tortured, beautiful face in the candlelight, and her heart twisted with pain for him. No more words between us tonight, she vowed, reaching to touch his shoulder. "Sleep, beloved, enslaved Pierce, sleep. Surely you who own slaves are more enslaved than the pathetic wretches you claim to own."

CHAPTER 64

JOHN COUPER WELCOMED HIS OLD FRIEND JAMES Gould on a cloudy, misty February morning and even braved the chill to cross the Cannon's Point veranda himself to greet the tall, gaunt man he'd come to trust as he trusted himself.

"I see July brought you up to visit me in your fine, new Boston-made carriage, James," Couper said as the men exchanged a warm handshake. "My Johnson will bring us something hot to drink, and one of my men from the stable will look after July and your team. Come in, come in. You're an answer to prayer, mon."

Reserved as usual, Gould had only smiled at his friend until they were seated across from each other in the Couper parlor, where a hot green oak blaze crackled in the huge fireplace. "It's been a while, Jock, since I've been the answer to anyone's prayer, but if I am, I'm glad. Something wrong?"

"No, only my aching, aging muscles and my heavy heart that such a cloud still hangs over our beloved St. Simons. It is as though we've lost not only young John Wylly but his accused killer as well.

"I doubt we'll really lose Dr. Hazzard from our midst. He's been charged only by the grand jury, remember. His trial in superior court is still coming up, and the way things look now, a mistrial could well be called and he'll get off scot-free."

"But surely by the time court convenes again in the spring, a jury trial will bring justice."

"*If* they can find a jury that can vote together on it," Gould said. "I look for an acquittal, because there's too much divided opinion for a unanimous verdict."

Couper sighed. "I make no bones about where my own sympathies lie. Nor do you, James. Our Island is split, but most like us are firmly on the side of our longtime neighbors the Wyllys. Still, I'm grieved because our vicinity needs the educated, good minds of the Hazzard brothers. And they shuffle in and out of church on Sundays as though they too were mere ghosts—speaking to no one, no one speaking to them. Even the Hazzard Negroes are shunned by those who, no matter their owners, call themselves Wylly people. Aye, my old heart is heavy for many reasons and filled with guilt that we didn't prevent it. Especially since the Almighty has been—is being—so kind to this old ram of His."

"Do you think it would help any if our standing committee— you, Dr. Grant, and I—held a meeting just to see if together we could find a way somehow to bring the ugly affair to a more harmonious conclusion?"

"Perhaps. Perhaps not. Two appointed members are now present in the two of us. Dr. Grant is a thoughtful gentleman, but do you think such a meeting would really help? I wonder. Another burden on my heart is the possible arrival of the new, young owner of Hampton across Jones Creek. My daughter Anne tells me that her Eve keeps hearing on her grapevine that Mr. Pierce Butler and his famous, opinionated, antislavery wife, Fanny Kemble Butler, and their two small children are indeed planning to spend some time here at his St. Simons place. Have you heard that?"

"Not I, but my son Horace expects it. In fact, he's quite excited that he might find a chance to speak with Mrs. Butler. The boy comes by his dislike of slavery honestly. I've told you many times of my own boyhood training under one of the best teachers and most truly Christian ministers I ever knew, the Reverend Lemuel Haynes, a Negro up in New England. It seems Mrs. Butler is an out-and-out abolitionist, like the Reverend Haynes."

"So I've heard," Couper said. "So I've read in the papers. It's been many years since you and I have broached the prickly subject, James."

"It has. I find life far more peaceful avoiding it. In my youth I marveled that you'd learned the trick of staying off the detested topic, Jock. You told me back then that I'd learn how it's done. I'm ashamed to say I have learned."

"Aye. I'm ashamed to have learned, too, James. By now even Thomas Spalding of Sapelo and I never touch on it."

"My boy Horace, since he's been at Yale, seems determined to free his boyhood playmate July."

"Aye. Horace told me himself."

"He can be outspoken like his father," James Gould mused.

"I may just find my outlook a bit more hopeful once Mr. Gowen is in charge at Hampton across Jones Creek," Couper said after a silence. " 'Tis said he'll be replacing Roswell Jr. any day now. The radical Fanny Butler won't find a more skillful, enterprising manager than King and his old father have been for the old major and for the young Butler heirs, but she may find the Gowens a bit easier to know." He chuckled. "You can see, I'm sure, James, that I'm grabbing on to any hint of tranquillity I can find, so filled with longing am I to return to the old amenable, cordial climate on our Island. Except for my son-in-law John Fraser and his family, my son at Hopeton, and, of course, beloved Rebecca, you are my point of comfort these days, and alas, we see each other too seldom. Who knows? Maybe a visit from the young Butlers might brighten things up a bit. I'm sure Anne and John will find them much to their liking. I've always believed John Fraser continues to miss the far more sophisticated society of his British past. My Anne as well." He took a deep breath and exhaled noisily. "Well now, Johnson will be bringing refreshment any minute and I'm an old goat to complain over anything. Have you any idea how grateful I am that my superior son James Hamilton found a way not only to save others but to live through the tragedy of the *Pulaski* explosion himself?"

For a long time James Gould sat watching the fire. Then, on a weary sigh he said, "Yes, I have an idea, Jock. There are days when I wonder if either my son Jim or Horace will be a productive man. You have reason to be proud."

" 'Tis said, James, that 'time flies over us but leaves its shadow behind.' "

"I love Jim, but he's not a happy man," Gould murmured, almost as to himself. "Horace means well and so far has left few shadows. You haven't mentioned your younger son, William Audley, since his brief visit last year, Jock. What do you hear from the boy? He has certainly grown into a fine-looking young man. Is he still doing well at Franklin College up in Athens, Georgia?"

Jock brightened. "I'm proud to say he is indeed! Just last week one of his professors took the trouble to let me know that the lad has evolved into a rather good scholar. I found it harder to believe than his mother did, but mothers can be like that." He chuckled. "Becca has always believed William Audley would mature into a dependable man. Has never stopped reminding me that I've always claimed I was such a rapscallion at sixteen, my own father sent me to America for the good of my native Scotland! My younger son is a man now at twenty-one and should be graduated and home to stay by early summer. To this day Rebecca, of course, invariably exaggerates my worth, but no one could exaggerate my troublesome conduct as a boy back in Scotland. William Audley does vow that he looks forward to taking over some here for me."

"You're blessed, Jock, by your children—all of them."

"Aye," he agreed, looking toward the parlor door. "And blessed by the paragon among all my people, this man who comes smiling toward us now with rich coffee and spicy buns as only Sans Foix can bake them and as only Johnson can serve them!"

After a brief, cheerful exchange, Johnson departed, and as though advanced age made them relish kind words and delicious food, the two old friends smilingly helped themselves. Johnson's pleasant entrance and Sans Foix's flaky buns not only lifted their hearts but roused them from mere mulling to talk of the current state of the country.

"James," Jock said, replacing his coffee cup in its saucer, "do you ever find yourself feeling a bit sorry for President Van Buren?"

"Sorry for him? Never felt much pity for a man born in the North who insists on favoring slavery. I've no room to talk, of course, being a slave owner myself. But a man has to feel a certain amount of sympathy for any politician who barely squeaked into office and then hit a nationwide financial panic. In that light, yes. I guess I do pity Martin Van Buren."

"It's always interested me that he and Henry Clay, political opponents in almost every area, remain such staunch friends. How does Clay stand in your estimation?" Couper asked.

"Fine, fiery orator. Always admired a man who could get his ideas across, but Clay flip-flops quite a lot. On one side one day and another the next."

"I can't help feeling he's a man of integrity, nevertheless. Worked in the law with the admirable Virginian George Wythe, teacher of Thomas Jefferson. Now, Jefferson was a great mon in my opinion. Did I ever tell you he's the gentleman who advised me to experiment with my olive trees, James?"

With a sly grin Gould answered, "Several times, Jock."

Couper laughed heartily. "Becca keeps reminding me that I do repeat myself on occasion." He passed the plate of spicy buns again. Gould refused. "By the way, our next edition of the *Intelligencer* should give us a report on how Senator Henry Clay fared in his speech this week on the people's right to petition Congress for the abolition of slavery in the District of Columbia. I am curious as to the side he'll take, aren't you?"

"That's what I mean about Clay," Gould mused. "He contributed so much to the concord between North and South right after the Missouri Compromise in 1820, but I'm never quite sure which side he'll come down on in any speech. Like you, I guess, I count on what I believe is the man's reputation for integrity. He and old John Quincy Adams did not deserve the criticism they both got when Clay backed Adams for President in 1824. Politicians are people like you and me. I never believed Adams made Clay his

Secretary of State in return for Clay's backing him for President. But a lot of folks did."

"It just could be," Jock said, "that Clay is coming to be known as the Great Pacificator—the Great Compromiser—because he has the courage to change his mind when changing it is good for the country."

"How do you hope he handles the problem of slavery in the District of Columbia, Jock?"

For a time Couper watched the fire burn. Then, looking straight at his friend, he said, "I know that outwardly we both appear to be proslavery, Gould. I thought you, of all people, knew in your heart that I'm *not*. Not deep down. I seldom find the courage to discuss it, but I'd like to see it abolished everywhere. Somehow I was sure you knew that."

James Gould's dry laugh added meaning to the few words he chose in response: "I do know, Jock. And I'm as guilty as you. We're both trapped in the system, but it's been good today for me, at least, that we're close enough as friends to face the issue together."

"I'm glad too, old friend, and anyway, there's little either of us can do about which side Henry Clay happens to take in his much-awaited speech this month. We're a long, long way down here from Washington City."

By mid-February, after seven-year-old Fanny Fraser seemed almost recovered from measles, Anne felt the urge to do something special for Eve, who had taken such excellent care of the nearly fatally ill girl.

"You my frien', ain't dat enough?" Eve asked Anne when she tried to find out what Eve specially longed for as the two gathered a bowl of white camellias for Fanny.

"That's a silly question and you know it," Anne said, clipping three pure-white blossoms to add to the bowl Eve held for her. "You really went far beyond the call of duty in your tender, loving care of my little daughter. Isn't there something you and June need for your cabin? Maybe a new chair or a length of cloth for new curtains?"

Flashing her radiant smile, Eve asked, "You notice dat Eve keep clean, iron curtains at de windows ob her cabin?"

"Of course I noticed! And I wish there was some way to convince some of our other people to scrub and sweep and dust and wash and iron the way you do."

"But you an' me's frien's, Miss Anne. Ain't none ob de others kin say dat lessen dey lie. I be here to look after you an' all your churn for de res' ob my life, but I be your frien' too. Dat make me clean an' tidy. Ain't gonna give you no chance to complain to dat stage woman, when she come to lib on S'n Simons, dat Eve be a lazy, no-good nigger only fit to be a slabe. She one nosy woman, dat Missus Butler. She go nosin' 'roun de cabins ober on de rice islan' makin' folks scrub wif soap an' water—makin' 'em scrub der faces an' hans an' feet an' backsides. Make 'em sweep de floors an' git off de las' dried bit ob food lef' on de dishes. She git down on their cabin floor herself an' scrub!" Eve laughed. "She be dead set *agin* slabery all right, too. She cry big ol' tears ober de womens dat hab to go back to de fiel's before dey kin walk good after a new baby be birthed."

Anne stared at her, wondering how on earth to respond to such loose talk. "I know you're just waiting for me to pin you down and demand to know *how* you know so much about Fanny Kemble Butler, but no matter how curious I am—and I am—I'm not going to ask because—"

"She got three names, dat stage lady?"

"Well, yes. Her maiden name was Frances Kemble. Then she married a wealthy man named Pierce Butler, so now her last name is Butler. Why?"

Eve's laughter was contagious most of the time. This time Anne was made uncomfortable by it.

"What's so funny?"

"June be such a fine, big, strong man, he don' need no name but June, no more'n I needs a name but Eve."

Again, Anne could only stare at the somehow suddenly superior look on Eve's even-featured, mysteriously beautiful dark face.

Was the gap between them always as wide as it seemed this moment? Was Eve actually daring to give her a superior look? Or was the enigmatic expression Anne saw now one of pure defense? Defense against what? Against Anne? Hadn't Eve always vowed that she'd care for Anne for as long as they both lived? Was Anne only imagining now that Eve had used that vow of friendship simply because she had no other choice but to look after the mistress who owned her very life?

"I—I don't think I like the way you've made me feel," Anne said, her voice sounding tight and nervous.

"Don' worry none, Miss Anne. Eve knows zactly what you're wonderin'."

"What?"

"I said don' worry none. Eve knows zactly what you're—"

"I heard what you said! I just don't think I know what you mean by not needing a last name. That June doesn't need a last name either. I get so confused. Help me, Eve! Can't you *help me?*"

"Eve here to try to help you. Dat be all they is."

"Is it?"

"Mos' ob de time I knows zactly how to help you, Miss Anne. You born to give me orders, though. I born to take 'em. How 'bout you tell me what kin Eve do to help you?"

Maybe, Anne thought, I should change the subject. Then all this will go away. But *what* do I want to go away? This is Eve. I own her. We're friends and my job, Mama says, is to be kind to Eve and help her grow inwardly into the kind of splendid house servant only Eve has the talent and intelligence to be. But I can't settle for that! I thought I could because I'm Anne Couper Fraser, but—but even that sets us apart in some funny way I suddenly deplore. *Why do I need three names?*

Eve's easy, bright smile loosened the tightness around Anne's heart enough for her to smile too. "You sho doin' a lot ob thinkin', Miss Anne. A lot ob wonderin'."

"I thought you said you knew what I was wondering about."

If Eve's smile eased Anne's heart a moment ago, it freed her now in a way even she didn't understand. "You seduced June with that amazing smile of yours, didn't you?"

The smile glowed without mercy. "Jus' so I got him," Eve said, her tone amused and airy. "Eve love June de way you love Mausa John. You know dat. Ain' no way you don' know, Miss Anne. Dat be where you not white at all!"

"What do you mean I'm not white?"

Eve merely tossed her head and laughed. "You knows the same as I does dat white folks don' put no stock in niggers lovin' the way dey loves."

"I don't know any such thing!"

"Sometime you be mulish like now, but you got lots ob brains, Miss Anne. You be the only white person anywhere wif de brains to know a nigger woman kin love the same as a white woman. A nigger man, too. June love me de same as Mausa John he love you. Eve don' lie to you. You know Eve neber lie to you. An' right now we best take these purty flowers upstairs to po' lil Fanny, an' don' you dast gib her a hint but dat you an' me's better frien's dan we eber was!"

Halfway to the house Eve stopped in the path, holding the glass bowl into which they would pour water so that the creamy white camellia blossoms could float pure, healing beauty for dear little Fanny's full recovery. "Dey is one mo' thing," Eve said. "Don' you worry none 'bout Missus Fanny Kemble Butler nosin' too much aroun' Eve's cabin. Me an' her's gonna do jus' fine together. She take one look at you an' know all dey is to know 'bout Eve."

Anne was speechless with amazement at Eve's intuition, her wisdom. The feeling inside her heart was only gratitude, when over her shoulder Eve tossed the words: "Dat stage lady, she gonna know for sho dat you an' me's got—worth!"

CHAPTER 65

JOCK COUPER WAS STANDING ALONE ON HIS WIDE porch at Cannon's Point the Saturday afternoon of February 16, when he heard oarsmen singing lustily and conch blasts from over at the Hampton dock. As the singing and rapid, wild blasts of the familiar signal ended and an even wilder whooping began among the Hampton people gathered on the dock, he knew that the Pierce Butlers had reached St. Simons Island at last.

"And what, I wonder, will their coming do to our Island?" he mumbled aloud to himself, a habit he'd fallen into as he approached his eightieth birthday. "It's been a long time since a famous person has graced our midst, and surely old Major Butler's grandson Pierce has taken him a wife whose name is known throughout the English-speaking world."

He hadn't noticed his own wife, Rebecca, watching him from their front door, so when she asked how he enjoyed conversation with himself, it startled him.

"Eh? Becca, my dear, you're married to a dauncy old goat

who's taken up talking to himself. Did you hear the Hampton conch blasting away?"

"I did," she said, joining him at the porch railing. "They're here and according to Anne's Eve, every one of the Butler people is ready and waiting. Mrs. Butler's reputation for generosity has surely preceded her. But where the Hampton people learned the word *abolitionist* I have no idea. Still, Anne vows that Eve's grapevine told her Mrs. Fanny Kemble Butler is an abolitionist, much against owning people but evidently not against spoiling them. I'm sure you'll know exactly how to converse with her, though."

He slipped an arm around her still-slim waist. "Becca, Becca, would that I were half as astute as you believe. We'll all simply be ourselves with the new arrivals from the North. Young Pierce Butler must not be an abolitionist. He certainly has no problem living high on the hog up in his grand Philadelphia mansion on the labors of the Hampton people. I wonder if the two—Miss Fanny and her husband—ever actually discuss our odd institution?"

"We'll find out soon enough, I expect. Now, it's chilly out here, Jock. Don't you think you've had enough fresh air for a while?"

"Almost," he said, his face lighting up. "I'll obey you, Becca, just as soon as I've doddered down the lane to find a hand free to drive me in the carriage down to Hamilton."

"But can't Johnson go down for you? There's a sharp wind off the river. And why does anyone need to ride all the way to Hamilton today?"

He smiled. "Because I promised our daughter to let her know the instant her Shakespearean idol, Fanny Kemble Butler, reached St. Simons, that's why. I've never broken a promise to my beloved daughter and this is surely no time to start."

THE HAMPTON HOUSE IN WHICH FANNY, PIERCE, their infant daughter, Frances, and three-year-old Sarah were to live with the children's cheerful Irish nurse, Marjorie, brought a dramatic exclamation from Fanny Kemble Butler on her first sight of it: *"Wretched!* Pierce, there are only two rooms downstairs and two upstairs. How in the name of decency will we learn to live in such a hovel?"

Alone in the mildewed, scruffy little entryway after Marjorie had taken the children upstairs to inspect the quarters where she and they would sleep, Pierce gave his wife a melting smile. "How will we learn, magnificent Fanny? By living here, I should imagine. How much more wretched do you find it than our Butler's Island mansion?"

In his arms, she laughed the bell-like laugh she knew he loved. "No more wretched at all, my prince. It galls me to admit it, but cramped as it is, already I can see that life on St. Simons Island could just possibly be a bit less repulsive than life lived practically underwater where your precious rice grows."

He kissed her and led her into what he laughingly called the drawing room. "You need a helping of Marjorie's flexible disposition, my sweet."

"No one treasures Marjorie as I do," Fanny said firmly. "What you hire her to do, she does to perfection. Our children, I sometimes think, are far more comfortable with Marjorie than with their mother. But darling Pierce, it's their mother you love." Before he could make a suitable response, she laid her hand playfully over his mouth. "Not another word until you've promised to go for a long walk with me. Never mind this hideous box of a house. What little we had time to see of nature on St. Simons, after being attacked by joy and shrieks from that mob of your dusky people, struck me as quite hopeful. A walk, please?"

Kissing the hand still clamped over his lips, he led her toward the narrow veranda.

"Sh!" Fanny gasped. "Not a word, love. But can you believe your eyes? There *is* strange, wild beauty here! How in the name of heaven could two almost neighboring islands be so different from each other? Ugliness must have been spawned in those turgid rice swamps of Butler Island. But Pierce, look! Stretching from that gum or maple tree into the very glooms of the woods themselves is a golden curtain! What on earth could it be?"

"Flowers?" he teased.

"But what *kind* of flowers?" She grabbed his hand, pulling him along the slightly overgrown path and plunged them both into the greenest tangle of thicket she'd seen anywhere on earth. "The yellow-curtain flowers grow on vines, dearest," she exulted, still running deeper into the undergrowth, Pierce following, his laughter unconvincing. "I must know their names—and Pierce! Shame on us both! We're trampling lovely purple violets under our feet. Can you believe violets in February? And everyone has vowed this is the coldest winter in history. Do you suppose we've died and gone to heaven?"

"I died and went to heaven when you married me, Fanny, but that once is enough. No! We are definitely *not* in heaven and quite probably all around us, writhing or coiled in wait under our feet in your violet beds or behind fallen logs, are a dozen poisonous snakes ready to fill us with venom. I tell you this must not happen again. Do you hear me? You are never, never again to race off like a wild thing into these untamed woods without protection. Never, never walk or ride a horse more than one yard off a well-cleared road!"

"What?"

"I mean it."

"But did I hear you say—ride? Do you really mean that the ground under our feet here on blessed St. Simons is firm enough for me to ride a horse? And when will you find one for me? I now declare that by nine tomorrow morning, I will be plunging where I please into this tangle of magic and beauty."

Carefully, firmly, he led her back to the open path, where Fanny kissed him soundly.

The pout returned to his mouth as he almost jerked her arms away. "Not out here where those peering, walleyed slaves can see us, wife."

"And don't you believe they kiss each other?"

"Fanny, hush!"

The laughter died in her throat. "I see."

"Well, I hope you do see. I am the owner and the master of this plantation. While we are here, you are the owner's wife and the plantation's mistress. Is it perfectly clear that you will behave in suitable fashion?"

"Nonsense," she snapped. "Do you believe you can deny me all pleasure on this dreary mission to your inherited lands? After the weeks spent in that rice swamp where the Altamaha River kept looking over the dikes at me every minute of every interminable day, do you think for a moment that I have any notion of not exploring terra firma again? Solid ground under my feet and stretches of water where water should be—in plain view to enjoy and not threatening to wash us away."

"You may of course ride to your heart's content," he said, his smile radiant now and, as always, making her weak. "After all, didn't I permit you to bring your dreamy-eyed Jack along from Butler Island just to please and pamper you, to keep you to cleared roads and protect you from rattlesnakes and wild boars?"

"I'll be happy to have Jack ride with me, especially if I need a path cut or at least until I've learned some of the terrain, but you may just as well know that I fully intend to ride alone at any time I choose and to prove my English breeding by calling on at least some of the other plantation mistresses." She stopped to look at him. "Pierce, what manner of white woman do you suppose *chooses* to live in such an isolated, primitive spot as this? Do you believe even one or maybe two can actually carry on an intelligent conversation?"

Before he could answer, she broke into a paean of praise and, skirts flying, raced ahead literally to embrace armfuls of silvery wild plum blossoms reaching toward her from one side of the path. "It's going to be rather good here—in some ways, beautiful Pierce. At least in some ways it's going to be good here because there is— oh, there is going to be beauty to discover. And"—her voice at its most enticing, she added—"you and I will find still more wonder together. You'll see. You'll see and feel and realize more magic in my arms than you knew existed on this old, crusty earth."

From behind them, they heard giggles, gasps, squeaky laughter. Five women of varying ages and notably varying skin colors had been watching and listening. One woman, her sooty skin far filthier than the others, had a child hung on her hip. Fanny spoke to them all as a group. "Good evening," she said, with dignity and warmth.

"Ha do, Missus," the group chorused. Then, still giggling, one or two jumping up and down, they hurried away into the woods toward their quarters.

"You didn't even greet them, Pierce. Shouldn't you have at least wished them a good evening? They belong to you."

"I—I meant to, Fanny," he muttered, sounding suddenly embarrassed. "But you did and that's sufficient."

"Did it cross your mind that the unbathed child on that woman's hip strongly resembled the mulatto Hampton driver, Bram? And now that I think of it, don't you agree that Bram is the exact image of your former overseer, Mr. Roswell King, Jr.?"

Casually, Pierce said, "Bram's probably King's brother. His father managed both plantations for old Major Butler, you know, for nearly twenty years."

Appalled, Fanny gasped, "Is—is that all you have to say about such a thing? When we first got here, didn't Bram introduce us to the blackest Negress named Minda?"

"She is his mother."

"I see."

"I hope you do see," Pierce said flatly, leading her back toward the house. "And that you say no more about it, since it's not at all unusual."

Walking in silence beside him, unable to push down an attack of anxiety, Fanny vowed to utter not one more word on the shocking subject. For a moment the unexpected anxiety dimmed her pleasure over having found so much beauty, but she would pray God to use her new anxiety as a warning to curb her words. Certainly with Pierce.

UP BEFORE PIERCE RETURNED FROM A CONFERENCE with Bram, his driver, Fanny, in an erratic but sincere effort, tried to record in a journal at least some of the beauty and horror she had experienced during their first week at Hampton. She had just begun to write when the door of her parlor creaked open and up to fourteen silent, bowing, barefoot Negro women filed in. No one spoke when Fanny nodded, and much as they had done on Butler Island, the group got down on their haunches and watched her.

I suppose it's best to be pleasant and to keep on writing, she thought. Evidently they're here to inspect me, to find out what I do inside my own house. So let them.

Now and then she would look up from her journal to smile, or long enough to sharpen a quill. Each time her eyes met theirs, they nudged each other, shook with laughter, somehow full of what appeared to be joy, and nodded.

"Did you come for some special reason?" Fanny asked finally, knowing full well they had come, as had the Butler Island women, for flannel, rice, sugar, to beg her to "pray Mausa not to send me back to de fiel' so soon arter my baby come," to plead for a piece of meat, and so on. Into her journal went each complaint, each plea. Solemnly, Fanny promised them all to take their needs straight to her husband, their master.

When one slim, big-eyed, gentle young woman began to crawl toward her on hands and knees, lifting her tattered skirts to expose lash marks, which revived the horror of the Butler Island "whipping for impudence," Fanny broke into tears.

"Enough!" she cried, getting to her feet, indicating with dramatic gestures that she could endure no more. "You have been good to visit me," she said as firmly as her tears allowed, "but please, I beg you—all of you—to leave me this minute. My husband will be here shortly and I promise, I do promise, to take your needs straight to him. I do *not* want you mistreated."

All stood now—some bent with age and labor, some straight and proud, others appearing almost frantic as they tried silently to decide how to please her. Diana, the horribly whipped girl, said, "We go, Missus. But we thanks you an' we thanks de Mausa fo' to visit us an' fo' to satisfy us wif two such pretty, lily-skinned lil' girls as Miss Sally an' de baby, Miss Frances. We be safe now dat Mausa an' Missus gib us churn. Mausa don' want us to die so he can't feed he own churn."

When Pierce strode into the parlor not five minutes after their hasty retreat, Fanny poured out her agony of soul and repeated each plea of the wretched women who had so recently left behind their spiritual and emotional and physical stenches.

"Their hard lives are a stench in the nostrils of God, Pierce," she declared, rushing to throw her arms about him. "There is only one way you can make the kind of miracle only you can make, my beloved husband. *You must better their lot!*"

"There is *no* way any miracle can be made and certainly not by me, Frances Anne." He had barked the words at her, his normally beautiful, petulant face hard and icy. "Day after day in the one week we've been on St. Simons Island, you have angered me far more deeply than at any point on Butler Island, and I want an end to it. I want an end to it *now*. I order you to stop listening to their lies. Niggers lie, Fanny. Niggers are born liars and I command that you close your ears forever to their trash talk of how they suffer. They are filling their lots in life and we fill ours. Let that be the end of it."

"But Pierce, your love for me should—"

"Not one more word. Not one more word! *Not one more word.*"

For a long, revealing moment, she stood as straight as a tree and stared him down. She uttered not one word. She obeyed Pierce to that point. For as long as he could stand, facing her down, she could stand. She would stand.

She did stand.

At first he stared in rage. Then, like pine kindling in a roaring fire, he started to curl and crumple. None of what was taking place in him showed. But she felt it. She felt this once-dashing, charming, pretty-talking, passionate young man—who had pursued her from city to city declaring eternal love, creating in her what she had been so sure was also love—shut her out. As firmly as though he had bolted a door behind him and left, he was gone. The chivalrous, romantic, sensuously tender man, who had drawn the very heart from her breast, had withdrawn his heart. Oh, he would devastate her again and again, she had no doubt, with his irresistible lovemaking, would make an idiotic fool of her, but as of this moment he was—gone.

And Fanny was alone—far, far from anything familiar enough

to be called home. Far, far removed even from her own familiar self.

Pierce still stood there, but he had brought down a great, weighted curtain between them. In public, even in the miserable presence of his slaves, he would act the gentleman, would even speak to her in privacy as though nothing had changed. But with the cold words forbidding her ever to speak to him again in behalf of his miserable human property, he had left her to love him— alone. She would never again return his love under the unthinking bliss of pleasing him. He would not be able to stop her from trying to better the lot of those wretches, but in her efforts, she would try alone.

Had she succeeded only in deluding herself that Pierce had in him a streak of human kindness that she, with her skills, could draw from him?

Through her being, this question burned: am I such an expert actress that I have misled myself? I have married this man. I have believed in my love for him, in his love for me. Is *my* love strong enough to sustain me? Will my two innocent babes upstairs in their lumpy little beds pay for the misguided actions of their mother? They will not. With all my heart I despise acting, but I can deceive and convince and twist hearts and give joy to strangers. Perfect strangers have bowed down to me by the thousands, and loathing it as I do, I will go on acting with him because I believe in the depths of my soul that slavery is not only wrong, wrong, wrong —it is against the very heart and will of the God I worship!

Pierce had let her long silence be. In fact, he was not even looking at her when she spoke at last. "I will be your wife, Pierce, and I will be the mother of your children, because they are my children too, but mark that I will also always remain myself." She crossed the cramped room to where he stood, head down. With one finger she lifted his chin so that he had no choice but to look at her. "I will remain myself, Pierce," she repeated.

In his usual courteous, soft-spoken way, he said, "I'm sure you will, Fanny."

CHAPTER 66

A FEW DAYS LATER, AFTER PERUSING THEIR COPY of the *National Intelligencer,* Jock Couper and Rebecca agreed on a day later in the week for inviting the Butlers to dinner. Then Couper sat alone in his parlor while Rebecca went to discuss the menu with Sans Foix and Johnson.

"I'm not sure I like my state of mind today," he said aloud to himself, indulging his habit of putting thoughts into words because loneliness assailed him each time Rebecca left his sight. "I'm not even sure of the nature of my state of mind," he informed himself. "A feeling of trouble is too close to the surface and there is no new trouble on my horizon, so I'm wool-gathering again. I must remind Rebecca to invite Anne and John when the Butlers come. After all, how much could an aging couple like Becca and me amuse or interest people of the world such as young Pierce Butler and his famous wife, Fanny Kemble? Never mind that my wife's distant cousin, Willy Maxwell, insists that she despises the theater, the lady is acclaimed everywhere in the English-speaking world."

His reverie was cut short by what sounded like two galloping horses, and smiling because he was beginning to bore himself, Couper pulled his stiff body to a standing position and made his way toward the Cannon's Point front door, standing open on this pleasant and unexpectedly mild February morning.

One glance out over his elegantly planted front garden brought him to an erect stance. He'd have to begin to watch his aging shoulders, keep them back, straight, especially when a guest was arriving, and without doubt a famous, somewhat startling guest had just reined her stallion—the beast still prancing—near Jock's wrought iron hitching post.

"Aye," he whispered excitedly, "that could be no other lady on earth but the great Fanny Kemble Butler come to call!" Escorted by a lean, attentive Negro on his own horse, the famous visitor to St. Simons Island made a picture Couper's old mind would never forget. Still sitting her huge stallion, Montreal, which Couper knew was now turned plow horse and probably excruciating to ride, he feasted his eyes on a woman of the highest caliber—handsome, arresting in the almost arrogantly good English form with which she sat the horse, and marvel of marvels for a true lady, she was wearing black broadcloth riding trousers strapped under the heel of her boots. She was riding sidesaddle, but her woman's saddle bore a horn with which to steady the rider on hard gallops. The elderly man chuckled to himself, trying to imagine the reaction among Island ladies because into their midst had blown a veritable hurricane exotic enough to keep them all in a state of shock for months to come.

Jock Couper hurried across his veranda to greet her. Before even one exchange, he knew he already liked this striking, dynamic creature, who, for all he knew, could be part druid, part British snob, part gentle heart, and part colorful vixen. That she would mean every word she uttered he had no doubt.

Like nothing so much as a veritable goddess, she moved briskly up his walkway toward the veranda, her clipped English-stage-trained voice calling to him as she neared his outstretched hands.

"I bid you good morning, sir! You must be the revered Mr. John Couper of Cannon's Point."

Before he could force his unruly legs to descend the steps, she had reached his side on the wide porch. As Jock bowed over her outstretched, noticeably large but graceful hand, he heard himself saying, "Aye, Mrs. Fanny Kemble Butler, I am John Couper, and never was a lady more welcome to my home! Come in, come inside if it's too chilly out here, please."

"One of the finest charms about your Island, Mr. Couper," she said on a rich, modulated laugh, "is that there is truly fresh air. But what of you, sir? Would you be more comfortable indoors?"

Couper, still holding on to her hand, said in a voice that sounded far younger than his normal tone, "Do ye ken, Mrs. Butler, that I am forced to restrain myself from applauding you, from the moment you dismounted?" He dropped her hand only to demonstrate by clapping his hands delightedly until she, laughing too, put an end to his antic.

"Sir, whether we sit in this glorious Island air or go inside, I can only beg you never, never to applaud me again! I loathe it."

"Indeed!"

"Indeed," she repeated, tossing her short, handsome whip onto a porch chair. "May I be truthful? And will you be truthful with me in return, sir? I'd love to spend a few moments with you out here in what must be the loveliest spot on this entire Island."

He made a gentlemanly performance of leading her to a rocker, seating her, and then eased himself down into the chair nearest hers. "Shall I send for my fair wife, Rebecca? Or do you feel quite safe alone out here in the St. Simons wilds with an old Scottish goat?"

"Send for her by all means if you like," Fanny said, "but I'm ever so pleased to have found you alone. You see, my husband tells me that you're one man who not only loves and reads his vast library of books but is probably the only gentleman in this godforsaken wilderness with both taste and intelligence." She dropped her slightly affected mannerisms and speech abruptly. "That is, if God, at least the God I love and struggle to follow, ever forsakes any spot or any single person, and no matter what rash thing I say, I know from my heart, sir, that He does not."

Couper stared at her, then smiled broadly, the one thing Fanny

Kemble Butler made him want to do most. "Except for my rather singular daughter Anne Couper Fraser, who lives at the south end of our Island with her British husband and lovely children, I believe I've never known a lady as—as direct as you, Mrs. Butler. Do you mind that I relish such directness?"

"Mind? I'm more relieved than I've been since our boat from Darien first scraped sand on Mr. Butler's dreary, waterlogged rice island on New Year's Eve last. I've never found myself in any place on earth where I felt so—alien, so lost, as I felt on Butler Island. I'm enamored of the beauty here, though, and how you've enhanced it at Cannon's Point!" For a brief moment she sat studying him, then added, "You've actually made me laugh and I'm deeply fond of you for that."

Then, before he could answer, her attention flew to the Negro still waiting beside the two mounts out at Couper's hitching posts. "Oh Jack, Jack, my dear," she called. "Will you kindly come here for a moment?"

Without batting an eye—at least he hoped he hadn't—Couper asked, "And did you call your boy 'Jack, my dear'?"

She looked a touch surprised, then tossed it off. "Did I? I suppose so, but how often do you truly think anyone ever addresses one of these miserable slaves in an even remotely affectionate way? Does it offend you if I called him 'Jack, my dear'? I know Mr. Butler's poor, mistreated wretches gape and gape and giggle and nudge each other each time I accidentally use the phrase 'my dear' with any one of them."

A devilish twinkle in his blue eyes, Couper said, "Of course I'm not offended. I'm an American by choice, Mrs. Butler. I was employed at the time by a Loyalist, but my heart cheered and fought for American freedom as best it could during our War for Independence, even as I fled to British Florida to protect my job."

Her laughter, controlled and lovely, nevertheless rang. "You and I may not agree on everything, Mr. Couper, but we are going to be friends. Your humor is delicious!"

Jack reached the bottom of the veranda steps just then, and after informing him that she would whistle when she was again ready for her horse, Fanny dismissed him. The young man grinned, thanked her profusely, bowed—even dared to smile at Couper—and left.

"He's from Butler Island, poor lad," Fanny said. "My husband stays suspicious of my every move, but he can be a kind man, so he gave me Jack for our entire stay here—for better or for worse. I admit there are times when I'd give almost anything for just one solitary ride. Mr. Butler insists, however, that Jack must protect me from myself—and from your poisonous snakes."

Couper was still pondering what she might have meant by actually telling him, a stranger, of her husband's suspicions, when his guest, sitting now on the edge of the rocker, asked, "By any chance, sir, do you subscribe to the *National Intelligencer,* published, I believe, in Washington City? I'd give almost anything to lay hands on the latest edition. Mr. Butler assured me that no one here would even know of it."

"Oh he did, eh? Well, 'tis true your husband has not met many of our St. Simons planters. Aye. If you'll excuse me, I'll place a copy of the latest *Intelligencer* right in your fair hands." Couper struggled out of his chair and made an effort to march briskly across the porch and into the parlor.

WHILE HER HOST WAS INSIDE HIS HOUSE, FANNY sat, absorbing the magnificent view across his gardens, the sun-dappled Hampton River, its stretching marshes, and the fringe of sea visible on such a clear day. Thank you, wonderful Lord, she breathed within herself, for this beauty and the beauty of my new friend, the gentle, good John Couper! I need this fine old man, Father. I need to feel free to empty my heart to him. Dare I? Dare I?

WHEN COUPER REAPPEARED, CARRYING THE *INTEL-ligencer* in one hand, he was chuckling. "Here you are, Mrs. Butler, and if I may be so forward, there are two questions I'd like you to answer for me if you don't object."

"Not at all, sir. Your first question?"

Easing himself back into his rocker, Couper asked, "Did I hear you correctly when you told your boy, Jack, that you'd *whistle* for him when you were ready to depart? Can you really whistle?"

Again the musical laughter came and Jock, though reddening a bit, laughed too. In response, Fanny, a little finger and a forefinger in her mouth, gave a noble, shrill whistle, which, if Jack could hear from the stable, meant that Couper's most welcome guest might be leaving.

"Oh dear," she exclaimed. "I didn't mean to whistle so loud. I'm not really ready to leave yet."

"Good. And the wind is from the west, so my guess is that 'Jack, my dear' did not hear."

When Couper handed her the *Intelligencer,* she thanked him profusely, began at once to search as though looking for a particular item.

"Hunting for something special, Mrs. Butler?" he asked.

"How rude of me to bury my face like that," she apologized. "But yes, I'm so eager to read Mr. Henry Clay's speech on the people's right to petition the Congress for abolition of slaves in the District of Columbia. Did you see it?"

"I did. Page three. I read it carefully. Word for word. I also had no idea which side the great orator Clay might take. To read what he said, one would think he had not contributed, as he most certainly did, to the working of the Missouri Compromise. We in the United States have Clay to thank for the measure of harmony between the North and the South, you know. But I fear he's using his persuasive skills in this latest speech against the cause of abolition."

"I pray not! What a cruel pity, Mr. Couper, what a cruel shame it is that such a man should either know no better or do no better for his country."

Couper cleared his throat. "You're an abolitionist, Mrs. Butler?"

"I'm an Englishwoman, sir! How could I be anything but sick at heart over the evil institution of slavery? Forgive me, I do long to be able to talk to you at length about it—freely. I can't, you know, with Mr. Butler. He begins to command me and grows quite red in the face and filled with fury when I even do some small thing such as give a length of flannel or an extra lump of sugar or a piece of meat to one of his poor, mistreated people." She sat up very straight. "I—I've been ordered never to report to him again when one of those miserable Hampton or Butler slaves comes pleading for me to secure one shred of his mercy for them."

"I see."

"You do? Mr. Couper, *what* do you see? Do you secretly wish I had never climbed those steps to your lovely veranda? Dare I pour out my heart to you? I can't believe your mind is closed on this or any subject, but—"

"But we're all like—foreigners to you down here on the coast, is that it?"

"In a way, yes. Still, am I imposing when I tell you I've already prayed—while you were in your house just now—that it might be possible for us to converse without the fear of offending? How free may I feel to unburden myself of this extreme melancholy? There are times when I truly fear that before my husband and I can make our escape back to the North, I will become ill. My poor husband feels ill much of the time these days and suffers, I know, from his stubborn refusal to admit that the ghastly conditions among his slaves even exist. Such denial can cause physical breakdowns."

"Undoubtedly," Couper said in a noncommittal voice. "But isn't Mr. Butler's Georgia property his main source of income?"

"Does that in any way alleviate the cruelty to these people?"

For a moment, Jock skirted close to irritation that his quiet morning had been so jarred by the arrival of this amazing woman. Still, he liked her, wanted her to like him, needed only an instant to collect himself, to calm his own turmoil that she was so outspoken. False, he thought.

My turmoil is not her outspokenness. It is that in my heart I know she's right about the Butler people. None of what she's said is new to me beyond the fact that the remarkable lady is forcing me to dig up what I myself have so long managed to keep buried —out of sight. Almost out of mind. Certainly out of conversation with anyone but James Gould, and that rarely.

He had but one choice. Her deep-set, magnificent dark eyes saw into him already. He would be as honest as possible with her and hope for the best. And so, for some surprising period of time, he told her of his own resistance to the methods used by both King overseers through the years. Told her of the Hampton rule that no Negro be allowed to cross little Jones Creek at the peril of a lashing. Confessed that he had heard those lashings and their accompanying cries and screams. Admitted that he had been able to live with his own conscience only because he had done all in his power to alleviate the hardship in the lives of his own people. He gave example after example, as though he were explaining to a superior. Ticked off those among his people who had been, against Georgia law, taught to read. Reported what he considered lenient working hours, humane tasks, rewards, assurance of ample food and housing even when his own financial straits were severe because of hurricanes and plummeting cotton prices and infestations of caterpillars. He came very close to telling her that he and his friend Thomas Spalding of Sapelo, when his daughter Anne was a mere child, had flagrantly broken a law, to which both their signatures had been affixed, by purchasing an illegal cargo of Ebo Negroes—many of them still at either Cannon's Point or Hamilton, his daughter's home now down the Island. He didn't admit to that dark deed, nor did he admit that twelve Ebos had committed suicide rather than submit to bondage, but the old guilt swept him again for the first time in many years. Fanny Kemble Butler had an almost uncanny way of causing him to hear the voice of God Himself saying, "Jock Couper, thou art the man."

When he stopped talking at last, his guest stood up, her hand out, and when he too had gotten to his feet, she said softly, with such effect that he cringed inwardly, "Dear Mr. Couper. Dear, good, well-meaning Mr. Couper. How I pity you. How I admire and pity you. My husband refuses to be honest about how his people are treated. I love him, but I cannot abide the weakness of dishonesty. You are a strong man. We can, we will be friends."

The smile that must have cast light into a hundred darkened theaters rendered Couper as helpless as an infant. "I like you. I trust you, even if you do turn to jelly when defending your benevolent practices. Probably because you turn to jelly, I trust you. I believe you do try to alleviate your people's lot. Perhaps only God Almighty can find a way to free them, but at least you try to allow them some semblance of human dignity. I heard that before I called on you today. The poor wretches at Hampton know it of you. Along with their incessant complaints and pleas for my intervention, they have let me know they would gladly change places with your people. We will be friends, Mr. Couper. We—are friends. I'm also friends with the Reverend William Ellery Channing of Boston, who, like me, is an abolitionist, praying daily that at least some slave owners will try as you try. I will tell him about you for his own edification. And I hope you and your family will visit us when you can."

She then accepted eagerly when Couper invited her and Butler to dinner at Cannon's Point, and with another handshake that required no words from either of them, she went slowly, regally down the front steps, whistled for Jack, and was gone.

CHAPTER 67

REBECCA COUPER, KNOWN UP AND DOWN THE COAST for her charm and expertise as a hostess, felt almost young again these days. Their first dinner in honor of Fanny and Pierce Butler had been, for Rebecca, a total success. There had been such a long hiatus in the Island's social life because of the Wylly tragedy and the explosion of the *Pulaski,* the entertaining she and Jock were doing again, especially with the Butlers, lifted her spirits. Her heart still ached for Eliza Mackay, who had lost her lovely daughter-in-law and both her small grandchildren on the *Pulaski,* but coming to know the altogether fascinating and famous Fanny Kemble helped divert her thoughts. Pierce Butler was charming, too, but despite his obvious social graces, good looks, and wealth, the young man struck Rebecca as being an oddly unhappy, even disturbed, gentleman.

That Anne and John enjoyed the Butlers was plain to see. Fanny Butler seemed pleased, not only that they knew Willy Maxwell as a friend, but that Anne and John actually remembered having seen her as an eight-year-old child on the stage of her father's Covent Garden theater in London. And there could be no doubt in anyone's mind that Mrs. Butler liked John exceedingly.

The Coupers and the Butlers and the Frasers had even made the boat trip to the mainland for a delightful weekend visit with James Hamilton and Caroline at Hopeton. Jock, these days, seemed in his favorite element. How the man loved people around him! Today, as Rebecca sat alone in the master bedroom busily at work on a new crewel cover for her parlor rocker, she found herself thinking a lot about Fanny Kemble Butler and wondered how St. Simons people struck this highly cultivated, outspoken woman.

Jock had told her some of what he and Mrs. Butler had talked about when he visited at Hampton. Fanny Kemble dropped by Cannon's Point often, too, on her many wild gallops about the woods or along the Island roads, dutifully paying her respects to the Wyllys, Mrs. Mary Abbott, the Goulds, the Demeres. There was no doubt in Rebecca's mind that her neighbors received Fanny graciously, but what, she couldn't help wondering, did they really think of her? Were they impressed, as was Rebecca, or irritated by her theatrical British accent? Perhaps someday, Mrs. Wylly or Mrs. Abbott or Mary Gould would tell her. If not, it would be as unthinkable for Rebecca to ask as it would be for any Island lady to ride out alone in trousers and visored riding cap as Mrs. Butler boldly did. Gossip was not a part of Rebecca Couper's nature, and except to wonder about the oddly strained atmosphere between Fanny Kemble Butler and her husband, Pierce, she was unaccountably attracted to the woman's stunning presence.

Plainly, Mrs. Butler was a devoted mother. A happy light filled her beautiful brown eyes each time she mentioned her children or her parents. The same light was not there when she looked at her oddly withdrawn husband.

Still, Rebecca thought, I'm sure she loves Pierce Butler in a way that he may not even know, in a way the polished, rather superficial gentleman may not have the capacity to understand. The two together, although they were flawlessly courteous to each other, seemed to bring out all the rough edges each possessed. I wonder if

Jock has noticed. Or Anne or John. There's no doubt at all about Anne's fondness for Mrs. Butler. Fanny Butler visits no one on the Island as often as she visits Anne, despite that long horseback ride to Hamilton.

Rebecca smiled as she smoothed the just-finished, graceful leaf design over her knee to examine it. I'm certainly not alone in noticing how Anne's John dotes on the colorful English woman. He looks younger and even finds more than usual to talk about when she's around. Dear John. The boy's pleased, I'm sure, that such a celebrated performer praises his lovely singing voice, never fails to urge him to sing. I was quite touched the last time we were all together down at Hamilton when Mrs. Butler asked him to sing "Amazing Grace." And how compellingly he sang it! Mrs. Butler's face was a study as she listened, seeming to drink in every word.

Alone in her room, Rebecca sang softly, remembering:

> *"Amazing grace, how sweet the sound*
> *That saved a wretch like me;*
> *I once was lost, but now I'm found,*
> *Was blind, but now I see. . . ."*

Mrs. Butler's manner is not exactly familiar to us, Rebecca thought, but unless I'm very wrong, she's a woman who sees much, a deeply spiritual lady. I did think she made a most unusual comment after profusely thanking John. She spoke sincerely and from her heart to John but then looked straight at her husband as she said, "I suppose it will always amaze me that God's grace could bring such a song from the heart of a man who once made his living by transporting slaves."

Pierce Butler had said nothing, merely looked away. John was naturally pleased that Mrs. Butler knew that the lyrics to "Amazing Grace" had been written by an English clergyman named John Newton, who in his youth had been captain of a slave ship. John had given Mrs. Butler his best smile when, only half humorously, he said, "Now and then, Fanny Kemble Butler, I have a strong feeling that you and I could write a book."

I wonder, Rebecca thought, how Anne felt about that exchange.

T HREE DAYS BEFORE SHE, PIERCE, MARJORIE, AND the children were to leave St. Simons for the North, Fanny Kemble awoke at dawn to find her husband already up and gone to work. She forced back the constant pain in her heart, intent by now on learning how to find peace in the one experience they could still share—the tender, physical intimacies—his touch, his clean, sweet body, his momentary possession of her when they were alone in their room at night. Her efforts, most of them secret of late, to help his poor slaves had come between them far more starkly than even Pierce seemed willing to admit.

We will pack and leave, she thought as she bathed and dressed in a fresh black broadcloth riding habit, and although I will try, I am somehow sure that he will never again permit me to visit this breathtakingly beautiful Island or to look into the faces of his people. There is but one way to stop me from trying to alleviate their suffering, and that is to imprison me at the North. I am far from ready to go, and yet I shall not miss their begging and pleading. They have made my life a misery from dawn to dark except when I have been able to ride out into the fragrant glory of St. Simons Island's tangled, shadowy, vining, blooming wilds. Thank God I have had rough old Montreal, always chafing at his bit to thud off with me into the thickets, road or no road. She sighed. Will I ever know the rhythm of a truly English-gaited horse again?

Fanny was certainly going to ride out today, after a visit with her children and breakfast. Each Island plantation had been marked off the list she kept for courtesy visiting. Today she could do what she most enjoyed doing—make the long, hard, sunlit and shadow-streaked trek all the way to the southwestern side of the Island, where Anne and John Fraser lived in what was surely St. Simons's finest property. She found herself hoping that John Fraser might by some chance be at home. Little had been said by either of them about it, but she had no doubt that she and Mr. Fraser were kindred spirits. He too hated slavery. She had sensed it time and time again from several of his expressive looks or remarks. Certainly she had known it in her very being the night he had sung old John Newton's "Amazing Grace." There had been no further talk between them, but today she longed for at least one frank exchange because most likely they would never meet again on this earth.

Like Fanny herself, John Fraser had spent much of his life in England, where slavery had blessedly been banished. He had somehow learned how to subdue his antipathy to the evil, and of course she knew why. He simply loved his wife, Anne, enough to keep it under control. But did he love Anne more than she loved Pierce? No. John Fraser was simply older. He was a man with a strict military background, who had somehow learned how to obey without losing his true self in the process.

I could sit here like a lady and write all my tumbling thoughts to blessed Willy Maxwell, she thought, but I'm not going to do it. A kind of relieved sickness has gripped me at the prospect of being forced to leave this place—a total failure in my mission—but the sickness is not all from having failed to better the conditions of my husband's human properties. Part of it is the loathing I feel in having to say, only a few days from now, that I shall never see the wild woodland beauty again no matter how long I live.

At the crude dressing table, she brushed and pinned up her hair, settled her riding cap in place, picked up her crop left lying on the candlestand yesterday, and headed outside to whistle for Jack to bring Montreal. Jack had not been riding with her for some time. Pierce hated that new custom, too, but for nearly a month, determined to be her own person, she had ridden freely and gladly alone wherever she pleased. Pierce was not entirely unyielding. He had scolded and then given up.

WAITING ALONE IN THE YARD FOR JACK TO BRING Montreal, the intense closeness of Pierce's overpowering, ecstatic lovemaking last night filled her with more awe than even the sight of another Island dawn—clear, high with color, fringed with the kind of light that could only be matched by the perplexing light of his physical nearness.

"How can that be?" she asked aloud into the coming day. "How can we be so close and so far apart?"

Surely, surely, were Pierce to come toward her this minute, they would, they could again be one whether he touched her or not. He wasn't coming toward her, though, and he wouldn't be. Her maddening, blind, gorgeous husband was off somewhere with Bram, his driver, seeing to maximum production from his human chattel.

MONTREAL'S UNGAINLY GALLOP JOLTED HER WILDLY along one of her favorite shortcuts she'd had Jack chop through the Hampton woods around the curve in Jones Creek, toward Couper Road, which would take her onto sun-dappled Frederica Road. Horse and rider were one in their shared abandon and equally shared perplexity that both had somehow allowed themselves to be thrust into the kind of life to which neither was suited. Montreal was no more the plow horse turned lady's mount than Fanny Kemble was the submissive wife Pierce Butler seemed bent on having.

If Jack was right that "budding snakes" were being scattered under the budding spring thickets as she crashed through wild blackberry brier hoops white with bloom and crushed wide, gleaming patches of starflowers and violets, so be it. She was heading eagerly, though sadly, for what she somehow knew was going to be an important last visit with her appealing friend Anne Fraser.

As she neared Frederica Road, its great live oak sentinels forming a shadowed green canopy between her and the brightening April sky, her heart sank. Another rider was galloping toward her from the south. And then her heart leaped. It was John Fraser himself!

As their horses thundered nearer each other, both Fanny and

John waved a welcome greeting, then slowed their mounts and brought them to a halt on the quiet, otherwise empty road.

"Mrs. Butler!" John called cheerfully as he dismounted and strode to where she sat Montreal.

"Good morning, Mr. Fraser," she said. "What great, good fortune that the lone rider I was dreading turned out to be you, sir. I'm truly delighted."

She reached her hand to John, who bowed over it. "And so am I, dear lady. Actually, I was headed for Cannon's Point to consult with Mr. Couper's driver, Tom, and to find out if my wife's maid, Eve, had heard correctly on her grapevine that you and Mr. Butler are leaving soon. You can't go, of course, until you've had at least one more visit with us at Hamilton. My beloved Anne will never allow it!"

"Nevertheless, evidently we must go. I was, until this fortunate meeting, galloping straight for your plantation to bid you both a reluctant goodbye."

"Then what fine luck this is meeting you! Had I been a few minutes later, you might have paid your final respects to Anne, sent a farewell message to me, and I'd never have had the chance to ask you what I find I must ask right now."

"Oh?"

"I realize how odd that sounded, but when time is running out, some matters are urgent enough to be dealt with directly. You see, it's extremely important to me for you to know that I agree with you wholly where slavery is concerned. But the most vital thing to find out, for myself alone, is whether you guessed that I, a slave owner and plantation master, nevertheless live and work through each day totally against the grain of my own beliefs."

For an instant, Fanny almost lost her poise. He had so disarmed her, so touched her heart by his unadorned honesty, she felt at a complete loss as to how to respond aside from the two actions she dared not take as a lady—weep for joy or throw her crop into the air and shout hurray! She was not being fair to this warmhearted gentleman by making him wait. Finally she said, not caring that tears filled her eyes, "Hearing you tell me such a thing is like receiving an entire mind full of hope and beauty, John Fraser."

"Hope and beauty?"

"Both hope and beauty. Except for a particularly confidential moment now and then with your intelligent, openhearted wife, Anne, and a few frank talks with her father, I haven't encountered such honesty from anyone since the moment I set foot on the coast of Georgia."

"My father-in-law, John Couper, in his heart of hearts, disapproves of being a slave owner," John said solemnly. "Perhaps when I'm eighty, I will have found a way to live as serenely with the evil practice as he seems to do." He dropped the intensely earnest look for a half-smile. "Notice I said *perhaps*. I doubt if I would ever possess the capacity for Mr. Couper's serenity, but I do love Anne enough to have made it almost to age forty-eight as a slave owner."

Fanny took her time. Time to try to think of exactly the right thing to say—the honest thing. As boy and man, John Fraser had surely shared her own English antipathy to slavery. Anne had told her that they returned from London some fourteen years ago. For fourteen long years he had somehow found a way to give his best efforts, not only to learn how to become a planter but to remain what certainly appeared to be a whole human being while at the same time despising what he had become.

Finally she asked, "Do you know at all *how* you have done what you've done for such a long time, Mr. Fraser? Have you come to like at least the planting role in your life? I fervently hope so, because if you despise that too, you must be of all men most miserable."

"I have learned to like my work, kind lady. Thank you for caring enough to ask. I have also learned, by keeping silent except before God, at least to live with the ugly aspect of my role. I can honestly tell you that so far as I know, I have not allowed my English dislike of the institution to mar Anne's happiness. Or that of my children."

"Mr. Fraser, you *are* honest. I confess I have no idea whatever how you participate in ruling the very lives of other human beings without despising yourself, but you don't despise yourself, do you?"

He laughed a little. "Not every day. And do you believe, as I do, that Anne is truly happy in her life with me?"

"I'd say she all but worships you and is spared worshiping you only because she truly worships Almighty God. If ever a man has made a woman's life complete, it is you. We women sense these things about each other, you know."

"Yes, I do know, and that of course is why I asked."

"Was my opinion of Anne's happiness part of why you hoped to see me again?"

"No. I truly didn't mean to burden you with my query about her. Still, your response has made me proud," he said with his wonderful smile. "There is something else though. Something impertinent. Because men usually don't outlive their wives, I find I need to know how the other ladies on St. Simons Island—most of them close friends of Anne's—have received you and your ideas."

"You *do* love your wife, don't you?"

"What a relief to find you as sensitive and as highly intelligent as I suspected," he said simply. "Yes, I love her with all my heart and soul and mind and body. Should I die first, I'd want to know, if by any chance Anne does come to agree with us concerning slavery, how they might treat her. Would they understand if, by then, she should decide to free those among our people left to her? Or would they ostracize her?"

Again, Fanny Kemble sat looking down at this amazing man, who was still looking up at her with an almost pleading expression. This part of his question was the hardest of all. Then gentle, soft-spoken Mrs. Abbott came to mind. Fanny had almost forgotten that she and Mrs. Mary Abbott had discussed slavery in depth. The widow Abbott had, as had the others, taken the usual ground of justifying slavery *as long as it was administered with kindness and indulgence.*

"How well does Anne know the widow Abbott, Mr. Fraser?"

"She's older, of course, but before his death, George Abbott was our postmaster. Both have been friends of Anne's family for years. Why do you ask?"

"I found Mrs. Abbott more patient with my strong objections

to the ugly system, and once, when she told me goodbye, she said that for all she could tell, I might be right. She even told me that I could have been led down here by Providence to be the means of some great change in the condition of the poor colored people."

"Mrs. Abbott said *that?*"

"My memory is fairly accurate," Fanny answered. "Those were very nearly her words. The next day I received a most enchanting bundle of flowers sent by Mrs. Abbott—pomegranate blossoms, roses, honeysuckle. Her bouquet spoke more clearly than her words. For a time after that one visit with Mrs. Abbott, I didn't feel quite so alone here. And Mary Gould would also understand. Her young brother Horace has influenced her greatly, I believe, since he returned from his years at Yale College."

"And have you discussed slavery with my Anne?"

"Yes."

"Is that all you can tell me?"

"She listened to my arguments in a most tolerant manner. I find her, if the truth be known, the most intelligent lady on the entire Island! You and I could have that brief, knowing exchange after you so sweetly sang 'Amazing Grace' that night with her parents present because Anne had already told me how you really feel about the ugly system."

He stared up at her. "Anne told you that I still feel guilt at being a slave owner?"

"She didn't mention guilt. But she did tell me of your dislike of it. She knows far more than you realize about the high cost to you of loving her as you do."

He looked away into the tangled, honeysuckle-choked woods. His voice more earnest than ever, he said, "Loving her is so fine, so good, most days it's as though it has cost me nothing, Mrs. Butler." He reached for her hand again, bowed over it, and said in the exact manner his mother must have taught him as a boy, "Thank you for stopping to talk with me. It has meant far more than you could possibly know."

"I refuse to say goodbye, Mr. Fraser. I am on my way to spend time with your fortunate—no, truly blessed—wife, but neither do

I plan to bid her goodbye. I'm going to believe that the three of us will somehow meet again."

Then, without another word, Fanny touched Montreal with her crop and raised a cloud of sand and shell dust as she galloped out of sight down Frederica Road.

CHAPTER 68

GREETED, AS SHE GALLOPED UP THE HAMILTON lane, by Anne Fraser's shouting, waving children, Fanny returned their greeting and made what she hoped was a pretty speech of gratitude when the tomboy, called Pete, elbowed her younger brother, John Couper, out of the way and took charge of Montreal.

When she saw the boy merely step courteously to one side, Fanny asked, smiling, "You don't mind when your sister takes over like that, John Couper?"

"No ma'am. She's a good sister. She's just a tomboy and can't help it."

"And who explained that to you, son?" Fanny asked.

"Eve. My mama's Eve."

"I see. What do you think of Eve? Do you obey her and do you respect her as a human being?"

The boy's handsome face crinkled into a merry laugh. "Oh yes, ma'am! Anybody had better respect Eve or Mama will lay down the law."

Right then Anne hurried out to the veranda and down the front steps. "Welcome, Mrs. Butler," she called. "What a lovely surprise!" When young Fanny Fraser took her mother's hand, Anne said, "Fanny, I see Pete hurrying back from the stable. You and John Couper, go with her to find Eve. This is the day when Eve teaches you all how to paint the Lord God Bird."

Fanny Kemble Butler laughed. "And what, pray tell, is a Lord God Bird?"

"That's what our people call a huge, pileated woodpecker," Anne said, taking her guest's arm to lead her up the steps to the veranda, where they both took chairs. "I do hope you can stay for dinner, Mrs. Butler. My husband won't want to miss seeing you. I also hope you'll tell me the rumors of your leaving are false."

"They're quite true, Mrs. Fraser, and your husband already knows we'll be departing in two or three days. You see, he and I met on Frederica Road this very morning."

"I—I don't want you to go!" Anne blurted. "I know our weather gets unbearably hot in summer, but—" she laughed a little. "I do hate giving in to Eve's grapevine again."

"You and your Eve are unlike any other mistress and servant on this Island, Mrs. Fraser. Did you know that?"

"I'm sure we are. Much of the time I act, I'm afraid, as though I were the servant and she the mistress. And that's despite the hours my dear mother has spent trying to teach me how to handle servants."

"The only response I can make to what you've just said is to urge you to give thanks that God created you exactly as you are— open, warmhearted, compassionate."

Anne's look, Fanny thought, was puzzled. "Compassionate?" her hostess asked.

"And intelligent. Your husband, at least, knows that I consider you the most intelligent lady on St. Simons Island. This morning, when we met on the road, we had a most interesting talk. Of course, among other things, he agrees with me about you." Her smile was playful.

"Here I thought Mr. Fraser was in his south field right here at Hamilton. He was on his way, I suppose, to see my father. There are times when I think my husband looks for excuses to visit Cannon's Point."

"Who could blame him? Your father is a most remarkable man. He and I have had some fascinating discussions, and he appears, at least, to go on regarding me warmly despite our fundamental disagreements. I shall miss my visits with him. I find your mother charming, too, but I fear a bit reserved, as though she's determined to be careful that I not be allowed to choose the topic for conversation."

Fanny was relieved to see the easy smile on her new friend's lovely face. "Mama *is* a discrete, careful lady," Anne said. "Tell me, Mrs. Butler, do you sing?"

On a surprised laugh, Fanny asked, "Sing? Why, I tried when I was young, much to my own mother's quite justified annoyance, I fear. My sister is the musician in our family, along with Mother. I love to sing, though. Why on earth do you ask?"

"Because I like to play the pianoforte, and I thought this sunny day might be just right for us to make some music together."

Taken with such an unexpected idea, and curious, Fanny agreed at once and followed Anne into the Hamilton parlor, where the sun was brighter than on the vine-draped veranda.

Seated at the keyboard of her small pianoforte, tastefully inlaid with fans and bows, Anne Fraser's small, strong hands rippled off a merry passage of an old Scottish ballad Fanny remembered as "Blue Bonnet." The only lines she could recall, though, were

"He wears a blue bonnet, blue bonnet, blue bonnet;
He wears a blue bonnet—a dimple in his chin."

They both stopped to laugh. "Is that a favorite of yours, Mrs. Fraser?"

"Please, won't you call me Anne? I know you're younger than I, only twenty-nine, but please agree."

"Very well. Is 'Blue Bonnet' a favorite?"

"In a way. John once wore a blue bonnet—on our honeymoon in Scotland."

"When you visited Willy Maxwell's old castle, called Caerlaverock?"

"Yes. Would you think me presumptuous if I called you Fanny?"

"It would please me greatly. I'm so glad we both know blessed Willy, Lord Herries. He's such a good man. And certainly devoted to you, Anne. Your husband too, of course."

Fingers resting on the keyboard, Anne looked up at her. "What do you truly think of us here on St. Simons, Fanny Kemble Butler?"

For a long moment Fanny could only stare down into the open, almost eager face of this unpredictable woman. First, out of a clear blue sky—music. Now this disarming question. "What do I truly think of Islanders? Ah, I fear no one should ever dare group people into a lump. Whatever I tell you must be between us, and I promise it will be truthful. Your parents, your father in particular, I find most lovable and engaging. Surely I find him as honest and direct as his advanced years allow. Your husband and you will live in my thoughts for as long as I live, not only because of those glorious English peas and prawns and drumfish you've been sending us, but individually, I can never forget either of you." She paused. "You see, as God in Heaven is my witness, Anne, I am convinced, as I've never been convinced, that John Fraser loves you with his entire being. Today he again showed me the bottomless depths of his love for you. I also see that there is nothing in this world he would not do to ensure your *happiness*. Even when it forces him to live daily against his own beliefs. Such a man is rare indeed."

Again surprising her, Anne said nothing. Then, with one finger, after a somewhat lengthy silence, she began to pick out the simple old melody of "Drink to Me Only with Thine Eyes."

"I know," Fanny said above the melody, "that you and John Fraser have cherished that song for as long as you've loved each other."

When the melody ended, Anne murmured, "Yes, it's our song. And did any man ever sing it as John does?"

"No one I've ever heard," Fanny said softly. "His voice is as golden as his great heart. I—envy you, Anne Fraser."

Anne looked up at her and asked, "You envy me? Truthfully, I wouldn't blame any woman for envying me John's love, but you and your charming husband seem so—"

"So close? We're both rather good actors, but somehow I don't believe your mother missed the truth about our marriage."

"My mother?"

"I've seen her watching Pierce and me. Do I love him? I love him beyond reason! Does he love me? I think yes, as much as Pierce Butler is capable of loving. I confuse him often. He isn't the world's most profound gentleman, you know. In fact, if one sees beneath his social graces and startling good looks, as does your perceptive mother, he's a somewhat shallow man, selfish, insensitive to the cruelty he imposes on his poor people, defensive to an impossible degree to the stark wickedness before God of being a slaveholder. You know that is not true of your John Fraser. I know you know because you've told me of his real beliefs about the system."

After a brief silence, Anne said, "And since you're being so honest, I must tell you that our leaving the veranda on such a glorious day to come inside for music was a ruse on my part. I'd hoped to keep you off that very subject. It's troublesome for me, as you must know." She held out both hands in an almost helpless gesture. "Fanny, I've lived my entire life—forty-two years—except for our time in London, in the hourly company of Negroes whose lot has been to serve me, to serve my family. I—I don't honestly know *how* I feel about any of it."

"Do you love your servant Eve as a friend?"

Anne gave a little self-conscious laugh. "Eve believes we're friends."

"And do you?"

"I—I'm not sure. No, that's a lie. I am sure. Yes. Yes, I'd do almost anything to make Eve happy."

"Would you set her free?"

"What?"

"Would you free her? Release her from the bondage under

which she has lived every day of her life, so that she could love you
naturally in return, stay with you if she chose, sass you, laugh at
you, boss you as you attempt to boss her?"

Anne flared a little. "How did you know? She does sass me.
She also bosses me. I told you there are times when I'm not sure
whether it is Eve or I who is in charge. Don't force me to answer
such a question, because I'm not sure I could live without Eve. All
the years we were in London I was almost helpless without her.
Ask John."

"I don't need to ask anyone. Perhaps I do need to ask your
forgiveness for having been intrusive, although I've never felt the
need to apologize to any other white woman on St. Simons for
expressing my true convictions." Fanny touched her shoulder ten-
tatively. "I beg you, Anne, do not let our different views come
between us." She felt the tears well up in her eyes and made no
effort to stop them. "I fear I'll give way to one of my fits of
weeping if we go on like this. I do cry, you know. I don't remember having wept so much in my entire twenty-nine years as I have
since we've been on your Island."

Wide-eyed, Anne looked at her. "You—you cry? Why, dear
Fanny? Why do you cry—here?"

"You really don't know, do you?"

"No and I want to. Is there any way I can help? Is there real
trouble between you and your sweet husband?"

Fanny's voice broke when she tried to explain what she already
feared was the impossible: "Anne, do you never grow weary of
slaves' everlasting complaints? God knows my heart aches for every poor, sooty wretch who must drag her weakened body too soon
back to the fields after childbirth, for every outstretched hand
begging for a piece of meat or a scrap of new cloth. You're never
faced with my dilemma of being forced to try to explain to them
that I have no ownership over them. That such ownership, to me,
is *sinful* in God's eyes and in mine. That they belong to me no
more than I belong to them." Weeping overwhelmed her and she
buried her face in both hands.

"Fanny," Anne said hoarsely. "Do you actually *tell* them that?"

"I try! Oh, how I try to help them understand my convictions.

Hour after hour they troop into my house, begging me to plead with Pierce in their behalf: '*you* tell Mausa an' he fix' . . . *you* tell Mausa we too weak to chop cotton . . . *you* tell Mausa . . . *you* tell Mausa.'" Fanny was sobbing now. "Some days I cry for hours!"

Anne, still seated at the keyboard, looked up at her for a long, long time in dumbfounded silence. The look was not hostile, just perplexed. "Fanny, you actually *told* your husband's people what you just told me?"

"Of course I told them!"

"And did any of them understand what you were saying?"

Finally, cheeks still wet with tears, Fanny gave Anne a weary, hopeless look. "You don't really know, do you."

"No. But if there's anything—anything at all I could do to—"

"Yes, there is something. After this intimate talk we've had, there *is* one thing you can do. Only one thing, if you will."

"Please tell me!"

"You can play the old John Newton hymn your greathearted John sang not long ago, like a saving angel. It's a healing song. Healing words and a healing melody. You and I need—healing. That's all you can do, I now know, but I beg you to play it."

" 'Amazing Grace'?" Anne asked.

Fanny could only nod yes.

"And will you sing it for me, Fanny?"

"I'll try. But not just for you—for us both. It could turn out to be our only eternal bridge, dear, dear Anne Fraser."

If someone had tried to force Fanny Kemble at gunpoint to explain to Anne what she really meant by their only chance to find an eternal bridge between them, she could not have explained it. At least not so that lovable, seemingly openhearted Anne Couper Fraser could understand. But she could and would sing the song.

As Anne played and Fanny sang, Anne seemed not to notice that some fifteen or twenty of John Fraser's slaves began to gather to listen on the front porch just outside the open parlor window. Not a foot shuffled, no throat cleared, no one coughed. Every dark face hungrily listened, and on some faces a kind of quiet glory shone as Fanny Kemble sang:

"Amazing grace, how sweet the sound
That saved a wretch like me;
I once was lost, but now I'm found,
Was blind, but now I see. . . .
'Twas grace that taught my heart to fear,
And grace my fears relieved,
How precious did that grace appear
The hour I first believed.
Through many troubles, toils and snares,
I have already come;
'Tis grace hath brought me safe thus far,
And grace will take me home. . . ."

PART VI

APRIL 19, 1839—
JULY 19, 1839

CHAPTER 69

THREE DAYS LATER, ON FRIDAY, APRIL 19, once Eve and the children had gone off crabbing after breakfast, Anne kissed John goodbye when he and Big Boy brought her horse for the ride she suddenly had to make all the way up the Island to Cannon's Point.

Tucked neatly in Big Boy's saddlebag was a muslin sack of Anne's prize English peas, picked just minutes before and sure to please Fanny Kemble Butler, *if* she and her husband hadn't already gone North.

Her new friend had told her they would be leaving in two or three days. Anne knew, on first opening her eyes at dawn this morning, that she might well miss seeing Fanny again, but she had to try. Packing and departing always took longer than anyone planned, so all the way up Frederica Road she hoped, even prayed, that the Butlers might still be on St. Simons.

If anyone had asked Anne to explain her reasons for having to see Fanny again, she would have no plausible answer. No answer more plausible than the one she'd given dear John: "It's just a need I have. And somehow it's an urgent need."

Her parting from Fanny Kemble, within minutes of Anne's realization that the Hamilton people had been listening from the veranda as Fanny sang, had affected Anne so deeply that she had not yet been able to bring herself to talk about it, even with John. Fanny, when her clear singing voice had ended the old hymn, had said little, but she had bent to kiss the top of Anne's head. "I will pray that somehow we shall meet again, dear Anne. And that when and if we do, you and I both will be better able to share our hearts. For a reason I don't quite fathom, I *want* very much to share yours."

And then she had walked away, out of Anne's parlor, across the veranda, down the front steps, without a glance back at the huddled knot of servants still in awe of what they had heard. In a moment, sitting alone at her pianoforte, Anne recognized Fanny's shrill whistle, and no other than June brought her big mount, Montreal, from the Hamilton stable.

Had Eve been in that knot of people gathered on the porch outside the open parlor window? And had *she* run to get June? Surely, if Eve had been anywhere near, she would have come right into the parlor to listen. Or would she have done that before a visitor?

Galloping now up Frederica Road, Anne knew that she saw so little clearly. As always, she sat her very own mount, Gentleman, as though she rested in her favorite rocker. Handling Gentleman was second nature to her. She was free to think but couldn't. Totally confusing thoughts had not stopped tumbling through her mind since her last sight of the famous young English lady, who had wept so piteously and then had eased both their hearts by singing that simple, old song.

From the mount ahead, as usual, Big Boy waved. Anne waved back and noticed that they were nearing the Gould place. She had fully intended to visit Mary Gould long before this but knew exactly why she hadn't done so. Because Mary was keeping her grief over John Wylly so close inside that few people knew about it, how could anyone think to comfort her?

If I stopped now, she thought, Mary would be the same, sweet, hospitable Mary she's always been, without one mention of John Wylly's tragic death. How, how, *how* does she do it?

She had no intention of visiting the Goulds. Only one thing mattered today and that was to reach Cannon's Point, beg Papa to take her immediately across Jones Creek in her now-desperate hope that Fanny Kemble might still be there.

"ANNE, DEAR GIR-R-L," PAPA CALLED AS, WITH Big Boy's help, Anne dismounted at the side of the river road in front of her childhood home, took a muslin sack from Big Boy's huge hand, and hurried toward her father. "What good fortune brings you here, Daughter?" he asked, giving her a loving hug.

"Mrs. Butler," she gasped, breathless from the long ride and returning his hug almost from habit. "Papa, is she still across the creek at Hampton? Mrs. Butler hasn't already gone, has she?"

"Aye, she and her little family left just after dawn today, my dear. Why? I believe she said she'd paid you a farewell visit."

Anne could only stand there biting her lips, trying hard for Papa's sake not to burst into tears. "Are you sure? Are you quite sure they've really gone?"

"I crossed the creek myself to give them a proper goodbye," the aging man said, his ruddy, expressive face a study in loving concern. "Is—is something wrong? Mrs. Butler did call on you, didn't she? I'm sure she told your mother she did and that you bid each other farewell with an old song. That it was your idea for you to play and for Mrs. Butler to sing."

"That's right. I played and she sang 'Amazing Grace.' Oh Papa!" Her arms around him again, Anne broke into tears and then, as the two had done through so much of her life, almost at the same instant they began to laugh. "Look at me," she said, eyes brimming, tears still pouring down her cheeks, but also laughing.

"You look about six-years-old, lass, standing there with that muslin bag in your hand, crying and laughing. Your old father's not as alert as he once was, so could you please explain a wee something to him? Was there a pressing reason for coming?"

"Probably not," she said, her tear-streaked face sheepish. "Making that long ride, when I knew there was little hope she would still be here, makes no more sense to me than it does to you —except that now I'm close enough for you to put your arms around me and comfort me."

Obeying, as always, he did just that.

Then, composing herself a bit, Anne held up her muslin bag. "I was bringing Mrs. Butler some of my English peas," she said, and that set them both off again into gales of laughter.

SEATED TOGETHER ON THE WIDE VERANDA AROUND which they had marched through every good rainstorm that had roared and blown over Cannon's Point when Anne was young, she of course wanted to know why her mother had not come out to greet her.

"She isn't here. Nothing would do once the Butler boat left the Hampton dock but that she be rowed across Jones Creek to call on the overseer's wife, Mrs. Gowen."

"But why? Why today? Mama has always liked Mrs. Gowen; still, they've never been close. Didn't she give you any idea of why she felt it necessary to call on her today?"

Papa leaned toward her. "I'd stake my life on the fact that she did not call on Mrs. Gowen to gossip. You know how she hates wagging tongues. I am fairly sure, however, that for a reason only she knows, her visit had to do with our extraordinary new friend, Mrs. Fanny Kemble Butler."

"Papa, do you think Mama liked her?"

"Mrs. Butler and her family—even her white nursemaid— were always welcome guests here."

"I know all about Mama's social graces. I'll never be the superb hostess she's always been, but surely you have at least a small clue as to her real feelings toward Fanny."

Chuckling, he asked, "So, you're calling her Fanny now, eh?"

"We agreed to use our first names, even though I'm twelve years older than she."

After a fairly long silence, his gaze moving out over the scenic stretch of marsh and water toward the sea, he said, "There's no doubt in anyone's mind, Anne, that your friend Fanny Kemble Butler stirred people up during her brief three months or so among those of us who, most of the time, feel only blessed by our serene Island life."

"Slavery," Anne said, also looking away.

"Aye, slavery. I find myself hoping, even praying, that no matter how she ruffled others' feathers, she was of some help to John."

"My John? I know he's terribly fond of her. I know also that they talked at least once about his discomfort at being a slave owner. Papa, you and Mother taught me never to use that word *slavery*. I'm in my forties and it's still hard for me to use it!"

" 'Tis likely your mother and I were wrong in that."

"Wrong?"

She caught just a hint of a smile when he said, "It's quite possible that even your well-meaning parents may have taught you and James Hamilton and Isabella and William Audley many things that may have been mainly for the protection of Jock and Rebecca Couper and not, as we chose to believe, for your benefit."

"Don't talk in riddles. I'm not in the mood for riddles. Fanny Butler and I were more outspoken with each other than I've ever dared be with anyone else, and I found it good. It scared me some, but it made me think. Papa, what it really did was confuse me!"

"I honestly don't know your mother's reason for calling on little Mrs. Gowen today, but I do have an inkling. Rebecca may want to know—feel that in her position among other Islanders she *needs* to know—if Fanny Butler went about preaching against slavery in every St. Simons home she visited. She did show great friendliness, you know, by making fairly frequent calls on our plantation families, at least on the ladyfolk."

"I'm so, so sorry Anna Matilda's still living at Monticello. I could talk to her without any hesitation about how strangely I was drawn to Fanny. At least I think I could. Papa, I was very drawn to Mrs. Butler. I still am and"—she held up the bag of peas—

"these stupid peas were the only way I could think of to show her how I felt. She did praise my English peas, you know."

"I truly believe Mrs. Butler would have been deeply touched by your offering. I'm sure they'll stop over on Butler Island tonight. They would both have enjoyed them, I know." He reached to pat her hand resting on the arm of the Cannon's Point old porch rocker. "Mrs. Butler and I didn't see eye-to-eye on everything, but I flatter myself that she enjoyed my company as much as I enjoyed hers. Perhaps we didn't even actually disagree on much. I'm just so many years older than she, and the years have subdued my crusading nature. She's a deeply spiritual lady, and although some will think her radical—extreme—she is truly compassionate."

"Papa, you once told John that in your heart you also disapprove of owning people. Do you still?"

"Yes. In my deepest heart. Your friend Mrs. Butler knows that too. She's a fair student of English history, I'd say. Leastwise she didn't seem surprised when I told her that our Scots over here fought to keep slavery out of colonial Georgia." He smiled wistfully. "I'd have been among them had I not been employed during the American Revolution in British Florida. The old Scots tried petitioning the governor. British General Oglethorpe was also against slavery."

"Is Mama against it in her heart of hearts?"

"I hear her boat down at our Jones Creek landing. Your mama's come home." He pulled himself up out of the big rocking chair. "Why don't you ask her yourself, Daughter? Alone. I need to inspect my own vegetable garden. Maybe we can compare green peas a bit later, eh?"

"I wish you'd stay. I always say things better when you're with me." Then she held out her muslin bag. "I'm inviting myself for dinner. Ask Sans Foix if he'll please cook my English peas for us?"

WHEN HER MOTHER GREETED HER ON THE VERANDA and learned that Anne had made the long ride hoping for one more brief visit with Fanny Butler, Anne began to talk rather nervously, keenly aware now that talking to Papa had always been easier.

"Mama, I can't tell you exactly why I so hoped to see Fanny again—yes, she asked me to call her Fanny. I can't tell you because I honestly don't know what I meant to say to her. But something happened inside me while she was singing 'Amazing Grace' at my house three days ago, when she came to tell me goodbye."

"Mrs. Butler *sang* the old song?"

"Only because I asked her to. It was my idea. She's a genuine Christian, Mama. Did you know that? Tears flowed down her cheeks through three stanzas of 'Amazing Grace' and, well, something seemed to happen inside me, too. I'm afraid, though, that it only left me confused about so much."

Her mother's quiet smile put Anne on guard. She hated being on guard with Mama, but there it was again. The sense that she had better be careful. That she mustn't overstep. Still, Papa's advice rang in her ears: *Why don't you ask her yourself, Daughter?* So far as she knew, no daughter was ever closer to her mother, except perhaps Anne and her own eldest, Annie. Still, hadn't she seen signs of her hesitant self showing in Annie lately? Did Annie feel the need to be guarded with her? Had she already said so much about wanting Annie to *think* before she married Paul Demere that her own beloved daughter—her real friend—was forced to stay on guard with her? More confusion. Seeing clearly had always been important to Anne. If her unforgettable visit with Fanny Kemble Butler meant so much, why had it left her so confused?

"Mama? Way down in your own heart, do you—do you disapprove of owning people?"

She could still hear, could almost *see* her own blunt question hanging right there in the sunlit air on the Cannon's Point veranda.

"Would you—ask that again, Anne, please?"

"I don't think I need to repeat it, Mama," she said, her voice, she thought, sounding surprisingly poised. "I'm sure you heard me. I need to know for myself what you truly think about—slavery. Am I being impertinent?"

After a brief silence her mother said, "Not at all, my dear. And you're nearing your midforties, so it's past time for me to stop being evasive with you. Time for me to stop being so conscious that you're my child and I'm your mother."

Anne could only stare at her. No words came.

"I don't blame you for staring, although that's one of the things I've tried to teach you children not to do. From now on, with you at least, I'm going to try to stop being only your parent. There comes a time, or I've always believed there should come a time, when mother and daughter mature into being real friends. And so, if you'll help me remember, I intend for the day Fanny Kemble Butler left us to be marked as the day Anne Couper Fraser and her mother, Rebecca Maxwell Couper, became—friends. One woman to another."

"Mama, I needed to hear you say that, but I never dreamed—"

Her mother smiled. "You never dreamed I'd ever actually say it?"

"I never dreamed how much I needed to hear you say it. Not only because it will make talking together easier, but because I'm suddenly afraid I'm not really being my Annie's friend!"

"I hope you can feel free enough with me to explain why you fear that, but I haven't yet answered your question concerning my own feelings about owning people. If I'm to keep up my part in our friendship, I must make an effort to answer you first. And it will be an effort, because I—well, until young Mrs. Butler came among us stirring her abolitionist winds about our Island, I've never really known what I think. Your father and I have always done all we could do under the circumstances to show our people kindness and to give them adequate care. But like you, I've simply lived my life in the midst of—the system, and I suppose it's been easier not to think about it one way or the other. Your thoroughly Scottish, thoroughly Christian father dislikes it. But by now he's probably as afraid as I am to say much more than that." She took a deep breath. "Your friend Mrs. Butler rather forced us to think, though, didn't she?"

"Oh, Mama, yes! And I'm not sure I like to dwell on any of it. Do you know she told me she'd never wept so much in her entire life as while she was living down here on our beloved Georgia coast?"

"I didn't know how much she'd wept, but Mrs. Gowen—poor, shy Mrs. Gowen—actually caught her sobbing twice."

"Do you think she talked about her ideas everywhere she visited, Mama?"

"I wouldn't be surprised. Did your father tell you why I insisted on calling on Mrs. Gowen today?"

"No. Maybe you didn't need a special reason."

"Now don't go back to being careful with me, Anne, because I did have a special reason. I too thought I needed to know how many of our neighbors had been exposed to Mrs. Butler's fury. After all, she's a theatrical person. I have no doubt that every thought that shoots through that fertile brain of hers is sharpened unconsciously by her dramatic technique. Don't ask if I doubt her sincerity. I don't doubt it for an instant. We just have to do the very best we can to keep level heads in all of this. Not to go to extremes in defending ourselves or in attacking her convictions. None of us will ever forget her time with us, but we must not allow her to create problems among us. Trouble."

"Did she preach to Mrs. Gowen?"

"Evidently she stayed completely off the subject with her."

"She did?"

"The famous lady *is* highly intelligent. If anyone knows that, you do. I know she talked freely with you, Anne. In fact, she told me herself that she considered you the most intelligent woman on St. Simons Island!" Mama laughed. "Of course, on that point I could agree with her wholeheartedly."

With a half-smile, Anne said, "That probably pleases me too much. Mama, she also talked a lot about owning people to Mrs. Abbott."

"Oh?"

"Fanny told John that Mary Abbott said she thought Providence might have sent her here to better the lot of our poor colored people."

"H-m-m. Well, I just hope we can all keep level heads. The

remarkable lady incensed some of us, I'm sure, and aroused the consciences of others like the Goulds, your dear father, John, you, evidently Mrs. Abbott. I have no idea how the Demeres felt about her."

"Annie hasn't said a word to me about any of them. In fact, she isn't telling her critical mother much of anything lately."

"Your dear Annie hasn't married Paul Demere yet. Don't make the mistake I made with you. Don't make it easier for Annie to be careful with you rather than to be truthful."

As spontaneously and as lovingly as she'd ever run to hug Papa, Anne jumped up and hugged her mother. "Mama, this is too perfect! Let's both hush this minute. I'm staying to dinner, of course." Then she laughed. "And one thing I know we're having is English peas."

CHAPTER 70

ANNE DATED HER DIARY FRIDAY, MAY 10, 1839, wrote only a few lines, laid down the quill, and closed the book. She was tired of her own complaining. Today she would have to mend for the children and John, then cut out dresses for some of the children in the quarters; she was already rebelling against all of it.

"I will not write down such ungrateful thoughts," she said aloud to herself in the quiet of the big master bedroom. "If I can't be grateful that all my family are healthy, if I can't give thanks for a soft, sunny May morning like this, I'll just stop. Now where's Eve? My hair's a mess and she's the only one who can do anything with it the day after it's been washed."

It still mattered that she look her best when John rode in from his fields for dinner each afternoon. The poor darling was working so hard these days, she felt that was the least she could do to give his spirits a lift. Unlike her, he stayed cheerful. The children wouldn't know what to think if their handsome father didn't laugh with them at mealtimes. No matter how long his hours, no matter how foreign he might still feel in his heart because planting wasn't his beloved military and he had no choice but to be a slave owner, he thought of ways to keep it all hidden. Still, when his driver, Cuffy, told John in no uncertain terms yesterday that young Bob had stolen a cured ham from their smokehouse and needed to be locked up by himself for a day or so, Anne thought she'd never seen John look so desperate, so helpless. He had given Cuffy orders to lock Bob in the tiny cabin used for punishment because John allowed no whippings, but Anne knew this morning, when he first opened his eyes, that he was worrying about young Bob.

"The boy craves ham as much as I sometimes crave it," John had mumbled, only half addressing Anne as he washed and dressed for work. "What gives me the right to deprive him of it? What gives me the right to lock him up for wanting a piece of ham?"

Since Fanny Butler's visit, John had spoken a little more often about his own problems in handling their people. As with Anne, the remarkable younger woman had plainly given John more courage, but what good did the new courage do either one of them? John did not own Hamilton Plantation. It was even being called Couper Plantation by many Islanders now, because old Mr. Hamilton had been dead for so long and everyone knew that she and John were only in charge as managers of her illustrious brother James's interests. None of these thoughts had ever bothered Anne before the Butlers visited St. Simons. All of life had seemed only a fine, successful, mostly happy dream. Yet nothing had really changed. Now and then she thought John did look more tired than usual, but he worked as hard as a man could work, and he would be forty-eight in October.

Where in the world is Eve? she wondered again and went out into the upstairs hall to call her. Of course Eve appeared almost at once, and when Anne began to fuss because she couldn't get her curls to behave, the lithe, too pert, bright-skinned servant laughed at her—dared to laugh at her.

"I wish I hadn't called you now," Anne grumbled, sitting

down at her dressing table while Eve took over, a smile still flickering on her attractive face.

"Den, why you call me, Miss Anne?"

"Because no one can make my hair do what you can make it
do, and how does it happen that you, only one year younger than I,
go on looking so youthful? I vow some days you don't look a day
over thirty!"

"Dat be because Eve so happy. Dat be because ob June."

"But look at us! Look at us both in my mirror this minute.
You're forty-one years old. It just isn't fair."

"Eve got a smile on her face, though. Look at yours."

That did it. No matter how Mama had tried, Anne still did not
know how to handle Eve. And the worst part was that Eve did
always seem to know exactly how to handle Anne.

"Sh! Listen, Miss Anne!" Eve hurried to the window, then
whirled around to announce that Miss Frances Anne Wylly Fraser
was riding up their lane all by herself.

"My sister-in-law?" Of course. Who else could it be? She felt
utterly foolish, because as usual, Eve, fascinated that white people
had so many names, had used Frances's entire name as she always
did with everyone. Even the children. Only yesterday Anne had
overheard her call Anne's youngest—not yet three—Selina Tunno
Fraser. Sometimes, because of Dr. Tunno's skill and kindness to
Anne when Selina was born, Eve even called the child Selina
Doctor Tunno Fraser!

"Stop fidgeting," Eve said, putting a final touch on Anne's
bangs. "It take Big Boy time to git down from our stables an' take
Miss Frances Anne Wylly Fraser's horse. By then, you be purty as a
pitcher and downstairs waitin' for her like you oughta be."

"F RANCES A NNE , YOU ' RE A GODSEND !" A NNE
called, running down the path to meet her friend. "I was going to
do a lot of dumb things today—mend, cut out dresses for the
quarters children—all things I hate to do. Now I can talk to you

instead. Come in, come in." She took Frances's arm and looked closely at her face. "You look so solemn. Has something happened?"

"It hasn't happened yet," Frances said as they headed, arm in arm, toward the house. "But I am so angry, I had to spout off to someone outside the family. It hurts poor Mama too much even to speak of—Dr. Thomas Hazzard."

Standing with Frances on the veranda, Anne asked, "What's he done now?"

"He's going to be married tomorrow, May 11, at St. Mary's to a woman named Sarah Stewart Richardson! Does he *have* to go on rubbing salt in our wounds like that? Hasn't he done enough to us? How would you feel if James Hamilton's killer fell happily in love and got married five months after he'd murdered your brother?"

"I—I'd be—livid! But let's not stand out here in this heat. The parlor must be at least a little cooler." Showing Frances to a chair near an open window, Anne took one nearby. "How did you find out that Dr. Hazzard is being married? Are you sure? The man's still under a grand jury charge of voluntary manslaughter."

"With his connections and prominence along the whole coast, he'll never be found guilty, Anne. Mr. Gould thinks they'll declare a mistrial and acquit him. They can't even get a jury together."

"I'd still like to know who told you about his marriage."

"That sweet, kind Dr. John Tunno, so we know it's true."

"Was Dr. Tunno on St. Simons?"

"No, but he wrote to Mama, thinking it might be less difficult for her to learn it from a friend."

"He is a real friend, but do you realize that even though he did so much for me during Selina's birth, I haven't seen him since? And she'll be three this fall."

"He stays busy in Darien, but in his letter to Mama, Dr. Tunno says he and his wife are planning, if he can get away, to spend some time with the Demeres at Mulberry Grove later this summer."

While Eve served lemonade—as usual, without being asked— Anne could tell that Frances was toying with a question.

Eve had barely left the room when Frances said, "Speaking of the Demeres, Anne, I—"

"That's one question you won't need to ask," Anne interrupted. "The answer is no. My Annie hasn't said another word about whether or not she plans to marry Paul Demere. Not to her mother anyway. Dear friend, am I being foolish?"

"For not being taken with young Paul? Foolish or not, if you don't like the boy, you don't like him."

"I can't honestly say I dislike him. He's just so terribly young —three years younger than Annie—and to my mind, irresponsible and spoiled."

"How many young men on St. Simons plantations do you know who aren't spoiled?"

"Not many. Fanny Butler agreed with me when I said that so far as I'm aware, only your late brother, John, and young Horace Gould seemed not to believe that life owes them a splendid living. There used to be a touch of that in my younger brother, William Audley, but Papa is sure he's changed a lot at college. Fanny Butler blamed that spoiled nature in some Island young men on their having been waited on hand and foot all their lives—by servants who dared *not* wait on them."

Frances Anne shrugged. "She may be right. Who knows? You liked Mrs. Butler a lot, didn't you?"

"I will always like her. She's certainly different from anyone I ever knew. Did she, as Mama says, preach to you and your family about the evil of our owning people, when she paid her courtesy calls to the Village?"

Frances laughed a little for the first time since her arrival. "She tried, but you know Mama. The fact that Mrs. Butler's a British lady and with Mama's overwhelming love of anything British, Mrs. Butler stopped trying to preach. Mama was so obviously honored and flattered by her visits, I think it rather took the wind out of Mrs. Butler's sails." After a moment, while they both sipped lemonade, Frances said, "My blessed William hated slavery. He and John were brought up that way. Even though Mama still considers herself a British Loyalist, you and I are of a very different culture, Anne. Especially those of us who grew up with our own special servant. Oh Anne, I haven't brain enough to discuss any of Mrs. Butler's views today. I'm too sick over Dr. Thomas Hazzard's wedding tomorrow. What a hard-hearted man he is!"

"And won't he be bringing his bride into a lonely, hostile, isolated existence at his place here? She'll be forced to live shut away from all Island society up there at Pike's Bluff. No one even speaks to either Hazzard brother at church. It's all being dreadfully hard for poor Theodore Bartow to preach the Gospel and pray for us all to the God of love. As sweet and tenderhearted as my sister Isabella is, she says her Theodore even avoids speaking with her about the ill will in our once-united little congregation. I can't help wondering if Dr. Hazzard will dare escort his new wife to worship with the rest of us Sunday after Sunday. Frances, *why* did such a violent thing have to happen?"

On a deep, hopeless sigh, her friend answered, "I don't know. Who really knows? I go to sleep every night of my life asking God *why*. I'm sure He hears, but I find no answer. Rather late, I fear, I've come to the conclusion that in this life—on earth—there simply is no answer to tragedy. No answer and usually no warning."

WHEN JOHN RODE IN FROM HIS FIELDS FOR DINNER, Anne thought he seemed almost too relieved to see Frances Anne there. He also appeared extremely tired. When young Fanny and John Couper raced out to meet him, each holding one of their little sister Selina's hands, their father only chucked Selina under the chin when she lifted her arms, expecting, as always, that he would hoist her high above his head.

The worst teething time just past, Selina, in the seemingly bad-tempered period of proving she was nearly three, set up a yowl of protest.

"What's the matter, Selina?" Frances Anne asked, stooping down to soothe the child. "Is your father too lazy to spoil you today?"

"Pick her up, Papa," Fanny scolded.

"She'll stop that yelling when you do," John Couper said in his disarmingly mature way. "You know she's gonna yell, Papa, till you give her a ride through the air way up over your head."

Anne saw John's quick frown vanish and replace itself with a big smile. Then he stooped down until his face was level with Selina's. "Selina, Eena, baby, listen to your old father. Do you think you could bring yourself to shut your mouth long enough to listen to me for just a minute?" When the curly-haired little girl shut off the yowl instantly, everyone, including John, laughed. Then he rubbed his head, closed his eyes for an instant, and said, "Now and then, little one, your aging father gets too tired to lift such a big girl up over his head. Didn't you know that?"

Anne stopped laughing. John was not playing a game! He *was* too tired. "John, do you feel—all right, darling?"

"Sure, Mama," Fanny piped. "Papa always feels good, don't you, Papa? He's just playing with Eena. Aren't you, Papa?"

Pete and Annie were at Cannon's Point this week, so Anne did what she always did when neither of her older children was nearby. She looked to John Couper for—for what? This minute, the only thing she needed was assurance that the children's father was all right. How would her only son, not yet seven, know?

The boy's quick smile came, lighting his rosy, even-featured face, calming his mother as John Couper's smile almost always did.

"Papa's fine, Mama," he said, sensing her need far more clearly than any child his age could possibly be expected to sense it. "Say, Papa, what did you plan to do this afternoon when we're finished with dinner?"

Anne thought John looked surprised. "What did I plan to do, Son? Why?"

"Oh, just askin'."

"Well, I need to have a consultation with your Grandfather Couper, Son. Why?"

"No reason, I guess," the boy said. "I was going to offer to ride for you wherever you had to go, but I don't know how to—have a consultation."

When John laughed proudly, Anne felt relieved but vowed to keep an eye on him throughout dinner.

"You've turned into such an expert horseman, you could certainly make a long ride like that, though," John said to his sturdy-shouldered son.

"Yes, sir, I could do that. Would you like me to escort you home to the Village, Aunt Frances?"

"I'd be honored, John Couper, but since I watched your mother's good friend Mrs. Butler ride all over this Island alone, I'm not a bit afraid. I do thank you, though. Maybe another time?"

AFTER MINA'S DELICIOUS, WELL-SERVED DINNER, Anne, John, all the children, and Eve, clutching the tiny hand of little Selina, as usual, walked with Frances to the mounting block on the shady side of the lane, where Big Boy waited with the Wylly horse. Goodbyes filled the warm afternoon air and everyone waved as Frances trotted up the lane toward home.

"Stay to the cleared roads, Aunt Frances," John Couper called after her. "Snakes don't like cleared spaces much."

"Aunt Frances is no dummy," Fanny scoffed at her brother.

Then, because the older children had begged Anne to go with them to the old shed, now called the studio, where Eve was teaching them with varying degrees of success to paint pictures on pieces of wood, John kissed Anne, watched her leave with John Couper and Fanny, and headed toward the stable for his own horse, Ginger.

Then he turned around abruptly. Eve was still standing there, holding Selina's hand. Still standing there as though she'd intended him to turn around. As though she'd willed him to do it.

"Eve?" he called, ambling slowly back to where she stood. "Did you want something?"

"Yes, Mausa John. Eve need to know somepin' only you kin tell her."

"All right, what is it?"

"You be—sick?"

"Sick?"

"You be—sick?"

"Why would you ask a foolish question like that?" His laugh was strained.

"I be Miss Anne's slave, sir, but firs' I be her frien'. Effen you be sick, Eve need to know *now*. Not later. Now."

"Sometimes you're too smart for your own good. You know that, don't you?"

"Yes, sir. But ceptin' for June, dey ain' nobody anywhere I loves lak I loves Miss Anne. I gotta right to know."

"Can you keep a secret? Can I trust you, the way Miss Anne trusts you?"

"Yes, sir."

"I honestly don't think I'm sick, Eve. But I've never, never felt so tired. That's all I can tell you. I feel exhausted—almost all the time these days. If my busiest days weren't up ahead with growing time all summer, I'd take my wife and make the water trip up to Saratoga for a rest. She needs a change too."

Selina, still holding tight to Eve's hand, seemed to be taking it all in.

"What chu think, Mausa John?" Eve asked, her mellow voice almost cross. "You think Eve an' June an' Cuffy an' Mina an' all yo' other niggers can't keep dis place with you gone?"

He laughed. This time, more naturally. "I'm sure you could, Eve, but I'm the one responsible for the productivity of this plantation. I have a far deeper obligation than anyone realizes, to my wife's generous brother Mr. James Hamilton Couper. Between us —and I mean just between us—for this year, anyway, he's allowing me to receive almost full profit from Hamilton. But that's a secret. So is my tiredness. I'll be fine, Eve. Don't worry, and I charge you not to allow Miss Anne to worry for one minute!"

CHAPTER 71

INTO THE GREEN, GREEN, FLOWERY MONTH OF June, life rocked along as usual, at least outwardly, except that Anne grew more and more worried over John's increasing fatigue. For the third or fourth evening he pled too much weariness to sing when she played her pianoforte for the children. Annie was teaching the four young ones to dance, including tiny, constantly jabbering Selina, who thankfully had finally learned that she received more praise by laughing when she fell down than from setting up her customary yowl.

The second week in June, Anne had begun to make secret check marks on each page of her diary on the days when John had appeared more like his old, merry, entertaining self. On the days when he talked little and seemed distracted by the children, too weary to do more than kiss her and hold her at night, she made an X. Only she would ever know the meaning of those diary marks because she tried hard to hide her anxiety over him. On the morning of the last day of the month, her heart squeezed when there were seven more *X*'s than check marks. He had been tired more often than not!

Anne thought she noticed Annie watching her father more closely, too, and longed to talk it over with her poised, eldest daughter. Falling into easy, confidential talk with Annie had once been so natural. Not now. It had been difficult since the day Anne recognized that she actually feared her daughter's attraction to Paul Demere. Did she really fear it? If she was honest, yes, she did fear for Annie's future happiness should she remain as drawn to the young man as she had been now for over a year. Was Paul really as aloof and self-centered as Anne believed him to be? She felt certain that her daughter also longed to talk to her in their old way. Why did the girl go on avoiding it?

"You worryin' 'bout Miss Annie an' Mr. Paul agin, ain't chu?" Eve asked early in July on the hottest morning Anne could remember.

"Do you *have* to read my mind every minute?" She had snapped at Eve again, heard herself do it and had to apologize. "Sometimes I wonder if you think up ways to force me to say I'm sorry. How did you know I worried half the night that any day now Annie is going to tell us that she and Paul plan to be married?"

As usual, Eve only shrugged. "Just so you not lettin' Mausa John worry you wif bein' tired so much," Eve answered, not looking up from her task of pouring exactly the right amount of cold water into a bowl of scalding hot water for Anne's sponge bath. "You an' me's got ourselves in hotter water dan dis wif bof dem mens. Me wif June, you wif Mausa John. June, he got a sore throat las' week so he couldn't even swallow my roas' oysters. He didn't like it one bit 'cause I kep' lookin' at 'im eber minute we was bof awake. Mens don' lak to be looked at cept in one way for one reason!"

Anne sighed. "I know. But Eve, when you love the way we love our men, how can we keep from watching over them? Worrying over sore throats, swollen ankles, tiredness. How can we keep from worrying for fear something serious might be wrong?"

Eve gave her an overly patient look, the kind she often gave Selina. "We don't keep from worryin', Miss Anne. We worries. We's livin', ain' we?"

"I don't know why we're discussing John, anyway. I think he seems much more like himself lately, don't you?" Her question was almost a plea. "Don't you, Eve?"

"Yes'm."

"You know I hate that noncommittal yes'm."

"Yes'm. You wanta worry today 'bout Miss Annie an' Mister Paul Demeres."

"No, I don't want to worry about them and there's no *s* on his last name. It's Demere."

"I tell you our Miss Annie, she neber been so happy an' peaceful inside her pretty lil self as lately. Dat be a sure sign she done found her man. But you ain' gonna help lessen you bring yo'self to lak him. How you feel effen Miss Rebecca, she treat Mausa John the way you treats Mister Paul Demeres?"

"*How* do I treat him?"

"Chilly. Oh you a lady, but eber time he come in dis house, you blows cold."

"I'm not a bit cold with Mr. Demere and I'll thank you to mind your own business."

"You be my bidness an' you jus' don' lak it cause I say Miss Rebecca, she show so much kindness to Mausa John back—lemme see—twenty-three years ago when you an' him was wakin' up of a morning an' breathin' all through the day for the sake ob lovin' each other."

Because Anne, too, had thought so often lately of those exciting, early days while performing some dull chore or lying beside John at night as he slept, Eve annoyed her still more. Did she have the friend she so desperately needed these days right under her nose in Eve? Why had Mama worked so hard to teach Anne how to keep a polite distance between her and any servant, when Eve was plainly not like any of the other people either at Hamilton or at Cannon's Point? Eve was wise. Smart. Aware, sympathetic. She *knew* that Anne and John had been madly in love for twenty-three years. Not only could Eve read, she could count. Anne herself had taught her. She could count and read and draw lifelike pictures—and read Anne's mind.

Well, what was wrong about remembering those old, romantic, laughter-filled times with John when they were both still young and foolish? Eve would declare there was nothing wrong with it. That because Anne still loved him in the same heart-stopping way, how could it be anything but good? How could she possibly find a more beautiful means of passing lonely or dull hours? She couldn't. Last night, with his arm across her body in his sleep because that's where it belonged, she had almost cried with longing, then smiled to herself, remembering the drenching, slashing, wind-driven rainstorm through which they'd sung and laughed their way to Dumfries, Scotland, on their honeymoon all those years ago. How the rain had come down and how John had loved amusing her with his Scottish tales about Papa's favorite poet, Bobby Burns, and how Anne had giggled at the mere, playful act of squeezing rainwater from her long skirt and bonnet ribbons as John recited the old Burns paen called "Scotch Drink." That merry, love-filled day still lived in her memory. She still felt this minute as though they had been quite alone in that crowded public carriage.

To bring it all back even more poignantly, to get her mind off wondering if her Annie ever played and laughed like that with Paul, she had lain beside John in the dark last night and recited the Burns stanza to herself:

> "Let other poets raise a fracas
> 'Bout vines, an' wines, an' drunken Bacchus,
> An' crabbit names an' stories wrack us
> An' grate our lug—
> I sing the juice Scotch bear can mak' us,
> In glass or jug. . . ."

"You thinkin' back, Miss Anne?" Eve asked, shaking out Anne's blue day skirt because she knew it was John's favorite. "Dat be good. You lookin' more lak you now. Mus' be thinkin' back to some good old times."

"Yes, I was, Eve. The kind of good times I long for my Annie to have for remembering someday when she's no longer young. Oh, I don't want to be a stuffy, chilly mother! I'm—*afraid* for her to marry Paul Demere. And don't ask me why. I just don't think he's good enough for Annie."

"Mausa John don' worry none. He lak 'im. He keep tellin' you the Demeres is a fine family."

"They are! They are, but—but this is Annie we're talking about. Annie, my firstborn." Tears stung her eyes suddenly and she heard herself almost cry out, "Help me, Eve! Help me. . . ."

CHAPTER 72

ON WEDNESDAY OF THE THIRD WEEK IN JULY, John, after swapping funny stories with June and giving him hoeing instructions to pass along to the Hamilton driver, Cuffy, mounted Ginger and walked her slowly toward the river bluff.

The last thing he intended was for Anne to see him ride off alone away from the house, when it was so near dinnertime. He therefore turned Ginger north, then trotted her past a thick stand of marsh myrtle and scrub oaks to a spot several yards from his carriage lane, until he was certain he could not be seen from any window of the Big House. Because Ginger had carried him for so long, knew him so well, the mare slowed again to a walk on her own, took him slowly and carefully toward the nearest spread of shade above the river, then stopped.

"Good girl," John said hoarsely, and for several minutes, until most of the shortness of breath plaguing him lately had passed, he sat the animal, not daring to dismount. Weeks ago he had stopped chasing John Couper or Fanny up the stairs as he'd always done, growling like a bear; he had experienced times of deep fatigue, but he had never felt afraid as now. Not once in his forty-seven years had he felt this kind of fear. Not in the nerve-racking minutes preceding battle. Not even in the thick of combat back in his days in the Royal Marines. Fear was foreign to him except where losing Anne was concerned. He had known varying degrees of choking fear each time she had given birth to one of their five children. Giving up the one accomplishment he held most dear, his officer's commission in the Royal Marines—moving to Georgia—had been possible only because he knew he could find no way to live without Anne, without Anne near enough to touch.

He had honestly been afraid of failure in his efforts to become a planter. Still, what he was experiencing now was different. Today he feared dying. Not actual death itself. He had fought through too many bloody battles for that. What he feared this minute was leaving Anne! No father adored his children more than he, but finally, the one thing he knew he could not endure was never being able to open his eyes again to see or feel Anne beside him.

For this black, desperate, trembling moment, only two people were alive in his world—he and Anne. He could almost hear his heart pounding; its irregular beat shook him. He remembered his father's telling him once that he, James Fraser, often willed his dizziness to stop. Willed his old heart to right itself. Father had died of heart failure. William's heart stopped in faraway New York. William and Father both lay now in Christ Churchyard.

"If Father could will his heart to right itself, so can I," he said aloud in a harsh whisper. Ginger's long, beautiful head switched back as though to look at him. She whinnied softly, telling him she was there. Then slowly, cautiously, picking her way carefully through the stubble and underbrush, she began to walk as smoothly as possible back toward the carriage lane. He gripped the reins, forcing himself to stay upright in the saddle by the pressure of his knees against Ginger's sides. Together they reached not just the hitching post, where he usually stopped, but with no help from him, Ginger took him all the way to the front porch, where his daughter Annie sat waiting.

John made himself smile at her, tried to raise his hand in

greeting. That small effort brought a return of the rapid, short breathing.

"Papa!" Annie had run to him, was steadying him in the saddle. "Don't try to dismount, Papa, please," she ordered. "You look so—pale!" Her shrill cry of "Mama!" left him feeling still more helpless. He wanted Anne protected.

"No, Daughter," he said, hearing the weakness in his own voice. "No, get help from—June. From Eve. Call John Couper. Get someone strong enough to help me to the ground and—and—"

At that moment Annie thanked God in an earnest, audible whisper and began to run toward the unmistakable sound of a clopping horse and the rattle of a flying buggy. "Paul!" she shouted. "Paul, hurry, please! Papa needs help!"

The buggy came to a stop and in what to John seemed only seconds, young, dapper Paul Demere had somehow gotten him to the ground and was leading him by one arm, Annie the other, upstairs to the master bedroom.

H IS BREATH COMING SO RAPIDLY HE STRUGGLED with each effort, John pushed himself bolt upright in the bed when he heard Anne scream.

"John, no! No, no!"

He could hear every move anyone made in the room, but at the same time they seemed far away, except for Anne's shrill, panic-stricken screams. There had to be some way to calm her. He had always found a way before.

"What happened, Annie?" Anne breathed. "What's Paul doing here? How did Paul know your father needed help?"

"Anne . . . Anne," John struggled to keep his voice light. He failed.

"What, dearest? What, John? What hurts you, my darling? Your face is white as chalk. You can't get your breath! What hurts you?"

"Nothing. Nothing at all," he mumbled. "You're—you're

blathering, Anne." Teasing wasn't going to work this time. "Paul?"

"Yes, sir. I'm right here. But I'm going to borrow your mare, if you don't mind, and ride home for Dr. John Tunno. He's visiting us at Mulberry Grove this month. I—I did come especially to have a talk with you, Mr. Fraser, but you need a doctor far more."

When John opened his eyes, he saw Paul lean down to give Annie a quick kiss and then Anne's voice was commanding Paul to go. "You're right, Paul," she almost shouted. "He—he must have a doctor! Thank you. I'll be forever grateful if you'll hurry right back with blessed Dr. Tunno. He'll know better than anyone exactly what to do for—my husband. Go, Paul Demere!" In her panic she even clapped her hands sharply as though Paul were a child. "Go *now,* do you hear me?"

SHE AND JOHN WERE NOT ALONE IN THEIR ROOM, Anne knew, but for some uncertain, unmeasurable length of time, she couldn't look around to see exactly who else stood there—in the shadows, away from the bed where he lay. Their bed. The bed that belonged, by dint of ecstasy and faithfulness and tears and laughter and God and love, only to the two of them.

It must have been almost dinnertime when he had come home, when Annie and Paul had somehow found him, when Paul had somehow just suddenly been there to help—to ride for Dr. Tunno.

Eve, she thought, where is Eve? There were no young children in the room, so Eve must not be there either. She's got them outside somewhere, maybe painting pictures in the old shed. Such chaotic thoughts roared inside her head. I need Eve here with me, not the children. Then slowly, for the first time since she'd run into the room screaming, she looked around her.

"I'm here, Mama," Pete said, standing straight in one dark corner. "I believe Papa's a lot better, don't you?"

"I'm here too, Mama," Annie whispered. "Papa's resting very well. Eve and the little children are out in the shed. Eve said to tell you that she'd send John Couper to find June, so he could keep them outside if you needed her here with you. If you need Eve for anything, just tell me, Mama."

"Yes," Anne said. "Yes, Annie, I'll tell you. And yes, Pete, I—I have to believe Papa's a lot better now. Dr. Tunno should be here from Mulberry Grove in an hour or so and then—and then everything will be all right."

"Do you suppose Papa ate something that made him sick?" Pete asked.

"Don't you dare let Mina hear you say a thing like that, Pete," Anne scolded, eyes fixed on John's face again. John's pale, handsome, quiet face. "John? Darling, I need terribly to—see your eyes. Can you—can you open your eyes, dearest one?"

He smiled first—his old, heart-lifting smile, broad enough so that she could see the strong, even, white teeth. "For you, beautiful Anne," he whispered, "I can do anything. Just—anything." When his eyes opened, he was looking directly at her with more love than any other man's eyes ever held for any woman. "I say, Anne?"

"Yes, dearest one?"

"Why do you think young Paul Demere wanted—to talk with me? Didn't—he say he'd hoped for a talk? Is Annie here in our room?"

"I'm here, Papa," Annie said. Her gentle voice broke with tenderness and caring as she took a step toward him. "Can't you guess why Paul came?"

"If I tried very hard, Annie, I'll bet I could guess. Wanta bet?"

Annie forced a laugh. "No. You and I know anyway, Papa."

"I'll wager—your beautiful—mother knows too," John said.

For all the endless time since she'd rushed into their room, Anne had been standing beside the bed. Now, when no adequate words came, she dropped to sit on it and threw both arms around John. "There," she murmured. "Isn't that better? Isn't that much better, beloved?"

"Much," he said and closed his eyes again. For a long time no one spoke, and Anne went on holding him, holding the wonderful head and shoulders—warm and living—close, close, close. "I'll— I'll hold you again in—just a while, dearest Anne, but because I know God is here I want to say—before God and our sweet Annie

—that I also know her mother wants *this* for her, too. For her and Paul. Tell her, Anne. Tell our firstborn."

His cheek, against which hers rested, was so warm, smelled so of the sunshine in which he'd worked too hard, Anne could not bring herself to lift her head. She could only hope that Annie was close enough to hear when she said, "We *do* want this kind of goodness and wonder—for Annie. Yes, John, we do. Oh, we do!"

From across the spacious room Annie's voice came in the silence that followed her mother's words. "Thank you, Papa. Forever and ever, I thank you. And Mama, dearest Mama, thank you, too."

ALMOST MIRACULOUSLY, PAUL HAD DR. JOHN Tunno there in a little less than an hour. Anne did poorly in thanking Paul for his kindness, but she tried. "I owe you so much, young man," she said as she waited with him, Annie, Pete, and John Couper in the hall outside the room where Dr. Tunno was examining John.

"Not at all, Mrs. Fraser," Paul said, looking as aloof as ever. "I happen to love your daughter Annie, you know. He is her father. There was really no trick to it, actually. I simply had one of our horses saddled for the good doctor and rode with him on Ginger. Dr. Tunno's a splendid horseman. Annie tells me your husband, in his inimitable way, gave us his blessing," Paul added with an almost impish smile. "And that he finagled you into giving yours too."

She'd misjudged Paul Demere. She still didn't like the boy, found him as condescending as ever, but if her parents had tried to teach her anything, it was not to judge anyone by looks and manner alone. She had judged Paul by both. "Yes, Paul. I—I also give you both my blessing," she said firmly.

"Just as soon as Papa's well again, we're going to be married, Mama," Annie whispered. "Do you think Dr. Tunno will be out of Papa's sickroom soon?"

It could not be called Papa's sickroom, Anne thought angrily. She wouldn't allow even Annie to call it that! She must have looked angry, because from the shadows at the far end of the upstairs hall where they'd allowed John Couper to join them, Eve came quickly toward her.

"It's all right, Eve," she said, sensing that Eve had caught her anger. "I'm going to be all right. Don't worry. I'm trying so hard." Abruptly, she threw herself into Eve's arms, something she had no memory of ever doing before. "Oh Eve, you'd understand if you could just imagine that it's—June lying in there so ill."

As Eve, without speaking, held her mistress as though she were a child, the bedroom door opened and Dr. Tunno stepped into the hallway.

"He's a very sick man, Mrs. Fraser. But he's strong in his body. Very strong in his spirit. Seems determined to make it for your sake. For the children. I'm going to need an able man to help me with my treatment. Your husband has what most call dropsy. It's his heart. He tells me there's a history of heart trouble in his family."

Anne jerked away from Eve's arms. "No," she snapped. "John, I know, has always been very much like his dear mother, and I'm sure she—she did *not* die of heart trouble!"

Dr. Tunno merely patted her shoulder and said, "I'll need to apply alternate tourniquets—cut off the blood flow from three extremities at a time in the hopes of preventing blood clots."

"No!"

"Hush, Miss Anne," Eve ordered.

"I'll bleed him, of course, so I'll need—"

"No! I forbid it, Dr. Tunno! I was so relieved that you were right here on St. Simons because you're the kindest, most skilled doctor anywhere, but I forbid you to—bleed him!"

"That's Dr. Tunno's decision, Mama," Annie pleaded. "Please don't make a fuss. Please, I beg you! It's for Papa's good. Paul's here. He can help."

The look Anne gave Eve was all desperation. Neither of them spoke. Then, when Eve took one step toward her, Anne, her pale, tear-filled eyes begging for help, said, "Get June, Eve! I—I want your June helping Dr. Tunno do—whatever he's going to do to—John."

"I'll find June, Mama," John Couper said. "I'll ride Papa's Ginger. When I come back, June will be with me."

John Couper's young, strong boy's voice—the tone of it, the strength in it—seemed to stiffen Anne's spine. She could feel her own body straighten. In some obscure, unexplainable way, her heart righted itself a little too. Their own son, John Couper, had just touched the innermost core of her being in a way only his father had ever touched it.

He wouldn't be seven until December, but Annie would be leaving her, so along with Eve, from now on she would be counting mainly on John Couper.

His little boots were already pounding down the stairs and when she heard the front door slam, she knew somehow that she could go on walking around, breathing, being the children's mother and John's wife, because from their singular love had come this boy.

CHAPTER 73

E VERYONE WHO VISITED H AMILTON, AND COULD
stay long enough to watch the sunset, vowed there had never been
a more glorious sight. Of course elegant old Mr. James Hamilton
had built the Big House to face the Frederica River, so that only
the thick, spiky border of yuccas and low, plump stands of marsh
and sea myrtle—its fall blossoms white puffs—stood between the
house and the water flowing through the marshes. Above and
across the wide sky, except on rainy, cloudy evenings, was spread
God's own pallet of color: brilliant and soft streakings, great
sweeps and mountains of clouds trailing their gold and bronze and
rose and yellow tints as though painted by divine fingers only
for the wonder and awe of those blessed enough to be there to
see.

For probably an hour or more, Anne had sat on her river
porch, Eve fanning her, stirring a bit of cool river breeze, saying
nothing unless Anne spoke to her. Fanny Kemble Butler, whose
awe at the Hamilton sunset had left Anne with an unforgettable

memory of the woman's truly spiritual nature, had been one of the few friends who seemed strong enough just to look and not to speak in the presence of such evening wonder. "Isn't it remarkable, Anne," Fanny had said just before she rode away, "how few human beings can endure—silence together?"

It was remarkable, Anne agreed then and remembered it now because she and Eve had always been able to be quiet together, both knowing exactly when to invite silence.

"It must be getting late," Anne said, her voice flat and almost lifeless. "Don't let your arm get too tired fanning."

"Do it feel good to you?" Eve asked, still waving the palmetto fan June had made just for cooling Miss Anne.

"Yes, thank you. Is June still—upstairs with Dr. Tunno?"

"No. De doctor, he done finished what he need June to help wif, but June, he be ridin' back in soon. You done forgot that him an' Miss Annie and Mr. Paul took Fanny an' lil Selina an' Pete up to stay wif Mausa Couper an' Miss Rebecca, so's you don' hab to think none 'bout dem."

"Oh yes, yes. I remember now. John Couper wouldn't hear of leaving, though, would he? I—remember that too. Where is he, Eve?"

"John Couper be wif Mausa John upstairs. What eber Dr. Tunno an' June do to Mausa John, he be a lot easier now."

"How do you know that? You've been right here with me."

"You mus' hab dropped off to sleep, Miss Anne, but John Couper, he been downstairs twice to give me a sign through the parlor window."

"Of course I didn't sleep! How could I?"

"Maybe not. But de boy, he tippytoe down to let us know his papa, he restin' good now. Kind ob dozin' off an' on when them two ain' talkin' to each other, John Couper say. De doctor, he takin' a rest too, in Miss Annie's bedroom. He plannin' to stay all night wif Mausa John."

Anne literally jumped in her chair to an upright position. *"What?* Eve, that must mean he's—he's very worried. Are you sure?"

"Dat what he tol' June, but he also stayin' so's you won' worry so much. De doctor say you got to sleep some too. He say this be de —waitin' time."

"Eve, if John can talk to our son, he can talk to me." Out of her rocker now, she started for the wide front door. "I'm going up there. John needs *me.*" Tears began to stream down her cheeks. "I thought a while ago that I had somehow turned a corner, that I'd found a way to—to keep on going for the children's sake, for John's sake, but I—I haven't, Eve."

"You ain't gonna climb dem steps by yo'self!"

Eve supported her into the house and up the wide stair in silence. When they reached the closed door to John's room, she gave her mistress a little shake. "Eve be right outside dis door. Don' you forget. I knows you gotta—be wif 'im, but I be right here."

"Dare I—send John Couper out here too, Eve?" Anne asked, as helpless as any child. "Will I hurt his feelings if I—if I tell him I need to be—alone with his father?"

Eve gave her a smile that again stiffened her resolve, again gave her an unexplainable confidence that somehow she could do whatever there would be to do once she was in their room again, alone with her beloved.

"You won' hab to tell John Couper nothin'," Eve whispered firmly. "Jus' walk on in an' you see Eve's right."

GOD'S FACE COULD BE IN A SMILE AS SURELY AS IT was everywhere in the sunset. The look on her small, sturdy son's face when she went softly into the shadowy room was proof of it.

"I'll be right outside with Eve, Mama," John Couper said. "Papa's resting just fine now. A few minutes ago, he even did his best to tell me how proud he is of my horsemanship."

The door closed almost soundlessly behind the boy, and Anne was once more blessedly alone with John. For an instant she stood rooted in the middle of the darkening room. Darkness does gather, she thought irrelevantly. *It gathers just the way you gather a piece of silk.*

Because of the heat, he was lying uncovered on their bed, the tall, familiar length of him motionless. His white, suddenly thin face made her think of a picture in one of her old storybooks of a Greek god—the straight, fine nose more prominent than she ever remembered, the perfect mouth parted slightly. His eyes were closed, and for the first time she noticed blue veins in his eyelids.

"I—I knew you'd—be here soon, beautiful Anne," he whispered without opening his eyes.

A kind of strangeness kept her from rushing to the bed, from throwing herself down beside him where she had always belonged. Instead, she heard the familiar squeaks in the floor under their handsome peacock-design carpet as she crept toward him—one hand out involuntarily. Still without opening his eyes, he reached for that extended hand.

"How did you know my hand was—right there?" she asked, her voice scarcely audible.

"I've—always known, haven't I?"

And then his eyes opened, and he gave her the smile that had turned her blood to water from the first moment they exchanged looks at Louisa Shaw's Dungeness on Cumberland Island those long, long years ago. The moment that now seemed to have happened only yesterday.

The hand to which she clung with both of hers was hot and bore a small white bandage. Dr. Tunno had bled him! *Dear God*, she thought, *this is John, this dear, silky body I love. This must not be happening! John* has *to get better. He has to get well. He's mine. He's my husband! He's—dear God, he's* John.

Aloud, she said, "You—you're better, John Couper says. And oh dearest, we can count on John Couper!"

"Anne?"

"Could I kiss you first?" she whispered. "Could I kiss you before you say one more word to me?"

The smile came again, a bit weaker than the earlier one. "That's—exactly what I was going to—ask you to do, wife."

His lips weren't John's. They were hot and dry and rough. And for the first time in all the years of their love, he couldn't really kiss her back.

When she moved away to look closely at him, with another courageous smile he murmured, "I'll—do better—the next time."

"And there *will* be lots of next times, sweet, wonderful John!"

Seconds after she heard the door open, Dr. Tunno lifted her to her feet and asked her to wait outside. "Only for a little while," he said calmly. "I won't keep you waiting too long. I just need to listen to his heart again. He may need a drop more tincture of digitalis. Please, Mrs. Fraser?"

Even Dr. Tunno didn't understand, she thought, hesitating for a few seconds before moving toward the open door. "I'm sorry, Doctor, but I—I can't leave now. Why must I go just for you to listen to my husband's heart?"

"Because I've asked you to, dear lady."

A hand grasped Anne's arm and pulled her firmly from the room and into the upstairs hall. It was Eve.

"You'd have to do this for me, Miss Anne, effen dat be June layin' on dat bed. You send for Doctor Tunno. You mind him."

"You're right, of course," Anne said, after Eve had reached to close the door again.

"I shouldn't have done that. I don't know half what I'm doing, I guess."

"What you needs to do is rest some."

"I couldn't rest!"

"Mausa John—an' the churn, dey needs you a lot more—later on maybe."

Fresh panic swept over Anne. "Why? Why on earth would you say such a thing, Eve?"

"Ain't no special reason. You jus' look lak you gonna drop ober. You b'lieve what I say?"

"Believe you? Of course I believe you. At least most of the time."

"Effen I vows to come get chu in jus' a few minutes, will you stretch yo' po' saggin' body out on John Couper's bed 'cross de hall an' jus' be quiet till I come back? It's almost dark outside. Mausa John, he be callin' fo' you to git yo'self back in his room in no time."

"Do you—do you really think he will?" Anne asked, grasping eagerly at any straw Eve held out to her. "Where is John Couper?"

"He say he goin' out by de river to think."

"Oh, poor little boy!"

"Come on now. Eve bed you down an' cover you up, jus' fo' a minute or two."

ONLY A FEW MINUTES WENT BY BEFORE ANNE AP-peared again at the door. Three times, within an hour, Eve sent her back to rest. Then, a longer time passed. Eve sat waiting on a straight chair, listening to the big downstairs clock tick, strike the quarter hour, the half hour. Eight o'clock, eight-thirty. She felt grown to the chair in the hall outside John Couper's small bed-room, while the clock struck nine and then ten. She could hear her own stomach growl from hunger. Neither she nor Miss Anne had eaten a bite of anything since morning. Mina would have left bread and rolls and jelly and milk in the kitchen, but wild horses couldn't have dragged Eve away from the chair now, not even long enough to run outside to the kitchen and hurry right back with a bite of food for both of them for when Miss Anne finally woke up. Was little John Couper still out by the river in the dark by himself? Eve had prayed to Jesus that Miss Anne would sleep, but without much faith that she would.

"So tuckered out, so full ob sorrows, so skeered, she drop off," Eve said softly to herself. Purposely, she had left the door to John Couper's room ajar. Her chair stood where she could keep an eye on her mistress every minute. Eve's own eyes were heavy, sandy. She dared not sleep. Time had never dragged by like this that she could remember. Why, she'd asked herself a hundred times, was Dr. Tunno still in John's room? He'd promised Miss Anne not to keep her waiting. Lord Jesus, Eve breathed. Lord Jesus, we's all leanin' hard, *hard*.

Quietly but quickly, the door to the sickroom opened, and at last there stood Dr. John Tunno, shoulders drooping, head down.

"Doctor?" Eve could scarcely hear her own voice.

"Is Mrs. Fraser resting?" the slender, weary man asked.

"Yes, sir." Eve jerked her head toward John Couper's room. "She be in dere. You want I should get her?"

Tunno straightened his back, looked at the ceiling, then down at the hall floor. Finally he said, "Mr. Fraser is—dead."

"Sh! Dat ain' no way fo' her to find out, sir!" Then she whispered, "Mausa John—be *dead?*"

Tunno nodded. "Should I be the one to tell Mrs. Fraser? Or should you?"

Anne's splintered sob shattered the quiet, night silence.

"Oh Lord Jesus," Eve moaned. "She done ober hear you!" And then Eve all but flew into John Couper's room and tried to get Anne's slippers on her bare feet, with no luck. "Miss Anne! Miss Anne!"

Her mistress, barefoot and dragging her thin summer robe over a chemise, was running down the hall, not even seeing Dr. Tunno standing there, Eve knew. Crying out John's name, she slipped on a small carpet, lost her balance, then regained it as she ran like a scared child into their bedroom.

"John! *John!*" There was a pleading keen in Miss Anne's voice Eve had never heard before.

"Eve be here, Miss Anne. Eve be—right chere. Calm yo'self. Try to calm yo'self jus' a little."

As though no one were in the room or even in the house but Mausa John, Miss Anne kept crying out, "John, don't leave me! Wait for me. Dearest, you can't—just leave me—like this! I haven't—I haven't told you—goodbye—or anything!"

CHAPTER 74

WHEN DR. TUNNO CLOSED THE FRONT DOOR DOWN-stairs an hour or so later, Eve supposed he'd been out to the kitchen for something to eat. Had he seen John Couper anywhere outside? All the children, except Miss Annie, were, in Eve's mind, her responsibility. But how could she be in two places at once? She took the care of her mistress's young ones to heart; still, even they held second place to Miss Anne.

In the chair outside the closed door to the master bedroom, she heard the doctor's slow, weary footsteps mount the stairs and sat waiting for him. "You done see young Mausa John Couper when you be outside, Doctor, sir?" she asked.

"No, I didn't see the boy anywhere, but I did hear a horse gallop off about an hour ago—maybe more."

"You hear a horse? I be sure I stayed awake! How a horse kin leave dis place wifout me hearin'? Oh Jesus, you don' think dat boy ride off by hisself, do you?"

"Yes I do, Eve. And I'd wager almost anything that he's most of the way to Cannon's Point by now. I've been around a lot of youngsters, but none quite like John Couper."

"In de dark? He jus' a lil boy! Not seben year old."

"But plenty old enough to know how close his mother is to her parents. I have no way of knowing this, but I'm sure the lad took a pine torch and rode to Cannon's Point with word of his father's death. His mother will need her parents. And Eve, you need to rest at least some."

When she flared at the doctor, she put herself in mind of Miss Anne. "I ain' sick! You ain' got no right to tell Eve what to do wif Miss Anne in de darkest shadow she eber been in."

"Very well. But I also need to go to Cannon's Point to explain everything to the Coupers. Could you get a horse saddled for me right away? Is your husband anywhere around?"

Eve stood to her full height. "June be near nuff dis minute, sir, so all I hab to do is give 'im a short whistle off de front porch an' he come runnin'. I done tol' 'im to stay close. June hab Mausa John's Ginger saddled ready fo' you to ride anytime you ready, lessen de boy done take Ginger hisself. But effen I leave my place here in dis hall to git June, you stay put. Miss Anne, she might need help ob some kind."

"I promise. I'll take your chair, Eve. Mrs. Fraser's blessed to have you."

Without another word, Eve ran down the stairs as softly as possible, wanting nothing to disturb Miss Anne's last minutes alone with Mausa John. From the veranda, she whistled for her own man.

But before she told him to saddle a horse for Dr. Tunno, she threw both arms around June and wept as though her own heart had just broken. It had.

"Eve, Eve, June be right chere," he murmured, holding her, his wide hand caressing her back. "You an' me, we knows how Miss Anne mus' feel now." Pulling her still closer, he whispered, "Dear Jesus, when I dies, put somebody close to my girl to hold 'er steady!"

Eve pulled away. "Hush! Don' you dare die. I be here to calm

Miss Anne, but dey ain' another nigger anywhere on S'n Simons could calm Eve if June let me go de way Mausa John let poor Miss Anne go!"

"But girl, he don' mean to let 'er go. A man can't help it when his time come to die."

In charge of herself again, Eve pushed him away, ordering him to saddle Ginger for Dr. Tunno.

"Huh-uh. Not Ginger. De boy done get me to saddle his papa's horse for him to ride to Mausa Couper's place."

Hands on her hips, Eve whispered sharply, still not wanting to disturb Miss Anne, "You be de one dat sent dat lil fella off by hisself in the dark to ride all dat way?"

"He be set on goin'. It be de bes' thing for him to hab our bes' horse an' a good, pitchy pine knot to see by. It be a dark night! What chu think, woman? Young Mausa John Couper kin ride!"

With no notion of staying away from Miss Anne one minute longer, Eve whirled and hurried back into the house, up the stairs, and took back her chair from Dr. Tunno. "June be saddlin' yo' horse, sir." She was still whispering. "It be good you ride to Cannon's Point, cause Mausa Couper got to git his bes' carpenter to buildin' poor Mausa John's coffin. We—we got to bury him tomorrow wif all dis heat hangin' on into de night lak dis!"

"Kindly tell Mrs. Fraser that if it's at all possible, I'll be back here with her father late this afternoon. That should give the Cannon's Point carpenter—"

"His name be Margin. Mausa James Gould teach him years ago."

"That should give Margin just enough time to build a good coffin and allow Mr. Jock Couper, the Fraser children, and me to bring it back down here in a wagon before dark this evening. And Eve, in case Mrs. Fraser needs some, I left smelling salts on the table beside the bed where her husband's body lies. You'll get someone to help you bathe and lay him out, I'm sure. Be sure to get some of the other women to help you. I know you're exhausted, too."

"I tell you who help me, sir. *She* help me! Miss Anne won' let no stranger lay a finger on her loved one, Mausa John." She lifted her chin almost imperceptibly. "Eve not be a stranger to him or to her."

BY NOON, WITH EVE'S MOSTLY SILENT BUT ATTEN-tive help, Anne had slowly, carefully, bathed the dear body. She also trimmed John's short, brown hair just a bit, stepping back to look every minute or so, as though the two were dressing to attend a fancy ball. Then, after she had sent Eve downstairs for a pitcher of hot water, Anne shaved him herself, touching the cleft in his strong chin again and then again.

"Men don't much like for anyone else to shave them, I've heard," Anne said as she worked, her voice almost steady. There was no peace in it, but she was calm. "I'm able to do all this, Eve, in case you're wondering, because it helps me to cross over to—to that strange, new place where I'll—have to live from now on. You see, it's very important that there are still some things I can do for him."

"Yes'm."

For just an instant Anne looked up from the still, motionless, half-lathered face straight at Eve. "I could have waited for Annie to come home to help me. I could have sent for June. I—wanted you. So don't just say yes'm."

"I knows you wanted only me, Miss Anne. An' I won' say yes'm agin."

Going ahead with the shaving, Anne, a half-smile on her face, said, as though she and Eve were planning a nice surprise for John, "Now, hanging in our wardrobe over there—probably way back in the far corner—you'll find his old military uniform, the one he wore so proudly as a British Marine officer. White trousers, red jacket with gold buttons. How he loved that uniform! And his black Hessian boots. Oh, he wore them so elegantly—gleaming with shine always." She wiped a blob of lather from John's side-burns. "Oh, Eve, I just realized we won't be able, I'm sure, to—to get his boots on. Look at his poor, swollen feet and ankles! The dropsy did that, Dr. Tunno said. Oh dear. He always had such slender, trim feet and ankles. But get the uniform now, please? I know it seems crazy, but I'd like to look at it for a while."

When she caught Eve staring at her, almost unbelieving, she added firmly, "Eve, I don't understand the way I am any more than you do, but so far, God is giving me all the grace I need. Get the white trousers and the red jacket. It's been years since he wore his uniform, but he's as muscular and trim today as the first day I laid eyes on him. The boots won't fit anymore, but his dress uniform will."

A MIDAFTERNOON RAIN HAD STOPPED AFTER AN hour or so, and the sky was clearing itself for what Anne feared would be a sunset too beautiful to bear alone.

But she *was* alone now, feeling tiny and insignificant in one of the big rockers on the river veranda. She was alone by choice. Even Eve, at Anne's insistence, had agreed to rest some in her own cabin. During the hollow, wooden hours while Anne waited for Dr. Tunno, her father, and her children to get there from Cannon's Point, the sky brightened to such a degree that she dreaded the moment when full sunlight would again bring the shadows back, spreading them across her green, tended yard. Where had the shadows gone while the sky was overcast and rainy?

Shadows and sun-streaks were as much a part of life on St. Simons as her family, as much a part of Island life as wrens and flycatchers and nonpareils and Lord God Birds and vines and moss and woods tangles. Anne had always, always loved sun-streaks and shadows, had waited for them both to return after a rain. Now, alone, she found herself fearing shadows. Dreading them. What would she do still later today? Later, after Papa and the children got there, so that the Hamilton Big House would no longer be so still and empty, when all the sun-streaks would go and the shadows would thicken into her first darkness alone. She needn't face that now, she told herself. Not yet, anyway. And as though looking at a painting, she began to picture a Lawrence *sunrise*—and somehow felt her heart lift a bit.

A glance at her gold watch on its ribbon around her neck told her it was already past time for John to have ridden in from his fields. He loved sharing their Hamilton sunsets so much, he seldom worked past their peaks of color. He also knew that she longed for him at sunset and John was her lover, so unless there was an emergency, he was always there.

A dry sob caught in her throat. She ached for a return of the tears that had flowed so freely, they'd wet John's face during their time alone before she and Eve began to bathe him. No tears would come now, and for a few moments, knowing how swiftly the time would fly once her family arrived, she reached for some kind of comfort in the fact that John was still in the house—John's dear, familiar form—upstairs, resting on their bed.

In order to go on breathing as the beauty spread more vividly above her, she would try giving thanks that he was all bathed and shaved and that his beloved uniform fit perfectly and that June was upstairs with him now, keeping watch. June and Eve had worked it all out together, so that not for one minute would he have to lie there alone. "Mausa John, he never stop fidgetin' when he by hisself," Eve had said one or maybe two hours ago. "Me an' June, we tak turns. June, he sit wif him while I brush up our cabin an' catch me forty winks. Then I take my turn. June wait wif him till I gets back."

With pain far worse than any pain of childbirth, the sharp regret came again: She, the woman he loved, had somehow fallen into an exhausted sleep during the long time Dr. Tunno stayed with John at the last, so that he had actually slipped away on his secret mission alone—with only a doctor there.

"When a hard thought come, don' dwell on it. Don't dwell on what chu can't stan' yet, Miss Anne," Eve had ordered. She hadn't suggested it, she had ordered Anne to push aside every thought of any kind that left her with guilt or without hope—a thought that hurt too much. She did her best now to obey Eve. "This be a hard goodbye, Miss Anne," Eve had said, "but there be an end to even this goodbye. You hold to dat, you hear me? Dere be an end even to dis—goodbye. You an' me, we hold to dat till we bof see Mausa John agin someday."

So far, on this afternoon of the first day without him, Anne had found small but available ways to obey Eve's order. Eve's news that both Dr. Tunno and blessed little John Couper had gone for Papa, who would send for James Hamilton, was holding her through these aching minutes now as the sky seemed to burst into color—John's kind of sunset. "Cataclysmic beauty," he had called it.

Papa was surely on his way to her now and with him, Dr. Tunno and her children. Of course Mama would come too, unless she decided to wait to see them at the church tomorrow. She may be keeping the younger ones at Cannon's Point tonight. Two-year-old Selina would be too young to grieve. Fanny, a year older than John Couper, would cry hard for her papa. Anne's head pounded now from her own weeping earlier, but she had always had bad headaches, so the pain in her head gave her some hope that things might someday be almost normal again. She was grabbing, she knew, at every tiny thought that might push her through these lonely minutes, but her still-unexplainable, solid hope was in their small son, John Couper. Somehow that hope remained real. As real as the feel of John's mother's brooch, which she touched again now, pinned to the collar of her dress as she'd pinned it every day through all the years since he'd sent it to her. The brooch felt real, as real as the knowledge that her young, stalwart son would make it possible for her to conduct herself through all that lay ahead in a way that would make his father proud.

The boy, who looked so much like them both, would keep them together in his own singular way. "With John Couper nearby," she whispered, addressing John directly, "you can never be too far away, can you? Oh dearest, you won't go—*too* far away, will you?"

IT WAS ALMOST DARK, THE SKY ONLY A SOMBER, bronze afterglow, when she and Eve finally heard the loaded Cannon's Point wagon rumble up the Hamilton lane. As Anne had thought, Mama kept Fanny and Selina with her for the night, but Papa was there when, leaning heavily on Eve's arm, she went to meet her loved ones. Annie clambered down out of the wagon seat where she had ridden with Papa and Dr. Tunno, who drove the team. Then she saw young John Couper and Pete jump to the ground from the wagon bed, where stood the freshly made coffin.

Without meaning to, Anne cried out. Until that minute, she hadn't remembered that, of course, they would be bringing John's coffin! A handsome, wooden box, which she knew had been tenderly, carefully built by Margin, Papa's carpenter, who had always made John laugh. Margin had made Anne laugh too. His humor and his ready chuckle were as much a part of Margin as his skilled hands. Eve whispered sharply, "Miss Anne, when a hard thought come, push it away!"

She tried, but one hard thought was always replaced by another: *Who would help June lift John's body into Margin's handsome box?* But Papa is here now, she reminded herself, and he'll think of a way to have it done when I don't know about it.

Without a word, the aging man was helped by John Couper and Dr. Tunno to climb down from the wagon seat, and finally she was in her father's arms. Beyond repeating her name, he said nothing. Just feeling the familiar embrace, knowing he was there to take charge, was enough. She only half heard it decided, by her loved ones and Eve, that she, Anne, would try to sleep tonight with Annie in her bed. So the last night with John's dear body under the same roof with her was ready to begin.

Somehow, it would also end.

PAPA HAD TOLD ANNE THAT HER BROTHER WILliam Audley had returned just that week from college, but she wasn't prepared for the grown-up, handsome, truly poised young gentleman who helped her mother from the carriage in the shell road at the entrance to the churchyard the next day.

"I'm so glad you got here—in time," she said to him when

William Audley gave her an affectionate hug, even before Anne greeted her mother, who was standing there holding tiny Selina's hand.

"I wanted us to be able to tell Selina when she's a little older," Mama explained, "that she was here—with us—today, Anne."

Mama's decision to bring Selina was the right one. Her words *almost* promised Anne that there would be ordinary, usual days, years, ahead when Selina would ask questions about her father. With all her heart Anne needed ordinary days ahead. Away from the sea, on the leeward side of St. Simons, there was no sunrise visible at Hamilton on any day. As proud as John was because James Hamilton had put him in complete charge of what Fanny Kemble Butler called the "finest estate on St. Simons Island," there had never been what Anne considered a real sunrise there. There were John's glorious sunsets rife with color and drama, but to Anne now, sunsets would always mark endings. Sunsets even marked the endings of shadows because light made shadows, and after the sun went down, even they turned to darkness. The aching heart can somehow survive peopled, light-filled days. Darkness, which Anne now felt had already become more familiar than light, had to her long been the symbol of loneliness, of being lost—the symbol of danger, dread, weeping.

Why, sitting on the aisle of the crowded church beside Papa, her children and Mama filling the remainder of the tiny wooden pew, was she allowing herself to think only of darkness, of the sun going *down?* Eve's order came flooding back: "When a hard thought come, push it away! *Don' dwell on it.*"

Good, faithful Eve was standing alone right beside Anne, the only person in the narrow church aisle, the only person of color inside the small church, fanning, fanning her mistress on this almost unbearably hot July day. Nothing would do Eve but that she be there with her—inside, where Anne needed her to be in all ways. Over a hundred other Hamilton and Cannon's Point people stood outside in the churchyard. In her nightmare state, she had glimpsed Big Boy and June and Cuffy. Many more, Papa said, had begged to come because they all felt a special bond with their friend Mausa John Fraser. At some point later, Anne knew, the people would sing, and at the thought of their music, which she had loved since childhood, her throat tightened.

Isabella's gentle husband, the Reverend Theodore Bartow, was standing now behind his pulpit, his sensitive, expressive voice speaking the words of Jesus: " 'I am the resurrection and the life . . . he that believeth in me, though he were dead, yet shall he live: and whosoever liveth and believeth in me, shall never die. . . .' "

O God, Anne breathed, please let that be true! Theodore went on to read more of what had been set down in *The Book of Common Prayer,* for Anne's strength and comfort, but on the last line about never dying, she stopped trying to listen with her mind. Rather, she *felt* Theodore's voice as though her soul were being rocked by it, gentled—not comforted—it was too soon for comfort. Facts got in her way. *John was dead.* Her mind went on declaring that it would always be a world without light and without comfort and without beauty because John was gone from it, but her soul stretched toward the sound of her brother-in-law's words and she felt *sunrise* light seep into her thoughts. . . . Odd to feel a sunrise in church, especially such a crowded, tiny, stuffy place, sitting on a stiff, hard bench—without John's shoulder pressing hers.

Then, as in the silence that comes when rain stops suddenly, she began to hear a few words too clearly: " 'Hear my prayer, O Lord, and with thine ears consider my calling; hold not thy peace at my tears; For I am a stranger with thee, and a sojourner. . . .' " Would she ever, out of such thick shadow as this, be anything but a stranger and a sojourner—walking, running, stumbling about— hunting for John?

After an especially sad funeral, she knew people inevitably commented on whether or not the bereaved widow "behaved like a true lady, kept her composure, managed somehow not to break down."

You will be proud of me, John, her heart said and knew he heard. Then, after some endless length of time, Theodore was no longer reading from "The Order for the Burial of the Dead." He was just talking. He was simply Theodore, Isabella's husband, standing up there talking straight to Anne:

"Anne Couper Fraser—and I speak also to your five children, Selina, John Couper, Fanny, Rebecca, whom we all know as Pete, and Annie; to your revered parents, Mr. and Mrs. John Couper; to Mr. and Mrs. James Hamilton Couper and their children; to my beloved wife, Isabella Couper Bartow; to William Audley Couper; and to each of your people who loved John Fraser in their way as you loved him in yours. Our cherished one is now and forever being cared for as none of us would know or understand how to care for him. Yet, we grieve, we weep, and there will be times when there seems no end to the weeping or the darkness. God Himself knows this. He knows the link we can't help making between loss and the shadow of darkness. Listen to God's own word on that very subject: 'Weeping may endure for a night, but joy cometh in the morning.' You have lost someone dear. A part of your very life has been chopped off by that loss, but we have the word of God that He knows all about it. Does it help enough to know that God knows? If we're honest, no, it does not. Desperately we need to know that the hard, grinding work of grieving will somehow, sometime end. That we will smile again because we *feel* like smiling, that we will, by some means, learn how to live without John, that you, Anne Fraser, will be a whole person again. That this long, shadow-filled night will end. It will end, because God says it will. You can be whole again, even though today it does not seem possible. Because God is a Redeemer God, there *will* someday—for you, Anne Fraser—be true beauty for these ashes. Joy for the oil of this mourning. We have His word for it that another morning and another sunrise will be yours. That there will be, in that sunrise, *joy.* Joy? Yes. Did God really mean that the grieving heart can know joy again? He did. He does. But the joy about which God speaks is far deeper than what we think of as— happiness. Don't confuse the two. There is as much difference between God's joy and human happiness as between night and day, shadow and sunlight. For you, once your night has ended, this joy can be an entirely new, never-before-realized experience, be- cause true joy is God in the marrow of your bones."

And then, from outside the church—all of them batting gnats and deerflies, Anne knew, in the sticky heat even under the shade

of the great oaks—the hundred or more people began to sing, first
to hum and then to sing in a buoyant, rhythmic, half-recitative:

> *"Day, day oh, see day's a com-in'*
> *Ha'k e ang-els,*
> *Day, day oh, see day's a com-in'*
> *Ha'k e ang-els,*
> *Oh, look at day, O Lord*
> *Look out de windah, O Lord,*
> *Look out de windah*
> *Ha'k e ang-els*
> *Throw off de cov-ah,*
> *Start that a-risin'*
> *Who dat a comin'?*
> *O Lord, look out de windah!*
> *O Lord!"*

T HROUGH THE WHOLE SERVICE, E VE HAD NOT
stopped fanning Anne. Because she had been in the singers' group
outside in the churchyard for other white funerals, she knew
Mausa Theodore Bartow would pray again any minute. But while
the other people outside were still humming, right there before the
whole congregation because she knew Anne loved the slave song,
Eve ever so softly began to hum the odd, offbeat alto melody to the
line "Look out de windah, O Lord . . . Look out de windah, O
Lord. . . ."

The first time the people had hit that one line with a beat white
folks never seemed to get quite right, Eve had seen Miss Anne lean
suddenly forward on the hard pew, almost as though she'd been
struck with a thought that gave her strength. Tears had Miss
Anne's cheeks so wet, Eve ached to wipe them dry for her. But
even now, in these minutes before Mausa James Hamilton Couper,
Captain James Frewin, Mausa William Audley Couper, Mausa Dr.
Robert Grant, young Mausa Horace Gould, and—because Miss
Anne had insisted—young Mausa Paul Demere would rise to pick

up the coffin to carry Mausa John out to where June done had the open grave dug and waiting, Eve felt almost hopeful for her beloved mistress. She couldn't have told anybody why, but Eve felt some kind of real hope for her.

She knew now that Miss Anne was not going to break down or yell like a colored might do when they carried the other half of her own life away from her forever. There wasn't any special reason, but Eve knew that inch by inch, Miss Anne was set on learning to walk way, way past wherever it is that shadows go.

CHAPTER 75

Sunset at Cannon's Point was never spectacular. It was gentle. Only the afterglow reflection of John's "cataclysmic beauty" ever took place on the eastern side of the Island. This minute, Anne thought as she rested after the few bites of supper she'd managed to force down with her family around her, the sunset is flaring over Hamilton.

The whole lot of them, except James Hamilton and his brood, who had taken their boat back to Hopeton from the Frederica dock when the service was over, sat in rockers on the Cannon's Point veranda. At Papa's insistence, June and Eve were also there, sitting together on the front steps, Eve watching Anne's every move. Except for one wren calling and a woodpecker at work nearby, it was quiet. Even Selina was not jabbering. The little girl, whose face still wore only a puzzled, confused look, was standing as motionless as a two-year-old could stand beside the chair of her newly discovered uncle, William Audley. As though they all waited for the roseate reflection of the setting sun to reach some indefinable glow, no one spoke until Papa cleared his throat and began one of his little speeches:

"Now that we're gathered here at the place where Anne and James Hamilton and Isabella and William Audley first took root," he said, "and now that we've celebrated, with the truly spiritual help of my son-in-law Theodore, the fine, light-filled life of my other son, John Fraser, in a proper Christian manner, it seems a good time for a look toward tomorrow. Perhaps not literally the day following this day, but a look toward a rather immediate tomorrow to come, after my beloved Anne has had a bit of time to rest her heart here in the loving care of her family."

Anne saw him reach with both hands to pick up one stiff, rheumatic leg in order to cross it over the other. Then he cleared his throat again and continued:

"At the churchyard, before James Hamilton and his family left to take their boat home from Frederica, he, his sister Anne, William Audley, and I had a brief but seemingly relieving and satisfying talk together. With the full consent of both James and William Audley, I believe Anne agrees that we formulated a plan that, even under the sorrowful circumstances of this day, will work for the benefit of all concerned."

"Papa," Anne interrupted, "could I please be the one to—to explain what we've decided to do?"

Out of the corner of her eye, Anne saw Eve start to jump up from the step where she sat beside June, then plainly change her mind. Good, Anne thought. Eve knows I'm up to telling them myself. Thank God, Eve knows.

"Why yes, Daughter," Papa said, masking his surprise. "That is, if you're equal to it. You're the very one who should do the telling."

Fresh tears stood in Anne's eyes, but she was sitting forward again, much as she'd been aware of doing in the church while Theodore was speaking to her from his heart and from his deep faith in God's eagerness to heal her agony. Anne's voice betrayed the hard weeping she'd done through all of last night and for much of the short time they'd been back at Cannon's Point this evening, but in her voice, even she could hear a kind of certainty, the promise of a coming strength no one on the wide porch could miss.

"Since James must hire another manager for Hamilton almost at once because it's growing season," she said, "William Audley will move into the Big House there just as soon as we can pack and move my family's belongings back up here to Lawrence. I—I haven't had a chance to talk this over with—with—"

Anne stopped, sure that everyone knew that from long-held habit, she'd almost said she hadn't had a chance to talk it over with John, but no one could think of anything to say, until Eve jumped up from the steps.

"You gotta mean me an' June. We packs up too, Miss Anne! You ain' gonna move back up here to Lawrence wifout me an' June, is you?"

Anne could almost hear John laugh at Eve's panic. Had there been any laughter in her, she would have joined him. "No, Eve, I wouldn't think of moving anywhere without both of you! I—I couldn't."

Eve didn't smile, but her face told Anne how relieved she was as she sank back down on the step beside June.

After waiting a moment for her thoughts to clear, Anne, looking straight at Theodore Bartow, went on: "While you were speaking from your pulpit directly to me today, Theodore, especially while you were talking about the morning God promises will come after the long night of weeping, I suddenly realized how terribly I've missed *sunrises* down at Hamilton. I missed them far more than I knew! So Papa says the children and I can move back to the dear little tabby house at Lawrence." One hard sob choked off her voice for an instant, but determined to make John proud of her, she squared her shoulders and continued. "You see, that little Lawrence house was the very first home of our own John and I—ever had. The very first place that belonged only to us. Papa says it still belongs to—us." Biting her lips, she looked from one of her children to another. "And so, children, we're moving back to be closer to your grandparents and so that we'll all be where we can actually watch each new day begin. I think I'll be able to be your mother again, at least in most ways, if only I can watch the sun come up in the mornings. Someday even Selina will be old enough to understand where all the shadows around us today—eventually go. And someday I pray that even I will learn to understand." She looked at Theodore again, who was holding tight to Isabella's hand. "Theodore, I know there will be times when I doubt every word of what you said to me today, but there will come a day—especially if I can live at Lawrence again—when I'll be able to believe, at least most of the time, in morning. Maybe I can come to believe in that *joy* you mentioned, even without John."

She heard a light, shuffling sound, then sensed rather than saw her son, John Couper, come to stand beside her chair. One arm around her shoulders, the boy said, "I guess maybe when there's enough light, Mama, the shadows just sort of go away, don't they?"

Tears were flowing too freely now for Anne to do more than grab and cling to his strong little hand and nod.

Afterword

I WILL GO ON FINDING IT DIFFICULT TO ENCOMPASS what must have been the depth of Anne's grief, but one thing seems sure—she gave no thought to marrying again. In all the many Couper-Fraser letters I have seen, there is no hint that she did anything but try her best to follow Miss Eliza Mackay's advice to other widows: "Begin to learn how to live the second half of your married life." All indications are that Anne did just that—for their children, for John, and for herself. And after some time spent with her parents at Cannon's Point, she moved her brood into the snug little cottage at Lawrence on St. Simons, watching for the sunrise, knowing it was there even on a rainy morning.

If the past thirty years are any sign, many of you have found, or will find, your way to Christ Churchyard on St. Simons Island in search of John Fraser's grave. Even though I had seen it once or twice before, his grave is not easy to find, as I learned one day while doing an interview for a TV station when *Bright Captivity* was published in 1991. For this reason, since you've just read of his burial (one of the most difficult scenes I ever tried!), it seems courteous for me to give you a little help in locating it.

Park in front of the church under the trees on Frederica Road and follow the old brick walkway that leads back to the entrance of the quaint, elegant little building. Take the path to the right, follow it past the granite slab on four legs above the grave of the Reverend Edmund Matthews, and within a few steps you will see to your right the broken marble column marker for young John Wylly, murdered in this book by a neighbor, Dr. Thomas Fuller Hazzard. Now look down where a slab bearing the name Armstrong is set in the sandy soil. From this sign, an older brick walkway runs ahead, more or less dividing the Wylly stones and the handsome Couper family markers. On your right, in line with the Wyllys, is the flat slab of granite where Anne's John was buried that hot July day in 1839. The graves were not as orderly as the walkways show, because no one believes either brick path was in place back then.

Near John, of course, lie his brother, William, his infant nephew, Clarence Brailsford, and Father James Fraser. Directly beside John you will see a smaller slab where lies one of the Fraser children, Sophia Julia, aged about five years, who, for the sake of the author's sanity and yours, I did not allow to be born. With great care my alert research assistant, Nancy Goshorn, and I checked events in the true Fraser story, and I took the novelist's liberty of whittling down the size of Anne and John's family from ten children to five. I simply found the loss of so many children an intolerable load of grief, and the actual flow of the story was in no way damaged by the decision. Therefore, in these pages you will not find mention of Sophia Julia, Susan, Elizabeth, James, or Margaret Mary Agnes Fraser. Only Margaret Mary Agnes married, so I have not omitted relevant descendants.

A little behind and to the left of the Coupers in Christ Church cemetery, you will find, surrounded by an iron fence, the graves of Anna Matilda Page King and her family. Characters familiar to the reader who knows my first trilogy of novels—*Lighthouse, New Moon Rising,* and *The Beloved Invader*—lie in the Gould plot near the Page-King section and behind the church itself. It is important to remember that at that time the cemetery was only gradually filling up—there was still plenty of room so, since the Couper tutor, William Browne, also taught Gould children, his grave may be found next to the old Gould plot.

After all, the Island was an authentic community. If one can somehow discount our huge influx of people now, it is still, in an almost mystical way, a community. I doubt that the early residents —the Coupers, Goulds, Caters, Armstrongs, Wyllys, Pages, Kings, Frasers, Abbotts, Frewins, Stevenses, or any of those others who lived on nineteenth-century St. Simons Island—thought much about the fact that they were making history of any kind. They simply shared one another in varying degrees of affection and loyalty—black and white—and as we do today, they shared the communal beauty of this singular Georgia barrier island. In a way, St. Simons is singular because it was never owned by only one family. It has always been a community, and much of its heart can still be found under the great oaks and the weathered markers of Christ Churchyard. I am not as free to wander the churchyard paths as I once was, because now the world has found it, too; because I'm sometimes recognized, my wanderings turn too quickly into guided tours. In the more than thirty years since my best friend, Joyce Blackburn, and I moved here, the number of headstones has increased as our dear neighbors and friends have died. Neither Joyce nor I was born here, but we will also have markers in Christ Churchyard one day, since we bought a small lot there months before we bought our own housesite at Frederica. I have experienced tears in the old cemetery, but the sense of community and Presence as our years spent here have turned into decades keeps the inevitable natural beauty comforting us in our losses.

As you will learn when you read the novel to follow this one, Anne Couper Fraser and four of her children—Pete, Selina, John Couper, and Fanny—are not in Christ Churchyard because they died elsewhere, but the grave of Anne's firstborn, Annie Fraser Demere, can be found nearby in the Demere plot. Although in Anne's efforts to learn how to live without John, history and circumstance took her personally into the tragedy of the Civil War and away from her adored St. Simons, I'm convinced that the Island itself never died in her memory or her heart.

In one definite sense, most writers, including this one, are loners. I love nothing so much as a day alone in the ever-changing, ever-stimulating, ever-mystical light of St. Simons Island. To some the sea is the Island's attraction. To me the essence of St. Simons has always been its deep, light-streaked, black-shadowed woods. Nowhere have I found both shadow and light so mingled. By now, in some secret recess of my being, I know—I still can't explain, but I know—*where shadows go.*

Even while starkly alone, as writers have to be, I live my days working in something like a communal atmosphere. Solitude in no way separates me from those who help me through the long months of writing, nor does it separate me from you who read. Many of you have bothered to let me know that you're out there waiting for the next book. And if you have read *Inside One Author's Heart*, the little extra, quite personal book I slipped in between *Bright Captivity* and this novel, you already know something of what my readers and my St. Simons Support Group (as my agent, Lila Karpf, calls my constant helpers) mean to me. I am certainly not writer enough to describe all they mean, but even in my writing solitude, I am in the warmest, most loyal community.

Since my longtime friend Nancy Goshorn now lives on St. Simons and stays beside me through every phase of historical research, along every twisting limb of every family tree as we search out the often obscure background material, I am, of course, in regular touch with her. We may not actually see each other for days, but we have an edge on Anne, John, Jock, and Rebecca—we have a telephone nearby. And through Nancy I stay in solid touch with archival experts in many fields: At the Glynn-Brunswick Regional Library, with Marcia Hodges, reference librarian, and with Dorothy Houseal, Diane Jackson, and Jim Darby, director. The same kind of community embraces those at our unusual St. Simons Public Library, supported, believe it or not, *only* by public contributions and now, since the death of our dear friend Fraser Ledbetter, under the high-caliber direction of Frances Kane. Also helpful there have been Kathleen Williams and Noelda Walker. At the

Clara Gould Library of Brunswick College, Director Al Spivey, Ginny Boyd, and Jamie Merwin have always been ready to assist us. Support is invariably on tap at our fine Coastal Georgia Historical Society archives on St. Simons through our friend Linda King, director, and Pat Morris, historian. There has been good, careful help too from Carolyn Crowder, manager of the Ida Hilton Library in Darien, Georgia, and not once through many novels have I been without both love and enthusiastic, professional assistance from my friends at Hodgson Hall in Savannah. For years my mainstay there was my political soul mate, Bobby Bennett, and now Director Anne Smith, Tracy Bearden, Jan Flores, Eileen Ielmini, Ryan Johnson, and Gloria Stover are always cheerfully on hand.

Also in my community and among my most expert helpers and advisers have been our friends Reed and the late Cornelia Ferguson of St. Simons; Malcolm Bell of Savannah (I find it still hard to believe that Malcolm and his Muriel have moved to North Carolina); Eloise Bailey of St. Marys, Georgia; Buddy Sullivan, author, real friend, and editor of the *Darien News,* of Darien; Anne Edwards of St. Simons; Mildred Huie, noted artist, historian, and longtime St. Simons friend; close, also longtime friends Frances Burns and Lucy Annand; relatively new but now dear friend, St. Simons artist Peggy Buchan, who lives and works with her husband, Danny, near the site of Anne's cottage at Lawrence. Through Eileen Humphlett, my own executive assistant, Dewey Benefield, vice president of the Sea Island Company, and Rachel Kelly, Sea Island executive assistant, kindly made available obscure Cannon's Point and Lawrence and Hamilton records. Rare-book woman~(rare in all ways!) and friend of years, Virginia Hobson Hicks of St. Simons, and my dear friend Dr. William Hitt, who guides me through my characters' medical quandaries, are both invaluable. And of Marietta, Georgia, Couper descendant (via Selina Fraser) Frances Daugherty, who seems to know almost everything and shares so freely, has me permanently in her debt because I am counting on her heavily for help with the next book. Her cousin—another Couper descendant—Elizabeth Zervas of Calabasas, California, has also been, through Frances, most generous. At

Ships of the Sea Museum in Savannah, Jeff Fulton was of real help, as were Cap Fendig of St. Simons and Rosa Mills of Sapelo Island.

I dedicated *Bright Captivity,* the first book of the Georgia Trilogy, to one of my most treasured friends anywhere—another Couper descendant—Jo Couper Cauthorn. An author never dedicates such a massive piece of work lightly. That, Jo, should tell you how important you are to me and in small measure demonstrate my gratitude for the way you go on caring. My thanks and affection go again also to your sister, Ann Fettner, of Washington, D.C.

The writing of a long novel is never without hardships and problems, at times even deep sorrow. Daily life has never been known to stop just because someone happens to be writing a book. I have to believe that there is, perhaps, more depth and scope in *Where Shadows Go* because much of its writing and research took place under a deep shadow of anxiety and dread as the light-filled life of one of my dearest friends and best encouragers was ebbing away. My beloved Easter Straker of Lima, Ohio, died just before I reached the end of *Shadows.* I'm sure she knows I'm finished now, but how I miss being able to call her so that I can tell her myself! Through this loss, though, I have made new, valued friends— Grover Blazer, Paul Knotts, Doug Adams, all the dear ones who cared for Easter—and an ever-deeper bond keeps growing with Easter's shared Lima friends, Doris Shuman and Mary Porter. Easter always vowed that each of my novels showed improvement over the one before. I hope she feels that way about *Where Shadows Go.* One thing I know: she understands fully now where they do go.

Through twelve novels since we found and seemed unable *not* to make St. Simons Island our home, I have tried to find words adequate to thank my dearest friend, Joyce Blackburn, not only for her line-by-line editing of my writing style—tough, careful, superbly critical—but for believing in me as she has unwaveringly done through more than thirty years in which we've shared life and our home here in the sun- and shadow-streaked woods. I have always failed to find adequate words. I'm failing again. Because she knows me as she does, it mattered so much that Joyce knew, perhaps even more than I, how I feared and dreaded the writing of the inevitable ending of this book. Both of us were sharply aware that I did *not* want Anne to lose John. The shadow of his going, even before I wrote it, hung for days over our lives. She also knew, as did I, that I feared I was not writer enough to bring it off, still managing to leave my readers with the small ray of hope I always try to find. These are basically true stories and John Fraser did die and he is buried in Christ Church cemetery. His name and the dates are on his marker. Knowing what lay ahead for book three of the Georgia Trilogy, I had no choice but to stick to the facts, heartbreaking as they were to us both. We were not the only ones with heavy hearts. My *absolutely necessary* assistant, Eileen Humphlett, Nancy Goshorn, and Sarah Bell Edmond also knew how I dreaded writing John's death. Believe me, they are, in all ways, my Support Group. Nancy seems never to tire of the long hours spent digging out obscure and needed research material, and Eileen not only manages my business *and* me but does almost everything else for me in my professional life except write my books. She does handle 90 percent of my sometimes heavy mail. She and I are so close that you who write to me seem to enjoy her cheerful comments about what I'm doing, and certainly her typing is more readable than I can manage on my old manual Olympia. Sarah Bell Edmond spends part of almost every day here in the house with Joyce and me and does far more to make life good than she seems able to believe. All four of these close ones went around on needles and pins until the day I could tell them that I had actually finished the final page! They love me despite all my quirks, and because I'm sure of their belief in me and in my ultimate intentions, I thoroughly enjoy that all four laugh at me much of the time. What, what, *what* would I do without each one of them— *God's handpicked gifts to me?*

So close to us all here on St. Simons, even though she lives and works her literary management magic for me in New York, my agent, Lila Karpf, is herself a central member of my absolutely essential Support Group. Lila and I talk almost every day long distance, and depending on her current efforts in my behalf, she and Eileen talk nearly as often. Lila, who is Joyce's agent, too, has been a vital part of our lives for years, but after the big, glowing

Eugenia Price Day Doubleday gave for me on St. Simons to celebrate the publication of *Bright Captivity* and my seventy-fifth birthday, a whole new dimension seemed to invade my already close relationship with Lila. We all feel it. She flew down from New York along with Carolyn Blakemore, my editor; Bebe Cole, my longtime friend who handles national sales at Doubleday; Ellen Archer, my happy-natured Doubleday publicist; dear, capable Steve Rubin, Doubleday's president; and Jayne Schorn, too attractive to be director of something as mysterious to me as marketing. Their actually seeing St. Simons Island and me in my own work environment seemed to make an enormous difference for us all. Lila now tells me she's *not* reading the *Where Shadows Go* manuscript in noisy old New York City "but on St. Simons under a great live oak tree. Because I've seen it all, I'm living every page!" Could an author ask for more, especially when truly superior agents are as rare as the proverbial hen's teeth? Certainly not this author. Thank you, dear Lila, for being you.

As I write this page of the Afterword, I have just opened a heavy Federal Express package containing the expert, careful, plainly caring editorial work of my longtime friend and favorite editor among all I've had, Carolyn Blakemore. There has been no time even to glance at the *Shadows* manuscript itself, but her cover letter told me everything an author needs to know at this stage of readying a piece of work for final submission to the publisher. Carolyn is a wise and sensitive woman. She wrote, "Most important of all—congratulations!" This any author needs. And Carolyn bothered to tell me again, even after a lengthy telephone conversation that left me on cloud nine, that I had made it. Right now I can't wait for tomorrow, when I'll have time to dig into her editing. I've heard authors say they dread this part. I don't. Perhaps I've simply been at it long enough, but I look forward to another journey through the nearly nine hundred pages of manuscript because I'll be making the journey with Carolyn, and to me she is the best company anywhere. Carolyn, again—thanks. How many more of these we'll be able to do I don't know, but I hope a bunch. I can't imagine writing a novel freely without you.

Doubleday, aside from retaining Carolyn Blakemore as editor, also makes it possible for Janet Falcone to do the expert, imaginative, and professional work of copy editing. I explained in *Inside One Author's Heart* the difference between an editor and a copy editor. At least, I explained it as well as I knew how, since copy editing is a complex area of readying a manuscript for the presses that is almost beyond my ken, as Jock Couper might say. A really good copy editor (and they too are rare these days) is born with a retentive mind sharper than any computer. Knowing Janet will be there to "fix me" gives me vast writing freedom. I am not a detail person, so even after Joyce, Eileen, Carolyn, and Nancy go over a manuscript with their varied expertise, I know that whatever is still wrong, wonderful Janet will correct. Janet is my final guardian over dates, births, deaths, spelling, grammar, punctuation, and more other mysteries than any author can keep front and center while writing. Best of all, she seems to like my books and lets me know that she does. Once more, Janet, heart-deep thanks for your special skills as well as your valued friendship.

Again, if you have read *Inside One Author's Heart,* you know that if things stay as good as they are now, I want to remain to the end of my writing life under contract to Bantam Doubleday Dell. Lila and I both hope for this, despite the dizzying pace at which publishing is changing in our changing world. One of the reasons I want to stay is that Steve Rubin, president of Doubleday, is my steady, perceptive, real booster. Along with retaining Carolyn Blakemore and Janet Falcone for me at my request, Steve, as busy as he is, gives all my work his own good attention; he has also given me a charming, talented young woman named Renée Zuckerbrot, whom we call my in-house editor. Not only is Renée there when Eileen and I need to know something quickly, she handles any and all of our glitches, checks manuscript, and writes my superb jacket and catalog copy. How many times during the writing do Eileen and I say, "Well, we'll call Renée. Then we'll know." Without Renée and Steve's wonderful right hand, Naomi Fields, life would indeed be rocky at times for this author hidden away on a coastal island so far from New York. Also at Doubleday, my thanks to Ginger Barton, another superb publicist, who has now added her special expertise to my books, and to blessed Emma Bolton, the receptionist who so competently and cheerfully handles my mail and our telephone calls when no one else is available. Renée Zuckerbrot is also the all-important liaison with my excellent art director, Whitney Cookman, when the time finally arrives for the vital communication needed in planning and executing the jacket art. The handsome jacket on *Where Shadows Go* is the superb creation of an artist new to me—Rob Wood—and selected for me by Whitney. Truthfully, I was sure I'd never like another book jacket as much as those for *Stranger in Savannah* and *Bright Captivity*. With help from photographs Eileen collected, Whitney and Rob combined their efforts to create what to me is the true physical and spiritual mystique of the St. Simons Island light and shadow I have loved for almost thirty-two years. I'm looking out my window at this light and shadow now and across my office at a copy of the jacket; the magic is in both places. Thank you, dear Whitney and Rob. Thanks also to cartographer Marty Holmer for the handsome endpaper maps.

If, like me, you've found the layout and type in my Doubleday books easier than usual to read, more artistically laid on the pages, we can all thank my expert designer, Marysarah Quinn, the very best. Once again, thank you, Marysarah.

And if you have looked at the dedication page of *Where Shadows Go,* you know that central in my life is my cherished friend Tina McElroy Ansa, considered by many, including me, to be one of our most important American writers. Of course, I am counting heavily on Tina's opinion of what I've done with one of my favorite characters in this novel—Eve. But I count on Tina for far more than that. I'm just plain honored that she considers me a good writer, and from my heart I thank her not only for her superb reviews of my stuff but for the widening readership she brings me. Most of all, I thank Tina for loving and trusting me. I certainly love and trust you, Tina. And all I know to do to prove it is to give you this book, which I do—from my heart.

Invariably, near the end of any Afterword, I find the need for one paragraph with space enough, unfortunately, for only a mention of certain persons, both near and far, whose varied contributions to my life go on keeping me everlastingly at it. First, I salute and thank each one of you who read when at last everything is between covers. This time I mention especially Jimmie Harnsberger of Macon, Georgia, and Charlene Tribble of Norcross, Georgia. I salute every bookseller everywhere and promise that here at least is one author who treasures all of you and recognizes your singular value to me and to my loyal readers. And now the names of you special "others" who add, in your own ways, to my every hour: my close, longtime friends Faith Brunson, Fred and Sara Bentley, Burnette Vanstory, Juanelle and John Edwards, State Senator Cathey Steinberg, and United States Senator Wyche Fowler, all among my close ones in the Atlanta area; beloved Dena Snodgass and Ann Hyman of Jacksonville, Florida; Helen Berg of Ypsilanti, Michigan; Neddy Mason and Eleanor Ratelle of Columbus, Ohio; my always encouraging sister-in-law, Millie Price, along with Mary Wheeler, Bob Summer, and Genon Neblett of Nashville, Tennessee; Sara Pilcher of Norfolk, Virginia; my special friend Gene Greneker of St. Simons; and my high school Spanish teacher, Mary Ann Hark of Hampton, Virginia. Too many other persons are important on St. Simons Island for separate mention, except for one—Ruby Wilson, whom I call every morning when I'm at home, because her voice is so rich and beautiful when she picks up the telephone to say "Good morning!"

At this writing I have one more novel under contract—the final book in the Georgia Trilogy about Anne Couper Fraser and her family. I even have a title for it—*Beauty from Ashes*. The human spirit, as I see it growing in Anne, goes on seeking that beauty even in the black, tortured shadows of the Civil War. Anyone who knows me at all already knows that by the time you read this, *Beauty from Ashes* is in progress. My super helpers have kept the *Shadows* publication right on schedule, leaving me three whole years before my eightieth birthday. And as Eve might ask, "Where is it written down in law that an author needs to stop work at eighty?"

So, because I am connected to the Creator God and by years and years of mutual devotion to you, my readers, I go on living and working and loving every minute of it.

Eugenia Price
St. Simons Island, Georgia

DATE DUE